# Broken Harbour

## TANA FRENCH

HACHETTE
BOOKS
IRELAND

First published in Ireland in 2012 by Hachette Books Ireland
An Hachette UK company

1

A CIP catalogue record for this title is available from the British Library

Trade paperback ISBN 978 1 444 70510 2

Typeset in Plantin Light by Hewer Text UK Ltd, Edinburgh

Printed and bound by Clays Ltd, St Ives plc

Hachette Books Ireland policy is to use papers that are natural, renewable
and recyclable products and made from wood grown in sustainable forests.
The logging and manufacturing processes are expected to conform
to the environmental regulations of the country of origin.

Hachette Books Ireland
8 Castlecourt Centre
Castleknock
Dublin 15

www.hachette.ie

# Broken Harbour

*Also by Tana French*

In the Woods
The Likeness
Faithful Place

For Darley, magician and gentleman

# ACKNOWLEDGEMENTS

I owe huge thank-yous to a lot of people: Ciara Considine at Hachette Books Ireland, Sue Fletcher at Hodder & Stoughton and Josh Kendall at Viking, for being the kind of editors every writer dreams of having; Breda Purdue, Ruth Shern, Ciara Doorley and everyone at Hachette Books Ireland; Swati Gamble, Emma Knight, Jaime Frost and everyone at Hodder & Stoughton; Clare Ferraro, Ben Petrone, Meghan Fallon and everyone at Viking; the wonderful fairy godmothers at the Darley Anderson Agency, especially Maddie, Rosanna, Zoe, Kasia, Sophie and Clare; Steve Fisher of Agency for the Performing Arts; Rachel Burd, for copyediting with a detective's eye for detail; Dr Fearghas Ó Cochláin, for answering questions that have probably got him on some kind of list; Alex French, for the computer-y bits, both on the page and off; David Walsh, who is responsible for all the correct bits of police procedure and none of the incorrect ones; Oonagh 'Sandbox' Montague, Ann-Marie Hardiman, Kendra Harpster, Catherine Farrell, Dee Roycroft, Mary Kelly, Susan Collins and Cheryl Steckel, for laughs, talks, pints, hugs and lots of other good things; David Ryan, ◆〰□ ○℥♋Ⅿ ○Ⅿ □◆ ◆ ◆〰⊱◆ ⊱■ ⊕⊱■♑♋⊱■♑◆; my parents, Elena Hvostoff-Lombardi (without whom this book would have been finished around 2015) and David French; and, as always and in more ways than I can count, my husband, Anthony Breatnach.

# I

Let's get one thing straight: I was the perfect man for this case. You'd be amazed how many of the lads would have run a mile, given the choice – and I had a choice, at least at the start. A couple of them said it to my face: *Sooner you than me, man*. It didn't bother me, not for a second. All I felt was sorry for them.

Some of them aren't wild about the high-profile gigs, the high-stakes ones – too much media crap, they say, and too much fallout if you don't get a solve. I don't do that kind of negativity. If you put your energy into thinking about how much the fall would hurt, you're already halfway down. I focus on the positive, and there's plenty of positive there: you can pretend you're above this stuff, but everyone knows the big cases are the ones that bring the big promotions. Give me the headline-grabbers and you can keep your drug-dealer stabbings. If you can't take the heat, stay in uniform.

Some of the lads can't handle kids, which would be fair enough except that, forgive me for asking, if you can't cope with nasty murders then what the hell are you doing on the Murder Squad? I bet Intellectual Property Rights would love to have your sensitive arse on board. I've handled babies, drownings, rape-murders and a shotgun decapitation that left lumps of brain crusted all over the walls, and I sleep just fine, as long as the job gets done. Someone has to do it. If that's me, then at least it's getting done right.

Because let's get another thing clear, while we're at it: I am bloody good at my job. I still believe that. I've been on the Murder Squad for ten years, and for seven of those, ever since I found my feet, I've had the highest solve rate in the place. This year I'm down to second, but the top guy got a run of slam-dunks, domestics, where the suspect practically slapped the cuffs on his own wrists and served himself up on a plate with applesauce. I pulled the tough ones, the nobody-seen-nothing junkie-on-junkie drudgery, and I still scored. If our superintendent had had one doubt, one single doubt, he could have pulled me off the case any time he wanted. He never did.

Here's what I'm trying to tell you: this case should have gone like clockwork. It should have ended up in the textbooks as a shining example of how to get everything right. By every rule in the book, this should have been the dream case.

The second it hit the floor, I knew from the sound that it was a big one. All of us did. Your basic murder comes straight to the squad room and goes to whoever's next in the rota, or, if he's out, to whoever happens to be around; only the big ones, the sensitive ones that need the right pair of hands, go through the Super so he can pick his man. So when Superintendent O'Kelly stuck his head around the door of the squad room, pointed at me, snapped, 'Kennedy, my office,' and vanished, we knew.

I flipped my jacket off the back of my chair and pulled it on. My heartbeat had picked up. It had been a long time, too long, since one of these had come my way. 'Don't go anywhere,' I said to Richie, my partner.

'Oooo,' Quigley called from his desk, mock-horrified, shaking a pudgy hand. 'Is Scorcher in the shit again? I never thought we'd see the day.'

'Feast your eyes, old son.' I made sure my tie was straight. Quigley was being a little bitch because he was next up in the rota. If he hadn't been a waste of space, O'Kelly might have let the case go to him.

'What've you done?'

'Shagged your sister. I brought my own paper bags.'

The lads snickered, which made Quigley purse up his lips like an old woman. 'That's not funny.'

'Too close to the bone?'

Richie was open-mouthed and practically hopping off his chair with curiosity. I flipped my comb out of my pocket and gave it a quick run through my hair. 'Am I good?'

'Lick-arse,' Quigley said, through his sulk. I ignored him.

'Yeah,' Richie said. 'You're grand. What . . . ?'

'Don't go anywhere,' I repeated, and went after O'Kelly.

My second hint: he was up behind his desk, with his hands in his trouser pockets, rolling up and down on the balls of his feet. This case had pumped up his adrenaline enough that he wouldn't fit in his chair. 'You took your time.'

'Sorry, sir.'

He stayed where he was, sucking his teeth and rereading the call sheet on his desk. 'How's the Mullen file coming along?'

I had spent the last few weeks putting together a file for the Director of Public Prosecutions on one of those tricky drug-dealer messes, making sure the little bastard didn't have a single crack to slime through. Some detectives think their job's done the second the charges are filed, but I take it personally when one of my catches wriggles off the hook, which they seldom do. 'Good to go. Give or take.'

'Could someone else finish it up?'

'Not a problem.'

He nodded and kept reading. O'Kelly likes you to ask – it shows you know who's boss – and since he is in fact my boss, I have no problem rolling over like a good little doggie when it makes things run more smoothly. 'Did something come in, sir?'

'Do you know Brianstown?'

'Haven't heard of it.'

'Neither had I. It's one of those new places; up the coast, past Balbriggan. Used to be called Broken Bay, something.'

'Broken Harbour,' I said. 'Yeah. I know Broken Harbour.'

'It's Brianstown now. And by tonight the whole country'll have heard of it.'

I said, 'This is a bad one.'

O'Kelly laid one heavy palm on the call sheet, like he was holding it down. He said, 'Husband, wife and two kids, stabbed in their own home. The wife's headed for hospital; it's touch and go. The rest are dead.'

We left that for a moment, listening to the small tremors it sent through the air. I said, 'How did it come in?'

'The wife's sister. They talk every morning, but today she couldn't get through. That got her het up enough that she got in her car and headed out to Brianstown. Car's in the driveway, lights are on in broad daylight, no one's answering the door, she rings the uniforms. They break the door down and surprise, surprise.'

'Who's on scene?'

'Just the uniforms. They took one look and figured they were out of their depth, called it straight in.'

'Beautiful,' I said. There are plenty of morons out there who would have spent hours playing detective and churning the whole case to shit, before they admitted defeat and called in the real thing. It looked like we had lucked into a pair with functioning brains.

'I want you on this. Can you take it?'

'I'd be honoured.'

'If you can't drop everything else, tell me now and I'll put Flaherty on this one. This takes priority.'

Flaherty is the guy with the slam-dunks and the top solve rate. I said, 'That won't be necessary, sir. I can take it.'

'Good,' O'Kelly said, but he didn't hand over the call sheet. He tilted it to the light, inspecting it and rubbing a thumb along his jawline. 'Curran,' he said. 'Is he able for this?'

Young Richie had been on the squad all of two weeks. A lot of the lads don't like training in the new boys, so I do it. If you know your job, you have a responsibility to pass the knowledge on. 'He will be,' I said.

'I can stick him somewhere else for a while, give you someone who knows what he's at.'

'If Curran can't take the heat, we might as well find out now.' I didn't want someone who knew what he was at. The bonus of newbie-wrangling is that it saves you a load of hassle: all of us who've been around a while have our own ways of doing things, and too many cooks etcetera. A rookie, if you know how to handle him, slows you down a lot less than another old hand. I couldn't afford to waste time playing after-you-no-after-you, not on this one.

'You'd be the lead man, either way.'

'Trust me, sir. Curran can handle it.'

'It's a risk.'

Rookies spend their first year or so on probation. It's not official, but that doesn't make it any less serious. If Richie made a mistake straight out of the gate, in a spotlight this bright, he might as well start clearing out his desk. I said, 'He'll do fine. I'll make sure he does.'

O'Kelly said, 'Not just for Curran. How long since you had a big one?'

His eyes were on me, small and sharp. My last high-profile one went wrong. Not my fault – I got played by someone I thought was a friend, dropped in the shit and left there – but still, people remember. I said, 'Almost two years.'

'That's right. Clear this one, and you're back on track.'

He left the other half unspoken, something dense and heavy on the desk between us. I said, 'I'll clear it.'

O'Kelly nodded. 'That's what I thought. Keep me posted.' He leaned forward, across the desk, and passed me the call sheet.

'Thank you, sir. I won't let you down.'

'Cooper and the Tech Bureau are on their way.' Cooper is the pathologist. 'You'll need manpower; I'll have the General Unit send you out a bunch of floaters. Six do you, for now?'

'Six sounds good. If I need more, I'll call in.'

O'Kelly added, as I was leaving, 'And for Jesus' sake do something about Curran's gear.'

'I had a word last week.'

'Have another. Was that a bloody *hoodie* he had on him yesterday?'

'I've got him out of trainers. One step at a time.'

'If he wants to stay on this case, he'd better manage a few giant steps before you hit the scene. The media'll be all over this like flies on shite. At least make him keep his coat on, cover up his tracksuit or whatever he's honoured us with today.'

'I've got a spare tie in my desk. He'll be fine.' O'Kelly muttered something sour about a pig in a tuxedo.

On my way back to the squad room I skimmed the call sheet: just what O'Kelly had already told me. The victims were Patrick Spain, his wife Jennifer, and their kids, Emma and Jack. The sister who had called it in was Fiona Rafferty. Under her name the dispatcher had added, in warning capitals, NB: OFFICER ADVISES CALLER IS HYSTERICAL.

Richie was up out of his seat, bobbing from foot to foot like he had springs in his knees. 'What . . . ?'

'Get your gear. We're going out.'

'I told you,' Quigley said to Richie.

Richie gave him the wide-eyed innocents. 'Did you, yeah? Sorry, man, wasn't paying attention. Other stuff on my mind, know what I mean?'

'I'm trying to do you a favour here, Curran. You can take it or leave it.' Quigley's wounded look was still on.

I threw my coat on and started checking my briefcase. 'Sounds like a fascinating chat you two were having. Care to share?'

'Nothing,' Richie said promptly. 'Shooting the breeze.'

'I was just letting young Richie know,' Quigley told me, self-righteously. 'Not a good sign, the Super calling you in on your own. Giving you the info behind our Richie's back. What does that say about where he stands on the squad? I thought he might want to have a little think about that.'

Quigley loves playing Haze the Newbie, just like he loves leaning on suspects one notch too hard; we've all done it, but he gets more out of it than most of us do. Usually, though, he has the brains to leave my boys alone. Richie had pissed him off somehow. I said, 'He's going to have plenty to think about, over the next while. He can't afford to get distracted by pointless crap. Detective Curran, are we good to go?'

'*Well*,' Quigley said, tucking his chins into each other. 'Don't mind *me*.'

'I never do, chum.' I slid the tie out of my drawer and into my coat pocket under cover of the desk: no need to give Quigley ammo. 'Ready, Detective Curran? Let's roll.'

'See you 'round,' Quigley said to Richie, not pleasantly, on our way out. Richie blew him a kiss, but I wasn't supposed to see it, so I didn't.

It was October, a thick, cold, grey Tuesday morning, sulky and tantrumy as March. I got my favourite silver Beemer out of the car pool – officially it's first come first served, but in practice no Domestic Violence kid is going to go near a Murder D's best ride, so the seat stays where I like it and no one throws burger wrappers on the floor. I would have bet I could still navigate to Broken Harbour in my sleep, but this wasn't the day to find out I was wrong, so I set the satnav. It didn't know where Broken Harbour was. It wanted to go to Brianstown.

Richie had spent his first two weeks on the squad helping me work up the file on the Mullen case and re-interview the odd witness; this was the first real Murder action he'd seen, and he was practically shooting out of his shoes with excitement. He managed to hold it in till we got moving. Then he burst out with, 'Are we on a case?'

'We are.'

'What kind of case?'

'A murder case.' I stopped at a red, pulled out the tie and passed it over. We were in luck: he was wearing a shirt, even if it was a cheapo white thing so thin I could see where his chest hair should have been, and a pair of grey trousers that would have been almost OK if they hadn't been a full size too big. 'Put that on.'

He looked at it like he had never seen one before. 'Yeah?'

'Yeah.'

For a moment I thought I was going to have to pull over and do it for him – the last time he had worn one had probably been for his confirmation – but he managed it in the end, give or take. He tilted the sun-visor mirror to check himself out. 'Looking sharp, yeah?'

'Better,' I said. O'Kelly had a point: the tie made bugger-all difference. It was a nice one, maroon silk with a subtle stripe in the weave, but some people can wear the good stuff and some just can't. Richie is five foot nine on his best day, all elbows and skinny legs and narrow shoulders – he looks about fourteen, although his file says he's thirty-one – and call me prejudiced, but after one glance I could have told you exactly what kind of neighbourhood he comes from. It's all there: that too-short no-colour hair, those sharp features, that springy, restless walk like he's got one eye out for trouble and the other one out for anything unlocked. On him, the tie just looked nicked.

He gave it an experimental rub with one finger. ''S nice. I'll get it back to you.'

'Hang on to it. And pick up a few of your own, when you get a chance.'

He glanced across at me and for a second I thought he was going to say something, but he stopped himself. 'Thanks,' he said, instead.

We had hit the quays and were heading towards the M1. The wind was blasting up the Liffey from the sea, making the pedestrians lean into it heads-first. When the traffic jammed up – some wanker in a 4x4 who hadn't noticed, or cared, that he wouldn't make it through the intersection – I found my BlackBerry and texted my sister Geraldine. *Geri, URGENT favour. Can you go get Dina from work ASAP? If she gives out about losing her hours, tell her I'll cover the money. Don't worry, she's fine as far as I know, but she should stay with you for a couple of days. Will ring you later. Thanks.* The Super was right: I had maybe a couple of hours before the media were all over Broken Harbour, and vice versa. Dina is the baby; Geri and I still look out for her. When she heard this story, she needed to be somewhere safe.

Richie ignored the texting, which was good, and watched the satnav instead. He said, 'Out of town, yeah?'

'Brianstown. Heard of it?'

He shook his head. 'Name like that, it's got to be one of those new estates.'

'Right. Up the coast. It used to be a village called Broken Harbour, but it sounds like someone's developed it since.' The wanker in the 4x4 had managed to get out of everyone's way, and the traffic was moving again. One of the upsides of the recession: now that half the cars are off the roads, those of us who still have somewhere to go can actually get there. 'Tell me something. What's the worst thing you've seen on the job?'

Richie shrugged. 'I worked traffic for ages, before Motor Vehicles. I saw some pretty bad stuff. Accidents.'

All of them think that. I'm sure I thought it too, once upon a time. 'No, old son. You didn't. That tells me just how innocent you are. It's no fun seeing a kid with his head split open because some moron took a bend too fast, but it's nothing compared to seeing a kid with his head split open because some prick deliberately smacked him off a wall till he stopped breathing. So far, you've only seen what bad luck can do to people. You're about to take your first good look at what people can do to each other. Believe me: not the same thing.'

Richie asked, 'Is this a kid? That we're going to?'

'It's a family. Father, mother and two kids. The wife might make it. The rest are gone.'

His hands had gone motionless on his knees. It was the first time I'd seen him absolutely still. 'Ah, sweet Jaysus. What age kids?'

'We don't know yet.'

'What happened to them?'

'It looks like they were stabbed. In their home, probably some-time last night.'

'That's rotten, that is. That's only bloody rotten.' Richie's face was pulled into a grimace.

'Yeah,' I said, 'it is. And by the time we get to the scene, you need to be over that. Rule Number One, and you can write this down: no emotions on scene. Count to ten, say the rosary, make sick jokes, do whatever you need to do. If you need a few tips on coping, ask me now.'

'I'm all right.'

'You'd better be. The wife's sister is out there, and she's not interested in how much you care. She just needs to know you're on top of this.'

'I am on top of it.'

'Good. Have a read.'

I passed him the call sheet and gave him thirty seconds to skim it. His face changed when he concentrated: he looked older, and smarter. 'When we get out there,' I said, once his time was up, 'what's the first question you're going to want to ask the uniforms?'

'The weapon. Has it been found at the scene?'

'Why not "Any signs of forced entry?"'

'Someone could fake those.'

I said, 'Let's not beat around the bush. By "someone", you mean Patrick or Jennifer Spain.'

The wince was small enough that I could have missed it, if I hadn't been watching for it. 'Anyone who had access. A relative, or a mate. Anyone they'd let in.'

'That's not what you had in mind, though, was it? You were thinking of the Spains.'

'Yeah. I guess.'

'It happens, old son. No point pretending it doesn't. The fact that Jennifer Spain survived puts her front and centre. On the other hand, when it plays out like this, it's usually the father: a woman just takes out the kids and herself, a man goes for the whole family. Either way, though, they don't normally bother to fake forced entry. They're way past caring about that.'

'Still. I figure we can decide that for ourselves, once the Bureau gets there; we won't be taking the uniforms' word for it. The weapon, though: I'd want to know about that straightaway.'

'Good man. That's top of the list for the uniforms, all right. And what's the first thing you'll want to ask the sister?'

'Whether anyone had anything against Jennifer Spain. Or Patrick Spain.'

'Well, sure, but that's something we're going to ask everyone we can find. What do you want to ask Fiona Rafferty, specifically?'

He shook his head.

'No? Personally, I'd be very interested to hear what she's doing there.'

'It says—' Richie held up the call sheet. 'The two of them talked every day. She couldn't get through.'

'So? Think about the timing, Richie. Let's say they normally talk at, what, nine o'clock, once the hubbies are off to work and the kids are off to school—'

'Or once they're in work themselves, the women. They could have jobs.'

'Jennifer Spain didn't, or the sister's problem would have been "She's not in work", not "I couldn't get through". So Fiona rings Jennifer at nine-ish, maybe half-eight at the earliest – up until then, they'd still be busy getting their day underway. And at ten thirty-six' – I tapped the call sheet – 'she's in Brianstown calling the uniforms. I don't know where Fiona Rafferty lives, or where she works, but I do know Brianstown is a good hour's drive away from just about anything. In other words, when Jennifer's an hour late for their morning chat – and that's an hour *maximum*, it could be a lot less – Fiona gets panicked enough to drop everything and haul her arse out to the back of beyond. That sounds a lot like overreacting to me. I don't know about you, my man, but I'd love to know what had her knickers in such a twist.'

'She mightn't be an hour away. Maybe she lives next door, just called round to see what the story was.'

'Then why drive? If she's too far away to walk, then she's far enough away that her going over there is odd. And here's Rule Number Two: when someone's behaviour is odd, that's a little present just for you, and you don't let go of it till you've got it unwrapped. This isn't Motor Vehicles, Richie. In this gig, you don't get to say, "Ah, sure, it's probably not important, she was just in a funny mood that day, let's forget it." Ever.'

There was the kind of silence that meant the conversation wasn't over. Finally Richie said, 'I'm a good detective.'

'I'm pretty sure you're going to be an excellent detective, someday. But right now, you've still got just about everything left to learn.'

'Whether I wear ties or not.'

I said, 'You're not fifteen, chum. Dressing like a mugger doesn't make you a big daring threat to the Establishment; it just makes you a prat.'

Richie fingered the thin cloth of his shirt front. He said, picking his words carefully, 'I know the Murder lads aren't usually from where I'm from. Everyone else comes from farmers, yeah? Or from teachers. I'm not what anyone expects. I understand that.'

His eyes in the rear-view mirror were green and level. I said, 'It doesn't matter where you come from. There's nothing you can do about it, so don't waste your energy thinking about it. What matters is where you're going. And that, mate, is something you *can* control.'

'I know that. I'm here, amn't I?'

'And it's my job to help you get further. One of the ways you take charge of where you're going is by acting like you're already there. Do you follow me?'

He looked blank.

'Put it this way. Why do you think we're driving a Beemer?'

Richie shrugged. 'Figured you liked the car.'

I took a hand off the wheel to point a finger at him. 'You figured my ego liked the car, you mean. Don't fool yourself: it's not that simple. These aren't shoplifters we're going after, Richie. Murderers are the big fish in this pond. What they do is a big deal. If we tool up to the scene in a beat-up '95 Toyota, it looks disrespectful; like we don't think the victims deserve our best. That puts people's backs up. Is that how you want to start off?'

'No.'

'No, it's not. And, on top of that, a beat-up old Toyota would make us look like a pair of losers. That matters, my man. Not just to my ego. If the bad guys see a pair of losers, they feel like their balls are bigger than ours, and that makes it harder to break them down. If the good guys see a pair of losers, they figure we'll never solve this case, so why should they bother trying to help us? And if *we* see a pair of losers every time we look in the mirror, what do you think happens to our odds of winning?'

'They go down. I guess.'

'Bingo. If you want to come out a success, Richie, you cannot go in smelling of failure. Do you get what I'm saying here?'

He touched the knot in his new tie. 'Dress better. Basically.'

'Except that it's not basic, old son. There's nothing basic about it. The rules are there for a reason. Before you go breaking them, you might want to have a think about what that reason might be.'

I hit the M1 and opened up wide, letting the Beemer do her thing. Richie glanced at the speedometer, but I knew without looking that I was bang on the limit, not a single mile over, and he kept his mouth shut. Probably he was thinking what a boring bollix I was. Plenty of people think the same thing. All of them are teenagers, mentally if not physically. Only teenagers think boring is bad. Adults, grown men and women who've been around the block a few times, know that boring is a gift straight from God. Life has more than enough excitement up its sleeve, ready to hit you with as soon as you're not looking, without you adding to the drama. If Richie didn't know that already, he was about to find out.

I'm a big believer in development – blame the property developers and their tame bankers and politicians for this recession if you want, but the fact is, if it wasn't for them thinking big, we'd never have got out of the last one. I'd rather see an apartment block any day, all charged up with people who go out to work every morning and keep this country buzzing and then come home to the nice little places they've earned, than a field doing bugger-all good to anyone except a couple of cows. Places are like people are like sharks: if they stop moving, they die. But everyone has one place that they like to think is never going to change.

I used to know Broken Harbour like the back of my hand, when I was a skinny little guy with home-cut hair and mended jeans. Kids nowadays grew up on sun holidays during the boom, two weeks in the Costa del Sol is their bare minimum. But I'm forty-two and our generation had low expectations. A few days by the Irish Sea in a rented caravan put you ahead of the pack.

Broken Harbour was nowhere, back then. A dozen scattered

houses full of families named Whelan or Lynch who'd been there since evolution began, a shop called Lynch's and a pub called Whelan's, and a handful of caravan spaces, just a fast barefoot run over slipping sand dunes and between tufts of marram grass to the cream-coloured sweep of beach. We got two weeks there every June, in a rusty four-bunker that my dad booked a year in advance. Geri and I got the top bunks; Dina got stuck on the bottom, opposite my parents. Geri got first pick because she was the oldest, but she always wanted the land-facing side so she could see the ponies in the field behind us. That meant I got to open my eyes every morning on white lines of sea-foam and leggy birds dashing along the sand, all of it glinting in the early light.

The three of us were up and out at daybreak with a slice of bread and sugar in each hand. We had all-day games of pirates with the kids from the other caravans, went freckly and peeling from salt and windburn and the odd hour of sunshine. For tea my mother would fry up eggs and sausages on a camping stove, and afterwards my father would send us to Lynch's for ice creams. We'd come back to find my mum sitting on his lap, leaning her head into the curve of his neck and smiling dreamily out at the water; he'd wind her hair around his free hand, so the sea breeze wouldn't whip it into her ice cream. I waited all year to see them look like that.

Once I got the Beemer off the main roads I started remembering the route, like I had known I would, just a faded sketch at the back of my head: past this clump of trees – taller, now – left at that kink in the stone wall. Right where the water should have risen into view over a low green hill, though, the estate came charging up out of nowhere and blocked our way like a barricade: rows of slate roofs and white gables stretching for what looked like miles in either direction, behind a high breezeblock wall. The signboard at the entrance said, in flamboyant curly lettering the size of my head, WELCOME TO OCEAN VIEW, BRIANSTOWN. A NEW REVELATION IN PREMIER LIVING. LUXURY HOUSES NOW VIEWING. Someone had spray-painted a big red cock and balls over it.

At first glance, Ocean View looked pretty tasty: big detached houses that gave you something substantial for your money, trim strips of green, quaint signposts pointing you towards LITTLE GEMS CHILDCARE and DIAMONDCUT LEISURE CENTRE. Second glance, the grass needed weeding and there were gaps in the footpaths. Third glance, something was wrong.

The houses were too much alike. Even on the ones where a triumphant red-and-blue sign yelled SOLD, no one had painted the front door a crap colour, put flowerpots on the windowsills or tossed plastic kiddie toys on the lawn. There was a scattering of parked cars, but most of the driveways were empty, and not in a way that said everyone was out powering the economy. You could look straight through three out of four houses, to bare rear windows and grey patches of sky. A heavyset girl in a red anorak was shoving a buggy along a footpath, wind grabbing at her hair. She and her moon-faced kid could have been the only people within miles.

'Jaysus,' Richie said; in the silence his voice was loud enough that both of us jumped. 'The village of the damned.'

The call sheet said 9 Ocean View Rise, which would have made more sense if the Irish Sea had been an ocean or even if it had been visible, but I guess you make the most of whatever you've got. The satnav was getting out of its depth: it took us down Ocean View Drive, dead-ended us down Ocean View Grove – which hit the trifecta by having no trees anywhere in sight – and informed us, 'You have reached your destination. Goodbye.'

I did a U-turn and went looking. As we got deeper into the estate, the houses got sketchier, like watching a film in reverse. Pretty soon they were random collections of walls and scaffolding, with the odd gaping hole for a window; where the house-fronts were missing the rooms were littered with broken ladders, lengths of pipe, rotting cement bags. Every time we turned a corner I expected to see a swarm of builders at work, but the nearest we got was a battered yellow digger in a vacant lot, listing sideways among churned-up mud and scattered mounds of dirt.

No one lived here. I tried to aim us back in the general direction of the entrance, but the estate was built like one of those old hedge-mazes, all cul-de-sacs and hairpin turns, and almost straightaway we were lost. A tiny dart of panic shot through me. I've never liked losing my bearings.

I pulled up at an intersection – reflex: it wasn't like anyone was going to dash out in front of me – and in the quiet where the noise of the motor had been, we heard the deep boom of the sea. Then Richie's head went up. He said, 'What's that?'

It was a short, raw, ripped-open shriek, repeating over and over, so regular it sounded mechanical. It spread out across mud and concrete and bounced off unfinished walls till it could have come from anywhere, or everywhere. As far as I could tell, that and the sea were the only sounds on the estate.

I said, 'I'm going to bet that's the sister.'

He gave me a look like he thought I was yanking his chain. 'That's a *fox* or something. Run over, maybe.'

'And here I thought you were Mr Streetwise who knew just how bad this was going to be. You're going to need to brace your-self, Richie. Big-time.'

I rolled down a window and followed the sound. The echoes led me off-course a few times, but we knew it when we saw it. One side of Ocean View Rise was pristine, bay-windowed white semi-ds lined up in pairs, neat as dominoes; the other side was scaffolding and rubble. Between the dominoes, over the estate wall, slivers of grey sea moved. A couple of the houses had a car or two in front of them, but one house had three: a white Volvo hatchback that had Family written all over it, a yellow Fiat Seicento that had seen better days, and a marked car. There was blue-and-white crime-scene tape along the low garden wall.

I meant what I said to Richie: in this job everything matters, down to the way you open your car door. Long before I say Word One to a witness, or a suspect, he needs to know that Mick Kennedy is in the house and that I've got this case by the balls. Some of it is luck – I've got height, I've got a full head of hair and it's still ninety-nine per cent dark brown, I've got decent looks if I say so myself, and all those things help – but I've put practice and treadmill time into the rest. I kept up my speed till the last second, braked hard, swung myself and my briefcase out of the car in one smooth move and headed for the house at a swift, efficient pace. Richie would learn to keep up.

One of the uniforms was squatting awkwardly by his car, patting at someone in the back seat who was pretty clearly the source of the screaming. The other one was pacing in front of the gate, too fast, with his hands clasped behind his back. The air smelled fresh, sweet and salty: sea and fields. It was colder out there than it had been in Dublin. Wind whistled half-heartedly through scaffolding and exposed beams.

The guy who was pacing was my age, with a paunch and a sandbagged look: he had obviously made it through twenty years on the force without seeing anything like this, and had been hoping to make it through twenty more. He said, 'Garda Wall. That's Garda Mallon, by the car.'

Richie was sticking out a hand. It was like having a puppy. I said, before he could start buddying up, 'Detective Sergeant Kennedy and Detective Garda Curran. You've been in the house?'

'Only when we got here first. As soon as we could, we got out and rang ye.'

'Good call. Tell me exactly what you did, entrance to exit.'

The uniform's eyes went to the house, like he could hardly believe it was the same place he had arrived at only a couple of hours earlier. He said, 'We were called in for a welfare check – the occupant's sister was worried. We reached the premises just after eleven o'clock and attempted to make contact with the residents by ringing the doorbell and by phone, but got no response. We saw no signs of forced entry, but when we looked in the front window, the lights on the ground floor were on and the sitting room appeared to be in some disorder. The walls—'

'We'll see the disorder for ourselves in a minute. Carry on.' Never let anyone describe the details before you get on the scene, or you'll see what they saw.

'Right.' The uniform blinked, pulled himself back on track. 'Anyhow. We attempted to go around to the back of the house, but you can see for yourselves, sure – a child couldn't get through there.' He was right: the gap between the houses was just wide enough for the side wall. 'We felt that the disorder and the sister's concerns warranted forcing entry through the front door. We found . . .'

He was shifting on his feet, trying to angle the conversation so that he could see the house, like it was a coiled animal that might pounce at any second. 'We entered the sitting room, found nothing to speak of – the disorder, but . . . We then proceeded to the kitchen, where we found a male and a female on the floor. Both stabbed, by the looks of it. One wound, on the female's face, was clearly visible to myself and Garda Mallon. It appeared to be a knife wound. It—'

'The doctors'll decide that. What did you do next?'

'We thought they were both dead. We were certain. There's a load of blood. Loads of . . .' He gestured vaguely towards his own body, a shapeless pecking movement. There's a reason why some guys stay in uniform. 'Garda Mallon checked their pulses all the same, just in case. The female, she was right up against the male, like curled up against him – she had her head, her head was on his arm, like she was asleep . . . When Garda Mallon checked, she had a pulse. He got the shock of his life. We never expected . . . He couldn't believe it, not till he put down his head and heard her breathing. Then we called for the ambulance.'

'And while you waited?'

'Garda Mallon stayed with the woman. Talked to her. She was unconscious, but . . . just telling her it was all right, we were the Guards, there was an ambulance coming and for her to hang on . . . I went upstairs. In the back bedrooms . . . There's two little children there, Detective. A young boy and a young girl, in their beds. I tried CPR. They're – they were cold, stiff, but I tried anyway. After what had happened with the mother, I thought, you never know, maybe they could still . . .' He rubbed his hands down the front of his jacket, unconsciously, like he was trying to wipe away the feel. I didn't give him a bollocking for wrecking evidence: he had only done what came naturally. 'No joy. Once I knew for definite, I rejoined Garda Mallon in the kitchen and we called for ye and the rest.'

I asked, 'Did the woman come to? Say anything?'

He shook his head. 'She didn't move. We kept thinking she was after dying on us, had to keep checking to make sure she was still . . .' He wiped his hands again.

'Do we have anyone at the hospital with her?'

'We called in to the station, had them send someone. Maybe one of us should have gone with her, but with the scene to be secured, and the sister – she was . . . Sure, you can hear.'

'You broke the news,' I said. I do the notification myself, any time I can. You can tell a lot from that first reaction.

The uniform said defensively, 'We told her to stay put, before we went in, but we'd no one to stay with her. She waited a good while, but then she came in. Into the house. We were with the victim, we were waiting for ye; the sister was at the kitchen door before we saw her. She started screaming. I got her outside again, but she was fighting . . . I had to tell her, Detective. It was the only way I could stop her trying to get back in, short of handcuffing her.'

'Right. We won't cry over spilt milk. What next?'

'I stayed outside with the sister. Garda Mallon waited with the victim until the ambulance arrived. Then he left the house.'

'Without doing a search?'

'I went back in, once he came out to stay with the sister. Garda Mallon, sir, he's all over blood; he didn't want to track it around the house. I performed a basic security search, just to confirm that there was no one on the premises. No one alive, like. We left the in-depth search for ye and the Bureau.'

'That's what I like to hear.' I flicked an eyebrow at Richie. The kid was paying attention: he asked, promptly, 'Did you find a weapon?'

The uniform shook his head. 'But it could be in there. Under the man's body, or . . . anywhere. Like I said, we tried not to disturb the scene any more than we had to.'

'How about a note?'

Another head-shake.

I nodded towards the marked car. 'How's the sister been doing?'

'We've been getting her calmed down a bit, off and on, but every time . . .' The uniform threw a harassed look over his shoulder at the car. 'The paramedics wanted to give her a sedative, but she wouldn't take it. We can get them back, if—'

'Keep trying. I don't want her sedated if we can help it, not till we've talked to her. We're going to take a look around the scene. The rest of the team are on their way: if the pathologist arrives, you can have him wait here, but make sure the morgue boys and the Tech Bureau keep their distance till we've had a go at the sister – one look at them and she'll flip out for real. Apart from that, keep her where she is, keep the neighbours where they are, and if anyone happens to wander up, keep him where he is too. Clear?'

'Grand,' said the uniform. He would have done the chicken dance if I'd told him to, he was so relieved that someone was taking this thing off his hands. I could see him itching to get down to his local and throw back a double whiskey in one gulp.

I didn't want to be anywhere except inside that house. 'Gloves,' I said to Richie. 'Shoe covers.' I was already flipping mine out of my pocket. He fumbled for his, and we started up the drive. The long boom and shush of the sea rushed up and met us head-on, like a welcome or a challenge. Behind us, those shrieks were still coming down like hammer-blows.

# 2

We don't get crime scenes to ourselves. They're off limits, even to us, till the Bureau techs give the all-clear. Until then, there are always other things that need doing – witnesses who need inter-viewing, survivors who need notifying – and you do those, check your watch every thirty seconds and force yourself to ignore the fierce pull from behind that crime-scene tape. This one was differ-ent. The uniforms and the paramedics had already trampled over every inch of the Spains' house; Richie and I weren't going to make anything worse by taking a quick look.

It was convenient – if Richie couldn't hack the bad stuff, it would be nice to find out without an audience – but it was more than that. When you get a chance to see a scene that way, you take it. What waits for you there is the crime itself, every screaming second of it, trapped and held for you in amber. It doesn't matter if someone's cleaned up, hidden evidence, tried to fake a suicide: the amber holds all that too. Once the processing starts, that's gone for good; all that's left is your own people swarming over the scene, busily dismantling it print by print and fibre by fibre. This chance felt like a gift, on this case where I needed it most; like a good omen. I set my phone on silent. Plenty of people were going to want to get hold of me, over the next while. All of them could wait till I had walked my scene.

The door of the house was a few inches open, swaying gently when the breeze caught it. When it was in one piece it had looked like solid oak, but where the uniforms had splintered it away from the lock you could see the powdery reconstituted crap under-neath. It had probably taken them one shove. Through the crack: a geometric black-and-white rug, high-trend with a high price tag to match.

I said to Richie, 'This is just a preliminary walk-through. The serious stuff can wait till the Bureau lads have the scene on record. For now, we don't touch anything, we try not to stand on anything, we try not to breathe on anything, we get a basic sense of what we're dealing with and we get out. Ready?'

He nodded. I pushed the door open with one fingertip on the splintered edge.

My first thought was that if this was what Garda Whatever called disorder, he had OCD issues. The hallway was dim and perfect: sparkling mirror, organised coat-rack, smell of lemon room freshener. The walls were clean. On one of them was a watercolour, something green and peaceful with cows.

My second thought: the Spains had had an alarm system. The panel was a fancy modern one, discreetly tucked away behind the door. The OFF light was a steady yellow.

Then I saw the hole in the wall. Someone had moved the phone table in front of it, but it was big enough that a jagged half-moon still poked out. That was when I felt it: that needle-fine vibration, starting in my temples and moving down the bones into my eardrums. Some detectives feel it in the backs of their necks, some get it in the hair on their arms – I know one poor sap who gets it in the bladder, which can be inconvenient – but all the good ones feel it somewhere. It gets me in the skull bones. Call it what you want – social deviance, psychological disturbance, the animal within, evil if you believe in that: it's the thing we spend our lives chasing. All the training in the world won't give you that warning when it comes close. You get it or you don't.

I took a quick look at Richie: grimacing and licking his lips, like an animal that's tasted something putrid. He got it in his mouth, which he would need to learn to hide, but at least he got it.

Off to our left was a half-open door: sitting room. Straight ahead, the stairs and the kitchen.

Someone had put time into doing up the sitting room. Brown leather sofas, sleek chrome-and-glass coffee table, one wall painted butter-yellow for one of those reasons that only women and interior designers understand. For the lived-in look, there was a good big telly, a Wii, a scattering of glossy gadgets, a little shelf for paperbacks and another one for DVDs and games, candles and blond photos on the mantelpiece of the gas fire. It should have felt welcoming, but damp had buckled the flooring and blotched a wall, and the low ceiling and the just-wrong proportions were stubborn. They outweighed all that loving care and turned the room cramped and dim, a place where no one could feel comfortable for long.

Curtains almost drawn, just the crack that the uniforms had looked through. Standing lamps on. Whatever had happened, it had happened at night, or someone wanted me to think it had.

Above the gas fire was another hole in the wall, about the size of a dinner plate. There was a bigger one by the sofa. Pipes and straggling wires half-showed from the dark inside.

Beside me Richie was trying to keep the fidgeting down to a minimum, but I could feel one knee jiggling. He wanted the bad moments over and done with. I said, 'Kitchen.'

It was hard to believe that the same guy who had designed the sitting room had come up with this. It was a kitchen-cum-dining-room-cum-playroom, running the whole length of the back of the house, and it was mostly made of glass. Outside the day was still grey, but the light in that room was full and dazzling enough to make you blink, with a lift and a clarity that told you the sea was very near. I've never been able to see why it's supposed to be a plus if your neighbours can check out what you're having for breakfast – give me net-curtain privacy any day, trendy or not – but that light almost made me understand.

Behind the trim little garden there were two more rows of half-built houses, crowding stark and ugly against the sky, a long banner of plastic flapping hard from a bare beam. Behind them was the estate wall, and then as the land fell away there it was, through the raw angles of wood and concrete: the view my eyes had been waiting for all day long, ever since I heard myself say *Broken Harbour*. The rounded curve of the bay, neat as the C of your hand; the low hills cupping it at each end; the soft grey sand, the marram grass bending away from the clean wind, the little birds scattered along the waterline. And the sea, high today, raising itself up at me green and muscled. The weight of what was in the kitchen with us tilted the world, sent the water rocking upwards like it was going to come crashing through all that bright glass.

That same care that had trendified the sitting room had gone into making this room cheerful and homey. Long table in pale wood, sunflower-yellow chairs; a computer on a wooden desk painted yellow to match; coloured plastic kid stuff, beanbags, a chalkboard. There were crayon drawings framed on the walls. The room was neat, especially for a place where kids played. Someone had tidied up, as the four of them moved onto the furthest edge of their last day. They had made it that far.

The room was an estate agent's dream, except that it was impossible to imagine anyone living there, ever again. Some frantic struggle had thrown the table over, slamming one corner into a window and cracking a great star across the glass. More holes in the walls: one high above the table, a big one behind an overturned Lego castle. A beanbag had burst open and spilled tiny white pellets everywhere; a trail of cookbooks fanned out across the floor, shards of glass glinted where a picture frame had smashed. The blood was everywhere: fans of spatter flying up the walls, crazy trails of drips and footprints crisscrossing the tile floor, wide smears on the windows, thick clumps soaked into the yellow fabric of the chairs. A few inches from my feet was one ripped half of a height chart, big beanstalk leaves and a climbing cartoon kid, *Emma 17/06/09* almost obliterated by clotting red.

Patrick Spain was at the far end of the room, in what had been the kids' play area, among the beanbags and crayons and picture books. He was in his pyjamas – navy top, navy-and-white-striped bottoms splotched with dark crusts. He was face down on the floor, one arm bent under him, the other stretched out over his head, like right up until the last second he had been trying to crawl. His head was towards us: trying to reach his kids, maybe, for whichever reason you choose. He had been fair-haired, a tall guy with broad shoulders; the build said maybe rugby, way back when, going to seed now. You would have wanted to be pretty strong, pretty angry or pretty crazy to take him on. Blood had turned sticky and dark in a puddle spreading from under his chest. It was smeared all around with a godawful tangle of swipes, hand-prints, drag-marks; a snarl of mixed footprints came out of the mess and headed towards us, fading to nothing halfway across the tiles, like the bloodstained walkers had dissolved into thin air.

To his left the pool of blood spread wider, thicker, with a rich gloss to it. We would have to double-check with the uniforms, but it was a pretty safe bet that that was where they had found Jennifer Spain. Either she had dragged herself over to die curled up against her husband, or he had stayed close after he was done with her, or someone had let them do this last thing together.

I stayed in the doorway longer than I needed to. It takes a while to wrap your head around a scene like that, the first time. Your inner world snaps itself away from the outside one, for protection: your eyes are wide open, but all that reaches your mind is streaks of red and an error message. No one was watching us; Richie could take all the time he needed. I kept my eyes off him.

A gust of wind crashed into the back of the house and kept coming straight through some crack, flooded around us like cold water. '*Jaysus*,' Richie said. The gust had made him jump, and he was a shade paler than usual, but his voice was steady enough. He was doing fine, so far. 'Feel that. What's this gaff made of? Jacks roll?'

'Don't knock it. The thinner the walls, the more likely the neighbours heard something.'

'If there's neighbours.'

'We'll keep our fingers crossed. Ready to move on?'

He nodded. We left Patrick Spain in his bright kitchen, with the thin streams of wind swirling around him, and went upstairs.

The top floor was dark. I flipped open my briefcase and found my torch – the uniforms had probably smeared their fat paws all over everything, but still, you never touch light switches: someone else could have wanted that light on or off. I turned on the torch and nudged the nearest door open with a toe.

The message had got garbled somewhere along the way,

because no one had stabbed Jack Spain. After the congealing red mess downstairs, this room was almost restful. Nothing was bloody; nothing had been broken or wrenched over. Jack Spain had a snub nose and blond hair, left to grow into curls. He was on his back, arms thrown up above his head, face turned to the ceiling, like he had collapsed asleep after a long day of football. You would almost have listened to hear him breathing, except something in his face told you. He had the secret calm that only dead children have, paper-thin eyelids sealed tight as unborn babies', as if when the world goes killer they turn inwards and backwards, back to that first safe place.

Richie made a small noise like a cat with a hairball. I trailed the torch around the room, to give him time to pull it together. There were a couple of cracks in the walls, but no holes, unless they were hidden by the posters – Jack had been into Manchester United. 'Got kids?' I asked.

'No. Not yet.'

He was keeping his voice down, like he could still wake Jack Spain, or give him bad dreams. I said, 'Neither do I. Days like this, that's a good thing. Kids make you soft. You get a detective who's tough as nails, can watch a post-mortem and order a rare steak for lunch; then his wife pops out a sprog and next thing you know he's losing the plot if a victim's under eighteen. I've seen it a dozen times. Every time, I thank God for contraception.'

I turned the torch back to the bed. My sister Geri has kids, and I spend enough time with them that I could take a rough guess at Jack Spain's age: around four, maybe three if he had been on the big side. The duvet was pulled back where the uniform had tried his useless CPR: red pyjamas twisted up, delicate rib cage underneath. I could even see the dent where the CPR, or I hoped it was the CPR, had snapped a rib or two.

There was blue around his lips. Richie said, 'Suffocated?'

He was working hard at keeping his voice under control. I said, 'We'll have to wait for the post-mortem, but it looks possible. If that's what we've got, it points towards the parents. A lot of the time they go for something gentle. If that's the word I'm looking for.'

I still wasn't looking at him, but I felt him tighten to hold back a wince. I said, 'Let's go find the daughter.'

No holes in the walls here either, no struggle. The uniform had pulled Emma Spain's pink duvet back up over her, when he gave up – preserving her modesty, because she was a girl. She had the same snub nose as her brother, but her curls were a sandy ginger and she had a faceful of freckles, standing out against the blue-white underneath. She was the older one, six, seven: her mouth was a touch open, and I could see the gap where a front tooth was gone. The room was princess-pink, full of frills and flounces; the bed was heaped with embroidered pillows, huge-eyed kittens and puppies staring up at us. Springing out of darkness in the torchlight, next to that small empty face, they looked like scavengers.

I didn't look at Richie till we were back out on the landing. Then I asked, 'Notice anything odd about both rooms?'

Even in that light he looked like he had a bad case of food poisoning. He had to swallow extra spit twice before he could say, 'No blood.'

'Bingo.' I nudged the bathroom door open with my torch. Colour-coordinated towels, plastic bath toys, the usual shampoos and shower gels, sparkling white fixtures. If someone had washed up in here, they had known how to be careful. 'We'll get the Bureau to hit this floor with luminol, check for traces, but unless we're missing something, either there was more than one killer or he went after the kids first. No one came from that mess' – I nodded downwards at the kitchen – 'and touched anything up here.'

Richie said, 'It's looking like an inside job, isn't it?'

'How's that?'

'If I'm some psycho that wants to wipe out a whole family, I'm not going to start with the kids. What if one of the parents hears something, comes in to check on them while I'm in the middle of doing the job? Next thing I know, I've got the ma and the da both beating the shite out of me. Nah: I'm going to wait till everyone's well asleep, and then I'm going to start by taking out the biggest threats. The only reason I'd start here' – his mouth twitched, but he kept it together – 'is if I know I'm not gonna get interrupted. That means one of the parents.'

I said, 'Right. It's far from definitive, but on first glance, that's how it looks. Did you notice the other thing pointing the same way?'

He shook his head. I said, 'The front door. It's got two locks, a Chubb and a Yale, and before the uniforms forced entry, both of them were on. That door wasn't just pulled closed as someone left; it was locked with a key. And I haven't seen any windows open or broken. So if someone got in from outside, or the Spains let someone in, how did he get back out? Again, it's not definitive – one of the windows could be unlocked, the keys could have been taken, a friend or associate could have a set; we'll have to check out all of those. But it's indicative. On the other hand . . .' I pointed with the torch: another hole, maybe the size of a paperback book, low over the skirting board on the landing. 'How would your walls end up with this kind of damage?'

'A fight. After the . . .' Richie rubbed at his mouth again. 'After the kids, or they'd have woken up. Looks to me like someone put up a good old struggle.'

'Someone probably did, but that's not what wrecked the walls. Get your head clear and look again. That damage wasn't done last night. Want to tell me why?'

Slowly, the green look started to get replaced by that concentration I had seen in the car. After a moment Richie said, 'No blood around the holes. And no bits of plaster underneath. No dust, even. Someone's tidied up.'

'Right you are. It's possible that the killer or killers stuck around to give the place a good hoover, for reasons of his own; but unless we find something to say that happened, the most likely explanation is that the holes were made at least a couple of days ago, could be a lot more. Got any ideas on where they might have come from?'

He looked better now that he was working. 'Structural problems? Damp, subsidence, maybe someone working on faulty wiring . . . There's damp in the sitting room – did you see the floorboards, yeah, and the patch on the wall? – and there's cracks all over the place; wouldn't be surprised if the wiring's banjaxed too. The whole estate's a tip.'

'Maybe. We'll get a building inspector to come down and take a look. But let's be honest, it'd take a pretty crap electrician to leave the place in this state. Any other explanations you can think of?'

Richie sucked on his teeth and gave the hole a long thoughtful stare. 'If I was just going off the top of my head,' he said, 'I'd say someone was looking for something.'

'So would I. That could mean guns or valuables, but usually it's the old reliables: drugs or cash. We'll have the Bureau check for drug residue.'

'But,' Richie said. He jerked his chin at the door of Emma's room. 'The kids. The parents were holding something that could get them killed? With the *kids* in the house?'

'I thought the Spains were top of your suspect list.'

'That's different. People snap, do mad things. That can happen to anyone. A K of smack behind the wallpaper, where your kids could find it: that doesn't just happen.'

There was a creak below us and we both spun around, but it was just the front door swaying in a snatch of wind. I said, 'Come on, old son. I've seen it a hundred times. I'm betting you have too.'

'Not with people like this.'

I raised my eyebrows. 'I wouldn't have taken you for a snob.'

'Nah, I'm not talking about class. I mean these people *tried*. Look at the place: everything's right, know what I mean? It's all clean; even down behind the jacks is clean. All the stuff matches. Even the spices in the rack, they're in date, all the ones where I could see the best-by. This family tried to get everything *right*. Messing about with the dodgy stuff . . . It just doesn't seem like their style.'

I said, 'It doesn't seem like it right now, no. But keep in mind, right now we know bugger-all about these people. They kept their house in good nick, at least occasionally, and they got killed. I'm telling you the second one means a lot more than the first. Anyone can hoover. Not everyone gets murdered.'

Richie, bless his innocent heart, was giving me a look that was pure scepticism with a touch of moral outrage thrown in. 'Loads of murder victims never did anything dangerous in their lives.'

'Some didn't, no. But loads? Here's the dirty secret about your new job, Richie my friend. Here's the part you never saw in interviews or documentaries, because we keep it to ourselves. Most victims went looking for exactly what they got.'

His mouth started to open. I said, 'Obviously not kids. The kids aren't what we're discussing here. But adults . . . If you try to sell smack on some other scumbag's turf, or if you go ahead and marry Prince Charming after he puts you in the ICU four times running, or if you stab some guy because his brother stabbed your friend for stabbing his cousin, then forgive me if this is politically incorrect, but you're just begging for exactly what you're eventually going to get. I know this isn't what we get taught on the detective course, but out here in the real world, my man, you would be amazed at how seldom murder has to break into people's lives. Ninety-nine times out of a hundred, it gets there because they open the door and invite it in.'

Richie shifted his feet – the draught was sweeping up the stairs to eddy round our ankles, rattle the handle of Emma's door. He said, 'I'm not seeing how anyone could ask for this.'

'Neither am I, at least not yet. But if the Spains were living like the Waltons, then who bashed their walls in? And why didn't they just call someone and get the place fixed – unless they didn't want anyone knowing what they were involved with? Or what one of them was involved with, at least.'

He shrugged. I said, 'You're right: this could be the one in a hundred. We'll keep an open mind. And if it is, that's just another reason why we can't get it wrong.'

Patrick and Jennifer Spain's room was picture-perfect, just like the rest of the house. It had been done up in flowery pink and cream and gold to look olde-fashionede. No blood, no signs of struggle, not a speck of dust anywhere. One small hole, where the wall met the ceiling above the bed.

Two things stuck out. First thing: the duvet and sheets were rumpled and thrown back, like someone had just jumped up. The rest of the house said that bed didn't get left unmade for long. At least one of them had been all tucked up, when it began.

Second thing: the bedside tables. Each of them had a little lamp with a tasselly cream shade; both the lamps were off. On the far table were a couple of girly-looking jars, face cream or whatever, a pink mobile phone and a book with a pink cover and kooky lettering. The near one was crammed with gadgets: what looked like two white walkie-talkies and two silver mobiles, all standing docked on chargers, and three empty chargers, all silver. I wasn't sure where the walkie-talkies came in, but the only people who have five mobiles are high-flying stockbrokers and drug dealers, and this didn't look like a stockbroker's pad to me. For a second there, I thought things were starting to come together.

Then: 'Jaysus,' Richie said, eyebrows going up. 'They went a bit over the top, didn't they?'

'How's that?'

'The baby monitors.' He nodded at Patrick's bedside table.

'That's what those are?'

'Yeah. My sister's got kids. Those white ones, that's the bit you listen to. The ones that look like phones, those are video. Watch the kid sleep.'

'*Big Brother*-style.' I moved the torch beam over the gadgets: white ones on, screens faintly backlit; silver ones off. 'How many do people normally have? One per kid?'

'Dunno about most people. My sister's got three kids and just the one monitor. It's in the baby's room, for when he's asleep. When the girls were small she just had the audio, like those' – the walkie-talkies – 'but the little fella was premature, so she got the video, keep an eye on him.'

'So the Spains were on the overprotective side. A monitor in every room.' Where I should have spotted them. It was one thing for Richie to get distracted by the big stuff and miss the details, but I was no virgin.

Richie shook his head. 'Why, but? They were big enough to

come get their ma if they needed her. And it's not like this is a massive huge mansion: if they hurt themselves, you'd hear them yelling.'

I said, 'Would you know the other halves of those things if you saw them?'

'Probably.'

'Good. Then let's go find them.'

On Emma's pink chest of drawers was a round white thing like a clock-radio, which according to Richie was an audio monitor: 'She's a little old for it, but the parents could've been heavy sleepers, wanted to be sure they'd hear her if she called . . .' The other audio monitor was on Jack's chest of drawers. No sign of the video cameras; not until we got back out onto the landing again. I said, 'We'll want the Bureau to check the attic, in case whoever was looking for—' and then I swung the torch beam up to the ceiling and stopped talking.

The hatch for the attic was there, all right. It was open onto blackness – the light caught the cover, propped up against something, and a flash of exposed roof-beam high above. Someone had nailed wire mesh over the opening, from below, without worrying too much about aesthetics: ragged edges of wire, big nailheads sticking out at violent angles. In the opposite corner of the landing, high on the wall, was something silver and badly mounted that I didn't need Richie to tell me was a video monitor. The camera was pointing straight at the hatch.

I said, 'What the holy hell?'

'Rats? The holes—'

'You don't set up bloody *surveillance* on rats. You keep the hatch down and call the exterminators.'

'Then what?'

'I don't know. A trap, maybe, in case whoever bashed in the walls came back looking for Round Two. The Bureau are going to want to be careful up there.' I held the torch high and moved it around, trying to get a glimpse of what was in the attic. Cardboard boxes, a dusty black suitcase. 'Let's see if the rest of the cameras give us any hints.'

The second camera was in the sitting room, on a little chrome-and-glass table beside the sofa. It was aimed at the hole over the fireplace, and a little red light said it was switched on. The third one had rolled into a corner of the kitchen, where it was surrounded by beanbag pellets and pointing at the floor, but it was still plugged in: it had been up and running. There was a viewer half-under the cooker – I had clocked it the first time round, taken it for a phone – and another under the kitchen table. No sign of the last one, or of the other two cameras.

I said, 'We'll give the Bureau a heads-up, have them keep an eye out. Anything you want another look at, before we bring them in?'

Richie looked unsure. I said, 'It's not a trick question, old son.'

'Oh. Right. Then no: I'm grand.'

'So am I. Let's go.'

Another gust of wind grabbed the house, and this time both of us jumped. I would have done a lot of things sooner than let young Richie see this, but the place was starting to get to me. It wasn't the kids, or the blood – like I said, I can handle both of those, no problem. Something about the holes in the wall, maybe, or the unblinking cameras; or about all that glass, all those skeleton houses staring in at us, like famine animals circled around the warmth of a fire. I reminded myself that I had dealt with worse scenes and never broken a sweat, but that shimmer moving through my skull bones said: *This is different.*

# 3

Unromantic little secret: half of being a Murder D is managerial skills. Trainees picture the lone wolf heading off into the wild after shadowy hunches, but in practice, guys who don't play well with others wind up in Undercover. Even a small investigation – and this wasn't going to be small – involves floaters, media liaisons, the Tech Bureau and the pathologist and the world and his auntie, and you need to make sure that at any given second all of them are keeping you up to speed, no one's getting in anyone's way and everyone is working to your big plan, because the buck stops with you. That slow-motion silence inside the amber was over: the second we stepped out of the house, before we even stopped walking quietly, it was time to start people-wrangling.

Cooper, the pathologist, was outside the gate, tapping his fingers on his case and not looking happy. Not that he would have anyway: at his best Cooper is a negative little bastard, and he's not at his best around me. I've never done anything to him, but for some reason all his own he doesn't like me, and when an arrogant bollix like Cooper doesn't like you, he does it right. One typo on a request form and he sends it back and makes me start over, and forget putting a rush on anything: my stuff waits its turn, urgent or not. 'Detective Kennedy,' he said, flaring his nostrils like I smelled. 'May I ask whether I resemble a waiter?'

'Not at all. Dr Cooper, this is Detective Curran, my partner.'

He ignored Richie. 'I am relieved to hear it. In that case, why am I waiting?'

He must have spent the delay coming up with that one. 'I apologise,' I said. 'There must have been some misunderstanding. Obviously I'd never waste your time. We'll leave you to it.'

Cooper gave me a withering look that said he wasn't falling for it. 'We can only hope,' he said, 'that you have managed not to contaminate the scene too extensively,' and he brushed past me, tugging his gloves more firmly into place, into the house.

No sign of my floaters yet. One of the uniforms was still hovering around the car and the sister. The other one was at the top of the road, talking to a handful of guys between two white vans: Tech Bureau, morgue. I said to Richie, 'What do we do now?'

As soon as we got outside he had started jiggling again: whipping his head back and forth to check out the road, the sky, the other houses, drumming a little two-fingered tattoo on his thighs. The question stopped him. 'Send the Bureau in?'

'Sure, but what are you planning on doing while they work? If we hang around asking "Are we there yet?" we'll just be wasting their time and ours.'

Richie nodded. 'If it was up to me, I'd talk to the sister.'

'You don't want to go see if Jenny Spain can tell us anything?'

'I figured it's gonna be a while before she can talk to us. Even if . . .'

'Even if she makes it. You're probably right, but we can't take that for granted. We need to keep on top of it.'

I was already dialling my phone. The reception felt like we were in Outer Mongolia – we had to head down to the bottom of the road, clear of the houses, so I could get a signal – and it took a bunch of complicated back-and-forth calls before I got hold of the doctor who had admitted Jennifer Spain and got him convinced I wasn't a reporter. He sounded young and viciously tired. 'She's still alive, anyway, but I can't promise anything. She's in surgery now. If she makes it through that, we'll have a better idea.'

I hit speakerphone so Richie could get this. 'Can you give me a description of her injuries?'

'I only examined her briefly. I can't be sure—'

The sea wind whipped his voice away; Richie and I had to bend close over the phone. I said, 'I'm just looking for a preliminary overview. Our own doctor will be examining her later, one way or the other. For now, all I need is a general idea of whether she was shot, strangled, drowned, you tell me.'

Sigh. 'You understand this is provisional. I could be wrong.'

'Understood.'

'OK. Basically, she was lucky to make it this far. She has four abdominal injuries that look like knife wounds to me, but that's for your doctor to decide. Two of them are deep, but they must have missed all the major organs and arteries, or she'd have bled out before she got here. There's another injury to her right cheek, looks like a knife slash, straight through into the mouth – if she makes it, she'll need considerable amounts of plastic surgery. There's also some kind of blunt trauma to the back of the skull. X-ray showed a hairline fracture and a subdural haematoma, but judging by her reflexes there's a decent chance she's escaped without brain damage. Again, she was very lucky.'

Which was probably the last time anyone would ever use that word about Jennifer Spain. 'Anything else?'

I could hear him swigging something, probably coffee, and swallowing a huge yawn. 'Sorry. There could be minor injuries – I wasn't looking for anything like that, my priority was getting her into surgery before we lost her, and the blood could have covered some cuts and contusions. There's nothing else major, though.'

'Any signs of sexual assault?'

'Like I said, that wasn't top priority. For what it's worth, I didn't see anything that would point that way.'

'What was she wearing?'

An instant of silence, while he wondered whether he had got it wrong and I was some specialised kind of pervert. 'Yellow pyjamas. Nothing else.'

'There should be an officer at the hospital. I'd like you to put her pyjamas in a paper bag and hand them over to him. Make a note of anyone who touched them, if you can.' I had chalked up two more points for Jennifer Spain being a victim. Women don't wreck their faces, and they sure as hell don't go in their pyjamas. They put on their best dresses, take time over their mascara and pick a method that they believe – and they're almost always wrong – will leave them quiet and graceful, all the pain washed away and nothing left but cool pale peace. Somewhere in what's left of their crumbling minds, they think that being found looking less than their best will upset them. Most suicides don't really believe that death is all the way. Maybe none of us do.

'We gave him the pyjamas. I'll make the list as soon as I get a chance.'

'Did she recover consciousness at any stage?'

'No. Like I said, there's a fair chance she never will. We'll know more after the surgery.'

'If she makes it, when do you think we'd be able to talk to her?'

Sigh. 'Your guess is as good as mine. With head wounds, nothing's predictable.'

'Thanks, Doctor. Can you let me know straightaway if anything changes?'

'I'll do my best. If you'll excuse me, I have to—'

And he was gone. I put in a quick call to Bernadette, the squad admin, to let her know that I needed someone to get started on pulling the Spains' financials and phone records, and put a rush on it. I was hanging up when my phone buzzed: three new voice messages, from calls that hadn't got through the shitty reception. O'Kelly, letting me know he had wangled me a couple of extra floaters; a journalist contact, begging for a scoop he wasn't going to get this time; and Geri. Only patches of the voicemail came through: '. . . can't, Mick . . . sick every five minutes . . . can't leave the house, even for . . . everything OK? Give me a ring when . . .'

'*Shit*,' I said, before I could bite it back. Dina works in town, in a deli. I tried to calculate how many hours it would be before I got anywhere near town again, and what the odds were of her making it that long without someone switching on a radio.

Richie cocked his head, questioning. 'Nothing,' I said. There was no point in ringing Dina – she hates phones – and there was no one else to ring. I took a fast breath and tamped it down at the back of my mind. 'Let's go. We've kept the Bureau boys waiting long enough.'

Richie nodded. I put my phone away, and we headed up to the top of the road to talk to the men in white.

The Super had come through for me: he had got the Tech Bureau to send out Larry Boyle, with a photographer and a scene-mapper and a couple of others in tow. Boyle is a round, pancake-faced little oddball who gives you the impression that he has a room at home packed with disturbing magazines, neatly alphabetised, but he runs a scene impeccably and he's the best we've got on blood spatter. I was going to need both of those.

'Well, about *time*,' he told me. He was already in his white hooded boiler suit, with his gloves and overshoes hanging ready from one hand. 'Who's this we've got here?'

'My new partner, Richie Curran. Richie, this is Larry Boyle from the Bureau. Be nice to him. We like him.'

'Stop that carry-on till we see if I'm any use to you,' Larry said, batting a hand at me. 'What's in there?'

'Father and two kids, dead. The mother's gone to hospital. The kids were upstairs and it looks like suffocation, the adults were downstairs and it looks like stabbing. We've got enough blood spatter to keep you happy for weeks.'

'Oh, lovely.'

'Don't say I never did anything for you. Apart from the usual, I'm looking for whatever you can tell me about the progression of events – who was attacked first, where, how much moving around they did afterwards, what the struggle might have looked like. As far as we could see, there's no blood upstairs, which could be significant. Can you check for us?'

'No problem to me. Any more special requests?'

I said, 'There was something very weird going on in that house, and I'm talking about well before last night. We've got a bunch of holes in the walls, and no clue who made them or why – if you can find us any indications, fingerprints or anything, we'd be very grateful. We've also got a load of baby monitors – at least two audio and five video, going by the chargers on the bedside table, but there could be more. We're not sure what they were for yet, and we've only located three of the cameras: upstairs landing, sitting-room side table, kitchen floor. I'd like photos of all of them *in situ*. And we need to find the other two cameras, or however many there are. Same for the viewers: we've got two charging, two on the kitchen floor, so we're short at least one.'

'Mmm,' Larry said, with relish. '*In*-teresting. Thank God for you, Scorcher. One more bedsit overdose and I think I'd have died of boredom.'

'I'm thinking we could have a drug connection here, actually. Nothing definite, but I'd love to know if there are drugs in that house, or if there used to be.'

'Oh, God, not drugs *again*. We'll swab anything that looks promising, but I'll be only delighted if it turns up negative.'

'I need their mobiles, I need any financial paperwork you run across, and there's a computer in the kitchen that'll need going over. And give the attic a good once-over for me, will you? We haven't been up there, but whatever was weird, it involved the attic somehow. You'll see what I mean.'

'Now that's more like it,' Larry said happily. 'I love a bit of weird. Shall we?'

I said, 'That's the injured woman's sister, in the uniforms' car. We're about to go have a chat with her. Can you hold off another minute, until we've got her out of view? I don't want her seeing you guys heading in, just in case she loses the plot.'

'I have that effect on women. Not a bother; we'll hang on here till you give us the nod. Have fun, boys.' He waved us goodbye with his overshoes.

Richie said grimly, as we headed back down the road towards the sister, 'He won't be so cheerful once he's been inside that house.'

I said, 'He will, though, old son. He will.'

I don't feel sorry for anyone I run across via work. Pity is fun, it lets you have a great wank about what a wonderful guy you are, but it does bugger-all good to the people you're feeling sorry for. The second you start getting gooey about what they've been through, your eye comes off the ball. You get weak. Next thing you know, you can't get out of bed in the morning because you can't face going in to work, and I have trouble seeing how that does anyone any good. I put my time and energy into bringing answers, not hugs and hot chocolate.

If I was going to feel sorry for someone, though, it would be the vics' families. Like I said to Richie, ninety-nine per cent of the vics have nothing to complain about: they got exactly what they went looking for. The families, about the same percentage of the time, never asked for anything like this kind of hell. I don't buy the idea that it's all Mummy's fault if Little Jimmy turns into a junkie smack dealer dumb enough to rip off his own supplier. Maybe she didn't exactly help him self-actualise, but my childhood left me with a few issues too, and did I wind up taking two in the back of the head from a pissed-off drug lord? I spent a couple of years seeing a counsellor, to make sure those issues weren't going to hold me back, and meanwhile I got on with things, because I'm a grown man now and that means my life is up to me. If I turn up one morning with my face blown off, that's all mine. And my family, for no good reason in the world, would be left picking out shrapnel.

I watch myself hardest of all around the families. Nothing can trip you up like compassion.

When she left home that morning, Fiona Rafferty had probably been a good-looking girl – I like them taller and a lot more groomed, myself, but there was a fine pair of legs in those faded jeans, and she had a good head of glossy hair, even if she hadn't taken the trouble to straighten it or to colour it something snazzier than plain mouse-brown. Now, though, she was a mess. Her face was red and swollen and covered in great streaks of snot and mascara, her eyes had turned piggy from crying and she had been wiping her face on the sleeves of her red duffel coat. At least she had stopped screaming, for the moment anyway.

The uniform was starting to look frayed around the edges, too. I said, 'We need a word with Ms Rafferty. Why don't you get onto your station, have them send someone out to take her to the hospital when we're done?' He nodded and backed away. I heard the sigh of relief.

Richie went down on one knee beside the car. 'Ms Rafferty?' he
said gently. The kid had bedside manner. Maybe a little too much:
his knee was smack in a muddy rut and he was going to be spending the rest of the day looking like he had fallen over his own feet,
but he didn't seem to notice.

Fiona Rafferty's head came up, slowly and wavering. She
looked blind.

'I'm very sorry for your trouble.'

After a moment her chin tilted down, a tiny nod.

'Can we get you anything? Water?'

'I need to ring my mam. How do I— Oh, God, the *babies*, I
can't tell her—'

I said, 'We're getting someone to accompany you to the hospital. They'll let your mother know to meet you there, and they'll
help you talk to her.'

She didn't hear me; her mind had already flinched off that and
ricocheted somewhere else. 'Is Jenny OK? She's going to be OK,
right?'

'We're hoping so. We'll let you know as soon as we hear anything.'

'The ambulance, they wouldn't let me go with her – I need to
be *with* her, what if she, I need to—'

Richie said, 'I know. The doctors are looking after her, though.
They know what they're at, those lads. You'd only get in their way.
You don't want that, no?'

Her head rocked from side to side: no.

'No. And anyway, we need you to help us out here. We'll need
to ask you some questions. Would you be able for that now, do you
think?'

Her mouth fell open and she gasped for air. '*No.* Questions,
Jesus, I can't— I want to go home. *I want my mam.* Oh, *God*, I
want—'

She was on the verge of breaking down again. I saw Richie start
to draw back, hands going up reassuringly. I said smoothly, before
he threw her away, 'Ms Rafferty, if you need to go home for a little
while and come back to us later on, we won't stop you. It's your
choice. But for every minute we lose, our chances of finding the

person who did this go down another notch. Evidence gets destroyed, witnesses' memories get blurry, maybe the killer gets farther away. I think you should know that, before you make your decision.'

Fiona's eyes were starting to focus. 'If I . . . You could lose him? If I come back to you later, he could be *gone*?'

I moved Richie out of her eyeline with a hard grip on his shoulder and leaned against the car door. 'That's right. Like I said, it's your choice, but personally I wouldn't want to live with that.'

Her face contorted and for a moment I thought she was gone, but she bit down hard on the inside of her cheek and pulled it together. 'OK. OK. I can . . . OK. I just . . . Can I just take two minutes and have a cigarette? Then I'll answer whatever you want.'

'I think you've made the right decision there. You take your time, Ms Rafferty. We'll be here.'

She pulled herself out of the car – clumsily, like someone standing up for the first time after surgery – and staggered off across the road, between the skeleton houses. I kept an eye on her. She found a half-built wall to sit on and managed to light her smoke.

Her back was to us, more or less. I gave Larry the thumbs-up. He waved cheerfully and came trundling towards the house, pulling his gloves on, with the rest of the techs trailing after him.

Richie's crappy jacket wasn't made for country weather; he was bouncing up and down with his hands in his armpits, trying not to look frozen. I said, keeping my voice down, 'You were about to send her home. Weren't you?'

He whipped his head around, startled and wary. 'I was, yeah. I thought—'

'You don't think. Not about something like that. Whether to cut a witness loose is my call, not yours. Do you understand?'

'She looked like she was about to lose it.'

'So? That's not a reason to let her leave, Detective Curran. That's a reason to make her pull it together. You almost threw away an interview that we can't afford to lose.'

'I was trying *not* to throw it away. Better get it in a few hours' time than upset her so bad we might not get her back till tomorrow.'

'That's not how it works. If you need a witness to talk, you find a way to make her do it, end of story. You don't send her *home* to have a bloody cup of tea and a biscuit and come back when it suits her.'

'I figured I should give her the choice. She just lost—'

'Did you see me putting handcuffs on the girl? Give her all the choice in the world. Just make damn sure she chooses the way you want her to. Rule Number Three, and Four and Five and about a dozen more: you do not go with the flow in this job. You make the flow go with *you*. Do I make myself clear?'

After a moment Richie said, 'Yeah. I'm sorry, Detective. Sir.'

Probably he hated me right then, but I could live with that. I don't care if my rookies take home photos of me to throw darts at, as long as when the dust settles they haven't done any damage, either to the case or to their careers. 'It won't happen again. Am I right?'

'No. I mean, yeah, you're right: it won't.'

'Good. Then let's go get that interview.'

Richie tucked his chin into his jacket collar and eyed Fiona Rafferty doubtfully. She was sagging on her wall, head almost between her knees, cigarette hanging forgotten from one hand. At that distance she looked like something discarded, just a crumple of scarlet cloth tossed away in the rubble. 'You think she can take it?'

'I haven't a clue. Not our problem, as long as she has the nervous breakdown on her own time. Now come on.'

I headed across the road without looking back to see if he was coming. After a moment I heard his shoes crunching on dirt and gravel, hurrying up behind me.

Fiona was a little more together: the occasional shudder still slammed through her, but her hands had stopped shaking and she had wiped the mascara off her face, even if it was with her shirt front. I moved her into one of the half-built houses, out of the stiff wind and out of view of whatever Larry and his buddies did next, found her a nice pile of breezeblocks to sit on and gave her another cigarette – I don't smoke, never have, but I keep a pack in my briefcase: smokers are like any other addicts, the best way to get them on side is with their own currency. I sat next to her on the breezeblocks; Richie found himself a windowsill at my shoulder, where he could watch and learn and take notes without making a big deal of it. It wasn't the ideal interview situation, but I've worked in worse.

'Now,' I said, when I'd lit her cigarette. 'Is there anything else we can get you? An extra jumper? A drink of water?'

Fiona was staring at the cigarette, jiggling it between her fingers and dragging it down in fast little gasps. Every muscle in her body was clenched; by the end of the day she was going to feel like she'd run a marathon. 'I'm fine. Could we just get this over with? Please?'

'No problem, Ms Rafferty. We understand. Why don't you start by telling me about Jennifer?'

'Jenny. She doesn't like Jennifer – she says it's prissy or something . . . It's always been Jenny. Since we were little.'

'Who's older?'

'Her. I'm twenty-seven, she's twenty-nine.'

I had figured Fiona for younger than that. Partly it was physical – she was on the short side, slight, with a pointed face and small irregular features under all the mess – but partly it was the gear, all that student-type scruffiness. Back when I was young, girls used to dress that way even after college, but nowadays they mostly put on a better show. Going by the house, I was willing to bet that Jenny had made more of an effort. I said, 'What does she do?'

'She's in PR. I mean, she was, up until Jack was born. Since then she stays home with the kids.'

'Fair play to her. She doesn't miss working?'

Something that could have been a head-shake, except Fiona was so rigid it looked more like a spasm. 'I don't think so. She liked her job, but she's not super-ambitious, or anything. She knew she wouldn't be able to go back if they had another baby – two sets of childcare, she'd have been working for, like, twenty euros a week – but they still went for Jack.'

'Any problems at work? Anyone she didn't get on with?'

'No. The other girls in the company sounded like total bitches to me – all these snide comments if one of them didn't top up her fake tan for a few days, and when Jenny was pregnant they were calling her *Titanic* and telling her she should be on a *diet*, for God's sake – but Jenny didn't think it was a big deal. She . . . Jenny doesn't like putting her foot down, you know? She'd rather go with the flow. She always figures . . .' A hiss of breath between her teeth, like physical pain had hit her. 'She always figures things work out OK in the end.'

'What about Patrick? How does he get on with people?' Keep them moving, keep them jumping from topic to topic, don't give them time to look down. If they fall, you might not be able to get them on their feet again.

Her face jerked towards me, swollen grey-blue eyes wide. 'Pat's— Jesus, you don't think he *did* this! Pat would never, he would *never*—'

'I know. Tell me—'

'*How* do you know?'

'Ms Rafferty,' I said, putting some stern into my voice. 'Do you want to help us here?'

'Of *course* I—'

'Good. Then you need to focus on the questions we're asking. The sooner we get some answers, the sooner you get some answers. OK?'

Fiona looked around wildly, like the room would vanish any second and she would wake up. It was bare concrete and sloppy mortar, with a couple of wooden beams propped against one wall like they were holding it up. A stack of fake-oak banisters covered in a thick coating of grime, flattened Styrofoam cups on the floor, a muddy blue sweatshirt balled up in one corner: it looked like an archaeological site frozen in the moment when the inhabitants had dropped everything and fled, from some natural disaster or some invading force. Fiona couldn't see the place now, but it was going to be stamped on her mind for the rest of her life. This is one of the little extras murder throws at the families: long after you lose hold of the victim's face or the last words she said to you, you remember every detail of the nightmare limbo where this thing came clawing into your life.

'Ms Rafferty,' I said. 'We can't afford to waste time.'

'Yeah. I'm OK.' She jammed out her cigarette on the breeze-blocks and stared at the butt like it had materialised in her hand out of nowhere. Richie leaned forward, holding out a foam cup, and said quietly, 'Here.' Fiona nodded jerkily; she dropped in her cigarette and kept hold of the cup, gripping it with both hands.

I asked, 'So what's Patrick like?'

'He's *lovely.*' Defiant flash of red-rimmed eyes. Under the wreckage was plenty of stubborn. 'We've known him forever – we're all from Monkstown, we always hung out with the same crowd, ever since we were kids. Him and Jenny, they've been together since they were sixteen.'

'What kind of relationship was it?'

'They were mad about each other. The rest of the gang, we thought it was a big deal if we went out with someone for more than a few weeks, but Pat and Jenny were . . .' Fiona caught a deep breath and jerked her head back, staring up through the empty stairwell and the haphazard beams at the grey sky. 'They knew straightaway that this was it. It used to make them seem older; grown-up. The rest of us were just messing about, just playing, you know? Pat and Jenny were doing the real thing. Love.'

The real thing has got more people killed than practically anything else I can think of. 'When did they get engaged?'

'When they were nineteen. Valentine's Day.'

'That's pretty young, these days. What did your parents think?'

'They were delighted! They love Pat too. They just said to wait till they finished college, and Pat and Jenny were fine with that. They got married when they were twenty-two. Jenny said there wasn't any point in putting it off any longer, it wasn't like they were going to change their minds.'

'And how did it work out?'

'It's worked out *great.* Pat, the way he treats Jenny – he still lights up when he finds out there's something she wants, because he can't wait to get it for her. Back when I was a teenager, I used to *pray* that I'd meet someone who'd love me the way Pat loves Jenny. OK?'

The present tense takes a long time to wear off. My mother died way back when I was a teenager, but every now and then Dina still talks about what perfume Mummy wears or what kind of ice cream she likes. It drives Geri crazy. I asked, not too sceptically, 'No arguments? In thirteen years?'

'That's not what I said. Everyone has arguments. But theirs aren't a big deal.'

'What do they argue about?'

Fiona was looking at me now, a thin layer of wariness solidifying over all the rest. 'Same as any couple. Stuff like, back when we were kids, Pat would get upset if some other guy fancied Jenny. Or when they were saving up towards the house, Pat wanted to go on holiday and Jenny thought everything should go into the savings. They always sort it out, though. Like I said, no big deal.'

Money: the only thing that kills more people than love. 'What does Patrick do?'

'He's in recruitment – was. He worked for Nolan and Roberts – they find people for financial services. They let him go in February.'

'Any particular reason?'

Fiona's shoulders were starting to tense up again. 'It wasn't anything he did. They let a few people go at the same time, not just him. Financial services companies aren't exactly recruiting these days, you know? The recession . . .'

'Did he have any problems at work? Any bad blood when he left?'

'*No!* You keep trying to make it sound like, like Pat and Jenny have all these *enemies* everywhere, they're *fighting* all the time— They're not like that.'

She was reared back away from me, the cup thrust out in two clenched hands like a shield. I said soothingly, 'Now, that's the kind of information I need. I don't know Pat and Jenny; I'm just trying to get an idea of them.'

'They're *lovely*. People like them. They love each other. They love the kids. OK? Does that give you enough of an *idea*?'

Actually that gave me shag-all idea about anything, but it was obviously the best I was going to get. 'Absolutely,' I said. 'I appreciate it. Does Patrick's family still live in Monkstown?'

'His parents are dead – his dad was back when we were kids, his mum was a few years ago. He's got a little brother, Ian, he's in Chicago— Ring Ian. Ask him about Pat and Jenny. He'll tell you the exact same thing.'

'I'm sure he will. Did Pat and Jenny keep any valuables in the house? Cash, jewellery, anything like that?'

Fiona's shoulders came down again, a little, while she considered that. 'Jenny's engagement ring – Pat paid a couple of grand for that – and this emerald ring that our granny left to Emma. And Pat has a computer; it's pretty new, he got it with his redundancy money, it might still be worth something . . . All that stuff, is it still there? Or did it get taken?'

'We'll check. That's it for valuables?'

'They don't *have* anything valuable. They used to have this big SUV, but they had to give it back; they couldn't make the repayments. And I guess there's Jenny's clothes – she used to spend a load on them, till Pat lost his job – but who's going to do *this* for a bunch of second-hand clothes?'

There are people who would do it for a lot less, but I didn't get the feeling that was what we were looking at. 'When did you last see them?'

She had to think about that. 'I met up with Jenny in Dublin, for coffee. This summer, maybe three or four months ago? I haven't seen Pat in ages – April, I guess. God, I don't know how it got to be that long—'

'What about the children?'

'April, the same as Pat. I was out here for Emma's birthday – she was turning six.'

'Did you notice anything out of the ordinary?'

'Like *what*?'

Head up, chin out, straight onto the defensive. I said, 'Anything at all. A guest who seemed out of place, maybe. A conversation that sounded odd.'

'No. Nothing was *odd*. There were a bunch of kids from Emma's class, and Jenny got a bouncy castle— Oh, God, Emma and Jack . . . Both of them, are you *sure* they're both . . . ? Could one of them not be just hurt, just, just . . .'

'Ms Rafferty,' I said, in my best gentle-but-firm, 'I'm pretty sure they're not just hurt. We'll let you know straightaway if anything changes, but right now I need you to stay with me. Every second counts, remember?'

Fiona pressed a hand over her mouth and swallowed hard. 'Yeah.'

'Well done.' I held out another cigarette and clicked the lighter. 'When did you last speak to Jenny?'

'Yesterday morning.' She didn't have to think about that one. 'I ring her every morning at half-eight, once I'm in work. We have our coffee and check in, just for a few minutes. Like a start to the day, you know?'

'It sounds nice. How was she yesterday?'

'*Normal!* She was completely *normal!* There was nothing, I swear to God, I've gone over it in my head and there was *nothing*—'

'I'm sure there wasn't,' I said soothingly. 'What did you talk about?'

'Just stuff, I don't know. One of my flatmates plays bass, her band has a gig coming up, I told Jenny about that; she was telling me how she was looking online for a toy stegosaurus, because Jack had brought home some friend from preschool on Friday and they went hunting a stegosaurus in the garden . . . She sounded *fine*. Totally *fine*.'

'Would she have told you if there was anything wrong?'

'Yeah, I think so. She would. I'm sure she would.'

Which didn't sound sure. I asked, 'Are you two close?'

Fiona said, 'There's just the two of us.' She heard herself and realised that wasn't an answer. 'Yeah. We're close. I mean, we were closer when we were younger, teenagers – we sort of went in different directions after that. And it's not as easy now that Jenny's out here.'

'How long has that been?'

'They bought the house like three years ago.' 2006: the height of the boom. Whatever they had paid, these days the gaff was worth half of that. 'There was nothing here then, though, just fields; they bought off the plans. I thought they were mental, but Jenny was over the moon, she was so *excited* – their own place . . .' Fiona's mouth contorted, but she got it back together. 'They moved out here maybe a year later. As soon as the house was finished.'

I asked, 'And what about you? Where do you live?'

'In Dublin. Ranelagh.'

'You said you share a flat?'

'Yeah. Me and two other girls.'

'What do you do?'

'I'm a photographer. I'm trying to get an exhibition together, but meanwhile I work at Studio Pierre – you know, Pierre, he was on that TV show about elite Irish weddings? I mostly do the baby shoots, or if Keith – Pierre – gets two weddings on the same day, I do one of them.'

'Were you doing a baby shoot this morning?'

She had to work to remember, it was so far away. 'No. I was going through shots, these shots from last week – the mother's coming in today to pick the album.'

'What time did you leave?'

'Like quarter past nine. One of the guys said he'd sort out the album for me.'

'Where's Studio Pierre?'

'By Phoenix Park.'

An hour from Broken Harbour, minimum, in morning traffic and in that shitty little car. I asked, 'Had you been worried about Jenny?'

That electric-shock head-shake.

'Are you sure? That's an awful lot of hassle to go to because someone doesn't answer her phone.'

A tense shrug. Fiona balanced the foam cup carefully beside her, tapped ash. 'I wanted to make sure she was OK.'

'Why wouldn't she have been?'

'*Because.* We always talk. Every day, for years. And I was right, wasn't I? She wasn't OK.'

Her chin wobbled. I leaned in close to give her a tissue, didn't lean back. 'Ms Rafferty,' I said. 'We both know there was more to it than that. You don't ditch work, possibly annoy a client, and drive for an hour, just because your sister's out of touch for forty-five minutes. You could have assumed that she'd gone to bed with a migraine, or that she'd lost her phone, or that the kids had come down with the flu, or any one of several hundred things, all of them a lot more likely than this. Instead, you jumped straight to the conclusion that something was wrong. You need to tell me why.'

Fiona bit down on her bottom lip. The air stank of cigarette smoke and singed wool – she had dropped hot ash on her coat, somewhere in there – and there was a dank, bitter smell coming off her, spreading on her breath and seeping out of her pores. Interesting fact from the front lines: raw grief smells like ripped leaves and splintered branches, a jagged green shriek.

'It wasn't anything,' she said, finally. 'It was ages ago – months. I'd practically forgotten about it, till . . .'

I waited.

'It was just . . . She rang me one evening. She said someone had been in the house.'

I felt Richie snap to attention at my shoulder, like a terrier ready to dash off after his stick. 'Did she report this?' I asked.

Fiona rubbed out her cigarette and dropped the butt into the cup. 'It wasn't like that. There was nothing to report. There wasn't, like, a window broken or the lock smashed or whatever, and there wasn't anything taken.'

'Then what made her think someone had been in the house?'

The shrug again, even tenser this time. Her head had gone down. 'She just thought. I don't know.'

I said, letting the firm start to edge out the gentle, 'This could be important, Ms Rafferty. What did she say, exactly?'

Fiona took a deep, shuddering breath and pushed hair behind

her ear. 'OK,' she said. 'OK. OK. So Jenny rings me, right, and she's like, "Did you make a copy of our keys?" I had their keys for about two *seconds* last winter, Jenny and Pat took the kids to the Canaries for a week and they wanted to know someone could get in if there was a fire or whatever. So I say no, course not—'

'Did you?' Richie asked. 'Make a copy?' He pulled it off – he managed to sound just plain interested, not the slightest bit accusing. Which was nice: it meant I wouldn't have to give him shit, or at least not too big a helping of it, for talking out of turn.

'No! Why would I?'

She had shot upright. Richie shrugged, gave her a deprecating little smile. 'Just checking. I've got to ask, you know?'

Fiona slumped back. 'Yeah. I guess.'

'And no one else could have made copies, that week? You didn't leave the keys where your flatmates could have taken them, or someone at work – nothing like that? Like I said, we have to ask.'

'I had them on my key ring. They weren't in a *safe* or anything – when I'm in work I have my keys in my bag, and when I'm home they're on a hook in the kitchen. But it's not like anyone would've known what they were, even if they cared. I don't think I even told anyone that I *had* them.'

Her flatmates and her workmates were going to be having in-depth chats all the same, not to mention background checks. 'Let's get back to the phone conversation,' I said. 'You told Jenny you hadn't copied her keys . . .'

'Yeah. Jenny says, "Well, someone's got them, and you're the only person we gave them to." It takes me like half an hour to convince her I don't have a clue what she's on about, so she'll even tell me what's the story. Finally she says her and the kids were out for the afternoon, at the shops or somewhere, and when she got back someone had been through the house.' Fiona had started picking the tissue to shreds, white wisps floating down on the red of her coat. She had small hands, slim-fingered, with bitten nails. 'I ask her how she knows, and at first she won't say, but finally I get it out of her: the curtains are hooked back all wrong, and she's missing half a packet of ham and the pen she keeps by the fridge for making shopping lists. I'm like, "You have *got* to be joking," and she nearly hangs up on me. So I talk her down, and once she stops giving me hassle, she sounds really freaked out, you know? Really *scared*. And Jenny isn't a wimp.'

This was one of the reasons I had come down hard on Richie for trying to postpone this interview. If you get someone talking right after his world ends, there's a decent chance he won't be able to stop. Wait till the next day and he'll already be starting to rebuild his pulverised defences – people work fast, when the stakes are that high – but catch him straight after the mushroom cloud unfurls and he'll spill anything from his tastes in porn to his secret nickname for the boss. 'Natural enough,' I said. 'That'd be pretty unsettling.'

'It was *ham slices* and a *pen*! If her jewellery was gone, or half her underwear or something, then yeah, sure, lose the head. But this stuff . . . I said to her, "OK, let's say somehow someone for some weird reason got in, he wasn't exactly Hannibal Lecter, was he?"'

I asked, before it could hit her what she had just said, 'What did Jenny think of that?'

'She got furious with me again. She said the big deal wasn't what he'd actually *done*; it was all the stuff she couldn't be sure about. Like if he'd been in the kids' rooms, gone through their stuff – Jenny said if they could afford it she'd throw away everything the kids had, start over, just in case. What he'd touched – she said everything looked like it was out of place all of a sudden, just an inch, or like it was smudged. How he got in. *Why* he got in – that was really getting to her. She kept saying, "Why us? What did he want off us? Do we look like a target? What?"'

Fiona shivered, a sudden jerk that almost doubled her over. I said easily, 'It's a good question. They have an alarm system; do you know if it was set that day?'

She shook her head. 'I asked. Jenny said no. She never used to bother, not during the day – I think they'd set it at night, when they went to bed, but that was because the local kids throw parties and stuff in the empty houses, they can get pretty out of control sometimes. Jenny said the estate was basically dead during the day – well, you can see for yourselves – so she hadn't been bothering. But she said she was going to start. She said, "If you've got those keys, you'd better not use them. I'm changing the alarm code *now* and after this it stays on, day and night, end of story." Like I said, she sounded really scared.'

But when the uniforms had broken down the door and the four of us had gone tramping all over Jenny's precious house, the alarm had been off. The obvious explanation was that, if anyone had come in from outside, the Spains had opened the door themselves; that Jenny, scared as she was, hadn't been scared of this person. 'Did she change the locks?'

'I asked that, too – was she going to. She went back and forth, but in the end she said no, probably not, it'd be a couple of hundred quid and the budget couldn't stretch to that. The alarm would be enough. She said, "I don't even mind that much if he tries to get in again. I'd almost rather he did. At least then we'd *know*." I told you: she's not a wimp.'

'Where had Pat been that day? Was this before he lost his job?'

'No, after. He'd gone down to Athlone, for a job interview – this was back when him and Jenny still had the two cars.'

'What did he think about the possible break-in?'

'I don't know. She never said. I thought . . . to be honest, I thought she hadn't told him. She was keeping her voice right down, on the phone – that could've been just because the kids were asleep, but in a house that size? And she kept saying "I" – "I'm changing the alarm code, I couldn't fit that in the budget, I'll sort the guy if I get him." Not "we".'

And there it was again: the little thing out of place, the gift I had told Richie to keep his eyes peeled for. 'Why wouldn't she tell Pat? Shouldn't that be the first thing she did, if she thought they'd had intruders?'

Another shrug. Fiona's chin was tucked down into her chest. 'Because she didn't want to worry him, I guess. He had enough on his plate. I thought that was probably why she wasn't planning on changing the locks, too. She couldn't do it without Pat knowing.'

'You didn't think that was a little odd – even risky? If someone had broken into his home, didn't he have the right to know?'

'Maybe, whatever, but I didn't actually think anyone had *been* in there. I mean, what's the simplest explanation? Pat took the pen and ate the bloody ham and one of the kids messed with the curtains, or they had a ghost burglar who could walk through walls and fancied a sandwich?'

Her voice was tightening up, getting defensive. I asked, 'Did you say that to Jenny?'

'Yeah, more or less. It just made her worse. She went off on this whole thing about how the pen was from the hotel where they'd stayed on honeymoon and it was special and Pat knew not to move it, and she knew exactly how much ham had been in the packet—'

'Is she the type of person who would know that kind of thing?'

After a moment Fiona said, like it hurt, 'Sort of, yeah. I guess. Jenny . . . she likes doing stuff right. So when she quit work, she got really serious about being a stay-at-home mum, you know? The place was spotless, she fed the kids on organic stuff that she made from scratch, she was doing these exercise DVDs every day so she'd get her figure back . . . Exactly what she had in her fridge – yeah, she might know.'

Richie asked, 'What hotel was the pen from, do you know?'

'Golden Bay Resort, in the Maldives—' Her head came back up and she stared at him. 'Do you seriously think . . . ? You think someone actually took it? You think that's the person who, who, you think they came back and—'

Her voice was starting to spiral dangerously. I asked, before she could lose hold, 'When was this incident, Ms Rafferty?'

She gave me a wild-eyed stare, squeezed hard on the lump of shredded tissue and pulled herself back. 'Like three months ago?'

'July.'

'Or it could've been earlier, maybe. During the summer, anyway.'

I made a mental note: check Jenny's phone records for evening calls to Fiona, and check the dates of any prowler reports from Ocean View. 'And since then, they've had no more problems along those lines?'

Fiona caught a fast breath, and I heard the painful rasp where her throat was closing up. 'It could have happened again. I wouldn't know. Jenny wouldn't have said anything to me, not after the first time.' Her voice had started to wobble. 'I told her to get a grip on herself. Stop talking crap. I thought . . .'

She made a sound like a kicked puppy, clapped her hands over her mouth and started to cry hard again. It took me a while to figure out what she was saying, through the tissue and the snot. 'I thought she was crazy,' she was gasping, over and over. 'I thought she was losing it. Oh, God, I thought she was crazy.'

# 4

And that was about as much as we were going to get out of Fiona that day. Calming her down would have taken a lot more time than we had to spare. The extra uniform had arrived; I told him to get names and numbers – family, friends, workplaces, workmates, going right back to when Fiona and Jenny and Pat were in nappies – take Fiona to the hospital, and make sure she knew not to open her mouth around the media. Then we handed her over. She was still crying.

I had my mobile out and was dialling before we even turned away – radio would have been simpler, but too many journos and too many weirdos have scanners these days. I got Richie by the elbow and drew him down the road. The wind was still coming off the sea, wide and fresh, raking Richie's hair into tufts; I tasted salt on my mouth. Where the footpaths should have been, there were thin dirt tracks in the uncut grass.

Bernadette got me through to the uniform who was at the hospital with Jenny Spain. He was about twelve, he was from some farm somewhere and he was the anal type, which was what I needed. I gave him his orders: once Jennifer Spain got out of surgery, if she made it that far, she needed a private room, and he needed to guard the door like a Rottweiler. No one was getting into that room without showing ID, no one was going in there unaccompanied, and the family wasn't going in at all. 'The victim's sister is going to be heading down there any minute, and their mother will show up sooner or later. They don't go into the room.' Richie was hovering and chewing on a thumbnail, head bent over the phone, but that made him glance up at me. 'If they want an explanation, and they will, you don't tell them these are my orders.

You apologise, you say this is standard procedure and you're not authorised to breach it, and you keep saying the same thing over and over till they back off. And get yourself a comfy chair, old son. You could be there for a while.' I hung up.

Richie squinted up at me, against the light. 'You think that's overkill?' I asked.

He shrugged. 'If it's true, what the sister was saying – about the break-in – it's pretty creepy, all right.'

I said, 'You figure that's why I'm going high-security? Because the sister's story is *creepy*?'

He stepped back, hands going up, and I realised my voice had risen. 'I just meant—'

'As far as I'm concerned, chum, there's no such thing as creepy. Creepy is for kids on Halloween. I'm making sure all my bases are covered. How stupid do you think we'd look if someone waltzed into that hospital and finished the job? You want to explain that one to the media? Or, come to that, do you want to explain yourself to the Super if tomorrow's front page is a close-up of Jenny Spain's injuries?'

'No.'

'No. Neither do I. And if it takes a little overkill to avoid that, then so be it. Now let's get you inside before the big bad wind freezes your itty bitty bollix off, shall we?'

Richie kept his mouth shut till we were heading back up the Spains' drive. Then he said, carefully, 'The family.'

'What about them?'

'You don't want them seeing her?'

'No, I don't. Did you spot the one big piece of actual info Fiona gave us, in with all your *creepy* stuff?'

He said, unwillingly, 'She had the keys.'

'Yeah,' I said. 'She had the keys.'

'She's in bits. Maybe I'm a sucker, but that looked genuine to me.'

'Maybe it is and maybe it isn't. All I know is, she had the keys.'

'"They're great, they love each other, they love the kids . . ." She talked like they were still alive.'

'So? If she can fake the rest, she can fake that. And her relation-ship with her sister wasn't as simple as she's trying to make out. We'll be spending a lot more time with Fiona Rafferty.'

'Right,' Richie said, but when I pushed the door open he hung back, fidgeting on the doormat and rubbing the back of his head. I asked, making sure the edge was gone out of my voice, 'What's up?'

'The other thing she said.'

'What's that?'

'Bouncy castles aren't cheap. My sister wanted to rent one for my niece's Communion. Couple of hundred squid.'

'Your point?'

'Their financial situation. In February Patrick gets laid off, right? In April, they're still flush enough that they're getting Emma a bouncy castle for her birthday party. But by somewhere around July, they're too skint to change the locks, even though Jenny thinks someone's been in the gaff.'

'So? Patrick's redundancy money was running out.'

'Yeah, probably. That's what I mean. And running out faster than it should've done. A good few of my mates are after losing their jobs. All of them who'd been at the same place a few years, they got enough to keep them going for a good while, if they were careful.'

'What are you thinking? Gambling? Drugs? Blackmail?' In this country's vice league, booze has all of those beat hands down, but booze doesn't wipe out your bank account in a few months flat.

Richie shrugged. 'Maybe, yeah. Or maybe they just kept spend-ing like he was still earning. A couple of my mates did that, too.'

I said, 'That's your generation. Pat and Jenny's generation. Never been broke, never seen this country broke, so you couldn't imagine it, even when it started happening in front of your eyes. It's a good way to be – a lot better than my generation: half of us could be rolling in the stuff and we'd still get paranoid about owning two pairs of shoes, in case we wound up on the side of the road. But it's got its downside.'

Inside the house the techs were working away: someone called

out something that ended in, '. . . Got any extra?' and Larry
shouted back cheerfully, 'I do of course, check in my . . .'

Richie nodded. 'Pat Spain wasn't expecting to be broke,' he
said, 'or he wouldn't've blown the dosh on the bouncy castle.
Either he was positive he'd have a new job by the end of summer,
or he was positive he'd have some other way of bringing in the
cash. If it started hitting him that that wasn't happening, and the
money was running out . . .' He reached out to touch the broken
edge of the door with one finger, drew his hand back in time.
'That's some serious pressure for a man, knowing he can't look
after his family.'

I said, 'So your money's still on Patrick.'

Richie said carefully, 'My money's nowhere till we see what Dr
Cooper thinks. I'm only saying.'

'Good. Patrick's the favourite, all right, but we've got plenty of
fences left; plenty of room for an outsider to come up and take it.
So the next thing we want to do is see if we can get anyone to
narrow the field. I suggest we start with a quick chat to Cooper,
before he heads, then go see if the neighbours have anything good
for us. By the time we're done there, Larry and his merry men
should be able to give us some kind of update, and they should
have the upstairs clear enough that we can go rooting around, try
and pick up a few hints about why the money might have been
running out. How does that sound to you?'

He nodded. 'Nice catch on the bouncy castle,' I said, giving him
a pat on the shoulder. 'Now let's go see what Cooper can do to the
odds.'

The house was a different place: that miles-deep silence had
vanished, blown away like fog, and the air was lit up and buzzing
with efficient, confident work. Two of Larry's lot were working
their way methodically through the blood spatter, one of them
dropping swabs into test tubes while the other one took Polaroids
to pinpoint where each swab had come from. A skinny girl with
too much nose was moving around with a video camera. The print
guy was peeling tape off a window handle; the mapper was

whistling between his teeth while he sketched. Everyone was going at a steady pace that said they were in for a long haul.

Larry was in the kitchen, squatting over a cluster of yellow evidence markers. 'What a *mess*,' he said, with relish, when he saw us. 'We're going to be here for*ever*. Did you come into this kitchen, when you were here before?'

'We stopped at the door,' I said. 'The uniforms were in here, though.'

'Of course they were. Don't let them go off duty without giving us their shoeprints, for elimination.' He straightened up, pressing a hand to the small of his back. 'Ow, bollix, I'm getting too old for this job. Cooper's upstairs with the kids, if you want him.'

'We won't interrupt him. Any sign of the weapon?'

Larry shook his head. 'Nada.'

'How about a note?'

'Does "Eggs, tea, shower gel" count? Because otherwise, no. If you're thinking this fella here, though' – a nod at Patrick – 'you know as well as I do, a lot of men don't. Strong silent types to the end.'

Someone had turned Patrick onto his back. He was white and slack-jawed, but you get the knack of seeing past that: he had been a good-looking guy, square chin and straight eyebrows, the type girls go for. I said, 'We don't know what we're thinking. Find anything unlocked? Back door, a window?'

'Not so far. The security wasn't bad, you know. Strong locks on the windows, double glazing, proper lock on the back door – not the type you can get past with a credit card. I'm not trying to do your job for you, or anything, but I'm just saying: not the easiest house to break into, specially without leaving marks.'

Larry's money was on Patrick too. 'Speaking of keys,' I said, 'let me know if you find any. We should have at least three sets of house keys. And keep an eye out for a pen that says "Golden Bay Resort". Hang on—'

Cooper was picking his way down the hall like it was dirty, holding his thermometer in one hand and his case in the other. 'Detective Kennedy,' he said, resignedly, like he had been hoping against hope that I would somehow vanish off the case. 'And Detective Curran.'

'Dr Cooper,' I said. 'I hope we're not interrupting.'

'I have just completed my preliminary examinations. The bodies may now be removed.'

'Can you provide us with any new information?' One of the things that pisses me off about Cooper is that when he's around I end up talking like him.

Cooper held up his case and raised his eyebrows at Larry, who said cheerfully, 'You can stick that by the kitchen door, nothing interesting going on over there.' He put the case down delicately and bent to put away his thermometer.

'Both children appear to have been smothered,' he said. I felt Richie's fidgeting go up a gear, at my shoulder. 'This is virtually impossible to diagnose definitively, but the absence of any obvious injuries or symptoms of poisoning inclines me towards oxygen deprivation as the cause of death, and they show no evidence of choking, no marks of ligature strangulation and none of the congestion and conjunctival haemorrhaging usually associated with manual strangulation. The Technical Bureau will need to examine the pillows for signs of saliva or mucus indicating that they were pressed over the victims' faces' – Cooper glanced at Larry, who gave him the thumbs-up – 'although, given that the pillows in question were on the victims' beds, the presence of bodily fluids would hardly constitute a smoking gun, so to speak. On post-mortem examination – which will begin tomorrow morning at precisely six o'clock – I will attempt to further narrow down the possible mechanisms of death.'

I said, 'Any sign of sexual assault?' Richie jerked like I was electric. Cooper's eyes slid over my shoulder to him for a second, amused and disdainful.

'On preliminary examination,' he said, 'there are no signs of sexual abuse, either recent or chronic. I will, of course, explore this possibility in more depth at the post-mortem.'

'Of course,' I said. 'And this victim here? Can you give us anything?'

Cooper pulled a sheet of paper out of his case and waited, inspecting it, till Richie and I went over to him. The paper was printed with two outlines of a generic male body, front and back. The first one was speckled with a precise, terrible Morse code of red-pen dots and dashes.

Cooper said, 'The adult male received four injuries to the chest from what appears to be a single-edged blade. One' – he tapped a horizontal red line halfway up the left side of the outline's chest – 'is a relatively shallow slash wound: the blade struck a rib near the midline and skidded outwards along the bone for approximately five inches, but does not appear to have penetrated farther. While this would have caused considerable bleeding, it would not have been fatal, even without medical treatment.'

His finger moved upwards, to three leaf-shaped red blots that made a rough arc from below the outline's left collarbone down to the centre of its chest. 'The other major injuries are puncture wounds, also from a single-edged blade. This one penetrated between the upper left ribs; this one struck the sternum; and this one entered the soft tissue by the edge of the sternum. Until the post-mortem is complete I cannot, of course, state the depths or trajectories of the wounds or describe the damage they caused, but unless the assailant was exceptionally strong, the blow directly to the sternum is unlikely to have done more than possibly flay off a chip of bone. I think we can safely posit that either the first or the third of these injuries is the one that caused death.'

The photographer's flash went off, leaving a flare of after-image hovering in front of my eyes: the squiggles of blood on the walls, bright and squirming. For a second I was sure I could smell it. I asked, 'Any defence injuries?'

Cooper flicked his finger at the scattering of red on the outline's arms. 'There is a shallow three-inch slash wound to the palm of the right hand, and a deeper one to the muscle of the left forearm – I would venture to guess that this wound is the source of much of the blood at the scene; it would have bled profusely. The victim also shows a number of minor injuries – small nicks, abrasions and contusions to both forearms – that are consistent with a struggle.'

Patrick could have been on either side of that struggle, and the cut palm could go either way: a defence wound, or his hand slipping down the blade as he stabbed. I asked, 'Could the knife wounds have been self-inflicted?'

Cooper's eyebrows lifted, like I was an idiot child who had somehow managed to say something interesting. 'You are correct, Detective Kennedy: that is indeed a possibility. It would require considerable willpower, of course, but yes: certainly a possibility. The shallow slash injury could have been a hesitation wound – a tentative preliminary attempt, followed by the deeper successful ones. The pattern is quite common in suicides by cutting the wrists; I see no reason why it should not be found in other methods as well. Assuming the victim was right-handed – which should be ascertained before we venture even to theorise – the positioning of the wounds on the left side of the body would be consistent with self-infliction.'

Little by little, Fiona and Richie's creepy intruder was falling out of the race, vanishing away over the horizon behind us. He wasn't gone, not yet, but Patrick Spain was front and centre and coming up the straight fast. This was what I'd been expecting all along, but out of nowhere I caught a tiny flash of disappointment. Murder Ds are hunters; you want to bring home a white lion that you tracked down in dark hissing jungle, not a domestic kitty-cat gone rabid. And under all that, there was a weak streak in me that had been feeling something like sorry for Pat Spain. Like Richie said, the guy had tried.

I asked, 'Can you give us a time of death?'

Cooper shrugged. 'As always, this is at best an estimate, and the delay before I was able to examine the bodies does not improve its accuracy. However, the fact that the thermostat is set to maintain the house's temperature at twenty-one degrees is helpful. I feel confident that all three victims died no earlier than three o'clock this morning and no later than five o'clock, with the balance of probability tilting towards the earlier time.'

'Any indication of who died first?'

Cooper said, spacing it out like he was talking to a moron, 'They died between three and five a.m. Had the evidence provided further details, I would have said as much.'

On every single case, just for kicks, Cooper finds excuses to diss me in front of people I need to work with. Sooner or later I'm going to work out what kind of complaint to file to make him back off, but so far – and he knows this – I've let it slide because, at the moments he picks, I have bigger things on my mind. 'I'm sure you would,' I said. 'What about the weapon? Can you tell us anything about that?'

'A single-edged blade. As I said.' Cooper was bent over his case again, sliding the sheet of paper away; he didn't even bother to give me the withering look.

'And this,' Larry said, 'is where we come in, *if* you don't mind, obviously, Dr Cooper.' Cooper waved a hand graciously – he and Larry get on, somehow. 'Come here, you, Scorcher. Look what my little friend Maureen found, just for you. Or didn't find, more like.'

The girl with the video camera and the nose moved away from the kitchen drawers and pointed. The drawers all had complicated kiddie-proof gadgets on them, and I could see why: in the top one was a neat moulded case, 'Cuisine Bleu' swooping across the inside of the lid in fancy lettering. It was made to hold five knives. Four of them were in place, from a long carving knife to a dinky little thing shorter than my hand: gleaming, honed hair-fine, wicked. The second-biggest knife was missing.

'That drawer was open,' Larry said. 'That's how we spotted them so soon.'

I said, 'And no sign of the fifth knife.'

Head-shakes all round.

Cooper was busy delicately detaching his gloves, finger by finger. I asked, 'Dr Cooper, could you take a look and tell us if this knife might be consistent with the victim's wounds?'

He didn't turn around. 'An informed opinion would

necessitate a full examination of the wounds, both at surface level and in cross-section, preferably with the knife in question available for comparison. Do I appear to have performed such an examination?'

When I was a kid I would have lost the rag with Cooper every time, but I know how to manage myself now, and it'll be a cold day in hell before I give him the satisfaction. I said, 'If you can rule this knife out somehow – the size of the blade, maybe, or the shape of the hilt – then we need to know now, before I send a dozen floaters off on a wild-goose chase.'

Cooper sighed and threw the box a half-second glance. 'I see no reason to exclude it from consideration.'

'Perfect. Larry, can we take one of the other knives with us, show the search team what we're looking for?'

'Be my guest. How about this one? Going by the holes in the box, it's basically the same as the one you're after, just smaller.' Larry picked out the middle knife, dropped it deftly into a clear plastic evidence bag and handed it over. 'Give it back when you're done.'

'Will do. Dr Cooper, can you give me any idea of how far the victim could have got after the wounds were inflicted? How long he could have stayed on his feet?'

Cooper gave me the fish-eye again. 'Less than a minute,' he said. 'Or possibly several hours. Six feet, or conceivably half a mile. Do take your pick, Detective Kennedy, since I am afraid I am unable to provide the kind of answer you want. Far too many variables are involved to permit an intelligent guess, and, regardless of what you might do in my place, I refuse to make an unintelligent one.'

'If you mean could the vic have got rid of the weapon, Scorcher,' Larry said helpfully, 'I can tell you he didn't go out the front, anyway. There's not a drop of blood in the hall, or on the front door. The bottoms of his shoes are *covered*, so are his hands, and he'd have had to hold himself up, wouldn't he, as he got weaker?' Cooper shrugged. 'Oh, he would. Besides, look around you: the poor fella was going like a sprinkler. He'd have left us smudges *everywhere*, not to mention a lovely Hansel-and-Gretel trail. No: once the drama had started, this fella didn't go into the front of the house, and he didn't go upstairs.'

'Right,' I said. 'If that knife shows up, let me know right away. Until then, we'll get out of your hair. Thanks, lads.'

The flash went off again. This time it slapped Patrick Spain's silhouette across my eyes: blazing white, arms flung wide like he was leaping into a tackle, or like he was falling.

'So,' Richie said, on our way down the drive. 'Not an inside job, after all.'

'It's not that simple, old son. Patrick Spain could have gone out into the back garden, maybe even over the wall – or he could have just opened a window and thrown that knife as far as he could. And remember, Patrick's not the only suspect here. Don't forget Jenny Spain. Cooper hasn't checked her out yet: for all we know, she could have been well able to leave the house, stash the knife, come back inside and arrange herself neatly next to her husband. This could be a suicide pact, or she could have been shielding Patrick – she sounds like the type who might well put her last few minutes into protecting the family reputation. Or this could have been her gig, from start to finish.'

The yellow Fiat was gone: Fiona was headed for the hospital to try and see Jenny – hopefully the uniform was driving, so she wouldn't wrap the car around a tree during a crying jag. Instead, we had a cluster of new cars, up at the end of the road by the morgue van. They could have been journalists, or residents who the uniforms were keeping away from the scene, but I was betting these were my floaters. I headed for them. 'And think about this,' I said. 'An outsider isn't going to go in there unarmed and hope he gets a chance to go through the kitchen drawers and find something good. He's going to bring his own weapon.'

'Maybe he did, and then he spotted those knives and figured he'd be better off with something that doesn't trace back to him. Or maybe he wasn't planning on killing anyone. Or maybe that knife isn't the weapon at all: he nicked it to throw us off.'

'Maybe. That's one reason why we need to find it fast: to make sure it doesn't lead us down the wrong track. Want to give me another one?'

Richie said, 'Before it's got rid of.'

'Right. Say this is an outside job: our man – or woman – probably threw the weapon in the water last night, if he has any sense, but if by any chance he's too thick to have thought of that off his own bat, all this activity's bound to tip him off that it might be an idea not to have a bloody knife hanging around. If he ditched it somewhere on the estate, we want to pick him up coming back for it; if he took it home with him, we want to catch him dumping it. All this is assuming he's in the area, obviously.'

Two seagulls exploded up from a heap of rubble, screaming at each other, and Richie's head whipped around. He said, 'He didn't find the Spains by accident. This isn't the kind of place where someone could be just passing by, just happen to spot a set of victims that pushed his buttons.'

'No,' I said. 'Not that kind of place at all. If he's not dead or local, then he came in here looking.'

The floaters were seven guys and a girl, all somewhere in their late twenties, hanging around their cars trying to look sharp and businesslike and ready for anything. When they saw us coming their way they straightened up, tugged jackets down, the biggest guy threw his cigarette away. I pointed to the butt and asked, 'What's your plan there?'

He looked blank. I said, 'You were going to leave it there, weren't you? On the ground, for the Bureau to find and file and send away for DNA testing. Which one were you hoping for? That you'd wind up at the top of our suspect list, or at the top of our time-waster list?'

He whipped up the butt and fumbled it back into his packet, and just that fast, all eight of them were on notice: as long as you're on my investigation, you do not drop the ball. Marlboro Man was scarlet, but someone had to take one for the good of the team.

I said, 'Much better. I'm Detective Kennedy, and this is Detective Curran.' I didn't ask for their names; no time for handshakes and chitchat, and I would only forget anyway. I don't keep track of my floaters' favourite sandwiches and their kids' birthdays, I keep track of what they're doing and whether they're doing it well. 'You'll get a full briefing later on, but for now, this is all you need to know: we're looking for a Cuisine Bleu brand knife, curved six-inch blade, black plastic handle, part of a matching set, a lot like this but slightly larger.' I held up the plastic evidence bag. 'All of you got camera phones? Take a picture, so you've got a reminder of exactly what you're looking for. Delete the photo before you leave the scene tonight. Don't forget.'

They whipped out phones and passed the evidence bag around, handling it like it was made of soap bubbles. I said, 'The knife I've described is a good bet for the murder weapon, but we don't get guarantees in this game, so if you come across another blade hanging around in the undergrowth, for God's sake don't skip on your merry way just because it doesn't fit the description. We're also keeping an eye out for bloody clothing, footprints, keys and anything else that looks remotely out of place. If you find something that's got potential, what do you do?'

I nodded at Marlboro Man – if you take someone down a peg, always give him a way to climb back up. He said, 'Don't touch it. Don't leave it unattended. Call the Bureau lads to photograph it and bag it.'

'Exactly. And call me, too. Anything you find, I want to see. Detective Curran and I will be interviewing the neighbours, so you'll need our mobile numbers, and vice versa – we'll be keeping this off the radio for now. The reception out here is shit, so if a call doesn't get through, text. Don't leave any voicemail messages. Everyone got that?' Down the road, our first reporter had set herself up against some picturesque scaffolding and was doing a piece to camera, trying to keep her coattails down against the wind. Within an hour or two there would be a few dozen like her. Plenty of them wouldn't think twice about hacking into a detective's voicemail.

We did the number-swap all round. 'There'll be more searchers joining us soon,' I said, 'and when they take over I'll have other jobs for you, but we need to get moving now. We're going to start from the back of the house. Start at the garden wall, work your way outwards, make sure you don't leave any gaps between your search areas, you know the drill. Go.'

The semi-d that shared a wall with the Spains' house was empty – permanently empty, nothing in the front room except a screwed-up ball of newspaper and an architectural-level spiderweb – which was a bastard. The nearest signs of human life were two doors down on the other side, in Number 5: the lawn was dead, but there were lace curtains in the windows and a kid's bike lying on its side in the drive.

Movement behind the lace, as we came up the path. Someone had been watching us.

The woman who answered the door was heavy, with a flat suspicious face and dark hair scraped back in a thin ponytail. She was wearing an oversized pink hoodie, undersized grey leggings that were a bad call, and a lot of fake tan that somehow didn't stop her looking pasty. 'Yeah?'

'Police,' I said, showing her my ID. 'Can we come in and have a word?'

She looked at the ID like my photo wasn't up to her high standards. 'I went out earlier, asked those Guards what was going on. They told me to go back inside. I've got a right to be on my own road. Yous can't tell me not to.'

This was going to be a real walk in the park. 'I understand,' I said. 'If you'd like to leave the premises at any point, they won't stop you.'

'Better not. And I wasn't trying to *leave the premises*, anyway. I only wanted to know what's after happening.'

'There's been a crime. We'd like to have a few words with you.'

Her eyes went past me and Richie to the action, and nosiness beat wariness. It usually does. She stood back from the door.

The house had started out exactly like the Spains', but it hadn't stayed that way. The hall had been narrowed down by heaps of gear on the floor – Richie caught his ankle on the wheel of a pram, bit back something unprofessional – and the sitting room was overheated and messy, with crowded wallpaper and a thick smell of soup and wet clothes. A chunky kid about ten was hunched on the floor with his mouth open, going at some PlayStation game that was obviously rated 18s. 'He's off sick,' the woman said. She had her arms folded defensively.

'Lucky for us,' I said, nodding to the kid, who ignored us and kept jamming buttons. 'He may be able to help us. I'm Detective Kennedy and this is Detective Curran. And you are . . . ?'

'Sinéad Gogan. Mrs Sinéad Gogan. Jayden, turn that thing off.' Her accent was some semi-rough outskirt of Dublin.

'Mrs Gogan,' I said, taking a seat on the flowery sofa and finding my notebook, 'how well do you know your neighbours?'

She jerked her head towards the Spains' house. 'Them?'

'The Spains, yes.'

Richie had followed me onto the sofa. Sinéad Gogan's small sharp eyes moved over us, but after a second she shrugged and planted herself in an armchair. 'We'd say hiya. We wouldn't be friendly.'

'You said she's a snobby cow,' said Jayden, not missing a beat blasting zombies.

His mother shot him a glare that he didn't see. 'You shut up.'

'Or?'

'Or else.'

I said, 'Is she a snobby cow?'

'I never said that. I saw an ambulance outside there. What's happened?'

'There's been a crime. What can you tell me about the Spains?'

'Did someone get shot?' Jayden wanted to know. The kid could multitask.

'No. What's snobby about the Spains?'

Sinéad shrugged. 'Nothing. They're grand.'

Richie scratched the side of his nose with his pen. 'Seriously?' he asked, a little diffidently. ''Cause – I mean, I haven't a clue, never met them before, but their gaff looked pretty poncy to me. You can always tell when people've got notions of themselves.'

'Should've seen it before. The big SUV outside, and him washing it and polishing it every weekend, showing off. That didn't last, did it?'

Sinéad was still slumped in her armchair, arms folded and thick legs planted apart, but the satisfaction was edging the snottiness out of her voice. Normally I wouldn't let new lads do the questioning on their first day out, but Richie's angle was good and his accent was getting us further than mine would. I left him to it.

'Not so much to show off about now,' he agreed.

'Doesn't stop them. Still think they're great. Jayden said something to that little young one—'

'Called her a stupid bitch,' Jayden said.

'—and your woman came over here giving it loads, all how the kids weren't getting *on* and was there any way to get them to *cooperate*? Like, so fake, know what I mean? Pretending to be all sweet. I said boys will be boys, deal with it. She wasn't happy about that; keeps her little princess away from us now. Like we're not good enough for them. She's just jealous.'

'Of what?' I asked.

Sinéad gave me a sour stare. 'Us. Me.' I couldn't think of a single reason why Jenny Spain would have been jealous of these people, but apparently that was beside the point. Our Sinéad probably figured she hadn't been invited to Beyoncé's hen party because Beyoncé was jealous.

'Right,' I said. 'When was this, exactly?'

'Spring. April, maybe. Why? Is she saying Jayden done something on them? Because he never—'

She was half out of her chair, heavy and threatening. 'No, no, no,' I said soothingly. 'When was the last time you saw the Spains?'

After a moment she decided she believed me and settled back down. 'To talk to, that was it. I see them around, but I've got nothing to say to them, not after that. Saw her going into the house with the kids yesterday afternoon.'

'At what time?'

'Around quarter to five, maybe. I'd say she was after getting the young one from school and going to the shops – she'd a couple of carrier bags. She looked grand. The little fella was throwing a tantrum 'cause he wanted crisps. Spoilt.'

'Were you and your husband home last night?' I asked.

'Yeah. Where would we go? There's nowhere. Nearest pub's in the town, twelve miles away.' Whelan's and Lynch's were presumably under concrete and scaffolding now, razed to make way for shiny new versions that hadn't materialised yet. For a second I smelled Sunday lunch at Whelan's: chicken nuggets and chips deep-fried from frozen, cigarette smoke, Cidona. 'Go all that way and then not be able to drink 'cause you've to drive home – there's no buses that go here. What's the point?'

'Did you hear anything out of the ordinary?'

Another stare, this one more antagonistic, like I had accused her of something and she was considering glassing me. 'What would we have heard?'

Jayden sniggered suddenly. I said, 'Did you hear something, Jayden?'

'What, like *screams*?' Jayden asked. He had even turned around.

'Did you hear screams?'

Pissed-off grimace. 'Nah.' Sooner or later some other detective was going to be running into Jayden in a whole different context.

'Then what did you hear? Anything at all could help us.'

Sinéad's face still had that look, antagonism cut with something like wariness. She said, 'We heard nothing. We'd the telly on.'

'Yeah,' Jayden said. 'Nothing.' Something on the screen exploded. He said, '*Shit*,' and dived back into the game.

I asked, 'What about your husband, Mrs Gogan?'

'He didn't hear nothing either.'

'Could we confirm that with him?'

'He's gone out.'

'What time will he be back?'

Shrug. 'What's after happening?'

I said, 'Can you tell us if you've seen anyone entering or leaving the Spains' house recently?'

Sinéad's mouth pursed up. 'I don't be spying on my

neighbours,' she snapped, which meant she did, as if I had had any doubts.

'I'm sure you don't,' I said. 'But this isn't about spying. You're not blind or deaf; you can't help it if you see people coming and going, or hear their cars. How many houses on this road are occupied?'

'Four. Us, and them, and two down the other end. So?'

'So if you see someone around this end, you can't help knowing they're here for the Spains. So have they had any visitors recently?'

She rolled her eyes. 'If they have, I didn't see them. All right?'

'Not as popular as they think,' Richie said, with a little smirk.

Sinéad smirked back. 'Exactly.'

He leaned forward. Confidentially: 'Does anyone bother coming out to them at all?'

'Not any more, they don't. When we first moved in, they'd have people over on a Sunday: the same kind as themselves, driving up in the big SUVs and all, swanning around with bottles of wine – a few cans weren't good enough for them. They used to have barbecues. Showing off again.'

'Not these days?'

The smirk got bigger. 'Not since he lost his job. They'd a birthday party for one of the kids, back in spring, but that's the last time I saw anyone go in there. Like I said, though, I don't be watching. But it just goes to show you, doesn't it?'

'It does, yeah. Tell us something: have you had any hassle with mice, rats, anything like that?'

That got Jayden's attention. He even hit Pause. 'Jesus! Did rats *eat* them?'

'No,' I said.

'Ahhh,' he said, disappointed, but he kept watching us. The kid was unnerving. He had flat, colourless eyes, like a squid.

His mother said, 'Never had rats. I wouldn't be surprised, the way the drains are in this place, but no. Not yet, anyway.'

Richie said, 'It isn't great out here, no?'

'It's a dump,' Jayden said.

'Yeah? Why?'

He shrugged. Sinéad said, 'Have you looked at the place?'

'Looks all right to me,' Richie said, surprised. 'Nice houses, loads of space, you've done the place up lovely . . .'

'Yeah, that's what we thought. Looked great on the plans. Hang on—'

She heaved herself out of the chair with a grunt and bent over – I could have lived without that view – to paw through the mess on a side table: celebrity magazines, spilled sugar, a baby monitor, half a sausage roll on a greasy plate. 'Here,' she said, shoving a brochure at Richie. 'That's what we thought we were buying.'

The front of the brochure said OCEAN VIEW, in the same curly writing as the signboard outside the estate, over a photo of a laughing couple hugging two catalogue kids in front of a snow-white house and Mediterranean-blue waves. Inside was the menu: four-bed, five-bed, detached, duplex, whatever your heart desired, all of them so pristine they almost glowed and so well Photoshopped you could barely tell they were scale models. The houses had names: the Diamond was a five-bed detached with garage, the Topaz was a two-bed duplex, the Emerald and the Pearl and the rest were some-where in between – it looked like we were in the Sapphire. More curly lettering cooed breathlessly about the beach, the crèche, the leisure centre, a corner shop, a playground, 'a self-contained haven with all the premier facilities of cutting-edge luxe living on your doorstep'.

It should have looked pretty damn sexy – like I said before, other people can get their kicks being snobby about new develop-ments if they want, but I love them; they feel positive, like big bets placed on the future. For some reason, though – maybe because I'd seen what was outside – this brochure struck me as what Richie would have called creepy.

Sinéad jabbed a stubby finger at the brochure. 'That's what we were promised. All that. Says it in the contract and everything.'

'And that's not what you got?' Richie asked.

She snorted. 'Does it look like it?'

He shrugged. 'It's not finished yet. Could be great when it is.'

'It's not going to *be* bleeding finished. People stopped buying, with the recession, so the builders stopped building. We went out one morning a few months back and they were gone. Everything, diggers and all. Never came back.'

'Jaysus,' Richie said, shaking his head.

'Yeah, Jaysus. Our downstairs toilet's banjaxed, but the plumber who put it in won't come and fix it 'cause he was never paid. Everyone does be saying we should go to court and get compensation, but who'd we bring?'

'The builders?' I suggested.

She gave me that flat stare again, like she was considering punching me for being such a thick. 'Um, yeah, we did actually think of that. Can't find them. They started hanging up on us; now they've changed their number. We went to yous lot, even. Yous said our toilet wasn't a *police matter.*'

Richie lifted the brochure to get her attention back. 'What about all this stuff, the crèche and that?'

'That,' Sinéad said. Her mouth squashed up in disgust. It made her even uglier. 'In there's the only place you'll ever see that. We complained about the crèche a load of times – that was one of the reasons we bought here, and then hello, nothing? It opened, in the end. Closed after a month 'cause there was only five kids going. Where the playground was supposed to be, that's like something out of Baghdad; kids'd take their life in their hands playing there. The leisure centre never even got built. We complained about that too, they put an exercise bike in an empty house and said there you go. Bike got robbed.'

'How about the shop?'

A humourless sniff of laughter. 'Yeah, right. I've to go five miles to buy milk, to the petrol station on the motorway. We haven't got *streetlights.* I'm afraid for my life to go out on me own after dark, there could be rapists or anything – there's a load of non-nationals renting a house over in Ocean View Close. And if something happened to me, would yous lot come out and do anything about it? My husband rang yous a few months back, when there was a bunch of knackers having a party in one of them houses across the road. Yous didn't show up till the morning. We could've been burnt out of it for all you'd care.'

In other words, getting anything out of Sinéad was always going to be this much fun. I said, 'Do you know if the Spains had been having any similar problems – with the development company, with the partiers across the road, with anyone?'

Shrug. 'Wouldn't know. Like I said, we weren't friendly, know what I mean? What happened to them, anyway? Are they dead, or what?'

Before long, the morgue boys were going to be bringing out the bodies. I said, 'Maybe Jayden should wait in another room.'

Sinéad eyed him. 'No point. He'll only listen at the door.' Jayden nodded.

I said, 'There's been a violent attack. I'm not in a position to give you details, but the crime in question is murder.'

'Jaysus,' Sinéad breathed, swaying forward. Her mouth stayed open, wet and avid. 'Who's been kilt?'

'We can't give you that information.'

'Did he go for her, did he?'

Jayden had forgotten about his game. On the screen a zombie was frozen splayed in mid-fall, with scraps of its head mushrooming everywhere. I asked, 'Do you have any reason to think he might go for her?'

That wary flick of her eyelids. She slumped back in the chair and folded her arms again. 'I was only asking.'

'If you do, Mrs Gogan, you need to tell us.'

'I don't know and I don't care.'

Bullshit, but I know that thick, lumpy stubborn: the harder I pushed, the more solid it would get. 'Right,' I said. 'In the last few months, have you seen anyone around the estate who you didn't recognise?'

Jayden let out a high, sharp snicker. Sinéad said, 'Never see anyone, hardly. And I wouldn't recognise most of them anyway. We're not, like, all buddy-buddy out here. I've friends of my own; I don't need to be hanging off the neighbours.'

Translated, you couldn't have paid the neighbours enough to hang out with the Gogans. They were probably all just jealous. 'Then have you seen anyone who looked out of place? Anyone who worried you for any reason?'

'Only the non-nationals in the Close. There's dozens of them in that house. I'd say the lot of them are illegal. You're not going to check that out either, though, are you?'

'We'll pass it on to the appropriate department. Has anyone called to the door? Selling something, maybe? Asking to check the pipes or the wiring?'

'Yeah, right. Like anyone cares about our wiring— *Jaysus!*' Sinéad shot upright. 'Was it, like, some psycho that broke in? Like on that show on the telly, like a *serial* killer?'

All of a sudden she looked alive. Fear had knocked the blankness off her face. I said, 'We can't give details of—'

''Cause if it's that, you better tell me *now*, right? I'm not staying here waiting for some sick bastard to come in and torture us, yous lot would stand there and watch him go at it before you'd do a bleeding thing—'

It was the first actual emotion we'd seen out of her. The ghost-blue children next door: nothing but gossip fodder, no more real than some TV show, right up until the danger might be personal. I said, 'I can promise you we won't stand there and watch.'

'Don't you disrespect me! I'll get onto the radio, I will, I'll ring the Joe Duffy Show—'

And we would spend the rest of this investigation battling our way through a media cyclone of cops-don't-care-about-the-little-guy hysteria. I've been there. It feels like someone's using a tennis-ball machine to fire starving pug dogs at you. Before I could come up with something soothing, Richie leaned forward and said earnestly, 'Mrs Gogan, you've got every right to be worrying. Sure, you're a mammy.'

'Exactly. I've got my kids to think about. I'm not gonna—'

'Was it a paedophile?' Jayden wanted to know. 'What'd he do to them?'

I was starting to see why Sinéad ignored him. 'Now, you know there's a load we can't be telling you,' Richie said, 'but I can't leave a mammy to worry, so I'm trusting you not to pass this on. Can I do that, yeah?'

I almost cut him off right there, but he had been working this interview well, so far. And Sinéad was calming down, that avid look creeping back up under the fear. 'Yeah. All right.'

'I'm gonna put it like this,' Richie said. He leaned closer. 'You've got nothing to be afraid of. If anyone dangerous is out there, and I'm only saying *if*, we're doing everything that needs doing about it.' He left an impressive pause and did something meaningful with his eyebrows. 'Do you get me, yeah?'

Confused silence. 'Yeah,' Sinéad said, in the end. 'Course.'

'You do, of course. Now remember: not a word.'

She said primly, 'I wouldn't.' She would tell everyone she knew, obviously, but she had shag-all to tell them: she would have to stick to a smug look and vague hints about secret info she couldn't share. It was a cute little trick. Richie went up a rung on my ladder.

'And you're not worried any more, sure you're not? Now that you know.'

'Ah, no. I'm grand.'

The baby monitor let out a furious shriek. 'For fuck's *sake*,' said Jayden, hitting Play and turning up the zombie volume.

'Baby's awake,' Sinéad said, without moving. 'I've to go.'

I said, 'Is there anything else you can tell us about the Spains? Anything at all?'

Another shrug. That flat face didn't change, but something flickered in her eyes. We would be coming back to the Gogans.

On our way down the drive I said to Richie, 'You want to talk about creepy? Take a look at that kid.'

'Yeah,' Richie said. He fingered his ear and glanced over his shoulder at the Gogans'. 'Something he's not telling us.'

'Him? The mother, sure. But the kid?'

'Definitely.'

'Right. When we come back to them, you can take a crack at him.'

'Yeah? Me?'

'You did a good job in there. Have a think about how you're going to go about it.' I tucked my notebook into my pocket. 'Meanwhile, who else do you want to ask about the Spains?'

Richie turned back to face me. 'D'you know something?' he

said. 'I haven't got a clue. Normally I'd say let's talk to the families, the neighbours, the victims' friends, the people they work with, the lads down the pub where he drinks, the people who saw them last. But they were both out of work. There's no pub for him to go to. Nobody calls round, not even their families, not when it means coming all this way. It could've been weeks since anyone even saw them, except maybe at the school gates. And *that*'s the neighbours.'

He jerked his head backwards. Jayden was pressed up against the sitting-room window, controller in one hand, mouth still hanging open. He saw me catch him looking, but he didn't even blink.

'The poor bastards,' Richie said softly. 'They'd no one.'

# 5

The two sets of neighbours at the other end of the road were out, at work or wherever. Cooper was gone, presumably off to the hospital to have a look at whatever was left of Jenny Spain. The morgue van was gone: the bodies would be headed for the same hospital to wait their turn for Cooper's attention, only a floor or two away from Jenny, if she had made it this far.

The Bureau team were still working hard. Larry flapped a hand at me from the kitchen. 'Come here, you, young fella. Have a look at this.'

'This' was the baby-monitor viewers, five of them, neatly laid out in clear evidence bags on the counter, all covered in black print dust. 'Found the fifth one in that corner over there, under a bunch of kiddie books,' Larry said triumphantly. 'His Lordship wants video cameras, His Lordship gets video cameras. And they're good ones, too. I'm no expert on the baby gear, but I'd say these are high-end. They pan, they zoom, they do colour during the daytime and black-and-white on automatic infrared in the dark, they probably make you poached eggs in the morning . . .' He walked two fingers along the line of monitors, clicking his tongue happily to himself, picked one and pressed the power button through the bag. 'Guess what that is. Go on, have a guess.'

The screen lit up in black and white: grey cylinders and rectangles crowding in at each side, floating white dust-motes, a shapeless patch of darkness hovering in the middle. I said, 'The Blob?'

'That's what I was thinking myself. But then Declan – that's Declan, over there; wave hello to the nice men, Declan – he noticed that this cupboard here was just a teeny crack open, so he took a look inside. And guess what he found?'

Larry flung open the cupboard with a flourish. 'Lookie, lookie.'

A ring of sullen red lights stared up at us for a second, then faded and vanished. The camera was stuck to the inside of the cupboard door with what looked like a full roll of duct tape. The cereal boxes and tins of peas had been pushed to the sides of the shelves. Behind them, someone had bashed a plate-sized hole in the wall.

'What the *hell*,' I said.

'Hold your horses right there. Before you say anything, take a look at this.'

Another monitor. The same fuzzy shades of monochrome: slanting beams, paint tins, some spiky mechanical tangle I couldn't make out. I said, 'The attic?'

'The very spot. And that thing on the floor? It's a *trap*. An animal trap. And not a sweet little mousey-catchey thingy, either. I'm not some kind of expert wilderness man, I wouldn't know, but that thing looks like it could take down a *puma*.'

Richie asked, 'Is there bait in it?'

'I like him,' Larry said, to me. 'Smart young fella; goes straight to the heart of things. He'll go far. No, Detective Curran, unfortunately no bait, so no way to guess what on earth they were trying to catch. There's a hole under the eaves where something could have got in – now don't get excited, Scorcher, we're not looking at a person here. Maybe a fox on a diet could just about have squeezed through, but nothing that would need a *bear* trap. We checked the attic for pawprints and droppings, see if we could get a hint that way, but there's nothing bigger than a spider's poo. If your vics had vermin, they're very, very *discreet* vermin.'

I said, 'Have we got prints?'

'Oh God yes, prints by the dozen. Fingerprints all over the cameras and the trap, and on that arrangement over the attic hatch. But young Gerry says don't quote him on this, but at a very preliminary glance there's no reason to think they're not consistent with your vic – this vic here, obviously, not the kiddies. Same for the footprints up in the attic: adult male, shoe size matches this boyo.'

'What about the holes in the walls – anything around there?'

'Again, bucketloads of prints – you weren't joking about keeping us busy, were you? A lot of them, going by the size, they're the kiddies exploring. Most of the rest, Gerry says same again: no reason to think they're not your victim, he'll need to get them into the lab to confirm. Offhand, I'd say the vics made the holes themselves, nothing to do with last night.'

I said, 'Look at this place, Larry. I'm a tidy kind of guy, but my gaff hasn't been in this good shape since the day I moved in. These people were beyond houseproud. They lined up their *shampoo* bottles. I'll give you fifty quid if you can find me one speck of dust. Why go to all that hassle keeping your house in perfect nick, and then bash holes in the walls? And if you have to bash holes, why not fix them? Or at least cover them up?'

'People are mad,' Larry said. He was losing interest; he cares about what happened, not why. 'All of them. You should know that, Scorch. I'm just saying, *if* someone from outside made those holes, it looks like either the walls have been cleaned since, or else he wore gloves.'

'Anything else around the holes? Blood, drug residue, anything?'

Larry shook his head. 'No blood, inside the holes or around them, except where they got in the way of spatter from this mess. No drug residue that we've found, but if you think we could be missing it, I'll get a drug dog in.'

'Hold off on that for now, unless something comes up pointing that way. What about in here, in the blood? No prints that couldn't have come from our vics?'

'Have you *seen* this place? How long do you think we've been here? Ask me again in a *week*. You can see for yourself, there's enough bloody footprints for Dracula's marching band, but I bet you most of them are the uniforms and the paramedics and their great big clumsy feet. We'll just have to hope that a few prints from the actual *crime* had dried enough to stay in shape even with that lot wandering back and forth all over them. Same for the bloody handprints: we've got loads, but whether there's any good ones left is anyone's guess.'

He was in his element: Larry loves complications and he loves grousing. 'And if anyone can salvage them, Lar, it's you. Any sign of the vics' phones?'

'Your wish is my command. Her mobile was on her bedside table, his was on the hall table, and we've bagged the landline just for funsies. Got the computer, too.'

'Beautiful,' I said. 'Send it all down to Computer Crime. What about keys?'

'A full set in her purse, on the hall table: two front door keys, back door key, car key. Another full set in his coat pocket. A set of spares for the house in the drawer of the hall table. No Golden Bay Resort pen, not so far, but we'll let you know.'

'Thanks, Larry. We'll go have a root around upstairs, if that's OK.'

'And here I was worried this would be just another boring over-dose,' Larry said happily, as we were leaving. 'Thank *you*, Scorcher. I owe you one.'

The Spains' bedroom was glowing a cosy, fuzzy gold – curtains stay closed, against salivating neighbours and journalists with zoom lenses, but Larry's lot had left the lights on for us when they were done printing the switches. The air had that indefinable intimate smell of a lived-in place: the faintest tint of shampoo, aftershave, skin.

There was a fitted wardrobe along one wall and two cream-coloured chests of drawers in the corners, the curly-edged kind that someone's gone at with sandpaper to make them look old and interesting. On top of the chest on Jenny's side were three framed eight-by-tens. Two were squashy red babies; the one in the middle was a wedding shot taken on the stairway of some fancy country-house hotel. Patrick in a tux with a pink tie and a pink rose in his buttonhole, Jenny in a fitted dress with a train that spread out over the stairs below them, bouquet of pink roses, lots of dark wood, lances of sunlight through the ornate landing window. Jenny was pretty, or had been. Average height, nice slim figure, with long hair that she had turned straight and blonde and twisted into some complicated thing on top of her head. Patrick had been in better shape then, broad-chested and flat-stomached. He had an arm around Jenny, and both of them were smiling from ear to ear.

I said, 'Let's start with the chests of drawers,' and headed for Jenny's. If one of this pair had secrets stashed away, it was her. The world would be a different place, a lot more difficult for us and a lot more ignorantly blissful for husbands, if women would just throw things away.

The top drawer was mainly makeup, plus a pill packet – Monday's pill was gone, she had been up to date – and a blue velvet jewellery box. She was into jewellery, everything from cheap bling through some nice tasteful pieces that looked pretty upmarket to me – my ex-wife liked her rocks, I know my way around carats. The emerald ring Fiona had mentioned was still there, in a battered black presentation box, waiting for Emma to grow up. I said, 'Look at this.'

Richie glanced across from Patrick's underwear drawer – he was working fast and neatly, giving each pair of boxers a quick shake and tossing it on a pile on the floor. He said, 'So, not robbery.'

'Probably not. Nothing professional, anyway. If things went wrong, an amateur might get spooked and run for it, but a professional – or a debt collector – wouldn't go without getting what he came for.'

'An amateur doesn't fit. Like we said before: this wasn't random.'

'True enough. Can you give me a theory that does cover what we've got?'

Richie unrolled pairs of socks and dumped them on the pile, getting his ideas straight. 'The intruder Jenny talked about,' he said, after a moment. 'Let's say he finds a way to get back in, more than once maybe. Fiona said herself, Jenny wouldn't have told her.'

No clandestine condoms at the bottom of the jewellery box, no wraps of Mummy's Little Helper tucked in with the makeup brushes. I said, 'But Jenny did tell Fiona she was going to start using the alarm. How does he get around that?'

'He got around the locks, the first time. Looks like Patrick thought he was coming in through the attic. He might've been right. Up through the house next door, maybe.'

'If Larry and his team had found an access point in the attic, they'd have told us. And you heard them: they looked.'

Richie started folding socks and boxers back into the drawer, taking care over it. We don't generally bother to leave things perfect; I couldn't tell whether he was thinking of Jenny having to come home to this place – which, given the odds of anyone buying it, was actually a possibility – or of Fiona having to clean it out. Either way, the empathy was something he was going to have to watch. He said, 'OK, so maybe your man's got a way around the alarm system. That could be what he does for a living. Could even be how he picked the Spains: he installed their system, got hung up on them . . .'

'The system came with the house, according to that brochure. It was here before they were. Dial back the *Cable Guy* there, old son.' Jenny's underwear drawer was divided neatly into special-occasion sexies, white exercise gear and what I assumed were everyday pink-and-white frillies; nothing kinky, no toys, apparently the Spains had been good old vanilla. 'But let's assume, just for a moment, that our man's found a way to gain access. Then what?'

'He starts getting more in-your-face, smashes those holes in the walls. No way to stop Patrick from finding out then. Maybe Patrick thinks like Jenny: he wants to know what the story is here, he'd rather catch the guy than shut him out or scare him off. So he sets up surveillance on the spots where he knows, or thinks, your man's been.'

'So that's a man-trap, up in the attic. To catch the guy in the act and keep him there till we arrive.'

Richie said, 'Or till Patrick was done with him. Depending.'

I raised my eyebrows. 'You've got a twisted mind, my son. That's a good thing. Don't let it run away with you, though.'

'If someone scared your wife, threatened your kids . . .' Richie shook out a pair of khakis; next to his scrawny arse they looked huge, like they had belonged to a superhero. He said, 'You might be on for doing some damage.'

'It hangs together, near enough. It hangs.' I slid Jenny's underwear drawer shut. 'Except for one thing: why?'

'You mean why would your man be after the Spains, like?'

'Why would he do any of it? We're talking about months of stalking, topped off with mass murder. Why pick this family? Why break in and do nothing worse than eat ham slices? Why break in again and bash the walls in? Why escalate to murder? Why take the risk of starting with the kids? Why suffocate them but stab the adults? Why any of it?'

Richie fished fifty cents out of the back pocket of the khakis and shrugged – he did it like a kid, shoulders jumping around his ears. 'Maybe he's mental.'

I stopped what I was doing. 'Is that what you're planning on putting in the file for the Director of Public Prosecutions? "I dunno, maybe he's, like, totally *mental*"?'

Richie flushed, but he didn't back down. 'I don't know what the doctors'd call it. But you know what I mean.'

'Actually, old son, I don't. "Mental" isn't a reason. It comes in an awful lot of flavours, most of them are non-violent, and every single one of them has some kind of logic, whether or not it makes sense to you and me. Nobody slaughters a family because, hey, I just felt mental today.'

'You asked for a theory that covers what we've got. That's the best I can come up with.'

'A theory that's built on "because he's mental" isn't a theory. It's a cheap cop-out. And it's lazy thinking. I expect better from you, Detective.'

I turned my shoulder to him and went back to the drawers, but I could feel him behind me, not moving. I said, 'Spit it out.'

'What I told your woman Gogan. That she didn't need to worry about some psycho. I just wanted to stop her ringing around the talk shows, but fact is, she's got a right to be scared. I don't know what word you want me to use, but if this fella's mental, then nobody has to go asking for trouble. He's bringing it with him.'

I slid the drawer shut, leaned back against the chest and stuck my hands in my pockets. 'There was a philosopher,' I said, 'a few hundred years back, who said you should always go for the simplest solution. And he wasn't talking about the easy answer. He meant the solution that involves throwing in the fewest extras on top of what you've actually got on hand. The fewest ifs and maybes, the fewest unknown guys who might possibly have just happened to wander up in the middle of the action. Do you see where I'm going with this?'

Richie said, 'You don't think there was any intruder.'

'Wrong. I think that what we've got on hand is Patrick and Jennifer Spain, and any solution that involves them needs fewer extras than a solution that doesn't. What happened here came from one of two places: inside this house, or outside. I'm not saying there was no intruder. I'm saying that even if the killer came from outside, the simplest solution is that the *reason* came from inside.'

'Hang on,' Richie said. 'You said: still room for an outsider. And that thing with the attic hatch: you said maybe to catch the guy who made the holes. What . . . ?'

I sighed. 'Richie. When I said *outsider*, I was talking about the guy who lent Patrick Spain gambling money. The guy Jenny was shagging on the side. Fiona Rafferty. I wasn't talking about Freddy bloody Krueger. Do you see the difference?'

'Yeah,' Richie said. His voice was even, but the set of his jaw said he was starting to get annoyed. 'I do.'

'I know this case looks – what's the word you used? – *creepy*. I know it's the kind of thing that gets the imagination working over-time. That's all the more reason to keep your feet on the ground. The most likely solution here is still what it was when we were driving up: your bog-standard murder-suicide.'

'That,' Richie said, pointing at the hole above the bed, 'that isn't bog-standard. Just for *starters*.'

'How do you know? Maybe all the free time was getting on Patrick Spain's nerves and he decided to go in for some kind of home improvement, or maybe there's something dicky in the electrics, just like you suggested, and he tried to fix it himself instead of paying an electrician – that could explain why the alarm wasn't on, too. Maybe the Spains had a rat after all, caught it, and left the trap up in case its mates came sniffing around. Maybe those holes get bigger every time a car goes past the house, and they wanted video to play in court when they sue the builders. For all we know, everything odd in this whole case comes down to shoddy building.'

'Is that what you think? Seriously, like?'

I said, 'What I think, Richie my friend, is that imagination is a dangerous thing. Rule Number Six, or whatever we're on now: stick with the nice boring solution that requires the least imagination, and you'll do fine.'

And I went back to digging through Jenny Spain's T-shirts. I recognised some of the labels: she had the same tastes as my ex. After a minute Richie shook his head, spun the fifty-cent piece onto the top of the chest and started folding Patrick's khakis. We left each other alone for a while.

The secret I had been waiting for was at the back of Jenny's bottom drawer, and it was a lump tucked into the sleeve of a pink cashmere cardigan. When I shook the sleeve, something skittered across the thick carpet: something small and hard, folded tightly in a piece of tissue paper.

'Richie,' I said, but he had already put down a jumper and come to look.

It was a round pin-badge, the cheapo metal kind you can buy at street stalls if you get the urge to wear a hash leaf or a band name. The paint on this one was worn patchy, but it had started out pale blue; to one side there was a smiling yellow sun, to the other something white that could have been a hot-air balloon or maybe a kite. In the middle it said, in bubbly yellow letters, I GO TO JOJO'S!

I said, 'What do you think of that?'

Richie said, 'Looks bog-standard to me,' and gave me a straight look.

'It does to me, too, but its location doesn't. Just offhand, can you give me a bog-standard reason for that?'

'Maybe one of the kids hid it there. Some kids are into hiding stuff.'

'Maybe.' I turned the badge over in my palm. There were two narrow bands of rust on the pin, where it had spent a long time stuck through the same piece of cloth. 'I'd like to know what it is, all the same. "JoJo's" ring any bells with you?'

He shook his head. 'Cocktail bar? Restaurant? Playschool?'

'Could be. I've never heard of it, but it could be long gone; this doesn't look new to me. Or it could be in the Maldives, or somewhere they went on holiday. I'm not seeing why Jenny Spain would need to hide anything like that, though. Something expensive, I'd be thinking lover's gift, but this?'

'If she wakes up . . .'

'We'll ask her what's the story. That doesn't mean she'll tell us, though.'

I folded the badge back into its tissue paper and found an evidence bag. From the chest of drawers Jenny smiled at me, tucked in the curve of Patrick's arm. Under the fancy hair and all the layers of makeup, she had been ridiculously young. The simple, shining triumph on her face told me that everything beyond that day had been just a golden blur in her mind: *And they lived happily ever after.*

Cooper's mood had improved, probably because this case was off the far end of the fucked-up scale. He rang me from the hospital once he had had a look at Jenny Spain. By that time Richie and I had moved on to the Spains' wardrobe, which was more of the same: mostly not designer stuff, but top-of-the-trend, and plenty of it – Jenny had three pairs of Uggs; no drugs, no cash, no dark side. In an old biscuit tin on Patrick's top shelf were a handful of withered stalks, a sea-worn piece of wood patchy with flaking green paint, a scattering of pebbles, bleached seashells: gifts from the children, collected on beach walks to welcome Daddy home.

'Detective Kennedy,' Cooper said. 'You will be pleased to know that the remaining victim still remains.'

'Dr Cooper,' I said. I hit speakerphone and held out the BlackBerry between me and Richie, who lowered a handful of ties – lots of Hugo Boss – to listen. 'Thanks for getting in touch. How's she doing?'

'Her condition is still critical, but her doctor feels she has an excellent chance of survival.' I mouthed *Yes!* at Richie, who did a noncommittal grimace: Jenny Spain surviving would be nice for us, not so much for her. 'I may say that I agree, although living patients are hardly my speciality.'

'Can you tell us about her injuries?'

There was a pause while Cooper considered making me wait for his official report, but the good mood held. 'She suffered a number of wounds, of which several are significant. A slash wound running from the right cheekbone to the right corner of the mouth. A stab wound beginning at the sternum and glancing off sideways into the right breast. A stab wound just below the bottom of the right shoulder blade. And a stab wound to the abdomen, just to the right of the navel. There are also a number of smaller cuts to the face, throat, chest and arms – these will be detailed and diagrammed in my report. The weapon was a single-edged blade or blades, consistent with the one used to stab Patrick Spain.'

When someone wrecks a woman's face, specially a woman who's young and pretty, it's almost always personal. I caught that smile and those pink roses out of the corner of my eye again, turned my shoulder to them.

'She was also struck on the back of the head, just to the left of the midline, with a heavy object whose striking surface was approximately the shape and size of a golf ball. There are fresh bruises to both wrists and forearms; the shapes and positions are consistent with manual restraint during a struggle. There is no sign of any sexual assault, and she has not had recent intercourse.'

Someone had gone to town on Jenny Spain. I said, 'How strong would the attacker or attackers have needed to be?'

'Judging by the edges of the wounds, the bladed weapon appears to have been extremely sharp, which means that no particular strength would have been required to inflict the stab and slash wounds. The blunt trauma injury to the head would depend on the nature of the weapon: if it was inflicted with an actual golf ball held in the attacker's hand, for example, it would have required a considerable amount of strength, whereas if it was inflicted by, let us say, a golf ball placed in the toe of a long sock, momentum would substitute for force, meaning that a child could have done it. The bruises to the wrists imply that a child did not, in fact, do it: the attacker's fingers slipped during the struggle, making it impossible for me to gauge the size of the hands that restrained Mrs Spain, but I can say that they did not belong to a small child.'

'Is there any way the injuries could have been self-inflicted?' Double-check everything, even the stuff that seems obvious, or some defence lawyer will do it for you.

'It would require a supremely talented would-be suicide,' Cooper said, using his Moron Whisperer voice again, 'to stab herself below the shoulder blade, hit herself on the back of the head and then, in the fraction of an instant before unconsciousness supervened, hide both weapons so thoroughly that they escaped discovery for at least a few hours. In the absence of proof that Mrs Spain is a trained contortionist and magician, I think we can probably exclude self-infliction.'

'Probably? Or definitely?'

'If you doubt me, Detective Kennedy,' Cooper said sweetly, 'do feel free to attempt the feat yourself,' and he hung up.

Richie was rubbing behind his ear like a dog scratching, thinking hard. He said, 'And that's Jenny out of the picture.'

I slid the phone back into my jacket pocket. 'But not Fiona. And if she was going after Jenny, for whatever reason, she might well have gone for the face. Being the plain one could've worn very thin after a lifetime. Bye-bye big sister, no open casket, no more being the family babe.'

He considered the wedding shot. 'Jenny's not actually prettier. Better groomed, just.'

'It works out to the same thing. If the two of them went

clubbing together, I bet I can tell you who got all the male attention and who was the consolation prize.'

'That there was Jenny's wedding, but. She mightn't be that done up normally.'

'I'll bet you anything she is. There's more makeup in that drawer than Fiona's used in her lifetime, and just about every piece of clothing here is worth more than Fiona's whole outfit put together – and she knew it: remember that comment about Jenny's expensive gear? Jenny's a looker, Fiona's not; simple as that. And while we're on male attention, think about this: Fiona got very, very protective about Patrick. She said the three of them go way back; I'd like to know a little more about the history there. I've seen stranger love triangles in my time.'

Richie nodded, still examining the photo. 'Fiona's only small. You think she could've taken out a big fella like Patrick?'

'With a sharp blade, and the element of surprise? Yeah, I think she probably could have. I'm not saying she's top of the list, but we can't cross her off it quite yet.'

Fiona moved another notch or two up the list when we got back to searching. Tucked away at the bottom of Patrick's wardrobe, behind the shoe rack, was the jackpot: a stocky grey filing box. Out of sight – it didn't go with the decor – but not out of mind: they had kept three years' worth of just about everything, all filed away in perfect order. I could have kissed the box. If I had to pick just one angle on a victim's life, give me financials any day. People wrap their e-mails and their friendships and even their diaries in multiple layers of bullshit, but their credit-card statements never lie.

All this stuff would be coming back to headquarters so we could get a lot better acquainted, but I wanted an overview straight away. We sat on the bed – Richie hesitated for a second, like he might contaminate it, or maybe vice versa – and spread out paper.

The big documents came first: four birth certs, four passports, marriage cert. They had a life insurance policy, up-to-date, that paid off the mortgage if either of them died. There had been another policy, two hundred grand on Patrick and a hundred on

Jenny, but that had lapsed over the summer. Their will left everything to each other; if they both died, everything including custody of the kids went to Fiona. There are plenty of people out there who would love a few hundred grand and a new house, and who would love it even more if it didn't come with a couple of kids attached.

And then we hit the financials, and Fiona Rafferty plummeted so far down the list I could barely see her. The Spains had kept things simple, everything into and out of one joint account, which was a bonus for us. And just like we had expected, they were flat broke. Patrick's old job had given him a nice little lump of redundancy money, but since then the only cash coming in had been his unemployment benefit and the children's allowance. And they had kept spending. February, March, April, the money had kept coming out of the account at the same rate as ever. May, they had started cutting back. By August, the whole family had been living on less than I do.

Too little too late. The mortgage was three months in arrears and there were two letters from the lender – some cowboy-sounding outfit called HomeTime – the second one a lot nastier than the first. In June the Spains had swapped their bill-pay mobiles for pay-as-you-go, and both of them had more or less stopped calling people – four months' worth of phone-credit receipts were paper-clipped together, barely enough to keep a teenage girl going for a week. The SUV had gone back where it came from at the end of July; they were a month behind on the Volvo, four months behind on the credit card and fifty quid behind on the electricity. As of their last statement, there had been three hundred and fourteen euros and fifty-seven cents in the current account. If the Spains had been into anything dodgy, they were either very bad at it or very, very good.

Even when they got careful, though, they had kept their wireless broadband. I needed to get Computer Crime to flag that computer every shade of urgent. Patrick and Jenny might have had no one in the flesh, but they had had the whole internet to talk to, and some people tell cyberspace the things they wouldn't tell their best friends.

In a way, you could probably say they had been broke even before Patrick lost his job. He had made good money, but their credit card had a six-grand limit and it had spent most of the time maxed out – there were a lot of three-figure charges to Brown Thomas, Debenhams, a few websites with vaguely familiar girly names – and then there were the two car loans and the mortgage. But only innocents think broke is made of how much you earn and how much you owe. Ask any economist: broke is made of how you feel. The credit crunch didn't happen because people woke up any poorer than they'd been the day before; it happened because people woke up scared.

Back in January, when Jenny had spent two hundred and seventy euros on some website called Shoe 2 You, the Spains had been doing just fine. By July, when she had been too scared to change the locks against an intruder, they had been broke as all hell.

Some people get hit by a tidal wave, dig in their nails and hold on; they stay focused on the positive, keep visualising the way through till it opens up in front of them. Some lose hold. Broke can lead people to places they would never have imagined. It can nudge a law-abiding citizen onto that blurred crumbling edge where a dozen kinds of crime feel like they're only an arm's reach away. It can scour away at a lifetime of mild, peaceful decency until all that's left is teeth and claws and terror. You could almost catch the stench of fear, dank as rotting seaweed, coming up from the dark space at the back of the closet where the Spains had kept their monsters locked down. I said, 'It looks like we might not need to go chasing after sister-history, after all.'

Richie ran a thumb through the bank statements again, came to rest on that pathetic last page. 'Jesus,' he said, shaking his head.

'Straight-up guy, wife and kids, good job, got his house and his life just the way he likes them; then out of the blue, hey presto, it's crumbling around his ears. His job's gone, his car's gone, his house is going – for all we know, Jenny could have been planning to leave him now that he wasn't providing, take the kids with her. That could have been what pushed him over the edge.'

'All in less than a year,' Richie said. He put the bank statements down on the bed next to the HomeTime letters, holding them between his fingertips like they were radioactive. 'Yeah. That could do it, all right.'

'We've still got plenty of ifs on the table. But if Larry's lads don't find any evidence of an outsider, and if the weapon turns up somewhere accessible, and if Jenny Spain doesn't wake up and give us a very plausible story about how someone other than her husband did this . . . This case could be over a lot sooner than we were expecting.'

That was when my phone rang again.

'And there you go,' I said, fishing it out of my pocket. 'How much do you want to bet this is one of the floaters to say we've got the weapon, somewhere nice and close?'

It was Marlboro Man, and he was so excited his voice was cracking like a teenager's. 'Sir,' he said. 'Sir, you need to see this.'

He was in Ocean View Walk, the double line of houses – you couldn't exactly call it a street – between Ocean View Rise and the water. The other floaters' heads popped out of gaps in walls as we passed, like curious animals'. Marlboro Man waved to us from a first-floor window.

The house had got as far as walls and roof, grey blocks heavy with tangled green creepers. The front garden was chest-high weeds and gorse, crowding up the drive and in at the empty doorway. We had to climb the rusted scaffolding, shaking creepers off our feet, and swing ourselves through a window-hole.

Marlboro Man said, 'I wasn't sure whether to . . . I mean, I know you were busy, sir, but you said to call you if we found anything that could be interesting. And this . . .'

Someone had, carefully and over plenty of time, turned the top floor of the house into his own private lair. A sleeping bag, one of the serious ones meant for semi-professional wilderness expeditions, weighted down at the bottom with a rough lump of concrete. Thick plastic sheeting tacked over the window-holes, to keep out the wind. Three two-litre bottles of water, neatly lined up against a wall. A clear plastic storage tub just big enough for a stick of Right Guard, a bar of soap, a washcloth, a toothbrush and a tube of toothpaste. A dustpan and brush in one clean corner: no spider-webs here. A supermarket bag holding another chunk of concrete, a couple of empty Lucozade bottles, a crumple of chocolate wrap-pers and a sandwich crust sticking out of squashed tinfoil. One of those plastic rain hoods that old women wear, hung on a nail in a beam. And a pair of black binoculars, lying on top of the sleeping bag next to their battered case.

They didn't look particularly high-end, but then they hadn't needed to be. The back window-holes looked straight down into Patrick and Jenny Spain's lovely glass kitchen, just thirty or forty feet away. Larry and his gang were discussing something to do with one of the beanbags.

'Sweet Jaysus,' Richie said softly.

I didn't say a word. I was so angry that all that would have come out was a roar. Everything I knew about this case had lifted itself high, heaved itself upside down and come slamming down on top of me. This wasn't the lookout post for some hitman hired to get back money or drugs – a professional would have cleaned up before he did the job, we would never have known he had been there. This was Richie's mentaller, bringing all his own trouble with him.

Patrick Spain was the one in a hundred, after all. He had done everything right. He had married his childhood sweetheart, they had made two healthy kids, he had bought a nice house and worked his arse off paying for it and packing it full and sparkling with all the stuff that would make it into the perfect home. He had done every single fucking thing he was supposed to do. Then this little piece of shit had strolled up with his cheap binoculars and nuked every atom of that to ashes, and left Patrick with nothing but the blame.

Marlboro Man was eyeing me anxiously, worried he had screwed up again. 'Well well well,' I said coolly. 'Looks like some of the heat's off Patrick.'

Richie said, 'It's like a sniper's nest.'

'It's exactly like a sniper's nest. All right: everybody out. Detective, ring your mates and tell them to pull back to the crime scene. Tell them to go casually, not like anything big's happened, but go *now*.'

Richie raised his eyebrows; Marlboro Man opened his mouth, but something in my face made him shut it again. I said, 'This guy could be watching us right now. That's the one thing we know about him, isn't it? He likes watching. I guarantee you he's been hanging around all morning, waiting to see how we liked his handiwork.'

Rows of half-formed houses, right and left and straight ahead, crowding to gawp at us. The beach at our backs, all sand dunes and great clumps of hissing grass; the hills at either end, with the jagged lines of rocks at their feet. He could have gone to ground anywhere. Every way I turned felt like crosshairs on my forehead.

I said, 'All the activity may have scared him into backing off for a while – if we're lucky, he's missed us finding this. But he'll be back. And when he shows, we want him thinking his little hidey-hole is still safe. Because the first chance he gets, he'll need to come up here. For that.' I nodded downwards at Larry and his team, moving around the bright kitchen. 'I'd bet every cent I've got: he won't be able to stay away.'

# 6

In every way there is, murder is chaos. Our job is simple, when you get down to it: we stand against that, for order.

I remember this country back when I was growing up. We went to church, we ate family suppers around the table, and it would never even have crossed a kid's mind to tell an adult to fuck off. There was plenty of bad there, I don't forget that, but we all knew exactly where we stood and we didn't break the rules lightly. If that sounds like small stuff to you, if it sounds boring or old-fashioned or uncool, think about this: people smiled at strangers, people said hello to neighbours, people left their doors unlocked and helped old women with their shopping bags, and the murder rate was scraping zero.

Sometime since then, we started turning feral. Wild got into the air like a virus, and it's spreading. Watch the packs of kids roaming inner-city estates, mindless and brakeless as baboons, looking for something or someone to wreck. Watch the business-men shoving past pregnant women for a seat on the train, using their 4x4s to force smaller cars out of their way, purple-faced and outraged when the world dares to contradict them. Watch the teenagers throw screaming stamping tantrums when, for once, they can't have it the second they want it. Everything that stops us being animals is eroding, washing away like sand, going and gone.

The final step into feral is murder. We stand between that and you. We say, when no one else will, *There are rules here. There are limits. There are boundaries that don't move.*

I'm the least fanciful guy around, but on nights when I wonder whether there was any point to my day, I think about this: the first thing we ever did, when we started turning into humans, was draw a line across the cave door and say: *Wild stays out.* What I do is what the first men did. They built walls to keep back the sea. They fought the wolves for the hearth fire.

I got everyone together in the Spains' sitting room – it was much too small, but there was no way we were having this chat in the fishbowl kitchen. The floaters clustered up shoulder to shoulder, trying not to stand on the rug or brush against the telly, like the Spains still needed their guests to have good manners. I told them what was behind the garden wall. One of the techs whistled, a long soft sound.

'Here, Scorcher,' Larry said. He had settled himself comfortably on the sofa. 'Now I'm not doubting you, we both know better than that, but is there no chance this is just some homeless guy who found himself a nice cosy place to doss down for a while?'

'With binoculars and an expensive sleeping bag, and bugger-all else? Not a chance, Lar. That nest was set up for one reason: so someone could spy on the Spains.'

'And he's not homeless,' Richie said. 'Or if he is, he's got somewhere he can have a wash, himself and the sleeping bag. No smell.'

I said to the nearest floater, 'Get onto the Dog Unit and have them send a general purpose dog out here ASAP. Tell them we're after a murder suspect and we need the best trailing dog they've got.' He nodded and backed into the hall, already pulling out his phone. 'Until that dog gets a chance at the scent, no one else goes into that house. All of you' – I nodded to the floaters – 'can pick up the search for the weapon, but this time keep well away from that hide – head out the front, around to both sides, and cut down to the beach. When the dog handler arrives, I'll text you all, and you'll come back here at a run. I'm going to need chaos outside the front of this place: people running, shouting, driving up on full lights and sirens, crowding around to look at something – give it as much drama as you can. Then pick a saint, or whatever you're into, and say a prayer that if our man's watching, the chaos lures him round to the front to see what's going on.'

Richie was leaning against a wall with his hands in his pockets.

He said, 'At least he's after leaving his binoculars behind. If he wants to see what's up, he can't just stay somewhere out the back and check it out long-distance; he'll have to come around the front, get in close.'

'There's no guarantee he hasn't got a second pair, but we'll hope. If he comes close enough, we might even get our hands on him, although that's probably too much to ask; this whole estate is a warren, he's got enough hiding places to keep him going for months. Meanwhile, the dog goes around to that nest, scents off the sleeping bag – the handler can bring the bag down to the ground, if he can't get the dog up there – and gets to work. *One* tech heads up there with them, *inconspicuously*, takes video and fingerprints, and leaves. Everything else can wait.'

'Gerry,' Larry said, pointing at a gangly young guy, who nodded. 'Fastest print tape in the West.'

'Good man, Gerry. If you get prints, you head straight back to the lab and do what you do. The rest of us will keep up the action out front for as long as you need it, and then we'll go back to what we were doing. We've got until six o'clock sharp. Then we clear the area. Anyone who's still working inside the house can keep going, but the outside needs to look like we've packed up and gone home for the night. I want the coast clear – literally – for our man.'

Larry's eyebrows were practically in his bald patch. It was a gamble, staking the whole evening's work on this one chance – witnesses' memories can change even overnight, rain showers can wash away blood and scent, tides can pull dumped weapons or bloody clothes out to sea forever – and gambling isn't like me, but this case wasn't like most cases. 'Once it gets dark,' I said, 'we re-deploy.'

'You're assuming the dog won't get him,' Larry pointed out. 'You think this fella knows what he's at?'

I saw the floaters shift as the thought sent a ripple of alertness through them. 'That's what we're aiming to find out,' I said. 'Probably not, or he'd have cleaned up after himself, but I'm not taking any chances. Sunset's around half-seven, maybe a little later. About eight or half past, as soon as we can't be seen, Detective

Curran and I will head up to that nest, where we'll spend the night.' I caught Richie's eye; he nodded. 'Meanwhile, two detectives will be patrolling the estate – again, inconspicuously – keeping an eye out for any action, in particular any action heading this way. Any takers?'

All of the floaters' hands shot up. I picked Marlboro Man – he had earned it – and a kid who looked young enough that one night with no sleep wouldn't wipe him out for the rest of the week. 'Keep in mind that he could come from outside the estate or from inside – he could be hiding out in a derelict house, or he could live here and that's how he targeted the Spains. If you spot anything interesting, ring me straight away. Still no radios: we have to assume that this guy is into his surveillance gear, deep enough that he owns a scanner. If someone looks promising, tail him if you can, but your top priority is making sure he doesn't spot you. If you get even the faintest sense that he's onto you, back right off and report to me. Got it?'

They nodded. I said, 'I'll also need a pair of techs to spend the night in here.'

'Not me,' Larry said. 'You know I love you, Scorcher, but I've got a previous engagement and I'm too old for the all-night carry-on, no double entendre intended.'

'No problem. I'm sure someone could do with the overtime, am I right?' Larry mimed his jaw hitting his chest – I have a rep for not authorising overtime. A few of the techs nodded. 'You can bring sleeping bags and take turns getting some kip in the sitting room, if you want to; I just need some kind of ongoing visible activity. Bring things back and forth from your car, swab things in the kitchen, take a laptop out there and pull up a graph that looks professional . . . Your job is to get our man interested enough that he can't resist the temptation to go up to his nest, get his binocu-lars and check out what you're doing.'

'Bait,' said Gerry the print tech.

'Exactly. We've got bait, trackers, hunters, and we'll just have to hope our man walks into the trap. We'll have a couple of hours off between six o'clock and nightfall; get something to eat, head back to the office if you need to check in, pick up anything you'll want for the stakeout. For now, I'll let you get back to what you're doing. Thanks, lads and ladies.'

They moved off – two of the techs were flipping a coin for the overtime, a couple of floaters were trying to impress me or each other by taking notes. The scaffolding had stamped smears of rust onto the sleeve of my overcoat. I found a tissue in my pocket and headed out to the kitchen to dampen it.

Richie followed me. I said, 'If you need something to eat, you can take the car and find that petrol station the Gogan woman talked about.'

He shook his head. 'I'm grand.'

'Good. And you're OK for tonight?'

'Yeah. No probs.'

'At six we'll head back to HQ, brief the Super, pick up anything we need, then meet up again and come back here.' If Richie and I could make it into town fast enough, and if the briefing didn't take too long, there was just a chance I would have time to get hold of Dina and put her in a taxi to Geri's. 'You're welcome to put in for overtime if you want. I'm not planning to.'

'Why not?'

'I don't believe in overtime.' Larry's boys had cut the water and taken out the sinktrap, in case our boy had washed up, but a left-over trickle came out of the tap. I caught it on the tissue and scrubbed at my sleeve.

'I heard that, all right. How come?'

'I'm not a babysitter, or a waiter. I don't charge by the hour. And I'm not some politician looking for ways to get paid three times over for every tap of work I do. I get paid my salary to do my job, whatever that happens to mean.'

Richie didn't comment. He said, 'You're pretty definite that this guy's watching us, aren't you?'

'On the contrary: he's probably miles away, at work, if he's got a job to go to and if he had the cool to go in today. But, like I said to Larry, I'm not taking any chances.'

In the corner of my eye something white flicked. I was facing the windows, braced ready to lunge at the back door, before I knew I had moved. One of the techs was out in the garden, squatting on a paving stone, swabbing.

Richie let that speak for itself while I straightened up and stashed the tissue in my briefcase. Then he said, 'So maybe "definite" isn't the right word. But you think he is.'

The great Rorschach blot on the floor where the Spains had lain was darkening, crusting at the edges. Above it, the windows ricocheted grey afternoon light back and forth, throwing off dislocated, off-kilter reflections: swirling leaves, a slice of wall, the heart-stopping nosedive of a bird against cloud. 'Yeah,' I said. 'I do. I think he's watching.'

And that left us with the rest of the afternoon to get through, on our way to that night. The media had started swarming up – later than I'd expected; clearly their satnavs didn't like the place any better than mine had – and were doing their thing, hanging over the crime-scene tape to get shots of the techs going in and out, doing pieces to camera in their best solemn voices. In my book, the media are a necessary evil: they live off the animal inside us, they bait their front pages with second-hand blood for the hyenas to snuffle up, but they come in useful often enough that you want to stay on their good side. I checked my hair in the Spains' bathroom mirror and went out to give them a statement. For a second I actually considered sending Richie. The thought of Dina hearing my voice talking about Broken Harbour sent heartburn flaring across my chest.

There were a couple of dozen of them out there, everything from broadsheets to red-tops and from national TV to local radio. I kept it as brief and as monotone as possible, on the off-chance that they might quote me instead of using the actual footage, and I made sure they got the impression that all four of the Spains were dead as dodos. My man would be watching the news, and I wanted him smug and secure: no living witnesses, the perfect crime, give yourself a pat on the back for being such a winner and then come on down to take another look at your prize work.

The search team and the dog handler arrived not long after-wards, which meant we had plenty of cast members for the drama in the front garden – the Gogan woman and her kid stopped pretending they weren't watching and stuck their heads out of the door, and the reporters practically burst the crime-scene tape trying to see what was going on, which I took as a good sign. I bent over something imaginary in the hall with the rest of the gang, shouted meaningless jargon out the door, jogged up and down the drive to get things from the car. It took all the willpower I had not to scan the tangle of houses for a blink of movement, a flash of light off lenses, but I never once looked up.

The dog was a shining, muscled Alsatian that picked up a scent off the sleeping bag in a split second, trailed it to the end of the road and lost it. I had the handler walk the dog through the house – if our man was watching, I needed him to think that was why we had called them in. Then I had the search team take over the weapon hunt, and sent the floaters out on new assignments. Go down to Emma's school – fast, before it lets out for the day – talk to her teacher, talk to her friends and their parents. Go down to Jack's preschool, ditto. Go around every shop near the schools, find out where Jenny got those carrier bags that Sinéad Gogan saw, find out if anyone saw someone following her, if anyone has CCTV footage. Go to the hospital where Jenny's being treated, talk to whichever relatives have shown, track down whichever ones haven't, make sure all of them know to keep their mouths shut and stay far from the media; go to every hospital within a sixty-mile radius, ask them about last night's crop of knife wounds, and hope our boy got cut in the struggle. Go ring HQ and find out if the Spains made any calls to the police in the last six months; go ring the Chicago PD and have them send someone to break the news to Pat's brother Ian. Go find anyone who lives in this godfor-saken place, threaten them with everything up to and including jail time if they tell the media anything they don't tell us first; find out if they saw the Spains, if they saw anything strange, if they saw anything at all.

Richie and I went back to the house search. It was a different

thing, now that the Spains had turned into that half-myth, rare as
a sweet-voiced hidden bird that no one ever sees alive: genuine
victims, innocent to the bone. We had been looking for the thing
they had done wrong. Now we were looking for the thing that they
could never have guessed they were doing wrong. The receipts
that would show who had sold them food, petrol, children's
clothes; the birthday cards that would tell us who had come to
Emma's party, the leaflet that would list the people who had
attended some residents' meeting. We were looking for the bright
lure that had hooked something clawed and simian, brought it
following them home.

The first floater to check in was the one I had sent to Jack's
preschool. 'Sir,' he said. 'Jack Spain didn't go here.'

We had pulled the number from a list, in bubbly girly handwriting, pinned above the phone table: doctor, Garda station, work
– crossed out – E school, J preschool. 'Ever?'

'No, he did up until June. When they finished up for the summer.
He was down on the list to come back this year, but in August
Jennifer Spain rang up and cancelled his place. She said they were
going to keep him at home instead. The lady who runs the place,
she thinks the problem was money.'

Richie leaned closer to the phone – we were still sitting on the
Spains' bed, getting deeper into paper. 'James, howya, it's Richie
Curran. Did you get the names of any kids Jack was friendly with?'

'Yeah. Three young lads in particular.'

'Good,' I said. 'Go talk to them and their parents. Then get back
to us.'

Richie said, 'Can you ask the parents when they last saw Jack?
And when they last brought their young fellas over to the Spains'
to play?'

'Will do. I'll be back in touch ASAP.'

'Do that.' I hung up. 'What's the story there?'

'Fiona said, when she was talking to Jenny yesterday morning,
Jenny told her about Jack bringing over a mate from preschool.
But if Jack wasn't in preschool . . .'

'She could have meant a friend he made last year.'

'Didn't sound like that, though, did it? It could've been a misunderstanding, but like you said: anything that doesn't fit. Can't see why Fiona would've lied to us about that, or why Jenny would've lied to Fiona, but . . .'

But if either of them had, it would be nice to know about it. I said, 'Fiona could have made it up because she and Jenny had a blazing row yesterday morning and she feels guilty about it. Jenny could have made it up because she didn't want Fiona to know how broke they were. Rule Number Seven, I think we're on: everyone lies, Richie. Killers, witnesses, bystanders, victims. Everyone.'

The other floaters called in, one by one. According to the Chicago boys, Ian Spain's reaction had been 'all good' – your standard mix of shock and grief, nothing to raise red flags; he said he and Pat hadn't been e-mailing much, but Pat hadn't mentioned any stalkers, any confrontations, anyone who was worrying him. Jenny had barely more family than he did – her mother had shown up at the hospital and there were some cousins in Liverpool, but that was it. The mother's reaction had been all good too, complete with a side order of near-hysteria about being kept away from Jenny. In the end the floater had managed to get a basic statement, for what it was worth; Jenny and her mother weren't close, and Mrs Rafferty knew less about the Spains' lives than Fiona did. The floater had tried to nudge her into going home, but she and Fiona had set up camp at the hospital, which at least meant we knew where to find them.

Emma had actually been going to primary school, where the teachers said she had been a nice kid from a nice family: popular, well-behaved, a people-pleaser, no genius but well able to keep up. The floater had a list of teachers and friends. No suspicious knife wounds at the nearby A&E departments, no phone calls to us from the Spains. The door-to-door had turned up nothing: out of maybe two hundred and fifty houses, fifty or sixty showed any signs of official occupation, about half of those had someone home, and no one in those couple of dozen knew much about the Spains. None of them thought they had seen or heard anything unusual, but they couldn't be sure: there were always joyriders, always half-wild teenagers prowling around the empty streets, setting bonfires and finding things to smash.

Jenny's shopping traced back to the supermarket in the nearest decent-sized town, where at about four o'clock the previous afternoon she had bought milk, mince, crisps and a few other things that the checkout girl didn't remember – the shop was working on pulling the receipt, and the CCTV footage. Jenny had seemed fine, the girl said, hurried and a bit stressed, but polite; no one had been talking to the family, no one had followed them out, at least not that the girl had seen. She only remembered them because Jack had been bouncing up and down in the trolley, singing, and while she swiped their shopping he had told her he was going to be a big scary animal for Halloween.

The search tossed up small things, low-tide flotsam and jetsam. Photo albums, address books, cards congratulating the Spains on their engagement, their wedding, their babies; receipts from a dentist, a doctor, a pharmacist. Every name and every number went into my notebook. Slowly, the list of question marks was getting shorter and the list of possible contact points was getting longer.

Computer Crime rang me late in the afternoon, to say they had taken a preliminary look at what we had sent them. We were in Emma's room: I had been going through her schoolbag (lots of pink-based crayon drawings, TODAY I AM A PRINCESS in careful, wobbly capitals), Richie had been down on his hunkers on the floor, flipping through the fairy tales on her bookshelf. With her gone and the bed stripped – the morgue boys had wrapped her sheets around her and taken the lot, in case our man had shed hairs or fibres while he did what he did – the room was so empty it sucked the breath out of you, as if she had been taken away a thousand years ago and no one had stepped in here since.

The techie was called Kieran or Cian or something. He was young and fast-talking, and he was enjoying himself: this was clearly a lot nearer to what he had signed on for than trawling hard drives for kiddie porn, or whatever he usually did with his day.

Nothing that stood out on the phones and nothing interesting about the baby monitors, but the computer was a different story. Someone had wiped it.

'So I'm not going to turn the machine on and wreck all the access times on the files, right? Plus, for all I know, someone's set a dead man's switch to wipe the whole thing when it gets powered up. So first thing I do, I take a copy of the hard drive.'

I put him on speakerphone. Above us, the insistent, nasty drone of a helicopter was circling, too low – media; one of the floaters would have to find out who, and warn them off showing footage of the hide.

'I plug the copy into my own machine and go for the browser history – if there's anything good in there, that's where you're going to find it. Except this computer doesn't *have* a browser history. Like, nothing. Not one page.'

'So they only used the internet for e-mail.' I already knew I was wrong: Jenny's online shopping.

'Bzzt, thanks for playing. Nobody uses the internet just for e-mail. Even my *granny* managed to find herself a Val Doonican fansite, and she only has a computer because I got it to stop her getting depressed after my granddad died. You can set your browser to delete your history every time you quit, but most people don't: you see that setting on public computers, internet cafés or whatever, not home machines. I checked anyway, and nope, the browser's not set to clear history. So I check for any deletions in the browser history and the temporary files, and voilà: four-oh-eight this morning, someone manually deleted the lot.'

Richie, still kneeling on the floor, caught my eye. We had been so focused on the lookout post and the break-in; it had never occurred to us that our man might have subtler ways of coming and going, less visible catflaps to let him wander through the Spains' lives. I had to stop myself glancing over my shoulder, to make sure nothing was watching me from Emma's wardrobe. 'Good catch,' I said.

The techie was still going. 'Now I want to know what else the dude did while he was messing around in there, right? So I do a scan for any other stuff that was deleted around the same time. And guess what pops up? The entire Outlook PST file. Nuked. At four-eleven in the a.m.'

Richie had his notebook propped on the bed and was taking notes. I said, 'That's their e-mail?'

'Oh yeah. *All* their e-mail, like everything they've ever sent and received. E-mail addresses, too.'

'Anything else get deleted?'

'No, that's it. There's a bunch of other stuff on the machine – all your basics, like photos and documents and music – but none of it's been accessed or modified in the last twenty-four hours. Your dude went in there, went straight for the online stuff, and got out.'

'"Our dude,"' I said. 'You're sure the owners didn't do it themselves?'

Kieran or Cian snorted. 'No chance.'

'Why not?'

'Because they aren't exactly computer geniuses. Do you know what's on that machine, like right on the desktop? A file named, I couldn't make this up, "Passwords". In which are, you'll never guess, *all* of these people's passwords. E-mail, online banking, everything. But that's not even the good part. They used the same password for a load of stuff, like a bunch of forums, eBay, the actual computer: "EmmaJack." I get a bad feeling about this straightaway, but I'm all about giving people the benefit of the doubt, so before I actually start banging my head off my keyboard, I phone Larry and ask him if the owners have rugrats and what they're called. He says – brace yourself – Emma and Jack.'

I said, 'They probably assumed if the computer got nicked, it would be by someone who didn't know the children's names, so he wouldn't be able to switch it on and read the file to begin with.'

The techie did a gusty sigh that said he had just dumped me in the same category as the Spains. 'Um, not the point. My girl-friend's called Adrienne, and I'd spork my own eyes out before I'd use that for a password to *anything*, because I have *standards*. Take it from me, right: anyone clueless enough to use his kids' freaking *names* as a password can barely wipe his own arse, never mind his hard drive. Someone else did this.'

'Someone with computer knowledge.'

'Well, some, yeah. More than the owners, anyway. We don't have to be talking about a professional, but he knew his way around a machine.'

'How long would it have taken?'

'The whole deal? Not long. He shut the machine down at four-seventeen. In and out in less than ten minutes.'

Richie asked, 'Would this fella have known you would work out what he'd done? Or would he figure he was after covering his tracks?'

The techie made a noncommittal noise. 'Depends. Plenty of guys out there think we're a bunch of muck savages with barely enough brains to find the On button. And plenty of guys are just about computer-savvy enough to land themselves in the shit, specially if they're in a hurry, which your dude could have been, right? If he was really serious about zapping the crap out of those files, or about covering his tracks so I'd never know anyone had touched the machine, there are ways – deletion software – but that takes more time and more smarts. Your dude was short on one or the other, or both. Overall, I'd bet he knew we'd be able to see the deletions.'

But he had made them anyway. There had been something crucial in there. I said, 'Tell me you can get this stuff back.'

'Some of it, sure, probably. The question is how much. We've got recovery software that I'm gonna try, but if this dude over-wrote the deleted files a few times – and I would've, if I was him – then they're gonna be kind of munged. The damn things get corrupted enough anyway, just through normal use; throw in a little malicious deletion, and we could end up with soup. Leave it with me, though.'

He sounded like he was itching to get stuck in. 'Give it every-thing you've got,' I said. 'We'll keep our fingers crossed.'

'Don't bother. If I can't beat some half-arsed amateur and his delete button, I might as well hang up the big-boy jockstrap and find myself a job in tech-support hell. I'll get you something. Trust me.'

'"Half-arsed amateur,"' Richie said, as I put my phone away. He was still kneeling on the floor, absently fingering a framed photo on the bookshelf: Fiona and a guy with floppy brown hair, holding up a tiny Emma swamped by her lace christening dress, all three of them smiling. 'But he managed to get past the login password.'

'Yeah,' I said. 'Either the computer was already on when he got here, in the middle of the night, or he knew the children's names.'

'*Scorcher,*' Larry said happily, bouncing over from the kitchen windows, when he saw us in the doorway. 'The very man I was thinking of. Come here, you, and bring that young fella with you. You're going to be very, very happy with me.'

'I could do with being very happy with something right now. What've you got?'

'What would make your day?'

'Don't be a tease, Lar. I don't have the energy. What have you magicked up?'

'No magic about it. This was good old-fashioned luck. You know how your uniforms went charging through here like a herd of buffalo in mating season?'

I wagged a finger at him. 'They're not *my* uniforms, my friend. If I had uniforms, they'd sneak through scenes on their tippytoes. You'd never even know they'd been there.'

'Well, I knew this lot had been here, all right. *Obviously* they had to save the living victim, but honest to God, I think they lay down on the floor and *wallowed,* or something. Anyway. I thought we'd need a miracle to get anything that didn't come from a great big clodhopping welly, but somehow, believe it or not, they managed not to wreck the entire scene. My lovely lads found handprints. Three of them. In blood.'

'You *gems,*' I said. A couple of the techs nodded to me. Their rhythm was starting to slow: they were getting near the end, gearing down to make sure they missed nothing. All of them looked tired.

'Keep your powder dry,' Larry told me. 'That's not the good bit. I hate to break it to you, but your fella wore gloves.'

'*Shit*,' I said. Even the most moronic criminal knows to wear gloves, these days, but you always pray for the exception, the one so carried away on his surge of desire that everything else gets washed out of his mind.

'Don't be complaining, you. At least we've found you proof that someone else was in this house last night. Here was me thinking that counted for something.'

'It counts for a lot.' The memory of me upstairs in Pat's bedroom, blithely dumping everything on his shoulders, slapped me with a rush of disgust. 'We won't hold the gloves against you, Lar. I'm sticking to my story: you're a gem.'

'Well, of course I am. Come here and have a look.'

The first handprint was a palm and five fingertips, at shoulder-height on one of the plate-glass windows looking out over the back garden. Larry said, 'See the texture to it, those little dots? Leather. Big hands, too. This wasn't some little runt of a guy.'

The second print was wrapped around the top edge of the children's bookcase, like our man had grabbed hold of it to keep his balance. The third one was flat on the yellow paint of the computer desk, next to the faint outline where the computer had stood, like he had rested a hand on there while he took his time reading what was on the screen.

I said, 'And that's what we came down to ask you about. That computer: did you pull any prints off it, before you sent it back to the lab?'

'We tried. You'd think a keyboard would be the dream surface, wouldn't you? You'd be so wrong. People don't use a whole fingertip to hit the key, just a tiny fraction of the surface, and then it gets hit over and over at slightly different angles ... It's like taking a piece of paper and printing a hundred different words on it, one on top of the other, and then expecting us to work out the sentence they came from. Your best bet is the mouse – we got a couple of partials that might be almost usable. Apart from that, nothing big enough or clear enough to hold up in court.'

'What about blood? On the keyboard or the mouse, specifically?'

Larry shook his head. 'There was some spatter on the monitor, a couple of drops on the side of the keyboard. No smudges on the keys or the mouse, though. No one used them with blood on his fingers, if that's what you're asking.'

I said, 'So it looks like the computer came before the murders – before the adults, anyway. That's some nerve he's got, if he sat here playing with their internet history while they were asleep upstairs.'

'The computer didn't have to come first,' Richie said. 'Those gloves – they were leather, they'd have been stiff, specially if they were all bloody. Maybe he couldn't type in them, took them off; they'd kept the blood off his fingers . . .'

Most rookies on their first outings keep their mouths shut and nod at whatever I say. Usually this is the right call, but every once in a while, watching other partners argue and bat theories back and forth and call each other every shade of stupid gives me a flash of something that could be loneliness. It was starting to feel good, working with Richie. 'Then he sat there playing with Pat and Jenny's internet history while they were bleeding out four feet from him,' I said. 'Some nerve, either way.'

'Hello?' Larry inquired, waving at us. 'Remember me? Remember how I told you the handprints weren't the good bit?'

'I like saving my dessert for last,' I said. 'Whenever you're ready, Larry, we would love the good bit.'

He got each of us by an elbow and turned us towards the sweep of congealing blood. 'Here's where the male victim was, amn't I right? Face down, head towards the hall door, feet towards the window. According to your buffaloes, the female was to his left, lying on her left side facing him, propped against his body, with her head on his upper arm. And here, just about eighteen inches from where her back would have been, we have *this*.'

He pointed to the floor, to the Jackson Pollock gibber of blood that radiated out around the puddle. I said, 'A shoeprint?'

'Actually, a couple of *hundred* shoeprints, God help us. But take a look at this one here.'

Richie and I bent closer. The print was so faint I could barely see it against the marbled pattern of the tiles, but Larry and his boys see things the rest of us don't.

'This one,' Larry said, 'is special. It's a print from a man's left trainer, size ten or eleven, made in blood. And get this: it doesn't belong to either of the uniforms, it doesn't belong to either of the paramedics – *some* people have the brains to wear their shoe covers – and it doesn't belong to either of your victims.'

The swell of satisfaction practically burst his boiler suit. He had every right to be pleased. 'Larry,' I said, 'I think I love you.'

'Take a number. I don't want to get your hopes up too high, though. For one thing, it's only half a print – one of your buffaloes obliterated the other half – and for another, unless your fella's a total eejit, that shoe's at the bottom of the Irish Sea by now. But *if* you should somehow get your hands on it, here's where the luck comes in: this print is perfect. I couldn't take a better one myself. When we get the pics back to the lab, we'll be able to tell you the size and, if you give us enough time, very possibly the make and model. Find me the actual shoe, and I'll have it matched for you inside a minute.'

I said, 'Thanks, Larry. You were right, as always: that's a good bit.'

I had caught Richie's eye and started moving towards the door, but Larry batted me on the arm. 'Did I say I was done? Now this is preliminary, Scorch, you know the drill, don't quote me on any of this or I may have to divorce you. But you said you wanted anything we could give you about what the struggle could have looked like.'

'Don't I always? All contributions gratefully accepted.'

'It's looking like the fight was confined to this room, just like you thought. In here, though, it was full-on. It went the whole width of the room – well, you can tell that yourselves from the way the place is wrecked, but I mean the part after the stabbing started. We've got a beanbag right over there at the far side that's been slashed open by a bloody knife, we've got a big spray of blood spatter on the wall on this side, above the table, and we've counted at least nine separate sprays in between.' Larry pointed and the sprays leapt out from the wall at me, suddenly vivid as paint. 'Some of those probably come from the male vic's arm – you heard Cooper, it was bleeding all over the place; if he swings his arm to defend himself, he's going to throw off blood – and some of them probably come from your boy swinging his weapon. Between the two of them, anyway, an awful lot of swinging went on. And the sprays are at different levels, different angles: your boy was stabbing while the vics were fighting back, while they were on the ground . . .'

Richie's shoulder jumped; he tried to cover it by scratching like something had bitten him. Larry said, almost gently, 'It's actually a big plus. The messier the fight, the more evidence gets left behind: prints, hairs, fibres . . . Give me a nice bloody scene any day.'

I pointed to the door into the hallway. 'What about over there? Did they get anywhere near there?'

Larry shook his head. 'Doesn't look like it. Not a sausage within about four feet of that door: no spatter, no bloody footprints except the uniforms' and the paramedics', nothing out of place. All just as God and the decorators intended.'

'Is there a phone in here? A cordless, maybe?'

'Not that we've found.'

I said, to Richie, 'You see what I'm getting at.'

'Yeah. The landline was out on the hall table.'

'Right. Why didn't Patrick or Jennifer go for it and hit 999, or at least try to? How did he restrain both of them at once?'

Richie shrugged. His eyes were still moving across the end wall, from blood-spray to blood-spray. 'You heard your woman Gogan,' he said. 'We don't have a great rep around this estate. They could've figured there was no point.'

The image pressed up against the inside of my skull: Pat and Jenny Spain throat-deep in terror, believing that we were too far away and too indifferent even to be worth calling, that all the world's protections had deserted them; that it was just the two of them, with the dark and the sea roaring up on every side, on their own against a man with a knife in one hand and their children's deaths in the other. Going by the tight movement of Richie's jaw, he was picturing the same thing. I said, 'Another possibility is two separate struggles. Our man does his thing upstairs, and then either Pat or Jenny wakes up and hears him on his way out – Pat would add up better, Jenny would be less likely to go investigating on her own. He goes after the guy, catches him in here, tries to hang onto him. That would explain the weapon of opportunity, and the extent of the struggle: our man's trying to get a big, strong, furious guy off of him. The fight wakes Jenny, but by the time she gets here, our man's taken Pat down, leaving him free to deal with her. The whole thing could have gone very fast. It doesn't take that long to make this kind of mess, not when there's a blade involved.'

Richie said, 'That'd make the kids the main targets.'

'It's looking that way anyhow. The children's murders are organised, neat: there was some kind of plan there, and everything went according to that plan. The adults were a bloody, out-of-control mess that could easily have ended very differently. Either he wasn't planning to cross paths with the adults at all, or he had a plan for them, too, and something went wrong. Either way, he started with the kids. That tells me they were probably his main priority.'

'Or else,' Richie said, 'it could be the other way round.' His eyes had slipped away from me again, back to the chaos 'The adults were the main target, or one of them was, and the bloody mess was the plan all along; that's what he was after. The kids were just something he had to get rid of, so they wouldn't wake up and get in the way of the good stuff.'

Larry had delicately worked one finger under his hood and was scratching where his hairline should have been. He was getting bored – all the psychological chitchat. 'Wherever he started, I'd say he finished up by leaving through the back door, not the front. The hall is clean, so's the drive, but we found three blood-smears on the paving stones in the back garden.' He beckoned us towards the window and pointed: neat strips of yellow tape, one just outside the door, two by the edge of the grass. 'The surface is uneven, so we're not going to be able to tell you what kind of smears – they could be shoeprints, or transfer where someone dropped a bloody object, or they could be droplets that got smudged somehow, like if he was bleeding and then stepped on the blood. One of the kids could have scraped its knee days ago, for all we know at this stage. All we're saying is, there they are.'

I said, 'So he's got a back-door key.'

'That or a teleporter. And we found one other thing in the garden that I thought you might want to know about. What with the trap in the attic and all.'

Larry wiggled his fingers at one of his boys, who picked an evidence bag off a pile and held it out. 'If you're not interested,' he said, 'we'll just bin it. Disgusting object.'

It was a robin, or most of one. Something had taken its head off, a couple of days back. There were pale things curling in the ragged dark hole.

'We're interested,' I said. 'Any way you can work out what killed it?'

'Really and truly not my area, but one of the boys back at the lab does outdoorsy things at weekends. Tracks badgers in his moccasins, or whatever. I'll see what he says.'

Richie was leaning in for a closer look at the robin: tiny clenched claws, crumbs of earth hanging from the bright breast-feathers. It was starting to stink, but he didn't seem to notice. He said, 'Most things, if they killed it they'd eat it. Cats, foxes, anything like that: they'd have had the guts out of it. They don't kill for the sake of it.'

'I wouldn't have taken you for the woodsman type,' Larry said, arching an eyebrow.

Richie shrugged. 'I'm not. I was posted down the country for a while, in Galway. Picked bits up from listening to the local lads.'

'Go on, then, Crocodile Dundee. What would take the head off a robin and leave the rest?'

'Mink, maybe? Pine marten?'

I said, 'Or human.' It wasn't the trap in the attic I had thought of, the second I saw what was left of that robin. It was Emma and Jack bouncing out into the garden to play, early one morning, and finding this, all among the grass and the dew. From that hide, someone would have had a perfect view. 'Those kill for the sake of it, all the time.'

By twenty to six, we were working our way through the playroom area and the light outside the kitchen windows was starting to cool towards evening. I said to Richie, 'Can you finish up here?'

He glanced up, didn't ask. 'No probs.'

'I'll be back in fifteen minutes. Be ready to head back to HQ.' I stood up – my knees jolted and cracked, I was getting too old for this – and left him crouching there, rummaging through picture books and plastic tubs of crayons, surrounded by the blood spatter that Larry and his team had no more use for. As I left my foot knocked over some kind of blue fluffy animal, which let out a high-pitched giggle and started to sing. Its thin, sweet, inhuman chant followed me down the hall and out the door.

As the day started to ebb, the estate was coming to life. The media had packed up and gone home, taking their helicopter with them, but in the house where we had talked to Fiona Rafferty a clutch of little boys were ricocheting about, swinging off the scaffolding and pretending to shove each other out of high windows, dancing black silhouettes against the burning sky. At the end of the road a huddle of teenagers were slouching on the wall around a weed-grown garden, not even pretending not to be smoking or drinking or staring at me. Somewhere someone was roaring furious circles on a big bike with no muffler; farther away, rap was pumping relentlessly. Birds dived in and out of empty window-holes, and by the roadside something scuttled in a heap of bricks and barbed wire, setting off a tiny avalanche of dust.

The back entrance of the estate was two great stone gateposts, opening onto a sweep of swaying long grass that had grown up thick in the gap where the gate should have been. The grass whispered soothingly and clamped tight around my ankles, tugging me back, as I moved down the gentle slope towards the sand dunes.

The search team was at the tideline, picking through seaweed and the bubbling holes where winkles were buried. They straightened up, one by one, when they saw me coming. I said, 'Any luck?'

They showed me their haul of evidence bags, like cold children straggling home with their finds at the end of a long day on some grotesque scavenger hunt. Cigarette butts, cider cans, used condoms, broken earphones, ripped T-shirts, food packets, old shoes: every empty house had had something to offer, every empty house been claimed and colonised by someone – kids looking for places to dare each other, couples looking for privacy or for thrills, teenagers looking for something to wreck, creatures looking for somewhere to breed and grow, mice, rats, birds, weeds, tiny busy insects. Nature doesn't let anything go empty, doesn't let anything go to waste. The second the builders and developers and estate agents had moved out, other things had started moving in.

There were a few finds worth having: two blades – a broken penknife, probably too small to be ours, and a switchblade that could have been interesting except that it was half rusted away – three door keys that would need checking against the Spains' locks, a scarf with a stiff dark patch that might turn out to be blood. 'Good stuff,' I said. 'Hand it all over to Boyle from the Bureau, and go home. At eight a.m. sharp, pick up where you left off. I'll be at the post-mortems, but I'll join you as soon as I can. Thank you, ladies and gentlemen. Nice work.'

They trudged up through the dunes towards the estate, pulling off gloves and rubbing at stiff necks. I stayed where I was. The team would assume I was taking a still moment to think about the case, working through the dark maths of the probabilities or letting small dead faces have their time to fill my mind. If our man was watching me, he would figure the same thing. I wasn't. I had budgeted these ten minutes into the day's schedule, to test myself against that beach.

I kept my back to the estate, all that strafed hope where there used to be bright swimming costumes fluttering on makeshift washing lines between caravans. There was an early moon, pale against the pale sky, flickering behind slim smoky clouds; below it the sea was grey and restless, insistent. Seabirds were reclaiming the tideline, now that the searchers were gone; I stood still, and after a few minutes they forgot me and went back to their skittering search for food and to their calls, high and clean as wind in fretted rock. Once, when a nightbird's squeal close outside the caravan window startled Dina awake, my mother quoted Shakespeare for her: *Be not afraid; the isle is full of noises: sounds and sweet airs that give delight and hurt not.*

The wind had grown a cold edge; I turned up my coat collar and dug my hands into my pockets. The last time I set foot on that beach, I had been fifteen: just starting to shave like I meant it, just getting used to my brand-new shoulders, just a week into going out with someone for the first time, a golden girl from Newry called Amelia who laughed at all my jokes and tasted like strawberries. I was different, back then: electric and reckless, body-slamming headlong onto any chance of a laugh or a dare, made out of enough momentum to shoot me straight through stone walls. When we guys arm-wrestled to impress the girls, I took on big Dean Gorry and beat him three times running, even though he was twice my size, because that was how badly I wanted to make Amelia clap for me.

I looked out over the water, into the night that was coming in on the tide, and I felt nothing at all. The beach looked like something I had seen in an old film, once upon a time; that hotheaded boy felt like a character from some book I had read and given away in childhood. Only, somewhere far inside my spine and deep in the palms of my hands, something hummed; like a sound too low to hear, like a warning, like a cello string when a tuning fork strikes the perfect tone to call it awake.

# 7

And of course, of bloody fucking *course*, Dina was waiting for me.

The first thing you notice about my little sister Dina is that she's the kind of beautiful that makes people, men and women both, forget what they were talking about when she came in. She looks like one of those old pen-and-ink sketches of fairies: slight as a dancer, with skin that never tans, full pale lips and huge blue eyes. She walks like she's skimming an inch above the ground. This artist she used to go out with once told her she was 'pure pre-Raphaelite', which would have been cuter if he hadn't dumped her flat on her arse two weeks later. Not that this came as a surprise. The second thing that stands out about Dina is that she is crazy as a bag of cats. Various therapists and psychiatrists have diagnosed various things along the way, but what it comes down to is that Dina is no good at life. It takes a knack that she's never quite got hold of. She can fake it for months at a stretch, sometimes even a year, but it takes concentration like she's tightrope-walking, and in the end she always wobbles and goes flying. Then she ditches her lousy McJob *du jour*, her lousy boyfriend *du jour* ditches her – men who like them vulnerable love Dina, right up until she shows them what vulnerable actually means – and she turns up on my doorstep or Geri's, generally at some ungodly hour of the morning, making bugger-all sense.

That night, to avoid becoming predictable, she showed up at my work instead. We work out of Dublin Castle, and since it's a tourist attraction – eight hundred years' worth of the buildings that have defended this city, in one way or another – anyone can walk straight in off the street. Richie and I were heading across the cobblestones towards the HQ building at a fast stride, and I was arranging the facts in my head ready to lay out for O'Kelly, when a slip of darkness detached itself from the corner of shadow by a wall and flew towards us. Both of us jumped. '*Mikey*,' Dina said, in a fierce undertone, fingers taut as wires clamping around my wrist. 'You have to come get me *now*. Everyone keeps pushing.'

Last time I had seen her, maybe a month before, she had had long rippling fair hair and some kind of floating flowery dress. Since then she had gone grunge: her hair was dyed glossy black and chopped off in a flapper-style bob – the fringe looked like she might have done it herself – and she was wearing a huge, ragged grey cardigan over a white slip, and biker boots. It's always a bad sign when Dina changes her look. I could have kicked myself for going so long without checking.

I moved her away from Richie, who was trying to get his jaw off the cobblestones. He looked like he was seeing me in a whole new light. 'I've got you, sweetheart. What's up?'

'I can't, Mikey, I can feel stuff in my hair, you know, the wind scraping into my hair? It hurts, it keeps hurting, I can't find the, not the off switch the button the way it stops.'

My stomach turned into one hard heavy lump. 'OK,' I said. 'OK. Do you need to come back to my place for a while, yeah?'

'We have to *go*. You have to listen.'

'We're going, sweetheart. Just hang on for one second, OK?' I steered her to the steps of one of the castle buildings, closed up for the night after the day's crop of tourists. 'Sit there for me.'

'*Why?* Where are you going?'

She was on the edge of panicking. 'Right over there,' I said, pointing. 'I need to get rid of my partner, so you and I can head home. It'll take me two seconds.'

'I don't want your partner. Mikey, there won't be room, how are we going to squash the fit?'

'Exactly. I don't want him either. I'll just send him on his merry way, and then we can get going.' I sat her down on the steps. 'OK?'

Dina pulled her knees up and shoved her mouth into the crook of her elbow. 'OK,' she said, muffled. 'Come on, OK?'

Richie was pretending to check his phone messages, to give me privacy. I kept one eye on Dina. 'Listen, Richie. I may not be able to make tonight. Are you still on for it?'

I could see the question marks bouncing up and down in his head, but he knew when to keep his mouth shut. 'Sure.'

'Good. Pick a floater. He – or she, if you want Whatshername – can put in for overtime, although you might try to get across the message that waiving it would be a better career move. If anything goes down out there, you ring me *at once*. It doesn't matter if you think it's unimportant, it doesn't matter if you think you can handle it, you ring me. Got that?'

'Got it.'

'In fact, if nothing goes down, ring me anyway, just so I know I'm up to speed. Every hour, on the hour. If I don't pick up, you keep ringing till I do. Got it?'

'Got it.'

'Tell the Super I had an emergency but not to worry, I'll have it under control and be back on the job by tomorrow morning at the latest. Brief him on today and on our plans for tonight – can you do that?'

'I can probably manage that, yeah.'

The twist to the corner of Richie's mouth said he didn't appreciate the question, but his ego was low on my priority list right then. 'No "probably", old son: manage it. Tell him the floaters have their assignments for tomorrow, so do the searchers, and we need a sub-aqua team to start work on the bay as early as possible. As soon as you're done with him, get moving. You'll need food, warm clothes, a packet of caffeine tabs – coffee's no good, you don't want to be pissing every half-hour – and a pair of thermal-imaging goggles: we have to assume this guy has some kind of night-vision gear, and I don't want him getting the jump on you. And check your gun.' Most of us go a full career without ever unholstering. Some people take that as a licence to get sloppy.

'Yeah, I've done a couple of stakeouts before,' Richie said, evenly enough that I couldn't tell whether he was giving me the finger. 'See you back here, tomorrow morning?'

Dina was getting antsy, biting off threads from the sleeve of her jumper. 'No,' I said. 'Not here. I'll try to get out to Brianstown at some point tonight, but that may or may not happen. If I don't make it, I'll meet you down at the hospital for the post-mortems. Six a.m., and for God's sake don't be late, or we'll spend the rest of the morning unknotting Cooper's knickers.'

'No probs.' Richie pocketed his phone. 'Might see you out there. Otherwise, we'll just have to do our best not to fuck up, yeah?'

I said, 'Don't fuck up.'

'We won't,' Richie said, more gently; he almost sounded like he was being reassuring. 'Good luck.'

He gave me a nod and headed for the door of HQ. He was smart enough not to glance back. '*Mikey*,' Dina hissed, clutching a fistful of the back of my coat. 'Can we *go*?'

I took a fraction of a second to look up at the dimming sky and throw out a hard urgent prayer to anything that was up there: *Let my man have more restraint than I'm giving him credit for. Don't let him go rushing into Richie's arms. Make him wait for me.*

'Come on,' I said, putting a hand on Dina's shoulder – she shoved herself up against my side, all sharp elbows and fast breath, like a spooked animal. 'Let's go.'

The first thing you need to do with Dina on days like this is get her indoors. A big part of what looks like madness is actually just tension, free-floating terror growing bigger as it gets buffeted around in currents and hooks onto everything that drifts past: she ends up frozen rigid by the immensity and the unpredictability of the world, like a prey animal trapped in the open. Get her into a familiar enclosed space with no strangers, no loud noises and no sudden movements, and she calms down, even has long lucid patches, while the two of you wait it out together. Dina was one of the factors I kept in mind when I was buying my apartment, after my ex and I sold our house. We picked a good time to split, or so I keep telling myself: the property market was on its way up, and my half of the equity got me a deposit on a fourth-floor two-bed in the Financial Services Centre. It's central enough that I can walk to work, trendy enough that it made me feel a little less like a loser for failing at marriage, and high enough that Dina won't be spooked by street noise.

'*Yes thank God about time*,' she said, on a wild rush of relief, when I unlocked the apartment. She shoved past me and pressed her back against the wall by the door, eyes closed, taking deep breaths. 'Mike, I need a towel shower, can I?'

I found her a towel. She dumped her handbag on the floor, vanished into the bathroom and slammed the door behind her.

Dina on a bad one could stay in the shower all night, as long as the hot water doesn't run out and she knows you're outside the door. She says she feels better in water because it makes her mind go blank, which is crammed with so many kinds of Jung that I wouldn't even know where to start. As soon as I heard the water running and her starting to sing to herself, I shut the living-room door and phoned Geri.

I hate making this call more than I hate almost anything in the world. Geri has three kids, ten and eleven and fifteen, a job doing the books for her best friend's interior design company, and a husband she doesn't see enough of. All those people need her. No one alive needs anything from me except Dina and Geri and my father, and what Geri needs most is for me not to make this phone call. I do everything in my power. It had been years since I had let her down.

'Mick! Hang on a sec for me, till I get this wash started—' Slam, click of buttons, mechanical hum. 'Now. Is everything OK? Did you get my message?'

'Yeah, I got it. Geri—'

'Andrea! I saw that! You give it back to him right now or I'll let him have your one, and you don't want that, do you? No, you do not.'

'*Geri*. Listen to me. Dina's losing it again. I have her over at my place, she's taking a shower, but I've got stuff I have to do. Can I drop her down to you?'

'Oh, God . . .' I heard the breath leak out of her. Geri is our optimist: she still hopes, after twenty years of this, that every time will be the last, that one morning Dina will wake up cured. 'Ah,

God, the poor little thing. I'd love to take her, but not tonight. Maybe in a couple of days, if she's still—'

'I can't wait a couple of days, Geri. I'm on a big case, I'm going to be working eighteen-hour shifts for the foreseeable, and it's not like I can bring her to work with me.'

'Oh, Mick, I *can't*. Sheila's got the stomach flu, that's what I was telling you, she's after giving it to her dad – the two of them were up all night getting sick, if it wasn't one it was the other – and I'd say Colm and Andrea'll come down with it any minute. I've been cleaning up sick and doing washing and boiling 7-Up all day, and it looks like I'll be doing the same again tonight. I couldn't manage Dina as well. I couldn't.'

Dina's episodes last anywhere between three days and two weeks. I keep some of my annual leave saved up just in case, and O'Kelly doesn't ask, but that wasn't going to work this time. I said, 'What about Dad? Just for once. Couldn't he . . . ?'

Geri left the silence there. When I was a kid Dad was straight-backed and lean, given to clean, square-edged statements with no wiggle room: *Women may fancy a drinking man, but they'll never respect him. There's no bad mood that fresh air and exercise can't mend. Always pay a debt before it's due and you'll never go hungry.* He could fix anything, grow anything, cook and clean and iron like a professional when he had to. Mum dying blew him right out of the water. He still lives in the house in Terenure where we grew up. Geri and I take turns calling down to him at the weekends, to clean the bathroom, put seven balanced meals in the freezer and check that the TV and the phone are still working. The kitchen wallpaper is the acid-trip orange swirl that Mum picked out in the seventies; in my room, my schoolbooks are dog-eared and cobwebbed on the bookshelf Dad made for me. Go into the sitting room and ask him a question: after a few seconds he'll turn from the telly, blink at you, say, 'Son. Good to see you,' and go back to watching Australian soap operas with the sound turned down. Occasionally, when he gets restless, he extracts himself from the sofa and shuffles around the back garden a few times, in his slippers.

I said, 'Geri, please. It's only for the night. She'll sleep all day tomorrow, and I'm hoping I'll have work sorted out by tomorrow evening. Please.'

'I would if I could, Mick. It's not that I'm too busy, you know I wouldn't mind that . . .' The background noise had faded: she had moved away from the kids, for privacy. I pictured her in their dining room strewn with bright jumpers and homework, tugging a strand of blonde out of its careful weekly set. We both knew I wouldn't have suggested our father unless I was desperate. 'But you know how she goes if you don't stay with her every minute, and I've Sheila and Phil to look after . . . What would I do if one of them started getting sick in the middle of the night? Just leave them to clean up their own mess? Or leave her and have her start carrying on, wake the house?'

I let my shoulders slump back against the wall and ran a hand over my face. My apartment felt airless, stuffed with the reek of whatever fake-lemon chemicals the cleaner uses. 'Yeah,' I said. 'I know. Don't worry about it.'

'Mick. If we can't cope . . . Maybe we should think about somewhere that can.'

'No,' I said. It came out sharp enough that I flinched, but Dina's singing didn't pause. 'I can cope. It'll be fine.'

'Will you be all right? Can you get someone to sub for you?'

'That's not how it works. I'll figure something out.'

'Oh, Mick, I'm sorry. I'm really sorry. As soon as they're a bit better—'

'It's OK. Tell them both I was asking for them, and you try not to catch whatever they've got. We'll talk soon.'

A distant yell of fury, somewhere on Geri's end. 'Andrea! What did I say to you? . . . Sure, Mick, Dina might be better herself by the morning, mightn't she? You never know your luck.'

'She might, yeah. We'll hope.' Dina yelped, and the shower shut off: the hot water had run out. 'Gotta go,' I said. 'Take care,' and I had the phone stashed away and myself neatly arranged in the kitchen, chopping vegetables, by the time the bathroom door opened.

I made myself a beef stir-fry for dinner – Dina wasn't hungry.

The shower had settled her: she curled up on the sofa, wearing a T-shirt and sweatpants that she had taken out of my wardrobe, gazing into space and rubbing dreamily at her hair with a towel. 'Shh,' she said, when I started to ask delicately about her day. 'Don't talk. Listen. Isn't it beautiful?'

All I could hear was the muttering of traffic, four floors down, and the synthesised tinkle of the music that the couple upstairs play every night to send their baby to sleep. I supposed it was peaceful, in its own way, and after a day keeping hold of every thread in that tangle of conversations, it was good to cook and eat in silence. I would have liked to catch the news, to see how the reporters were spinning things, but that was out.

After dinner I brewed coffee, a lot of it. The sound of the beans grinding sent Dina off on a fresh fidget: padding restless barefoot circles around the living room, taking books off my shelves and flipping the pages and putting them back in the wrong places. 'Were you supposed to be going out tonight?' she asked, with her back to me. 'Like on a date or something?'

'It's Tuesday. No one goes on dates on Tuesdays.'

'God, Mikey, get some spontaneity. Go out on school nights. Go wild.'

I poured myself a mug of espresso-strength and headed for my armchair. 'I don't think I'm the spontaneous type.'

'Well, does that mean you go on dates at the weekends? Like, you've got a girlfriend?'

'I don't think I've called anyone my girlfriend since I was twenty. Adults have partners.'

Dina mimed sticking two fingers down her throat, with sound effects. 'Middle-aged gay guys in 1995 have partners. Are you going out with anyone? Are you shagging anyone? Are you giving anyone a blast from the yoghurt bazooka? Are you—'

'*No*, Dina, I'm not. I was seeing someone until recently, we broke up, I'm not planning on getting back in the saddle for a while. OK?'

'I didn't know,' Dina said, a lot more quietly. 'Sorry.' She subsided onto one arm of the sofa. 'Do you still talk to Laura?' she asked, after a moment.

'Sometimes.' Hearing Laura's name filled up the room with her perfume, sharp and sweet. I took a big swallow of coffee to get it out of my nose.

'Are you guys going to get back together?'

'No. She's seeing someone. A doctor. I'm expecting her to ring me any day to tell me that they're engaged.'

'Ahhh,' Dina said, disappointed. 'I like Laura.'

'So do I. That's why I married her.'

'So why did you divorce her, then?'

'I didn't divorce her. She divorced me.' Laura and I have always done the civilised thing and told people the break-up was mutual, nobody's fault, we grew in different directions and all the usual meaningless rubbish, but I was too tired.

'Seriously? Why?'

'Because. I don't have the energy tonight, Dina.'

'Whatever,' Dina said, rolling her eyes. She slid sinuously off the sofa and padded into the kitchen, where I heard her opening things. 'Why don't you have anything to *eat*? I'm *starving*.'

'There's plenty to eat. The fridge is full. I can make you a stir-fry, or there's lamb stew in the freezer, or if you want something lighter you can have porridge, or—'

'Ew, please. I don't mean stuff like that. Fuck the five food groups and antioxidant blah blah blah. I want like ice cream, or one of those shitty burgers you stick in the microwave.' A cupboard door slammed and she came back into the living room holding out a granola bar at arm's length. '*Granola?* What are you, a girl?'

'No one's making you eat it.'

She shrugged, threw herself on the sofa again and started nibbling a corner of the bar, making a face like it might poison her. She said, 'When you were with Laura you were happy. It was sort of weird, because you're not one of those naturally happy people, so I wasn't used to seeing you that way. It actually took me a while to figure out what was going on. But it was nice.'

I said, 'Yes, it was.'

Laura is the same kind of sleek, highlighted, labour-intensive pretty as Jennifer Spain. She was on a diet every day I knew her, except birthdays and Christmases; she tops up her fake tan every three days, straightens her hair every morning of her life, and never goes out of the house without full makeup. I know some men like women to leave themselves the way nature intended, or at least to pretend they do, but the gallantry with which Laura fought nature hand to hand was one of the many things I loved about her. I used to get up fifteen or twenty minutes early in the mornings so I could spend that time just watching her get ready. Even on days when she was running late, dropping things and swearing to herself, for me it was the most restful thing life had to offer, like watching a cat put the world in order by washing itself. It always seemed to me that a girl like that, a girl who worked that hard at being what she was supposed to be, was likely to want what she was supposed to want: flowers, good jewellery, a nice house, holidays in the sun, and a man who would love her and put his heart into taking care of her for the rest of their lives. Girls like Fiona Rafferty are complete mysteries to me; I can't imagine where you would start trying to figure them out, and that makes me nervous. With Laura, it seemed to me that I had a chance at making her happy. It was moronic of me to be taken by surprise when she, with whom I had felt safe for exactly that reason, turned out to want precisely what women are supposed to want.

Dina said, without looking at me, 'Was it because of me? That Laura dumped you?'

'No,' I said, instantly. It was true. Laura found out about Dina early on, in much the way you would expect. She never once said or hinted, I believe she never once thought, that Dina wasn't my responsibility, that I should keep her crazy out of our home. When I came to bed, late on nights when Dina was finally asleep in our spare room, Laura would stroke my hair. That was all.

Dina said, 'Nobody wants to deal with this shit. *I* don't want to deal with this shit.'

'Maybe some women wouldn't. They're not women I'd marry.'

She snorted. 'I said I *liked* Laura. I didn't say I thought she was a *saint*. How stupid do you think I am? I *know* she didn't want some crazy bitch showing up on her doorstep, fucking up her whole week. That one time, candles, music, wineglasses, both of your hair all messed up? She must have hated my guts.'

'She didn't. She never has.'

'You wouldn't tell me if she did. Why else would she have dumped you? Laura was mad about you. And it's not like it was your fault, like you hit her or called her a slag, I know how you treated her, like some kind of princess. You'd have brought her the moon. *Her or me*, did she say that? *I want my life back, get that loony out of here?*'

She was starting to wind tight, her back pressed against the arm of the sofa. There was a flare of fear in her eyes.

I said, 'Laura left me because she wants children.'

Dina stopped in mid-breath and stared, open-mouthed. 'Oh, shit, Mikey. Can you not have kids?'

'I don't know. We didn't try.'

'Then . . . ?'

'I don't want to have children. I never have.'

Dina thought about that in silence, sucking her granola bar absently. After a while she said, 'Laura would probably chill out a lot if she had kids.'

'Maybe. I hope she gets the chance to find out. But it was never going to be with me. Laura knew that when she married me. I made sure she did. I never misled her.'

'Why don't you want kids?'

'Some people don't. It doesn't make me a freak.'

'I didn't call you a freak. Did I call you a freak? I just asked why.'

I said, 'I don't believe in Murder Ds having kids. They turn you soft: you can't take the heat any more, and you end up making a bollix of the job and probably the kids too. You can't have both. I'll take the job.'

'Oh my God, great big bullshit. Nobody doesn't have kids because they don't *believe* in it. You always blame everything on your job, it's so *boring*, you have no idea. Why don't you want kids?'

'I don't *blame* things on my job. I take it seriously. If that's boring, I apologise.'

Dina rolled her eyes and did a huge fake-patient sigh. 'OK,' she said, slowing down so that the idiot could keep up. 'I'd bet everything I've got, which is fuck-all but there you go, that your entire squad doesn't get *sterilised* their first day on the job. You work with guys who have kids. They do the exact same job you do. They can't be letting murderers go all the time, or they'd get fired. Right? Am I right?'

'Some of the guys have families. Yeah.'

'Then why don't you want kids?'

The coffee was kicking in. The apartment felt small and ugly, harsh with artificial light; the urge to get out, start driving too fast back to Broken Harbour, nearly launched me right out of my chair. I said, 'Because the risk is too big. It's so enormous that just thinking about it makes me want to puke my guts. That's why.'

'The risk,' Dina said, after a moment's silence. She turned the wrapper of the granola bar inside out, carefully, and examined the shiny side. 'Not from the job. You mean me. That they'd turn out like me.'

I said, 'You're not who I'm worried about.'

'Then who?'

'Me.'

Dina watched me, the lightbulb reflecting tiny twin will-o'-the-wisps in those inscrutable milky-blue eyes. She said, 'You'd make a good father.'

'I think I probably would. But probably's not good enough. Because if we're both wrong and I turned out to be a terrible father, what then? There would be absolutely *nothing* I could do. Once you find out, it's too late: the kids are there, you can't send them back. All you can do is keep on fucking them up, day after day, and watch while these perfect babies turn into wrecks in front of your eyes. I can't do it, Dina. Either I'm not stupid enough or I'm not brave enough, but I can't take that risk.'

'Geri's doing OK.'

'Geri's doing great,' I said. Geri is cheerful, easygoing, and a natural at motherhood. After each of her kids was born, I rang her every day for a year – stakeouts, interrogations, fights with Laura, everything else in the world got put on hold for that phone call – to make sure she was all right. Once she sounded hoarse and subdued enough that I made Phil leave work and check on her. She had a cold and obviously thought I should feel like an idiot, which I didn't. Better safe, always.

'I want kids someday,' Dina said. She balled up the wrapper, threw it in the general direction of the bin and missed. 'I bet you think that's a really shit idea.'

The thought of her showing up pregnant next time made my scalp freeze. 'You don't need my permission.'

'But you think it anyway.'

I asked, 'How's Fabio?'

'His name's Francesco. I don't think it's going to work out. I don't know.'

'I think it would be a better idea to wait to have kids until you're with someone you can rely on. Call me old-fashioned.'

'You mean, in case I lose it. In case I'm minding this little tiny three-week-old baby and my head starts to explode. Someone should be there to watch me.'

'That's not what I said.'

Dina stretched out her legs on the sofa and inspected her toenail polish, which was pearly pale blue. She said, 'I can tell when I'm going, you know. Do you want to know how?'

I don't want to know anything, ever, about the inner workings of Dina's mind. I said, 'How?'

'Things start sounding all wrong.' A quick glance at me, under cover of her hair. 'Like I take off my top at night and drop it on the floor, and it goes *plop*, like a rock falling into a pond. Or once I was walking home from work and my boots, every time my boots hit the ground they *squealed*, like a mouse in a trap. It was horrible. In the end I had to sit down on the footpath and take them off, to make sure there wasn't a mouse stuck inside – I did know there wasn't, I'm not stupid, but just to make sure. I figured it out then; what was happening, I mean. But I still had to take a taxi home. I couldn't stand hearing that, all the way. It sounded like it was in *agony*.'

'Dina. You should go to someone about it. As soon as it happens.'

'I do go to someone. Today I was in work and I opened one of the big freezers to get more bagels, and it crackled; like a fire, like there was a forest fire in there. So I walked out and came to you.'

'Which is great. I'm delighted you did. But I'm talking about a professional.'

'Doctors,' Dina said, with her lip curling. 'I've lost count. And how much use have they ever been?'

She was alive, which counted for a lot to me and which I felt should count for at least something to her, but before I could point that out, my mobile rang. As I went for it, I checked my watch: nine on the dot, good man Richie. 'Kennedy,' I said, getting up and moving away from Dina.

'We're in place,' Richie said, so softly I had to press my ear to the phone. 'No movement.'

'Techs and floaters doing their thing?'

'Yeah.'

'Any problems? Run into anyone along the way? Anything I should know?'

'Nah. We're good.'

'Then we'll talk in an hour, or sooner if there's any action. Good luck.'

I hung up. Dina was twisting the towel into a tight knot and watching me sharply, through that wing of glossy hair. 'Who was that?'

'Work.' I pocketed the mobile, inside pocket. Dina's mind has paranoid corners. I didn't want her hiding my phone so that I couldn't discuss her with imaginary hospitals, or, even better, answering it and telling Richie that she knew what he was up to and she hoped he died of cancer.

'I thought you were off.'

'I am. More or less.'

'What's "more or less" supposed to mean?'

Her hands were starting to tense up on the towel. I said, keeping my voice easy, 'It means that sometimes people need to ask me something. There's no such thing as "off" in Murder. That was my partner. He'll probably ring a few more times tonight.'

'Why?'

I got my coffee mug and headed for the kitchen to top up. 'You saw him. He's a rookie. Before he makes any big decisions, he needs to check with me.'

'Big decisions about what?'

'Anything.'

Dina started using one thumbnail to pick at a scab on the back of her other hand, in short hard scrapes. 'Someone was listening to the radio this afternoon,' she said. 'In work.'

Oh, shit. 'And?'

'And. It said there was a dead body, and police were treating the death as suspicious. It said Broken Harbour. They had some guy talking, some cop. It sounded like you.'

And then the freezer had started making forest-fire noises. I said carefully, taking a seat in my armchair again, 'OK.'

The scraping picked up force. 'Don't *do* that. Don't bloody *do* that.'

'Do what?'

'Put on that face, that stupid poker-up-your-arse cop face. Talk like I'm some idiot witness you can play little games with because I'm too intimidated to call you on it. You don't intimidate me. Do you get that?'

There was no point in arguing. I said calmly, 'Got it. I'm not going to try to intimidate you.'

'Then stop fucking about and *tell* me.'

'You know I can't discuss work. It's not personal.'

'*Jesus*, how the hell is this not personal? I'm your *sister*. How much more personal does it *get*?'

She was jammed tight into her corner of the sofa, feet braced like she was getting ready to come flying at me, which was unlikely but not impossible. I said, 'True enough. I meant I'm not hiding anything from you personally. I have to be discreet with everyone.'

Dina chewed at the back of her forearm and watched me like I was her enemy, narrowed eyes alight with cold animal cunning. 'OK,' she said. 'So let's just watch the news.'

I had been hoping that wouldn't occur to her. 'I thought you liked the peace and quiet.'

'If it's public enough that the whole damn country can see it, surely to jumping Jesus it can't be too confidential for me to watch. Right? Considering that it's not *personal*.'

'For God's sake, Dina. I've been in work all day. The last thing I want to do is come home and look at work on TV.'

'Then tell me *what the fucking fuck is going on*. Or I'm going to turn on the news and you'll have to hold me down to stop me. Do you want to do that?'

'All right,' I said, hands going up. 'OK. I'll give you the story, if you'll calm down for me. That means you need to stop biting your arm.'

'It's my bloody arm. What do you care whose business is it?'

'I can't concentrate while you're doing that. And as long as I can't concentrate, I can't tell you what's going on. It's up to you.'

She shot me a defiant glare, bared small white teeth and bit down once more, hard, but when I didn't react she wiped her arm on her T-shirt and sat on her hands. 'There. Happy?'

I said, 'It wasn't just one body. It was a family of four. They were living out in Broken Harbour – it's called Brianstown now. Someone broke into their house last night.'

'How'd he kill them?'

'We won't be sure till the post-mortem. It looks like he used a knife.'

Dina stared at nothing and didn't move, didn't even breathe, while she thought that over. 'Brianstown,' she said finally, abstractedly. 'What a stupid fucking cretin name. Whoever came up with that, someone should push his head underneath a lawnmower and hold it there. Are you positive?'

'About the name?'

'No! Je-*sus*. About the *dead people*.'

I rubbed at the hinge of my jaw, trying to work some of the tension out of it. 'Yeah. I'm positive.'

The focus had come back into her eyes: they were on me, unblinking. 'You're positive because you're working on it.'

I didn't answer.

'You said you didn't want to look at it on the news because you'd been working on it all day. That's what you said.'

'Looking at a murder case is work. Any murder case. That's what I *do*.'

'Blah blah blah whatever, *this* murder case is *your* work. Right?'

'What difference does that make?'

'It makes a difference because if you tell me, I'll let you change the subject.'

I said, 'Yeah. I'm on the case. Me and a bunch of other detectives.'

'Hmm,' Dina said. She threw the towel in the general direction of the bathroom door, slid off the sofa and started moving around the room again, forceful automatic circles. I could almost hear the hum of the thing that lives inside her starting to build, a thin mosquito whine.

I said, 'And now we change the subject.'

'Yeah,' Dina said. She picked up a little soapstone elephant that Laura and I brought back from holiday in Kenya one year, squeezed it hard and examined the red dents it left in her palm with interest. 'I was thinking, before. While I was waiting for you. I want to change my flat.'

'Good,' I said. 'We can go look for something online right now.' Dina's flat is a shithole. She could afford a perfectly decent place, I help her with the rent, but she says purpose-built apartment blocks make her want to bang her head off the walls, so she always ends up in some decrepit Georgian house that was converted into bedsits in the sixties, sharing a bathroom with some hairy loser who calls himself a musician and needs regular reminders that she has a cop for a brother.

'No,' Dina said. '*Listen*, for God's sake. I want to change it like *change* it, I hate its guts because it itches. I already tried to move, went to the upstairs girls to ask them to swap, I mean it's not like it's going to itch them insides of the corners of their elbows and up their fingernails same as it does me. It's not bugs, I'm you should take a look at how clean, I think it's just that shitty carpet pattern. I told them that but those bitches wouldn't listen, they got all goggle-mouthed, big stupid fish, I wonder if they have pet fish for pets? So since I can't move out I have to *change* things, I want to move the rooms. I think we hammered them down before but I don't remember, Mikey, do you did you?'

Richie rang every hour on the hour, just like he had promised, to tell me that more nothing had happened. Sometimes Dina let me answer on the first ring, chewed on one of her fingers while I talked and waited till I hung up before she kicked it up another gear: *Who was that, what did he want, what did you tell him about me* . . . Sometimes I had to listen to it ring out two or three times, while she circled faster and talked louder to cover it, until she exhausted herself and slumped on the sofa or the carpet, and I could pick up. At one o'clock she slapped the phone out of my hand, voice rising towards a scream, when I went to answer: *You don't give a fucking I'm trying to tell you something, trying to talk to you, don't you ignore me for that whoever, you listen listen listen* . . .

Just after three she fell asleep on the sofa in mid-sentence, curled in a tight ball with her head burrowed between the cushions. She had the hem of my T-shirt wrapped around one fist and she was sucking on the cloth.

I got the duvet from the spare room and tucked it around her. Then I dimmed the lights, got a mug of cold coffee, and sat at the dining table playing solitaire on my phone. Far below us a truck beeped rhythmically, backing up; down the corridor a door slammed, muffled by the heavy carpeting. Dina whispered in her sleep. For a while it rained, a soft swish and patter at the windows, dimming back to silence.

I was fifteen, Geri was sixteen and Dina was almost six when our mother killed herself. For as long as I could remember, a part of me had been waiting for the day it would happen; with the cunning that comes to people whose minds have been stripped to one desire, she picked the only day we weren't waiting for. All year round we took her as a full-time job, my father and Geri and me:

watching like undercover agents for the first signs, coaxing her to eat when she wouldn't get out of bed, hiding the painkillers on days when she drifted around the house like a cold spot in the air, holding her hand all night long when she couldn't stop crying; lying as brightly and slickly as grifters to neighbours, relatives, anyone who asked. But for two weeks in the summer, all five of us were set free. Something about Broken Harbour – the air, the change of scenery, sheer determination not to ruin our holiday – changed my mother into a laughing girl lifting her palms to the sun, tentative and amazed, as if she couldn't believe its tenderness on her skin. She ran races with us on the sand, kissed the back of my father's neck when she rubbed in his sunscreen. For those two weeks, we didn't count the sharp knives or sit bolt upright at the tiniest nighttime noise, because she was happy.

The summer I was fifteen, she was happiest of all. I didn't understand why, until afterwards. She waited till the last night of our holiday before she walked into the water.

Up until that night Dina was a sparky little scrap of contrariness and mischief, always ready to explode into her high bubbling giggle and always able to pull you in too. Afterwards, the doctors warned us to watch her for 'emotional consequences' – these days she would have been shot straight into therapy, probably we all would, but this was the eighties, and this country still thought therapy was for rich people who needed a good kick up the arse. We watched – we were good at that; at first we watched 24/7, took turns sitting by Dina's bed while she twitched and murmured in her sleep – but she didn't seem to be in any worse shape than me or Geri, and she definitely looked a lot better off than our father. She sucked her thumb, cried a lot. Over a long while she went back to normal, as far as we could see. The day she woke me by shoving a wet facecloth down my back and running away screaming with laughter, Geri lit a candle to the Blessed Virgin, in thanksgiving that Dina was back.

I lit one too. I held on to the positive as hard as I could and told myself I believed it. But I knew: a night like that one doesn't just disappear. I was right. That night burrowed deep inside Dina's softest spot and stayed curled up, biding its time, for years. When it had swollen fat enough, it stirred, woke up and ate its way back to the surface.

We had never left Dina on her own during an episode. Occasionally she somehow got sidetracked before she reached my place or Geri's; she had come to us bruised, coked off her face, once with an inch-wide clump of hair pulled out by the roots. Every time, Geri and I tried to find out what had happened, but we never expected her to tell us.

I thought about ringing in sick. I almost did it; I had the phone in my hand, ready to dial the squad room and tell them I had picked up a nasty dose of gastric flu from my niece and someone else would have to take on this case till I could step away from the bathroom. It wasn't the instant career nosedive that stopped me, regardless of what everyone I know would have thought. It was the picture of Pat and Jenny Spain, fighting to the death alone because they believed we had abandoned them. I couldn't find a way to live with making that the truth.

At a few minutes to four I went into my bedroom, switched my mobile to silent and watched the screen till it lit up with Richie's name. More nothing; he was starting to sound sleepy. I said, 'If there's no action by five, you can start winding it up. Tell Whatshisname and the other floaters to go get some kip and report back in at noon. You can manage another few hours with no sleep, am I right?'

'No bothers. I've got some caffeine tabs left.' There was a moment's pause while he looked for the right way to word it. 'Will I see you at the hospital, yeah? Or . . . ?'

'Yes, old son, you will. Six sharp. Have Whatshisname drop you off on his way home. And make sure you get some breakfast into you, because once we get moving, we're not going to be stopping for tea and toast. See you soon.'

I showered, shaved, found clean clothes and had a quick bowl of muesli, as quietly as I could. Then I wrote Dina a note: *Good morning, dormouse – had to go to work but I'll be back ASAP. Meanwhile, eat anything you can find in the kitchen, read/watch/listen to anything you can find on the shelves, have another shower – the place is all yours. Ring me/Geri any time if you have any hassle or if you just feel like a chat. M.*

I left it on the coffee table, on top of a fresh towel and another granola bar. No keys: I had spent a long time thinking about that, but in the end it came down to a choice between the risk that the apartment would catch fire while she was locked in there and the risk that she would go wandering down some dodgy street and run into the wrong person. It was a bad week to have to trust in either luck or humanity, but if I'm backed into that corner, I'll go with luck every time.

Dina twisted on the sofa, and for a moment I froze, but she only sighed and nuzzled her head deeper into the cushions. One slim arm hung outside the duvet, pale as milk, printed with neat, faint half-circles of red toothmarks. I eased the duvet up to cover it. Then I pulled on my overcoat, slipped out of the apartment and closed the door behind me.

# 8

Richie was waiting outside the hospital at a quarter to six. Normally I would have sent one of the uniforms – officially, all we were there for was to identify the bodies, and I have more productive ways to spend my time – but this was Richie's first case, and he needed to watch the PM. If he didn't, word would get around. As a bonus, Cooper likes you to watch, and if Richie managed to get on his good side, we would have a shot at the fast track if we needed it.

It was still night, just that cold pre-dawn thinning of the darkness that leaches the last strength out of your bones, and the air had a bite to it. The light of the hospital entrance was a warmthless, stuttering white. Richie was leaning against the railing, with an industrial-size paper cup in each hand, kicking a crumple of tinfoil back and forth between his feet. He looked pale and baggy-eyed, but he was awake and wearing a clean shirt – it was just as cheap as the one before, but I gave him points for having thought of it at all. He even had my tie on over it.

'Howya,' he said, handing me one of the cups. 'Thought you might want this. Tastes like washing-up liquid, though. Hospital canteen.'

'Thanks,' I said. 'I think.' It was coffee, give or take. 'How was last night?'

He shrugged. 'Would've been better if our fella'd shown up.'

'Patience, old son. Rome wasn't built in a day.'

Another shrug, down at the tinfoil that he was kicking harder. I realised that he had wanted to have our guy ready to present to me first thing this morning, all trussed up and oven-ready, the kill to prove that he was a man. He said, 'The techs say they got a load done, anyway.'

'Good.' I leaned against the railings next to him and tried to get the coffee into me: one hint of a yawn and Cooper would boot me out the door. 'How did the patrol floaters do?'

'Grand, I think. They picked up a few cars coming into the estate, but all the plates checked out to Ocean View addresses: just people heading home. A bunch of teenagers met up in one of the houses down the other end from us, brought a couple of bottles with them, played their music loud. Around half-two there was a car going around and around, slow, but it was a woman driving and she had a baby crying in the back, so the lads figured she was trying to get it to sleep. That was the lot.'

'You're satisfied that if someone dodgy had been prowling around, they'd have spotted him?'

'Unless he was really lucky, yeah. I'd say so.'

'No more media?'

Richie shook his head. 'I thought they'd be going after the neighbours, but nah.'

'Probably off looking for loved ones to hassle; juicier stuff there. It looks like the press office has them under control, for now anyway. I had a quick skim of the early editions: nothing we didn't already know, and nothing about Jenny Spain being alive. We won't be able to keep that to ourselves much longer, though. We need to get our hands on this guy fast.' Every front page had run with a howl-sized headline and an angelic blond shot of Emma and Jack. We had a week, two at the outside, to get this guy before we turned into worthless incompetents and the Super turned into a very unhappy camper.

Richie started to answer, but a yawn cut him off. 'Get any sleep?' I asked.

'Nah. We talked about doing shifts, but the countryside's bleeding *noisy*, did you know that? Everyone gives it loads about the peace and quiet, but that's a load of bollix. The sea, and there were like a hundred bats throwing a party, and mice or something running around, all through the houses. And something went for a wander down the road; sounded like a tank, charging through all those plants. I tried checking it out with the goggles, but it headed down between the houses before I could get it. Something big, anyway.'

'Too creepy for you?'

Richie gave me a wry sideways grin. 'I managed not to crap my kacks. Even if it'd been quiet, I wanted to be awake. In case.'

'I'd have been the same. How are you doing?'

'All right. A bit wrecked, like, but I'm not gonna crash out halfway through the post-mortem or anything.'

'If we get you a couple of hours' kip somewhere along the way, can you take another night?'

'Little more of this' – he tilted the coffee cup – 'and yeah, sure I can. Same as last night, yeah?'

'No,' I said. 'One of the definitions of insanity, my friend, is doing the same thing again and again and hoping for different results. If our man could resist the bait last night, he can resist it tonight. We need better bait.'

Richie's head turned towards me. 'Yeah? I thought ours was pretty decent. Another night or two and I'd say we'll have him.'

I raised my cup to him. 'Vote of confidence appreciated. But the fact is, I misjudged our boy. He's not interested in us. Some of them can't stay away from the cops: they insert themselves into the investigation every way they can find, you can't turn around without tripping over Mr Helpful. Our guy isn't like that, or we'd have him by now. He doesn't give a damn what we do, or what the Bureau lads do. But you know what he's *very* interested in, don't you?'

'The Spains?'

'Ten points for you. The Spains.'

'We haven't got the Spains, but. I mean, Jenny, yeah, but—'

'But even if Jenny was able to help us out, I want to keep her under wraps for as long as I can. True enough. What we do have, though, is Whatshername, that floater – what *is* her name?'

'Oates. Detective Janine Oates.'

'Her. You may not have noticed this, but from a distance, in the right context, Detective Oates could quite probably pass for Fiona Rafferty. Same height, same build, same hair – Detective Oates's is a lot neater, luckily, but I'm sure she could mess it up if we asked her to. Get her a red duffel coat and Bob's your uncle. It's not that they're actually anything alike, but to spot that you'd have to get a proper look, and for that, you'd need a decent vantage point and your binoculars.'

Richie said, 'We clear out at six again, she drives up – have we got a yellow Fiat in the pool, yeah?'

'I'm not sure, but if we don't, we can just have a marked car drop her off. She goes into the house and spends the night doing whatever she thinks Fiona Rafferty would do, as obviously as possible – wandering around looking distraught with the curtains open, having a read of Pat and Jenny's papers, that kind of thing. And we wait.'

Richie drank his coffee, with an unconscious grimace on each sip, and considered that. 'You think he knows who Fiona is?'

'I think there's a damn good chance he does, yeah. Remember, we don't know where he came into contact with the Spains; it could have been somewhere that involved Fiona too. Even if it wasn't, she may not have been out here in a few months, but for all we know he's been watching them for a lot longer than that.'

On the horizon the outline of low hills was starting to take shape, darker against darkness. Somewhere beyond them, the first light was moving up the sand in Broken Harbour, seeping into all those empty houses, into the emptiest one of all. It was five to six. I said, 'Have you ever been to a post-mortem?'

Richie shook his head. He said, 'There's a first time for everyone.'

'There is, yeah, but it's not usually like this. This is going to be bad. You should be there, but if you're seriously not on for it, this is when you need to speak up. We can say you're getting some kip after the stakeout.'

He crushed his paper cup into a wad and tossed it at the bin with a hard downward snap of his wrist. 'Let's go,' he said.

The morgue was in the hospital basement, small and low-ceilinged, with dirt and probably worse things ground into the grout between the floor tiles. The air was chilly and damp, motionless. 'Detectives,'

Cooper said, eyeing Richie with a faint anticipatory smirk. Cooper is maybe fifty, but in the tube lighting, against white tile and metal, he looked ancient: greyish and shrivelled, like an alien stepped out of some hallucination, probes at the ready. 'How nice to see you. We will begin, I think, with the adult male: age before beauty.' Behind him, his assistant – heavy build, stolid stare – pulled open a storage drawer with a horrible grating screech. I felt Richie brace his shoulders beside me, a tiny jerk.

They broke the seals on the body bag, unzipped it to reveal Pat Spain in his blood-stiffened pyjamas. They photographed him clothed and naked, took blood and fingerprints, bent close while they picked at his skin with tweezers and clipped his fingernails for DNA. Then the assistant swung the instrument tray around to Cooper's elbow.

Post-mortems are brutal things. This is the part that always catches rookies off guard: they expect delicacy, tiny scalpels and precision cuts, and instead they get bread knives sawing fast careless gashes, skin ripped back like sticky paper. Cooper at work looks more like a butcher than a surgeon. He doesn't need to take care to minimise scarring, hold his breath making sure not to nick an artery. The flesh he works on isn't precious any more. When Cooper is done with a body, no one else will need it, ever again.

Richie did well. He didn't flinch when the pruning shears snapped Pat's ribs open, or when Cooper folded Pat's face downwards on itself, or when the skull saw sent up a thin acrid smell of scorched bone. The squelching sound when the assistant dumped the liver on the weighing scales made him jump, but that was all.

Cooper moved deftly and efficiently, dictating into the hanging mike and ignoring us. Pat had eaten a cheese sandwich and some crisps, three or four hours before he died. Traces of fat in his arteries and around his liver said he should have been getting fewer crisps and more exercise, but overall he had been in good shape: no illnesses that showed, no abnormalities, a long-ago broken collarbone and thickened ears that could have been rugby injuries. I said quietly, to Richie, 'Healthy man's scars.'

Finally Cooper straightened, stretching his back, and turned to us. 'To summarise,' he informed us, with satisfaction, 'my preliminary statement at the scene was correct. As you will remember, I posited that the cause of death was either this wound' – he prodded the gash in the middle of Pat Spain's chest with his scalpel – 'or this one.' A poke to the slit below Pat's collarbone. 'In point of fact, each of these was potentially fatal. In the first, the blade glanced off the central edge of the sternum and nicked the pulmonary vein.'

He folded back Pat's skin – delicately, holding the flap between thumb and finger – and pointed with his scalpel, to make sure Richie and I both saw exactly what he meant. 'Absent any other wounds or any medical treatment, this injury would have resulted in death within approximately twenty minutes, as the subject gradually bled out into the chest cavity. As it happened, however, this sequence of events was interrupted.'

He let the skin drop back into place and reached to pry up the flap below the collarbone. 'This is the wound that proved fatal. The blade entered between the third and fourth ribs, at the mid-clavicular line, causing a one-centimetre laceration to the right ventricle of the heart. Blood loss would have been rapid and extensive. The drop in blood pressure would have led to unconsciousness within fifteen or twenty seconds, and to death perhaps two minutes later. The cause of death was exsanguination.'

So there was no way Pat had been the one who got rid of the weapons; not that I thought he had been, not any more. Cooper tossed his scalpel into the instrument tray and nodded to the assistant, who was threading a thick, curved needle and humming softly to himself. I said, 'And the manner of death?'

Cooper sighed. He said, 'I understand that you currently believe a fifth party was present in the house at the time of the deaths.'

'That's what the evidence tells us.'

'Hmm,' Cooper said. He flicked something unthinkable off his gown, onto the floor. 'And I am sure this leads you to assume that this subject' – a nod at Pat Spain – 'was a victim of homicide. Unfortunately, some of us do not have the luxury of assumption. All of the wounds are consistent with either assault or self-infliction. The manner of death was either homicide or suicide: undetermined.'

Some defence lawyer was going to love that all over. I said, 'Then let's leave that blank on the paperwork for now, and come back to it when we've got more evidence. If the lab finds DNA under his fingernails—'

Cooper leaned over to the hanging mike and said, without bothering to look at me, 'Manner of death: undetermined.' That little smirk slid over me, to Richie. 'Do cheer up, Detective Kennedy. I doubt there will be any ambiguity as to the next subject's manner of death.'

Emma Spain came out of her drawer with her bedsheets folded neatly around her like a shroud. Richie twitched, at my shoulder, and I heard the fast rasp as he started scratching at the inside of a pocket. She had curled up all cosy in those same sheets, two nights ago, with a good-night kiss. If he started thinking along those lines, I would have a new partner by Christmas. I shifted, nudging against his elbow, and cleared my throat. Cooper gave me a long stare across that small white shape, but Richie got the message and went still. The assistant unfolded the sheets.

I know detectives who learn the knack of unfocusing their eyes at the bad parts of post-mortems. Cooper violates dead children searching for signs of violation, and the investigating officer stares intently at nothing but a blur. I watch. I don't blink. The victims didn't get to choose whether or not to endure what was done to them. I'm spoilt enough, next to them, without claiming to be too delicate even to endure looking.

Emma was worse than Patrick not just because she was so young, but because she was so unblemished. Maybe this sounds twisted, but the worse the injuries, the easier the autopsy. When a body comes in macerated to something from an abattoir, the Y incision and the grating snap as the top of the skull comes off don't pack much punch. The injuries give the cop in you something to focus on: they turn the victim from a human being into a specimen, made out of urgent questions and fresh clues. Emma was just a little girl, tender-soled bare feet and freckled snub nose,

sticking-out belly button where her pink pyjama top had ridden
up. You would have sworn that she was only a hairsbreadth from
alive; that if you had just known the right words to say in her ear,
the right spot to touch, you could have woken her. What Cooper
was about to do to her in our name was a dozen times more brutal
than anything her murderer had done.

The assistant took off the paper bags tied over her hands to
preserve evidence, and Cooper bent over her with a palette knife
to take fingernail scrapings. 'Ah,' he said suddenly. 'Interesting.'

He reached for tweezers, did something finicky at her right
hand, and straightened up holding the tweezers high. 'These,' he
said, 'were between the index and middle fingers.'

Four fine, pale hairs. A blond man crouched over the pink
ruffled bed, that tiny girl fighting— I said, 'DNA. Is there enough
there for a shot at DNA?'

Cooper shot me a thin smile. 'Control your excitement,
Detective. Microscopic comparison will, of course, be necessary,
but judging by colour and texture, there appears to be every probability that these hairs come from the head of the victim herself.'
He dropped them into an evidence bag, pulled out his fountain
pen and bent to scribble something on the label. 'Assuming the
evidence bears out the preliminary theory of suffocation, I would
theorise that her hands were trapped beside her head by the pillow
or other weapon, and that, unable to claw at the attacker, she
pulled at her own hair in her final moments of consciousness.'

That was when Richie left. At least he managed not to put a fist
through the wall, or puke his guts onto the floor. He just turned on
his heel, walked out and closed the door behind him.

The assistant sniggered. Cooper gave the door a long, chilly
stare. 'I apologise for Detective Curran,' I said.

He transferred the stare to me. 'I am not accustomed,' he told
me, 'to having my post-mortems interrupted without an excellent
reason. Do you, or does your colleague, have an excellent reason?'

So much for Richie getting on Cooper's good side. And that
was the least of our problems. Whatever flak Quigley had been
giving Richie in the squad room was nothing to what he could

expect from now on, if he didn't get his arse back into the morgue and see this thing through. We were talking lifetime nickname here. Cooper probably wouldn't spread the word – he likes being above gossip – but the glint in the assistant's eye said he couldn't wait.

I kept my mouth shut while Cooper worked his way through the external examination. No more nasty surprises along the way, thank Christ. Emma was a little above average height for six, average weight, healthy in every way that Cooper could check. There were no healed fractures, no burn marks or scars, none of the hideous spoor of abuse, physical or sexual. Her teeth were clean and healthy, no fillings; her nails were clean and clipped; her hair had been trimmed not long ago. She had spent the little life she had being well taken care of.

No conjunctival haemorrhages in her eyes, no bruising to her lips where something had been pressed over her mouth, nothing that could tell us anything about what he had done to her. Then Cooper, shining his pencil torch into Emma's mouth like he was her GP, said, 'Hm.' He reached for his tweezers again, tilted her head farther back and manoeuvred them deep into her throat.

'If I remember correctly,' he said, 'the victim's bed held a number of ornamental pillows, embroidered with anthropomorphic animals in multicoloured wool.'

Kittens and puppies, staring in the torchlight. 'That's correct,' I said.

Cooper pulled the tweezers out of her mouth with a flourish. 'In that case,' he said, 'I believe we have evidence of cause of death.'

A wisp of wool. It was sodden and darkened, but when it dried out it would be rose-pink. I thought of the kitten's pricked ears, the puppy's hanging tongue.

'As you have seen,' Cooper said, 'smothering often leaves so few signs that it is impossible to diagnose definitively. In this case, however, if this wool matches that used in the pillows, I will have no difficulty in stating that the victim was smothered with one of the pillows from her bed – the Bureau may well be able to identify the specific weapon. She died either from anoxia or from cardiac arrest pursuant to anoxia. The manner of death was homicide.'

He dropped the tag of wool into an evidence bag. As he sealed it, he gave it a nod and a brief, satisfied smile.

The internal exam gave us more of the same: a healthy little girl, nothing to say she had ever been ill or hurt in her life. Emma's stomach contained a partially digested meal of minced beef, mashed potato, vegetables and fruit: cottage pie, with fruit salad for dessert, eaten about eight hours before she died. The Spains seemed like the family-dinner type, and I wondered why Pat and Emma hadn't eaten the same meal that night, but that was a small enough thing that it could easily go unexplained forever. A queasy stomach that couldn't take cottage pie, a kid being given the meal she had refused at lunchtime: murder means that little things get swept away, lost for good on the ebb of that red tsunami.

When the assistant started stitching her up, I said, 'Dr Cooper, could you give me two minutes to go get Detective Curran? He'll want to see the rest of this.'

Cooper stripped off his bloody gloves. 'I am unsure what gives you that impression. Detective Curran had every opportunity to see *the rest of this*, as you call it. He apparently feels himself to be above such mundanities.'

'Detective Curran came here directly from an all-night stakeout. Nature called, as it does, and he didn't want to interrupt your work again by coming back in. I don't think he should be penalised for having spent twelve straight hours on duty.'

Cooper threw me a disgusted glance that said I could at least have come up with something more creative. 'Detective Curran's theoretical innards are hardly my problem.'

He turned away to drop his gloves into the biohazard bin; the clang of the lid said this conversation was over. I said evenly, 'Detective Curran will want to be here for Jack Spain's post-mortem. And I think it's important that he should be. I'm willing to go out of my way to make sure that this investigation gets everything it needs, and I'd like to think that everyone involved will do the same.'

Cooper turned around, taking his time, and gave me a shark-eyed stare. 'Simply out of interest,' he said, 'let me ask: are you attempting to tell me how to run my post-mortems?'

I didn't blink. 'No,' I said gently. 'I'm telling you how I run my investigations.'

His mouth was pursed up tighter than a cat's arse, but in the end he shrugged. 'I plan to spend the next fifteen minutes dictating my notes on Emma Spain. I will then move on to Jack Spain. Anyone who is in the room when I begin the process may remain. Anyone who is not present at that point will refrain from disturbing yet another post-mortem by entering.'

We both understood that I was going to pay for this, sooner or later. 'Thank you, Doctor,' I said. 'I appreciate that.'

'Believe me, Detective, you have no reason to thank me. I have no plans to deviate one iota from my usual routine, either for your sake or for Detective Curran's. That being the case, I feel I should inform you that my usual routine does not include small talk between post-mortems.' And he turned his shoulder to me and started talking into the hanging mike again.

On my way out, behind Cooper's back, I caught the assistant's eye and pointed a finger at him. He tried to do perplexed innocence, which didn't suit him, but I held the eye contact till he blinked. If this story got around, he knew where I was going to come looking.

The frost was still on the grass, but the light had brightened to a pearly pale grey: morning. The hospital was starting to wake up for the day. Two old women in their best coats were supporting each other up the steps, talking loudly about stuff I would have been happier not hearing, and a young guy in a dressing gown was leaning beside the door and having a smoke.

Richie was sitting on a low wall near the entrance, staring at the toes of his shoes, with his hands dug deep in the pockets of his jacket. It was actually a pretty decent jacket, grey, with a good cut. He managed to make it look like denim.

He didn't look up when my shadow fell across him. He said, 'Sorry.'

'Nothing to apologise for. Not to me.'

'Is he done?'

'He's done with Emma. He's about to move on to Jack.'

'Jesus *Christ*,' Richie said softly, to the sky. I couldn't tell whether he was swearing or praying.

I said, 'Kids are hell. No way round that. We all act like it's not a problem, but the fact is, it kills every single one of us, every time. You're not alone there.'

'I was sure I could handle it. Definite.'

'And that's the right way to think. Always go in thinking positive. Doubts will kill you in this game.'

'I've never gone to bits like that before. I swear. At the scene, even: I was *grand*. Not a problem.'

'Yeah, you were. The scene's different. The first look is bad, and then the worst's over. It doesn't keep coming at you.'

I saw his Adam's apple jump as he swallowed. After a moment he said, 'Maybe I'm not cut out for this.'

The words sounded like they hurt his throat. I said, 'Are you sure you want to be?'

'All I ever wanted. Since I was a kid. Saw a programme on the telly – documentary, not made-up crap.' A quick squint my way, to check if I was laughing at him. 'Some old case, a girl that got killed down the country. The detective was talking about how they solved it. I thought he was the smartest guy I'd ever seen, you know? Way smarter than college professors and people like that, because he got things *done*. Things that mattered. I just thought . . . *That. I want to do that.*'

'And now you're learning to do that. Like I told you yesterday, it takes time. You can't expect to have the whole thing sussed on your first day.'

'Yeah,' Richie said. 'Or else your man Quigley's right, and I should fuck off back to Motor Vehicles and spend some more time arresting my cousins.'

'Is that what he was saying to you yesterday? When I was in with the Super?'

Richie rubbed a hand over his hair. 'It doesn't matter,' he said tiredly. 'I don't give a damn what Quigley says. I only give a damn if he's right.'

I dusted off a piece of wall and sat down beside him. 'Richie, old son,' I said. 'Let me ask you something.'

His head turned towards me. He had that food-poisoned look again. I gambled that he wouldn't puke on my suit.

'I'm betting you know I have the highest overall solve rate on this squad.'

'Yeah. I knew coming in. When the Super said he was putting me with you, I was only delighted.'

'And now you've had a chance to watch me work, where do you think that solve rate comes from?'

Richie looked uncomfortable. Clearly he had asked himself the same question, and hadn't managed to come up with an answer.

'Is it because I'm the smartest guy in the squad room?'

He did something between a shrug and a wriggle. 'How would I know?'

'In other words, no. Is it because I'm some kind of psychic wonder boy, like you see on TV?'

'Like I said. I wouldn't—'

'You wouldn't know. Right. Then let me say it for you: my brain and my instincts are no better than anyone else's.'

'I didn't say that.'

In the thin morning light his face looked pinched and anxious, desperately young. 'I know. It's true just the same: I'm no genius. I would have liked to be. For a while, when I started out, I was sure I was something special. Not a doubt in my mind.'

Richie watched me, wary, trying to work out if he was getting told off here. He said, 'When . . . ?'

'When did I figure out that I'm not Superboy?'

'I guess. Yeah.'

The hills were hidden in mist, just snatches of green appearing and disappearing. There was no way to tell where land ended and sky began. 'Probably a lot later than I should have,' I said. 'There wasn't one moment that sticks out. Let's just say I got older and wiser, and it became obvious. I made a few mistakes I shouldn't have made, missed a few things that Superboy would have spotted. Most of all, I worked with a couple of guys along the way who were the real thing: what I wanted to be. And it turns out I'm just about smart enough to spot the difference when it's right in front of my nose. Smart enough to see how smart I'm not, I guess.'

Richie said nothing, but he was paying attention. That alertness was rising in his face, edging out the rest; he almost looked like a cop again. I said, 'It was a nasty surprise, finding out that I was nothing special. But like I said to you before, you work with what you've got on hand. Otherwise you might as well buy yourself a one-way ticket on the train to failure.'

Richie said, 'Then the solve rate . . . ?'

'The solve rate,' I said. 'My solve rate is what it is for two reasons: because I work my arse off, and because I keep control. Over situations, over witnesses, over suspects, and most of all, over myself. If you're good enough at that, you can compensate for just about anything else. If you're not, Richie, if you lose control, then it doesn't matter how much of a genius you are: you might as well go home. Forget your tie, forget your interrogation technique, forget all the things we've talked about over the last couple of weeks. They're just symptoms. Get down to the core of it, and every single thing I've said to you boils down to control. Do you understand what I'm telling you?'

Richie's mouth was starting to set into a tough line, which was what I wanted to see. 'I have control. Sir. Cooper got me off guard, is all.'

'Then don't be off guard.'

He bit down on the inside of his cheek. 'Yeah. Fair enough. It won't happen again.'

'I didn't think it would.' I gave him a quick clap on the shoulder. 'Focus on the positive here, Richie. There's a decent chance that this is the worst way you'll ever spend a morning, and you're still standing. And if it only takes you till your third week on the job to find out that you're not Superboy, you're a lucky man.'

'Maybe.'

'Believe me. You've got the rest of your career to bring yourself into line with your goals. That's a gift, my friend. Don't throw it away.'

The day's worth of damage was starting to roll into the hospital: a guy in overalls pressing a blood-soaked cloth over his hand, a girl with a thin, strained face carrying a dazed-looking toddler. Cooper's clock was ticking, but this needed to come from Richie, not from me.

He said, 'Am I never going to live this down in the squad, no?'

'Don't worry about that. I'm on it.'

He looked at me full face, for the first time since I'd got out there. 'I don't want you watching out for me. I'm not a kid. I can fight my own battles.'

I said, 'You're my partner. It's my job to fight them with you.'

That took him by surprise. I watched something change in his face as it sank in. After a moment he nodded. He said, 'Can I still . . . ? I mean, will Dr Cooper let me back in?'

I checked my watch. 'If we move fast, he will.'

'Right,' Richie said. He blew out a long breath, ran his hands over his hair and stood up. 'Let's go.'

'Good on you. And Richie?'

'Yeah.'

'Don't let this get to you. This is a blip. You've got everything it takes to be a Murder D.'

He nodded. 'I'm going to give it my best shot, anyway. Thanks, Detective Kennedy. Thank you.' Then he tugged his tie straight and the two of us headed back into the hospital, side by side.

Richie made it through Jack's post-mortem. It was a bad one: Cooper took his time, he made sure we got an eyeful of every detail, and if Richie had glanced away once he would have been toast. He didn't. He watched steadily, not twitching, barely even blinking. Jack had been healthy, well-nourished, big for his age; active, judging by all the scabs on his knees and elbows. He had eaten cottage pie and fruit salad around the same time as Emma. Residue behind his ears said he had had a bath, wiggled too hard for the shampoo to be rinsed away properly. Then he had gone to bed, and deep in the night someone had killed him – presumably by suffocating him with a pillow, but this time there was no way to be sure. He had no defensive injuries, but Cooper made sure to point out that that meant nothing: he could have slipped over the line in his sleep, or he could have screamed his last seconds away into the pillow that stopped him fighting. Richie's face had sunk in around the mouth and nose, like he had lost ten pounds since we walked into that morgue.

When we got out it was lunchtime, not that either of us felt like eating. The mist had burned off, but it was still dark as dusk; the sky was heavy with cold clouds, and on the horizon the hills were a smoky, sullen green. Hospital traffic had picked up: people going in and out, an ambulance unloading a young guy in motorcycle leathers with one leg at a bad angle, a clutch of girls in scrubs helpless with laughter over something on one of their phones. I said, 'You made it. Well done, Detective.'

Richie made a hoarse sound halfway between a cough and a retch, and I whipped my coat out of his way, but he wiped a hand over his mouth and pulled it together. 'Just about. Yeah.'

I said, 'You're thinking that, next time you get a chance at some sleep, you'll need a couple of shots of straight whiskey first. Don't do it. The last thing you want is to have dreams and not be able to wake up.'

'Jesus,' Richie said softly, not to me.

'Keep your eye on the prize. The day our boy goes down for life, it'll be the icing on the cake, knowing you ticked every box along the way.'

'That's if we get him. If we don't . . .'

'No ifs, my friend. That's not how I roll. He's ours.'

Richie was still looking at nothing. I made myself comfortable on the wall again and pulled out my mobile, to give him a chance to take a few deep breaths. 'Let's get ourselves updated,' I said, when the phone was ringing. 'See what's been going down in the real world,' and he woke up and came over to sit beside me.

I checked in with headquarters first: O'Kelly was going to want a full update and a chance to tell me to stop fucking about and catch someone, both of which I was happy to give him, and I wanted updates of my own. The searchers had turned up a small stash of hash, a woman's razor and a cake tin. The sub-aqua team had found a badly rusted bicycle and a pile of building rubble; they were still going, but the currents were strong enough that they didn't hold out much hope of anything smaller having stayed put for more than an hour or two. Bernadette had assigned us an incident room – one of the good ones, with plenty of desks and a decent-sized whiteboard and a working DVD-cum-VCR player, so someone could watch CCTV footage and the Spains' home movies – and a couple of the floaters were setting it up, covering the walls with crime-scene shots, maps, lists, organising a roster for the tip line. The rest were out in the field, starting the long process of talking to anyone whose path had ever crossed the Spains'. One of them had tracked down Jack's friends from preschool: most of them hadn't heard from the Spains since June, when the school closed for the summer. One mother said Jack had come over a couple of times since then, to play with her son, but sometime in August Jenny had stopped returning her calls. The woman had added something about that not being like Jenny at all.

'So,' I said, as I hung up. 'One of the sisters is a liar: Fiona or Jenny, take your pick. Well spotted. And starting this summer, Jenny was being odd about Jack's little friends. That'll need explaining.'

Richie was looking healthier, now that he had something to concentrate on. 'Maybe your woman did something that pissed Jenny off. Simple as.'

'Or maybe Jenny was just embarrassed to admit they'd had to pull Jack out of preschool. But there could have been something else bothering her. Maybe this woman's husband was a little too friendly, or maybe one of the employees at the preschool had done something that scared Jack, and Jenny wasn't sure what to do about it . . . We need to find out, either way. Remember Rule Number Two, or whatever it was: odd behaviour is a present, just for us.'

I was dialling my message minder when the mobile rang. It was the computer whiz, Kieran or whatever, and he was talking before I got my name out. 'So I've been trying to recover the browser history, see what was such a big deal that someone wanted it gone. So far, I've gotta be honest with you, it's been kind of disappointing.'

'Hold on,' I said. No one was within earshot; I put the phone on speaker. 'Go.'

'I've got a handful of URLs or partial URLs, but we're talking eBay, we're talking some mommies-and-kiddies board, we're talking a couple of sports boards and a home-and-garden forum and some site that sells women's underwear. Which was fun for me, but not a lot of help to you. I was expecting, I don't know, like a smuggling operation or a *dog*fighting ring or something. I can't see any reason why your dude would want to wipe the vic's bra size.'

He sounded intrigued, more than disappointed. I said, 'Her bra size, maybe not. The forums are a different story. Any sign of the Spains having problems out in cyberspace? Anyone they pissed off, anyone who was giving them hassle?'

'How would I know? Even when I've got a hit on a site, it's not like I can check what they *did* on there. Each forum's got like a few thousand members, minimum. Even if we assume your vics were members, not just lurkers, I don't know who I'm supposed to be looking at.'

Richie said, 'They had a file of all their passwords, yeah? Can you not use that?'

Kieran was starting to lose patience with the idiot laypeople. The kid had a low boredom threshold. 'Use it how? Throw the passwords at every ID on every website in the world till I wind up logging in to something? They didn't put their forum IDs in the password file; half the time they didn't even put down the name of the website, just initials or something. So, like, I've got a line here that says "WW – EmmaJack", but I don't have a bog whether WW is Weight Watchers or World of Warcraft, or what ID they used on whatever site we're talking about. I got her eBay ID because I turned up a couple of hits on the feedback page for "sparkly-jenny", so I tried logging in and boom, away we went. Kids' clothes and eyeshadow, in case you're interested. No leads like that on any other site, though, or not so far.'

Richie had his notebook out, writing. I said, 'Check all the sites for a sparklyjenny, or variations on that – jennysparkly, that kind of thing. If they didn't get clever with their passwords, odds are they didn't get clever with their IDs.'

I could almost hear Kieran rolling his eyes. 'Um, yeah, that had actually occurred to me. No other sparklyjennys yet, but we'll keep looking. Any chance of, like, just getting the IDs off the vic? Save us a load of time.'

'She hasn't come round yet,' I said. 'Our guy wiped that history for a reason. I'm thinking maybe he'd been stalking Pat or Jenny online. Check out the last few days' worth of posts on each forum. If there's been any drama in the last while, it shouldn't be hard to find.'

'Who, *me*? Are you for reals? Get a random *eight*-year-old to read forums till his brain cells commit mass suicide. Or, like, a chimpanzee.'

'Have you seen the amount of media attention this case is getting, old son? We need our best and our brightest on this one, every step of the way. No chimpanzees here.' Kieran did a long, exasperated sigh, but he didn't argue. 'Focus on the last week, to start with. If we need to go deeper, we can.'

'Who's this "we", Kemosabe? I mean, not being smart, but remember, I'll probably turn up more sites as the recovery software does its thing. If your vics hit a bunch of different forums, me and my boys can check them out fast or we can check them out in depth. Take your pick.'

'Fast should do it for the sports boards, unless you spot something good. Just have a quick skim for any recent drama. On the mums-and-kids and the home-and-garden one, go into depth.' Online as well as off, women are the ones who talk.

Kieran groaned. 'I was afraid you'd say that. The mommy board is like Armageddon; there's some kind of nuclear war going on about "controlled crying". I'd have been totally fine living the entire rest of my life without finding out what that is.'

'Like the man says, chum, education is never a waste. Grin and bear it. You're looking for a stay-at-home mum with a background in PR, a six-year-old daughter, a three-year-old son, a mortgage in arrears, a husband who got laid off in February, and a full set of financial problems. Or we'll assume you are. We could be very wrong, but we'll go with that for now.'

Richie glanced up from his notebook. 'What d'you mean?'

I said, 'Online, Jenny could have had seven kids, a stockbroking firm and a mansion in the Hamptons. She could've been living in a hippie commune in Goa. People lie on the Net. Surely that doesn't come as a surprise.'

'Lie like rugs,' Kieran agreed. 'All the time.'

Richie was giving me a sceptical look. 'On dating sites, yeah, they do. Add a few inches, knock off a few pounds, give yourself a Jag or a PhD, means you get to shop in the luxury section. But feeding crap to a bunch of other women you're never gonna meet? Where's the percentage in that?'

Kieran snorted. 'I've got to ask, Kemosabe. Has your other half ever *been* online?'

I said, 'If you can't stand your own life, these days, you go online and get a new one. If everyone you're talking to believes you're a jet-set rock star, then they treat you like one; and if that's how everyone treats you, then that's how you feel. When you come right down to it, how is that different from actually being a jet-set rock star, at least part-time?'

The sceptical look had grown. 'Because you're *not* a bleeding jet-set rock star. You're still Bobby Bollix from Accounting. You're still sitting in your one-bed apartment in Blanchardstown eating Scooby Snax, even if you have the world thinking you're drinking champagne in a five-star hotel in Monaco.'

'Yes and no, Richie. Human beings aren't that simple. Life would be a lot more straightforward if all that mattered was what you actually are, but we're social animals. What other people think you are, what *you* believe you are: those matter too. Those make a difference.'

'Basically,' Kieran said cheerfully, 'people talk crap to impress each other. Nothing new there. They've done it in meatspace since forever; cyberspace just makes it easier.'

I said, 'Those boards could have been the place where Jenny got away from everything that was wrong in her life. She could have been anyone, out there.'

Richie shook his head, but it had gone from disbelieving to baffled. Kieran asked, 'So what do you want me to look for?'

'Keep an eye out for anyone who fits her stats, but if no one matches, that doesn't mean she's not there. Look for anyone who's having serious trouble with another poster, anyone who mentions being stalked or harassed – online or off – anyone who mentions her husband or her kid being stalked or harassed. If you find anything good, call us. Any luck on the e-mails?'

Keys clicking in the background. 'So far, just a bunch of fragments. I've got a mail from someone called Fi, back in March, wanting to know if Emma has the Ultimate Box Set of *Dora the Explorer*, and I've got someone in the house submitting a CV for a recruitment job in June, but apart from that it's basically spam spam spam. Unless "Make your rod harder for her pleasure" is some kind of secret code, we've got nothing.'

I said, 'Then keep looking.'

Kieran said, 'Chillax. Like you said, your dude didn't wipe the machine just to show off his mad skills. Sooner or later, something's gonna show.'

He hung up. Richie said softly, 'Sitting out there, middle of nowhere, playing rock star for people you'll never meet. How bloody *lonely* would you have to be?'

I left my mobile off speaker while I checked my voicemail, just in case – Richie took the hint and slid away from me on the wall, squinting into his notebook like the killer's home address was in there somewhere. I had five messages. The first one was from O'Kelly, bright and early, wanting to know where I was, why Richie hadn't managed to pull in our man last night, whether he was wearing something that wasn't a shiny tracksuit, and whether I wanted to change my mind and partner up with an actual Murder D on this one. The second one was from Geri, apologising all over again about last night and hoping work was all right and hoping Dina felt better: 'And listen to me, Mick, if she's still not doing great, I can take her tonight, no bother – Sheila's on the mend and Phil's practically grand, he's only got sick the once since midnight, so you just drop her over to ours as soon as you get the chance. I mean it, now.' I tried not to think about whether Dina had woken up yet, and what she had thought of being locked in.

The third message was from Larry. He and his boys had run the prints from the sniper's nest through the computer, got nothing: our man wasn't in the system. The fourth one was O'Kelly again: same message as before, this time with free bonus swearing. The fifth one had come in just twenty minutes earlier, from some doctor, upstairs. Jenny Spain was awake.

One of the reasons I love Murder is that the victims are, as a general rule, dead. The friends and relations are alive, obviously, but we can palm them off on Victim Support after an interview or two, unless they're suspects, in which case talking to them doesn't run your mind through a shredder quite the same way. I don't make a habit of sharing this, in case people take me for a sicko or – worse – a wimp, but give me a dead child, any day, over a child sobbing his heart out while you make him tell you what the bad man did next. Dead victims don't show up crying outside HQ to beg for answers, you never have to nudge them into reliving every hideous moment, and you never have to worry about what it'll do to their lives if you fuck up. They stay put in the morgue, light-years beyond anything I can do right or wrong, and leave me free to focus on the people who sent them there.

What I'm getting at is that going to see Jenny Spain in hospital was my worst work-related nightmare come true. A part of me had been praying that we would get the other phone call, the one to say she had let go without ever regaining consciousness, that there had been a borderline to her pain.

Richie's head had turned towards me, and I realised my hand was clenched around the phone. He said, 'News, yeah?'

I said, 'Looks like we can ask Jenny Spain for those IDs after all. She's awake. We're going upstairs.'

The doctor outside Jenny's room was fair and skinny, trying hard to make himself older with a middle-aged parting and the beginnings of a beard. Behind him, the uniform at the door – maybe because I was tired, everyone looked about twelve – took one look at me and Richie and snapped to attention, chin tucked in.

I held up my ID. 'Detective Kennedy. Is she still awake?'

The doctor gave the ID a careful going-over, which was good. 'She is, yeah. I doubt you'll get a lot of time with her, though. She's on powerful painkillers, and injuries on this scale are exhausting in themselves. I'd say she'll be falling asleep soon.'

'She's out of danger, though?'

He shrugged. 'No guarantees. Her prognosis is brighter than it was a couple of hours ago, and we're cautiously optimistic about her neurological function, but there's still a massive risk of infection. We'll have a better idea in a few days.'

'Has she said anything?'

'You know about the facial injury, don't you? She has a hard time talking. She told one of the nurses she was thirsty. She asked me who I was. And she said, "It hurts," two or three times, before we upped the painkillers. That's it.'

The uniform should have been in there with her, in case that changed, but I had told him to guard the door, and by God he was guarding it. I could have kicked myself for not using an actual detective with a functioning brain, instead of some pubescent drone. Richie asked, 'Does she know? About her family?'

The doctor shook his head. 'Not as far as I can tell. I'm guessing there's a certain amount of retrograde amnesia. It's common enough after a head injury; usually transient, but again, no guarantees.'

'And you didn't tell her, no?'

'I thought you might want to do that yourselves. And she hasn't asked. She . . . well, you'll see what I mean. She's not in great shape.'

He had been keeping his voice low, and on that his eyes slid over my shoulder. I had missed her, up until then: a woman, asleep in a hard plastic chair up against the corridor wall, with a big flowered purse clutched on her lap and her head canted back at a painful angle. She didn't look twelve. She looked at least a hundred – white hair falling out of its bun, face swollen and discoloured from crying and exhaustion – but she couldn't have been over about seventy. I recognised her from the Spains' photo albums: Jenny's mother.

The floaters had taken a statement from her the day before. We would have to come back to her sooner or later, but at that moment there was more than enough agony waiting for us inside Jenny's room, without stocking up in the corridor. 'Thanks,' I said, a lot more quietly. 'If anything changes, let us know.'

We gave our IDs to the drone, who examined them from every angle for about a week. Mrs Rafferty shifted her feet and moaned in her sleep, and I almost shouldered the uniform out of our way, but luckily he picked that moment to decide we were legit. 'Sir,' he said smartly, handing back the IDs and stepping away from the door, and then we were inside Jenny Spain's room.

No one would ever have known her for the platinum girl shining in those wedding photos. Her eyes were closed, eyelids puffy and purple. Her hair, straggling on the pillow from under a wide white bandage, was stringy and darkened to mouse-brown by days without washing; someone had tried to get the blood out of it, but there were still matted clumps, strands sharpened into hard points. A pad of gauze, stuck down with sloppy strips of tape, covered her right cheek. Her hands, small and fine like Fiona's, were slack on the bobbled pale-blue blanket, a thin tube running into a great mottled bruise; her nails were perfect, filed to delicate arcs and painted a soft pinkish-beige, except the two or three that had been ripped away down to the quick. More tubing ran from her nose up around her ears, snaked down her chest. All around her machines beeped, clear bags dripped, light flashed off metal.

Richie closed the door behind us, and her eyes opened.

She stared, dazed and dull-eyed, trying to figure out whether we were real. She was fathoms deep in the painkillers. 'Mrs Spain,' I said, gently, but she still flinched, hands jerking up to defend herself. 'I'm Detective Michael Kennedy, and this is Detective Richard Curran. Would you be able to talk to us for a few minutes?'

Slowly Jenny's eyes focused on mine. She whispered – it came out thick and clotted, through the damage and the bandage – 'Something happened.'

'Yes. I'm afraid so.' I turned a chair to the side of the bed and sat down. Across from me, Richie did the same.

'What happened?'

I said, 'You were attacked, in your home, two nights ago. You were seriously wounded, but the doctors have been taking good care of you, and they say you're going to be fine. Can you remember anything about the attack?'

'Attack.' She was struggling to swim to the surface, through the vast weight of drugs bearing down on her mind. 'No. How . . . what . . .' Then her eyes came alive, flaring incandescent blue with pure terror. '*The babies. Pat.*'

Every muscle in my body wanted to fling me out the door. I said, 'I'm so sorry.'

'*No.* Are they – where—'

She was fighting to sit up. She was much too weak to do it, but not too weak to rip stitches trying. 'I'm so sorry,' I said again. I cupped a hand around her shoulder and pressed down, as gently as I could. 'There was nothing we could do.'

The moment after those words has a million shapes. I've seen people howl till their voices were scraped away, or freeze like they were hoping it would pass them over, prowl on to rip out someone else's rib cage, if they just stayed still enough. I've held them back from smashing their faces off walls, trying to knock out the pain. Jenny Spain was beyond any of that. She had done all her defending two nights before; she had none left for this. She dropped back on the worn pillowcase and cried, steadily and silently, on and on.

Her face was red and contorted, but she didn't move to cover it. Richie leaned over and put a hand on hers, the one without the IV line, and she gripped it till her knuckles whitened. Behind her a machine beeped, faintly and steadily. I focused on counting the beeps and wished to God I had brought water, gum, mints, anything that would let me swallow.

After a long time, the crying wore itself away and Jenny lay still, cloudy red eyes staring at the flaking paint on the wall. I said, 'Mrs Spain, we're going to do everything we can.'

She didn't look at me. That thick, ragged whisper: 'Are you sure? Did you . . . see them yourself?'

'I'm afraid we're sure.'

Richie said gently, 'Your babies didn't suffer, Mrs Spain. They never knew what was happening.'

Her mouth started to convulse. I said quickly, before she could get lost in it again, 'Mrs Spain, can you tell us what you remember about that night?'

She shook her head. 'I don't know.'

'That's OK. We understand. Could you take a moment and think back, see if anything comes to you?'

'I don't . . . There's nothing. I can't . . .'

She was tensing up, her hand tightening on Richie's again. I said, 'That's fine. What's the last thing you do remember?'

Jenny gazed at nothing and for a moment I thought she had drifted away, but then she whispered, 'The babies' bath. Emma washed Jack's hair. Got shampoo in his eyes. He was going to cry. Pat . . . his hands in the sleeves of Emma's dress, like it was dancing, to make Jack laugh . . .'

'That's good,' I said, and Richie gave her hand an encouraging squeeze. 'That's great. Any little thing could help us. And after the children's bath . . . ?'

'I don't know. I don't know. The next thing was here, that doctor—'

'OK. It might come back to you. Meanwhile, can you tell me whether there's anyone who's bothered you, over the past few months? Anyone who worried you? Maybe someone you knew was acting a bit odd, or you saw someone around who made you nervous?'

'No one. Nothing. Everything's been *fine*.'

'Your sister Fiona mentioned that you had a break-in during the summer. Can you tell us about that?'

Jenny's head stirred on the pillow, like something hurt. 'That was nothing. Not a big deal.'

'Fiona sounded like it was a pretty big deal at the time.'

'Fiona exaggerates. I was just stressed that day. I got worried about nothing.'

Richie's eyes met mine, across the bed. Somehow, Jenny was managing to lie.

I said, 'There are a number of holes in the walls of your home. Do those have anything to do with the break-in?'

'*No*. Those are . . . They're nothing. They're just DIY stuff.'

'Mrs Spain,' Richie said. 'Are you sure?'

'Yeah. I'm positive.'

Through all the fog of drugs and damage, something in her face glinted dense and hard as steel. I remembered what Fiona had said: *Jenny isn't a wimp.*

I asked, 'What kind of DIY stuff?'

We waited, but Jenny's eyes had clouded over again. Her breathing was so shallow that I could barely see her chest rise and fall. She whispered, 'Tired.'

I thought about Kieran and his ID hunt, but there was no way she would be able to find those in the wreckage of her mind. I said gently, 'Just a few more questions, and we'll let you rest. A woman called Aisling Rooney – her son Karl was a friend of Jack's from preschool – she mentioned that she tried to get in touch over the summer, but you stopped returning her calls. Do you remember that?'

'Aisling. Yeah.'

'Why didn't you ring her back?'

A shrug; barely a twitch, but it made her wince. 'I just didn't.'

'Had you had problems with her? With any of that family?'

'No. They're fine. I just forgot to ring her.'

That flash of steel again. I pretended I hadn't seen it, moved on. 'Did you tell your sister Fiona that Jack had brought home a friend from preschool last week?'

After a long moment, Jenny nodded. Her chin had started to tremble.

'Had he?'

She shook her head. Her eyes and lips were squeezed tight. I said, 'Can you tell me why you told Fiona he had?'

Tears leaked onto Jenny's cheeks. She managed, '. . . *Should have*—' before a sob jackknifed her like a punch. 'So tired . . . please . . .'

She pushed Richie's hand away and covered her face with her arm. He said, 'We'll let you get some rest. We're going to send someone from Victim Support to talk to you, OK?'

Jenny shook her head, gasping for breath. Blood had dried in the creases of her knuckles. 'No. Please . . . no . . . just . . . by myself.'

'I promise, they're good. I know nothing's going to make this better, but they can help you get through it. They've helped out a load of people who've had this happen. Would you give them a shot?'

'I don't . . .' She managed to catch her breath, in a deep, shaky heave. After a moment she asked, dazed, 'What?' The painkillers were closing over her head again.

'Never mind,' Richie said gently. 'Is there anything we can get you?'

'I don't . . .'

Her eyes were closing. She was slipping into sleep, which was the best place for her. I said, 'We'll be back when you're feeling stronger. For now, we're going to leave our cards here with you. If you remember anything, anything at all, please call either one of us.'

Jenny made a sound between a moan and a sob. She was asleep, tears still sliding down her face. We put our cards on her bedside table and left.

Out in the corridor, everything was the same: the uniform was still standing to attention, and Jenny's mother was still asleep in her chair. Her head had dropped to one side and her fingers had loosened on her purse, twitching against the worn handle. I sent the uniform into the room as quietly as I could and got us around the corner, walking fast, before I stopped to put away my notebook.

Richie said, 'That was interesting, yeah?' He sounded subdued, but not shaken up: the live ones didn't get to him. Once that empathy had somewhere to go, he was fine. If I had been in the market for a long-term partner, we would have been perfect for each other. 'A lot of lies, for just a few minutes.'

'So you noticed that. They might or might not be relevant – like I told you, everyone lies – but we'll need to find out. We'll come back to Jenny.' It took me three tries to get my notebook into my coat pocket. I turned my shoulder to Richie to hide it.

He hovered, squinting up at me. 'You all right?'

'I'm fine. Why do you ask?'

'You look a bit . . .' He wavered one hand. 'That was rough enough, in there. I thought maybe . . .'

I said, 'Why don't you go ahead and assume that anything you can take, I can take. That wasn't rough. That was just another day on the job – as you'll know, once you get a little experience under your belt. And even if it had been rough as all hell, I'd be fine. That chat we had earlier, Richie, about control: did that not go in?'

He backed away, and I realised my tone had been a notch sharper than I wanted it to be. 'Only asking.'

It took a second to sink in: he genuinely had been. Not prodding for weak spots, or trying to even things out after the post-mortem incident; just looking out for his partner. I said, more gently, 'And I appreciate it. Sorry for snapping at you. How about you? Are you all right?'

'I'm grand, yeah.' He flexed his hand, wincing – I could see deep purple dents where Jenny's nails had dug in – and glanced back over his shoulder. 'The mother. Are we . . . when do we let her go in?'

I headed down the corridor, towards the exit stairs. 'Whenever she wants, as long as she's supervised. I'll ring the uniform and let him know.'

'And Fiona?'

'Same goes for her: she's more than welcome, once she doesn't mind having company. Maybe they'll be able to get Jenny to pull it together a bit, get more out of her than we could.'

Richie kept pace and said nothing, but I was starting to get the hang of his silences. I said, 'You think I should be concentrating on how they can help Jenny, not how they can help us. And you think I should have let them go in yesterday.'

'She's in hell. They're *family*.'

I took the stairs fast. 'Exactly, old son. E-fucking-xactly. They are family, which means we don't have a hope of understanding the dynamics there, not yet anyway. I don't know what a couple of hours with Mum and Sis would have done to Jenny's story, and I didn't want to find out. Maybe the mother's a guilt-tripper, she makes Jenny feel even worse about ignoring the intruder, so when Jenny talks to us she skips over the fact that he broke in a few more times along the way. Maybe Fiona warns her that we were looking at Pat, and by the time we get to Jenny she won't talk to us at all. And don't forget: Fiona may not be top of our suspect list, but she's not off it – not till we find out how our man picked the Spains – and she's still the one who would have inherited if Jenny had died. I don't care how badly the vic needs a hug, I'm not letting the heir talk to her before I do.'

'I guess,' Richie said. At the bottom of the stairs he moved aside to let a nurse go past, pushing a trolley of coiled plastic and glinting metal, and watched her bustle down the corridor. 'Probably you're right.'

I said, 'You think I'm a cold bastard, don't you?'

He shrugged. 'Not for me to say.'

'Maybe I am. It depends on your definition. Because you see, Richie, to me, a cold bastard is someone who could look Jenny Spain in the eye and tell her, *Sorry, ma'am, we won't be catching the person who butchered your family, because I was too busy making sure everybody liked me, see you around*, and then waltz off home for a nice dinner and a good night's sleep. That's something I can't do. So if I have to do some minor cold shit along the way, to make sure that doesn't happen, so be it.' The exit doors juddered open, and a wave of cool rain-drenched air rolled over us. I crammed as much of it into my lungs as I could.

Richie said, 'Let's talk to the uniform now. Before the ma wakes up.'

In the heavy grey light he looked terrible, eyes bloodshot, face flat and haggard; if it hadn't been for the half-decent clothes, Security would have taken him for a junkie. The kid was exhausted. It was heading for three o'clock. Our night shift started in five hours.

'Go ahead,' I said. 'Give him a bell.' Richie's face told me I looked as bad as he did. Every breath I took was still clotted with disinfectant and blood, like the hospital air had closed around me and soaked into my pores. I almost wished I smoked. 'And then we can get away from this place. Time to go home.'

# 9

I dropped Richie outside his place, a beige terraced house in Crumlin – the tattered paintwork said it was rented, the bikes chained to the railings said he was sharing with a couple of mates. 'Get some sleep,' I said. 'And remember what I said: no booze. We need to be on the ball for tonight. I'll see you outside HQ at a quarter to seven.' As he put his key in the door, I saw his head drop forward like he had nothing left to hold it up.

Dina hadn't rung me. I had been trying to take that as a sign that she was peacefully reading or watching telly, or maybe still asleep, but I knew she wouldn't ring even if she was bouncing off the walls. When Dina's doing well, she'll answer texts and the occasional call; when she's not, she doesn't trust her mobile enough to touch it. The closer I got to home, the more that silence seemed to turn dense and volatile, an acrid fog I had to fight through to reach my door.

Dina was sitting cross-legged on my living-room floor, with my books strewn around her like a hurricane had flung them off the shelves, ripping a page out of *Moby-Dick*. She stared me in the eye, tossed the page on a pile in front of her, threw the Melville against the opposite wall with a bang, and reached for another book.

'What the *fuck*—' I dropped my briefcase and grabbed the book out of her hand; she kicked out at my shin, but I leaped back. 'What the *hell*, Dina?'

'*You*, you fuckety bastarding prick, you *locked* me, what was I supposed going to do, sit here good girl like your *dog*? You don't *own* you can't make me!'

She made a dive for another book; I dropped on my knees and

caught her wrists. 'Dina. Listen to me. Listen. I couldn't leave you the keys. I don't have a spare set.'

Dina laughed, a high yelp that bared her teeth. 'Yeah yeah yeah right, *you* don't, Mr Anal with your books are *alphabetised* but no spare keys? You know what I was going to? Put this on *fire*.' She jerked her chin fiercely at the heap of torn pages in front of her. 'Then let's see if someone doesn't let me out, smoke alarm going good and loud, all your snobby yuppie neighbours wouldn't be happy then, would they, ooh darlings the *noise*, in a residential area—'

She would have done it. The thought made my stomach curl. Maybe it weakened my grip: Dina lunged sideways, nearly ripping her wrists free, going for the books again. I clamped my hands tighter and shoved her back against the wall; she tried to spit at me, but nothing came out. '*Dina*. Dina. Look at me.'

She fought, twisting and kicking and making a furious humming sound between her clenched teeth, but I hung on till she froze stiff and her eyes met mine, blue and wild as a Siamese cat's. 'Listen to me,' I said, close into her face. 'I had to go to work. I thought you'd still be asleep when I got home. I didn't want to wake you up to let me in. So I took the keys with me. That's all. That's all there is to it. OK?'

Dina thought that over. Gradually, fraction by fraction, her wrists relaxed in my hands. 'Ever do that again,' she said coolly, 'ever. I'll ring your cops and say you keep keeping me locked here and you rape me every day, every way. See how your *job* does then. Detective Sergeant.'

'Christ, Dina.'

'I will.'

'I know you will.'

'Oh, don't give me that look. If you lock me up like I'm some animal, some crazy, then it's your fault if I have to get out some way. Not my fault. Yours.'

The fight was over. She flicked my hands off like she was batting away midges and started combing her hair into place with her fingertips. 'All right,' I said. My heart was hammering. 'All right. I'm sorry.'

'Seriously, Mikey. That was a stupid thing to do.'

'Apparently. Yeah.'

'Not apparently. *Obviously.*' Dina got up off the floor and shoved past me, dusting off her hands and wrinkling her nose in distaste as she picked her way through the scattered books. 'God, what a *mess*.'

I said, 'I have work tomorrow, too, and I haven't had a chance to get spare keys cut. I figured you might want to stay with Geri till I do.'

Dina groaned. 'Oh, God, Geri. She'll tell me about the kids. I mean, I love them and whatever, but, like, Sheila's periods and Colm's spots? *Way* TMI.' She thumped down on the sofa, with a bounce, and started shoving her feet into her biker boots. 'I'm not staying here if you seriously have only one set of keys, though. I might go stay with Jezzer. Can I use your phone? I'm out of credit.'

I had no idea who or what Jezzer was, but it didn't sound like my kind of person. I said, 'Sweetheart, I need a favour from you. I really do. I've got a lot on my plate right now, and I'd feel much better if I knew you were at Geri's. I know it's stupid and I know you'll be bored out of your twist, but it'd make a big difference to me. Please.'

Dina's head came up and she stared at me, that unblinking Siamese stare, her shoelace wrapped around her hands. 'This case,' she said. 'The Broken Harbour one. It's getting to you.'

Dammit, stupid stupid stupid: the last thing I wanted her thinking about was this case. 'Not really,' I said, keeping my voice casual. 'It's more that I've got Richie to keep an eye on – my partner, the rookie I told you about? It's hard work.'

'Why? Is he thick?'

I picked myself up off the floor. Somewhere in the struggle I had whacked my knee, but letting Dina see that would be a bad idea. 'Not thick at all, just new. He's a good kid, he's going to make a good detective, but he's got a lot to learn. It's my job to teach it to him. Throw in some eighteen-hour shifts, and it's going to be a long week.'

'Eighteen-hour shifts in Broken Harbour. I think you should swap cases with someone else.'

I extracted myself from the mess, trying not to limp. There had to be a hundred torn-out pages in the heap, presumably each from a different book. I tried not to think about it. 'It doesn't work that way. I'm fine, sweetheart. Really.'

'Hmm.' Dina went back to her lace, tugging it tight with quick sharp jerks. 'I worry about you,' she said. 'Do you know that?'

'Don't. If you want to help me out, the best thing you can do is humour me and spend a night or two at Geri's. OK?'

Dina tied her lace in some kind of fancy double bow and pulled back to examine it. 'OK,' she said, on a long-suffering sigh. 'You have to give me a lift there, though. Buses are too scratchy. And hurry up and get those keys cut.'

I dropped Dina off at Geri's and made excuses to avoid going in – Geri wanted me to stay for dinner, on the grounds that 'you won't catch it, sure Colm and Andrea haven't, I thought Colm's bowels were at him earlier on but he says he's grand – Pookie, *down*! – I don't know what he was doing in the toilet all that time, but that's his business . . .' Dina threw me a silent-scream face over her shoulder and mouthed *You owe me* as Geri shepherded her into the house, still talking, with the dog bouncing and yapping around them.

I went home again, threw a few things into a holdall and grabbed a fast shower and an hour's sleep. I got dressed like a kid on a first date, all thumbs and heartbeat, dressing just for him: shirt and tie in case I got a chance to interview him, two thick jumpers so I could wait for him through the cold, heavy dark coat to shield me from him till the right moment came. I imagined him, somewhere, dressing for me and thinking about Broken Harbour. I wondered if he still thought he was the stalker, or if he understood that he had turned to prey.

Richie was outside the back gate of Dublin Castle at a quarter to seven, carrying a sports bag and wearing a padded jacket, a woolly hat and, going by his shape, every fleece he owned. I rode the speed limit all the way to Broken Harbour, as the fields dimmed around us and the air turned sweet with turf smoke and ploughed earth. It was getting dark when we parked in Ocean View Parade – across the estate from the Spains', nothing but scaffolding, no one to spot an unfamiliar car – and started walking.

I had memorised the route from a map of the estate, but I still felt like we were lost the moment we stepped away from the car. Dusk was closing in: the day's clouds had blown away and the sky was a deep blue-green, with a faint white glow over the rooftops where the moon was rising, but the streets were dark, chunks of garden wall and unlit street-lamps and sagging chicken wire looming out of nowhere and gone a few steps later. When our shadows showed faintly they were twisted and unfamiliar, turned hunchbacked by the holdalls slung over our shoulders. Our footsteps came back to us like followers', bouncing off bare walls and across stretches of churned mud. We didn't talk: the dusk that was helping to cover us could be covering someone else, anywhere.

In the near-darkness the sound of the sea was bigger, stronger, disorientating, rising up at us from every direction at once. The patrol floaters' old dark-blue Peugeot materialised behind us like a ghost car, so close that we both jumped, its engine noise hidden in that long dull roar. By the time we realised who it was, they were gone, slipping away between houses that showed stars through their window-holes.

Down Ocean View Rise, rectangles of light fell across the road. One of them lit up a yellow Fiat parked outside the Spains' house: our fake Fiona was in place. At the top of Ocean View Walk, I moved Richie into the shadow of the corner house, put my mouth close to his ear and whispered, 'Goggles.'

He squatted over his holdall and pulled out a pair of thermal-imaging goggles. Supplies had given him the good ones, newbie or no. The stars vanished and the dark street leaped into ghostly half-life, creepers hanging pale on tall blocks of grey wall, wild plants crisscrossing white and lacy where the pavements should have been. In a couple of the gardens, small glowing shapes crouched in corners or scurried through the weeds, and three phantom wood-doves slept high in a tree, heads tucked under their wings; no warm thing bigger than that, anywhere in sight. The street was silent, just sea-sounds and wind fingering through the creepers and a lone bird crying out on the beach, over the wall. 'Looks clear,' I said, into Richie's ear. 'Let's go. Carefully.'

The goggles said nothing was alive in our man's lair, at least not in the corners I could see. The scaffolding was rough with rust, and I felt it shake under our weight. Upstairs, the moon blazed in through a window-hole where the plastic was pinned back like a curtain. The room had been stripped bare; the Bureau had taken everything, to test for prints, fibres, hairs, body fluids. There were black swipes of print dust on the walls and the windowsills.

Every light in the Spains' house was on, turning the place into a great beacon signalling to our man. Our fake Fiona was in the kitchen, still wrapped in her red duffel coat; she had filled the Spains' kettle and was leaning against the counter waiting for it to boil, cupping her mug in both hands and staring blankly at the finger-paintings stuck to the fridge. In the garden, moon-light caught on glossy leaves, turned them white and shivering so that it looked like all the trees and hedges had burst into flower at once.

We set up our stuff where our man had set up his: against the back wall of the hide, for clear views of both the Spains' kitchen – just in case – and the front window-hole, looking out over the beach, that he had used as a door. The plastic sheeting over the other holes would screen us from a watcher hidden in the jungle all around. The night was coming down cold, there would be frost before dawn; I spread out my sleeping bag to sit on, added another jumper under my coat. Richie knelt on the floor pulling stuff out of his holdall like a kid on a camping trip: a thermos, a packet of chocolate Hobnobs, a slightly squashed tower of sandwiches wrapped in tinfoil. '*Starving*,' he said. 'Sandwich, yeah? I brought enough for the two of us, in case you didn't get a chance.'

I was about to say no automatically when I realised that he was right, I hadn't remembered to bring food – Dina – and that I was starving too. 'Thanks,' I said. 'I'd love one.'

Richie nodded and pushed the sandwich tower towards me. 'Cheese and tomato, turkey, or ham. Take a few.'

I took cheese and tomato. Richie poured strong tea into the thermos cap and tilted it at me; when I held up my water bottle, he downed the tea in one and poured himself another capful. Then he made himself comfortable with his back against the wall and got stuck into his sandwich.

He didn't look like he was under the impression that tonight would involve deep and meaningful conversation, which was good. I know other detectives get into heart-to-hearts on stakeouts. I don't. One or two newbies had tried, either because they genuinely liked me or because they wanted to nuzzle up to the boss, I didn't bother to find out which before I nipped that in the bud. 'These are good,' I said, taking another sandwich. 'Thanks.'

Before it got dark enough for action stations, I checked in with the floaters. Our fake Fiona's voice was steady, maybe too steady, but she said she was fine, thanks, no backup needed. Marlboro Man and his friend said we were the most exciting thing they'd seen all evening.

Richie was working his way methodically through the sandwiches, gazing out past the last row of houses to the dark beach. The comforting fragrance of his tea made the room feel warmer. After a while he said, 'I wonder did it actually use to be a harbour.'

'It did,' I said. He would take it for granted that I had been researching, Mr Boring using his scraps of free time to comb the internet. 'This was a fishing village, a long time back. You might still be able to see what's left of the pier, down at the south end of the beach, if you go looking.'

'Is that why Broken Harbour, yeah? The broken-down pier?'

'No. It's from *breacadh*: daybreak. I suppose because it would have been a good place to watch the dawn.'

Richie nodded. He said, 'I'd say it was lovely out here, back before all this.'

'It probably was,' I said. The smell of the sea swept over the wall and in through the empty window-hole, wide and wild with a million intoxicating secrets. I don't trust that smell. It hooks us somewhere deeper than reason or civilisation, in the fragments of our cells that rocked in oceans before we had minds, and it pulls till we follow mindlessly as rutting animals. When I was a teenager, that smell used to set me boiling, spark my muscles like electricity, bounce me off the walls of the caravan till my parents sprang me free to obey the call, bounding after whatever tantalising once-in-a-lifetimes it promised. Now I know better. That smell is bad medicine. It lures us to leap off high cliffs, fling ourselves on towering waves, leave behind everyone we love and face into thousands of miles of open water for the sake of what might be on the far shore. It had been in our man's nose, two nights before, when he climbed down the scaffolding and went over the Spains' wall.

Richie said, 'They'll say it's haunted now. Kids.'

'Probably.'

'Be daring each other to run up and touch the door of the house. Go inside.'

Below us, the lampshades Jenny had bought for her cosy family kitchen were bright with yellow butterflies. One of them was missing, gone to Larry's lab. 'You're talking like it's going to be abandoned for good,' I said. 'Dial down the negativity there, old son. Jenny'll need to sell up, once she's able. Wish her luck. She could do with it.'

Richie said bluntly, 'A few more months and the whole estate'll be abandoned. It's dead in the water. No one's gonna buy out here, and even if they were, there's hundreds of houses to choose from. Are you telling me you'd pick that one?' He jerked his chin towards the window.

'I don't believe in ghosts,' I said. 'And neither do you, not while you're on the job, anyway.' I didn't tell him: the ghosts I believe in weren't trapped in the Spains' bloodstains. They thronged the whole estate, whirling like great moths in and out of the empty doorways and over the expanses of cracked earth, battering against the sparse lighted windows, mouths stretched wide in silent howls:

all the people who should have lived here. The young men who had dreamed of carrying their wives over these thresholds, the babies who should have been brought home from the hospital to soft nurseries in these rooms, the teenagers who should have had their first kisses leaning against lampposts that would never be lit. Over time, the ghosts of things that happened start to turn distant; once they've cut you a couple of million times, their edges blunt on your scar tissue, they wear thin. The ones that slice like razors forever are the ghosts of things that never got the chance to happen.

Richie had demolished half the sandwiches and was rolling a piece of tinfoil into a ball between his palms. He said, 'Can I ask something?'

He practically raised his hand. It made me feel like I was sprouting grey hair and bifocals all over. I said, hearing the stuffy note in my voice, 'You don't need to ask my permission, Richie. That's part of my job, answering any questions you've got.'

'Right,' Richie said. 'Then I was wondering how come we're here.'

'On this earth?'

He didn't know whether he was supposed to laugh. 'No, I mean . . . Like, here. Doing the stakeout.'

'You'd rather be at home in bed?'

'No! I'm grand where I am; nowhere I'd rather be. I only wondered. Just . . . it doesn't make any difference who's here, does it? If our fella shows, he shows; anyone can bring him in. I would've expected you to . . . I don't know. Delegate.'

I said, 'It probably won't make any difference to the arrest, no. But it might make a difference to what comes next. If you're the one who puts the cuffs on your guy, it gets the relationship off on the right foot: shows him who's his daddy now, straight from the off. In an ideal world, I'd always be the one who made the collar.'

'You're not, but. Not every time.'

'I'm not magic, my friend. I can't be everywhere. Sometimes I have to give someone else a chance.'

Richie said, 'Not this time, but. No one else's getting a look-in on this one till we both get tired enough that we fall over. Amn't I right?'

The grin in his voice felt good, the solid taking it for granted that we were in this together. 'Right,' I said. 'And I've got enough caffeine tabs to last us a while.'

'Is it because it's kids?'

The grin had faded. 'No,' I said. 'If it were just the kids, then it'd be no big deal to let some floater take our guy down. But I want to be the one who gets the man who killed Pat Spain.'

Richie waited, watching me. When I left it there, he said, 'How come?'

Maybe it was my cracking knees and the stiffness in my neck as I had pulled myself up the scaffolding, the dragging sense that I was moving towards old and tired; maybe that was what made me all of a sudden want to know what the other lads talk about, into the long tedious nights, that brings them into the squad room the next day walking in step, making shared decisions with just a tilt of the head or a lift of an eyebrow. Maybe it was those moments, over the past couple of days, when I had caught myself feeling like I wasn't just showing a rookie the ropes; when it had felt like Richie and I were working together, side by side. Maybe it was that treacherous sea-smell, eroding all my why-nots to shifting sand. Maybe it was just fatigue. 'Tell me this,' I said. 'What do you think would have happened if our guy had been just a little better at what he did? Cleaned up this place before he went hunting, got rid of his footprints, left the weapons on the scene?'

'We'd have stuck with Pat Spain.'

In the darkness I could barely see him, just the angle of his head against the window, the tilt of his chin towards me. 'Yeah. Probably we would have. And even if we'd had a hunch that someone else was involved . . . What do you think other people would have thought, if we couldn't put out a description, couldn't come up with one piece of evidence that he even existed? That Gogan woman, the whole of Brianstown, the man on the street watching this case on the news. Pat and Jenny's families. What would they have assumed?'

Richie said, 'Pat.'

'Exactly like we did.'

'And the real guy would've still been out there. Maybe getting ready to do it again.'

'Maybe, yeah. But that's not my point. Even if he went home last night and found a nice place to hang himself, this guy would have made Pat Spain into a murderer. In the eyes of everyone who'll ever hear his name, Pat would have been a man who killed the woman who lay down with him. The children they made together.' Even saying the words set that high hum moving in my skull: evil.

Richie said, almost gently, 'He's dead. It couldn't hurt him.'

'Yeah, he's dead. Twenty-nine years of life are all he'll ever have. He should have had fifty more, sixty, but this guy decided to take them all away. And even that wasn't enough for him: he wanted to go back in time and take away those pathetic twenty-nine years, too. Take away everything Pat had ever been. Leave him with nothing.' I saw that evil like a low cloud of sticky black dust spreading slowly out from this room to cover the houses, the fields, blotting out the moonlight. 'That's fucked up,' I said. 'That's so fucked up I don't even have words for it.'

We sat there, not talking, while our Fiona found the dustpan and swept up shards of a plate that had smashed in a corner of the kitchen floor. After a while Richie opened his Hobnobs, offered me one and, when I shook my head, munched his way steadily through half the packet. After a while he said, 'Can I ask something?'

'Seriously, Richie, you're going to have to knock that off. It's not going to inspire confidence in our man if you put up your hand in the middle of an interrogation and ask me if you're allowed to talk now.'

This time he did grin. 'Something personal, but.'

I don't answer personal questions, not from trainees, but then the whole conversation was one I don't have with trainees. It took me by surprise, how good it felt, and how easy: to let go of veteran and rookie and all the boundaries that come with them, slip into being just one of two men talking. 'Fire away,' I said. 'If you're over the line, I'll tell you.'

'What does your da do?'

'He's retired. He was a traffic warden.'

Richie let out a snort of laughter. I said, 'What's funny there?'

'Nothing. Just . . . I figured something a bit more posh. A teacher at a private school, like; geography, maybe. Now that you say it, though, it makes sense.'

'Should I take that as a compliment?'

Richie didn't answer. He shoved another Hobnob in his mouth and rubbed crumbs off his fingers, but I could feel him thinking. After a while he said, 'What you said at the scene the other day: how you don't get killed unless you go looking for it. Bad things mostly happen to bad people. That's a luxury, thinking that. D'you know what I mean?'

I pushed away the nudge of something more painful than irritation. 'Can't say I do, old son. In my experience – and I don't want to rub this in your face, but I've had more of that than you have – what you get out of life is mostly what you planted. Not always, no, but mostly. If you think you're a success, you will be a success; if you think you deserve nothing but crap, you'll get nothing but crap. Your inner reality shapes your outer one, every day of your life. Do you follow me?'

Richie watched the warm yellow lights of the kitchen below us. He said, 'I don't know what my dad does; he wasn't around.' He said it matter-of-factly, like it was something he had had to say too many times before. 'I grew up in the flats – probably you knew that already. I saw loads of bad stuff happen to people who never asked for it. Loads.'

I said, 'And here you are. A detective on a top squad, doing the job you always wanted, working the biggest case of the year and damn close to a solve. Wherever you come from, that counts as success. I think you're proving my point here.'

Richie didn't turn his head. 'I'd say Pat Spain thought the same way as you.'

'Maybe he did. So?'

'So he still lost his job. Worked his arse off, thought positive, did everything right, ended up on the dole. How did he plant that?'

'That was unfair as all hell, and I'll be the first to say it shouldn't have happened. But come on: there's a recession on. Exceptional circumstances.'

Richie shook his head. 'Sometimes bad things just happen,' he said.

The sky was rich with stars; it had been years since I had seen so many. Behind us, the sound of the sea and the sound of wind sweeping the long grass fused into one long soothing caress down the back of the night. I said, 'You can't think that way. Whether it's true or not. You have to believe that somewhere along the way, somehow, most people get what they deserve.'

'Or . . . ?'

'Or how do you get up in the morning? Believing in cause and effect isn't a luxury. It's an essential, like calcium, or iron: you can go without it for a while, but in the end you'll start eating yourself up from inside. You're right: every now and then, life isn't fair. That's where we come in. That's what we're *for*. We get in there and we fix it.'

Below us, the light went on in Emma's room – our Fiona, keeping things interesting. It turned the curtains a soft translucent pink, lit the silhouettes of little animals prancing across the cloth. Richie nodded down at the window. He said, 'We're not going to fix that.'

That morning in the morgue filled up his voice. 'No,' I said. 'That can't be fixed. But at least we can make sure that the right people pay and the right people get a chance to move on. At least we can manage that much. I know we're not saving the world. But we're making it better.'

'You believe that?'

His upturned face, white and young in the moonlight: he so badly wanted me to be right. 'Yeah,' I said. 'I do. Maybe I'm naïve – I've been accused of that before, a couple of times – but I believe it. You'll see what I mean. Wait till we get this guy. Wait till you go home that night and get into bed, knowing he's behind bars and he's going to stay there for three life sentences. See if the world you're in then doesn't feel like a better place than this one.'

Our Fiona opened Emma's curtains and gazed out into the garden, a slight dark silhouette against the pink wallpaper. Richie watched her. He said, 'I hope.'

The frail web of lights stretched across the estate had started to disintegrate, the bright threads of inhabited streets snapping into blackness. Richie rubbed his gloved hands together, blew into them. Our Fiona moved back and forth through the empty rooms, turning lights on and off, opening and closing curtains. The cold settled into the concrete of the hide, struck through the back of my coat into my spine.

The night went on and on. A handful of times, a noise – a long slither through the undergrowth below us, a burst of scrabbling and scuffling in the house across the road, a shrill wild squeal – had us on our feet and pressed back against walls, ready for action, before our minds understood that we had heard anything. Once the thermal goggles picked out a fox, luminous and poised in the road, head up, something small drooping from its mouth; another time they caught a sinuous streak of light whipping away through the gardens, between bricks and weeds. A few times we were too slow, caught nothing except the last rattle of pebbles, creepers swaying together, a vanishing flicker of white. Each time, it took longer before our heart rates eased to normal and we could sit down again. It was getting late. Our man was close by, tugged two ways and concentrating hard, deciding.

'I forgot,' Richie said suddenly, after one o'clock. 'I brought these.' He leaned over to his sports bag and pulled out a set of binoculars in a black plastic case.

'Binoculars?' I held out my hand for them, opened the case to have a look. They looked low-end, and they weren't from Supplies; the case still had that new-plastic smell. 'Did you go out and buy those specially?'

'They're the same model our fella had,' Richie said, a touch sheepishly. 'I figured we should have them too. See what he saw, yeah?'

'Oh, Jesus. Tell me you're not one of these touchy-feely types who get all into the idea of seeing through the killer's eyes while they have a good rub of their intuition.'

'*No*, I'm bleeding not. I meant literally. Like could he make out facial expressions, could he see anything on the computer – the names of the websites they were on, or whatever. That kind of thing.'

Even in the moonlight I could see his fierce blush. It touched me: not just the idea of him spending his own money and time to track down the right binoculars, but how openly he cared what I thought. I said more gently, holding them out, 'It's a good idea. Have a look; you never know what might turn up.'

He looked like he wished the binoculars would disappear, but he adjusted them and leaned his elbows on the windowsill to focus on the Spains' house. Our Fiona was at the sink, rinsing her mug. I said, 'What are you getting?'

'I can see Janine's face, really clearly; like if I could lip-read, I could see anything she said. I couldn't see the screen on the computer, if it was there – wrong angle – but I can read the titles on the bookshelf, and that little whiteboard with the shopping list: eggs, tea, shower gel. That could be something, yeah? If he could read Jenny's shopping list every night, then he'd know where she was gonna be the next day . . .'

'It's worth checking out. We'll pay special attention to CCTV from her shopping route, see if anyone keeps cropping up.' At the sink, our Fiona's head flicked round sharply, like she felt our eyes on her. Even without the binoculars, I saw her shiver.

'Man,' Richie said suddenly, loud enough that I jumped. 'Shit; sorry. But look at this.'

He passed me the binoculars. I trained them on the kitchen and adjusted them for my eyesight, which was a depressing notch worse than Richie's. 'What am I looking at?'

'Not the kitchen. Past there, down the hall. You can see the front door.'

'So?'

'So,' Richie said, 'just left of the front door.'

I shifted the binoculars to the left and there it was: the alarm panel. I whistled, low. I couldn't see the numbers, but I didn't need to: watching someone's fingers move would have told me everything I needed to know. Jenny Spain could have changed the code every day, if she wanted to, and just a few minutes up here while she or Patrick locked up would have undone all her caution. 'Well well well,' I said. 'Richie, my friend, I apologise for slagging your binoculars. I guess we know how someone could have got past the alarm system. Good work. Even if our man doesn't show up, tonight hasn't been a waste of time.'

Richie ducked his head and rubbed at his nose, looking somewhere between embarrassed and pleased. 'We still don't know how he got the keys, sure. Alarm code's no good without those.'

That was when my phone vibrated, in my coat pocket: Marlboro Man. 'Kennedy,' I said.

His voice was a shade above a whisper. 'Sir, we've got something. We spotted a guy coming out of Ocean View Lane. It's a cul-de-sac, backs onto the north wall of the estate, nothing but building sites; the only reason for anyone to be there is if he came in over the wall. On the tall side, dark clothing, but we didn't want to get too close, so that's all we've got. We tailed him at a distance until he turned down Ocean View Lawns. Again, that's a cul-de-sac, none of the houses are finished, there's no legit reason why anyone would want to go there. We didn't want to follow him down there, obviously, but we're maintaining surveillance on the end of Ocean View Lawns. So far, no sign of anyone coming out, but he could have gone over a wall again. We were going to do a circuit and see if we can pick him up.'

Richie had turned around and was watching me, binoculars hanging forgotten in his hands. I said, 'Good catch, Detective. Yes, stay on the line and do a quick tour of the area. If you can get a proper look at the man and give us a description, that'd be great, but for Jesus' sake don't risk scaring him off. If you spot anyone, don't slow down, don't make it obvious that you're checking him out, just keep driving and chat away between yourselves and pick up what you can. Go.'

I couldn't put the phone on speaker, not with our man loose and anywhere, everywhere, every stirring amongst the creepers. I pointed to it and motioned to Richie to come closer. He squatted beside me, ear cocked close.

Murmurs from the floaters, one of them rustling a map and working out directions, the other one easing the car into gear; the low purr of the engine. Someone was drumming his fingertips on the dash. Then, a minute later, a sudden burst of loud, confused gabble – 'And the wife says to me, go on, you can keep it in the bin with the rest!' – and an explosion of artificial laughter.

Richie and I, heads almost touching over the phone, weren't breathing. The gabble rose, died away. After a pause that felt like a week, Marlboro Man said, even more softly but with a rising current of excitement pulling at his voice, 'Sir. We've just passed a male, about five foot ten or eleven, slim build, heading east on Ocean View Avenue – that's just over the wall from Ocean View Lawns. There's no street lighting, so we didn't get a great look, but he's wearing a dark mid-length coat, dark jeans, dark wool hat. Going by the walk, I'd say twenties to thirties.'

I heard Richie's quick hiss of breath. I asked, just as quietly, 'Did he suss you?'

'No, sir. I mean, I can't swear to it, but I honestly don't think so. He looked round fast when he heard us behind him, and then he put his head right down, but he didn't do a legger, and as long as we had him in the rear-view he was still just walking along the street, same pace, same direction.'

'Ocean View Avenue. Is that inhabited?'

'No, sir. Just walls.'

So no one could say we were putting the inhabitants in danger, by letting this thing go free through the night to find its own way to us. Even if Ocean View Avenue had been teeming with rosy families and unlocked doors, I wouldn't have worried. This wasn't a spree killer, blazing away at anything that came on his screen. No one mattered to this guy, no one existed, except the Spains.

Richie had moved over to his holdall, crouching low so he wouldn't be silhouetted against the window-holes, and pulled out a folded piece of paper. He spread it on the floor in front of us, in a pale rectangle of moonlight: a map of the estate.

'Good,' I said. 'Get onto Detective . . .' I clicked my fingers at Richie and pointed down at the Spains' kitchen; he mouthed *Oates*. 'Detective Oates. Let her know it looks like action stations. Tell her to make sure the doors are locked, the windows are locked and her gun is loaded. Then she needs to start moving stuff – papers, books, DVDs, I don't care – from the front of the house to the kitchen, as visibly as possible. You two, fall back to the point where you first spotted this guy. If he chickens out and tries to head back past you, pick him up. Don't ring me again unless it's urgent. Otherwise, we'll let you know if anything happens.'

I pocketed my phone. Richie brought a finger down on the map: Ocean View Avenue, up in the north-west corner of the estate. 'Here,' he said, very quietly, just a murmur under the powerful murmur of the sea. 'If he's heading for us, and he's sticking to the empty streets and going over walls for short cuts, it'll take him ten, maybe fifteen minutes.'

'Sounds about right. I don't see him coming straight here: he's got to be worried that we've found this place. He'll have a nose around first, decide whether he's going to risk coming up here: look for cops, for unfamiliar cars, see if there's any activity . . . Let's say twenty-five minutes, all told.'

Richie glanced up at me. 'If he decides it's too risky, does a legger, then it's the floaters who get to pick him up. Not us.'

'Fine with me. Unless he comes up here, he's just some guy out for a night walk in the middle of nowhere. We can find out who he is and have a nice chat with him, but unless he's stupid enough to wear the bloody trainers or come out with a full confession, we won't be able to hold him. And I'm happy to let someone else be the guy who picks him up and has to throw him back a few hours later. We don't want him feeling like he's got one up on you and me.' What we would do if he ran didn't matter: I knew he was coming to us, knew as surely as if I could smell him, a sharp hot musk steaming off the rooftops and rubble, curling closer. Since the moment I had seen that lair, I had known he would come back to it. Sooner or later, an animal on the run runs for home.

Richie's mind had been moving in the same direction. He said, 'He'll come. He's already closer than he ever got last night; he's dying to find out what's the story. Once he sees Janine . . .'

I said, 'That's why we've got her moving stuff to the kitchen. I'm betting the first thing he'll do is check out the front of the Spains' house, from the building sites across the road. The idea is that he'll spot her from there, he'll want to know what she's doing with all the stuff, but in order to find out, he'll have to come back here. The houses are too close together for him to squeeze in between, so he can't come over the wall and in by the back. He'll have to come down Ocean View Walk.'

The top of the road was dark, shadowed by houses; the bottom stretch curved into moonlight. I said, 'I'll take the top of the road and the goggles. You take the bottom. Any movement, any at all, you let me know. If he does come up here, we'll do our best to keep things quiet – it'd be nice not to alert the residents that some-thing's going on – but he may not give us the choice. The one thing we don't forget for a second is that this guy is dangerous. Going on past form, there's no reason to think he's armed, but we're going to act like he is. Armed or not, this is a rabid animal and we're in his den. Remember exactly what he did down there, and take it for granted that, given the chance, he'd do the same to you and me.'

Richie nodded. He passed me the thermal-vision goggles and started tossing his things back into his holdall, fast and efficiently. I folded the map, stuffed Richie's food wrappers into a plastic bag and tucked it away. A few seconds later the room was bare floor-boards and breeze-block again, like we had never been there. I slung our holdalls into a dark corner, out of the way.

Richie set himself up by the window-hole facing the bottom of the road, squatting in a slant of shadow by the sill, and pried a corner of plastic sheeting loose so he could see out. I checked the Spains' house: our Fiona came into the kitchen carrying an armful of clothes, put them on the table and left again. Upstairs I could see, faint through Jack's window, the glow of a light in Pat and Jenny's bedroom. I pressed myself against the wall by the window overlooking the top of the road, and lifted the goggles.

They turned the sea invisible, a bottomless black. At the top of the street, the flat grey crisscross of scaffolding stretched away into the distance; an owl floated across the road, drifting on the air currents like a sheet of burning paper. The stillness went on and on.

I thought my eyelids were frozen wide open, but I must have blinked. There was no sound. One moment the top of the street was empty; the next he was standing there, blazing white and fierce as an angel between the shadowy ruins on either side. His face was almost too bright to look at. He stood still, listening, like a gladiator at the entrance to the ring: head up, arms held free from his sides, hands half-closed, ready.

I didn't breathe. I kept one eye on him and lifted a hand to catch Richie's attention. When his head turned towards me, I pointed out the window and beckoned.

Richie crouched low and slid across the floor to the other side of my window like he was weightless. As he pressed his back against the wall, I saw his hand go to the butt of his gun.

Our man came down the road slowly, placing his feet carefully, his head turning to every tiny sound. There was nothing in his hands, no night-vision gear on his face; just him. In the gardens, the small glowing animals uncurled and bounded away from his approach. Radiant against that web of metal and concrete, he looked like the last man left on earth.

When he was one house away I put the goggles down, and that tall shining figure flicked to a huddle of black, trouble sliding down the night to land on your doorstep. I signalled to Richie and backed away from the window-hole, into the shadows. Richie eased himself into the far corner opposite me; for a moment I heard his fast breathing, till he caught it and stilled it. The first weight of our man's hand on the metal bar sent a shiver vibrating all through the scaffolding, circling the house like a dark shimmer.

It grew as he climbed, a low thrumming like the pulse of a drum, and then it faded to silence. His head and shoulders appeared in the window, darker against dark. I saw his face turn to the corners, but the room was wide and the shadows hid us.

He swung in through the window with an ease that said he had done it a thousand times. The second his feet hit the floor and his body turned towards his lookout window, I came out of my corner and slammed into him from behind. He let out a hoarse shot of breath and staggered forward across the floor; I got an elbow around his neck, twisted his arm high behind his back with the other hand and slammed him up against a wall. The air went out of him in one sharp grunt. When his eyes opened, he was looking at Richie's gun.

I said, 'Police. Don't move.'

Every muscle in his body was rigid; he felt like he was made of steel rods. I said, and my voice sounded cool and clipped and like someone else's, 'I'm going to handcuff you for everyone's safety. Do you have anything on you that we should know about?'

He didn't seem to hear me. I eased my hands off him, watching; he didn't move, didn't even flinch when I wrenched his wrists behind him and snapped the cuffs tight. Richie patted him down, fast and hard, tossing what he found into a small pile on the floor: a torch, a packet of tissues, a roll of mints. Wherever he had hidden his car, he had left his ID and his money and his keys with it. He had been travelling light, making sure there was nothing to give him away with even a clink.

I said, 'I'm going to take the handcuffs off, so that you can climb down the scaffolding. I don't expect you to try anything stupid; if you do, it won't do anything except put me and my partner in a very bad mood. We're going back to headquarters for a chat. Your belongings will be returned to you there. Any problems with any of that?'

He was somewhere else, or fighting hard to be. His eyes, narrowed against the moonlight, were fixed somewhere on the sky outside the window, over the Spains' rooftop. 'Great,' I said, when it was obvious I wasn't going to get an answer. 'I'm going to take that to mean there's no problem. If anything changes, you can go right ahead and let me know. Now let's go.'

Richie climbed down first, awkwardly, with one of the holdalls slung over each shoulder. I waited, holding the handcuff chain between our man's wrists, till Richie gave me the thumbs-up from the ground; then I clicked the cuffs open and said, 'Go. No sudden moves.'

When I took his shoulder and pointed him in the right direction, he woke up and stumbled across the bare floor. In the window-hole he stood still for a moment; I saw the thought go through his mind, but before I could say anything he must have realised that from that height he would be lucky to break anything more than his ankles. He swung himself out of the window and started climbing, docile as a dog.

This guy I used to know gave me the nickname back in training college, when I scored a scorcher of a goal in some football match. I let it stick because I thought it would give me something to live up to. In the second when I was alone, in that terrible room filled with moonlight and sea-roar and months of waiting and watching, a tiny part at the back of my mind thought: *Forty-eight hours, four solves. Now there's a scorcher.* I understand how many people would call that sick, and I understand why, but that doesn't change the fact: you need me.

# 10

We stuck to the uninhabited streets, Richie and me with our hands tucked through our man's elbows, like we were helping our buddy home after a long night's bad drinking. None of us said a word – most people would have at least a few questions if you slapped cuffs on them and hauled them off to a cop car, but not this guy. Slowly the sound of the sea subsided and left room for the rest of the night, bats shrilling, wind tugging at forgotten scraps of canvas; for a while teenagers' jagged shouts reached us, thin and faraway, bounced back and forth off concrete and brick. Once I heard a harsh swallow that made me think our man might be crying, but I didn't turn my head to look. He had called enough shots.

We put him in the back of the car, and Richie leaned on the bonnet while I moved out of earshot to make phone calls: sending the patrol floaters to hunt for a car parked somewhere not far from the estate, telling the bait floater she could go home, letting the night admin know we would need an interview room ready. Then we drove back to Dublin in silence. The haunted blackness of the estate, scaffolding bones looming up out of nowhere, stark against the stars; then the smooth speed of the motorway, cat's-eyes flicking in and out of existence and the moon keeping pace off to one side, huge and watchful; then, gradually, the colours and movement of town building up around us, drunks and fast-food joints, the world coming back to life outside our sealed windows.

The squad room was quiet, just the two guys on call looking up from their coffees as we passed the door, to see who had been out night-hunting and was bringing something home. We put our man in the interview room. Richie undid the cuffs and I talked the guy through the rights sheet, in a bored drone like this was just meaningless paperwork. The word 'solicitor' got a violent shake of his head; when I put the pen in his hand, he signed without a single question. The signature was a jerky squiggle that gave away nothing but an initial C. I picked up the sheet and left.

We watched him from the observation room, through the one-way glass. It was the first time I had had a proper look at him. Short-cropped brown hair, high cheekbones, a jutting chin with a couple of days' worth of reddish stubble; he was wearing a black duffel coat that had seen plenty of use, a heavy roll-neck grey jumper and faded jeans, all dressed up for a night's stalking. He had on hiking boots: the trainers were gone. He was older than I had thought, and taller – late twenties, and not far off six foot – but he was so thin that he looked like the last stages of a hunger strike. It was the thinness that had minimised him into something younger, smaller, harmless. That illusion could have got him in the Spains' door.

No cuts or bruises that I could see, but anything could be hidden under all those clothes. I turned the interview-room thermostat up higher.

It felt good, seeing him in that room. Most of our interview rooms could do with a shower, a shave and a full makeover, but I love every inch of them. Our territory fights on our side. In Broken Harbour he had been a shadow that moved through walls, an iodine scent of blood and seawater, with shards of moonlight stuck in his eyes. Now he was just a guy. They all are, once you get them between those four walls.

He sat hunched rigidly in the uncomfortable chair, staring down at his fists on the table like he was bracing himself for torture. He hadn't even glanced around the room – linoleum pocked with old cigarette burns and lumps of chewing gum, walls scored with graffiti, bolted-down table and filing cabinet, the video camera's dull red light watching him from a high corner – to get his bearings. I said, 'What do we know about him?'

Richie was watching so intently that his nose was practically touching the glass. 'He's not on anything. At first I was thinking he could be on the gear, 'cause he's so skinny, but no.'

'Not right now, anyway. That's good for us: if we get anything, we don't want him saying it was the drugs talking. What else?'

'Loner. Nocturnal.'

'Right. Everything says he's more comfortable keeping his distance from other people, rather than making close contact – he got his kicks by watching, broke in when the Spains were out rather than when they were asleep. So when it comes time to push him, we want to get in close, get in his face, both of us at once. And since he's nocturnal, we want the push to come towards dawn, when he's starting to fade. Anything else?'

'No wedding ring. More than likely he lives alone: no one to notice when he's out all night, ask him what he's at.'

'Which would have its upside and its downside, as far as we're concerned. No flatmate to testify that he got in at six on Tuesday morning and ran the washing machine for four hours straight, but on the other hand, no one for him to bother hiding things from. When we find his gaff, there's a chance he'll have left us a little present – the bloodstained clothes, that honeymoon pen. Maybe a trophy he took the other night.'

The guy stirred, groped at his face, rubbed clumsily at his mouth. His lips were swollen and cracked, like he had gone a long time without water.

Richie said, 'He's not working a nine-to-five. He could be unemployed, or self-employed, or maybe he does shift work or a part-time gig – something that means he can spend the night up in that nest when he wants to, without banjaxing himself for work the next day. Just going by the clothes, I'd say middle-class.'

'So would I. And he's never been in the system before – his prints came up clean, remember. He probably doesn't even know anyone who's ever been in the system. He's got to be disorientated and scared. That's good stuff, but we want to save it for when we need it. We want to get him as relaxed as we can, see how far that takes us, then scare the living shite out of him when it comes to the big push. The good thing is, he won't walk out on us before then. Middle-class guy, probably got respect for authority, doesn't know the system . . . He'll stay till we kick him out.'

'Yeah. Probably he will.' Richie was drawing absent, abstract patterns in the mist his breath had left on the glass. 'And that's all I can figure out about him. You know that? This fella's organised enough to set up that nest, disorganised enough that he doesn't even bother taking it down again. Clever enough to get himself into that house, thick enough to take the weapons away with him. He's got enough self-control that he waited for months, but he can't even wait two nights after the murder before he's back up to his hide – and he must've known we'd be on the lookout, must've done. I can't get a handle on him.'

On top of all that, the guy looked much too frail to have done this. I wasn't fooled. Plenty of the most brutal predators I've caught looked soft as kittens, and they're always at their tamest just after the kill, spent and sated. I said, 'He's got no more self-control than a baboon. None of them do. We've all wanted to kill someone, at some point in our lives – don't tell me you haven't. What makes these guys different from us is that they don't stop themselves from actually doing it. Scratch the surface and they're animals: screaming, shit-flinging, throat-ripping animals. That's what we deal with. Never forget that.'

Richie didn't look convinced. I said, 'You think I'm being hard on them? Society's given them a raw deal, and I should have a little more empathy?'

'Not exactly. Just . . . if he's got no control, then how'd he manage to hold back for so long?'

I said, 'He didn't. We're missing something.'

'How d'you mean?'

'Like you said, this guy spent at least a few months, probably more, just watching the Spains, maybe occasionally sneaking into the house when they weren't around. That wasn't his amazing self-control in action: it was because that was all he needed to get his fix. And then, all of a sudden, he comes *charging* out of his comfort zone: jumps from binoculars straight to full-on close contact. That didn't come out of nowhere. Something happened, in this last week or so; something big. We'll need to find out what that was.'

In the interview room, our man knuckled his eyes, stared at his hands like he was looking for blood, or tears. 'And I'll tell you one more thing,' I said. 'He feels very emotionally connected to the Spains.'

Richie stopped drawing. 'You think? I was thinking it wasn't personal. The way he kept his distance . . .'

'No. If he were a professional, he'd be home by now: he'd have clocked that he's not under arrest, and he'd never even have got into our car. And he isn't a sociopath who saw them as just random objects that looked like fun, either. The soft kill on the kids, the close-contact kill on the adults, wrecking Jenny's face . . . He had feelings for them. He thinks he was close to them. More than likely the only actual interaction they ever had was when Jenny smiled at him in the queue at Tesco; but in his head, at least, there was a connection there.'

Richie breathed on the glass again and went back to his patterns, more slowly this time. 'You're taking it as a definite that he's our man,' he said. 'Yeah?'

I said, 'It's early days to call anything definite.' There was no way to tell him that the drumming in my ears had swelled so high, in the car with this man at my shoulder, I had almost been afraid I would have us off the road. The man permeated the air around him with wrongness, strong and repellent as naphtha, as if he had been soaked in it. 'But if you're asking for my personal opinion, then yes. Hell yes. This is our man.'

The guy raised his head as if he had heard me, and his eyes, rimmed with painful-looking swells of red, skidded around the room. For a second they rested on the one-way glass. Maybe he watched enough cop shows to know what it was; maybe the thing that had fluttered through my skull in the car moved both ways, shrilled like a bat at the back of his neck to warn him I was there. For the first time, his eyes focused, like they were staring straight into mine. He took a quick deep breath and set his jaw, ready.

The tips of my fingers were prickling with how much I wanted to get in there. 'We'll let him wonder for another fifteen minutes,' I said. 'Then you go in.'

'Just me?'

'He'll see you as less of a threat than me. Nearer his age.' And there was the class gap, too: a nice middle-class boy could easily discount an inner-city kid like Richie as some idiot skanger. The lads would have been gobsmacked if they had seen me letting a brand-new newbie loose on this interrogation, but Richie wasn't quite your ordinary rookie, and this felt like a two-man job. 'Just settle him, Richie. That's all. Find out his name, if you can. Get him a cup of tea. Don't go anywhere near the case, and for the love of all that's holy don't let him ask for a lawyer. I'll give you a few minutes with him, and then I'll come in. OK?'

Richie nodded. He said, 'You think we'll get a confession out of him?'

Most of them never confess. You can show them their prints all over the weapon, the victim's blood all over their clothes and CCTV footage of them whacking her over the head, and they'll still be spewing out injured innocence and howling about frame-ups. In nine people out of ten, self-preservation goes deeper than sense, deeper than thought. You pray to get the tenth person, the one built with a crack in the self-preservation where something else runs deeper still – the need to be understood, the need to please you, sometimes even conscience. You pray for the one who, somewhere darker than the inside of bone, doesn't want to save himself; for the one who stands at the top of the cliff and has to fight the urge to leap. Then you find that crack, and you press.

I said, 'That's what we're aiming for. The Super comes in at nine; that gives us six hours. Let's have this ready to hand over to him, all wrapped up and tied with a bow.'

Richie nodded again. He pulled off his jacket and three heavy jumpers and dropped them on a chair, leaving him narrow and gangly as a teenager in a long-sleeved navy T-shirt that had been washed thin. He stood at the glass, no fidgeting, and watched the guy hunch lower over the table until I checked my watch and said, 'Go.' Then he ran a hand through his hair so it stood up on end, got two cups of water from the cooler, and went.

He did it nicely. He went in holding out a cup and saying,

'Sorry, man, I meant to bring this in to you before, only I got caught up . . . Is that all right for you? Would you have a cup of tea instead, yeah?' His accent had got thicker. The class thing had occurred to him, too.

Our man had jumped half out of his skin when the door opened, and he was still catching his breath. He shook his head.

Richie hovered, looking fifteen. 'You sure? Coffee?'

Another head-shake.

'Grand. You'll let me know if you need more of this, yeah?'

The guy nodded and reached for the water. The chair rocked under his weight. 'Ah, hang on,' Richie said. 'He's after giving you the dud chair.' Quick surreptitious glance at the door, like I might be behind it. 'Go on: swap over. Have this one.'

Our man shuffled awkwardly across. Probably it made no difference – all the chairs in the interview rooms are chosen to be uncomfortable – but he said, so low I barely heard him, 'Thanks.'

'No problem. Detective Richie Curran.' He held out a hand.

Our man didn't take it. He said, 'Do I have to tell you my name?' His voice was low and even, good to listen to, with a slight rough edge like it hadn't got much use lately. The accent gave me nothing; he could have been from anywhere.

Richie looked surprised. 'Do you not want to? Why not?'

After a moment he said, to himself, '. . . make any difference . . .' To Richie, with a mechanical handshake: 'Conor.'

'Conor what?'

A fraction of a second. 'Doyle.' It wasn't, but that didn't matter. Come morning we would find either his house or his car, or both, and strip them to the bones looking for, among other things, his ID. All we needed for now was something to call him.

'Nice to meet you, Mr Doyle. Detective Kennedy'll be here in a while, then yous can get started.' Richie balanced the edge of his arse on a corner of the table. 'I'll tell you now, I'm only delighted you showed up. I was dying to get out of there, I was. I know people pay good money to go camping up by the sea and all, but the countryside isn't my style, know what I mean?'

Conor shrugged, a small, jerky movement. 'It's peaceful.'

'I'm not mad about peaceful. City boy, me; give me the noise and the traffic any day. And I was freezing my bollix off, as well. Are you from up there, are you?'

Conor glanced up sharply, but Richie was slugging at his water and watching the door, just making small talk while he waited for me. Conor said, 'No one's from Brianstown. They just move there.'

'That's what I meant: are you living there, yeah? Jaysus, you couldn't pay me enough.'

He waited, all mild innocuous curiosity, till Conor said, 'No. Dublin.'

Not local. Richie had knocked out one angle and saved us a lot of hassle right there. He raised his cup in a cheerful toast. 'Up the Dubs. No better place. And wild horses couldn't drag us away, amn't I right?'

Another shrug. 'I'd live down the country. Depending.'

Richie hooked an ankle around a spare chair and pulled it over for his feet, getting comfortable for an interesting chat. 'Would you, seriously? Depending on what?'

Conor wiped a palm up his jaw, hard, trying to pull it together: Richie was nudging him off balance, poking little holes in his concentration. 'Dunno. If you had a family. Space for the kids to play.'

'Ah,' Richie said, pointing a finger at him. 'There you go, see. I'm a single man: I need somewhere I can get a few drinks in, meet a few girls. Can't live without that, know what I mean?'

I had been right to send him in. He was relaxed as a sunbather and doing a beautiful job. I was willing to bet that Conor had gone into that room with the intention of keeping his lip firmly zipped, for years if necessary. Every detective, even Quigley, has knacks, little things that he does better than anyone else around: we all know who to call if we want a witness reassured by the expert, or a quick bit of intimidation done right. Richie had one of the rarest knacks of all. He could make a witness believe, against all the evidence, that they were just two people talking, the same way the two of us had talked while we waited in that hide; that Richie was seeing not a solve in the making, not a bad guy who needed locking up for the good of society, but another human being. It was good to know.

Conor said, 'That gets old, the going out. You stop wanting it.'

Richie's hands went up. 'Take your word for that, man. What do you start wanting instead?'

'Something to come home to. A wife. Kids. A bit of peace. The simple stuff.'

It moved through his voice, slow and heavy, like a shadow looming under dark water: grief. For the first time, I felt a flick of empathy for the guy. The disgust that came with it almost shot me into the interview room to get to work on him.

Richie held up crossed index fingers. 'Sooner you than me,' he said cheerfully.

'Wait.'

'I'm twenty-three. Long while to go before the biological clock kicks in.'

'Wait. Nightclubs, all the girls made up to look exactly like each other, everyone pissed off their heads so they can act like someone they're not. After a while, it'll make you sick.'

'Ah. Got burned, yeah? Brought home a babe and woke up with a hound?'

Richie was grinning. Conor said, 'Maybe. Something like that.'

'Been there, man. The beer goggles are a bastard. So where do you go looking for chicks, if the clubs don't do it for you?'

Shrug. 'I don't go out much.'

He was starting to turn his shoulder to Richie, block him out: time to change things up. I went for the interview room with a bang: sweeping the door open, spinning a chair over to face Conor – Richie slid off the table and into a chair next to me, fast – throwing myself back in it, shooting my cuffs. 'Conor,' I said. 'I don't know about you, but I'd love to get this sorted out fast enough that we can all get some sleep tonight. What do you say?'

Before he could come up with an answer, I held up a hand. 'Whoa, hang on there, Speedy Gonzalez. I'm sure you've got plenty to say, but you'll get your turn. Let me share a few things with you first.' They need to be taught that you own them now; that from this moment on, you're the one who decides when they talk, drink, smoke, sleep, piss. 'I'm Detective Kennedy, this is Detective Curran, and you're just here to answer some questions for us. You're not under arrest, nothing like that, but we need a chat. I'm pretty sure you know what all this is about.'

Conor shook his head, one heavy shake. He was dropping back towards that weighted silence, but I was fine with that, for the moment anyway.

'Ah, man,' Richie said reproachfully. 'Come *on*. What d'you *think* it's about? The Great Train Robbery?'

No response. 'Leave the man alone, Detective Curran. He's only doing what he was told, aren't you, Conor? Wait your turn, I said, and that's what he's doing. I like that. It's good to have the ground rules clear.' I steepled my fingers on the table and examined them thoughtfully. 'Now, Conor, I'm sure spending your night like this doesn't make you a happy man. I can see your point there. But if you look at this properly, if you really look at it, this is your lucky night.'

He shot me a look of pure jagged incredulity.

'It's true, my friend. You know and we know that you shouldn't have been setting up camp in that house, because it's not yours, now is it?'

Nothing. 'Or maybe I'm wrong,' I said, with the corner of a grin. 'Maybe if we check with the developers, they'll tell us you put down a nice big chunk of deposit, will they? Do I owe you an apology, fella? Are you on that property ladder after all?'

'No.'

I clicked my tongue and wagged a finger at him. 'I didn't think so. Naughty, naughty: just because no one's living there, son, that doesn't mean you get to move in, bag and baggage. That's still breaking and entering, you know. The law doesn't take a day off just because you fancy a holiday home and no one else was using it.'

I was piling on the patronising as thick as I could, and it was needling Conor out of his silence. 'I didn't *break* anything. Just walked in.'

'Why don't we let the lawyers explain why that's beside the point? If things go that far, of course, which' – I raised a finger – 'they don't need to. Because like I said, Conor, you're a very lucky young man. Detective Curran and I aren't actually that interested in a pissant B and E charge – not tonight. Let's put it this way: when a couple of hunters go out for the night, they're looking for big game. If a rabbit, say, is all they can find, they'll take that; but if the rabbit puts them on the trail of a grizzly bear, they're going to let the bunny hop along home while they go chasing the grizzly. Are you following me?'

That got me a disgusted glance. Plenty of people take me for a pompous git way too fond of the sound of his own voice, which is absolutely fine with me. Go ahead and dismiss me; go right ahead and drop your guard.

'What I'm saying, son, is that you are, metaphorically speaking, a bunny. If you can point us at something bigger, off you hop. Otherwise, your fuzzy little head's going over our mantelpiece.'

'Point you at what?'

The flare of aggression in his voice would have told me, all on its own, that he didn't need to ask. I ignored it. 'We're on the hunt for info, and you're the very man to give it to us. Because when you were picking a house for your bit of breaking and entering, you struck it lucky. As I'm pretty sure you've noticed, your little nest looks straight down into the kitchen of Number Nine Ocean View Rise. Like you had your very own reality-show channel, playing twenty-four-seven.'

'World's most *boring* reality-show channel,' Richie said. 'Would you not have found, like, a strip club? Or a bunch of girls that go around topless?'

I pointed a finger at him. 'We don't know it was boring, now do we? That's what we're here to find out. Conor, my man, you tell us. The people who live at Number Nine: boring?'

Conor turned the question over, testing for dangers. In the end he said, 'A family. Man and woman. Little girl and little boy.'

'Well, no shit, Sherlock, pardon my French. That much we've worked out for ourselves; there's a reason they call us detectives.

What are they like? How do they spend their time? Do they get on? Is it snuggles or screaming matches down there?'

'Not screaming matches. They used to . . .' That grief stirring again, dark and massive, under his voice. 'They'd play games.'

'What kind of games? Like Monopoly?'

'Now I see why you picked them,' Richie said, rolling his eyes. 'The excitement, yeah?'

'Like once they built a fort in that kitchen, cardboard boxes and blankets. Played Cowboys and Indians, all four of them; kids climbing all over him, her lipstick for war paint. Evenings, him and her used to sit out in the garden, after the kids were in bed. Bottle of wine. She'd rub his back. They'd laugh.'

Which was the longest speech we'd heard him make. He was dying to talk about the Spains, gagging for the chance. I nodded away, pulled out my notebook and my pen and made squiggles that could have been notes. 'This is good stuff, Conor my man. This is exactly what we're after. Keep it coming. You'd say they're happy? It's a good marriage?'

Conor said quietly, 'I'd say it was a beautiful marriage. Beautiful.'

*Was.* 'Never saw him do anything nasty to her?'

That snapped his head round towards me. His eyes were grey and cold as water, amid the swollen red. 'Like *what*?'

'You tell me.'

'He used to bring her presents all the time: small stuff, fancy chocolate, books, candles – she liked candles. They'd kiss when they passed in the kitchen. All those years together, and they were still mad about each other. He'd have *died* sooner than hurt her. OK?'

'Hey, fair enough,' I said, raising my hands. 'A man's got to ask.'

'There's your answer.' He hadn't blinked. Under the stubble his skin had a rough, windburned look, like he had spent too much time in cold sea air.

'And I appreciate it. That's what we're here for: to get the facts straight.' I made a careful note in my book. 'The kids. What are they like?'

Conor said, 'Her.' The grief surged in his voice, close to the surface. 'Like a little doll, little girl in a book. Always in pink. She had wings she'd wear, fairy wings—'

'"She"? Who's "she"?'

'The little girl.'

'Oh, come on, fella, don't play games. Of course you know their names. What, they never yelled to each other in the garden? The mum never called the kids in for dinner? Use their names, for God's sake. I'm too old to keep all this him-her-she-he stuff straight.'

Conor said quietly, like he was being gentle with the name, 'Emma.'

'That's right. Go on about Emma.'

'Emma. She loved stuff around the house: putting on her little apron, making Rice Krispie buns. She had a little chalkboard; she'd line up her dolls in front of it and play teacher, teach them their letters. Tried to teach her brother, too, only he wouldn't stay still long enough; knocked over the dolls and legged it. Peaceful, she was. Happy-natured.'

*Was* again. 'And her brother? What's he like?'

'Loud. Always laughing, shouting – not even words, just shouting to make noise, because that was so funny it creased him up. He—'

'His name.'

'Jack. He'd knock over Emma's dolls, like I said, but then he'd come help her pick them back up, kiss them better. Give them sips of his juice. Once Emma was home sick, a cold or something: he brought her stuff all day long, his toys, his blanket. Sweet kids, both of them. Good kids. Great.'

Richie's feet shifted, under the table: he was working hard to let that go by. I tapped my pen off my teeth and examined my notes. 'Let me tell you something interesting that I've noticed, Conor. You keep saying "used to". They used to play family games, Pat used to bring Jenny presents . . . Did something change?'

Conor stared at his reflection in the one-way glass like he was measuring a stranger, volatile and dangerous. He said, 'He lost his job. Pat.'

'How do you know?'

'He was there during the day.'

And so had Conor been, which didn't exactly point to him being a productive little worker bee. 'No more Cowboys and Indians after that? No more cuddles in the garden?'

That cold grey flash again. 'Being out of work wrecks people's heads. Not just him. Plenty of people.'

The quick leap to the defence: I couldn't tell whether that was on Pat's behalf or his own. I nodded thoughtfully. 'Is that how you'd describe him? Head-wrecked?'

'Maybe.' That sediment of wariness was starting to build up again, stiffening his back.

'What gave you that impression? Give us a few examples.'

A one-shouldered jerk that could have been a shrug. 'Don't remember.' The finality in his voice said he wasn't planning to.

I leaned back in my chair and took leisurely fake notes, giving him time to settle. The air was heating up, pressing around us dense and scratchy as wool. Richie blew out air loudly and fanned himself with his top, but Conor didn't seem to notice. The coat was staying on.

I said, 'That's going back a few months, Pat losing his job. When did you start spending time out at Ocean View?'

A second's silence. 'A while back.'

'A year? Two?'

'Maybe a year. Maybe less. I didn't keep track.'

'And how often do you get up there?'

A longer silence, this time. The wariness was starting to crystal-lise. 'Depends.'

'On what?'

Shrug.

'I'm not looking for a stamped timesheet here, Conor. Just give us a ballpark. Every day? Once a week? Once a month?'

'Couple of times a week, maybe. Less, probably.'

Which meant every other day, at least. 'What time? Day or night?'

'Nights, mostly. Sometimes daytime.'

'What about night before last? Did you head up to your little holiday home?'

Conor leaned back in his seat, folded his arms and focused on the ceiling. 'I don't remember.'

End of conversation. 'OK,' I said, nodding. 'You don't want to talk about that just yet, fine with us. We can talk about something else instead. Let's talk about you. What do you do, when you're not kipping in abandoned houses? Got a job?'

Nothing. 'Ah, for God's sake, man,' Richie said, rolling his eyes. 'Like pulling teeth. What d'you think we're gonna do? Arrest you for being in IT?'

'Not IT. Web design.'

And a web designer would have known more than enough about computers to wipe the Spains'. 'See, Conor? How hard was that? Web design's nothing to be ashamed of. There's good money in it.'

A humourless sniff of a laugh, up at the ceiling. 'You think?'

'Recession,' Richie said, snapping his fingers and pointing at Conor. 'Am I right? You were doing grand, all up and coming and web-designing away, and then the crash came and bang, just like that, on the dole.'

That hard almost-laugh again. 'I wish. I'm self-employed. No dole for me; when the work went, the money went.'

'Shit,' Richie said suddenly, eyes widening. 'Are you homeless, man? Because we can give you a hand there. I'll make a few calls—'

'I'm not bloody homeless. I'm grand.'

'No reason to be embarrassed. These days there's loads of people—'

'Not me.'

Richie looked sceptical. 'Yeah? D'you live in a house or a flat?'

'Flat.'

'Where?'

'Killester.' Northside: just right for a regular commute up to Ocean View.

'Sharing with who? Girlfriend? Flatmates?'

'No one. Just me. All right?'

Richie turned up his hands. 'Only trying to help.'

'I don't need your help.'

'I've got a question, Conor,' I said, twirling my pen between my fingers and watching it with interest. 'Your flat got running water?'

'What's it to you?'

'I'm a cop. I'm nosy. Running water?'

'Yeah. Hot *and* cold.'

'Electricity?'

Conor said, 'For fuck's *sake*,' to the ceiling.

'Mind your language, son. Got electricity?'

'Yeah. Electricity. Heating. A cooker. Even a microwave. What are you, my mum?'

'Couldn't be further from it, fella. Because my question is, if you've got a nice cosy bachelor pad with all mod cons and even a microwave, why the hell are you spending your nights pissing out the window of a freezing rat-trap in Brianstown?'

There was a silence. I said, 'I'm going to need an answer, Conor.'

His chin set hard. 'Because. I like it.'

Richie stood up, stretched and started moving around the edges of the room, in the loose-kneed, bobbing lope that says *trouble* on any backstreet. I said, 'That's not going to do the job, fella. Because – and stop me if this isn't news to you – two nights ago, when you *don't remember* what you were doing, someone got into the Spains' house and murdered the lot of them.'

He didn't bother to pretend that came as a shock. His mouth tightened like a vicious cramp had wrenched through him, but nothing else moved.

I said, 'So, naturally, we're interested in anyone who has links to the Spains – especially anyone whose link is what you might call out of the ordinary, and I'd say your playhouse qualifies there. You could even say we're *very* interested. Am I right, Detective Curran?'

'Fascinated,' Richie said, from behind Conor's shoulder. 'Is that the word I'm after, yeah?' He was making Conor edgy. The bad-news walk wasn't intimidating him, nothing like that, but it was breaking his concentration, keeping him from slamming his silence shut around himself. I realised that I was liking working with Richie, more and more.

'"Fascinated" would work, all right. Even "obsessed" wouldn't be out of place. Two little kids are dead. Personally, and I don't think I'm alone here, I'm willing to do whatever it takes to put away the cocksucking bastard who killed them. I'd like to think any decent member of society would do the same.'

'Dead right,' said Richie approvingly. The circles were getting tighter, faster. 'Are you with us on that, Conor, yeah? You're a decent member of society, aren't you?'

'Haven't got a clue.'

I said pleasantly, 'Well, let's find out, shall we? We'll start with this: in the course of your year or so of breaking and entering – you didn't keep track, of course, you just liked it out there – did you happen to notice anyone unsavoury hanging around Ocean View?'

Shrug.

'Is that a no?'

Nothing. Richie sighed noisily and started skimming the sides of his shoe soles off the linoleum on each step, with a horrible squealing noise. Conor winced. 'Yeah. It's a no. I saw no one.'

'What about the night before last? Because we need to cut the crap, Conor: you were out there. See anyone interesting?'

'I've got nothing to tell you.'

I raised my eyebrows. 'You know, Conor, I doubt that. Because I'm only seeing two options here. Either you saw what happened, or you are what happened. If it's Door Number One, then you need to start talking right now. If it's Door Number Two . . . well, that's the only reason why you would want to keep your mouth shut. Isn't it?'

People tend to react, when you accuse them of murder. He sucked his teeth, stared at a thumbnail.

'If you can see an option I've missed, old son, then by all means share it with us. All donations gratefully accepted.'

Richie's shoe squealed inches behind Conor, and he jumped.

He said, and there was an edge to his voice, 'Like I said: I've got nothing to tell you. Pick your own options; not my problem.'

I swept my pen and notebook out of my way and leaned forward across the table, into his face, leaving him nowhere else to look. 'Yeah, it is, old son. It bloody well is. Because me and Detective Curran and the entire police force of this country, every single one of us is out to bring down the fucker who slaughtered this family. And you're right smack in our crosshairs. You're the guy who's on the spot for no good reason, who's been spying on the Spains for a year, who's filling us up with bullshit when any innocent man in the world would be helping us out . . . What do you think that says to us?'

Shrug.

'It says you're a murdering scumbag, fella. I'd say that's very much your problem.'

Conor's jaw tightened. 'If that's what you want to think, there's nothing I can do about it.'

'Jesus,' Richie said, rolling his eyes. 'Self-pity much?'

'Call it what you want.'

'Come *on*. There's loads you can do about it. You could give us a hand, just for starters: tell us everything you saw going down around the Spains' gaff, hope something in there helps us out. Instead, you're gonna sit here and sulk like some kid who's got caught smoking hash? Grow up, man. Seriously.'

That got Richie a filthy look, but Conor wasn't biting. He kept his mouth shut.

I eased back into my seat, adjusted the knot in my tie and changed the note to something gentler, almost curious. 'Do we have it wrong, Conor? Maybe it wasn't like it looks. We weren't there, me and Detective Curran; there could have been a lot more to it than we realise. This might not be murder at all; it could have been manslaughter. I can even see how it could have started out as self-defence, and then things got out of hand. I'm willing to accept that. But we can't do that unless you tell us your side of the story.'

Conor said, to the air somewhere over my head, 'There's *no fucking story.*'

'Oh, but there is. That's not really up for debate, is it? The story might be "I wasn't in Brianstown that night, and here's my alibi." Or it might be "I was out there and I saw someone dodgy hanging about, and here's a description." Or "The Spains caught me breaking in, they went for me and I had to defend myself." Or "I was up in my hide getting good and stoned when everything went black, and the next thing I remember I was sitting in my bathtub, covered in blood." Any one of those could fly with us, but we need to hear it. Otherwise, we're going to assume the worst. Surely you can see that. Can't you?'

Silence, so packed with stubborn that you could feel it elbowing you. There are detectives, even nowadays, who would have fixed this problem with a few rabbit-punches to the kidneys, either on a toilet trip or while the video camera was mysteriously on the blink. I had been tempted once or twice, when I was younger, had never given in – handing out slaps is for morons like Quigley, who have nothing else in their arsenal – and I had had that under control for a long time. But in that thick, overheated stillness I understood for the first time exactly how fine the line was, and how very easily crossed. Conor's hands holding the edge of the table were long-fingered and strong, big capable hands with the tendons standing out and the cuticles bitten bloody. I thought of what they had done, of Emma's cat pillow and the gap in her front teeth and Jack's soft pale curls, and I wanted to pound a lump hammer down on those hands until they were crunching pulp. The thought of doing it made the blood shake in my throat. It horrified me, how deep in my gut I wanted it, how simple and natural a desire it seemed.

I tamped it down hard and waited until my heart rate subsided. Then I sighed and shook my head, more in sorrow than in anger. 'Conor, Conor, Conor. What do you think this is going to accomplish? Tell me that, at least. Do you seriously believe we're going to be so impressed by your little act that we'll send you off home and forget the whole thing? "I like a man who sticks to his guns, old son, don't you worry about those nasty murders"?'

He stared at the air, narrow-eyed and intent. The silence

stretched. I hummed to myself, adding a beat with my fingertips on the table, and Richie perched on the edge of the table jiggling his knee and cracking his knuckles with real dedication, but Conor had gone past that. He barely knew we were there.

Finally Richie did an ostentatious stretch-groan-yawn routine and checked his watch. 'Here, man, are we going to be doing this all night?' he wanted to know. ''Cause if we are, I need coffee to keep up with the pace. Thrill a minute, this.'

I said, 'He's not going to answer you, Detective. We're getting the silent treatment.'

'Can we get it while we're in the canteen, yeah? I swear, I'm gonna fall asleep right here if I don't get some coffee into me.'

'No reason why not. This little shit is making me sick to my stomach anyway.' I clicked my pen shut. 'Conor, if you need to get your sulk out of the way before you can talk to us like an adult human being, be our guest, but we're not going to sit around and watch you do it. Believe it or not, you're not the centre of the universe. We've got plenty of more urgent things to do than watch a grown man act like a spoilt kid.'

Not a blink. I clipped my pen to my notebook, tucked them back in my pocket and gave it a pat. 'We'll be back when we get a moment. If you need to go to the jacks, you can give the door a bang and hope someone hears. See you around.'

On the way out Richie whipped Conor's cup off the table, catching the bottom delicately between thumb and fingertip. I pointed at it and told Conor, 'Two of our favourite things: prints and DNA. Thanks, fella. You saved us a load of time and hassle, right there.' Then I gave him a wink and a thumbs-up, and slammed the door behind us.

In the observation room, Richie asked, 'Was that all right, me getting us out of there? I just thought . . . I mean, we'd hit a wall, like. And I figured it was easier for me to pull the plug without losing face, yeah?'

He was rubbing one foot off the opposite ankle and looking apprehensive. I pulled an evidence bag out of the cabinet and tossed it to him. 'You did fine. You're right: time to regroup. Any thoughts?'

He dropped the cup into the evidence bag and looked around for a pen; I passed him mine. 'Yeah. Know something? He's ringing a bell. The face.'

'You've been looking at him for a long time, it's late, you're shattered. Sure your mind's not playing tricks?'

Richie squatted beside the table to label the bag. 'Yeah, I'm sure. I've seen him before. I'm wondering was it back when I was in Vice, maybe.'

The observation room is on the same thermostat as the interview room. I tugged my tie looser. 'He's not in the system.'

'I know. I'd remember if I'd arrested him. But you know yourself: some guy catches your eye and you can tell he's up to something, but there's nothing you can pin on him, so you just hang on to that face and wait till it shows up again. I'm wondering . . .' He shook his head, dissatisfied.

'Put it on the back burner. It'll come to you. When it does, let me know; we need to ID this guy, and soon. Anything else?'

Richie initialled the bag, ready to hand in to the evidence room, and gave my pen back. 'Yeah. Winding him up won't get us anywhere, not with this fella. We had him pissed off there, all right, but the angrier he gets, the quieter he gets. We need another angle.'

I said, 'We do. The distraction stuff was good – nicely done there – but it's taken us as far as it can. And intimidation won't work, either. I was wrong about one thing: he's not afraid of us.'

Richie shook his head. 'Nah. He's on guard, all right, big-time, but scared . . . Nah. And the thing is, he should be. I'd still say he's a virgin; he's not acting like he knows the drill. This whole thing should have him crapping his kacks by now. Why doesn't it?'

In the interview room Conor was still and taut, hands spread flat on the table. There was no way he could have heard us, but I lowered my voice all the same. 'Over-confidence. He thinks he covered his tracks, figures we've got nothing on him unless he talks.'

'Maybe, yeah. But he has to know we've got a full team going over that house with a fine-tooth comb, looking for anything he left behind. That should be worrying him.'

'They're arrogant bastards, a lot of them. Think they're smarter than we are. Don't let that bother you; it'll work for us, in the long run. Those are the ones that go to pieces when you whip out something they can't ignore.'

'What if . . .' Richie said diffidently, and stopped. He was twirling the bag back and forth, looking at it, not at me. 'Never mind.'

'What if what?'

'I was only going to say. If he's got a solid alibi, something like that, and he knows sooner or later we'll run up against it . . .'

I said, 'You mean, what if he's feeling safe because he's innocent.'

'Yeah. Basically.'

'Not a chance, chum. If he had an alibi, why not just tell us and go home? You think he's pulling our chains for kicks?'

'Could be. He's not mad about us.'

'Even if he were innocent as a baby – and he's not – he shouldn't be this cool. The innocent ones get just as frightened as the guilty ones – more, a lot of the time, because they're not arrogant pricks. They shouldn't, obviously, but there's no telling them that.'

Richie glanced up and lifted a noncommittal eyebrow. I said, 'If they've done nothing wrong, then the fact is, they've got nothing to be afraid of. But the facts aren't always the point.'

'I guess. Yeah.' He was rubbing at the side of his jaw, where stubble should have been by this stage. 'Another thing, but. Why isn't he pointing us at Pat? We've given him a dozen openings. It'd be easy as pie: "Yeah, Detective, now that you mention it, your man Pat went loopy after he lost his job, used to smack his wife around, beat the shite out of his kids, saw him threaten them with a knife just last week . . ." He's not thick; he must've seen his chance. Why didn't he grab it?'

I said, 'Why do you think I've been giving him those openings?'

Richie shrugged, a complicated, embarrassed squirm. 'I dunno.'

'You thought I was being sloppy, and I just got lucky that this guy didn't take advantage. Wrong, old son. I told you before we went in there: our man Conor thinks he has some connection to the Spains. We needed to know what kind of connection. Did Pat Spain cut him off on the motorway and now he thinks all his troubles are Pat's fault and his luck won't turn till Pat's dead and gone, or did he chat to Jenny at some party and decide the stars wanted them to be together?'

Conor hadn't moved. The white strip-lighting caught the sheen of sweat on his face; it turned him waxy and alien, something shipwrecked from another planet, light-years more lost than we could imagine.

I said, 'And we got our answer: in his own fucked way, Conor Whatever cares about the Spains. All four of them. He didn't point us at Pat because, even to save himself, he wouldn't drop Pat in the shit. He believes he loved them. And that's how we're going to take him down.'

We left him there for an hour. Richie took the cup down to the evidence room and picked up faded coffee on his way back – the canteen coffee works mainly by the power of suggestion, but it's better than nothing. I checked in with the patrol floaters: they were working their way out from the estate, they had spotted about a dozen parked cars, all of which came back with legit reasons for being in the area, and they were starting to sound tired. I told them to keep looking. Then Richie and I stayed in the observation room, with our sleeves pushed up and the door wide open, and we watched our man.

It was almost five o'clock. Down the corridor the two lads on night duty were tossing a basketball back and forth and slagging each other's aim, to keep themselves awake. Conor sat still in his chair, hands cupping his knees. For a while his lips moved, like he was reciting something under his breath, in a regular, steadying rhythm. 'Praying?' Richie asked softly, beside me.

'We'll hope not. If God's telling him to keep his mouth shut, we're in for a rough ride.'

In the squad room the ball knocked something off a desk with a crash, one of the lads said something creative and the other one started to laugh. Conor sighed, a deep wave of breath that lifted and dropped his whole body. He had stopped whispering; he looked like he was slipping into some kind of trance. I said, 'Let's go.'

We went in loud and cheerful, fanning ourselves with statement sheets and bitching about the heat, handing him a cup of luke-warm coffee and warning him that it tasted like piss: bygones are bygones, all friends again now. We rewound to the safe ground before we'd lost him, spent a while poking around the edges of stuff we'd already covered – did you ever see Pat and Jenny arguing, ever see either of them shouting, ever see either of them smack the kids ... The chance to talk about the Spains lured Conor out of his silent zone, but as far as he was concerned, they had made the Brady Bunch look like something off *Jerry Springer*. When we moved on to his schedule – what time do you usually get to Brianstown, what time do you fall asleep – his memory went glitchy again. He was starting to feel safe, starting to think he knew how this worked. It was time to move things forward.

I said, 'When was the last time you can confirm that you were in Ocean View?'

'Don't remember. Could be last—'

'Whoa,' I said, sitting up fast and raising a hand to cut Conor off. 'Hang on.'

I went for my BlackBerry, hit a button to make the screen light up, pulled it out of my pocket and whistled. 'Hospital,' I said to Richie in a quick undertone, and saw in the corner of my eye Conor's head snapping up like he had been kicked in the back. 'This could be what we've been waiting for. Suspend the inter-view till I get back.' And, on my way out the door: 'Hello, Doctor?'

I kept one eye on my watch and the other on the one-way glass. Five minutes had never lasted so long, but they were lasting even longer for Conor. That taut control had exploded into pieces: he was shifting his arse like the seat was heating up, drumming his feet, biting his cuticles bloody. Richie watched him with interest and said nothing. Finally Conor demanded, 'Who was that?'

Richie shrugged. 'How would I know?'

'What you've been waiting for, he said.'

'We've been waiting for a lot of things.'

'Hospital. What hospital?'

Richie rubbed at the back of his neck. 'Man,' he said, halfway between amused and embarrassed, 'don't know if you've missed this, but we're working on a *case* here, yeah? We don't go around telling people what we're at.'

Conor forgot Richie existed. He propped his elbows on the table, folded his fingers across his mouth and stared at the door.

I gave him another minute. Then I came in fast, slammed the door and told Richie, 'We're in business.'

He raised his eyebrows. 'Yeah? Beautiful.'

I swung a chair around to Conor's side of the table and sat down, my knees practically touching his. 'Conor,' I said, slapping the phone down in front of him. 'Tell me who you think that was.'

He shook his head. He was staring at the phone. I could feel his mind speeding, caroming at wild angles like a race car gone out of control.

'Listen carefully, fella: as of now, you do not have time to dick me around. You may not know it yet, but all of a sudden you are in a big, big hurry. So tell me: who do you think that was?'

After a moment Conor said, low, into his fingers, 'Hospital.'

'What?'

A breath. He made himself straighten up. 'You said. A hospital.'

'That's better. And why do you think a hospital would be ringing me?'

Another head-shake.

I slapped the table, just hard enough to make him jump. 'Did you hear what I just said about dicking me around? Wake up and pay attention. It's five in the bloody a.m., there's nothing in my world except the Spain case, and I just got a call from a hospital. Now why the *fuck* do you think that might be, Conor?'

'One of them. One of them's in that hospital.'

'That's right. You fucked up, son. You left one of the Spains alive.'

The muscles in his throat were clenched so tight that his voice came out a hoarse rasp. 'Which one?'

'You tell me, fella. Who would you like it to be? Go on. If you had to choose, which one of them would it be?'

He would have answered anything to make me go on. After a moment he said, 'Emma.'

I leaned back in my chair and laughed out loud. 'That's adorable. Really, it is. That sweet little girl: you figure maybe she deserved a shot at life? Too late, Conor. The time to think about that was two nights ago. Emma's in a morgue drawer right now. Her brain's in a jar.'

'Then who—'

'Were you out at Brianstown night before last?'

He was half out of his chair, clutching the edge of the table, crouched and wild-eyed. '*Who*—'

'I asked you a question. Night before last. Were you out there, Conor?'

'Yeah. Yeah. I was there. Who – which—'

'Say please, fella.'

'*Please.*'

'That's better. The one you missed was Jenny. Jenny's alive.'

Conor stared at me. His mouth opened wide, but all that came out was a great rush of breath, like he had been punched in the stomach.

'She's alive and kicking, and that was her doctor on the phone, telling me she's awake and wants to talk to us. And we all know what she's going to say, don't we?'

He barely heard me. He gasped for air, again and again.

I shoved him down into his seat; he went like his knees had turned liquid. 'Conor. Listen to me. I told you that you've got no time to waste, and I wasn't joking. In just a couple of minutes, we're going to head over to the hospital to talk to Jenny Spain. And as soon as that happens, I will never again in my life give a damn about anything you have to say. This is it: your last chance.'

That reached him. He stared, slack-jawed and wild.

I pulled my chair even nearer, leaned in till our heads were almost touching. Richie slid around and sat on the table, close enough that his thigh pressed against Conor's arm. 'Let me explain something to you,' I said, quiet and even, straight into his ear. I could smell him, sweat and a wild tang like split wood. 'I happen to believe that basically, deep down, you're a decent guy. Everyone else you meet from here on in, every single person, is going to believe you're a sick, sadistic, psychopathic bastard who should be skinned alive and hung out to dry. I may be losing the bit I have, and I may end up regretting this, but I don't agree. I think you're a good guy who somehow ended up in a shit situation.'

His eyes were blind, but that got a tiny twitch of his eyebrows: he was hearing me. 'Because of that, and because I know nobody else is going to give you a break, I'm willing to make you a deal. You prove me right, tell me what happened, and I'll tell the prosecutors you helped us out: you did the right thing, because you felt remorse. When it comes time for your sentencing, that's going to matter. In a courtroom, Conor, remorse equals concurrent sentences. But if you show me that I'm wrong about you, if you keep on dicking me around, that's what I'm going to tell the prosecutors, and the whole lot of us are going to go for broke. I don't like being wrong about people, Conor; it pisses me off. We'll charge you with everything we can think of, and we'll go for consecutive sentences. Do you know what that means?'

He shook his head: clearing it or saying no, I couldn't tell which. I get no say in the sentencing and not a lot in the charges, and any judge who would give out concurrent sentences on dead children needs a straitjacket and a punch in the gob, but none of that mattered. 'That means three life sentences in a row, Conor, plus a few years on top for the attempted murder and the burglaries and the destruction of property and whatever else we can whip out. We're talking about sixty years, *minimum*. How old are you, Conor? What are your odds of seeing a release date that's sixty years away?'

'Ah, he might see it,' Richie objected, leaning in to examine him critically. 'They look after you, in prison: don't want you getting out early, even if it's in a coffin. I've gotta warn you, man, the company's gonna be shite – you won't be let into the general population 'cause you'd last about two days, you'll be in the secure unit with all the paedos, so the conversation's gonna be pretty fucked-up – but at least you'll have loads of time to make friends.'

That twitch of his eyebrows again: that had got through. 'Or,' I said, 'you could save yourself a lot of hell, right here. With concurrent sentences, do you know how many years we're talking about? Around *fifteen*. That's bugger-all. How old will you be in fifteen years?'

'My maths isn't great,' Richie said, giving him another interested once-over, 'but I'd say maybe forty-four, forty-five? And I don't have to be Einstein to figure out there's a massive difference between getting out at forty-five and getting out at *ninety*.'

'My partner the human calculator is spot on, Conor. Forty-whatever is still young enough to have a career, get married, have half a dozen kids. Have a life. I don't know if you realise this, old son, but that's what I'm putting on the table here: your life. But this is a one-time-only offer, and it expires in five minutes. If your life's worth anything to you, son, anything at all, better start talking.'

Conor's head fell back, exposing the long line of his throat, the soft spot at its base where the blood beats just below the skin. 'My life,' he said, and his lip curled in something that could have been a snarl or a terrible smile. 'Do whatever you want to me. I don't give a damn.'

He planted his fists on the table, set his jaw and stared straight ahead, into the one-way glass.

I had fucked up. Ten years earlier I would have grabbed for him wildly, thinking I'd lost him, and ended up pushing him further away. Now I know, because I've fought hard to learn, how to let other things work with me; how to stay still, stay back, and let the job do its job. I eased back in my chair, examined an imaginary spot on my sleeve and left the silence to stretch while that last conversation dissipated out of the air, absorbed into the graffitied particleboard and the scored linoleum, gone. Our interview rooms have seen men and women pushed over the rims of their own minds, heard the thin dull crack of them breaking, watched while they spilled out things that should never be in the world. These rooms can soak up anything, close around it without leaving a trace behind.

When the air had emptied itself of everything but dust I said, very softly, 'But you do give a damn about Jenny Spain.'

A muscle flicked, at the corner of Conor's mouth.

'I know: you didn't expect me to understand that. You didn't think anyone would, did you? But I do, Conor. I understand just how much you cared about all four of them.'

That tic again. 'Why?' he asked, the words forcing themselves out against his will. 'Why do you think that?'

I rested my elbows on the table and leaned in towards him, my clasped hands next to his, like we were two best mates in the pub having a late-night session of I-love-you-man. 'Because,' I said gently, 'I understand you. Everything about the Spains, every-thing about that room you set up, everything you've said tonight: all of it tells me what they meant to you. There's no one in the world who means more, is there?'

His head turned towards me. Those grey eyes were clear as still water, all the night's tension and turmoil drained away. 'No,' he said. 'No one.'

'You loved them. Didn't you?'

A nod.

I said, 'Let me tell you the biggest secret I've ever learned, Conor. All we really need in life is to make the people we love happy. We can do without anything else; you can live in a card-board box under a bridge, as long as your woman's face lights up when you get home to that box in the evening. But if you can't manage to do that . . .'

Out of the corner of my eye I saw Richie easing backwards, off the table, leaving the two of us in our circle. Conor said, 'Pat and Jenny were happy. The happiest people alive.'

'But then that went, and you couldn't give it back to them. Probably someone or something out there could have made them happy again, but it wasn't you. I know exactly what it's like, Conor:

loving someone so much that you'd do anything, you'd rip out your own heart and serve it to them with barbecue sauce if that was what it took to make them OK, but it's not. It wouldn't do one fucking bit of good. And what do you do when you realise that, Conor? What can you do? What's left?'

His hands lay spread on the table, palms upturned, empty. He said, so low I barely heard him: 'You wait. All you can do.'

'And the longer you wait, the angrier you get. At yourself, at them, at this whole terrible fucked-up mess of a world. Till you can't think straight any more. Till you barely know what you're doing.'

His fingers curled inward, fists tightening.

'Conor,' I said: so softly, words falling weightless as feathers through the hot still air. 'Jenny's been through enough hell for a dozen lifetimes. The last thing I want to do is put her through any more. But if you don't tell me what happened, then I have to go over to that hospital and make her tell me instead. I'll have to force her to relive every moment of the other night. Do you think she's strong enough to take that?'

His head swayed, side to side.

'Neither do I. For all I know, it'll push her mind so far over the edge that she'll never find her way back, but I don't have a choice. You do, Conor. You can save her from that, at least. If you love her, now's your time to show it. Now's your time to get it right. You'll never have another chance.'

Conor vanished, somewhere behind that face as angular and immobile as a mask. His mind was going like a race car again, but he had it under control now, working efficiently and at furious speed. I didn't breathe. Richie, pressed back against the wall, was still as stone.

Then Conor took a quick breath, ran his hands over his cheeks and turned to look at me. 'I broke into their house,' he said, clearly, matter-of-factly, as if he was telling me where he had parked a car. 'I killed them. Or thought I had, anyway. Is that what you were after?'

I heard Richie let his breath out, with a tiny unconscious

whimper. The hum in my skull rose, screamed like a whirl of diving wasps, and died.

I waited for the rest, but Conor was waiting too: just watching me, with those swollen red-edged eyes, and waiting. Most confessions begin with *It wasn't like you think* and go on forever. Killers fill up the room with words, trying to coat over the razor edges of the truth; they prove to you over and over that it just happened or that he asked for it, that in their place anyone would have done the same. Most of them will keep proving it till your ears bleed, if you let them. Conor was proving nothing. He was done.

I said, 'Why?'

He shook his head. 'Doesn't matter.'

'It's going to matter to the victims' family. It's going to matter to the sentencing judge.'

'Not my problem.'

'I'll need a motive to go in your statement.'

'Make one up. I'll sign whatever you want.'

Mostly they loosen, after the river's been crossed. Everything they had went into clinging to their safe bank of lies. Now the current's ripped them away, buffeted them dizzy and gasping, smashed them down with a tooth-cracking jolt on the far bank, and they think the hard part is over and done with. It leaves them unravelled and boneless; some of them shake uncontrollably, some of them cry, a few can't stop talking or can't stop laughing. They haven't noticed yet that the landscape is different here; that things are transforming around them, familiar faces dissolving, landmarks vanishing into the distance, that nothing will ever be the same again. Conor was different. He was still gathered like a waiting animal, made of concentration. In some way that I couldn't spot, the battle wasn't over.

If I got into it with him over the motive, he would win, and you don't let them win. I said, 'How did you get into the house?'

'Key.'

'To which door?'

A splinter of a pause. 'Back.'

'Where'd you get that?'

That splinter again, bigger this time. He was being careful. 'Found it.'

'When?'

'A while back. Few months, maybe more.'

'Where?'

'Street outside. Pat dropped it.'

I could feel it on my skin, the sideslipping twist to his voice that said *Lie*, but I couldn't put my finger on where or why. Richie said, from the corner behind Conor's shoulder, 'You couldn't see the street from your hide. How'd you know he'd dropped the key?'

Conor thought that over. 'Saw him come in from work in the evening. Later that night, I went for a wander around, spotted the key, figured he had to be the one that lost it.'

Richie wandered over to the table, pulled out a chair facing Conor. 'No you didn't, man. There's no street lighting. What are you, Superman? See in the dark?'

'It was summer. Bright till late.'

'You were prowling round their gaff while it was still bright? While they were still awake? Come on, man. What were you, *looking* to get arrested?'

'So maybe it was dawn. I found the key, I got it copied, I got in. End of story.'

I said, 'How many times?'

That tiny pause again, while he tested answers in his head. I said crisply, 'Don't waste your time, old son. There's no point in bullshitting me. We're well past that. How many times were you in the Spains' house?'

Conor was rubbing at his forehead with the back of his wrist, trying to hold it together. That sheetrock wall of stubbornness was starting to waver. Adrenaline can only keep you going for so long; any minute now, he was going to be too exhausted to sit up straight. 'A few. A dozen, maybe. What's it matter? I was there night before last. I've told you.'

It mattered because he knew his way around the house: even in darkness, he would have been able to find his way up the stairs, into the children's rooms, to their beds. Richie asked, 'Ever take anything away with you?'

I saw Conor dig for the energy to say no, and give up. 'Little things, only. I'm not a thief.'

'What kind of stuff?'

'A mug. Handful of rubber bands. A pen. Nothing worth anything.'

I said, 'And the knife. Let's not forget the knife. What did you do with it?'

That should have been one of the tough questions, but Conor turned towards me like he was grateful for it. 'Into the sea. The tide was up.'

'Where'd you throw it from?'

'The rocks. South end of the beach.'

We were never getting that knife back. It was halfway to Cornwall by now on some long cold current, rocking fathoms deep among seaweed and soft blind creatures. 'And the other weapon? The one you used to hit Jenny?'

'Same.'

'What was it?'

Conor's head fell back and his lips parted. The grief that had been looming under his voice, all night long, had made its way to the surface. It was that grief, not fatigue, that was leaching the willpower out of him, scouring his concentration away. It had eaten him alive, from the inside out; it was all that was left.

He said, 'It was a vase. Metal one, silver, with a heavy base on it. Simple thing, it was; beautiful. She used to put a couple of roses in it, have it on the table when she made fancy dinners for the two of them . . .'

He made a small sound between a swallow and a gasp, the sound of someone sliding underwater. I said, 'Let's rewind a little, shall we? Start from the point when you entered the house. What time was it?'

Conor said, 'I want to sleep.'

'As soon as you've talked us through it. Was anyone awake?'

'I want to sleep.'

We needed the full story, blow by blow and packed with details that only the killer would know, but it was heading for six o'clock and he was heading for the level of fatigue that a defence attorney could use. I said gently, 'OK. You're nearly there, son. I'll tell you what: we'll just get what you've told us in writing, and then we'll take you somewhere you can get a bit of kip. Fair enough?'

He nodded, a lopsided jerk, like his head had suddenly turned too heavy for his neck. 'Yeah. I'll write it down. Just leave me alone while I do it. Can you do that?'

He was at the end of his strength, way past trying to get smart with his statement. 'Sure,' I said. 'If that's what works for you, not a problem. We'll need to know your real name, though. For the statement sheet.'

For a second I thought he was going to stonewall us again, but all the fight was gone. 'Brennan,' he said, dully. 'Conor Brennan.'

I said, 'Well done.' Richie moved quietly to the corner table and passed me a statement sheet. I found my pen and filled in the header, in strong block capitals: CONOR BRENNAN.

I put him under arrest, cautioned him again, went through the rights sheet again. Conor didn't even look up. I put the statement sheet and my pen into his hands, and we left him there.

'Well well well,' I said, tossing my notebook onto the table in the observation room. Every cell in my body was fizzing like champagne with pure triumph; I felt like throwing a Tom Cruise, jumping up on the table shouting *I love this job!* 'Now that was a whole lot easier than I was expecting. Here's to us, Richie my friend. Do you know what we are? We're a bloody great team.'

I gave him a pumping handshake and a clap on the shoulder. He was grinning. 'Felt like that, all right.'

'No two ways about it. I've had a lot of partners in my time, and I can tell you, hand on heart: that was the real thing. There are guys who partner for years and still don't work together that smoothly.'

'It's good, yeah. It's good stuff.'

'By the time the Super gets in, we'll have that statement signed, sealed and delivered to his desk. I don't need to tell you what this is going to do for your career, do I? Let's see that prick Quigley give you hassle now. Two weeks on the squad, and you're part of the biggest solve of the year. How does it feel?'

Richie's hand slid out of mine too fast. He still had the grin, but there was something unsure in it. I said, 'What?'

He nodded at the one-way glass. 'Look at him.'

'He'll write it up just fine. Don't you worry about that. He'll have second thoughts, of course he will, but they won't kick in till tomorrow: emotional hangover. By then, we'll have our file half ready to send to the DPP.'

'It's not that. The state of that kitchen . . . You heard Larry: the struggle was full-on. Why isn't he more beat up?'

'Because he isn't. Because this is real life, and sometimes it doesn't go exactly the way you'd expect it to.'

'I just . . .' The grin was gone. Richie was digging his hands into his pockets, staring at the glass. 'I have to ask, man. You're positive he's our guy?'

The fizz started to fade out of my veins. I said, 'That's not the first time you've asked me that.'

'I know, yeah.'

'So let's hear it. What's got up your arse?'

He shrugged. 'Dunno. You've been awful sure all along, is all.'

The anger shot through me like a muscle spasm. 'Richie,' I said, very carefully keeping my voice under control. 'Let's review for a second, shall we? We've got the sniper's nest that Conor Brennan set up to stalk the Spains. We've got his own admission that he broke into their house multiple times. And now, Richie, now we've got a fucking *confession*. Go ahead and tell me, old son: what the fuck else do you want? What the *fuck* would it take to make you sure?'

Richie was shaking his head. 'We've got plenty. I'm not arguing there. But even back when we had nothing, only that hide, you were positive.'

'So *what*? I was *right*. Did you miss that part? You're getting your knickers in a knot because I got there ahead of you?'

'Makes me nervous, being too sure too early. It's dangerous.'

The jolt hit me again, hard enough to clench my jaw. 'You'd rather keep an open mind. Is that it?'

'Yeah. I would.'

'Right. Good idea. For how long? Months? Years? Till God sends choirs of angels to sing you the guy's name in four-part harmony? Do you want us to be standing here in ten years' time, telling each other, "Well, it could be Conor Brennan, but then again, it could be the Russian Mafia, we might want to explore that possibility a little more thoroughly before we make any rash decisions"?'

'*No.* I'm only saying—'

'You *have* to get sure, Richie. You have to. There is no other option. Sooner or later, you shit or you get off the pot.'

'I *know* that. I'm not talking about any ten years.'

The heat was the kind you get in a cell in a bad August: thick, motionless, clogging your lungs like wet cement. 'Then what the hell *are* you talking about? What'll it take? In a few hours' time, when we get our hands on Conor Brennan's car, Larry and his boys are going to find the Spains' blood all over it. Around the same time, they're going to match his fingerprints to the prints they found all over that hide. And a few hours after that, assuming that please God we get hold of the trainers and the gloves, they're going to prove that that bloody shoeprint and those bloody hand-prints were made by Conor Brennan. I'd bet a month's salary on it. Will that make you sure?'

Richie rubbed at the back of his neck and grimaced. I said, 'Oh, for Christ's sake. Right. Let's hear it. I guaran-damn-tee you, by the end of today, we'll have physical proof he was in that house when that family got killed. How are you planning to explain that away?'

Conor was writing, head bent low over the statement sheet, arm curved protectively around it. Richie watched him. He said, 'This guy loved the Spains. Like you said. Say, let's just say, he's up in his hide the other night – maybe Jenny's on the computer, he's watching her. Then Pat comes downstairs and goes for her. Conor freaks out, goes to break up the fight: legs it down from his hide and over the wall, lets himself in through their back door. But by then it's too late. Pat's dead or dying, Conor thinks Jenny is too – probably he doesn't check too carefully, not with all the blood and the panic. Maybe he's the one that brought her over to Pat, so they could be together.'

'Touching. How do you explain the wiped computer? The missing weapons? What's all that about?'

'Same again: he cares about the Spains. He doesn't want Pat taking the rap. He wipes the computer 'cause he thinks maybe whatever Jenny was doing on there could be what triggered Pat – or he knows for definite that it was. Then he takes the weapons and dumps them, so it'll look like an intruder.'

I took a second and a breath, to make sure I wouldn't bite his head off. 'Well, it's a pretty little fairy story, old son. Poignant, is that the word I'm looking for? And that's all it is. It's fine as far as it goes, but you're skipping right past this: why the holy hell did Conor confess?'

'Because. What happened in there.' Richie nodded at the glass. 'Man, you practically told him you were going to put Jenny Spain in a straitjacket if he didn't give you what you were after.'

I said, and my voice was cold enough to warn a much stupider man than Richie, 'Do you have a problem with the way I'm doing my job, Detective?'

His hands went up. 'I'm not picking holes. I'm only saying: that's why he confessed.'

'No, Detective. No, it bloody well isn't. He confessed *because he did it*. All that crap I gave him about loving Jenny, all that did was pick the lock; it didn't put anything behind the door that wasn't *already fucking there*. Maybe your experience has been different from mine, maybe you're just better at this job, but I have a hard enough time getting my suspects to confess to what they *did*. I can safely say I've never, in all my career, managed to get one of them to confess to something he *didn't* do. If Conor Brennan says he's our man, then it's because he is.'

'He's not like most of them, though, is he? You said it yourself, we've both been saying: he's different. There's something weird going on there.'

'He's weird, yeah. He's not *Jesus*. He's not here to give his life for Pat Spain's sins.'

Richie said, 'It's not just him that's weird. What about the baby monitors? Those weren't your man Conor's doing. And the holes in the walls? There was something going on *inside* that house.'

I leaned back against the wall with a thump and folded my arms. It might have been just the fatigue, or the thin yellowy-grey dawn smearing the window, but that champagne fizz of victory was well and truly gone. 'Tell me, old son: why the hate for Pat Spain? Is this some kind of chip on your shoulder, because he was a good solid pillar of the community? Because if it is, I'm warning you now: get rid of it, sharpish. You're not always going to be able to find a nice middle-class boy to pin things on.'

Richie came at me fast, finger pointing; for a second I thought he was going to jab me in the chest, but he had enough sense left to stop himself. 'It's got nothing to do with class. *Nothing.* I'm a cop, man. Same as yourself. I'm not some thicko skanger you brought in as a favour because it's Take A Knacker To Work Day.'

He was too close and much too angry. I said, 'Then act like a cop. Step back, Detective. Get a grip on yourself.'

Richie stared me out of it for another second; then he wheeled away, flung himself back against the glass and shoved his hands deep into his pockets. 'You tell me, man: why are you so dead set that it *isn't* Patrick Spain? Why the love?'

I had no obligation to explain myself to some jumped-up little newbie, but I wanted to; I wanted to say it, shove it deep into Richie's head. 'Because,' I said, 'Pat Spain followed the rules. He did everything people are supposed to do. That's not how killers live. I told you from the start: things like this don't come out of nowhere. All that crap the families give the media – "Oh, I can't believe he would do this, he's such a Boy Scout, never done anything bad in his life, they were the happiest couple in the world" – that's garbage. Every time, Richie, every single time, it turns out that the guy was a Boy Scout except for a record as long as your arm, or he'd never done anything bad except for his little habit of terrorising the shit out of his wife, or they were the happiest couple in the world except for the minor fact that he was banging her sister. There's not one hint, anywhere, that any of that applied to Pat. You're the one who said it: the Spains did their best. Pat was a trier. He was one of the good guys.'

Richie didn't move. 'Good guys break.'

'Seldom. Very, very seldom. And there's a reason for that. It's because the good guys have stuff to hold them in place, when the going gets tough. They've got jobs, families, responsibilities. They've got the rules they've been following their whole lives. I'm sure all that stuff sounds uncool to you, but here's the fact: it works. Every day, it keeps people from crossing over the line.'

'So,' Richie said flatly, 'because Pat was a nice middle-class boy. A pillar of the community. That's why he couldn't be a killer.'

I didn't want to have this argument, not in an airless observation room at some ungodly hour of the morning with sweat sticking my shirt to my back. I said, 'Because he had things to love. He had a home – OK, it was in the arsehole of nowhere, but one look at it should have told you that Pat and Jenny loved every inch of the place. He had the woman he'd been loving ever since they were sixteen; *still mad about each other,* that's what Brennan said. He had two kids who climbed all over him. That's what holds the good guys together, Richie. They've got places to put their hearts into. They've got people to take care of. People to love. That's what stops them from going over the edge, when a guy who wasn't weighted down would be in freefall. And you're trying to convince me that Pat just turned around one day and blew all that away, for no reason at all.'

'Not for no reason. You said yourself: he could've been about to lose the lot. The job was gone, the gaff was going; the wife and kids could've been about to go as well. It happens. All over this country, it's been happening. The triers are the ones that snap, when trying doesn't do any good.'

All of a sudden I was exhausted, two sleepless nights digging their claws in and dragging me down with all their weight. I said,

'The one who snapped was Conor Brennan. Now there's a man who's got nothing left to lose: no work, no home, no family, not even his own *mind*. I'll bet you any amount of money you want, when we start looking into his life we're not going to find a close-knit circle of friends and loved ones. Nothing's holding Brennan in place. He's got nothing to love; nothing except the Spains. He's spent the last *year* living like some kind of cross between a hermit and the Unabomber, all so he could stalk them. Even your own little theory hinges on the fact that Conor was a delusional freakshow who was spying on them at three in the bloody morning. The guy's not right, Richie. He's not OK. There's no way around that.'

Behind Richie, in the harsh white light of the interview room, Conor had put down the pen and was pressing his fingertips into his eyes, rubbing them in a grim, relentless rhythm. I wondered how long it had been since he had slept. 'Remember what we talked about? The simplest solution? It's sitting behind you. If you find evidence that Pat was a vicious sonofabitch who was beating the shit out of his family while he got ready to leave them for a Ukrainian lingerie model, then come back to me. Until then, I'm putting my money on the psycho stalker.'

Richie said, 'You told me yourself: "psycho" isn't a motive. All that about being upset because the Spains weren't happy, that's nothing. They'd been in trouble for months. You're telling me the other night he just decided out of the blue, so fast he didn't even have time to clean out his hide: *There's nothing on the telly, I know what I'll do, I'll head on down to the Spains' and kill the lot of them*? Come *on*, man. Here's you saying Pat Spain didn't have a motive. What the hell was this fella's motive? Why the hell would he want any of them dead?'

One of the many ways that murder is the unique crime: it's the only one that makes us ask why. Robbery, rape, fraud, drug dealing, all the filthy litany, they come with their filthy explanations built in; all you have to do is slot the perp into the perp-shaped hole. Murder needs an answer.

Some detectives don't care. Officially, they're right: if you can prove whodunit, nothing in the law says you need to prove why. I care. When I pulled what looked like a random drive-by, I spent weeks – after we had the shooter in custody, after we had enough evidence to sink him ten times over – having in-depth conversations with every monosyllabic cop-hating lowlife in his shithole neighbourhood, until someone let slip that the victim's uncle worked in a shop and had refused to sell the shooter's twelve-year-old sister a packet of cigarettes. The day we stop asking why, the day we decide that it's acceptable for the answer to a severed life to be *Just because*, is the day we step away from that line across the cave entrance and invite the wild to come howling in.

I said, 'Trust me: I'm going to find out. We've got Brennan's associates to talk to, we've got his flat to search, we've got the Spains' computer – and Brennan's, if he's got one – to go through, we've got forensic evidence waiting to be analysed . . . Somewhere in there, Detective, there's a motive. Forgive me if I don't have every piece of the puzzle in place within forty-eight hours of getting the bloody *case*, but I promise you, I will find them. Now let's get this fucking statement and go home.'

I headed for the door, but Richie stayed put. He said, 'Partners. That's what you said this morning, remember? We're partners.'

'Yes. We are. So?'

'So you don't make the decisions for the both of us. We make them together. And I say we keep looking at Pat Spain.'

The stance – feet planted apart, shoulders squared – told me he wasn't going to budge without a fight. We both knew that I could shove him back in his box and slam the lid on his head. One bad report from me and Richie was off the squad, back to Motor Vehicles or Vice for another few years, probably forever. All I had to do was touch on that, one delicate hint, and he would back off: finish Conor's paperwork, leave Pat Spain to rest in peace. And that would be the end of that tentative thing that had begun in the hospital car park, less than twenty-four hours earlier.

I closed the door again. 'All right,' I said. I let myself slump back against the wall and tried to squeeze tension out of my shoulder. 'All right. Here's what I suggest. We'll need to spend the next week or so investigating Conor Brennan, to waterproof our case – that's assuming he's our man. I suggest that, during that time, you and I also conduct a parallel investigation into Pat Spain. Superintendent O'Kelly would like that idea even less than I do – he'd call it a waste of time and manpower – so we won't make a song and dance about it. If and when it does come up, we're just making sure Brennan's defence isn't going to find anything on Pat that they can use as a red herring in court. It'll mean a lot of very long shifts, but I can handle that if you can.'

Richie already looked ready to fall asleep standing up, but he was young enough that a few hours would fix that. 'I can handle it.'

'I thought so. If we turn up anything solid on Pat, then we'll regroup and review. How does that strike you?'

He nodded. 'Good,' he said. 'Sounds good.'

I said, 'The word for this week is *discreet*. Until and unless we come up with solid evidence, I'm not going to spit on Pat Spain's body by calling him a murderer to the people who loved him, and I'm not going to watch you do it either. If you let any of them twig that he's being treated as a suspect, we're done. Do I make myself clear?'

'Yeah. Crystal.'

In the interview room, the pen was still down on the scribbled statement sheet and Conor was sagging over them, the heels of his hands pressed into his eyes. I said, 'We all need sleep. We'll hand him over for processing, get the report typed up, leave instructions for the floaters, and then we'll go home and crash for a few hours. We'll meet back here at noon. Now let's go see what he's got for us.'

I scooped my jumpers off the chair and bent to stuff them back into the holdall, but Richie stopped me. 'Thanks,' he said.

He was holding out his hand and looking me straight in the face, steady green eyes. When we shook, the strength in his grip took me by surprise.

'No thanks needed,' I said. 'It's what partners do.'

The word hung in the air between us, bright and fluttering as a lit match. Richie nodded. 'Sound,' he said.

I gave him a quick clap on the shoulder and went back to packing up. 'Come on. I don't know about you, but I'm dying for some kip.'

We threw our stuff into our holdalls, binned the litter of paper cups and coffee stirrers, switched off the lights and closed the observation-room door. Conor hadn't moved. At the end of the corridor the window was still bleary with that tired city dawn, but this time the chill didn't touch me. Maybe it was all that youthful energy beside me: the victory fizz was back in my veins and I felt wide awake again, straight-backed and strong and rock-solid, ready for whatever came next.

# 11

The phone dragged me up from the deep-sea bottom of sleep. I came up gasping and flailing – for a second I thought the shrieking noise was a fire alarm, telling me Dina was locked in my flat with flames swelling. 'Kennedy,' I said, when my mind found its footing.

'This could have nothing to do with your case, but you did say to ring if we picked up any other forums. You know what a private message is, right?'

Whatshisname, the computer tech: Kieran. 'More or less,' I said. My bedroom was dark; it could have been any hour of the day or night. I rolled over and fumbled for the bedside lamp. The sudden flare of light jabbed me in the eyes.

'OK, on some boards, you can set your preferences so that, if you get a private message, a copy of it comes to your e-mail. Pat Spain – well, it could be Jennifer, but I'm assuming it's Pat, you'll see what I mean – he had that setting activated, on one board at least. Our software recovered a PM that came through a forum called Wildwatcher – that's the "WW" in the password file, gotta be, not World of Warcraft.' Kieran apparently worked to the soothing rhythm of cranked-up house music. My head was already pounding. 'It's from some dude called Martin, sent the thirteenth of June, and it says, quote, "Not looking to get in any arguments but seriously if it's a mink I would def lay down poison esp if you have kids those bastards are vicious" – spelled wrong – "would attack a kid no problem." Unquote. Any mink in the case?'

My alarm clock said ten past ten. Assuming it was still Thursday morning, I had been asleep for less than three hours. 'Have you checked out this Wildwatcher site?'

'No, I decided to get a pedicure instead. Yeah, I've checked it out. It's a site where people can talk about wild animals they've spotted – I mean, not *that* wild, it's a UK-based site so we're mostly talking, like, urban foxes? – or ask what's that darling little brown birdie nesting in their wisteria. So I ran a search for "mink", right, and it turned up a thread started by a user called Pat-the-lad on the morning of June twelfth. He was a new user; looks like he registered specifically to post this. Want me to read it to you?'

'I'm in the middle of something,' I said. My eyes felt like someone had rubbed sand into them; so did my mouth. 'Can you e-mail me the link?'

'No problemo. What do you want me to do with Wildwatcher? Check it out fast, or in depth?'

'Fast. If no one gave Pat-the-lad any hassle, you can probably move on, for now anyway. That family didn't get killed over a mink.'

'Sounds good to me. See you around, Kemosabe.' In the second before Kieran hung up, I heard him turn up his music to a volume that could pulverise bone.

I took a fast shower, turning the water colder and colder till my eyes were focusing again. My face in the mirror irritated me: I looked grim and intent, like a man with his eyes on the prize, not a man whose prize was safe and sound in his display cabinet. I got my laptop, a pint glass of water and a few pieces of fruit – Dina had taken a bite out of a pear, changed her mind and put it back in the fridge – and sat on the sofa to check out Wildwatcher.

Pat-the-lad had registered at 9.23 a.m. on 12 June, and started his thread at 9.35. It was the first time I had heard his voice. He came across as a good guy: down-to-earth, straight to the point, knew how to lay out the facts. *Hi guys, got a question. Living on the east coast of Ireland, right by the sea if that makes a difference. Last few weeks been hearing weird noises in the attic. Running, lots of scratching, something hard rolling about, sound I can only describe as tapping/ticking. Went up there but no sign of any animal. There's a slight smell, hard to describe, kind of smoky/musky, but could be just something to do w the house (?pipes overheating?). Found one hole under eaves leading outside but only about 5 inches by 3. Noises sound like something bigger than that. Checked the garden, no sign of a den, no sign of any holes where something could have dug under the wall (5 feet high). Any ideas what it could be/suggestions what to do about it? Got young kids so if it could be dangerous need to know. Thanks.*

The Wildwatcher board wasn't a hotbed of action, but Pat's thread had got noticed: over a hundred replies. The first few told him he had rats or possibly squirrels and he should call an exterminator. He came back a couple of hours later to answer: *Thanks guys think its just 1 animal, never hear noises in more than 1 place at a time. Don't think its a rat or a squirrel – thought that at first but put down mousetrap w big lump of peanut butter, no go, plenty of action that nite but trap not touched in the morn. So something that doesn't eat peanut butter!*

Someone asked what time of day the animal was most active. That evening Pat posted: *At first only heard it at night after we went to bed, but could be because I wasn't listening for it during the day. Started paying attention about a week ago and its all times of day/ night, no pattern. Last 3 days noticed a real uptick in noise when my wife is cooking, specially meat — thing goes mental. Sort of creepy to be honest w you. Tonight she was making dinner (beef casserole) + I was w the kids in my sons room which is over kitchen. Thing was scrabbling + banging like trying to get through ceiling. Right above my sons bed so am a bit worried. Any more ideas?*

People were starting to get interested. They thought it was a stoat, a mink, a marten; they posted photos, slim sinuous animals, mouths wide to show delicate, wicked teeth. People suggested that Pat put down flour in the attic to get the animal's pawprints, take pictures of those and its scat and post them on the board. Then someone wanted to know what the big deal was: *Why r u even here??? Just get rat poison put it in the attic n bobs ur uncle. Or r u 1 of those bleedin hearts that dont beleive in killing vermin?? If u r then u deserve wat u get.*

Everyone forgot all about Pat's attic and started yelling at each other about animal rights. It got heated – everyone called everyone else a murderer – but when Pat came back the next day, he kept a level head and stayed well away from the flames. *Rather not go for poison except as total last resort. There are gaps in attic floor leading down into space (?8 inches deep?) between beams + ceiling of rooms below. Have had a look in w torch + couldn't see anything dodgy but don't want it crawling in there and dying, or it'll stink the place out + I'll have to take up attic floor to get it. Same reason why I didn't just board up hole under eaves, don't want to trap it inside by mistake. Haven't seen any scat but will keep a lookout + take advice on prints.*

Nobody paid any attention to him – someone had, inevitably, compared someone to Hitler. Later that day, the admin locked the thread. Pat-the-lad never posted again.

This was obviously where the cameras and the holes in the walls came in, somehow, but they still didn't quite add up. I couldn't picture that level-headed guy chasing a stoat around his house with a lump hammer like something out of *Caddyshack*, but neither could I picture him sitting back and watching on a baby monitor while something gnawed chunks out of his walls, especially with his kids just a few feet away.

Either way, this should have meant we could leave the monitors and the holes behind. Like I had told Kieran, a mink hadn't convinced Conor Brennan to commit mass murder; the problem belonged to Jenny or to her estate agent, not to us. But I had given Richie my word: we were going to investigate Pat Spain, and anything odd in his life needed explaining. I told myself there was plenty of silver lining – the more loose ends we tied up, the fewer chances for the defence to create confusion in court.

I made myself tea and cereal – the thought of Conor eating his jail breakfast gave me a hard-edged thump of grim pleasure – and took my time rereading the thread. I know Murder Ds who go searching for mementoes like that, for any thread-fine echo of the victim's voice, any watery reflection of his living face. They want him to come alive for them. I don't. Those torn scraps won't help me solve the case, and I've got no time for the cheap pathos of it, the easy, excruciating poignancy of watching someone meander happily towards the cliff edge. I let the dead stay dead.

Pat was different. Conor Brennan had tried so hard to deface him, weld a killer's mask onto his wrecked flesh for all eternity. Catching a glimpse of Pat's own face felt like a blow on the side of the angels.

I left a message on Larry's phone, asking him to get his outdoorsy man to check out the Wildwatcher thread, head down to Brianstown ASAP and see what he thought of the wildlife possibilities. Then I e-mailed Kieran back. *Thanks for that. After that reception, looks like Pat Spain took his wildlife issues to some other site. We need to find out where. Keep me updated.*

It was twenty to noon when I got into the incident room. All the floaters were either out working or out on coffee break, but Richie was at his desk, ankles wrapped around the legs of his chair like a teenager, nose to nose with his computer screen. 'Howya,' he said, without looking up. 'The lads picked up your man's car. Dark-blue Opel Corsa, 03D.'

'Style icon that he is.' I handed him a paper cup of coffee. 'In case you didn't get a chance. Where'd he have it parked?'

'Thanks. Up on that hill overlooking the south end of the bay. He had it stashed off the road, in among the trees, so the lads missed it till daylight.'

A good mile from the estate, maybe more. Conor had been taking no chances. 'Beautiful. It's gone to Larry?'

'Towing it now.'

I nodded at the computer. 'Anything good?'

Richie shook his head. 'Your man's never been arrested, under Conor Brennan, anyway. Couple of speeding tickets, but the dates and locations don't match anywhere I was posted.'

'Still trying to work out why he rings a bell?'

'Yeah. I'm thinking it could be from a long time back, 'cause in my head he's younger, like maybe twenty. Might be nothing, but I just want to know.'

I tossed my coat over the back of my chair and took a swig of my coffee. 'I'm wondering if someone else knows Conor from before, too. Pretty soon we need to pull in Fiona Rafferty, give her a look at him and see how she reacts. He got his hands on the Spains' door key somehow – I don't believe that crap he gave us about finding it on a dawn wander – and she's the only one who had it. I'm having a hard time seeing that as coincidence.'

At that point Quigley oiled up behind me and tapped me on the arm with his morning tabloid. '*I* heard,' he breathed, like it was a dirty secret, 'that you got someone for your big-deal case last night.'

Quigley always gives me the urge to straighten my tie and check my teeth for scraps. He smelled like he had eaten breakfast at a fast-food joint, which would explain a lot, and there was a sheen of grease on his upper lip. 'You heard right,' I said, taking a step back from him.

He widened his pouchy little eyes at me. 'That was quick, wasn't it?'

'That's what we're paid for, chum: getting the bad guys. You should try it sometime.'

Quigley's mouth pursed up. 'God, you're awful defensive, Kennedy. Are you having doubts, is it? Thinking maybe you've got the wrong fella?'

'Stay tuned. I doubt it, but go ahead and keep your champagne on ice, just in case.'

'Now hang on there. Don't take out your insecurities on me. I'm only being pleased for you, so I am.'

He was pointing his paper at my chest, all puffed up with injured outrage – feeling hard done by is the fuel that keeps Quigley running. 'Sweet of you,' I said, turning away to my desk to let him know we were finished. 'One of these days, if I'm bored, I'll take you out on a big case and show you how it's done.'

'Oh, that's right. Bring this one in and you'll be getting all the big fancy cases again, won't you? Ah, that'd be great for you, so it would. Some of us' – to Richie – 'some of us just want to solve murders, the media attention doesn't matter to us, but our Kennedy's a little different. He likes the spotlight.' Quigley waggled the newspaper: ANGELS BUTCHERED IN THEIR BEDS, a blurry holiday shot of the Spains laughing on some beach. 'Well, nothing wrong with that, I suppose. As long as the job gets done.'

'You want to solve murders?' Richie asked, puzzled.

Quigley ignored that. To me: 'Wouldn't it be great altogether if you got this one right? Then maybe everyone would put that *other time* behind them.' He actually had a hand lifted to pat my arm, but I gave him a stare and he thought better of it. 'Good luck, eh? We'll all be hoping you've got the right fella.' He shot me a smirk and a little wave of his crossed fingers, and waddled off to try and bring down someone else's morning.

Richie waved bye-bye with a manic cheesy grin, and watched him go out the door. He said, 'What other time?'

The stack of reports and witness statements on my desk was shaping up nicely. I flicked through them. 'One of my cases went pear-shaped, a couple of years back. I put my money on the wrong guy, ended up missing the collar. Quigley was talking shite, though: at this stage, no one except him even remembers that. He's hanging on to it for dear life because it made his year.'

Richie nodded. He didn't look one bit surprised. 'The face on him, when you said that about showing him how it's done: pure poison. Bit of history there, yeah?'

One of the floaters had a nasty habit of typing in all caps, which was going to have to go. 'No history. Quigley is shit at his job, and he figures that's everyone's fault but his. I get cases he'll never get, which makes it my fault he gets stuck with the dregs, and I take them down, which makes him look worse, which makes it my fault that he couldn't solve a game of Cluedo.'

'Two more brain cells and he'd be a Brussels sprout,' Richie said. He was leaning back in his chair, biting a thumbnail and still watching the door where Quigley had gone out. 'Good thing, too. He'd only love a chance to put the boot into you. If he wasn't thick as pig shite, you'd be in trouble.'

I put the statement sheets down. 'What's Quigley been saying about me?'

Richie's feet started a soft-shoe shuffle under his chair. 'Just that. What you heard there.'

'And before that?' Richie tried to look blank, but his feet were still going. 'Richie. This isn't about my tender feelings. If he's undermining our working relationship here, I need to know.'

'He's not. I don't even remember what he said. Nothing you could put your finger on.'

'There never is, with Quigley. What did he say?'

A twitchy shrug. 'Just some crap about the emperor not wearing as many clothes as he thinks, and pride goes before a fall. It didn't even make any sense.'

I wished I had smacked that little shit down harder when he gave me the chance. 'And?'

'And nothing. That's when I got rid of him. He was giving it "Slow and steady does it"; I asked him why slow and steady wasn't doing it for him. He didn't like that.'

It startled me, the small ridiculous dart of warmth at the thought of this kid fighting my corner. I said, 'And that's not why you were worried that I was jumping the gun with Conor Brennan.'

'*No!* Man, that was nothing to do with Quigley. *Nothing.*'

'It'd better not be. If you think Quigley's on your side, you're in for a big shock. You're young and promising, which makes it your fault that he's a middle-aged loser. Given the choice, I'm not sure which of us he'd throw under a bus first.'

'I know that, too. That fat fuck told me the other day I might *feel more at home* back in Motor Vehicles, unless I have too many *emotional connections* with suspects there. I don't listen to anything he says.'

'Good. Don't. He's a black hole: get too close and he'll drag you down with him. Always stay far away from negativity, old son.'

'I stay far away from useless *pricks*. He's not dragging me anywhere. How the hell is he on this squad?'

I shrugged. 'Three possibilities: he's related to someone, he's shagging someone, or he's got something on someone. Take your pick. Personally, I figure if he was connected I'd know by this time, and he doesn't look like much of a femme fatale to me. That leaves blackmail. Which gives you another good reason to leave Quigley alone.'

Richie's eyebrows went up. He said, 'You think he's dangerous? Seriously? That thick bastard?'

'Don't underestimate Quigley. He's thick, all right, but not as thick as you're thinking, or he wouldn't be here. He's not danger- ous to me – or to you, for that matter, as long as you don't do anything stupid – but that's not because he's a harmless idiot. Think of him as the gastric flu: he can make your life smell pretty bad and he takes forever to shake off, so you try to avoid him, but he can't do you any serious damage, not unless you're weak already. Here's the thing, though: if you're vulnerable, if he gets a chance to take hold, then yeah. He could be dangerous.'

'You're the boss,' Richie said cheerfully – the image had made him happy, even if he still didn't sound particularly convinced. 'I'll stay away from Diarrhoea Man.'

I didn't bother trying not to grin. 'And that's the other thing. Don't go poking him with sticks. I know the rest of us do it, and we shouldn't either, but we're not new boys. No matter how much of an arse Quigley is, giving him cheek makes you look like an uppity little brat – not just to him, but to the rest of the squad. You're playing straight into Quigley's hands.'

Richie grinned back. 'Fair enough. He asks for it, but.'

'He does. You don't have to answer.'

He put a hand over his heart. 'I'll be good. Honest. What's the plan for today?'

I went back to my stack of paper. 'Today we're going to find out why Conor Brennan did what he did. He's entitled to his eight hours' sleep, so we can't touch him for another couple of hours, minimum. I'm in no hurry. I say we let him wait for us this time.' Once they're under arrest, you have up to three days before you have to charge them or cut them loose, and I was planning on taking as much of that as we needed. It's only on TV that the story ends when the confession's on tape and the hand- cuffs click home. In a real investigation, that click is just the beginning. What it changes is this: your suspect goes tumbling from the top of your priority list straight to the bottom. You can go for days without seeing his face, once you have him where you want him. All you care about is building the walls to keep him there.

I said, 'We'll go talk to O'Kelly now. Then we'll have chats with the floaters, have them start working through Conor's life and the Spains'. They need to find an overlap point where the Spains might have caught his eye – a party they all went to, a company that hired Pat to do their recruitment and Conor to do their web design. He said he's been stalking them for about a year now, which means we want the floaters focusing on 2008. Meanwhile, you and I are going to search Conor's gaff, see if we can fill in a few cracks – pick up anything that might give us a motive, anything that might point us towards how he got hold of either the Spains or the keys.'

Richie was fingering a nick on his jaw – the shave had been unnecessary, but at least it showed the right attitude – and trying to find the right way to ask. I said, 'Don't worry: I'm not ignoring Pat Spain. I've got something to show you.'

I switched on my computer and pulled up Wildwatcher. Richie scooted his chair across so he could read over my shoulder.

'Huh,' he said, when he was finished. 'I guess that could maybe explain the video monitors. You get people like that, yeah? People who get way into watching animals. Set up whole CCTV systems to keep an eye on the foxes in their back garden.'

'Like watching *Big Brother*, only with smarter contestants. I don't see that happening here, though. Pat's obviously worried about the animal coming into contact with the kids; he wouldn't encourage it just for kicks. He sounds like he just wants to get rid of the thing.'

'He does, yeah. Long way from that to half a dozen cameras.' A silence, while Richie reread. 'The holes in the walls,' he said, carefully. 'It'd take a pretty big animal to make those.'

'Maybe, maybe not. I've got people on that. Has someone brought in a building inspector to look at the gaff, check for subsidence and whatever?'

'Report's in the pile. Graham got it done.' Whoever that was. 'Short version, the house is in bits: damp going up half the walls, subsidence – the cracks – and something's wrong with the plumbing, I couldn't work out what, but the gist is the whole place would've needed re-plumbing within a year or two. Sinéad Gogan wasn't wrong about the builders: load of bloody chancers. Slap the houses up, sell them and get out before anyone could suss their game. But your man says none of the problems would account for the holes in the walls. The one in the eaves, that could've been the subsidence; the ones in the walls, nah.' Richie's eyes came up to meet mine. 'If Pat made those holes himself, chasing after a squirrel . . .'

I said, 'It wasn't a squirrel. And we don't know that he did. Who's jumping the gun now?'

'I'm only saying *if*. Knocking holes in your own walls . . .'

'It's drastic, all right. But you tell me: there's a mysterious animal running around your gaff, you want it gone, you don't have the dosh for an exterminator. What do you do?'

'Board up the hole under the eaves. If you've trapped the yoke inside by mistake, you give it a couple of days to get hungry, take off the boards so it can do a legger, then try again. If it still won't leave, you put down poison. If it dies in the walls and stinks the place out, *then* you bring out the hammer. Not before.' Richie shoved himself off my desk so that his chair rolled back towards his own. 'If Pat made those holes, man, then Conor's not the only one whose mind wasn't OK.'

'Like I said. We'll find out. Until then—'

'I know. Keep my gob shut about it.'

Richie swung his jacket on and started poking at the knot in his tie, trying to check it without ruining it. I said, 'Looking good. Let's go find the Super.'

He had forgotten all about Quigley. I hadn't. The part I hadn't told Richie: Quigley doesn't go near a fair fight. His personal talent is a hyena's nose for anything weak or bleeding, and he doesn't take people on unless he's positive he can take them down. It was obvious why he was targeting Richie. The newbie, the working-class boy who needed to prove himself half a dozen different ways, the smart-arsed kid who couldn't keep a leash on his tongue: it was easy and safe, to goad him along while he talked himself into trouble. What I couldn't work out, what might have worried me if I hadn't been floating on such a good mood, was why Quigley was targeting me.

O'Kelly was a happy camper. 'The very men I've been waiting for,' he said, swivelling his chair to face us, when we knocked on his office door. He pointed at chairs – we had to clear away stacks of e-mail printouts and holiday applications before we could sit down; O'Kelly's office always looks like the paperwork is on the verge of winning – and held up his copy of our report. 'Go on. Tell me I'm not dreaming.'

I gave him the rundown. 'The little fucker,' O'Kelly said, when I was done, but without much heat. The Super's worked Murder for a long time and seen a lot of things. 'The confession checks out?'

I said, 'What we've got checks out, yeah, but he started looking for his sleep break before we could get into details. We'll take another shot at him later, or tomorrow.'

'But the little fucker's our man. You've got enough that I can go to the media, tell them the people of Brianstown are safe in their beds again. Is that what you're telling me?'

Richie was looking at me too. I said, 'It's safe out there.'

'That's what I like to hear. I've been beating back the reporters with a stick; I swear half the little bastards are hoping the fucker'll strike again, keep them in a job. This'll put a stop to their gallop.' O'Kelly leaned back in his chair with a satisfied sigh and aimed a stubby forefinger in Richie's direction. 'Curran, I'm going to hold my hand up and say I didn't want you on this one. Did Kennedy tell you that?'

Richie shook his head. 'No, sir.'

'Well, I didn't. Thought you were too green to wipe your own arse without someone holding the jacks roll for you.' In the corner of my eye I caught the twitch of Richie's mouth, but he nodded gravely. 'I was wrong. Maybe I should use rookies more often, give those lazy lumps out there something to think about. Fair play to you.'

'Thanks, sir.'

'And as for this fella' – a thumb-jerk at me – 'there's men out there that would've told me not to let him within a mile of this one, either. Make him work his way back up, they said. Make him prove he's still got what it takes.'

A day earlier I would have been starving to find the fuckers and stuff that down their throats. Now the six o'clock news would do it for me. O'Kelly was watching me, sharp-eyed. 'And I hope I've done that, sir,' I said smoothly.

'I knew you would, or I wouldn't have risked it. I told them where they could stick it, and I was right. Welcome back.'

'Good to be back, sir,' I said.

'I bet it is. I was right about you, Kennedy, and you were right about this young fella here. There's plenty of lads on this squad that would still be holding their dicks in their hands and waiting for a confession to land in their laps. When are you charging your little fucker?'

I said, 'I'd like the full three days. I want to be sure we don't leave any cracks in this one.'

'That,' O'Kelly told Richie, 'that's our man Kennedy all over. Once he's got his teeth into someone, God help the poor bastard. Watch and learn. Go on, go on' – a magnanimous wave of his hand – 'take all the time you need. You've earned it. I'll get you the extensions. Anything else you want, while you're at it? More men? More overtime? Just say the word.'

'We're all right for the moment, sir. If anything changes, I'll let you know.'

'Do that,' O'Kelly said. He nodded at us, squared off the pages of our report and tossed it onto a stack: conversation over. 'Now get out there and show the rest of that shower how it's done.'

Out in the corridor, a safe distance from O'Kelly's door, Richie caught my eye. He said, 'So does this mean I'm allowed to wipe my own arse now, yeah?'

Plenty of people take the piss out of the Super, but he's my boss and he's always looked out for me, and I take both of those seriously. 'It's a metaphor,' I said.

'I got that. What's the jacks roll meant to be?'

'Quigley?' I said, and we went back into the incident room laughing.

Conor's place was a basement flat, in a tall brick house with the paint peeling off the window-frames; his door was at the back, down a flight of narrow steps with rusted railings. Inside, the flat – bedroom, tiny living-room-cum-kitchen, tinier bathroom – looked like he had forgotten it existed a long time ago. It wasn't filthy, or not quite, but there were cobwebs in the corners, food scraps in the kitchen sink and things ground into the linoleum. The fridge was ready-meals and Sprite. Conor's clothes were good quality but a couple of years old, clean but half-folded in crumpled heaps at the bottom of the wardrobe. His paperwork was in a cardboard box in a corner of the living room – bills, bank statements, receipts, all tossed in together; some of the envelopes hadn't even been opened. With a little work, I could probably have put my finger on the exact month when he had let go of his life.

No obviously bloody clothes, no clothes in the washing machine, no clothes hanging up to dry; no bloody trainers – no trainers at all – but the two pairs of shoes in the wardrobe were a size ten. I said, 'I've never seen a guy his age who doesn't own a single pair of trainers.'

'Ditched them,' Richie said. He had flipped Conor's mattress up against the wall and was running a gloved hand over the under-side. 'I'd say that was the first thing he did, when he got home Monday night: got some clean clothes on and dumped the dirty ones as quick as he could.'

'Which means nearby, if we're lucky. We'll get a few of the lads to start searching the neighbourhood bins.' I was going through the heaps of clothes, checking pockets and feeling seams for damp. It was cold in there: the heating – a plug-in oil heater – was off, and a chill struck straight up through the floor. 'Even if we never find the bloody stuff, though, it could still come in useful. If young Conor tries to go for some kind of insanity defence – and let's face it, that's basically the only option he's got left – then we point out that he tried to cover up what he'd done, which means he knew it was wrong, which means he was as sane as you and me. Legally, anyway.'

I put in a call for some lucky searchers to do bin duty – the flat was near enough to underground that I had to go outside to get a signal on my phone; Conor wouldn't have been able to talk to his friends even if he had had any. Then we moved on to the sitting room.

Even with the lights on, the room was dim. The window, at head-level, looked out on a flat grey wall; I had to crane my neck sideways to catch a narrow rectangle of sky, birds whirling against heavy cloud. The most promising stuff – a monster computer with cornflakes in the keyboard, a battered mobile – was on Conor's desk, and it was stuff we couldn't touch without Kieran. Beside the desk was an old wooden fruit crate, with a tattered label of a dark-haired girl holding up an orange and smiling. I flipped the lid off. Inside was Conor's stash of souvenirs.

A blue checked scarf, faded from washing, with a few long pale hairs still caught in the weave. A half-burnt green candle in a glass jar, filling the box with the sweet, nostalgic scent of ripe apples. A page from a palm-sized notepad, crumples carefully smoothed out: a phone doodle, fast strong strokes, a rugby player running with the ball in his elbow. The mug, a cracked tea-stained thing painted with poppies. The handful of elastic bands, arranged as neatly as treasure. A kid's crayon drawing, four yellow heads, blue sky, birds overhead and black cat sprawled in a flowering tree. A green plastic magnet shaped like an X, faded and chewed. A dark-blue pen with gold curly writing: *Golden Bay Resort – your door to Paradise!*

I reached out one finger and pushed the scarf away from the bottom corner of the drawing. EMMA, in those wobbly capitals, and beside it the date. The rust-brown that smeared the sky and the flowers wasn't paint. She had drawn the picture on Monday, probably in school, with a handful of hours left in her life.

There was a long silence. We knelt on the floor, smelling wood and apples.

'So,' I said. 'There's our proof. He was in the house the night they died.'

Richie said, 'I know that.'

Another silence, this one stretched tighter, while we each waited for the other to break it. Upstairs, high heels went clicking sharply across a bare floor. 'OK,' I said, and fitted the lid gently onto the crate. 'OK. Let's bag it, tag it and move on.'

The ancient orange sofa was just about visible under jumpers, DVDs, empty plastic bags. We worked our way through the layers, checking for blood and shaking things out and dumping them onto the floor. 'For Christ's sake,' I said, unearthing a TV guide for the beginning of June and a half-full packet of salt and vinegar crisps. 'Look at this.'

Richie gave a wry grin and held up a wad of paper towel that had been used to clean up something like coffee. 'Seen worse.'

'So have I, but there's still no excuse. I don't care if the guy was skint: self-respect is free. The Spains were just as broke as he was, and their gaff was spotless.' Even at my lowest, just after Laura and I split, I never left chunks of food to rot in my sink. 'It's hardly as if he was too busy to pick up a J cloth.'

Richie had got down to the sofa cushions; he pulled one out and ran his hand around the edges of the frame, in among the crumbs. 'Twenty-four hours a day in this place, no job to go to, no money to go out: that'd have your head melted. Not sure I'd be arsed cleaning, either.'

'He wasn't stuck here twenty-four-seven, remember. Conor still had places to go. He was a busy boy, out at Brianstown.'

Richie unzipped the cushion cover and slid a hand inside. 'True enough,' he said. 'And you know something? That's why this place is a tip. It wasn't his home. That hide on the estate, that was his home. And that was as clean as you like.'

We did the search right: undersides of drawers, backs of book-shelves, inside the boxes of out-of-date processed crap in the freezer – we even used Conor's charger to plug Richie's phone into every socket in the place, to make sure none of them was a dud hiding a cache spot. The paperwork box was going back to

HQ with us, in case Conor had used an ATM two minutes after Jenny or kept a receipt for designing Pat's company's website, but we took a quick look just for kicks. His bank statements followed the same general depressing pattern as Pat and Jenny's: a decent income and solid savings, then a smaller income and shrinking savings, then broke. Since Conor was self-employed, he had tanked less dramatically than Pat Spain – gradually the cheques got smaller, the gaps between them got larger – but he had done it earlier. The slide had started in late 2007; by the middle of 2008, he had been dipping into his savings. It had been months since anything went into his account.

By half-two we were finishing up, putting stuff back where it belonged, which in this case meant rearranging it from our focused mess to Conor's unfocused one. It had looked better our way.

I said, 'You know what strikes me about this place?'

Richie was shoving books back onto the bookshelf by the handful, setting little eddies of dust swirling. 'Yeah?'

'There's no trace of anyone else in here. No girlfriend's toothbrush, no photos of Conor with his mates, no birthday cards, no "Ring Dad" or "8pm, meet Joe at the pub" on the calendar: nothing that says Conor's ever met another human being in his life.' I slid DVDs onto their rack. 'Remember what I said about him having nothing to love?'

'Could be all digital. Loads of people our age, they keep everything on their phones, or on the computer – photos, appointments—' A book went down on the shelf with a flat bang and Richie whirled round to me, his mouth open, his hands going up to clasp the back of his head. '*Shit*,' he said. '*Photos.*'

'Is there a rest of that sentence, old son?'

'*Shit*. I *knew* I'd seen him. No bleeding wonder he cared about them—'

'Richie.'

Richie rubbed his hands over his cheeks, caught a deep breath and blew it out again. 'Remember last night, yeah, you asked Conor which one of the Spains did he hope had made it? And he said Emma? No bleeding wonder, man. He's her godfather.'

The framed photo on Emma's bookshelf: a featureless baby in white lace, Fiona all dressed up, a floppy-haired guy at her shoulder. I remembered him boyish, smiling; I couldn't see his face. I said, 'Are you sure?'

'I am, yeah. I'm sure. That picture in her room, remember? He was younger, he's lost a load of weight since, got his hair cut short, but I swear to God, it's him.'

The photo had gone to HQ, along with everything else identifying anyone who had known the Spains. 'Let's double-check,' I said. Richie was already pulling out his phone. We almost ran up the steps.

Inside five minutes, the floater on tipline duty had dug out the picture, taken a photo of it on his phone and e-mailed it to Richie's. It was small and starting to pixelate, and Conor looked happier and better rested than I could ever have pictured him, but it was him, all right: solid in his grown-up suit, holding Emma like she was made of crystal, with Fiona reaching across him to put a finger into one tiny hand.

'Fucking hell,' Richie said softly, staring down at the phone.

'Yeah,' I said. 'That about sums it up.'

'No wonder he knew all about Pat and Jenny's relationship.'

'Right. The little prick: he was sitting back laughing at us, the whole time.'

A corner of Richie's mouth twitched. 'Didn't look like he was laughing to me.'

'He won't be when he sees that picture, anyway. But he's not going to see it till we're good and ready. I want all our ducks in a row before we go anywhere near Conor again. You wanted a motive? I'd bet a lot of money that trail starts right here.'

'It could go back a long way.' Richie tapped the screen. 'That there, that's six years ago. If Conor and the Spains were best buds back then, they'd already known each other for a while. We're talking college at least, probably school. The motive could be anywhere along the way. Something happens, everyone forgets all about it, then Conor's life goes to shite and all of a sudden something from fifteen years ago feels like a huge big deal again . . .'

He was talking like he believed, at last, that Conor was our boy. I bent closer over the phone, to hide a smile. 'Or it could be a lot more recent. Sometime in the last six years, the relationship went so far south that the only way Conor could see his goddaughter was through binoculars. I'd love to know what happened there.'

'We'll find out. Talk to Fiona, talk to all their old mates—'

'Yeah, we will. We've got the little bastard now.' I wanted to grab Richie in a headlock, like we were a pair of idiot teenagers bonding by giving each other dead arms. 'Richie, my friend, you just earned your whole year's salary.'

Richie grinned, reddening. 'Ah, no. We'd have worked it out sooner or later.'

'We would, yeah. But sooner is an awful lot better. We can take half a dozen floaters off trying to work out if Conor and Jenny bought petrol at the same station in 2008, and that gives us half a dozen extra chances at finding those clothes before a bin lorry takes them away . . . You're the Man of the Match, my friend. Give yourself a big pat on the back.'

He shrugged, rubbing his nose to cover the blush. ''S just luck.'

'Bollix. There's no such thing. Luck only comes in useful on the back of good solid detective work, and that's exactly what you had there. You tell me: what do you want to do next?'

'Fiona Rafferty. Fast as we can.'

'Hell yes. You ring her; she liked you better than me.' Admitting it didn't even sting. 'See how soon you can get her to come in to HQ. Get her down there inside two hours, and lunch is on me.'

Fiona was at the hospital — in the background, that machine was steadily beeping away — and even her 'Hello?' sounded exhausted to breaking point.

Richie said, 'Ms Rafferty, it's Detective Curran. Have you got a minute?'

A second's silence. 'Hang on,' Fiona said. Muffled, through a hand over the phone: 'I've got to take this. I'll only be outside, OK? Call me if you want me.' The click of a door, and the beeping vanished. 'Hello?'

Richie said, 'Sorry to take you away from your sister. How's she getting on?'

A moment's silence. 'Not great. Same as yesterday. That's when you talked to her, right? Before we were even allowed in.'

There was an edge to Fiona's voice. Richie said, calmly, 'For a few minutes, yeah, we did. We didn't want to tire her out too much.'

'Are you going to come back and keep asking her questions? Because don't. She hasn't got anything to tell you. She doesn't remember anything. Mostly she can't even *talk*. She just cries. All of us just cry.' Fiona's voice was shaking. 'Can you just . . . leave her alone? *Please?*'

Richie was learning: he didn't answer that. He said, 'I rang because we've got some news for you. It'll be on the telly later, but we figured you'd rather hear this from us. We're after arresting someone.'

Silence. Then: 'It wasn't Pat. I told you. I *told* you.'

Richie's eyes met mine for a second. 'Yeah, you did.'

'Who— Oh, God. Who is he? *Why* did he? *Why?*'

'We're still working on that. We figured maybe you could give us a hand. Can you come into Dublin Castle, have a talk about it? We'll give you the details there.'

Another second of dead air, while Fiona tried to get hold of all this. 'Yeah. Yeah, absolutely. Just, can I, can it wait a while? My mum went home, she's getting some sleep, I don't want to leave Jenny by herself – Mum's coming back at six, I could be down to you by like seven. Would that be too late?'

Richie raised his eyebrows at me; I nodded. 'That's perfect,' he said. 'And listen, Ms Rafferty: do us a favour and don't say it to your sister yet. Make sure your mother doesn't, either. OK? Once the suspect's been charged and all, we can tell her, but it's still early days; we don't want to be upsetting her if anything goes wrong. Will you promise me that?'

'Yeah. I won't say anything.' A quick catch of breath. 'This guy. Please. Who is he?'

Richie said gently, 'We'll talk later. Take care of your sister, yeah? And of yourself. See you soon.' He hung up before Fiona could keep asking.

I checked my watch. It was coming up to three o'clock: four hours to wait. 'No free lunch for you, sunshine.'

Richie tucked his phone away and gave me a quick grin. 'And here I was going to order the lobster.'

'Would you settle for tuna salad? I'd like to head up to Brianstown, check in with the search teams and give you another shot at the Gogan kid, but we should pick up something to eat on the way. It looks bad for me if you drop dead from starvation.'

'Tuna salad's good. Wouldn't want to wreck your rep.'

He was still grinning. Modesty or no, Richie was a happy man. 'I appreciate your concern,' I said. 'You finish up inside. I'll give Larry a bell, tell him to bring his boys down here, and then we can get moving.'

Richie went bouncing back down the stairs two at a time. '*Scorcher*,' Larry said delightedly. 'Have I told you lately that I love you?'

'It never gets old. What've I done now?'

'That car. Everything a man could want, and it's not even my birthday.'

'Fill me in. If I'm sending you pressies, I deserve to know what's in them.'

'Well, the first bit wasn't *in* the car, exactly. When the boys went to tow it, a key ring fell out of the wheel well. We've got the car keys, we've got what looks like a pair of house keys – one Chubb, one Yale – and, drum roll please, we've got a key to the Spains' back door.'

'Now that,' I said, 'is sweet.' The alarm code, and now this: all we needed was where Conor had got the key – and one obvious answer was coming in for a chat in a few hours' time – and the whole tangled question of access would be neatly tied up in a bow. Pat and Jenny's nice solid house had been as secure as a tent on the open strand.

'I thought you'd like it. And once we actually got into the car, oh my. How I love cars. I've seen guys who practically took baths in pure bleach after they finished doing their business, but did they bother to clean their cars? No, they did not. This one's an absolute *nest* of hairs and fibres and dirt and all things nice, and if I were a betting man, I'd bet you plenty that we'll get at *least* one match between the car and the crime scene. We've also got a muddy shoeprint on the driver's floor mat: we'll have to work it up to see how much detail we can get, but it's from a man's trainer, size ten or eleven.'

'Even sweeter.'

'And then, of course,' Larry said demurely, 'there's the blood.'

By that stage I wasn't even surprised. Every once in a while this job gives you a day like that, a day when all the dice roll your way, when you just have to stretch out your hand and a plump juicy piece of evidence drops into it. 'How much?'

'Smears *everywhere*. Only a couple of smudges on the door handle and the steering wheel, he'd taken his gloves off by the time he got back to the car, but the driver's seat is covered – we'll send it all off for DNA, but I'm going to go out on a limb and guess it might just match up to your vics. Tell me I make you happy.'

'Happiest man in the world,' I said. 'And in exchange, I've got another pressie for you. Richie and I are at the suspect's flat, having a quick look around. Whenever you've got a moment, we'd love you to come down here and give it a proper going-over. No blood as far as we can see – sorry about that – but we've got another computer and another phone, to keep young Kieran busy, and I'm sure you'll find something to interest you too.'

'My cup runneth over. I'll be down as fast as I can skip. Will you and your new friend still be around?'

'Probably not. We're heading back to the crime scene. Is your badger-tracking guy out there?'

'He is indeed. I'll tell him to hang on for you. And I'll save your great big hug for later. Ciao ciao.' Larry hung up.

The case was coming together. I could feel it, an actual physical sensation, as if it were my own vertebrae slipping into alignment with small confident clicks, letting me straighten and take a belly-deep breath for the first time in days. Killester is near the sea, and for a second I thought I caught a whiff of salt air, vivid and wild, slicing straight through all the city smells to find me. As I pocketed my phone and started down the stairs, I caught myself smiling, up at the grey sky and the turning birds.

Richie was piling crap back onto the sofa. I said, 'Larry's having a blast with Conor's car. Hairs, fibres, a footprint, and – get this – a key to the Spains' back door. Richie, my friend, this is our lucky day.'

'Great. That's great, yeah.' Richie didn't look up.

I said, 'What is it?'

He turned around like he was dragging himself up from a sucking dream. 'Nothing. I'm grand.'

His face was pinched and focused, turned inwards on itself. Something had happened.

I said, 'Richie.'

'I just need that sandwich. Felt a bit crap all of a sudden, you know that way? Low blood sugar, probably. And the air in here, and all—'

'Richie. If something's up, you need to tell me.'

Richie's eyes came up to meet mine. He looked young and wildly lost, and when his lips parted I knew it was to ask for help. Then something in his face clicked shut and he said, 'Nothing's up. Seriously. Will we go, yeah?'

When I think about the Spain case, from deep inside endless nights, this is the moment I remember. Everything else, every other slip and stumble along the way, could have been redeemed. This is the one I clench tight because of how sharp it slices. Cold still air, a weak ray of sun glowing on the wall outside the window, smell of stale bread and apples.

I knew Richie was lying to me. He had seen something, heard something, fitted a piece into place and caught a glimpse of some brand-new picture. It was my job to keep pushing until he came clean. I understand that; I understood it then, in that low-ceilinged flat with the dust prickling my hands and clogging the air. I understood – or I would have, if I had pulled myself together, through the fatigue and all the other things that are no excuse – that Richie was my responsibility.

I thought he had twigged something that proved once and for all that Conor was our man, and he wanted to nurse the sting to his pride in private for a little while. I thought something had pointed him towards a motive and he wanted to move a few steps further down that road, till he was sure, before he brought me with him. I thought of the other partners on the squad, the ones going strong after longer than most marriages: the deft balance with which they moved around each other; the trust as solid and practical as a coat or a mug, something never talked about because it was always in use.

I said, 'Yeah. You could probably do with some more coffee, too; I know I could. Let's get out of here.'

Richie tossed the last of Conor's crap onto the sofa, picked up the big evidence bag that held the orange crate and brushed past me, pulling off a glove with his teeth. I heard him heaving the crate up the steps.

Before I switched off the light I took one last look around, scanning every inch for the mysterious thing that had blazed up at him out of nowhere. The flat was silent, sullen, already closing back in on itself and turning deserted again. There was nothing there.

# 12

Richie made a big effort, on the drive to Broken Harbour: keeping the chat going, telling me some long rueful story about when he was a uniform and had to deal with two ancient brothers beating the shite out of each other for some reason to do with sheep – the brothers were both deaf, their mountainy accents were too thick for Richie, no one had a clue what was going on and the story ended with them joining forces against the city boy and Richie leaving their house with a walking stick jabbing him in the arse. He was clowning it up, trying to keep the conversation on safe ground. I played along: minor uniform fuckups of my own, things a friend and I shouldn't have got up to in training college, stuff with punchlines. It would have been a good drive, a good laugh, except for the slim shadow lying between us, dimming the windscreen, thickening whenever we left a silence.

The sub-aqua team had found a fishing boat that had been at the bottom of the harbour for a long time, and they made it clear that that was the most interesting thing they were expecting to find. They were faceless and sleek in their dive suits, turning the harbour military and sinister. We thanked them, shook their slick gloved hands and told them to go home. The searchers, who had been working their way across the estate, were dirty, tired and pissed off: they had found eight knives of varying shapes and sizes, all of which had clearly been planted overnight by teenagers who thought they were hilarious geniuses sticking it to the man, and all of which would have to be checked out. I told the team to move the search up to the hill where Conor had hidden his car. According to his story, the weapons had gone into the water, but Richie was right about this much: Conor was playing games with

us. Until we knew exactly what games and why, everything he said
needed checking.

A rangy guy with blond dreadlocks and a dusty parka was
sitting on the Spains' garden wall, smoking a rollie and looking
dodgy. I said, 'Can we help you?'

'Howya,' he said, mashing out his smoke on the sole of his shoe.
'Detectives, yeah? Tom. Larry said you wanted me to hang on for
you.'

What with lab coats and crime-scene overalls and not dealing
with the public, the Bureau has lower sartorial standards than we
do, but this guy was still something special. I said, 'Detective
Kennedy and Detective Curran. You're here about the animal in
the attic?'

'Yeah. Want to come inside, see what's up?'

He looked like he was stoned off his tits, but Larry is fer-
ociously picky about who he works with, so I tried not to write the
kid off yet. 'Let's do that,' I said. 'Your boys found a dead robin in
the back garden. Did you take a look?'

Tom stashed his cigarette butt in his tobacco pouch, ducked
under the tape and shambled up the drive. 'Yeah, sure, but not a
lot there to see. Lar said you wanted to know was it an animal kill
or a human one, but all the insect activity wrecked the wound. All
I can tell you is it was kind of ragged, yeah? Like, it wasn't done by
a sharp blade. It could've been a serrated blade, probably a dull
one, or it could've been teeth. No way to tell.'

Richie said, 'What kind of teeth?'

Tom grinned. 'Not human. What, you were thinking your guy
was, like, Ozzy?'

Richie grinned back. 'Right. Happy Halloween, I'm too old for
bats, here's a robin.'

'That's so fucked up,' Tom said cheerfully. Someone had
mended the Spains' door – roughly, with a few screws and a
padlock – to keep out ghouls and journalists; he dug into his
pocket for the key. 'Nah. Animal teeth. We could be looking at a
rat, or a fox, except both of those would've probably eaten the
guts and stuff, not just the head. If it was an animal, I'm gonna say

probably a mustelid. Like stoats and mink, right? One of that family. They're into surplus killing.'

I said, 'That was Detective Curran's guess, too. Would a mustelid fit with whatever was going on in the attic?'

The padlock clicked, and Tom pushed the door open. The house was cold – someone had switched the heat off – and the faint tang of lemon in the air had faded: instead it smelled of sweat, the plasticky chemical scent of crime-scene overalls, and old blood. Cleaning up crime scenes isn't in our job description. We leave the debris behind, the killer's and our own, until the survivors either call in a professional crew or do it themselves.

Tom headed for the stairs. 'Yeah, I read your vic's Wildwatcher thread. He's probably right about ruling out mice and rats and squirrels – they'd have been all over the peanut butter. First thing I thought: hey, any of the neighbours got a cat? A couple of things don't fit, though. A cat wouldn't just take the head off that robin, and a cat wouldn't spend a lot of time hanging around the attic without giving itself away – meowing to get down through the attic hatch, or something. They're not careful about humans the way wild animals are. Plus, your vic said he smelled something musky, yeah? Musky or smoky? Doesn't sound like cat spray to me. Most of the mustelids, though: yeah, they'll let off a musky smell.'

He had dug up a stepladder somewhere and put it on the landing, under the hatch. I found my torch. The bedroom doors were still half open; I caught a glimpse of Jack's stripped bed.

'Careful,' Tom said, swinging himself up through the hatch. Above us, his torch came on. 'Pull left, yeah? Don't want to hit this.'

The trap was on the attic floor, just a few inches to the right of the hatch. I had only seen it in pictures. Solid, it was more powerful and more obscene, wicked teeth splayed wide, torchlight sliding in smooth arcs along the jaws. One look and you heard it, the savage whisk of air, the bone-crunching thud. None of us moved closer.

A long chain straggled across the floor, anchoring the trap to a metal pipe in a low corner, among dusty candlesticks and outgrown plastic toys. Tom nudged the chain with one toe, keeping his distance. 'That,' he said, 'that's a leghold trap. Nasty bastards. A couple of extra quid gets you one with padding or offset jaws, so it'll do less damage, but this one's old-style, none of your fancy stuff. The animal goes in after the bait, puts pressure on the pan, the jaws bite down and they don't let go. After a while the animal bleeds out or dies of stress and exhaustion, unless you come back and get it. It could maybe gnaw its own leg off, but it'd probably bleed to death first. This trap's got a seven-inch jaw spread: it could handle anything up to, like, a wolf. Your vic wasn't sure what he was chasing, but he was bloody serious about getting it.'

'What about you?' I said. I wished Pat had had the sense to install a light in his attic. I didn't want to take my torch beam off that trap — it felt like it might slide closer, in the blackness, till someone misjudged a step — but neither was I crazy about all those invisible corners. I could hear the sea, loud through the thin membrane of roof tiles and insulation. 'What do you think he was chasing?'

'OK. First question, right, is access. No problems there.' Tom tilted his chin upwards. At the top of the back wall – above Jack's bedroom, as far as I could figure – was a patch of weak grey light.

I saw what the building inspector had meant: the hole was a ragged gap that looked like the wall had simply ripped away from the roof. Richie let out a mirthless little breath of something like laughter. 'Look at that,' he said. 'No wonder the builders won't take the Gogans' phone calls. Give me enough Lego and I'd build a better estate myself.'

Tom said, 'Most of the mustelids, they're agile little buggers. They could get over the garden wall and up there, no problem, if they were attracted by escaping heat or cooking smells. Doesn't look to me like an animal actually made the hole, but an animal could've expanded it, maybe. See that?' The top edge of the hole, jagged and crumbling; the nibbled insulation. 'Teeth and claws could've done that, or it could just be weather wear. No way to know for sure. We've got the same kind of thing going on over here, too.'

The bar of torchlight swung down and back, over my shoulder. I almost leaped around, but he was only picking out a roof beam in the far corner. He said, 'Cool or what?'

The wood was crisscrossed with a frenzy of deep score-marks, in parallel sets of three or four. Some of them were a foot long. The beam looked like it had been attacked by a jaguar. Tom said, 'Those could come from claws, come from some kind of machine, come from a knife or like a piece of wood with nails stuck in it. Take your pick.'

The kid was pissing me off – the whoa-dude-chillax attitude to something that I personally wasn't taking lightly, or maybe just the fact that everyone assigned to this case appeared to be fourteen and I had missed the memo that said we were recruiting at skateboard parks. I said, 'You're the expert here, old son. You're the one who's here to tell us what you think. Why don't *you* take your pick.'

Tom shrugged. 'If I had to bet, I'd go with an animal. No way I can tell you whether it was ever actually up here, though. The marks could've been made back when this was a building site and the beam was exposed, or lying around on the ground outside. That might make more sense, seeing as it's just the one beam, yeah? If something made them up here, though: whoa. See the spaces between the marks?'

He tilted the torch beam to the gouges again. 'They're like an inch apart. That's not a stoat or a mink. Something with fuck-off big paws did that. If that's what your vic was hunting, then the trap size wasn't overkill after all.'

The conversation was getting to me more than it should have. The hidden corners of the attic felt crammed, seething with near-inaudible ticking noises and pinpoint red eyes; all my instincts were prickle-backed and bare-toothed, coiled to fight. I said, 'Is there anything elsc we need to see up here? Or can we finish this chat somewhere that won't double my dry-cleaning bill every sixty seconds?'

Tom looked faintly surprised. He examined the front of his parka, which looked like he had been wrestling dustballs. 'Oh,' he said. 'Right. Nah, that's all the good stuff: I had a look for scat,

hairs, any signs of nesting activity, but no dice. We'll head downstairs, yeah?'

I went down last, keeping my torch focused on the trap. Richie
and I both leaned away from it, involuntarily, on our way through
the hatch.

'So,' I said, on the landing, getting out a tissue and starting work
on my coat – the dust was nasty stuff, brown and sticky, like some
kind of toxic industrial by-product. 'Tell me what we're dealing
with.'

Tom got comfortable with his arse propped on the stepladder,
held up a hand and started ticking off fingers. 'OK, so we're going
with the mustelids, yeah? There's no weasels in Ireland. We've got
stoats, but they're tiny, like half a pound: I'm not sure they could
make the kind of noise your guy talked about. Pine martens are
heavier, and they're big-time climbers, but there's no woodland
nearer than that hill down at the end of the bay, so he'd be kind of
off his patch, and I couldn't find any marten sightings around
here anyway. A mink, though: a mink could work. They like living
near water, so' – he tilted his chin towards the sea – 'happy days,
yeah? They're surplus killers, they're climbers, they're not scared
of anything including humans, and they stink.'

I said, 'And they're vicious little bastards. They'd attack a kid,
no problem. If you had one in your house, you'd be bloody serious
about getting rid of it. Am I right?'

Tom did something noncommittal with his head. 'I guess, yeah.
They're crazy aggressive – I've heard of mink going for a fifty-
pound lamb, eating straight through the eye socket into the brain,
moving on to the next one, taking out a couple of dozen in one
night. And when they're cornered, they'll take on anything. So
yeah, you wouldn't be too happy about one moving in. I'm not
totally convinced that's what we've got, though. They're maybe
the size of a big house cat, tops. No reason why they'd need to
enlarge the entry hole, no way they could leave those claw-marks,
and no reason you'd need a trap that size to catch them.'

I said, 'Those aren't dealbreakers. According to you, we can't
assume the animal in the attic was responsible for either the hole

or the beam. As for the trap, our vic didn't know what he was hunting, so he erred on the side of caution. A mink's still in the running.'

Tom examined me with mild surprise, and I realised there had been a bite to my voice. 'Well, yeah. I mean, I can't even swear *anything* was ever in here, so nothing's a dealbreaker; it's all hypothetical, yeah? I'm just saying which pieces could fit where.'

'Great. And plenty of them fit with a mink. Any other possibilities?'

'Your other maybe is an otter. The sea's right there, and they've got massive territories, so one of them could live down on the beach and count this house as part of his range. They're big buggers, too, like two or three feet long, maybe twenty pounds: an otter could've left those marks on the beam, and he might've needed to enlarge that access hole. And they can get kind of playful, so those rolling noises would make sense – if it found, like, one of those candleholders or those kiddie toys or something, and it was batting it around the attic floor . . .'

'Three feet, twenty pounds,' I said, to Richie. 'Running around your home, right above your kids. That sounds like something that could get a reasonable, sane guy fairly worried. Am I right?'

'Whoa,' Tom said placidly, holding up his hands. 'Slow down. It's not, like, a perfect fit. Otters scent-mark, all right, but they do it with droppings, and your guy didn't find any. I had a nose around, and I can't see any either. None in the attic, none under the attic floor, none in the garden.'

Even outside the attic, the house felt restless, infested. The wall at my back, the thought of how thin the plaster was, made me itch. I said, 'And I didn't smell anything, either. Did you?' Richie and Tom shook their heads. 'So maybe it wasn't droppings that Pat smelled: it was the otter itself, and now it hasn't been around in a while, so the scent's faded. '

'Could be. They smell, all right. But . . . I don't know, man.' Tom squinted off into the distance, working one finger in between the dreadlocks to scratch his scalp. 'It's not just the scent thing. This whole deal, this isn't otter behaviour. End of story. They're seriously not climbers – I mean, I've *heard* of otters climbing, but that's like headline news, you know what I mean? Even if it did, something that size going up and down the side of a house, you've gotta figure it'll get seen. And they're *wild*. They're not like rats or foxes, the urbanised stuff that's OK with living right up against humans. Otters stay away from us. If you've got an otter here, he's a fucking weirdo. He's the one that the other otters tell their cubs to stay out of his garden.'

Richie tilted his chin at the hole above the skirting board. 'You've seen these, yeah?'

Tom nodded. 'Freaky or what? The vics had the whole place this fancy, all their shit *matched*, but they were OK with massive holes in their walls? People are weird.'

'Could an otter have made those? Or a mink?'

Tom squatted on his haunches and examined the hole, cocking his head at different angles, like he had all week. 'Maybe,' he said, in the end. 'It'd help if we had some debris left, so we could at least tell whether these were made from inside the walls or outside, but your vics were serious about clean-up. Someone's even sanded down the edges – see there? – so if there were clawmarks or tooth-marks, they're gone. Like I said: weird.'

I said, 'I'll ask our next vics to be sure and live in a hovel. Meanwhile, work with what we've got.'

'No hassle,' Tom said cheerfully. 'Mink, I've gotta say they couldn't do it. They're not really into digging, unless they have to, and with those little paws . . .' He waved his hands. 'The plaster's pretty thin, but still, it'd take them ages to get that kind of damage done. Otters dig, and they're strong, so yeah, an otter could've done it, easy. Except somewhere along the way he'd get stuck inside the wall, or he'd chew on an electrical wire and bzzt, otter barbecue. So maybe yeah, but probably no. Does that help?'

'You've been a great help,' I said. 'Thanks. We'll let you know if any more info comes in.'

'Oh yeah,' Tom said, straightening and giving me a double thumbs-up and a big grin. 'This is some mad shit, yeah? Love to see more.'

I said, 'I'm delighted we could make your day. I'll take that key, if you don't have plans for it.'

I held out my hand. Tom pulled a tangle of crap out of his pocket, picked out the padlock key and dropped it into my palm. 'Pleasure's all mine,' he said cheerfully, and bounced off down the stairs, dreadlocks flapping.

At the gate, Richie said, 'I'd say the uniforms left copies of that key at HQ for us, no?'

We were watching Tom slouch off to his car, which inevitably was a green VW camper van in urgent need of a coat of paint. 'They probably did,' I said. 'I didn't want that little tosser bringing his mink-spotting mates on a tour of the scene. "Like, dude, how totally cool is that?" This isn't bloody *entertainment*.'

'Techs,' Richie said absently. 'You know what they're like. Larry's the same, sure.'

'That's different. A *teenager* is what this guy's like. He needs to cop himself on and grow up. Or maybe I'm just not down with the kids these days.'

'So,' Richie said, digging his hands deep into his pockets. He wasn't looking at me. 'The holes, yeah? Not subsidence. And not any animal that your man can put his finger on.'

'That's not what he said.'

'Just about.'

'"Just about" doesn't count in this game. According to Dr Dolittle over there, mink and otter are both still in.'

Richie said, 'Do you think one of those did the job? Honest to God, like. Do you?'

The air held the first whiff of winter; in the half-houses across the road, the kids trying to get themselves killed were wearing padded jackets and woolly hats. 'I don't know,' I said. 'And honest to God, I don't really care, because even if Pat made the holes, I don't see how that makes him a homicidal maniac. Like I asked you inside: let's say you had twenty pounds' worth of mystery animal running around your attic. Or let's say you had one of the most *crazy aggressive* predators in Ireland hanging out right above your son's bed. Would you be willing to bash a couple of holes in your walls, if you thought that was your best shot at getting rid of this thing? Would that mean there was something wrong with your mind?'

'That wouldn't be your best shot, but. Poison—'

'Say you'd tried poison, and the animal was too smart to take it. Or, even more likely: say the poison worked just fine, but the animal died somewhere down inside your walls, you couldn't work out exactly where. Then would you get out the hammer? Would that mean you were fucked-up enough to slaughter your own family?'

Tom started up his van, which belched out a cloud of non-wildlife-friendly fumes, and waved out the window to us as he headed off. Richie waved back automatically, and I saw those skinny shoulders rise and fall in a deep breath. He checked his watch and said, 'Have we got time for that word with the Gogans, yeah?'

The Gogans' front window had sprouted a bunch of plastic bats and, with the level of taste I would have expected, a life-sized plastic skeleton. The door opened fast: someone had been watching us.

Gogan was a big guy, with a wobbly belly hanging over his navy tracksuit bottoms and a pre-emptive head-shave, and he was where Jayden had got that flat-eyed stare. He said, 'What?'

I said, 'I'm Detective Kennedy, and this is Detective Curran. Mr . . . ?'

'Mr Gogan. What d'you want?'

Mr Gogan was Niall Gogan, he was thirty-two, he had an eight-year-old conviction for chucking a bottle through the window of his local, he had driven a forklift in a warehouse off and on for most of his adult life and he was currently out of work, officially anyway. I said, 'We're investigating the deaths next door. Could we come in for a few minutes?'

'You can talk to me here.'

Richie said, 'I promised Mrs Gogan we'd keep her up to speed. She was worried, yeah? We've got a bit of news.'

After a moment Gogan stepped back from the doorway. He said, 'Make it quick. We're busy.'

This time we got the whole family. They had been watching some soap opera and eating something involving hard-boiled eggs and ketchup, going by the plates on the coffee table and by the smell. Jayden was sprawled on one sofa; Sinéad was on the other, with the baby propped up in a corner, sucking on a bottle. The kid was living proof of Sinéad's virtue: the spit of its dad, bald head and pale stare and all.

I moved to one side and let Richie have centre stage. 'Mrs Gogan,' he said, leaning over to shake hands. 'Ah, no, don't get up. Sorry to interrupt your evening, but I promised to keep you updated, didn't I?'

Sinéad was practically falling off the sofa with eagerness. 'Have you got the fella, have you?'

I moved to a corner armchair and got out my notebook – taking notes turns you invisible, if you do it right. Richie went for the other armchair, leaving Gogan to shove Jayden's legs out of the way on the sofa. He said, 'We've got a suspect in custody.'

'Jaysus,' Sinéad breathed. That avid look was brightening her eyes. 'Is he a psychopath?'

Richie shook his head. 'I can't tell you a lot about him. The investigation's still going on.'

Sinéad stared at him with her mouth open, disgusted. The look on her face said, *You made me mute the telly for this?*

Richie said, 'I figured yous have a right to know this fella's off the street. As soon as I can give you more, I will. Right now, though, we're still trying to make sure we can keep him where he is, so we have to play it close to the chest.'

Gogan said, 'Thanks. Was that it, yeah?'

Richie made a face and rubbed at the back of his head, looking like a bashful teenager. 'Look . . . OK, here's the story. I haven't been doing this long, yeah? But I know one thing for definite: the best witness you can get is a smart young kid. They get everywhere, see everything. Kids don't overlook stuff, the way adults do: anything that goes on, they spot it. So when I met your Jayden, I was only delighted.'

Sinéad pointed a finger at him and started, 'Jayden didn't see—' but Richie raised his hands to cut her off.

'Give us a sec, yeah? Just so I don't lose my train of thought. See, I know Jayden *thought* he saw nothing, or he'd've told us last time we were here. But I figured, maybe he was thinking back, over the last couple of days. That's the other thing about a smart kid: it all stays up here.' He tapped his temple. 'I thought maybe, if I was lucky, something might've come back to him.'

Everyone looked at Jayden. He said, 'What?'

'Did you remember anything that could help us out?'

Jayden took just a second too long to shrug. Richie had been right: he knew something.

'There's your answer,' Gogan said.

'Jayden,' Richie said. 'I've got a load of little brothers. I know when a young fella's keeping something to himself.'

Jayden's eyes slid sideways and up, to his father, asking.

'There a reward?' Gogan wanted to know.

This wasn't the moment for the speech about the rewards of helping the community. Richie said, 'Nothing so far, but I'll let yous know if one gets offered. I know you don't want your young fella mixed up in this – I wouldn't either. All I can tell you is, the man who did this was going solo: he doesn't have any pals who might go after witnesses, nothing like that. As long as he's off the street, your family's safe.'

Gogan scratched the stubble under his chins and took that in, the unspoken part as well. 'He mental, yeah?'

That knack of Richie's again: little by little, this was easing over the boundary between an interview and a conversation. Richie spread his hands. 'Can't talk about him, man. I'm only saying: you've gotta go out of the house sometimes, yeah? Work, interviews, meetings . . . It was me, I'd be happier leaving my family if I knew this guy was well out of the way.'

Gogan eyed him and kept up the steady scratching. Sinéad snapped, 'I'm telling you now, if there's a mad serial killer running around, you can forget about going to the pub, I'm not staying here on my own waiting for some lunatic to—'

Gogan glanced over at Jayden, who was slouching low on the sofa and watching with his mouth open, and jerked his head towards Richie. 'Go on. Tell the man.'

'Tell him what?' Jayden wanted to know.

'Don't act thick. Whatever he's asking about.'

Jayden sank deeper into the sofa and watched his toes dig into the carpet. He said, 'There was just this guy. Like, ages ago.'

Richie said, 'Yeah? When?'

'Before summer. At the end of school.'

'See, that's what I'm talking about. Remembering the little things. I knew you were a smart one. June, yeah?'

Shrug. 'Probably.'

'Where was he?'

Jayden's eyes went to his father again. Richie said, 'Man, you're doing something good here. You're not gonna get in trouble.'

Gogan said, 'Tell him.'

'I was in Number Eleven. Like, the one that's attached to the murder house? I was—'

Sinéad demanded, 'What the fuck were you doing in there? I'll bleeding clatter you—'

She saw Richie's lifted finger and subsided, chin shoved out at an angle that said all of us were in big trouble. Richie asked, 'How'd you get into Number Eleven?'

Jayden squirmed. His tracksuit made a farting noise on the fake leather and he snickered, but he stopped when no one joined in. Finally he said, 'I was only messing. I had my keys, and . . . I was just messing, right? I just wanted to see if it worked.'

Richie said, 'You tried your keys on other houses?'

Jayden shrugged. 'Kind of.'

'Fair play to you. That's dead clever, that is. We never even thought of that.' And we should have: it would have been right in character for these builders, to pick up a cut-price lot of one-key-fits-all dud locks. 'Do they all work on any house, yeah?'

Jayden was sitting up straighter, starting to enjoy how smart he was. 'Nah. The front-door ones, they're useless; ours didn't work on anywhere else, and I tried loads. The back-door one, though, right? It opens, like, half the—'

Gogan said, 'That's enough. Shut up.'

'Mr Gogan,' Richie said. 'I'm serious: he's not in any trouble.'

'D'you think I'm thick? If he'd been in other houses – and he wasn't – it'd be breaking and entering.'

'I'm not even thinking about that. No one else will, either. Do you know how much of a favour your Jayden is after doing us? He's helping us put away a *murderer*. I'm over the *moon* that he was messing about with that key.'

Gogan stared him out of it. 'You try coming back at him with something later on, he'll take back every word.'

Richie didn't blink. 'I won't. Believe me. I wouldn't let anyone else, either. This is way too important.'

Gogan grunted and gave Jayden the nod. Jayden said, 'Seriously? You guys never even thought of that?'

Richie shook his head. 'Thick,' Jayden said, under his breath.

'This is what I'm talking about: we're lucky we found you. What's the story with the back-door key?'

'It opens, like, half the back doors around. I mean, obviously I didn't try anywhere there's people living' – Jayden tried to look virtuous; no one fell for it – 'but the empty houses, like down the road and all up Ocean View Promenade, I got into *loads*. Easy. I can't even believe no one else thought of it.'

Richie said, 'And it opens Number Eleven. That's where you met this guy?'

'Yeah. I was in there, like just hanging out, and he knocked on the back door – I guess he came over the garden wall, or something.' He had come from his hide. He had spotted an opportunity. 'So I went out to him. I mean, I was *bored*. There was nothing to do in there.'

Sinéad snapped, 'What've I told you about talking to strangers? Serve you right if he got you in a van and—'

Jayden rolled his eyes. '*Duh*, do I look stupid? If he'd tried to grab me, I would've *run*. I was only like two seconds from *here*.'

Richie asked, 'What did yous talk about?'

Jayden shrugged. 'Not much. He said what was I doing there. I said just hanging around. He said how did I get in. So I explained about the keys.'

He had been showing off to impress the stranger with his cleverness, the same way he was showing off to impress Richie. 'And what did he say?' Richie asked.

'He said that was really smart. He said he wished he had a key like that. He lived down the other end of the estate, only his house was all flooded 'cause the pipes burst or something, so he was looking for an empty house where he could sleep till his got fixed.'

It was a good story. Conor had known enough about the estate to come up with something plausible – Jayden had every reason to believe in burst pipes and repairs that dragged on forever – and he had done it fast. Thinking on his feet, lying plausibly, taking advantage of what came to hand: the guy was good, when he wanted something badly enough.

'Only he said all the houses, either they didn't have doors and windows or whatever, so they were freezing, or else they were locked up and he couldn't get into them. He asked could he borrow my key and make a copy, so he could get into somewhere good. He said he'd give me a fiver. I said a tenner.'

Sinéad burst out, 'You gave some pervert our key? You fucking *thick—*'

'I'll change the lock tomorrow,' Gogan said brusquely. 'Shut up.'

Richie said easily, ignoring them both, 'Makes sense. So he gave you a tenner and you lent him the key, yeah?'

Jayden kept one eye on his mother for trouble. 'Yeah. So?'

'Then what happened?'

'Nothing. He said don't tell anyone or he could get in trouble with the builders because they own the houses. I said OK.' Another smart call: the builders weren't likely to be popular with anyone in Ocean View, even the kids. 'He said he'd put the key under a rock – he showed me which one. Then he went away. He said thanks. I had to go home.'

'Did you see him again?'

'Nah.'

'Did he get the key back to you?'

'Yeah. The day after. Under the rock, like he said.'

'Do you know does your key fit the Spains' door?'

Which was a tactful way of putting it. Jayden shrugged, too easily and not vehemently enough for a lie. 'Never tried.'

In other words, he hadn't wanted to risk getting caught by someone who knew where he lived. 'Did your man get in by the back door?' Sinéad wanted to know. Her eyes were wide.

'We're exploring all the possibilities,' Richie said. 'Jayden, what did this fella look like?'

Jayden shrugged again. 'Thin.'

'Older than me? Younger?'

'I guess the same as you. Younger than him.' Me.

'Tall? Short?'

Shrug. 'Normal. Maybe sort of tall, like him.' Me again.

'Would you recognise him if you saw him again, would you?'

'Yeah. Probably.'

I leaned over to my briefcase and found the photo array. One of the floaters had put it together for us that morning, and he had done a good job: six twenty-somethings, all lean, with close-cropped brown hair and plenty of chin. Jayden would need to come down to HQ for a formal lineup, but we could at least eliminate the possibility that he had given his key to some unrelated weirdo.

I passed the array to Richie, who held it out to Jayden. 'Is he in here?'

Jayden milked it for all it was worth: tilting the sheet at different angles, holding it up to eye level and squinting at it. Finally he said, 'Yeah. This guy.'

His finger was on the middle shot in the bottom row: Conor Brennan. Richie's eyes met mine for a second.

'Jaysus Christ,' Sinéad said. 'He was talking to a *murderer*.' She sounded somewhere between awestruck and outraged. I could see her trying to work out who to sue.

Richie said, 'You're sure, Jayden?'

'Yeah. Number Five.' Richie reached to take back the array sheet, but Jayden was still staring at it. 'Was he the guy that killed them all?'

I saw the quick flicker of Richie's eyelids. 'It'll be up to the court and the jury to decide what he did.'

'If I hadn't've given him the key, would he have killed me?'

His voice sounded fragile. The ghoulishness was gone; all of a sudden he just looked like a scared little kid. Richie said gently, 'I don't think so. I can't swear to it, but I'd bet you were never in any danger, not even for a second. Your mammy's right, though: you shouldn't talk to strangers. Yeah?'

'Is he gonna come back?'

'No. He's not coming back.'

Richie's first slip: you don't make that promise, at least not when you still need leverage. 'That's what we're trying to make sure of,' I said smoothly, stretching out a hand for the sheet. 'Jayden, you've been a great help, and it'll make a big difference. But we need all the help we can get, to keep this guy where he is. Mr Gogan, Mrs Gogan: you've also had a couple of days to think back and see whether you know something that might help us. Does anything come to mind? Anything you've seen, heard, anything out of place? Anything at all?'

There was a silence. The baby started to make small complaining snuffles; Sinéad reached out a hand, without looking, and jiggled its cushion till it stopped. Neither she nor Gogan was looking at anyone.

In the end Sinéad said, 'Can't think of anything.' Gogan shook his head.

We let the silence grow. The baby wriggled and set up a high, protesting whine; Sinéad picked it up and bounced it. Her eyes across its head were cold, flat as her husband's, defiant.

Finally Richie nodded. 'If you think of anything, yous have my card. Meanwhile, do us a favour, yeah? There's a few newspapers out there that might be interested in Jayden's story. Keep it to yourselves for a few weeks, OK?'

Sinéad went lipless with outrage; obviously she had already been planning her shopping spree and deciding where to get her makeup done for the photo shoot. 'We can talk to whoever we like. You can't stop us.'

Richie said calmly, 'The papers'll still be there in a couple of weeks' time. When we have this fella sorted, I'll give you the go-ahead and you can give them a ring. Until then, I'm asking you to do us a favour and not impede our investigation.'

Gogan got the threat, even if she didn't. He said, 'Jayden'll talk to no one. Is that all, yeah?'

He stood up. 'One last thing,' Richie said, 'and we'll be out of your way. Can we borrow your back-door key for a minute?'

It opened the Spains' back door like it had been oiled. The lock clicked open and the last link in that chain clicked into place, a taut glinting thread running from Conor's hide straight into the violated kitchen. I almost raised a hand to high-five Richie, but he was looking out over the garden wall, at the empty window-holes of the hide, not at me.

'And that's how the blood-smears got on the paving stones,' I said. 'He went out the same way he came in.'

Richie's fidgets had come back; his fingertips were drumming a fast tattoo on the side of his thigh. Whatever was bothering him, the Gogans hadn't fixed it. He said, 'Pat and Jenny. How'd they end up here?'

'What do you mean?'

'Three in the morning, both of them in their pyjamas. If they were in bed and Conor came after them, how'd they end up struggling down here? Why not in the bedroom?'

'They caught him on the way out.'

'That'd mean he was only after the kids. Doesn't fit with the confession: he was all about Pat and Jenny. And wouldn't they have checked on the kids first thing when they heard noise, stayed trying to help them? Would you care about an intruder getting away, if your kids were in trouble?'

I said, 'There's still plenty about this case that needs explaining. I'm not denying that. But remember, this wasn't just any intruder.

This was their best mate – or their ex-best mate. That could have made a difference to the way things went down. Let's wait and see what Fiona has to tell us.'

'Yeah,' Richie said. He pushed the door open and cold air swept into the kitchen, stripping away the stagnant layer of blood and chemicals, turning the room, for a breath, fresh and stirring as morning. 'Wait and see.'

I found my phone and rang the uniforms – they needed to send down whoever was handy with the padlocks, before the Gogans decided to set up a nice little sideline selling souvenirs. While I waited for someone to pick up, I said to Richie, 'That was a good interrogation.'

'Thanks.' He sounded nowhere near as pleased with himself as he should have. 'We know why Conor made up that story about finding Pat's key, anyway. Keep Jayden out of trouble.'

'Sweet of him. Plenty of killers feed stray puppies, too.'

Richie was looking out at the garden, which had already started to take on an abandoned feel – weeds pushing up above the grass, a blue plastic bag left to flap from the bush where it had blown. 'Yeah,' he said. 'Probably they do.' He slammed the back door – the final rush of cold air fluttered the stray papers left to drift on the floor – and turned the key again.

Gogan was waiting at his front door to get his key back. Jayden was behind him, hanging off the door handle. When Richie handed over the key, Jayden squirmed out, under his father's arm. 'Mister,' he said, to Richie.

'Yeah?'

'If I hadn't have given your man the key. Would they not have got kilt?'

He was staring up at Richie with real, sharp horror in those pale eyes. Richie said, gently but very firmly, 'This wasn't your fault, Jayden. It's the fault of the person who did the job. End of story.'

Jayden twisted. 'But how would he have got in if he didn't have the key?'

'He would've found a way. Some stuff is gonna find a way to happen; once it's got started, you can't stop it, no matter what you do. This whole thing got started a long time before you ever met this fella. Yeah?'

The words slid down my skull, dug in at the back of my neck. I shifted, trying to get Richie moving, but he was focused on Jayden. The kid looked about half convinced. After a moment, he said, 'I guess.' He slipped back under his father's arm and vanished into the dim hall. In the moment before Gogan shut the door, he caught Richie's eye and gave him a small, reluctant nod.

The two sets of neighbours at the bottom of the road were in, this time. They were the Spains, three days back: young couples, little kids, clean floors and saved-for fashionable touches, houses ready and welcoming for visitors who wouldn't come. None of them had seen or heard anything. We were discreet about telling them to get their back-door locks changed: just a precaution, a possible manufacturing fault we had stumbled on in the course of the investigation, nothing to do with the crime.

One of each couple had a job, long hours and long commutes; the other man had been made redundant a week ago, the other woman back in July. She had tried to make friends with Jenny Spain – 'We were both stuck out here all day, I thought it'd be less lonely if we had someone to talk to . . .' Jenny had been polite, but she had kept her distance: a cup of tea always sounded lovely, but she was never free and never sure when she would be. 'I thought maybe she was shy, or she didn't want me to think we were best friends and start dropping in every day, or maybe she was annoyed because I never tried before – I never had a chance, I was barely even home . . . But if she was worried about . . . I mean, was it . . . ? Can I ask?'

She had taken it for granted that it was Pat, just like I had told Richie everyone would. I said, 'We have someone in custody in connection with the crime.'

'Oh, God.' Her hand went to her husband's, on the kitchen table. She was pretty, slim and blond and nicely put together, but she had been crying before we arrived. 'Then it wasn't . . . It was just . . . some guy? Like a burglar?'

'The person in custody isn't a resident of the house.'

That made the tears started leaking out again. 'Then . . . Oh, God . . .' Her eyes went over my shoulder, to the far end of the kitchen. Their daughter was about four, cross-legged on the floor with her smooth fair head bent over a plush tiger, murmuring away. 'Then it could've been *us*. There was nothing to stop it being us. You want to say, "There but for the grace of God," only you can't, can you? Because that's like saying God wanted them to be . . . It wasn't God. It was just an accident; just luck. Only for luck . . .'

Her hand was white-knuckled on her husband's and she was working hard to hold in a sob. It hurt my jaw, how much I wanted to be able to tell her that she was wrong: that the Spains had sent out some call on the sea wind and Conor had answered, that she and hers had made a life that was safe.

I said, 'The suspect is in custody. He'll be staying that way for a long time.'

She nodded, not looking at me. Her face said I didn't get it.

The husband said, 'We were wanting to get out anyway. We'd have been gone months ago, only who'd buy this? Now . . .'

The wife said, 'We're not staying here. We're *not*.'

The sob broke through. Her voice and her husband's eyes held the same splinter of helplessness. They both knew they were going nowhere.

On our way back to the car, my phone buzzed to tell me I had a message. Geri had rung me just after five.

'Mick . . . God, I hate to bother you, I know you're only up to your ears, but I thought you'd want to know – maybe you already do, sure, but . . . Dina's after walking out on us. Mick, I'm so sorry, I know we were supposed to be looking after her – and we *were*, I only left her with Sheila for fifteen minutes while I went down to the shops . . . Is she after coming to you? I know you're probably annoyed with me, I wouldn't blame you, but Mick, if she's with you, please, could you ring me and let me know? I'm really sorry, honestly, I am . . .'

'*Shit,*' I said. Dina had been missing for an hour, minimum. There was nothing I could do it about it for at least another couple of hours, until Richie and I were done with Fiona. The thought of what could happen to Dina in that amount of time made me feel like my heart was trying to beat against thick mud. 'Shitfucking *fuck.*'

I didn't realise I had stopped moving till I saw Richie, a couple of steps ahead, turned around to watch me. He said, 'Everything OK, yeah?'

'Everything's fine,' I said. 'It's not work-related. I just need a minute to clear things up.' Richie opened his mouth to say something else, but before he could get it out I had turned my back on him and was heading back down the footpath, at a pace that told him not to follow.

Geri picked up on the first ring. 'Mick? Is she with you?'

'No. What time did she leave?'

'Oh, God. I was hoping—'

'Don't panic. She could be at my place, or at my work – I've been out in the field all afternoon. What time did she leave?'

'Half past four, about. Sheila's mobile rang and it was Barry, that's her boyfriend, so she went up to her room just for privacy, and when she came down Dina was gone. She wrote, "Thanks, bye!" on the fridge with her eyeliner, and this outline of her hand underneath, waving, like. She took Sheila's wallet, it had sixty euros in it, so she's got money, anyway . . . As soon as I got home and Sheila told me, I drove all round the neighbourhood, looking for her – I swear I looked everywhere, I was going into shops and looking into people's gardens and all – but she was gone. I didn't know where else to look. I've rung her a dozen times, but her phone's off.'

'How did she seem, this afternoon? Was she getting pissed off with you, or with Sheila?' If Dina had got bored . . . I tried to remember whether she had mentioned Jezzer's surname.

'No, she was *better*! *Much* better. Not angry, not scared, not getting wound up – she was even making sense, most of the time. She seemed a bit distracted, like, not really paying attention when you talked to her; like she had something on her mind. That was *all*.' Geri's voice was spiralling higher. 'She was practically grand, Mick, honest to God she was, I was positive she was on her way up or I'd never have left her with Sheila, never . . .'

'I know you wouldn't. I'm sure she's fine.'

'She's not fine, Mick. She's not. Fine is the *last* thing she is.'

I glanced over my shoulder: Richie was leaning against the car door with his hands in his pockets, facing up into the building sites to give me privacy. 'You know what I mean. I'm sure she just got bored and headed to a friend's house. She'll turn up tomorrow morning, with croissants to show you she's sorry—'

'That doesn't make her fine. Someone who's *fine* doesn't steal her niece's babysitting money. Someone who's *fine* wouldn't need all of us to walk on eggshells all the—'

'I know, Geri. But that's not something we can deal with tonight. Let's just focus on one day at a time. OK?'

Over the estate wall the sea was darkening, rocking steadily towards night; the small birds were out again, scavenging at the water's edge. Geri caught her breath, exhaled with a shake in it. 'I'm so bloody *sick* of this.'

I had heard that note a million times before, in her voice and in my own: exhaustion, frustration and annoyance, cut with pure terror. No matter how many dozen times you go through the same rigmarole, you never forget that this could be the time when, finally, it ends differently: not with a scribbled apology card and a bunch of stolen flowers on your doorstep, but with a late-night phone call, a rookie uniform practising his notification skills, an ID visit to Cooper's morgue.

'Geri,' I said. 'Don't worry. I've got one more interview to get through before I can leave, but then I'll sort this out. If I find her waiting for me at work, I'll let you know. You keep trying her mobile; if you get through, tell her to meet me at work, and give me a text so I know she's coming. Otherwise, I'll track her down the second I finish up. OK?'

'Yeah. OK.' Geri didn't ask how. She needed to believe it would be that simple. So did I. 'Sure, she'll be fine on her own for another hour or two.'

'Get some sleep. I'll keep Dina at mine tonight, but I might have to bring her over to you again tomorrow.'

'Do, of course. Everyone's grand, Colm and Andrea haven't caught it, thank God . . . And I won't leave her out of my sight this time. I promise. Mick, I'm really sorry about this.'

'I mean it: don't worry. Tell Sheila and Phil I hope they're feeling better. I'll be in touch.'

Richie was still leaning against the car door, gazing up at the sharp crisscross of walls and scaffolding against a cold turquoise sky. When I beeped the car unlocked, he straightened up and turned. 'Howya.'

'Sorted,' I said. 'Let's go.'

I opened my door, but he didn't move. In the fading light his face looked pale and wise, much older than thirty-one. He said, 'Anything I can do?'

In the second before I could open my mouth, it surged up inside me, sudden and powerful as flood waters and just as danger-ous: the thought of telling him. I thought of those ten-year partners who knew each other by heart, what any of them would have said: *That girl the other night, remember her? That's my sister, her mind's fucked, I don't know how to save her . . .* I saw the pub, the partner getting the pints in and tossing out sports arguments, dirty jokes, half-true anecdotes, till the tension fell out of your shoulders and you forgot your mind was shorting out; sending you home at the end of the night with a hangover in the making and the feeling of him solid as a rockface at your back. The picture was so clear I could have warmed my hands at it.

The next second I got my grip back and it turned my stomach, the thought of splaying my private family business in front of him and begging him to give me a pat on the head and tell me it would all be OK. This wasn't some ten-year best buddy, some blood brother; this was a near-stranger who couldn't even be arsed sharing whatever had struck him in Conor Brennan's flat. 'No need,' I said crisply. I thought, briefly, of asking Richie to interview Fiona on his own, or asking him to type up the day's report and postponing Fiona till morning – Conor wasn't going anywhere – but both of those felt disgustingly pathetic. 'The offer's appreciated, but I've got everything under control. Let's go see what Fiona has to tell us.'

# 13

Fiona was waiting for us outside HQ, drooping against a lamp-post. In the circle of smoky yellow light, with the hood of her red duffel coat pulled up against the cold, she looked like some small lost creature out of fireside stories. I ran a hand over my hair and locked Dina down in the back of my mind. 'Remember,' I said to Richie, 'she's still on the radar.'

Richie caught a deep breath, like the exhaustion had blindsided him all of a sudden. He said, 'She didn't give Conor the keys.'

'I know. But she knew him. There's history there. We need to know a lot more about that history before we can rule her out.'

Fiona straightened up as we came closer. She had lost weight in the last two days; her cheekbones poked out sharply, through skin that had faded to a papery grey. I could smell the hospital off her, disinfected and polluting.

'Ms Rafferty,' I said. 'Thank you for coming in.'

'Could we just . . . Would it be OK if we made this quick? I want to get back to Jenny.'

'I understand,' I said, stretching out an arm to guide her towards the door. 'We'll be as fast as we can.'

Fiona didn't move. Her hair straggled around her face in limp brown waves; it looked like she had washed it in a sink with hospital soap. 'You said you got the man. The man who did this.'

She was talking to Richie. He said, 'We've got someone in custody in connection with the crimes. Yeah.'

'I want to see him.'

Richie hadn't spotted that coming. I said smoothly, 'I'm afraid he's not here. We've got him in jail at the moment.'

'I need to see him. I need . . .' Fiona lost her train of thought, shook her head and shoved back hair. 'Can we go there? To the jail?'

'It doesn't really work that way, Ms Rafferty. It's out of hours, we'd have to fill in the paperwork, then it could take a few hours to bring him over here, depending on the available security . . . If you want to get back to your sister, we'll need to leave that for another time.'

Even if I had left her room to argue, she didn't have the energy. After a moment she said, 'Another time. I can see him another time?'

'I'm sure we can work something out,' I said, and held out my arm again. This time Fiona moved, out of the circle of lamplight and into the shadows, towards the door of HQ.

One of the interview rooms is set up to be gentle: carpet instead of linoleum, clean pale-yellow walls, non-institutional chairs that don't leave your arse bruised, a water cooler, an electric kettle and a basket of little sachets of tea and coffee and sugar, actual mugs instead of foam cups. It's for victims' families, fragile witnesses, suspects who would take the other rooms as an affront to their dignity and stalk out. We put Fiona there. Richie settled her – it was nice, having a partner who could be trusted with someone that shaky – while I went down to the incident room and threw a few bits of evidence into a cardboard box. By the time I got back, her coat was on the back of her chair and she was curled around a steaming mug of tea like her whole body needed warming. Without the coat she was slight as a child, even in the loose jeans and over-sized cream cardigan. Richie was sitting opposite her, elbows propped on the table, halfway through a long reassuring story about an imaginary relative who had been saved from some dramatic combination of injuries by the doctors at Jenny's hospital.

I slid the box unobtrusively under the table and took a chair next to Richie. He said, 'I was just telling Ms Rafferty, her sister's in good hands.'

Fiona said, 'The doctor said in a couple of days they're going to lower the dose of painkillers. I don't know how Jenny's going to cope.

She's in really bad shape anyway – obviously – but the painkillers help, half the time she thinks it's just a bad dream. When she comes off them, and the whole thing hits her . . . Can they give her something else? Antidepressants, or something?'

'The doctors know what they're at,' Richie said gently. 'They'll help her get through.'

I said, 'I'm going to ask you to do something for us, Ms Rafferty. While you're here, I need you to forget about what happened to your family. Put it out of your mind; just concentrate, one hundred per cent, on answering our questions. Believe me, I know that sounds impossible, but it's the only way you can help us put this man away. This is what Jenny needs from you right now – what they all need from you. Can you do that for them?'

This is the gift we offer them, people who loved the victims: rest. For an hour or two they get to sit still and – guilt-free, because we gave them no choice – stop hurling their minds on the jagged shards of what happened. I understand how immense that is, and how priceless. I saw the layers in Fiona's eyes, like I'd seen them in hundreds of others': relief, and shame, and gratitude.

She said, 'OK. I'll try.'

She would tell us things she had never wanted to mention, to give herself a reason to keep talking. 'We appreciate that,' I said. 'I know it's difficult, but you're doing the right thing.'

Fiona balanced her tea on her thin knees, cupping it between her hands, and gave me her full attention. Already her spine had uncurled a notch. I said, 'Let's start at the beginning. There's a good chance none of this will be relevant, but it's important for us to get all the information we can. You said Pat and Jenny got together when they were sixteen, isn't that right? Can you tell me how they met?'

'Not exactly. We're all from the same area, so we knew each other from around, ever since we were little kids, like in primary school; I don't remember the exact first time any of us met. When we got to like twelve or thirteen, a bunch of us started hanging out together – just messing about on the beach, or roller-blading, or we'd go down to Dun Laoghaire and hang out on the pier. Sometimes we went into town, for the cinema and then Burger King, or on the weekends we'd go to the school discos if there was a good one on. Just kid stuff, but we were close. Really close.'

Richie said, 'There's no one like the mates you make when you're a teenager. How many in the gang?'

'Jenny and me. Pat and his brother Ian. Shona Williams. Conor Brennan. Ross McKenna – Mac. There were a couple of others who hung out with us sometimes, but that was the real gang.'

I rummaged in my cardboard box, found a photo album – pink cover, flowers made of sequins – and flipped it open at a Post-it. Seven teenagers perched on a wall, squashed together to fit in the shot, laughter and brandished ice-cream cones and bright T-shirts. Fiona had braces, Jenny's hair was a shade darker; Pat had his arms wrapped around her – his shoulders were already as broad as a man's, but his face was a boy's, open and ruddy – and she was taking a huge mock-bite out of his ice cream. Conor was all gangly legs and arms, doing a goofy chimpanzee impression, falling off the wall. I said, 'Is this the gang?'

Fiona put her tea down on the table – too quickly; a few drops slopped out – and reached out a hand to the album. She said, 'That's Jenny's.'

'I know,' I said gently. 'We needed to borrow it, just for a while.'

It made her shoulders jump, the sudden feel of our fingers probing deep into their lives. 'God,' she said, involuntarily.

'We'll have it back to Jenny as soon as possible.'

'Can you . . . If you get done with it in time, maybe could you just not tell her you had it? She doesn't need anything else to deal with. This . . .' Fiona spread her hand across the photo. She said, so quietly I barely heard her, 'We were really happy.'

I said, 'We'll do our best. You can help there, too. If you can give us all the info we need, then we can avoid asking Jenny these questions.'

She nodded, without looking up. 'Well done,' I said. 'Now, this has to be Ian. Am I right?' Ian was a couple of years younger than Pat, skinnier and brown-haired, but the resemblance was obvious.

'Yeah, that's Ian. God, he looks so young there . . . He was really shy, back then.'

I tapped Conor's chest. 'And who's this?'

'That's Conor.'

It came out promptly and easily, no tension around it. I said, 'He's the guy holding Emma in her christening photo, the one in her room. He's her godfather?'

'Yeah.' The mention of Emma made Fiona's face tighten up. She pressed her fingertips on the photo like she was trying to push herself into it.

I said easily, moving on to the next face, 'Which makes this guy Mac, right?' Chubby and bristle-haired, outflung arms and pristine white Nikes. You could have told what generation these kids were just from their clothes: no hand-me-downs, nothing mended, everything was brand-new and brand name.

'Yeah. And that's Shona.' Red hair, the kind that would have been frizzy if she hadn't spent a lot of time with the straighteners, and skin that I would have bet was freckled under the fake tan and careful makeup. For a strange second I almost felt sorry for these kids. When I was that age, my friends and I were all poor together; it had very little to recommend it, but at least it had involved less effort. 'Her and Mac, they were the ones who could always make us laugh. I'd forgotten her looking like that. She's blond now.'

I asked, 'So you all stay in touch?' I caught myself hoping the answer was yes – not for investigative reasons, but for Pat and Jenny, stranded on their cold deserted island, sea winds blowing. It would have been good to know that some roots had held strong for them.

'Not really. I have the others' phone numbers, but it's been ages. I should ring them, tell them, but I just . . . I can't.'

She brought her mug to her mouth to hide her face. 'Leave the numbers with us,' Richie said helpfully. 'We'll do it. No reason you should have to break the news.'

Fiona nodded, without looking at him, and fumbled in her pockets for her phone. Richie ripped a page out of his notebook and passed it to her. As she wrote I asked, moving her back towards safer ground, 'It sounds like you were a pretty close-knit bunch. How did you get out of touch?'

'Just life, mostly. Once Pat and Jenny and Conor went to college . . . Shona and Mac are a year younger than them, and me and Ian are another year, so we weren't on the same buzz any more. They could go to pubs, and proper clubs, and they were meeting new people at college – and without the three of them, the rest of us just didn't . . . It wasn't the same.' She handed the paper and pen back to Richie. 'We all tried – at first we all still saw each other all the time. It was weird because suddenly we had to schedule stuff days in advance and someone was always pulling out at the last minute, but we did hang out. Gradually, though, it just got to be less and less. Even up until a couple of years ago, we still met up for a pint every few weeks, but it just . . . it stopped working.'

She had her hands wrapped around the mug again, tilting it in circles and watching the tea swirl. The smell of it was doing its job, making this alien place feel homey and safe. 'Actually, it probably stopped working a long time before that. You can see it in the photos: we stop being jigsawed together like in that one there, instead we're just these elbows and knees stuck out at each other, all awkward . . . We just didn't want to see it. Pat, especially. The less it worked, the harder he tried. We'd be sitting on the pier or somewhere, and Pat'd be spread out till he was practically stretching, trying to keep close to all of us, make it feel like one big gang again. I think he was proud of it, that he still hung out with the same friends he'd had since he was a kid. That meant something to him. He didn't want to let it go.'

She was unusual, Fiona: perceptive, acute, sensitive; the kind of girl who would spend a long time alone thinking about something she didn't understand, picking away at it until the knot unravelled. It made her a useful witness, but I don't like dealing with unusual people. 'Four guys, three girls,' I said. 'Three couples and an odd man out? Or just a gang of mates?'

Fiona almost smiled, down at the photo. 'A gang of mates, basically. Even when Jenny and Pat started going out, it didn't change things as much as you'd think. Everyone had seen it coming for ages, anyway.'

I said, 'I remember you saying you dreamed about someone loving you the way Pat loved Jenny. The other lads were no prizes, no? You didn't bother giving it a go with any of them?'

She blushed. The rosiness drove the grey out of her face, turned her young and vivid. For a moment I thought it was for Pat, that he had been filling up the place other boys could have had, but she said, 'I actually did. Conor . . . we went out, just for a while. Four months, the summer I was sixteen.'

Which was practically marriage, at that age. I caught the tiny shift of Richie's feet. I said, 'But he treated you badly.'

The blush brightened. 'No. Not badly. I mean, he was never mean to me, nothing like that.'

'Really? Most kids that age, they can be pretty cruel.'

'Conor never was. He was . . . he's a sweet guy. Kind.'

I said, 'But . . . ?'

'But . . .' Fiona rubbed at her cheeks, like she was trying to wipe the flush away. 'I mean, I was kind of startled when he even asked me out – I always wondered if maybe he was into Jenny. Nothing he said, just . . . you know how you get a vibe? And then, once we were going out, he . . . it felt like . . . I mean, we had a great time, we had a laugh, but he always wanted to do stuff together with Pat and Jenny. Like go to the cinema with them, or go hang out on the beach with them, or whatever. All his body, all the angles of him always pointed Jenny's way. And when he looked at her . . . he lit up. He'd tell some joke, and on the punchline he'd look at her, not at me . . .'

And there was our motive, the oldest one in the world. In a strange way, it was comforting, knowing that I had been right, way back at the beginning: this hadn't blown in off the wide sea like some killer gale and crashed into the Spains at random. It had grown out of their own lives.

I could feel Richie practically thrumming, beside me, with how badly he wanted to move. I didn't look at him. I said, 'You thought it was Jenny he wanted. He was going out with you to get closer to her.'

I tried to soften it, but it came out brutal all the same. She flinched. 'I guess. Sort of. I think maybe partly that, and partly he was hoping, if we were together, we'd be like them; like Jenny and Pat. They were . . .'

On the page facing the group shot was a photo of Pat and Jenny – taken the same day, going by the clothes. They were side by side on the wall, leaning into each other, faces turned together, close enough that their noses brushed. Jenny was smiling up at Pat; his face looking down at her was absorbed, intent, happy. The air around them was a hot, sweet summer-white. Far behind their shoulders, a slip of sea was blue as flowers.

Fiona's hand hovered over the photo, like she wanted to touch but couldn't do it. She said, 'I took that.'

'It's very good.'

'They were easy to shoot. Most of the time, when you're taking a shot of two people, you have to be careful with the space in between them, how it breaks up the light. With Pat and Jenny, it was like the light didn't break, just kept going straight across the gap . . . They were something special. They both had a load going for them anyway – they were both really popular at school, Pat was great at rugby, Jenny always had a load of guys after her – but together . . . They were golden. I could've watched them all day. You looked at them and you thought, *That. That's how it's supposed to be.*'

Her fingertip brushed their clasped hands, skated away. 'Conor . . . his parents were separated, his dad was over in England or somewhere – I'm not positive, Conor never talked about him. Pat and Jenny were the happiest couple he'd ever known. It was like he wanted to *be* them, and he thought if we went out together, we might . . . I didn't put all this stuff into words at the time, or anything, but afterwards, I thought maybe . . .'

I asked, 'Did you talk to him about it?'

'No. I was too embarrassed. I mean, my *sister* . . .' Fiona ran her hands through her hair, pulling it forward to hide her cheeks. 'I just broke it off. It wasn't that big a deal. It wasn't like I was in *love* with him. We were just kids.'

But it must have been a big deal, all the same. *My sister* . . . Richie shoved back his chair and headed across to switch on the electric kettle again. He said easily, over his shoulder, 'I remember you told us Pat got jealous of other guys fancying Jenny, back when you were teenagers. Was that Conor, yeah?'

That brought Fiona's head up, but he was shaking a coffee sachet and looking at her with simple interest. She said, 'He wasn't jealous like you mean. He just . . . he'd noticed it, too. So when I broke up with Conor, Pat got me on my own a couple of days later and asked me was that why. I didn't want to tell him, but Pat . . . he's really easy to talk to. I always told him stuff. He was like my big brother. So we ended up talking about it.'

Richie whistled. 'When I was a young fella,' he said, 'I would've been raging if my mate was after my girlfriend. I'm not the violent type, but he'd've got a smack in the puss.'

'I think Pat thought about it. I mean' – a sudden flash of alarm – 'he wasn't the violent type either, not ever, but like you said . . . He was pretty angry. He'd called round to our house to see me – Jenny was out shopping – and when I told him he just walked out. He was *white*; his face looked like it was made out of something solid. I was actually scared – not that I thought he'd *do* anything to Conor, I knew he wouldn't, but I just . . . I thought what if everyone found out, it'd smash the gang to pieces, everything would be horrible. I wished . . .' She ducked her head. More quietly, down to her mug: 'I wished I'd kept my stupid mouth shut. Or just never gone near Conor to begin with.'

I said, 'It was hardly your fault. You couldn't have known. Or could you?'

Fiona shrugged. 'Probably not. I felt like I could've, though. Like, why would he be into me when Jenny was around?' Her head was tucked down lower.

There it was again, that glimpse of something deep and tangled, stretched between her and Jenny. I said, 'That must have been pretty humiliating.'

'I survived. I mean, I was sixteen; everything was humiliating.'

She was trying to turn it into a joke, but it fell flat. Richie gave her a grin, as he leaned over her shoulder to take her mug, but she passed it to him without catching his eye. I said, 'Pat wasn't the only one who had a right to be pissed off. Weren't you angry, too? With Jenny, or Conor, or both?'

'I wasn't that kind of kid. I just felt like it was my own fault. For being such an idiot.'

I asked, 'And Pat didn't get physical with Conor after all?'

'I don't think so. Neither of them had bruises or anything, not that I saw. I don't know exactly what happened. Pat phoned me the next day and said not to worry about it, forget we ever had the conversation. I asked him what happened, but all he'd say was that it wasn't going to be a problem any more.'

In other words, Pat had kept control, dealt neatly with a nasty situation and kept the drama to a minimum. Conor, meanwhile, had been smacked down good and hard by Pat, humiliated even more excruciatingly than Fiona, and left in no doubt that he didn't have a chance in hell with Jenny. This time I did look at Richie. He was messing with tea bags.

I asked, 'And was it a problem after that?'

'No. Never. None of us ever said anything about it. Conor was extra nice to me for a while, like maybe he was trying to make up for things going wrong – except he always was nice to me anyway, so . . . And I got the feeling he was keeping his distance from Jenny – nothing too obvious, but he made sure it was never just the two of them going anywhere, stuff like that. Basically, though, every-thing went back to normal.'

Fiona had her head bent, picking bobbles of fluff off the sleeve of her cardigan, and the residue of that blush was still on her cheeks. I asked, 'Did Jenny find out?'

'That I'd broken up with Conor? She couldn't exactly miss it.'

'That he had been interested in her.'

The tinge of red deepened again. 'I think she did, actually. I mean, I actually think she might have known all along. I never told her, and no way would Conor have, or Pat – he's really protective, he wouldn't have wanted to worry her. But one night, a couple of weeks after that stuff with Pat happened, Jenny came into my room – we were getting ready for bed, she was already in her pyjamas. She was just standing there, messing with my hair clips, sticking them on the ends of her fingers and stuff. In the end I was like, "What?" She goes, "I'm really sorry about you and Conor." I said something like, "I'm fine, I don't care" – I mean, it had been weeks, she'd already said it a load of times, I didn't know what she was getting at – but she went, "No, seriously. If it was my fault – if I could've done anything differently . . . I mean, I'm so, so sorry, that's all."'

Fiona laughed, a small wry breath. 'God, we were both *dying* of embarrassment. I was like, "No, it wasn't your fault, why would it be your fault, I'm fine, good night . . ." I just wanted her to leave. Jenny – for a second I thought she was going to say something else, so I stuck my head in the wardrobe and started throwing clothes around, like I was getting out stuff for the next day. When I looked around, she'd gone. We never talked about it again, but that's why I figured she knew. About Conor.'

'And she was worried that you felt she'd been leading him on,' I said. 'Did you?'

'I never even thought about it.' Fiona caught my questioning eyebrow, and her eyes skipped away. 'Well. I mean, I thought about it, but I never blamed her for . . . Jenny liked flirting. She liked getting attention from guys – she was eighteen, of course she did. I don't think she encouraged Conor, exactly, but I think she knew he was into her, and I think she enjoyed it. That's all.'

I asked, 'Do you think she did anything about it?'

Fiona's head snapped up and she stared at me. 'Like what? Like telling him to back off? Or like getting *together* with him?'

I said blandly, 'Either one.'

'She was going out with *Pat*! Like seriously going out, not just kid stuff. They were in *love*. And Jenny's not some kind of two-timing— That's my *sister* you're talking about.'

I raised my hands. 'I'm not doubting for a second that they were in love. But a teenage girl, just starting to realise that she's going to spend the rest of her life with the same man: she could panic, feel like she needed one little moment with another guy before she settled down. That wouldn't make her a slapper.'

Fiona was shaking her head, hair flying. 'You don't get it. Jenny— When she does something, she does it *properly*. Even if she hadn't been crazy about Pat – and she was – she'd never cheat on anyone. Not even a kiss.'

She was telling the truth, but that didn't mean she was right. Once Conor's mind started breaking loose from its moorings, one old kiss could have grown into a million sweet possibilities, swaying just out of reach. 'Fair enough,' I said. 'What about confronting Conor? Would she have done that?'

'I don't think so. I mean, what for? What good would it have done? It would've just embarrassed everyone, and maybe messed up Pat and Conor. Jenny wouldn't have wanted that. She's not some drama queen.'

Richie poured boiling water. 'I'd have said Pat and Conor were already well messed up, no? I mean, even if Pat didn't give Conor a few slaps that day, he wasn't a holy martyr. He couldn't exactly keep on being mates like nothing had happened.'

'Why not? It's not like Conor had *done* anything. They were best friends; they weren't going to let something like that wreck everything. Is any of this . . . ? Why . . . ? I mean, it was like eleven years ago.'

Fiona was starting to look wary. Richie shrugged, dumping a tea bag in the bin. 'I'm only saying: they must've been pretty close, if they got past something like that. I've had good mates in my time, but I've got to say, any of that carry-on and they'd've been on their bikes.'

'They were. Close. We all were, but Pat and Conor, they were different. I think . . .' Richie handed her a fresh mug of tea; she swirled the spoon in it absently. She was concentrating, feeling for the words. 'I always thought it was because of their dads. Conor's dad, like I told you, he wasn't around, and Pat's dad died when he was like eight . . . That makes a difference. To guys, especially. There's something about guys who had to be the man of the family when they were just kids. Guys who had to be too responsible, too early. It shows.'

Fiona glanced up; our eyes met, and for some reason hers skipped away, too quickly. 'Anyway,' she said. 'They had that in common. I guess it was a big deal to them both, having someone around who understood. Sometimes they used to go for walks, just the two of them – like down the beach, or wherever. I used to watch them. Sometimes they wouldn't even talk; just walk, like close together, so their shoulders were practically touching. In step. They'd get back looking calmer; smoothed out. They were *good* for each other. When you've got a friend like that, you'd do a lot to hang on to him.'

The sudden, painful flare of envy caught me by surprise. I was a loner, my last few years in school. I could have done with a friend like that.

Richie said, 'You would, all right. I know you said college got in the way, but I'd say it took more than just that to make you lot drop each other.'

Fiona said, unexpectedly, 'Yeah, it did. I think when you're kids, you're less . . . defined? Then you get older and you start deciding what kind of person you want to be, and it doesn't always match up with what your friends are turning into.'

'I know what you mean. Me and my mates from school, we still meet up, but half of us want to talk about gigs and Xbox, and the other half want to talk about the colour of baby shite. Lots of long silences, these days.' Richie slid into his seat, handed me a mug of coffee and took a big slug of his own. 'So who went what way, in your gang?'

'At first it was mostly Mac and Ian. They wanted to be, like, rich guys about town – Mac works for an estate agent, Ian does something in banking, I'm not even sure what. They started going to all the super-trendy places, like drinking in Café en Seine and then on to Lillie's, places like that. When we'd all meet up, Ian would be telling you how much he paid for every single thing he was wearing, and Mac would be, like, *shouting* about how some girl had been all over him the night before and the tide wouldn't take her out, but he was in the mood for some charity work so he threw her a length . . . They thought I was an idiot for going into photography – specially Mac – and he kept *telling* me I was an idiot and I was never going to make the big bucks and I should grow up, and I needed to buy myself some decent clothes so I'd have a chance at bagging a guy who could look *after* me. And then Ian's company sent him to Chicago and Mac was mostly in Leitrim, selling apartments in these big developments down there, so we got out of touch. I figured . . .'

She turned pages in the album, gave a wry little smile to a shot of the four lads making duckfaces and faux-gangster hand signs. 'I mean, an awful lot of people went like that during the boom. It's not like Mac and Ian were going out of their way to be tossers; they were just doing what everyone else was. I figured they'd outgrow it. Up until then, they're no fun to be around, but they're still good guys, underneath. People you knew when you were teenagers, the ones who saw your stupidest haircut and the most embarrassing things you've done in your life, and they still cared about you after all that: they're not replaceable, you know? I always thought we'd get back on track, someday. Now, after this . . . I don't know.'

The smile was gone. I asked, 'Conor didn't go to Lillie's with them?'

A momentary shadow of the smile flitted back. 'God, no. Not his style.'

'He's more of a loner?'

'Not a loner. I mean, he'd be down the pub having a laugh as much as anyone, but the pub wouldn't be Lillie's. Conor's kind of intense. He never had any time for trendy stuff; he said that was letting other people make your decisions for you, and he was old enough to make his own. And he thought all the my-credit-card-is-bigger-than-your-credit-card stuff was idiotic. He said that to Ian and Mac, that they were turning into a pair of brain-dead sheep. They didn't take it too well.'

'An angry young man,' I said.

Fiona shook her head. 'Not angry. Just . . . what I said before. They didn't match up any more, and that bothered all three of them. They took it out on each other.'

If I stayed on Conor much longer, she was going to start wondering. 'What about Shona? Who did she stop matching up with?'

'Shona . . .' Fiona shrugged, eloquently. 'Shona's somewhere out there being the girl version of Mac and Ian. A lot of fake tan, a lot of labels, a lot of friends with fake tans and labels, and they're bitchy – not once in a while, the way everyone is, but all the *time*. When we met up, she'd keep on making little snide comments about Conor's haircut, or my clothes, and she'd get Mac and Ian laughing along – she was funny, she always was, but it didn't use to be *vicious* funny. Then this one time a few years ago I texted her to see if she was on for pints, just like normal, and she basically texted me back saying she had got engaged – we hadn't even met her boyfriend, all we knew was he was loaded – and she would die of embarrassment if her *fiancé* ever saw her with someone like me, so keep an eye on the Social and Personal sections for her wedding photos, bye!' Another dry little shrug. 'Her, I'm not positive she's going to outgrow it.'

'What about Pat and Jenny?' I asked. 'Did they want to be cool kids about town, too?'

Pain arced across Fiona's face, but she gave her head a quick jerk and shook it away, reached for her mug. 'Sort of. Not like Ian and Mac, but yeah, they liked going to the in places, wearing the right stuff. For them, though, the big deal was always each other. Getting married, getting a house, having kids.'

'Last time we talked, you mentioned that you and Jenny spoke every day, but you hadn't seen each other in a long time. You drifted too. Was that why? She and Pat were on their own little domestic buzz, and it didn't match with yours?'

She flinched. 'That sounds awful. But yeah, I guess that was it. The further they got down that road, the further they got from the rest of us. Once Emma came, they were all about bedtime routines and putting her name down for schools, and it's not like the rest of us knew anything about that.'

'Like my lot,' Richie said, nodding. 'Baby shite and curtains.'

'Yeah. At first they could get a babysitter and come for a few pints, so at least we saw them, but once they moved out to Brianstown . . . I'm not sure they really wanted to come out, anyway. They were busy doing the family thing, and they wanted to do it right; they weren't into getting pissed in pubs and falling home at three in the morning, not any more. They invited us around all the time, but the distance, and with everyone working long hours . . .'

'Nobody could make it. Been there. When was the last time they invited you, do you remember?'

'Months ago. May, June. After all the times I couldn't make it, Jenny kind of gave up.' Fiona's hands were starting to clench around her mug. 'I should've made more of an effort.'

Richie shook his head easily. 'No reason why you should've. You were doing your thing, they were doing theirs, everyone was well and happy – they were happy, yeah?'

'Yeah. I mean, the last few months they were worried about money, but they knew they'd be OK in the end. Jenny said it to me a couple of times, that she wasn't going to let herself get all hyper because she knew they'd come out all right somehow or other.'

'And you figured she was right?'

'I actually did, yeah. That's what Jenny's like: things do work out for her. Some people, they're just good at life. They do it right, without even thinking about it. Jenny always had the knack.'

For a flash I saw Geri in her savoury-smelling kitchen, examining Colm's homework and laughing at Phil's joke and keeping an eye on the ball that Andrea was batting around; and then Dina, wild-haired and claw-fingered, fighting me for no reason she could ever have named. I managed not to look at my watch. 'I know what you mean,' I said. 'I would have envied that. Did you?'

Fiona thought about that, wrapping hair around her finger. 'When we were younger, maybe. Probably. You know when you're teenagers, no one has a clue what they're at? Jenny and Pat always knew what they were doing. Probably that was one of the reasons I went out with Conor – I was hoping if I did the same stuff Jenny did, I'd be like that. Certain about stuff. I would've liked that.' She unspiralled the lock of hair and examined it, twisting it to catch and lose the light. Her nails were bitten down to the quick. 'But once we grew up ˙. . . no. I didn't want Jenny's life: working in PR, getting married that early, having kids straightaway – none of that. Sometimes I kind of *wished* I wanted it, though. It would've made life a lot simpler. Does that make sense?'

'Absolutely,' I said. Actually it sounded like some teenager's whine, *I wish I could do things the normal way but I'm just too special,* but I kept the zap of irritation to myself. 'What about the designer gear, though? The expensive holidays? That must have stung, watching Jenny enjoy all that while you were stuck sharing a flat and counting your pennies.'

She shook her head. 'I'd only look stupid in designer clothes. I'm not that into money.'

'Come on, Ms Rafferty. Everyone wants money. That's nothing to be ashamed of.'

'Well, I don't want to be *broke*. But it's not the most important thing in my entire universe. What I want is to be a really good photographer – like good enough that I wouldn't have to try and explain to you about Pat and Jenny, or about Pat and Conor; I could just show you my photos, and you'd see. If that takes a few years of working at Pierre's for crap money while I learn, then OK, fair enough. My flat's nice, my car works, I go out every weekend. Why would I want more money?'

Richie said, 'That's not how the rest of the gang thought, but.'

'Conor did, kind of. He doesn't care that much about money either. He does web design, and he's really into it – he says in a hundred years' time it'll be one of the great art forms – so he'd do stuff for free, if it was something that got him interested. But the others . . . no. They never got it. They thought – I think even Jenny thought – I was just being immature, and sooner or later I'd get a grip.'

I said, 'That must have been infuriating. Your oldest friends, your own sister, and they thought everything you wanted was worthless.'

Fiona exhaled and pushed her fingers through her hair, trying to find the right words. 'Not really. I mean, I've got plenty of friends who do get it. The old gang . . . yeah, I wished we were on the same wavelength, but I didn't blame them. Everything in the papers, in magazines, on the news . . . it was like you were a moron, or a freak, if you just wanted to be comfortable and do stuff you love. You weren't supposed to be thinking about that; you were only supposed to be thinking about getting rich and buying property. I couldn't really get all pissed off with the others for doing exactly what they were supposed to do.'

She ran her hand over the album. 'That's why we drifted. Not the age gap. Pat and Jenny and Ian and Mac and Shona, they were all doing the things you're supposed to do. In different ways, so they drifted apart too, but they all wanted what we're supposed to want. Conor and me, we wanted something else. The others couldn't understand that. And we didn't understand them, not really. And that was the end of that.'

She had turned the pages back to that shot of the seven of them on the wall. There was no bitchiness in her voice, just a kind of sad, bewildered wonder at how strange life could be, and how final. I said, 'Pat and Conor obviously managed to stay close, though, didn't they? If Pat picked Conor to be Emma's godfather. Or was that Jenny's call?'

'No! That was Pat. I told you, they were best friends. Conor was Pat's best man. They stayed close.'

Right up until something changed, and they hadn't been close any more. 'Was he a good godfather?'

'Yeah. He was great.' Fiona smiled, down at the gangly boy in the photo. The thought of telling her made me wince. 'We used to bring the kids to the zoo together, him and me, and he'd tell Emma stories about the animals having mad adventures after the zoo got locked up for the night . . . One time she lost her teddy, the one she had in bed at night? She was devastated. Conor told her the teddy had won a round-the-world trip, and he got all these postcards of places like Surinam and Mauritius and Alaska, I don't even know where he got them – I guess online – and he cut out photos of a teddy like hers and stuck them on the cards, and wrote messages from the teddy, like, "Today I went skiing on this mountain and then drank hot chocolate, I'm sending you a big hug, love, Benjy" and he'd post them to Emma. Every single day, till she got all into this new doll and she wasn't upset about the bear any more, she got one of those cards.'

'When was that?'

'Like three years ago? Jack was only a baby, so . . .'

That ripple of pain darted across Fiona's face again. Before she could start thinking, I asked, 'When was the last time you saw Conor?'

There was a sudden wary flicker in her eyes. The safe shell of concentration was starting to thin; she knew something was up, even if she couldn't tell what. She sat back in her chair and wrapped her arms around her waist. 'I'm not sure. It's been a while. A couple of years, I guess.'

'He wasn't at Emma's birthday party, this April?'

The tension in her shoulders went up a notch. 'No.'

'Why not?'

'I guess he couldn't make it.'

I said, 'You've just told us Conor was willing to go to a lot of trouble for his goddaughter. Why wouldn't he bother with her birthday party?'

Fiona shrugged. 'Ask him. I don't know.'

She was picking at the sleeve of her jumper again and not looking at either of us. I leaned back, got comfortable and waited.

It took a few minutes. Fiona glanced at her watch and ripped at fragments of fluff, until she realised that we could wait longer than she could. Finally she said, 'I think they could have maybe had some kind of argument.'

I nodded. 'An argument about what?'

An uncomfortable shrug. 'When Jenny and Pat bought the house, Conor thought they were nuts. I did too, but they didn't want to hear that, so I tried a couple of times and then I kept my mouth shut. I mean, even if I wasn't sure it would work out, they were happy, so I wanted to be happy for them.'

'But Conor didn't. Why not?'

'He's not great at keeping his mouth shut and just nodding and smiling, even when that's the best thing he could do. He thinks it's hypocritical. If he thinks something's a crap idea, he'll say it's a crap idea.'

'And that annoyed Pat, or Jenny? Or both of them?'

'Both. They were like, "How else are we supposed to get on the property ladder? How else are we supposed to buy a decent-sized house with a garden for the kids? It's a brilliant investment, in a few years it'll be worth enough that we can sell it and buy somewhere in Dublin, but for now . . . If we were millionaires, yeah, we'd get a great big place in Monkstown straight off, but we're not, so unless Conor wants to lend us a few hundred grand, this is what we're getting." They were really pissed off that he wasn't supportive. Jenny kept saying, "I don't want to listen to all that negativity, if everyone thought that way then the country would be in ruins, we want to be around positivity . . ." She was genuinely upset. Jenny's a big believer in positive mental attitude; she felt like Conor would wreck everything if they kept listening to him. I don't know the details, but I think in the end there was some kind of big blowup. After that Conor wasn't around, and they didn't mention him. Why? Does it matter?'

I asked, 'Did Conor still have feelings for Jenny?'

It was the million-dollar question, but Fiona just gave me a look like I hadn't heard a word she had said. 'That was forever ago. It was kid stuff, for God's sake.'

'Kid stuff can be pretty powerful. There are plenty of people out there who never forget their first loves. Do you think Conor was one of them?'

'I don't have a clue. You'd have to ask him.'

'What about you?' I asked. 'Do you still have feelings for him?'

I had expected her to snap at me on that one, but she thought about it, her head bent over his face in the album, her fingers tangling in her hair again. 'It depends what you mean by feelings,' she said. 'I miss him, yeah. Sometimes I think about him. We'd been friends since I was, like, eleven. That's important. But it's not like I get all wistful and pine for the one who got away. I don't want to get back *together* with him. If that's what you wanted to know.'

'It didn't occur to you to stay in touch after he had the blowup with Pat and Jenny? It sounds like you had more in common with him than they did, after all.'

'I thought about it, yeah. I left it a while, in case Conor needed to simmer down – I didn't want to get in the middle of anything – but then I rang him a couple of times. He didn't get back to me, so I didn't push it. Like I said, he wasn't the centre of my world or anything. I figured, same as with Mac and Ian, we'd find each other again, somewhere down the line.'

This wasn't where or how she had pictured the reunion. 'Thanks,' I said. 'That could be helpful.'

I reached to take the album, but Fiona's hand came out to stop me. 'Can I just – for a second . . . ?'

I moved back and left her to it. She pulled the album closer, circled it with her forearms. The room was still; I could hear the faint hiss of the central heating moving through the walls.

'That summer,' Fiona said, barely to us. Her head was bent over the photo, hair tumbling. 'We laughed so *much.* The ice cream . . . There was this little ice-cream kiosk, down near the beach – our parents used to go there when they were kids. That summer the landlord said he was raising the rent to something astronomical, there was no way the guy could pay it – the landlord wanted to force him out, so he could sell the land for, I don't know, offices or apartments or something. Everyone around was *outraged* – the place was like an institution, you know? Kids got their first ice cream there, you went on first dates there . . . Pat and Conor, they said, "There's only one way to keep him in business: we'll see how much ice cream we can get into us." We ate ice cream every single day, that summer. It was like a mission. We'd only be finished one lot, and Pat and Conor would disappear and they'd come back with *another* big handful of cones, and we'd all be screaming at them to get those away from us; they'd be cracking up laughing, telling us, "Go on, you have to do it, it's for the cause, rage against the machine . . ." Jenny kept saying she was going to turn into a great big lump of lard and then Pat would be sorry, but she ate them anyway. We all did.'

Her fingertip brushed across the photo, lingering on Pat's shoulder, Jenny's hair, coming to rest on Conor's T-shirt. She said, on a sad whisper of a laugh, '"I go to JoJo's."'

For a second Richie and I didn't breathe. Then Richie said, easily, 'JoJo's was the ice-cream shop, yeah?'

'Yeah. He gave out these little badges, that summer, so you could show you supported him. "I go to JoJo's," and a picture of an ice-cream cone. Half of Monkstown was wearing them – old women and everything. We saw a *priest* with one once.' Her finger shifted, moving off a pale spot on Conor's T-shirt. It was small and blurry enough that we hadn't looked at it twice. Each bright T-shirt and top had one somewhere, the chest, the collar, the sleeve.

I bent to fish in the cardboard box, pulled out the little evidence bag that held the rusted pin we had found hidden in Jenny's drawer. I passed it across the table. 'Is this one of the badges?'

Fiona said softly, 'Oh my God. God, look at that . . .' She tilted the badge to the light, searching for the image through the wear and the print dust that had turned up nothing. 'Yeah, it is. Is this Pat's or Jenny's?'

'We don't know. Which of them would have been more likely to keep it?'

'I'm not sure. I would've said neither of them, actually. Jenny doesn't like clutter, and Pat doesn't really get sentimental like that. He's more practical. He'll *do* stuff, like the ice creams, but he wouldn't keep the badge just for the sake of it. Maybe he could've forgotten it in with a bunch of other things . . . Where was it?'

'In the house,' I said. I reached out a hand for the bag, but Fiona held on to it, fingers pressed on the badge through the thick plastic.

'What . . . why do you need it? Does it have something to do with . . . ?'

I said, 'In the early stages, we have to go on the assumption that anything could be relevant.'

Richie asked, before she could press harder, 'Did the campaign work? Yous got the landlord off JoJo's back?'

Fiona shook her head. 'God, no. He lived in Howth or some-where; he didn't care if the whole of Monkstown was sticking pins in his voodoo doll. And even if we'd all eaten ice cream till we dropped dead of heart attacks, JoJo wouldn't have been able to pay what the guy was looking for. I think we sort of knew that all along, that he was going to lose. We just wanted . . .' She turned the bag in her hands. 'That was the summer before Pat and Jenny and Conor were going to college. We knew that, too, deep down: that everything was going to start changing when they went. I think Pat and Conor started the whole thing because they wanted to make that summer special. It was the last one. I think they wanted us all to have something good to look back on. Silly stories to tell, years down the line. Stuff so we could say, "Do you remember . . . ?"'

She would never say it about that summer again. I asked, 'Do you still have your JoJo's badge?'

'I don't know. Maybe somewhere. I've got a bunch of stuff in boxes in my mum's attic – I hate throwing stuff away. I haven't seen it in years, though. Forever.' She smoothed the plastic over the badge for a moment, then held it out to me. 'When you're done with it, if Jenny doesn't want it, could I have it?'

'I'm sure we can work something out.'

'Thanks,' Fiona said. 'I'd like that.' She took a breath, pulling herself out of someplace wrapped in warm sunlight and helpless laughter, and checked her watch. 'I should go. Is that . . . ? Was there anything else?'

Richie's eyes met mine, with a question in them.

We would need to talk to Fiona again: we needed Richie to stay the good guy, the safe one who didn't hit her on every bruise. 'Ms Rafferty,' I said quietly, leaning forward on my elbows, 'there's something I need to tell you.'

She froze. The look in her eyes was terrible: *Oh God, not more.* 'The man we've got under arrest,' I said. 'It's Conor Brennan.'

Fiona stared. When she could, she said, panting for breath, 'No. Hang on. *Conor?* What . . . Under arrest for *what?*'

'We've arrested him for the attack on your sister and the murders of her family.'

Fiona's hands jumped; for a second I thought she was going to slap them over her ears, but she pressed them on the table again. She said, flat and hard as a brick slamming down on stone, 'No. Conor didn't.'

She was as certain as she had been about Pat. She needed to be. If either of them had done this, then her past as well as her present was a mauled, bleeding ruin. All that bright landscape of ice creams and in-jokes, screams of laughter on a wall, her first dance and her first drink and her first kiss: nuked, humming with radio-activity, untouchable.

I said, 'He's made a full confession.'

'I don't care. You— What the *fuck*? Why didn't you tell me? You just let me sit here talking about him, let me yap away and hoped I'd say something that would make things worse for him— That's *shit. If* Conor actually confessed, then it's only because you messed with his head the way you've been messing with mine. He *didn't do this.* This is *insane.*'

Good middle-class girls don't talk to detectives that way, but Fiona was too furiously intent for caution. Her hands were fisted on the table and her face looked bleached and friable, like a shell dried out on sand. She made me want to do something, anything, the stupider the better: take it all back, push her out the door, spin her chair to the wall so I wouldn't have to see her eyes. 'It's not just the confession,' I said. 'We have evidence backing it up. I'm so sorry.'

'What kind of evidence?'

'I'm afraid we can't go into that. But we're not talking about little coincidences that can be explained away. We're talking about solid, unarguable, incriminating evidence. Proof.'

Fiona's face shut down. I could see her mind speeding. 'Right,' she said, after a minute. She pushed her mug away on the table and got up. 'I have to get back to Jenny.'

I said, 'Until Mr Brennan is charged, we won't be releasing his name to the press. We'd prefer that you don't mention it to anyone, either. That includes your sister.'

'I wasn't planning to.' She pulled her coat off the back of her chair and swung it on. 'How do I get out of here?'

I opened the door for her. 'We'll be in touch,' I said, but Fiona didn't look up. She headed down the corridor fast, with her chin tucked into her collar like she was already shielding herself against the cold.

# 14

The incident room had emptied, just the kid manning the tipline and a couple of others working late, who upped the paper-shuffling when they saw me. Richie said bluntly, as we got to our desks, 'I don't think she had anything to do with it.'

He was all geared up to fight his corner. I said, giving him a quick grin, 'Well, that's a relief. At least we're on the same page on this one.' He didn't grin back. 'Relax, Richie. I don't think she did, either. She envied Jenny, all right, but if she was going to flip out on her, it would've been back when Jenny had the perfect picket-fence life, not now that it was all in ruins and Fiona got to say *I told you so*. Unless her phone records come back with a bunch of calls to Conor, or her financials come back with some massive debt, I think we can cross her off our list.'

Richie said, 'Even if it turns out she's skint. I believe her: she's not into money. And she was doing her best to give us all the info she could, even when it hurt. Whoever did this, she wants him locked up.'

'Well, she did, until she found out it was Conor Brennan. If we need to talk to her again, she won't be anywhere near as helpful.' I pulled my chair up to my desk and found a report form, for the Super. 'And that's another mark for her being innocent. I'd bet a lot of money that was genuine, her reaction when we told her. That hit her right out of the clear blue sky. If she was behind all this, she'd have been panicking about Conor ever since she found out we had someone in custody. And she sure as hell wouldn't be pointing us in his direction by giving him a motive.'

Richie was copying Fiona's phone numbers into his notebook. He said, 'Not much of a motive.'

'Oh, come on. Spurned love, with a dose of humiliation thrown in? I couldn't have asked for a better one if I'd ordered it from a catalogue.'

'I could. Fiona thought *maybe* Conor might've fancied Jenny, ten years back. That's not a lot of motive in my book.'

'He fancied her *now*. What else do you think the JoJo's badge was about? Jenny wouldn't have kept hers, neither would Pat, but I bet I know someone who would have. And one day, when he was wandering around the Spains' house, he decided to leave Jenny a little present – the creepy bastard. *Remember me, from back when everything was lovely and your life didn't suck dick in hell? Remember all the happy times we had together? Don't you miss me?*'

Richie pocketed his notebook and started flicking through the pile of reports on his desk, but he wasn't reading them. 'Still doesn't point to him killing her. Pat's the jealous type, he's already warned Conor off Jenny once, and he's got to be feeling pretty insecure right now. If he found out Conor was leaving Jenny presents . . .'

I kept my voice down. 'He didn't find out, though, did he? That badge wasn't thrown across the kitchen, or stuffed down Jenny's throat. It was hidden away in her drawer, safe and sound.'

'The badge was. We don't know what else Conor could've left.'

'True enough. But the more little treats he left Jenny, the more it points to him still being mad about her. That's evidence against Conor. Not against Pat.'

'Except Jenny must've known who left that badge. Must've. How many people would own a JoJo's badge, and know to leave it for her? And she kept it. Whatever Conor felt about her, it wasn't just one-way. It's not like she was binning his presents and he flipped out. Pat's the one who would've flipped over what was going on.'

I said, 'As soon as Jenny's doctor cuts down the painkillers, we'll need to have another chat with her, find out exactly what the story was there. She may not remember the other night, but she can't have forgotten that badge.' I thought of Jenny's ripped face, her wrecked eyes, and caught myself hoping that Fiona would convince the doctors to keep her doped up to the gills for a good long time.

Richie flipped pages faster. He asked, 'What about Conor? Were you planning on having another go at him tonight?'

I checked my watch. It was past eight o'clock. 'No. Let him stew a while longer. Tomorrow we'll hit him with everything we've got.'

That made Richie's knees start jiggling, under his desk. He said, 'I'll give Kieran a ring before I head. See if he's come up with anything new on Pat's websites.'

He was already reaching for the phone. 'I'll do it,' I said. 'You do the report for the Super.' I shoved it onto his desk before he could argue.

Even at that hour, Kieran actually sounded pleased to hear from me. 'Kemosabe! I was just thinking about you. One question: am I da man, or am I totally da man?'

For a second I thought matching the jaunty tone would take more than I had left. 'I'm going to go out on a limb and say you're totally da man. What have you got for me?'

'You would be correctamundo. To be honest, when I got your e-mail I was like, yeah, right, even if your guy did take his weasel issues somewhere else, the web's a big place; how am I meant to find him, Google "weasel"? But remember that partial URL the recovery software tossed up? The home-and-garden forum?'

'Yeah.' I gave Richie the thumbs-up. He left the form on his desk and scooted his chair over to mine.

'We checked it out back when I first told you about it: went through the last two months of posts. Closest we got to drama was a couple of guys on the DIY board having a dick-measuring contest about drywalling, whatever the hell that is, which frankly I don't actually care? No one was harassing anyone – there's a decent chance this could be *the* most boring forum ever – no one matched your victim and no one was called anything like sparklyjenny, so we moved on. But then I got your e-mail and I had a brainwave: we could've been looking for the wrong thing, at the wrong time.'

I said, 'It wasn't Jenny who posted there. It was Pat.'

'Bada-bing. And not in the last two months, either. It was back in June. He last posted on Wildwatcher on the thirteenth, right? If he tried anywhere else in the next couple of weeks, I haven't found it yet, but on the twenty-ninth of June he shows up on the "Nature and Wildlife" section of the home-and-garden site, going under Pat-the-lad again. He'd posted on the site before, like a year and a half ago – something to do with his toilet backing up – so probably that's why it occurred to him. Want me to forward the link?'

'Please. Now, if you can.'

'Once more with feeling, Kemosabe: am I da man?'

'You are totally da man.' The corner of Richie's mouth twitched. I gave him the finger. I knew I couldn't get away with talking like that, but I didn't care.

'Music to my ears,' Kieran said. 'Link coming atcha,' and he hung up.

Pat's thread on the home-and-garden site started the same way as his Wildwatcher thread: a rundown of the facts, quick and neat, the kind of rundown I would have been pleased to get from any of my floaters. Where the Wildwatcher thread had ended, though, this one kept going.

*I've checked for scat a few times but no dice, the thing must be going outside to do its business. I put down flour to try and get pawprints but no joy there either, when I went back up to check the flour was sort of smudged and brushed around (can post pix if that helps) but no prints. Only physical sign I've seen is about 10 days ago the thing was going nuts, so I went up in the attic + right under the hole were four long stalks w leaves on, still green (??looked like something off one of the plants from down by the beach? no clue, city guy here) + a piece of wood about 4in x 4 – worn down, w bits of green paint peeling off, like maybe a piece of plank out of a boat. Have no clue a) why any animal would want it or b) how it got it into attic, hole under eaves is only barely big enough. Again can post pix if they could help.*

'We saw that lot,' Richie said quietly. 'In his wardrobe. Remember?'

The biscuit tin, tucked away on Pat's wardrobe shelf. I had

taken it for granted they were gifts from the kids, saved for their sweetness. 'Yeah,' I said. 'I remember.'

*Put out another trap that nite w piece of chicken in it but no joy. Have had people suggest a mink, marten, stoat, but all of those would go for chicken wouldn't they? + why would they be bringing in leaves + wood? Would really like to know what's up there.*

He caught the board's interest straightaway, just like he had caught Wildwatcher's. Within minutes he had replies. Someone thought the animal was moving in and bringing the whole family: *Stockpiling leaves and wood could indicate nesting behaviour. June is late in the year for that . . . but you never know. Have you checked whether any more nesting materials have been added since then?*

Someone else thought he was making a fuss over nothing. *If I were you I wouldnt worry about it. If it was a predator (in other words – anything dangerous) then it would of had to be something smart enough to stay away from free meat. I cant think of anything that would do that. Have you thought about squirrels?? Mice?? Or could be birds? Magpies? Maybe since your near the sea something like seagulls??*

When he checked back in, the next day, Pat sounded unconvinced. *Hi yeah, could be squirrels all right, but have to say from the noises it sounds way bigger. I'm not taking this as definite, cos the acoustics in the house are really weird (someone can be at the other end of the house + sound like they're right next to you) but when its stamping around up there, sounds the size of like a badger to be honest w you – I know there's no way a badger could get up there but defo bigger than a squirrel or a magpie + way bigger than a mouse. Not mad about the idea of having a predator that's too clever to fall for traps. Also not mad about the idea of it nesting up there. Haven't been up recently but guess I'll have to go check it out.*

The guy who had suggested mice still wasn't impressed. *You said yourself the acoustics are weird. Their probably just amplifing the noises from a couple of mice or something. Your not in Africa or somewhere that it could be a leopard or whatever. Seriously keep going with the mouse traps try different kinds of bait and forget it.*

Pat was still online: *Yeah that's what my wife thinks, actually she*

*thinks prob some kind of bird (wood pigeons?) cos pecking would
explain the tapping noises. Thing is she hasn't actually heard it – noises
are always either a) late at night when she's asleep (haven't been sleeping great the last while myself so awake at odd hours) or b) when she's
cooking + I'd have the kids upstairs out of her way. So she doesn't
realise how loud + basically impressive it is. Trying not to mention it
too often/make a big deal out of it cos I don't want to freak her out but
starting to get to me a bit to be honest. No I'm not worried its going to
like rip us limb from limb but would be a big relief to just know what
it is. Will check out attic + update asap, any + all advice appreciated.*

The floaters were packing up, making sure to do it just loudly
enough that I would notice how late they had stayed. 'Good night,
Detectives,' one of them said, when they were hovering in the
doorway. Richie said automatically, 'Safe home, see yous tomorrow'; I raised a hand and kept scrolling.

It was late the next night, coming up to midnight, before Pat got
back online. *OK went up to the attic and checked it out, no more
nesting materials or whatever. Only thing is one of the roof beams is
covered all over in what looks like claw marks. Have to say I'm kind of
freaked out because they look like they're from something pretty big.
Thing is though, not positive I'd actually checked out that beam before
(its way off in back corner) so they could have been there for ages, like
even before we moved in – that's what I'm hoping anyway!*

The guy who had suggested nesting was watching the thread:
within a few minutes of Pat's post, he was on with another suggestion. *I assume you have a hatch going up to the attic. In your situation
I would leave the hatch open, mount a camcorder pointing at the hatch
and I would press Record just before you go to bed or before your wife
begins to cook dinner. Sooner or later the animal will get curious . . . and
you will get footage. If you are worried that it will come down into the
main house and be dangerous if trapped then you can nail some chicken
wire over the opening. Hope this helps.*

Pat came back fast and buoyant: just the thought of having the
animal in his sights had lifted his spirits. *Brilliant idea – thanks a
mill! At this stage its been in + out of the house for like a month + a
half, so not too worried it'll suddenly decide to attack at this point.*

*Actually wouldn't mind if it did, I'd give it something to think about, if I can't take it down then I deserve whatever it can dish out right?* He followed that up with three little emoticons rolling back and forth, laughing. *I'd just like to get a good look at the thing, don't mind how, just want to see what I'm dealing with. Also kind of wondering if my wife should see it – if she sees its not just a bird I figure we can get on the same page + work out what to do between the 2 of us. Also would be nice not to have her worrying that I'm losing the bit I have! Camcorder is a little out of our budget at the mo but we've got a video baby monitor I could rig up. Can't believe I didn't think of it before – actually even better than a camcorder cos it does infrared so no need to leave the hatch open – I'll just rig it up in the attic + away we go. I'll give my wife the receiver to watch while dinner is on + keep my fingers xd. She might even let me do the cooking for once!! Wish us luck!* And a small yellow smiley face, waving.

'"Losing the bit I have,"' Richie said.

'It's a figure of speech, old son. This guy kept his head when his best mate fell for his future *wife*: dealt with the situation, no drama, cool as a cucumber. You think he'd have a nervous breakdown over a mink?' Richie, gnawing on his pen, didn't answer.

And that was it from Pat, for a couple of weeks. A few of the regulars wanted updates, there was some sniffiness about blow-ins who came looking for help and never said thank you, and the thread tailed off.

On the fourteenth of July, though, Pat was back, and things had gone up a notch. *Hi guys, me again, really need a hand here. Just to update, I'm trying the video monitor but so far no good. Tried setting camera to catch different bits of the attic but still no go. I know the animal's not gone cos I'm still hearing it like every day/night. Its getting louder – think its got more confident or else maybe its grown bigger. My wife still hasn't heard it ONCE, if I didn't know better I'd swear its deliberately waiting til she isn't around.*

*Anyway here's the update, this aft went up to the attic to see if any more leaves/wood/whatever + in one corner were four animal skeletons. Not an expert here but they looked like rats or maybe squirrels. Heads were gone. Maddest thing is they were lined up really neatly, like someone had arranged them ready for me to find – know that sounds crazy but I swear that's what it looked like. Don't want to say anything to my wife in case she freaks out but guys this IS a predator and I NEED to find out what kind.*

This time the regulars were unanimous: Pat was out of his depth here, he needed a professional and fast. People posted links to pest control services and, less helpfully, to sensationalist news stories where small children had been maimed or killed by unexpected wildlife. Pat sounded a little reluctant (*I was kind of hoping to deal with this myself – don't like getting people in to fix stuff I should be able to sort*), but in the end he handed out thanks all round and headed off to ring the pros.

'Not cool as a cucumber there,' Richie said. I ignored him.

Three days later, Pat was back. *OK so pest control guy came out this morn. Took 1 look at skeletons + said can't help you out man, biggest he deals w is rats + no way is this a rat, rats don't line up bodies like that + rats won't take the head off a squirrel + leave the rest – he's pretty sure all 4 skeletons are squirrels. Never seen anything like it he said. He said maybe a mink or could be some exotic pet that some idiot had to get rid of + let go into the wild. Possibly something like a bobcat or even a wolverine, he said you'd be amazed the tiny spaces these things can slip through. He said could be specialists that would deal w it but I'm not keen on spending loads of dosh to have someone else come out here + tell me not his problem either. Also at this stage starting to feel kind of like its personal – this house ain't big enough for the two of us!!* Those little faces again, rolling and laughing.

*So am looking for ideas on how to trap it/flush it out/what to use for bait/how to get proof it exists for my wife. Night before last thought I had it, was giving my son a bath + the thing started going nuts right over our heads – at first just like a few scratches but gradually built up till it sounded like it was spinning round in circles trying to scratch a hole in the ceiling or something. My son heard it too, wanted to know what it was. Told him it was a mouse – never lie to him normally but he was getting scared and what was I supposed to say?? Legged it downstairs to get my wife to come hear it, by the time we got back upstairs the noise had totally stopped, not another peep out of the little bastard all night. Swear to God it was like it knew. Lads I NEED HELP here. This thing is scaring my son in his own home. My wife looked at me like I was some kind of total looper. I need to get this fucker.*

The desperation rose off the screen, hot fumes like tar smoking in ruthless sun. The scent of it stirred up the board, turned them restless and aggressive. They started jostling Pat: had he shown the skeletons to his wife? What did she think about the animal now? Did he know how dangerous wolverines were? Was he going to call in the specialist? Was he going to put down poison? Was he going to board up the hole under the eaves? What was he going to do next?

They – or, more likely, all the other things crowding in on his life – were getting to Pat: that level-headed ease was fraying at the edges. *To answer your questions no my wife doesn't know about the skeletons, I scheduled pest control guy for when she was going to the shops w the kids + he took them away. I don't know about you but I believe its my job to take care of my wife not scare the shit out of her. Its one thing for her to hear scratching, totally other deal showing her skeletons w heads gone. Once I've got my hands on this thing then obviously I'll tell her everything. Don't exactly like her thinking I'm going mental meanwhile, but I'd rather that than have her petrified every time she has to be in the house on her own, hope that's OK w you but if not basically tough shit.*

*About specialist etc: haven't decided yet but no I'm not planning on boarding up the hole + I'm not planning on poison. Sorry if that's not what you guys would advise but again tough, I'm the one living with this + I am GOING TO find out what it is + I'm going to teach it to fuck w my family, THEN it can bugger off + die wherever it wants but til then I'm not gonna risk losing it. If you have an actual helpful idea then yeah please feel free to contribute I'd be delighted to hear it, but if you're just here to give me hassle for not having this under control then screw you. To everyone who isn't being a shit thanks again + I'll keep you updated.*

At this point someone with a couple of thousand posts to his name said: *Guys. Don't feed the troll.*

Richie asked, 'What's a troll?'

'Seriously? Jesus, have you never been on the internet? I thought you were the wired generation.'

He shrugged. 'I buy music online. Looked stuff up a few times. Message boards, though: nah. Happier with real life.'

'The internet is real life, my friend. All those people on here, they're as real as you and me. A troll is someone who posts bollix to stir up drama. This guy thinks Pat's messing about.'

Once their suspicions were raised, none of the posters wanted to look like suckers: everyone had, apparently, been wondering all along if Pat-the-lad was a troll, an aspiring writer looking for inspiration (*Remember that guy last year on the Structural Issues board with the walled-up room and the human skull? The short story showed up on his blog a month later? Piss off, troll*), a scammer building towards a pitch for money. Within a couple of hours, the general consensus was that if Pat had been for real, he would have put down poison a long time ago, and that any day now he would be back to announce that the mysterious animal had eaten his imaginary kids and ask for help paying for their funerals.

'Jaysus,' Richie said. 'They're a bit harsh.'

'This? Hardly. If you got online more, you'd know this is nothing. It's a wilderness out there; the normal rules don't apply. Decent, polite people who don't raise their voices from one year's end to the next buy a modem and turn into Mel Gibson on tequila slammers. Compared to a lot of the stuff you see, these guys were being real sweethearts.'

Pat had seen it Richie's way, though: when he came back, he came back furious. *Look you pack of wankers I am NOT A FUCKING TROLL OK???? I know you spend all your time on this board but I actually have a fucking LIFE, if I was going to waste my time messing w someones head it wouldnt be you lot of losers, just trying to deal w WHAT IS IN MY ATTIC + if you useless twats cant help me w that then you can FUCK OFF. And he was gone.*

Richie whistled softly. 'That there,' he said, 'that's not just the internet talking. Like you said, Pat was a level-headed guy. To get like that' – he nodded at the screen – 'he must've been well freaked out.'

I said, 'He had reason to be. Something nasty was in his home, scaring his family. And everywhere he turned, people refused to help him. Wildwatcher, the pest-control guy, this board here: all of them basically told him to bugger off, it wasn't their problem; he was on his own. In his place, I think you'd be *well freaked out* too.'

'Yeah. Maybe.' Richie reached out to the keyboard, glancing at me for permission, and scrolled back up to reread. When he was done he said, carefully, 'So. No one but Pat ever actually heard this yoke.'

'Pat and Jack.'

'Jack was three. Kids that age, they're not the best with what's real and what's not.'

'So you're with Jenny,' I said. 'You figure Pat was imagining it.'

Richie said, 'Your man Tom. He wouldn't swear to it that there was ever an animal in the attic.'

It was after half-eight. Down the corridor, the cleaner was playing chart music on her radio and singing along; outside the incident-room windows, the sky was solid black. Dina had been AWOL for four hours. I didn't have time for this. 'And he wouldn't swear there wasn't, either. But you feel that this somehow supports your theory that Pat slaughtered his family. Am I right?'

Richie said, picking the words, 'We know he was under plenty of stress. There's no two ways about that. From what he says on here, sounds like the marriage wasn't doing great, either. If he was in bad enough shape that he was imagining things . . . Yeah, I think that'd make it more likely he went off the deep end.'

'He didn't imagine those leaves and that piece of wood that appeared in the attic. Not unless we did too. I may have my issues, but I don't believe I'm hallucinating quite yet.'

'Like the lads on the board said, those could've been a bird. They're not proof of some mad animal. Any man who wasn't stressed to fuck would've thrown them in the bin, forgotten all about them.'

'And the squirrel skeletons? Were those a bird too? I'm not a wildlife expert, any more than Pat was, but I have to tell you: if we've got some bird in this country that'll decapitate squirrels, eat the flesh and line up the leftovers, nobody told me.'

Richie rubbed the back of his neck and watched my screensaver spiral in slow geometric patterns. He said, 'We didn't see the skeletons. Pat didn't keep those. The leaves, yeah; the skeletons, the bit that would've actually proved there was something dangerous up there, no.'

The flash of irritation made me clamp my jaw tight for a second. 'Come on, old son. I don't know what you keep in your bachelor pad, but I promise you, a married man who tells his wife he wants to store squirrel skeletons in the wardrobe is in for a short sharp shock and a few nights on the sofa. And what about the kids? You think he wanted the kids finding those?'

'I don't know *what* the man wanted. He's all about showing his wife that this yoke exists, but when he gets solid proof, he backs right off: ah, no, couldn't do that, wouldn't want to freak her out. He's dying to get a look at it, but when the pest-control fella says he should get in a specialist: ah, no, waste of money. He's begging this board to help him figure out what's up there, he offers to post photos of the flour on the attic floor, photos of the leaves, but when he finds the skeletons – and they could've had teethmarks on them – not a word about pics. He's acting . . .' Richie glanced sideways at me. 'Maybe I'm wrong, man. But he's acting like, deep down, he knows there's nothing there.'

For a strong, fleeting second I wanted to grab him by the neck and shove him away from the computer, tell him to piss off back to Motor Vehicles, I would handle this case myself. According to the floaters' reports, Pat's brother Ian had never heard anything about any animal. Neither had his old workmates, the friends who had been at Emma's birthday party, the few people he had still been e-mailing. This explained why. Pat couldn't bring himself to tell them, in case they reacted like everyone else, from strangers on discussion boards to his own wife; in case they reacted like Richie.

I said, 'Just asking, son. Where do you think the skeletons materialised from? The pest-control guy saw them, remember.

They weren't all in Pat's mind. I know you think Pat was going off his rocker, but do you seriously think he was biting the heads off squirrels?'

Richie said, 'I didn't say that. But no one except Pat saw the pest-control guy, either. We've only that post to say that he ever called someone in. You said yourself: people lie, on the internet.'

I said, 'So let's find the pest-control guy. Get one of the floaters on to tracking him down. Have him start with the numbers Pat got from the board; if none of those pan out, then he needs to check every company in a hundred-mile radius.' The thought of a floater coming in on this angle, another cool pair of eyes reading through those posts and another face slowly taking on the same look Richie had worn, tightened my neck again. 'Or, better yet, we'll do it ourselves. First thing tomorrow morning.'

Richie tipped my mouse with one finger and watched Pat's posts flick back to life. He said, 'Should be easy enough to find out.'

'Find out what?'

'Whether the animal exists. Couple of video cameras—'

'Because that worked so well for Pat?'

'He didn't have cameras. The baby monitors, they don't record; he could only catch what was happening in real time, when he had a chance to keep an eye out. Get a camera, set it up to record that attic round the clock . . . Inside a few days, if there's anything there, we ought to get a look at it.'

For some reason the idea made me want to bite his head off. I said, 'That's going to look just great on the request form, isn't it? "We'd like to request a valuable piece of department equipment and a massively overworked technician, on the off-chance that we might possibly catch a glimpse of some animal that, *whether it exists or not*, has absolutely sweet fuck-all to do with our case."'

'O'Kelly said, anything we need—'

'I know he did. The request would be approved. That's not the point. You and me, we've got a certain amount of brownie points with the Super right now, and personally I'd rather not blow the lot on having a look at a mink. Go to the fucking zoo.'

Richie shoved his chair back and started circling the incident room restlessly. 'I'll fill out the form. That way it's only me blowing my brownie points.'

'No you bloody won't. You'll make it sound like Pat was some kind of gibbering maniac seeing pink gorillas in his kitchen. We had a deal: no pointing the finger at Pat until and unless you've got evidence.'

Richie whirled on me, both hands slamming down on someone's desk, sending papers flying. 'How am I supposed to *get* evidence? If you put the brakes on, any time I start off on something that could go somewhere—'

'Calm down, Detective. And lower your voice. You want Quigley popping in to find out what's going on?'

'The deal was we *investigate* Pat. Not I *mention* investigating Pat once in a while and you shoot me down. If the evidence is out there, how the fuck am I supposed to get to it? Come on, man. Tell me. How?'

I pointed at my monitor. 'What does this look like we're doing? Investigating Pat bloody Spain. No, we're not calling him a suspect to the world. That was the deal. If you feel like it's not fair on you—'

'*No.* Fuck not being fair on me. I don't care. It's not fair on Conor Brennan.'

His voice was still rising. I made mine stay even. 'No? I'm not seeing what a video camera would do for him. Say we set up and catch nothing: how does the lack of otters invalidate Brennan's confession?'

Richie said, 'Tell me this. If you believe Pat, why aren't you all for the cameras? One shot of a mink, a squirrel, even a *rat*, and you can tell me to fuck off. You sound the same as Pat, man: you sound like you know there's nothing there.'

'No, chum. I don't. I sound like I don't give a damn whether there's anything there or not. If we pick up nothing, what does that prove? The animal could have been scared off, could have got killed by a predator, could be hibernating . . . Even if it never existed, that doesn't put this on Pat. Maybe the noises were something to do with the subsidence, or the plumbing, and he overreacted and read too much into them. That would make him a guy under stress, which we already knew. It wouldn't make him a killer.'

Richie didn't argue with that. He leaned back on a desk, pressing his fingers into his eyes. After a moment he said, more quietly, 'It'd tell us something. That's all I'm asking for.'

The argument, or fatigue, or Dina, had heartburn rolling up into my throat. I tried to swallow it down without grimacing. 'OK,' I said. 'You fill out the request form. I've got to head, but I'll sign it before I leave – better have both our names on there. Don't go requesting any strippers.'

'I'm doing my best here,' Richie said, into his hands. There was a note in his voice that caught at me: something raw, something lost, something like a wild call for help. 'I'm just trying to get this right. Man, I swear to God, I'm trying.'

Every rookie feels like the world is going to stand or fall on his first case. I didn't have time to hand-hold Richie through it, not with Dina out there, wandering, shooting off the kind of fractured strobe-light glitter that draws predators from miles around. 'I know you are,' I said. 'You're doing fine. Double-check your spelling; the Super's picky about that.'

'Yeah. OK.'

'Meanwhile, we'll forward this link to Whatshisname, Dr Dolittle – he might spot something in there. And I'll have Kieran check out Pat's account on this board, see if he sent or received any private messages. A couple of these guys sounded like they were getting pretty invested in his story; maybe one of them got into some kind of correspondence with him, and Pat gave him a few more details. And we'll need to find the next discussion board he went to.'

'There mightn't be a next one. He tried two boards, neither one of them was any use . . . He could've given up.'

'He didn't give up,' I said. On my monitor, cones and parabolas moved gracefully in and out of one another, folded in on themselves and vanished, unfurled and began their slow dance all over again. 'The man was desperate. You can take that any way you want to, you can say it was because he was losing his marbles if that's what you want to believe, but the fact remains: he needed help. He'd have kept looking online, because he had nowhere else to look.'

I left Richie writing up the request form. I already had a mental list of places to look for Dina, left over from the last time and the time before that and the time before that: her exes' flats, pubs where the barman liked her, dive clubs where sixty quid would get you plenty of ways to fry your brain for a while. I knew the whole thing was pointless – there was every chance in the world that Dina had caught a bus to Galway because it looked so pretty in some documentary, or entranced some guy and gone back to look at his etchings – but I didn't have a choice. I still had my caffeine tablets in my briefcase, from the stakeout: a few of those, a shower, a sandwich, and I would be good to go. I slapped down the cold little voice telling me that I was getting too old for this, and much too tired.

When I put my key in the door of my flat, I was still running through addresses in my head, working out the fastest route. It took me a second to realise that something was wrong. The door was unlocked.

For a long minute I stood still in the corridor, listening: nothing. Then I put down my briefcase, unsnapped my holster and slammed the door open.

Debussy's *Sunken Cathedral* chiming softly through the dim sitting room; candlelight catching in the curves of glasses, glowing rich red in dark wine. For one incredible, breath-robbing second, I thought: *Laura*. Then Dina uncurled her legs from the sofa and leaned forward to pick up her wineglass.

'Hi,' she said, raising the glass to me. 'About bloody time.'

My heart was slamming at the back of my throat. 'What the *fuck*?'

'Jesus, Mikey. Take a chill pill. Is that a *gun*?'

It took me a couple of tries to get the snap done up again. 'How the hell did you get in here?'

'What are you, Rambo? Overreact much?'

'Christ, Dina. You scared the shit out of me.'

'Pulling a gun on your own sister. And here I thought you'd be happy to see me.'

The pout was a mock one, but the glitter of her eyes in the candlelight said to be careful. 'I am,' I said, bringing my voice down. 'I just wasn't expecting you. How did you get in?'

Dina gave me a little smug grin and shook her cardigan pocket, which jingled merrily. 'Geri had your spare keys. Actually, you know something, Geri has the whole of Dublin's spare keys – Little Miss Reliable, sorry, *Mrs* Reliable, isn't she *exactly* who you'd want checking your house if you got burgled on holiday or something? Like if you were making *up* the person who has every-one's spare key, wouldn't she be exactly like Geri? God, you should've seen it, give you a laugh: she's got them lined up on hooks in the utility room, all nice and labelled in her best hand-writing. I could've robbed half her neighbourhood if I'd felt like it.'

'Geri's going out of her mind worrying about you. We both were.'

'Well, duh, that's why I came here. That and to cheer you up. You looked so stressed the other day, I swear if I had a credit card I'd have booked you a hooker.' She leaned over to the table and held out the other wineglass. 'Here. I brought you this instead.'

Either bought out of Sheila's babysitting money, or shoplifted – Dina finds it irresistible to try and trick me into drinking stolen wine, eating hash brownies, going for a ride in her latest boyfriend's untaxed car. 'Thanks,' I said.

'So sit down and drink it. You're making me nervous, hovering like that.'

My legs were still shaking from the bang of adrenaline and hope and relief. I retrieved my briefcase and closed the door. 'Why aren't you at Geri's?'

'Because Geri could bore the tits off a bull, is why. I was there, what, like a day, and I've heard every single thing that Sheila and Colm and Thingy have ever done in their lives. She makes me want to get my tubes tied. Sit *down*.'

The faster I got her back to Geri's, the more sleep I would get, but if I didn't show some appreciation for this little scene, she would blow a fuse until God knew what hour of the morning. I dropped into my armchair, which folded around me so lovingly that I thought I would never be able to get up again. Dina leaned over the coffee table, balancing herself on one hand, to give me the wine. 'Here. I bet Geri thought I was dead in a ditch.'

'You can't blame her.'

'If I'd been feeling too crap to go out, then I wouldn't have *gone* out. God, I feel sorry for Sheila, don't you? I bet whenever she goes to her friends' houses, she has to ring home every half-hour or Geri'll think she's been sold into slavery.'

Dina has always been able to make me smile even when I'm trying my best not to. 'Is that what this is in honour of? One day with Geri, and all of a sudden you appreciate me?'

She curled back up in the corner of the sofa and shrugged. 'I felt like being nice to you, that's what it's in honour of. You don't get enough taking care of, since you and Laura split up.'

'Dina, I'm fine.'

'Everyone needs someone to take care of them. Who's the last person that did anything nice for you?'

I thought of Richie holding out coffee, smacking Quigley down when he tried to bad-mouth me. 'My partner,' I said.

Dina's eyebrows shot up. 'Him? I thought he was some itty-bitty baby newbie that couldn't find his arse with both hands. He was probably just licking up to you.'

'No,' I said. 'He's a good partner.' Hearing myself say the word sent a quick wave of warmth through me. None of my other trainees would have argued with me over the camera: once I said no, that would have been the end of that. Suddenly the argument felt like a gift, the kind of shoving match that partners can have every week for twenty years.

'Hmm,' Dina said. 'Good for him.' She reached for the wine bottle and topped up her glass.

'This is nice,' I said, and a part of me meant it. 'Thanks, Dina.'

'I know it is. So why aren't you drinking that? Are you scared

I'm trying to poison you?' She grinned, little white cat teeth bared at me. 'Like I'd be obvious enough to put it in the wine. Give me some credit.'

I smiled back. 'I bet you'd be very creative. I can't get pissed tonight, though. I've got work in the morning.'

Dina rolled her eyes. 'Oh God, here we go, work work work, shoot me now. Just throw a sickie.'

'I wish.'

'So do it. We'll do something nice. The Wax Museum just opened up again, do you know in my whole entire life I've never been to the Wax Museum?'

This wasn't going to end well. 'I'd love to, but it'll have to be next week. I need to be in bright and early tomorrow, and it could be a long one.' I took a sip of the wine, held up the glass. 'Lovely. We'll finish this, and then I'm going to take you back to Geri's. I know she's boring, but she does her best. Cut her some slack, OK?'

Dina ignored that. 'Why can't you throw a sickie tomorrow? I bet you've got like a year of holidays saved up. I bet you've never thrown a sickie in your whole life. What are they going to do, fire you?'

The warm feeling was vanishing fast. I said, 'I've got a guy in custody, and I've got till early Sunday morning to either charge him or release him. I'm going to need every minute of that to get my case sorted. I'm sorry, sweetheart. The Wax Museum's going to have to wait.'

'Your case,' Dina said. Her face had sharpened. 'The Broken Harbour thing?'

There was no point in denying it. 'Yeah.'

'I thought you were going to swap with someone else.'

'Can't be done.'

'Why not?'

'Because it doesn't work that way. We'll catch the Wax Museum as soon as I've wrapped things up, OK?'

'Fuck the Wax Museum. I'd rather stab myself in the eyes than go stare at some stupid doll of Ronan Keating.'

'Then we'll do something else. Your choice.'

Dina shoved the wine bottle closer to me with the toe of her boot. 'Have more.'

My glass was still full. 'I have to drive you to Geri's. I'll stick with what I've got. Thanks.'

Dina flicked a fingernail off the edge of her glass, a sharp monotonous pinging, and watched me under her fringe. She said, 'Geri gets the papers every morning. Of bloody course. So I read them.'

'Right,' I said. I pushed down the bubble of anger: Geri should have been paying more attention, but she's a busy woman and Dina is a slippery one.

'What's Broken Harbour like now? In the photo it looked like shit.'

'It is, pretty much. Someone started building what could have been a nice estate, but it never got finished. At this stage, it probably never will. The people living there aren't happy.'

Dina stuck a finger in her wine and swirled it. 'Fuck's sake. What a totally shitty thing to do.'

'The developers didn't know things were going to turn out like this.'

'I bet they did, too, or anyway they didn't care, but that's not what I meant. I meant what a shitty thing to do, getting people to move out to Broken Harbour. I'd rather live in a landfill.'

I said, 'I've got a lot of good memories of Broken Harbour.'

She sucked her finger clean with a pop. 'You just think that because you always have to think everything's lovely. Ladies and gentlemen, my brother Pollyanna.'

I said, 'I've never seen what's so bad about focusing on the positive. Maybe it's not cool enough for you—'

'What positive? It was OK for you and Geri, you got to go hang out with your friends; I was stuck sitting there with Mum and Dad, getting sand up my crack, pretending I was having fun paddling in water that practically gave me frostbite.'

'Well,' I said, very carefully. 'You were only five, the last time we went there. How well do you remember it?'

A flash of blue stare, under the fringe. 'Enough that I know it sucked. That place was *creepy*. Those hills, I always felt like they were staring at me, like something crawling on my neck, I kept wanting to—' She smacked the back of her neck, a vicious reflexive slap that made me flinch. 'And the *noise*, Jesus Christ. The sea, the wind, the gulls, all these weird noises that you could never figure out *what* they were . . . I had nightmares practically every night that some sea-monster thing stuck its tentacles in the caravan window and started strangling me. I bet you anything someone died building that shitty estate, like the *Titanic*.'

'I thought you liked Broken Harbour. You always seemed like you were having a good time.'

'No I didn't. You just want to think that.' For a second, the twist to Dina's mouth made her look almost ugly. 'The *only* good thing was that Mum was so happy there. And look how that turned out.'

There was a moment of silence that could have sliced skin. I almost dropped the whole thing, went back to drinking my wine and telling her how delicious it was – maybe I should have, I don't know – but I couldn't. I said, 'You make it sound like you were already having problems.'

'Like I was already crazy. That's what you mean.'

'If that's how you want to put it. Back when we were going to Broken Harbour, you were a happy, stable kid. Maybe you weren't having the holiday of a lifetime, but overall, you were fine.'

I needed to hear her say it. She said, 'I was never fine. This one time I was digging a hole in the sand, little bucket and spade and everything all adorable, and at the bottom of the hole there was a face. Like a man's face, all squashed up and making faces, like he was trying to get the sand out of his eyes and his mouth. I screamed and Mum came, but by then he was gone. And it wasn't just at Broken Harbour, either. Once I was in my room and—'

I couldn't listen to any more of this. 'You had a great imagination. That's not the same thing. All little kids imagine things. It wasn't till after Mum died—'

'It was, Mikey. You didn't know because when I was little you could just put it down to "Oh, kids imagine stuff," but it was always. Mum dying had nothing to do with it.'

'Well,' I said. My mind felt very strange, juddering like a city in an earthquake. 'So maybe it wasn't Mum dying, exactly. She'd been depressed all your life, off and on. We did our best to keep it away from you, but kids sense things. Maybe it would actually have been better if we hadn't tried to—'

'Yeah, you guys did your best, and you know what? You did a great job. I hardly remember being worried about Mum ever, at all. I knew she got sick sometimes, or sad, but I didn't have a clue that it was a big deal. It's not because of that, the way I am. You keep trying to *organise* me, file me away all neat and make sense, like I'm one of your cases— I'm not one of your fucking *cases.*'

'I'm not trying to organise you,' I said. My voice sounded eerily calm, artificially generated somewhere far away. Tiny memories fell through my mind, blooming like flakes of flaming ash: Dina four years old and shrieking blue murder in her bath, clinging to Mum, because the shampoo bottle was hissing at her; I had thought she was trying to dodge having her hair washed. Dina between me and Geri in the back of the car, fighting her seatbelt and gnawing her fingers with a hideous worrying sound till they were lumpy and purple and bleeding, I couldn't even remember why. 'I'm just saying of course it was because of Mum. What else would it be? You were never abused, I'd swear to that on my life, you were never beaten or starved or— I don't think you ever even got a smack on the backside. We all loved you. If it wasn't Mum, then why?'

'There isn't any *why*. That's what I mean, trying to organise me. I'm not crazy *because* anything. I just am.'

Her voice was clear, steady, matter-of-fact, and she was looking at me straight on, with something that could almost have been compassion. I told myself that Dina's hold on reality is one-fingered at best, that if she understood the reasons why she was crazy then she wouldn't be crazy to begin with. She said, 'I know that's not what you want to think.'

My chest felt like a balloon filling with helium, rocking me dangerously. My hand was clamped on the arm of my chair as if it could anchor me. I said, 'If you believe that. That this just happens to you for no reason. How do you live with that?'

Dina shrugged. 'Just do. How do you live with it when you have a bad day?'

She was slouching into the corner of the sofa again, drinking her wine; she had lost interest. I took a breath. 'I try to understand why I'm having a bad day, so I can fix it. I focus on the positive.'

'Right. So if Broken Harbour was so great and you have all these great memories and everything's so positive, then why is it wrecking your head going back there?'

'I never said it was.'

'You don't need to say it. You shouldn't be doing this case.'

It felt like salvation, to be having the same old fight, back on familiar ground, with that slantwise glitter waking in Dina's eyes again. 'Dina. It's a murder case, just like all the dozens of others I've worked. There's nothing special about it, except the location.'

'Location location location, what are you, an estate agent? This location is *bad* for you. I could tell the second I saw you the other night, you were all wrong; you smelled funny, like something burning. Look at you now, go look in mirrors, you look like something shat on your head and set you on fire. This case is fucking you up. Phone your work tomorrow and tell them you're not doing it.'

In that instant I almost told her to fuck off. It astonished me, how suddenly and how hard the words slammed up against my lips. I have never, in all my adult life, said anything like that to Dina.

I said, when I could be sure that my voice was wiped empty of any hint of anger, 'I'm not going to give up this case. I'm sure I do look like shit, but that's because I'm exhausted. If you want to do something about that, stay put at Geri's.'

'I can't. I'm *worried* about you. Every second you're out there thinking about that *location*, I can feel it making your head go bad. That's why I came back here.'

The irony was enough to make anyone howl with laughter, but Dina was dead serious: bolt upright on the sofa, legs folded under her, ready to fight me all the way. I said, 'I'm fine. I appreciate you looking out for me, but there's no need. Seriously.'

'Yes there is. You're just as much of a mess as I am. You just hide it better.'

'Maybe. I'd like to think I've put in enough work that I'm not actually a mess at this point, but who knows, maybe you're right. Either way, the upshot is that I'm well able to deal with this case.'

'No. No way. You like thinking you're the strong one, that's why you love when I go off the rails, because it makes you feel all Mr Perfect, but it's bullshit. I bet sometimes when you're having a bad day you hope I'll show up on your doorstep talking crap, just so you'll feel better about yourself.'

Part of the hell of Dina is that even when you know it's rubbish, even when you know it's the dark corroded spots on her mind talking, it still stings. I said, 'I hope you know that's not true. If I could help you get better by having an arm amputated, I'd do it like a shot.'

She sat back on her heels and thought about that. 'Yeah?'

'Yeah. I would.'

'Awww,' Dina said, with more appreciation than sarcasm. She sprawled on her back on the sofa and swung her legs over the arm, watching me. She said, 'I don't feel good. Ever since I read those newspapers, things are sounding funny again. I flushed your jacks and it made a noise like popcorn.'

I said, 'I'm not surprised. That's why we need to get you back to Geri's. If you feel like crap, then you're going to want someone around.'

'I do want someone around. I want you. Geri makes me want to get a brick and hit myself in the head. One more day of her and I'll do it.'

With Dina, you don't have the luxury of taking anything as hyperbole. I said, 'So find a way to ignore her. Take deep breaths. Read a book. I'll lend you my iPod and you can block Geri out altogether. We can load it up with whatever music you want, if my taste isn't trendy enough for you.'

'I can't use earphones. I start hearing stuff and then I can't tell if it's in the music or inside my ears.'

She was banging one heel off the side of the sofa in a relentless, infuriating rhythm that jarred against the fluid sweep of the Debussy. I said, 'Then I'll lend you a good book. Take your pick.'

'I don't need a good book I don't need a DVD box set I don't need a nice fucking cup of tea and a sudoku magazine. I need *you*.'

I thought of Richie at his desk, chewing a thumbnail and spell-checking his request form, of that desperate call for help in his voice; of Jenny in her hospital bed, wrapped in a nightmare that wasn't going to end; of Pat, gutted out like a trophy animal, waiting in one of Cooper's drawers for me to make sure he wouldn't be stamped *Killer* in a few million minds; of his children, too young even to know what dying was. That surge of anger heaved up again, shoving at me. I said, 'I know that. Right now, other people need me more.'

'You mean this Broken Harbour thing is more important than your family. That's what you mean. You don't even see how fucked-up that is, do you, you don't even see that no normal guy in the world would *say* that, no one would say that unless he was obsessed with some hellhole place that was pumping shit into his brain. You know perfectly bloody well if you send me back to Geri's then she'll bore me till I lose my mind, and I'll walk out and she'll be going crazy worrying, but you don't even care, do you? You're still going to make me go back there.'

'Dina, I don't have time for this shit. I've got, what, fifty-odd hours to charge this guy. In fifty-odd hours' time I'll do whatever you need, come get you from Geri's at the crack of dawn, go to any museum you want, but until then, you're right: you're not the centre of my universe. You can't be.'

Dina stared, propped up on her elbows. She had never heard that whipcrack in my voice before. The gobsmacked look on her face swelled that balloon inside my chest. For a terrifying instant I thought I was going to laugh.

'Tell me something,' she said. Her eyes had narrowed: the gloves were coming off. 'Do you sometimes wish I would die? Like when my timing is shit, like now. Do you wish I would just die? Do you hope someone'll ring you in the morning and go, "I'm so sorry, sir, a train just splattered your sister"?'

'Of course I don't want you to die. I'm hoping *you'll* ring me in the morning and go, "Guess what, Mick, you were right, Geri isn't actually a form of torture banned by the Geneva Convention, somehow I've survived—"'

'Then why are you acting like you wish I would die? Actually I bet you don't want a train, you want it to be all *neat*, don't you, all nicey-neat – how do you hope it? Hang myself, is that what you'd like, or an overdose—'

I didn't feel like laughing any more. My hand was clenched around the wineglass, so tight I thought it would smash. 'Don't be bloody ridiculous. I'm acting like I want you to have a little self-control. Just enough to put up with Geri for two fucking days. You really think that's too much to ask?'

'Why should I? Is this some kind of stupid *closure* thing, you fix this case it makes up for what happened to Mum? Because if it is then *puke*, I can't even *stand* you, I'm going to puke all over your sofa right this—'

'This has fucking *nothing* to do with her. That's one of the stupidest things I've ever heard. If you can't come up with anything that makes more sense than that, maybe you should keep your big yap shut.'

I hadn't lost my temper since I was a teenager, not like this and definitely not at Dina, and it felt like doing a hundred down a motorway on six straight vodkas, immense and lethal and delicious. Dina was sitting up, leaning forward across the coffee table, fingers stabbing at me. 'See? This is what I'm talking about. *This* is what this thing is doing to you. You never get mad at me, and now look at you, just look, the state of you, you want to hit me, don't you? Say it, come on, how badly do you want to—'

She was right: I did, I wanted to slap her right across the face. Some fraction of me understood that if I hit her then I would stay with her, and that she knew it too. I put my glass down on the coffee table, very gently. 'I'm not going to hit you.'

'Go on, go ahead, you might as well. What's the difference? If you throw me away into Geri's House of Hell and I run away and then I can't come to you and I can't hold it together and I end up jumping in the river, how is that better?' She was half on the coffee table, face shoved at me, right within arm's reach. 'You won't give me one little slap because God no you're too good for that, fuck forbid you might feel like the bad guy just once, but it's OK to make me jump off a bridge, right, that's fine, that's just—'

A sound halfway between a laugh and a yell came out of me. 'Sweet Jesus! I can't begin to tell you how sick I am of hearing that. You think *you're* going to puke? How about me, getting this shit shoved down my throat every time I bloody turn around? *You won't take me to the Wax Museum, I think I'll kill myself. You won't help me move all my stuff out of my flat at four in the morning, I think I'll kill myself. You won't spend the evening listening to my problems instead of taking one last shot at saving your marriage, I think I'll kill myself.* I know it's my own fault, I know I've always caved the second you whipped out this crap, but this time: no. You want to kill yourself? Do it. You don't want to, then don't. It's up to you. Nothing I do will make any difference anyway. So *don't fucking dump it on my lap.*'

Dina stared at me, open-mouthed. My heart was ricocheting off my ribs; I could barely breathe. After a moment she threw her wineglass on the floor – it bounced on the rug, rolled away in an arc of red like flung blood – got up and headed for the door, scooping up her bag on the way. She deliberately passed so close to me that her hip barged into my shoulder; she was expecting me to grab her, fight her to make her stay. I didn't move.

In the doorway, she said, 'You'd better find a way to tell your work to fuck off. If you don't come find me by tomorrow evening, you're going to be sorry.'

I didn't turn around. After a minute the door slammed behind her, and I heard her give it a kick before she ran off down the corridor. I sat very still for a long time, gripping the arms of my chair to stop my hands shaking. I listened to my heart banging in my ears and to the hiss of the speakers after the Debussy ran out, listened for Dina's footsteps coming back.

My mother almost took Dina with her. It was sometime after one in the morning, on our last night at Broken Harbour, when she woke Dina, slipped out of the caravan and headed for the beach. I know because I came in at midnight, dazzled and breathless from lying in the dunes with Amelia under a sky like a great black bowl full of stars, and when I eased the caravan door open the bar of moonlight lit up all four of them, rolled up tight and warm in their bunks, Geri snoring delicately. Dina turned and murmured something as I slid into my bed with my clothes still on. I had bribed one of the older guys to buy us a flagon of cider, so I was half drunk, but it must have been an hour before that stunned delight stopped humming in my skin and I could fall asleep.

A few hours later I woke up again, to make sure it was all still true. The door was swinging open, moonlight and sea-sounds rushing in to fill up the caravan, and two bunks were empty. The note was on the table. I don't remember what it said. Probably the police took it away; probably I could go looking for it in Records, but I won't. All I remember is the P.S. It said, *Dina is too little to do without her mum.*

We knew where to look: my mother always loved the sea. In the few hours since I had been there, the beach had turned inside out, transformed itself into something dark and howling. A rising wind blustering, clouds scudding over the moon, sharp shells cutting my bare feet as I ran and no pain. Geri gasping for breath beside me; my father lunging towards the sea in the moonlight, flapping pyjamas and flailing arms, a grotesque pale scarecrow. He was shouting, 'Annie Annie Annie,' but the wind and the waves bowled it away into nothing. We hung on to his sleeves like kids. I shouted in his ear, 'Dad! Dad, I'll get someone!'

He grabbed my arm and twisted. My dad had never hurt any of us. He roared, '*No!* No one, don't you bloody dare!' His eyes looked white. It was years before I realised: he still thought we were going to find them alive. He was saving her, from all the people who would take her away if they knew.

So we looked for them by ourselves. No one heard us shouting, *Mummy Annie Dina Mummy Mummy Mummy*, not through the wind and the sea. Geraldine stayed on land, up and down the beach, scrabbling through the sand dunes and clawing at clumps of grass. I went in the water with my father, thigh-deep. When my legs got numb it was easier to keep going.

For the rest of that night – I never figured out how long it lasted, longer than we should have been able to survive – I fought the current to stay standing and groped blind at it as it surged past. Once my fingers tangled in something and I howled because I thought I had one of them by the hair, but it came up out of the water a great lump like a chopped-off head and it was just seaweed, wrapping round my wrists, clinging when I tried to throw it away from me. Later I found a cold ribbon of it still bound around my neck.

When dawn started turning the world a bleak bleached grey, Geraldine found Dina, burrowed headfirst like a rabbit into a clump of marram grass, arms dug into the sand up to her elbows. Geri bent back long blades of grass one by one and scooped away handfuls of sand like she was freeing something that could shatter. Finally Dina was sitting up on the sand, shivering. Her eyes focused on Geraldine. 'Geri,' she said. 'I had bad dreams.' Then she saw where she was and started to scream.

My father wouldn't leave the beach. In the end I wrapped my T-shirt around Dina – it was heavy with seawater, her shivering got worse – hoisted her over my shoulder and carried her back to the caravan. Geraldine stumbled along beside me, holding Dina up when my grip slid.

We pulled off Dina's nightie – she was cold as a fish and gritted all over with sand – and wrapped her in everything warm we could find. Mum's cardigans smelled of her; maybe that was what made Dina yelp like a kicked puppy, or maybe our clumsiness hurt her. Geraldine stripped like I wasn't there and climbed into Dina's bunk with her, pulled the duvet over both their heads. I left them there and went to find someone.

The light was turning yellow and the other caravans were

starting to wake up. A woman in a summer dress was filling her kettle at the tap, with a couple of toddlers dancing around her, splashing each other and screaming with giggles. My dad had dropped to the sand by the waterline, hands hanging uselessly at his sides, staring at the sun rising over the sea.

Geri and I were covered head to toe in cuts and scrapes. The paramedics cleaned up the worst ones – one of them let out a low whistle when he saw my feet; I didn't understand why until much later. Dina got taken to hospital, where they said she was physically fine apart from mild hypothermia. They let Geri and me take her home and look after her, until they decided my father wasn't planning to 'do anything silly' and they could let him out. We made up aunts and told the doctors they would help.

After two weeks, our mother's dress came up in a Cornish fishing boat's nets. I identified it – my father couldn't get out of bed, I wasn't about to let Geri, that left me. It was her best summer dress, cream silk – she had saved up – with green flowers. She used to wear it to Mass, when we were in Broken Harbour, then for Sunday lunch at Lynch's and our walk along the strand. It made her look like a ballerina, like a laughing tiptoe girl off an old postcard. When I saw it laid out on a table in the police station, it was streaked brown and green from all the nameless things that had woven around it in the water, fingered it, caressed it, helped it on its long journey. I might not even have recognised it, only I knew what to look for: Geri and I had spotted it missing, when we packed away her things to leave the caravan.

That was what Dina had heard on the radio, with my voice swirling around it, the day I caught this case. *Dead, Broken Harbour, discovered the body, State pathologist is at the scene.* The near-impossibility of it would never have occurred to her; all the rules of probability and logic, the neat patterns of centre lines and cat's-eyes that keep the rest of us on the road when the weather is wild, those mean nothing to Dina. Her mind had spun out into a smoking wreck of bonfire noises and gibberish, and she had come to me.

She had never told us what happened that night. Geri and I

tried a couple of thousand times to catch her off guard – asked when she was half asleep in front of the telly, or daydreaming out the car window. All we got was that flat 'I had bad dreams,' and her blue eyes skittering away to nothing.

When she was thirteen or fourteen we started to realise – gradually, and without any real surprise – that there was something wrong. Nights when she sat on my bed or Geri's talking full speed until dawn, revved up into a frenzy about something we could barely translate, raging at us for not caring enough to understand; days when the school rang to say she was staring and glazed, terrified, like her classmates and her teachers had turned into meaningless shapes gesturing and jabbering; fingernail tracks scabbing on her arms. I had taken it for granted, always, that that night was the embedded thing corroding at the bottom of Dina's mind. What else could have done it?

*There isn't any why.* That dizziness took hold of me again. I thought of balloons unmoored and soaring, exploding in the thinning air under the pressure of their own weightlessness.

Footsteps came and went in the corridor, but none of them paused outside my door. Geri rang twice; I didn't answer. When I could stand up, I blotted the rug with kitchen roll until I had soaked up as much of the wine as I could. I spread salt on the stain and left it to work. I poured the rest of the wine down the sink, threw the bottle in the recycling bin and washed the glasses. Then I found Sellotape and a pair of nail scissors and sat on my living-room floor, taping pages back into books and trimming the tape to within perfect hairsbreadths of the paper, until the heap of wrecked books was a neat stack of mended ones and I could start putting them back on my shelves, in alphabetical order.

# 15

I slept on the sofa, to make sure that even the quietest turn of a key in the lock would wake me. Four or five times that night I found Dina: curled asleep on my father's doorstep, shrieking with laughter at a party while someone danced barefoot to wild drums; wide-eyed and slack-jawed under a glassy film of bathwater, fan of hair swaying. Every time I woke up already on my feet and halfway to the door.

Dina and I had fought before, when she was on a bad one. Never like this, but every now and then something I thought was innocuous had sent her whirling out in a fury, usually throwing something at me on her way out the door. I had always gone after her. Mostly I caught her within seconds, dawdling outside for me. Even the few times when she had given me the slip, or fought me and screamed till I backed off before someone called the police and she landed in a locked ward, I had followed and searched and phoned and texted till I got hold of her and coaxed her back to my place or Geri's. That was all she wanted, deep down: to be found and brought home.

I got up early, showered, shaved, made some breakfast and a lot of coffee. I didn't ring Dina. Four times I had a text half typed, but I deleted them all. On my way to work I didn't detour past her flat, or risk crashing the car while I craned my neck at every slim dark-haired girl I passed: if she wanted me, she knew how to find me. My own daring left me breathless. My hands felt shaky, but when I looked at them on the wheel they were steady and strong.

Richie was already at his desk, with his phone clamped to his ear, swinging his chair back and forth and listening to perky hold music loud enough that I could hear it too. 'Pest-control companies,' he said, nodding at a printout in front of him. 'Tried all the numbers

Pat got off the discussion board: no joy. This here, this is every exterminator in Leinster, so we'll see what shows up.'

I sat down and picked up my phone. 'If you get nothing, we can't assume that means there's nothing to get. A lot of people out there are doing nixers, these days. If someone didn't declare a job to the Revenue, you think he's going to declare it to us?'

Richie started to say something, but then the hold music cut out and he swung around to his desk. 'Good morning, this is Detective Garda Richard Curran, I'm looking for some information . . .'

No message from Dina – not that I had expected one, she didn't even have my work number, but a part of me had been hoping anyway. One from Dr Dolittle and his dreadlocks, saying he had checked out the home-and-garden board and, whoa, some mad shit there or what? According to him, the lined-up skeletons sounded like something a mink would be into, but the idea of an abandoned exotic pet was also way cool, and there were totally guys out there who would smuggle in a wolverine and worry about the pet-care angle later. He was planning to have a wander around Brianstown over the weekend and see if he could find any signs of 'something fun'. And a message from Kieran, who at eight on a Friday morning had already started pumping his world full of drum and bass, telling me to call him.

Richie hung up, shook his head at me and started dialling again. I rang Kieran back.

'Kemosabe! Hang on there.' A pause, while the music went down to a volume that meant he barely even had to shout. 'I checked out your guy Pat-the-lad's account on that home-and-garden board: no private messages, in or out. He could have deleted them, but to check that out, we'd need a subpoena to the site owners. Basically, that's what I called to tell you: we're running out of road here. The recovery software's finished doing its thing, and we've checked out everything it gave us. No more posts about weasels or whatever, anywhere that's in the computer history. Literally *the* most interesting thing we've got is some idiot forwarding Jenny Spain an e-mail about *non-nationals* kidnapping a kid in a shopping centre and cutting its hair in the jacks, which is only interesting because it's like the world's oldest urban legend and I can't believe people actually still fall for it? If you really want to know what was living in your guy's attic, and you figure he told the net, then your next step is to put in a request to the vics' service provider and keep your fingers crossed they hold info on visited sites.'

Richie hung up again; he kept one hand on the phone, but instead of redialling he watched me, waiting. 'We don't have time for that,' I said. 'We've got less than two days to charge Conor Brennan or release him. Anything on his computer that I should know about?'

'Not so far. No links to the vics – none of the same websites, no e-mails to or from. And I'm not seeing any deletions over the last few days, so it's not like he wiped the good stuff when he knew we were coming – unless he wiped it so well I can't even see that, and excuse me if this sounds arrogant but I don't *think* so? Basically, he's barely even touched his machine in the last six months. Occasionally he checked his e-mail, he did some design upkeep on a couple of websites, and he watched a bunch of *National Geographic* animal documentaries online, but that's about it. Real thrill-seeker, this guy.'

'Right,' I said. 'Keep looking through the Spains' computer. And keep me posted.'

I could hear the shrug in Kieran's voice. 'Sure, Kemosabe. One needle in a haystack coming up. Catch you later.'

For a treacherous second I thought of leaving it. Whatever else Pat had said about his vermin problem, out there in cyberspace, what difference did it make? All it would do was give people yet another excuse to write him off as some nutter. But Richie was watching me, hopeful as a puppy watching his leash, and I had promised. 'Stay on that,' I said, nodding at the pest-control list. 'I've got an idea.'

Even under stress, Pat had been an organised guy, efficient. In his place, I wouldn't have bothered to re-type my whole saga when I switched discussion boards. Pat might not have been a computer genius, by Kieran's standards, but I was willing to bet he had known how to copy and paste.

I pulled up his original posts, the Wildwatcher one and the home-and-garden one, and started pasting sentences into Google. It only took four tries before a post by Pat-the-lad came up.

'Richie,' I said. He was already scooting his chair over to my desk.

The website was an American one, a forum for hunters. Pat had shown up there on the last of July, almost two weeks after he flamed out on the home-and-garden site: he had spent a while licking his wounds, or searching for the right place, or it had just taken that long for his need for help to reach a pitch he couldn't ignore.

Not much had changed. *I hear it most days but no real pattern – sometimes could be 4/5 times in a day/night, sometimes nothing for 24 hours. Have had a video baby monitor rigged up in the attic for a while now but no joy – am wondering if maybe the animal's actually in the space between the attic floor/the ceiling underneath – tried to check w torch but can't see anything. So I'm planning to leave the attic hatch open and point another video monitor at the opening, see if this thing gets ballsy + decides to go exploring. (I'll put chicken wire over the hatch so it doesn't show up on one of my kids pillow, don't worry, I'm not totally mental . . . yet anyway!)*

'Hang on,' Richie said. 'Back on that home-and-garden site, Pat went apeshit about how he didn't want Jenny knowing any of this; he didn't want her scared. Remember? Now, but, he's putting up that monitor on the landing. How was he planning on hiding that from her?'

'Maybe he wasn't. Married couples do talk occasionally, old son. Maybe Pat and Jenny had a good heart-to-heart somewhere along the way, and she knew all about the thing in the attic.'

'Yeah,' Richie said. One of his knees had started jiggling. 'Maybe.'

*But since the first monitor hasn't been a big success I was wondering if anyone has any other ideas? Like species it could be or bait it might go for? PLEASE for Christ's sake don't tell me to use poison or get an exterminator or any of that shit because those are out, end of story. Apart from that any ideas welcome!!!*

The hunters gave him the usual list of suspects, this time with a heavy slant towards mink – they agreed with Dr Dolittle about the lined-up skeletons. When it came to solutions, though, they were a lot more hard-core than the other boards. Within a few hours, one guy had told Pat: *OK so fuck this mousetrap bullshit. Time to grow a pair and break out the serious weaponry. What you need here is a real trap. Check this out.*

The link went to a site like a trapper's candy store, pages and pages of traps aimed at everything from mice to bear and every-one from animal-lovers to full-on sadists, each one described in loving, semi-comprehensible jargon. *Three choices. 1. You can go for a live trap, the ones that look like wire cages. Won't hurt your target. 2. Go for a foothold trap, the one you probly picture from the movies. Will hold your target till you get back to it. Watch out though. Depending what you've got, the animal could make a lot of noise. If that would bug your wife or kids then maybe forget it. 3. Go for a Conibear trap. Breaks the target's neck, kills it pretty much right away. Whatever you pick you want like a four inch jaw spread. Good luck. Watch your fingers.*

Pat came back sounding a lot happier: again, the prospect of a plan had made all the difference. *Man thanks a mil, you're saving my arse here, I owe you big time. Think I'm going to go w the foothold – sounds weird but I don't want to kill this thing, at least not till I've had a good look at it, I've got a right to come face to face with it after all this. At the same time though after all the hassle it's given me, I don't feel like going all out to make sure I don't hurt a hair on its precious little head! To be honest I'm like fuck it, I've spent long enough taking shit from this thing, now its my turn to give it some shit for a change and I'm not going to waste my chance right?*

Richie's eyebrows were up. He said, 'Lovely.'

I almost wished I had given in to temptation and left this whole thing to Kieran. I said, 'Trappers use leghold traps all the time. It doesn't make them psycho sadists.'

'You remember what Tom said, yeah? You can get ones that do less damage, don't hurt the animal as much, but Pat didn't go for one of those. Tom said they cost a couple of quid extra; I figured it was that. Now . . .' Richie sucked on his teeth and shook his head. 'I'm thinking I was wrong, man. It wasn't the money. Pat wanted to do damage.'

I scrolled down. Someone else wasn't convinced: *Foothold is a dumb idea for indoors. Think it through OK. What are you gonna do with your catch?? Fine you want to look at it or whatever but then what?? You can't just pick it up and take it outside or it's gonna take your hand off. Out in the woods you just shoot it but I don't recommend that in your attic. Doesn't matter how great your old lady is . . . women don't like bullet holes in their pretty ceilings.*

That didn't faze Pat. *Have to be honest you're right, hadn't even thought about what I'm gonna do with it once I've caught it! Just been focusing on how it'll feel when I go up there and see it in the trap – I swear I can't remember the last time I was looking forward to something this much, its like being a little kid waiting for Santa!! Not sure what I'll do after that. If I decide to kill it I could just hit it on the head with something hard I guess?*

'"Hit it on the head with something hard,"' Richie said. 'Like someone did to Jenny.'

I kept reading. *Otherwise if I decide to let it go, I could leave it in the trap till it gets too worn out to attack me, then wrap a blanket or something around it + take it out into the hills + release it there right? How long would it take for it to wear itself out enough to be harmless? Like a few hours or like a few days?* My spine twitched. I felt Richie's eyes on me – Pat, the pillar of society, daydreaming about something dying a three-day death above his family's heads. I didn't look up.

The guy who had doubts about the foothold trap still wasn't convinced: *No way to tell. Way too many varaibles. Depends what the catch is, when it last ate/drank, how much damage the trap does, whether it tries to chew off its paw to escape. And even if it looks safe it could come round one last time when you try to release it and take a chunk out of you. Seriously bro . . . I've been doing this a long time and I'm telling you this is a shit idea. Get something else. Not a foothold.*

It was a couple of days before Pat came back to answer that. *Too late, already ordered it! Went for something a little bigger than you guys recommended, I figure what the hell, better safe than sorry am I right?* Little faces, laughing and rolling. *I'll just have to wait till I catch the animal + figure out what to do with it then. Probably just watch it for a while + see if inspiration strikes.*

This time Richie didn't look up. The same sceptic pointed out that this wasn't meant to be a spectator sport: *Look a trap isn't for torturing. Any decent trapper picks up his catch as soon as he can. Sorry bro but this is fucked up. Whatever's in your walls, you got way bigger problems.*

Pat didn't care. *Yeah no shit, but this is the one I'm working on now OK? Who knows, maybe when I see the animal in there I'll feel sorry for it. Seriously doubt it though. My son is three, he's heard it a few times, he's a gutsy little fella doesn't scare easy but he was terrified. Today he said to me You can go kill it with a gun Daddy, right? What was I supposed to say to him, No, sorry son, I can't even get a look at the little fucker? I said Yeah course I will. So yeah I'm kind of having a hard time picturing me getting up much pity for whatever this is. I never deliberately hurt anything in my life (well, my little brother when we were kids, but hey who hasn't) but this is different. If you don't get that then tough.*

The trap took a while to arrive, and the wait got to Pat. On the twenty-fifth of August he was back: *OK I kind of have a problem (well, more of a problem). This thing has got out of the attic. Its going down inside the walls. Started hearing it in the sitting room, always in one specific spot by the sofa, so I made a hole in the wall right there + set up a monitor. Nothing, just the thing moved to the hallway wall – when I set up another monitor there it moved to the kitchen – etc etc etc. I swear its like its deliberately messing with my head for a laugh – I know it cant be but thats how it feels. Either way its definitely getting braver. In some ways I kind of think thats good, cos if it comes out of the walls into the open I'm more likely to get a look at it, but should I be worried that its going to attack us??*

The guy who had suggested the trap website was impressed. *Jesus! Holes in the walls? Your old lady is out of this world. If I told my girl I wanted to bust up the walls, my sh!t would be out on the street.*

Pat was pleased – a row of grinning green faces. *Yeah man, she's a total gem all right. One in a million. Shes not too pleased, specially since she STILL hasn't heard any of the really serious noises, just the odd bit of scraping that could be a mouse or a magpie or anything. But she's like OK, if thats what you need to do then go for it. Now you see why I HAVE to catch this thing yeah? She deserves it. Actually she deserves a mink coat not a half dead mink/whatever, but if thats the best I can get her then shes bloody well getting it!*

'Look at the times,' Richie said quietly. His fingertip hovered by the screen, moved down the time-stamps beside the posts. 'Pat's up awful late, isn't he?' The board was set to American West Coast time. I did the maths: Pat was posting at four in the morning.

The sceptic wanted to know, *What's all this shit with baby monitors? Believe me I'm not some expert on those but they don't record right? So the animal could like dance a polka in your attic but if you've gone to take a leak and your not actually there to see it then tough shit. Why don't you get video cameras and get some actual footage??*

Pat didn't like that. *Because I don;t WANT 'actual footage'. OK? I want to actually catch the actual animal actually in my actual house. I want to actually show it to my actual wife. Anyone can get footage of some animal, YouTube is full of it. I need THE ANIMAL. Anyway I didnt ask you for advice on my technology OK? Just on what to do about this thing being in the walls. If you dont feel like helping me out thwn fine that's your perogative, I'm sure there are plenty of other threads that could use your genius.*

The trap guy tried to soothe him down. *Hey man, don't worry about it getting into the walls. Just fix up the holes and forget the whole thing till you get your trap. Till then anything you can do is just pissing into the wind. Just chill and wait.*

Pat didn't sound convinced. *Yeah maybe. I'll keep you updated. Thanks.*

Richie said, 'He didn't fix up the holes, though, did he? If he'd had chicken wire or something over them, we'd have seen the marks. He left them open.' He left the rest unsaid: somewhere along the way, Pat's priorities had shifted.

I said, 'Maybe he moved furniture in front of them.' Richie didn't answer.

On the last of August, Pat's trap finally arrived. *Got it today!!!!*

*Its a beauty. I actually went for one of the old-style ones with the teeth – hey, what's the point of getting a trap if you can't get the kind you saw in movies when you were a kid? I want to just sit here stroking it like some James Bond baddy – more* laughing faces *– but I better get it set up before my wife gets home. She's a bit dodgy about the idea already + it looks pretty lethal which I think is a good thing but she might not feel the same way! Any advice?*

A couple of people told him not to get caught with that thing: apparently they were illegal in most of the civilised world. I wondered how it had made it through Customs. Probably the seller had marked it 'antique ornament' and kept his fingers crossed.

Pat didn't seem worried. *Yeah well, I'll take my chances – its still my house (up until the bank comes and takes it back) and Im protecting it, I can put out any trap I want. I'll let you know how it goes down. Can't WAIT for this.* I was so tired that my senses were getting their wires crossed. The words leapt off the screen like a voice in my ears, young, intent, overexcited. I caught myself leaning closer, listening.

He came back a week later, but this time he was sounding a lot more subdued. *OK tried raw mince for bait, no dice. Even tried raw steak cos its bloodier so I thought maybe that might help but no. Left it there for three days so it would smell good + rank, nothing. Kind of starting to get worried – not sure what the hell Im going to do if this doesnt pan out. Going to try live bait next. Seriously guys please keep your fingers crossed that it works OK?*

*OK heres the other weird thing. This morn when I went up to take the steak away (before it could get rank enough that my wife smelled it, that wouldn't go down well) there was this little pile of stuff in a corner of the attic. Six pebbles, smooth ones like they came off the beach, and three seashells, old white dried out ones. I'm 110% sure they were never there before. What the fuck?!*

Nobody on the board seemed to care. Their general opinion was that Pat was putting way too much time and thought into this and who cared how a few rocks had got into his attic? The sceptic wanted to know why the whole saga was still going on: *Seriously dude why are you making this into some big soap opera? You need to put down some damn poison go for a couple beers and forget the whole thing. You could have done that like months ago. Is there some huge secret reason why you don't just do it?*

At two the next morning, Pat came back and blew his top. *OK you want to know why I wont use poison, heres why. My wife thinks Im insane. OK? She keeps saying Oh no I dont you're just stressed you'll be fine, but I know her + I can tell. She doesnt get it, she tries but she thinks I'm inagining this whole thing. I need to show her this animal, just hearing the noises isn]t going to be good enough at this stage, she has to SEE it in the actual flesh so she knows I'm not a) hallucinating the whole thing or b) exagerating something stupid like mice or whatever. Otherwise shes goign to leave me and take the kids with her. NO WAY AM I LETTING THAT AHPPEN. Her + those kids are everything Ive got. If I put down poison then the animal could go off somewhere to die + my wife will never know it actually existed, she'll just think I was crazy + then I got better + she]ll always be watching for the next time I go off the rails. Before you say anything YES Ive thought of boarding up the hole before I put down poison, but then what if I shut it out instead of in and it fucks off for good???? So since you ask I'm not using poison because I love my family. Now FUCK OFF.*

A tiny hiss of breath from Richie, leaning in close beside me, but neither of us looked up. The sceptic posted a smiley rolling its eyes; someone else posted one tapping its temple; someone else told Pat to take the blue ones before the red ones. Trap Guy told them all to back off: *You guys, quit it. I want to know what he's got. If you piss him off so bad he never comes back then what? Pat-the-lad, ignore these dumb shits. Their mamas never taught them manners. You get yourself some live bait and give that a try. Mink like killing. If it's a mink it won't be able to pass that up. Then come back and tell us what you got.*

Pat was gone. Over the next few days there was some banter about Trap Guy going over to Ireland to catch this thing himself, some semi-sympathetic speculation about the state of Pat's mind and his marriage (*This type shit is why I stay single*), and then everyone moved on. The exhaustion was making things sideslip inside my mind: for a jumbled split second I worried about Pat not posting, wondered if we should go out to Broken Harbour and check on him. I found my water bottle and pressed its cold side against my neck.

Two weeks later, on the twenty-second of September, Pat was back and he was in much worse shape. *PLEASE READ!!! Had some trouble getting live bait – finally got to a pet shop + got a mouse. Stuck it down on one of those glue baords + put it in the trap. Poor little bastard was squeaking like crazy, felt like shit about it but hey a guy's gotta do what a guys gotta do right?? I watched the monitor practically EVERY SINGLE SECOND ALL BLOODY NIGHT – swear on my mothers grave I only closed my eyes for like twnety minutes around 5 am, didn't mean to but I was shattered + just nodded off. When I woke up IT WAS GONE. Mouse + glue trap GONE. Foothold trap WAS NOT TRIGGGERED it was STILL WIDE OPEN. Soon as my wqife took the kids out this morning for school I went up there to chekc + yeah trap is open + mouse/glue board are NOWHERE IN THE ATTIC. Like what the fuck??!!? How the hell could ANYTHING do that??? And what thje fuck do I do now??? I cant tell my wife this, she doesnt understnad – if I tell her shes gonna think I'm a lunatic. WHAT DO I DO????*

I had a sudden wild flood of nostalgia for just three days earlier, that first walk-through of the house, when I had thought Pat was some loser stashing drugs in his walls and Dina was safely making sandwiches for suits. If you're good at this job, and I am, then every step in a murder case moves you in one direction: towards order. We get thrown shards of senseless wreckage, and we piece them together until we can lift the picture out of the darkness and hold it up to the white light of day, solid, complete, clear. Under all the paperwork and the politics, this is the job; this is its cool shining heart that I love with every fibre of mine. This case was different. It was running backwards, dragging us with it on some ferocious ebb tide. Every step washed uo deeper in black chaos, wrapped us tighter in tendrils of crazy and pulled us downwards.

Dr Dolittle and Kieran the techie were having a wonderful time – insanity always seems like a great big adventure when all you have to do is dabble a fingertip here and there, gawk at the mess, wash off the residue in your nice safe sane home and then go to the pub and tell your friends the cool story. I was having a lot less fun than they were. It slid into my mind, with a quick pinch of unease, that Dina might have had something almost like a point about this case, even if it wasn't in the way she thought.

Most of the hunters had given up on Pat and his saga – more head-tapping smileys, someone wanting to know whether it was a full moon over in Ireland. A few of them started taking the piss: *Oh shit man I think u have 1 of these!!!! Whatever u do don't let it near water!!!* The link went to a picture of a snarling gremlin.

Trap Guy was still trying to be reassuring. *Hang in there, Pat-the-lad. You just think about the upside. At least now you know what kind of bait it goes for. Next time just stick it down harder. You're getting there.*

*One more thing to think about. I'm not accusing anyone of anything, just thinking here – how old are your kids? Are they old enough to think that messing with their daddy could be a funny joke?*

At 4.45 the next morning Pat said, *Never mind. Thanks man I know youre' trying to help but this trap thing isnt working. Got no clue what to try next. Basically I'm fucked.*

And that was the end of that. The regulars played 'What's in Pat-the-lad's attic?' for a while – pictures of Sasquatch, leprechauns, Ashton Kutcher, the inevitable Rickroll. When they got bored, the thread sank.

Richie leaned back from the computer, rubbing a crick out of his neck, and glanced at me sideways. I said, 'So.'

'Yeah.'

'What do you make of that?'

He chewed his knuckle and stared at the screen, but he wasn't reading; he was thinking hard. After a moment he took a long breath. 'What I make of that,' he said, 'is that Pat had lost it. Doesn't even matter any more whether there actually was something in his gaff or not. Either way, he was well off the rails.'

His voice was simple and grave, almost sad. I said, 'He was under a lot of stress. That's not necessarily the same thing.'

I was playing devil's advocate; underneath, I knew. Richie shook his head. 'No, man. No. That there' – he flicked the edge of my monitor with a fingernail – 'that's not the same guy from this summer. Back in July, on that home-and-garden board, Pat's all about protecting Jenny and the kids. By the time he gets to this stuff here, he doesn't give a damn if Jenny's scared, doesn't give a damn if this yoke can get at the kids, as long as he gets his hands on it. And then he's going to leave it in a trap – a trap he picked specifically to hurt it as much as possible – and he's going to watch it take its time dying. I don't know what the doctors would call it, but he's not OK, man. He's not.'

The words rang like an echo in my head. It took me a moment to remember why: I had said them to Richie, just two nights before, about Conor Brennan. My eyes wouldn't focus; the monitor looked off-kilter, like a dense lump of dead weight sending the case rocking at dangerous angles. 'No,' I said. 'I know.' I took a swig of water; the cold helped, but it left a foul, rusty aftertaste on my tongue. 'You need to bear in mind, though, that that doesn't necessarily make him a murderer. There's nothing in there about hurting his wife or children, and plenty about how much he loves them. That's why he's so set on getting his hands on the animal: he thinks that's the only way to save his family.'

Richie said, '"It's my job to take care of her." That's what he said, on that home-and-garden board. If he felt like he couldn't do that any more . . .'

'"What the fuck do I do now?"' I knew what came next. The thought rolled through my stomach with a dull heave, as if the water had been tainted. I closed my browser and watched the screen flash to a bland, innocuous blue. 'Finish your phone calls later. We need to talk to Jenny Spain.'

She was alone. The room felt almost summery: the day was bright, and someone had opened the window a crack, so that a breeze toyed with the blinds and the fug of disinfectant had dissipated to a faint clean tang. Jenny was propped up on pillows, staring at the shifting pattern of sun and shadow on the wall, hands loose and unmoving on the blue blanket. With no makeup she looked younger and plainer than she had in the wedding photos, and somehow less nondescript, now that the little quirks showed – a beauty spot on the unbandaged cheek, an irregular top lip that made her look ready to smile. It wasn't a remarkable face in any way, but it had a clean-lined sweetness that brought up summer barbecues, golden retrievers, soccer games on new-mown grass, and I have always been caught by the pull of the unremarkable, by the easily missed, infinitely nourishing beauty of the mundane.

'Mrs Spain,' I said. 'I don't know if you remember us: Detective Michael Kennedy and Detective Richard Curran. Would it be all right if we came in for a few minutes?'

'Oh . . .' Jenny's eyes, red-rimmed and puffy, moved over our faces. I managed not to flinch. 'Yeah. I remember. I guess . . . yeah. Come in.'

'No one's here with you today?'

'Fiona's at work. My mum had an appointment about her blood pressure. She'll be back in a while. I'm fine.'

Her voice was still hoarse and thick, but she had looked up quickly when we came in: her head was starting to clear, God help her. She seemed calm, but I couldn't tell whether it was the stupe-faction of shock or the brittle glaze of exhaustion. I asked, 'How are you feeling?'

There was no answer to that. Jenny's shoulders moved in some-thing like a shrug. 'My head hurts, and my face. They're giving me painkillers. I guess they help. Did you find out anything about . . . what happened?'

Fiona had kept her mouth shut, which was good, but interest-ing. I shot Richie a warning glance – I didn't want to bring up Conor, not while Jenny was so slowed and clouded that her reac-tion would be worthless – but he was focusing on the sun coming through the blinds, and there was a tense set to his jaw. 'We're following a definite line of inquiry,' I said.

'A line. What line?'

'We'll keep you posted.' There were two chairs by the bed, cushions squashed into their angles where Fiona and Mrs Rafferty had tried to sleep. I took the one closest to Jenny and pushed the other towards Richie. 'Can you tell us anything more about Monday night? Even the smallest thing?'

Jenny shook her head. 'I can't remember. I've been trying, I'm trying all the time . . . but half the time I just can't think, because of the drugs, and the other half my head hurts too much. I think probably once I'm off the painkillers and they let me out of here – once I'm home . . . Do you know when . . . ?'

The thought of her walking into that house made me wince. We were going to have to talk to Fiona about hiring a cleaning team, or having Jenny stay at her flat, or both. 'I'm sorry,' I said. 'We don't know anything about that. What about before Monday night? Can you think of anything out of the ordinary that happened recently – anything that worried you?'

Another shake of Jenny's head. Only fragments of her face showed, behind the bandage; it made her hard to read. 'The last time we spoke,' I said, 'we started discussing the break-ins you had over the past few months.'

Jenny's face turned towards me, and I caught a spark of wariness: she knew something was off – she had only told Fiona about one – but she couldn't find what. 'That? Why does that matter?'

I said, 'We have to examine the possibility that they could be connected to the attack.'

Jenny's eyebrows pulled together. She could have been drifting, but some immobility said she was struggling hard to think, through that fog. After a long minute she said, almost dismissively, 'I told you. It wasn't a big deal. To be honest, I'm not sure there even were any break-ins. It was probably just the kids moving things.'

I said, 'Could you give us the details? Dates, times, things you noticed missing?' Richie found his notebook.

Her head moved restlessly on the pillow. 'God, I don't remember. Back in, I don't know, maybe July? I was tidying up, and there was a pen and some ham slices missing. Or I thought there might be, anyway. We'd all been out that day, so I just got a bit nervous in case I'd forgotten something unlocked and someone had come in – there's squatters living in some of the empty houses, and sometimes they come poking around. That's all.'

'Fiona said you accused her of using her keys to get in.'

Jenny's eyes went to the ceiling. 'I told you before: Fiona turns everything into a big deal. I didn't *accuse* her of anything. I *asked* if she'd been in our house, because she's the only one who had the keys. She said no. End of story. It wasn't, like, some big drama.'

'You didn't ring the local police?'

Jenny shrugged. 'And say what? Like, "I can't find my pen, and someone's eaten some ham slices out of the fridge"? They'd have laughed. Anyone would've laughed.'

'Did you change the locks?'

'I changed the alarm code, just in case. I wasn't going to get all the locks done when I didn't even know if anything had *happened*.'

I said, 'But even after you changed the alarm code, there were other incidents.'

She managed a little laugh, brittle enough to shatter against the air. 'Oh my God, *incidents*? This wasn't a *war* zone. You make it sound like someone was, like, bombing our sitting room.'

'I might have the details wrong,' I said smoothly. 'What exactly did happen?'

'I don't even remember. Nothing big. Could this wait? My head's killing me.'

'We just need a few more minutes, Mrs Spain. Could you set me straight on the details?'

Jenny put her fingertips gingerly to the back of her head, winced. I felt Richie shift his feet and glance at me, ready to leave, but I didn't move. It's a strange sensation, being played by the victim; it goes against the grain to look at the wounded creature we're supposed to be helping, and see an adversary we need to outwit. I welcome it. Give me a challenge any day, over a mass of flayed pain.

After a moment Jenny let her hand fall back into her lap. She said, 'Just the same kind of thing. Smaller, even. Like a couple of times the curtains in the sitting room were pulled back all wrong – I straighten them out when I hook them behind the hold-back, so they'll fall right, but a couple of times I found them all twisted up. See what I mean? It was probably the kids playing hide-and-seek in them, or—'

The mention of the children made her catch her breath. I said quickly, 'Anything else?'

Jenny let her breath out slowly, got herself back. 'Just . . . stuff like that. I keep candles out, so the house always smells nice – I've got a bunch of them in one of the kitchen cupboards, all different smells, and I change them every few days. Once in the summer, maybe August, I went to get the apple one and it was gone – and I knew I'd had it just the week before, I remembered seeing it. But Emma always loved that one, the apple one; she could have taken it to play with in the garden or something, and forgotten it.'

'Did you ask her?'

'I don't remember. It was months ago. It wasn't a big *deal.*'

I said, 'Actually, it sounds quite disturbing. You weren't frightened?'

'*No.* I wasn't. I mean, even if we did have some weird burglar, he was only after, like, candles and ham; that's not exactly terri-fying, is it? I thought *if* there was someone, it was probably just one of the children from the estate – some of them run completely wild; they're like apes, screaming and throwing stuff at your car when you drive past. I thought maybe one of them, on a dare. But probably not even that. Things go missing, in houses. Do you ring the police every time one of your socks disappears in the wash?'

'So even when the incidents kept happening, you still didn't change the locks.'

'No. I didn't. If there was anyone coming in, just *if*, then I wanted to catch them. I didn't want them heading off to bother someone else; I wanted them stopped.' The memory brought Jenny's chin up, gave a tough set to her jaw and a cool, fight-ready intentness to her eyes; it swept away that nondescript quality, turned her vivid and strong. She and Pat had been a good match:

fighters. 'After a while, sometimes when we went out I didn't even set the alarm, on purpose – so if someone did get in, they might stay till I came back and caught them. See? I wasn't *frightened*.'

'I understand,' I said. 'At what point did you tell Pat about this?' Jenny shrugged. 'I didn't.'

I waited. After a moment she said, 'I just didn't. I didn't want to bother him.'

I said gently, 'I'm not second-guessing you, Mrs Spain, but that seems like an odd decision. Wouldn't you have felt safer if Pat had known? Wouldn't he have been safer, in fact, if he had known?'

A shrug that made her wince. 'He had enough on his mind.'

'For example?'

'He'd been made redundant. He was doing his best to get another job, but it wasn't happening. We were . . . we didn't have a load of money. Pat was a bit stressed.'

'Anything else?'

Another shrug. 'That's not enough?'

I waited again, but this time she wasn't budging. I said, 'We found a trap in your attic. An animal trap.'

'Oh my God. *That.*' That laugh again, but I had caught the zap of something bright – terror, maybe, or fury – that brought her face alive for an instant. 'Pat thought we might have a stoat or a fox or something coming in and out. He was dying to have a look at it. We're city kids; even the rabbits down in the sand dunes had us all excited, when we first moved in. Catching a real live fox would've been, like, the coolest thing ever.'

'And did he catch anything?'

'Oh, God, no. He didn't even know what kind of bait to use. Like I said, city kids.'

Her voice was cocktail-party light, but her fingers were clawed into the blanket. I asked, 'And the holes in the walls? A DIY project, you said. Was it anything to do with this stoat?'

'No. I mean, a little bit, but not really.' Jenny reached for the glass of water on the bedside table, took a long drink. I could see her fighting to speed up her mind. 'The holes just happened, you know? Those houses . . . there's something wrong with the foundations. Holes just, like, *appear*. Pat was going to fix them, but he wanted to work on something first – the wiring, maybe? I don't remember. I don't understand that stuff.' She threw me a self-deprecating glance, all helpless little woman. I kept my face wooden. 'And he wondered if maybe the stoat, or whatever, might come down into the walls and we could catch it that way. That's all.'

'And that didn't bother you? The delay in mending the walls, the possibility of vermin in the house?'

'Not really. To be honest, I didn't believe for a second it was actually a stoat or anything big, or I wouldn't have let it near the kids. I thought maybe a bird, or a squirrel – the kids would've loved to see a squirrel. I mean, obviously it would've been nice if Pat had decided to build a garden shed or something, instead of messing about in the walls' – that laugh again, such hard work that it hurt to hear – 'but he needed something to keep him occupied, didn't he? So I thought, OK, whatever, there are worse hobbies.'

It could have been true, could have been just a refracted version of the same story Pat had poured out onto the internet; I couldn't read her, through all the things getting in the way. Richie moved in his chair. He said, picking the words, 'We've got information that says Pat was pretty upset about the squirrel, or the fox, or whatever it was. Could you tell us about that?'

That zap of some vivid emotion shot across Jenny's face again, too quick to catch. 'What information? From who?'

'We can't go into details,' I said smoothly.

'Well, sorry, but your *information* is wrong. If this is Fiona again, then this time she's not just being a drama queen, she's making the whole thing up. Pat wasn't even sure there *was* anything getting in – or it could've been just mice. A grown man doesn't get *upset* about mice. I mean, come on, would you?'

'Nah,' Richie admitted, with a touch of a smile. 'Just checking. Another thing I was meaning to ask: you said Pat needed something to keep him occupied. What did he do all day, after he was made redundant? Apart from the DIY?'

Jenny shrugged. 'Looked for a new job. Played with the kids. He went running a lot – not so much since the weather turned, but this summer; there's some lovely scenery out at Ocean View. He'd been working like mad ever since we left college; it was nice for him to have a little time off.'

It came out just a touch too smoothly, like she had recited it before. 'You said earlier he was stressed about it,' Richie said. 'How stressed?'

'He didn't like being out of work – *ob*viously; I mean, I know there are people who do, but Pat's not like that. He would've been happier if he'd known when he'd get a new job, but he made the best of it. We believe in positive mental attitude. PMA all the way.'

'Yeah? There's a lot of fellas these days that are out of work and having a tough time adjusting; no shame in that. Some of them get depressed, or get irritable; maybe they drink that bit too much, or lose their tempers that bit easier. It's natural enough, sure. Doesn't make them weak, or mental. Did Pat have any of that stuff, yeah?'

He was struggling for the easy intimacy that had got him under Conor's guard and the Gogans', but it wasn't working: his rhythm was off and his voice had a forced note, and instead of relaxing Jenny had managed to haul herself upright, her eyes blazing a furious blue. 'Oh my God, *no*. He wasn't, like, having a nervous *break*down or whatever. Whoever's been saying—'

Richie raised his hands. 'It'd be fair enough if he was, is all I'm saying. It could happen to the best of us.'

'Pat was fine. He needed a new job. He wasn't crazy. OK, Detective? Is that OK with you?'

'I'm not saying he was crazy. I'm only asking: were you ever worried about him? That he'd hurt himself, like? Maybe even hurt you? With the stress—'

'*No!* Pat would never. Not in a million years. He – Pat was . . . What are you doing? Are you trying to . . .' Jenny had fallen back onto the pillows, breathing in shallow gasps. She said, 'Could we just . . . leave this till some other time? Please?'

Her face was grey and fallen-in, all of a sudden, and her hands had gone limp on the blanket: she wasn't putting it on this time. I glanced at Richie, but he had his head down over his notebook and didn't look up.

'Absolutely,' I said. 'Thank you for your time, Mrs Spain. Please accept our sympathies, again. I hope you're not in too much pain.'

She didn't answer. Her eyes had dulled; she was nowhere near us any more. We eased out of the chairs and out of the room as quietly as we could. As I closed the door behind us, I heard Jenny starting to cry.

Outside, the sky was patchy, just enough sunshine to trick you into thinking you were warm; the hills were dappled with moving splotches of light and shade. I said, 'What happened there?'

Richie was tucking his notebook back into his pocket. He said, 'I made a bollix of it.'

'Why?'

'Her. The state of her. Put me off my game.'

'You were fine with her on Wednesday.'

He twitched a shoulder. 'Yeah. Maybe. It was one thing when we thought this was some stranger, you know? But if we're gonna have to tell her that her own husband did that to her, to their kids . . . I guess I was hoping she already knew.'

'*If* he did it. Let's worry about one step at a time.'

'I know. I just . . . I fucked up. Sorry.'

He was still messing with his notebook. He looked pale and shrunken, like he was expecting a bollocking. A day earlier he would probably have got one, but that morning I couldn't remember why I should put in the energy. 'No real harm done,' I said. 'Anything she says now won't hold up anyway; she's on enough painkillers that any statement would get thrown out in a heartbeat. That was a good moment to leave.'

I thought that would reassure him, but his face stayed tight. 'When do we give her another go?'

'When the doctors take down her dosage. From what Fiona said, it shouldn't be long. We'll check in tomorrow.'

'Could be a good while before she's in decent enough shape to talk. You saw her: she was practically unconscious there.'

I said, 'She's in better shape than she's trying to make out. At the end, yeah, she faded fast, but up until then . . . She's foggy and in pain, all right, but she's come a long way since the other day.'

Richie said, 'She looked like shite to me.'

He was heading for the car. 'Hang on,' I said. He needed a few breaths of fresh air, and so did I; I was much too tired to have this conversation and drive safely at the same time. 'Let's take five.'

I headed for the wall where we had sat the morning of the post-mortems – that felt like a decade ago. The illusion of summer didn't hold up: the sunlight was thin and tremulous, and the air had an edge that cut through my overcoat. Richie sat beside me, running the zip of his jacket up and down.

I said, 'She's hiding something.'

'Maybe. Hard to be sure, through all the drugs.'

'I'm sure. She's trying much too hard to act like life was perfect up until Monday night. The break-ins were no big deal, Pat's animal was no big deal, everything was just fine. She was chatting away like we'd all met up for a nice coffee.'

'Some people, that's how they operate. Everything's always fine. Doesn't matter what's wrong, you never admit it; just grit your teeth, keep saying it's all grand, and hope it comes true.'

His eyes were on me. I couldn't hold back a wry grin. 'True enough. Habits die hard. And you're right, that sounds like Jenny. But at a time like this, you'd think she'd be spilling everything she's got. Unless she's got a bloody good reason not to.'

Richie said, after a second, 'The obvious one is that she remembers Monday night. If it's that, then it says Pat. For her husband, she might keep her mouth shut. For someone she hadn't even seen in years, no way.'

'Then why is she playing down the break-ins? If she genuinely wasn't frightened, then why not? Any woman in the world, if she suspects someone's got access to the house where she and her babies are living, she *does* something about it. Unless she knows perfectly well who's coming in and out, and she doesn't have a problem with it.'

Richie bit at a cuticle and thought that over, squinting into the weak sunlight. A little colour was coming back to his cheeks, but his spine was still curled with tension. 'Then why'd she say anything to Fiona?'

'Because she didn't know at first. But you heard her: she was trying to catch the guy. What if she did? Or what if Conor got ballsy and decided to leave Jenny a note, somewhere along the way? There's history there, remember. Fiona thinks there was never anything romantic between the two of them – or that's what she says she thinks, anyway — but I doubt she'd know if there had been. At the very least, they were friends; close friends, for a long time. If Jenny found out Conor was hanging around, she might have decided to rekindle the friendship.'

'Without telling Pat?'

'Maybe she was afraid he'd fly off the handle and beat the shite out of Conor – he had a history of jealousy, remember. And maybe Jenny knew he had something to be jealous about.' Saying it out loud sent a shot of electricity through me, a charge that almost lifted me off the wall. Finally, and about bloody time, this case was starting to fit itself into one of the templates, the oldest and best-worn one of all.

Richie said, 'Pat and Jenny were mad about each other. If there's one thing everyone agrees on, it's that.'

'You're the one saying he tried to kill her.'

'Not the same thing. People kill people they're mad about; happens all the time. They don't cheat on someone they're mad about.'

'Human nature is human nature. Jenny's stuck in the middle of nowhere, no friends around, no job to go to, up to her ears in money worries, Pat's obsessing over some animal in the attic; and all of a sudden, just when she needs him most, Conor shows up. Someone who knew her back when she was the golden girl with the perfect life; someone who's adored her for half their lives. You'd have to be a saint not to be tempted.'

'Maybe,' Richie said. He was still ripping at that cuticle. 'But say you're right, yeah? That doesn't take us any closer to a motive for Conor.'

'Jenny decided to break off the affair.'

'That'd be a motive to kill her, just. Or maybe just Pat, if Conor thought it'd make Jenny come back to him. Not the whole family.'

The sun was gone; the hills were fading into grey, and the wind punched fallen leaves in dizzy circles before slapping them back to the damp ground. I said, 'Depends how much he wanted to punish her.'

'OK,' Richie said. He took his nail away from his mouth and shoved his hands into his pockets, pulled his jacket closer around him. 'Maybe. But then how come Jenny's saying nothing?'

'Because she doesn't remember.'

'Doesn't remember Monday night, maybe. But the last few months: she remembers those just grand. If she'd been having an affair with Conor, or even just hanging out with him, she'd remember that. If she'd been planning on dumping him, she'd know.'

'And you think she'd want that splashed across the headlines? "Murdered Children's Mother Had Affair with Accused, Court Told." You think she's going to volunteer to be the media's Whore of the Week?'

'Yeah, I do. You're saying he killed her *kids*, man. No way would she cover for that.'

I said, 'She might if she felt guilty enough. An affair would make it her fault Conor was in their lives, which would make it her fault he did what he did. A lot of people would have a pretty tough time getting their own heads around that, never mind telling it to the police. Never underestimate the power of guilt.'

Richie shook his head. 'Even if you're right about an affair, man, it doesn't say Conor. It says Pat. He was already losing the plot – you said that yourself. Then he finds out his wife's having it off with his old best mate, and he snaps. He takes Jenny out as punishment, takes the kids along so they won't have to live without their parents, finishes off with himself because he's got nothing left to live for. You saw what he said on that board: *Her and those kids are everything I've got.*'

A couple of med students who should have known better had brought their eyebags and stubble outside for a cigarette. I felt a sudden rush of impatience, so violent that it smashed the fatigue away, with everything around me: the pointless reek of their smoke, the tactful little dance steps of our interview with Jenny, the image of Dina tugging insistently at the corner of my mind, Richie and his stubborn, tangled mess of objections and hypotheticals. 'Well,' I said. I stood up and dusted off my coat. 'Let's start by finding out whether I'm right about the affair, shall we?'

'Conor?'

'No,' I said. I wanted Conor so badly I could almost smell him, the sharp resiny tang of him, but this is where control comes in useful. 'We're saving him for later. I'm not going near Conor Brennan till I can go in with a full clip of ammo. We're going to talk to the Gogans again. And this time I'll do the talking.'

Ocean View looked worse every time. On Tuesday it had looked like a battered castaway waiting for its saviour, like all it needed was some property developer with plenty of cash and plenty of get-up-and-go to stride in and kick it into all the bright shapes it was meant to be. Now it looked like the end of the world. I half-expected feral dogs to slink up around the car when I stopped, last survivors to come staggering and moaning out of skeleton houses. I thought of Pat jogging circles around waste ground, trying to run those scrabbling noises out of his mind; of Jenny listening to the wind whistle around her windows, reading pink-covered books to keep up her PMA and wondering where her happy ending had gone.

Sinéad Gogan was home, of course. 'What d'yous want?' she demanded, in the doorway. She was wearing the same grey leggings from Tuesday. I recognised a grease stain on one wobbly thigh.

'We'd like a few words with you and your husband.'

'He's out.'

Which was a pisser. Gogan was what passed for the brains of this outfit; I had been relying on him to figure out that they needed to talk to us. 'That's all right,' I said. 'We can come back and talk to him later, if we need to. For now, we'll see how much you can help us.'

'Jayden's already told you—'

'Yeah, he has,' I said, brushing past her and heading for the sitting room, with Richie in my wake. 'It's not Jayden we're interested in, this time. It's you.'

'Why?'

Jayden was sitting on the floor again, shooting zombies. He said promptly, 'I'm off sick.'

'Switch that off,' I told him, making myself comfortable in one of the armchairs. Richie took the other one. Jayden made a disgusted face, but when I pointed at the controller and snapped my fingers, he did as he was told. 'Your mother's got something to tell us.'

Sinéad stayed in the doorway. 'I don't.'

'Sure you do. You've been keeping something back ever since we first walked in here. Today is when you come clean. What was it, Mrs Gogan? Something you saw? Heard? What?'

'I don't know anything about that fella. I never even seen him.'

'That's not what I asked you. I don't care if it's got nothing to do with that *fella*, or any fella; I want to hear it anyway. Sit down.'

I saw Sinéad consider going into a don't-give-me-orders-in-my-own-house routine, but I gave her a stare that said this would be a very bad idea. In the end she rolled her eyes and plumped down on the sofa, which groaned. 'I've to get Baby up in a minute. And I don't know anything that's got to do with anything. OK?'

'You don't get to decide that. The way it works is, you tell us what you know; *we* figure out how it's relevant. That's why we're the ones with the badges. So let's go.'

She sighed noisily. 'I. Don't. Know. Anything. What am I supposed to say?'

I said, 'Just how stupid are you?'

Sinéad's face turned uglier and she opened her mouth to hit me with some stale drivel about respect, but I kept slamming the words at her till she shut it again. 'You make me want to puke. What the hell do you think we're investigating? Shoplifting? Littering? This is a *murder* case. Multiple murder. How has that not sunk into your thick head?'

'Don't you call me—'

'Tell me something, Mrs Gogan. I'm curious. What kind of scum lets a kid-killer walk away because she doesn't like cops? Just how far below human do you have to be, to think that's OK?'

Sinéad snapped, 'Are you going to let him talk to me like that?'

She was talking to Richie. He spread his hands. 'We're under a load of pressure here, Mrs Gogan. You've seen the papers, yeah? The whole country's looking for us to get this sorted. We've got to do whatever it takes.'

'No shit,' I said. 'Why did you think we kept coming back? Because we can't stay away from your pretty face? We're here because we've got a guy in custody, and we need the evidence to keep him there. Think hard, if you're able. What do you figure is going to happen if he gets out?'

Sinéad had her arms folded across her flab and her lips pinched into a tight, outraged knot. I didn't wait. 'The first thing is that I'm going to be very bloody pissed off, and even you have to know that pissing off a cop is a bad idea. Does your husband ever do nixers, Mrs Gogan? Do you know how long he could get for welfare fraud? Jayden doesn't look sick to me; how often does he skip school? If I put in the effort – and believe me, I will – just how much trouble do you think I could make for you?'

'We're a decent family—'

'Save it. Even if I believed you, I'm not your biggest problem. The second thing that's going to happen, if you keep messing us around, is that *this guy is going to get out.* God knows I don't expect you to give a damn about justice or the good of society, but I thought at least you had the brains to look after your own family. This man knows that Jayden could tell us about the key. Do you think he doesn't know where Jayden lives? If I tell him that someone's got the goods on him and they could talk any minute, who do you think is going to spring to his mind?'

'Ma,' Jayden said, in a small voice. He had bum-shuffled back against the sofa and was staring at me. I could feel Richie's head turned towards me, too, but he had the sense to keep his mouth shut.

'Is all of this clear enough for you? Do you need me to explain it in smaller words? Because unless you're literally too stupid to live, the next thing out of your mouth is going to be whatever you've been keeping back.'

Sinéad was pressed back into the sofa, mouth hanging open. Jayden was holding on to the hem of her leggings. The fear on their faces brought back last night's giddy, tilting rush, sent it speeding through my blood like a drug with no name.

I don't talk to witnesses this way. My bedside manner may not be the finest, I may have a rep for being cold or brusque or whatever people want to call it, but I had never in my career done anything like this. It wasn't because I hadn't wanted to. Don't fool yourself: we all have a cruel streak. We keep it under lock and key either because we're afraid of getting punished or because we believe this will somehow make a difference, make the world a better place. No one punishes a detective for giving a witness a little scare. I've heard plenty of the lads do worse, and nothing ever happened.

I said, 'Talk.'

'*Ma.*'

Sinéad said, 'It was that yoke there.' She nodded at the baby monitor, lying on its side on the coffee table.

'What was?'

'Sometimes they get their wires crossed, or whatever you call it.'

'Frequencies,' Jayden said. He looked a lot happier, now that his mother was talking. 'Not wires.'

'You shut up. This is all your fault, you and your bleeding tenner.' Jayden shoved himself away from her, along the floor, and slumped into a sulk. 'Whatever you call them, they get crossed. Sometimes – not all the time; maybe every couple of weeks, like – that yoke picked up their monitor, instead of ours. So we could hear what was going on in there. It wasn't on purpose or nothing, I don't be listening in on people' – Sinéad managed a self-righteous look that didn't suit her – 'but we couldn't help hearing.'

'Right,' I said. 'And what did you hear?'

'I told you, I don't be earwigging on other people's

conversations. I paid no notice. Just switched the monitor off and then on again, to reset it. I only ever heard a few seconds, like.'

'You listened for ages,' said Jayden. 'You made me turn down my game so you could hear better.'

Sinéad shot him a glare that said he was in deep shit as soon as we left. For this, she had been ready to let a murderer walk free: so she could look like a good respectable housewife, to herself if not to us, instead of a nosy, petty, furtive little bitch. I'd seen it a hundred times, but it made me want to slap the fourth-hand look of virtue right off her ugly face. I said, 'I don't give a damn if you spent your days under the Spains' window with an ear trumpet. I just want to know what you heard.'

Richie said matter-of-factly, 'Anyone would've listened, sure. Human nature. At first you'd no choice, anyway: you needed to figure out what was going on with your monitor.' His voice had that ease again: he was back on form.

Sinéad nodded vigorously. 'Yeah. Exactly. The first time it happened, I nearly had a heart attack. Middle of the night, all of a sudden there's a kid calling, "Mummy, Mummy, come here," right in my ear. First I thought it was Jayden, only it sounded way too young, and he doesn't call me Mummy anyway; and Baby was only born. Scared the life out of me.'

'She screamed,' Jayden told us, smirking. He had apparently recovered. 'She thought it was a ghost.'

'I did, yeah. So? My husband woke up then, and he figured it out, but anyone would've been freaking. So what?'

'She was going to get a psychic out. Or one of those ghost hunters.'

'You shut up.'

I said, 'When was this?'

'Baby's ten months now, so January, February.'

'And after that you heard it every couple of weeks, for a total of about twenty times. What did you hear?'

Sinéad was still furious enough to glass me, but a gossip about the uppity neighbours was impossible to resist. 'Mostly just boring sh— stuff. The first few times, it was himself reading some *story* to put one of the kids to sleep, or it was the young fella jumping on his bed, or the young one talking to her dollies. Around the end of summer, but, they must've moved the monitors downstairs or something, 'cause we started hearing other stuff. Like them watching the telly, or her showing the young one how to make chocolate chip cookies – wouldn't just buy them from the shop like the rest of us, she was too good for that. And once – middle of the night again – I heard her say, "Just come to bed. Please," like she was begging, and him saying, "In a minute." Didn't blame him; it'd be like shagging a bag of potatoes.' Sinéad tried to catch Richie's eye for a shared smirk, but he stayed blank. 'Like I said. Boring.'

I said, 'And the ones that weren't boring?'

'There was only the once.'

'Let's hear it.'

'It was one afternoon. She was just after getting in, I guess from picking up the young one from school. We were in here, Baby was having his nap so I'd the monitor out, and all of a sudden there's your woman, yapping away. I almost switched it off, 'cause I swear she'd make you sick, but . . .'

Sinéad gave a defiant little shrug. I said, 'What was Jennifer Spain saying?'

'Talking her head off. She's like, "Now let's get ready! Your daddy's going to be home from his walk any minute, and when he gets in, we're going to be happy. Very very happy." She's all *perky*' – Sinéad's lip curled – 'like some American cheerleader. Don't know what she had to be perky about. She's, like, *arranging* the kids, telling the little girl to sit right here and have a dolly picnic, and the young fella to sit over here and not be throwing his Lego, ask nicely if he wants a hand. She goes, "Everything's going to be lovely. When your daddy gets in, he's going to be sooo happy. That's what you want, isn't it? You don't want Daddy to be unhappy, do you?"'

'"*Mummy* and *Daddy*,"' said Jayden, under his breath, and snorted.

'She was going on like that for ages, till the monitor cut out. See what I mean about her? She was like your woman off *Desperate*

*Housewives*, the one that has to have everything perfect or she loses the head. It was like, Jaysus, re*lax*. My husband goes, "D'you know what that one needs? She needs a good—"'

Sinéad remembered who she was talking to and cut herself off, with a stare to show she wasn't afraid of us. Jayden sniggered.

'To be honest with you,' she said, 'she sounded bleeding mental.'

I asked, 'When was this?'

'A month back, maybe. Middle of September. See what I mean? Nothing to do with anything.'

Not like anyone off *Desperate Housewives*; like a victim. Like every battered woman and man I had dealt with, back in Domestic Violence. Every one of them had been sure that their partners would be happy and everything in the garden would be rosy, if they could just get it right. Every one of them had been terrified, to a point somewhere between hysteria and paralysis, of getting it wrong and making Daddy unhappy.

Richie had gone still, no more foot-jiggling: he had spotted it too. He said, 'That's why the first thing you thought, when you saw our lot outside, was that Pat Spain had killed his wife.'

'Yeah. I thought maybe if she didn't have the house clean, or if the kids were bold, he gave her the slaps. Just goes to show you, doesn't it? There she was, all up herself, with her fancy gear and her posh accent, and all the time he's beating the bollix out of her.' Sinéad couldn't keep the smirk off the corners of her mouth. She had liked the idea. 'So when yous showed up, I figured it had to be that. She burned the dinner or something, and he went ballistic.'

Richie asked, 'Anything else that made you think he could be hurting her? Anything you heard, anything you saw?'

'Those monitors being downstairs. That's weird, know what I mean? At first I couldn't think of any reason why they'd be anywhere but the kids' bedrooms. When I heard her going on like that, though, I thought maybe he put them all around, so he could keep tabs on her. Like if he went upstairs or out in the garden, he could bring the receivers with him, so he'd hear everything she did.' Satisfied little nod: she was delighted with her own investigative genius. 'Creepy or what?'

'Nothing else, no?'

Shrug. 'No bruises or nothing. No yelling, that I heard. She did have a face on her, but, whenever I saw her outside. She used to be all *cheerful* – even when the kids were acting up or whatever, she'd this big fake smile on her. That went out the window, the last while: she looked down in the dumps the whole time. Spacy, like – I thought maybe she was on the Valium. I figured it was 'cause of him being out of work: she wasn't happy about having to live like the rest of us, no more SUV and no more designer gear. If he was battering her, though, could've been that.'

I asked, 'Did you ever hear anyone else in the house, other than the four Spains? Visitors, family, tradesmen?'

That lit up Sinéad's whole pasty face. 'Jesus! Was your woman playing away, yeah? Getting some fella in while her husband was out? No wonder he was keeping tabs. The cheek of her, acting like we were something she'd scrape off her shoe, when she was—'

I said, 'Did you hear or see anything that would indicate that?'

She thought that over. 'Nah,' she said, regretfully. 'Only ever heard the four of them.'

Jayden was messing about with his controller, flicking at buttons, but he didn't quite have the nerve to switch it back on. 'The whistling,' he said.

'That was some other house.'

'Wasn't. They're too far away.'

I said, 'We'd like to hear about it, either way.'

Sinéad shifted on the sofa. 'It was only the one time. August, maybe; could've been before. Early morning. We heard someone whistling – not a song or nothing, just like when a fella whistles to himself while he's doing something else.' Jayden demonstrated, a low, tuneless, absent sound. Sinéad shoved his shoulder. 'Stop that. You're giving me a headache. Them in Number Nine, they were all gone out – her too, so it couldn't have been her bit on the side. I thought it had to be from one of them houses down at the end of the road; there's two families down there, and they've both got kids, so they'd have the monitors.'

'No you didn't,' Jayden said. 'You thought it was a ghost. Again.'

Sinéad snapped, to me or Richie or both, 'I'm entitled to think what I like. Yous can go ahead and look at me like I'm thick; yous don't have to live out here. Try it for a while, then come back to me.'

Her voice was belligerent, but there was real fear in her eyes. 'We'll bring our own Ghostbusters,' I said. 'Monday night, did you hear anything on the monitors? Anything at all?'

'Nah. Like I said, it only happened every few weeks.'

'You'd better be sure.'

'I am. Positive.'

'What about your husband?'

'Him neither. He'd have said.'

I said, 'Is that the lot? Nothing else we might want to hear about?'

Sinéad shook her head. 'That's it.'

'How do I know that?'

''Cause. I don't want yous coming back here again, calling me names in front of my son. I've told you everything. So you can eff off and leave us *alone*. OK?'

'My pleasure,' I said, getting up. 'Believe me.' The arm of the chair left something sticky on my hand; I didn't bother hiding the look of distaste.

As we left, Sinéad planted herself in the doorway behind us, doing something that was meant to be an imposing stare but came off looking like an electrocuted pug dog. When we were a safe distance down the drive, she shouted after us, 'You can't talk to me like that! I'll be putting in a complaint!'

I pulled my card out of my pocket without breaking stride, waved it above my head and dropped it on the drive for her to pick up. 'See you then,' I called back over my shoulder. 'I can't wait.'

I was expecting Richie to say something about my new interview technique – calling a witness a scumbag moron isn't anywhere in the rulebook – but he had sunk back somewhere in his mind; he trudged back to the car with his hands deep in his pockets, head bent into the wind. My mobile had three missed calls and a text, all from Geri – the text started, *Sorry mick but any news abt* . . . I deleted them all.

When we got onto the motorway, Richie resurfaced far enough to say – carefully, to the windscreen – 'If Pat was hitting Jenny . . .'

'If my aunt had balls, she'd be my uncle. The Gogan cow doesn't know everything about the Spains, no matter what she'd like to think. Luckily for us, there's one guy who does, and we know exactly where to find him.'

Richie didn't answer. I took one hand off the wheel to give him a clap on the shoulder. 'Don't worry, my friend. We'll get the goods out of Conor. Who knows, it might even be fun.'

I caught his sideways glance: I shouldn't have been this upbeat, not after what Sinéad Gogan had given us. I didn't know how to tell him that it wasn't good humour, not the way he thought; it was that wild rush still careening around my veins, it was the fear on Sinéad's face and Conor waiting for me at the end of this drive. I got my foot on the pedal and kept it there, watching the needle creep up. The Beemer handled better than ever, flew straight and hard as a hawk diving on prey, like this speed was what it had been aching for all along.

# 16

Before we had Conor brought over to us, we skimmed through everything the tide had washed up in the squad room: reports, phone messages, statements, tips, the lot. Most of it was a whole lot of nothing – the floaters looking for Conor's friends and family had turned up no one but a couple of cousins, the tip line had attracted the usual swarm of freaks who wanted to talk about the Book of Revelations and complicated maths and immodest women – but there were a couple of gems in there. Fiona's old pal Shona was in Dubai this week and would sue us all personally if anyone printed her name in connection with this mess, but she did share her opinion that Conor had been mad about Jenny when they were kids and that nothing had changed since, otherwise why had he never had a relationship longer than six months? And Larry's boys had found a rolled-up overcoat, a jumper, a pair of jeans, a pair of leather gloves and a pair of trainers, size ten, shoved in the bin of an apartment block a mile from Conor's flat. They were all covered in blood. The blood types matched Pat and Jenny Spain. The left trainer was consistent with the print in Conor's car, and a perfect match to the one on the Spains' kitchen floor.

We waited in the interview room, one of the tiny cramped ones with no observation room and barely enough space to move, for the uniforms to bring Conor up. Someone had been using it: there were sandwich wrappers and foam cups scattered on the table, a faint smell of citrus aftershave and sweat and onion in the air. I couldn't stay still. I moved around the room, balling up rubbish and tossing it into the bin.

Richie said, 'He should be well nervous by now. A day and a half sitting in there, wondering what we're waiting for . . .'

I said, 'We need to be very clear on what we're after. I want a motive.'

Richie stuffed empty sugar sachets into a foam cup. 'We might not get one.'

'Yeah. I know.' Saying it hit me with another wave of that light-headedness; for a second I thought I would have to lean on the table till my balance steadied. 'There might not be one. You were right: sometimes shit just happens. But that's not going to stop me giving it my best shot.'

Richie thought about that, examining a plastic wrapper he had picked off the floor. 'If we might not get a motive,' he said. 'What else are we after?'

'Answers. What Conor and the Spains fought about, a few years back. His relationship with Jenny. Why he wiped that computer.' The room was as clean as it was going to get. I made myself lean against the wall and stay put. 'I want us to be sure. When you and I leave this room, I want both of us on the same page and both of us sure who we're chasing. That's all. If we can just get that far, the rest will fall into place.'

Richie watched me. His face was unreadable. He said, 'I thought you were sure.'

My eyes were gritty with fatigue. I wished I had got an extra coffee, when we stopped for lunch. I said, 'I was.'

He nodded. He tossed the cup into the bin and came to lean against the wall next to me. After a while he dug a packet of mints out of his pocket and held it out. I took one and we stayed there, sucking mints, shoulder to shoulder, until the interview-room door opened and the uniform brought Conor in.

He looked bad. Maybe it was just because he wasn't wearing the duffel coat this time, but he seemed even thinner, thin enough that I wondered if we should get him checked out by a doctor, bones jutting painfully through the reddish stubble. He had been crying again.

He sat hunched over the table, staring at his fists planted in front of him, not moving even when the central heating kicked on with a clang. In a way, that reassured me. The innocent ones fidget and jitter and almost leap out of their seats at the slightest noise; they're itching to talk to you and get the whole thing straightened out. The guilty ones are concentrating, marshalling all their forces tight around the inner stronghold and bracing themselves for battle.

Richie stretched up to switch on the video camera and told it, 'Detective Kennedy and Detective Curran interviewing Conor Brennan. Interview commenced at four forty-three pm.' I ran through the rights sheet; Conor signed without looking, sat back and folded his arms. As far as he was concerned, we were done.

'Oh, Conor,' I said, leaning back in my chair and shaking my head sadly. 'Conor, Conor, Conor. And here I thought we were getting on so well, the other night.'

He watched me and kept his mouth shut.

'You weren't being honest with us, fella.'

That sent a zip of fear across his face, too sharp to hide. 'I was.'

'No you weren't. Ever heard of the truth, the whole truth and nothing but the truth? You let us down on at least one of those. Now why would you go and do that?'

Conor said, 'Don't know what you're talking about.' His mouth clamped shut in a hard line, but his eyes were still fixed on me. He was afraid.

Richie, lounging against the wall under the camera, clicked his tongue reproachfully. I said, 'Let's start with this: you gave us the impression that, up until Monday night, the closest you'd got to the Spains was through binoculars. You didn't think it might be an idea to mention that you'd been best buddies since you were kids?'

A faint red sprang up on his cheekbones, but he didn't blink: this wasn't what he was afraid of. 'None of your business.'

I sighed and wagged a finger at him. 'Conor, you know better than that. You name it, it's our business now.'

'And how much difference did it make?' Richie pointed out. 'You had to know Pat and Jenny had photos, man. All you did was set us back a couple of hours and piss us off.'

'My colleague speaks the truth,' I said. 'Can you remember that, next time you're tempted to dick us around?'

Conor said, 'How's Jenny?'

I snorted. 'What's it to you? If you were so concerned about her health, you could have just, I don't know, not stabbed the poor woman. Or are you hoping she's finished the job for you?'

His jaw had tightened, but he held on to his cool. 'I want to know how she's doing.'

'And I don't care what you want. Tell you what, though: we've got a few questions for you. If you answer them all like a nice boy, without any more messing, then maybe I'll be in a better mood and I'll feel like sharing. Does that sound fair enough?'

'What do you want to know?'

'Let's start with the easy stuff. Tell us about Pat and Jenny, back when you were all kiddies together. What was Pat like?'

Conor said, 'He was my best mate, since we were fourteen. You probably know that already.' Neither of us answered. 'He was sound. That's all. The soundest bloke I've ever known. Liked rugby, liked having a laugh, liked hanging out with his mates; he liked most people, everyone liked him. A lot of popular blokes are wankers, when you're that age, but I never saw Pat be a bastard to anyone. Maybe all that doesn't sound like anything special to you. But it is.'

Richie was tossing a sugar sachet in the air and catching it. 'You were close, yeah?'

Conor's chin pointed from Richie to me. 'You're partners. That means you've got to be ready to trust each other with your lives, right?'

Richie caught his sachet and stayed still, letting me answer. I said, 'Good partners do. Yeah.'

'Then you know what Pat and me were like. There's some stuff I told him, I think I might've done myself in if anyone else had found out. I told him anyway.'

He had missed the irony, if it was there. The flash of unease almost sent me out of my chair and circling the room again. 'What kind of stuff?'

'You must be joking. Family stuff.'

I glanced across at Richie – we could find out somewhere else, if we needed to – but his eyes were on Conor. I said, 'Let's talk about Jenny. What was she like, back then?'

Conor's face softened. 'Jenny,' he said gently. 'She was something special.'

'Yeah, we've seen the photos. No awkward phase going on there.'

'That's not what I mean. She came into a room and made things better. She always wanted everything lovely, everyone happy, and she always knew the right thing to do. She had this touch, I've never seen anything like it. Like once we were all at a disco, one of those underage things, and Mac – this guy we used to hang out with – he was hovering around some girl, kind of dancing around her and trying to get her to dance with him. And she made this face at him and said something, I don't know what, but her and her mates all collapsed laughing. Mac came back to us scarlet. Devastated. The girls were still pointing and giggling; you could tell he just wanted to disappear. And Jenny turns around to Mac and holds out her hands and says, "I love this song, only Pat hates it. Would you dance with me? Please?" And off they go, and next thing you know Mac's smiling, Jenny's laughing at something he said, they're having a ball. That shut the girls up. Jenny was ten times prettier than your woman, any day.'

I said, 'That didn't bother Pat?'

'Jenny dancing with Mac?' He almost laughed. 'Nah. Mac was a year younger. Fat kid with bad hair. And anyway, Pat knew what Jenny was doing. I'd say he just loved her more for doing it.'

That softness had seeped into his voice. It sounded like a lover's, a voice for low light and drifting music, for only one listener. Fiona and Shona had been right.

I said, 'Sounds like a good relationship.'

Conor said simply, 'They were beautiful. Only word for it. You know when you're a teenager, a lot of the time it feels like the whole world is shite? The two of them'd give you hope.'

'That's lovely,' I said. 'Really, it is.'

Richie had started playing with the sugar sachet again. 'You went out with Jenny's sister Fiona, yeah? When you were, what, eighteen?'

'Yeah. For a few months, only.'

'Why'd you break up?'

Conor shrugged. 'It wasn't working out.'

'Why not? She was a geebag? You had nothing in common? She wouldn't do the do?'

'No. She was the one that broke it off. Fiona's great. We got on great. It just wasn't working out.'

'Yeah, well,' Richie said dryly, catching the sugar, 'I can see where it wouldn't. If you were in love with her sister.'

Conor went still. 'Who said that?'

'Who cares?'

'I care. Because they're full of shite.'

'Conor,' I said, warning. 'Remember our deal?'

He looked like he wanted to kick both of our teeth in, but after a moment he said, 'It wasn't the way you make it sound.'

And if that wasn't a motive then at least, at the very least, it was only one step away. I couldn't stop myself from glancing over at Richie, but he had thrown the sugar too far and was lunging for it. 'Yeah?' he wanted to know. 'How do I make it sound?'

'Like I was some dirtbag trying to get between the two of them. I wasn't. If I could've pushed a button and split them up, I would never have done it. Anything else, what I felt: that was my business.'

'Maybe,' I said. I was pleased with the sound of my voice, lazy, amused. 'Up until Jenny found out, anyway. She did find out, didn't she?'

Conor had reddened. After all these years, this should have healed over. 'I never said a word to her.'

'You didn't need to. Jenny guessed. Women do, old son. How did she feel about it?'

'Wouldn't know.'

'Did she give you the old brush-off? Or did she enjoy the

attention, lead you on? Ever have a little kiss and a cuddle, when Pat wasn't looking?'

Conor's fists were clenched on the table. '*No*. I told you, Pat was my best mate. I told you what the two of them were like together. You think either of us, me or Jenny, would *ever* have done that?'

I laughed out loud. 'Oh, God, yeah. I've been a teenage bloke myself. I'd have sold my own mother downriver for a bit of tit.'

'Probably you would've. I wouldn't.'

'Very honourable of you,' I said, with only a flicker of a smirk. 'But Pat didn't understand that you were just worshipping nobly from afar, did he? He confronted you about Jenny. You want to tell us your version of what went down?'

Conor demanded, 'What do you *want*? I've told you I killed them. All this, back when we were kids, this had nothing to do with it.'

His knuckles were white. I said coolly, 'Remember what I told you? We like deciding for ourselves what's relevant. So let's hear what went down between you and Pat.'

His jaw moved, but he kept control. 'Nothing *went down*. I'm at home one afternoon, a few days after Fiona broke up with me, and Pat calls round and says, "Let's go for a walk." I knew something was up – he had this grim face on him, wouldn't look at me. We went walking down the beach, and he asked me if Fiona dumped me because I was into Jenny.'

'Man,' said Richie, making a cringe face. 'Awkward.'

'You think? He was really upset. So was I.'

I said, 'Restrained kind of guy, Pat, wasn't he? Me, I'd have knocked your teeth out.'

'I thought probably he would. I was OK with that. Figured I deserved it. But Pat – he wasn't the type to lose his temper, ever. He just went, "I know loads of guys fancy her. I don't blame them. Not a problem, as long as they keep their distance. But you . . . Jesus, man, I never even thought of worrying about you."'

'And what did you tell him?'

'Same as I told you. That I'd die before I'd get between them.

That I'd never let Jenny know. That all I wanted was to find some other girl, be like the two of them, forget I'd ever felt this way.'

The shadow of old passion in his voice said he had meant every word, for whatever that was worth. I raised an eyebrow. 'And that was all it took? Seriously?'

'It took hours. Walking up and down that beach, talking. But that's the bones of it.'

'And Pat believed you?'

'He knew me. I was telling the truth. He believed me.'

'And then?'

'Then we went to the pub. Got locked, ended up staggering home holding each other up. Saying all the shite that guys say on nights like that.'

*I love you, man, not in a gay way, but I love you, you know that, I'd do anything for you, anything . . .* That unease flared through me, fiercer this time. I said, 'And everything in the garden was rosy again.'

Conor said, 'Yeah. It bloody was. I was Pat's best man, a few years later. I'm Emma's godfather. Check the paperwork, if you don't believe me. You think Pat would've picked me if he'd thought I was trying to be with his wife?'

'People do strange things, fella. If they didn't, me and my partner here would be out of a job. But I'll take your word for it: best buds again, brothers in arms, all that good stuff. And then, a few years ago, the friendship went tits-up. We'd like to hear your version of what happened there.'

'Who said it went tits-up?'

I grinned at him. 'You're getting predictable, fella. A: we ask the questions. B: we don't reveal our sources. And C: you said, among other people. If you'd still been all matey with the Spains, you wouldn't have needed to freeze your balls off on a building site to see how they were doing.'

After a moment Conor said, 'It was that fucking place. Ocean View. I wish to Jesus they'd never heard of it.'

His voice had a new, savage undercurrent to it. 'I knew straight away. Right from the off. Maybe three years ago, not long after

Jack was born, I went over to Pat and Jenny's place for dinner one night – they were renting this little townhouse in Inchicore, back then; I was ten minutes down the road, I was over all the time. I get there, and the two of them, they're over the moon. I'm barely in the door, they shove this brochure of houses at me: "Look! Look at this! We put down our deposit this morning, Jenny's mum minded the kids so we could camp outside the estate agent's overnight, we were tenth in the queue, we got the exact one we wanted!" They'd been dying to buy somewhere ever since they got engaged, so I was all ready to be delighted for them, yeah? But then I look at the brochure and the estate's in *Brianstown*. Never heard of it; sounds like one of those nowhere dives that the developer's named after his kid or himself, playing little emperor. And it says something like "Just forty minutes from Dublin," only I take one look at the map and that's if you've got a helicopter.'

I said, 'Long way from Inchicore. No more calling round for dinner every few days.'

'That wasn't a problem. They could've found somewhere in *Galway* and I'd've been happy for them, as long as it was going to make them happy.'

'Which they thought this place was.'

'There *was* no place. I look closer at this brochure, and those aren't houses; they're models. I say, "Is the estate even built?" and Pat goes, "It will be when we move in."'

Conor shook his head, a corner of his mouth twisting. Something had changed. Broken Harbour had slammed into this conversation like a battering gust of wind, turning all of us tense and intent. Richie had put the sugar sachet away. 'Betting years of their lives on a field in the middle of nowhere.'

I said, 'So they were optimists. That's a good thing.'

'Yeah? There's optimistic, and then there's plain crazy.'

'You didn't think they were old enough to make that decision for themselves?'

'Yeah. I did. So I kept my gob shut. Said congratulations, I'm delighted for you, can't wait to see the place. Nodded and smiled whenever they talked about it, when Jenny showed me bits of curtain material, when Emma drew a picture of what her room was going to look like. I *wanted* it to be wonderful. I was *praying* it'd be everything they'd ever wanted.'

I said, 'But it wasn't.'

Conor said, 'The two of them brought me down to see the place, when the house was ready. A Sunday: the day before they were signing the final contracts. Two years ago – bit more, because it was summer. It was hot, sticky-hot – cloudy, and the cloud pressing the air down on top of you. The place was . . .' A grim sound that could have been a laugh. 'You've seen it. It was better then – the weeds hadn't come up, and there was still loads of work going on, so at least it didn't feel like a graveyard – but still: it wasn't somewhere anyone would want to *live*. When we get out of the car, Jenny goes, "Look, you can see the sea! Isn't it gorgeous?" I go, "Yeah, great view," but it wasn't. The water looked dirty, greasy; there should have been a breeze coming off of it, cool us down, but it was like the air had died. The house was pretty enough, if you like Stepford, but straight across the road was waste ground and a bulldozer. The whole place was fucking horrendous. Made me want to turn around and get out as fast as I could, drag Pat and Jenny with me.'

Richie said, 'What about them? Were they happy enough?'

Conor shrugged. 'Sounded like. Jenny goes, "They'll be finished building across the road in just a couple of months" – didn't look like that to me, but I kept my mouth shut. She goes, "It's going to be so lovely. The mortgage people are giving us a hundred and ten per cent, so we can furnish the place. I was thinking about a maritime theme for the kitchen, to go with the sea? Don't you think a maritime theme would be nice?"

'I go, "Might be safer to take just the hundred per cent, furnish as you go along." Jenny laughs – it sounded fake, but that could've been just the way the air flattened everything out – and she goes, "Oh, Conor, relax. We can afford it. So we won't eat out as much; there's nowhere nearby anyway. I want everything to be nice."

'I go, "I'm just saying, it'd be safer. In case." Maybe I should've said nothing, but that place . . . It felt like a big dog watching you, starting to come closer, and you know right now is when you need to get the fuck out. Pat just laughs and goes, "Man, do you know how fast property prices are rising? We haven't even moved in yet, and the gaff's already worth more than we're paying. Any time we decide to sell, we'll come out with a profit."'

I said, hearing the pompous note in my voice, 'If they were crazy, then so was the rest of the country. Nobody saw the crash coming.'

Conor's eyebrow flicked. 'You think?'

'If anyone had, the country wouldn't be in this mess.'

He shrugged. 'I don't have a clue about financial stuff. I'm just a web designer. But I knew nobody wanted thousands of houses out in the middle of nowhere. People only bought them because they got told that in five years' time they could sell up for double what they'd paid, and move somewhere decent. Like I said, I'm just some idiot, but even I knew a pyramid scheme eventually runs out of suckers.'

'Well, look at Alan Greenspan here,' I said. Conor was starting to piss me off – because he had been right, and because Pat and Jenny had had every right to believe that he was wrong. 'It's easy to be right in hindsight, fella. It wouldn't have killed you to be a little more positive for your friends.'

'You mean, give them a little more bullshit? They were getting plenty of that already. The banks, the developers, the government: *Go on, buy, best investment of your lives—*'

Richie balled up the sugar sachet and sank it in the bin with a sharp rustle. He said, 'If I'd seen my best mates running towards that cliff, I'd've said something, too. Might not have stopped them, but it might've meant the fall came as less of a shock.'

The two of them were looking at me like they were the ones on the same side, like I was the outsider. Richie was only nudging Conor towards what the crash had done to Pat, but it grated just the same. I said, 'Keep talking. What happened next?'

Conor's jaw moved. The memory was winding him tighter and tighter. 'Jenny – she always hated fights – Jenny goes, "You should see the size of the back garden! We're thinking about getting a slide for the kids, and in the summer we'll have barbecues – you can stay over afterwards, so you won't have to worry about having a few cans—" Only just then there's this huge *crash* across the road, like a whole bale of slates falling off the top of the scaffolding, something like that. We all jump a mile. When our hearts start beating again, I say, "You're positive about this. Yeah?" Pat goes, "Yeah. We are. We'd better be: the deposit's non-refundable.'"

Conor shook his head. 'He's trying to make it into a joke. I say, "Fuck the deposit. You can still change your minds." And Pat, he blows *up* at me. He yells, "Fuck's sake! Can't you just *pretend* to be happy for us?" And that wasn't Pat, not at all – like I said, he never lost his temper. So I knew he was having second thoughts, major ones. I go, "Do you actually want this gaff? Just tell me that."

'He goes, "Yeah, I do. I always did. You know that. Just because you're happy renting some bachelor pad for the rest of your life—" I go, "No. Not *a* gaff. *This* gaff. Do you want it? Do you even like it? Or are you only buying it because you're supposed to?"

'Pat goes, "So it's not perfect. I bloody well knew that already. What the fuck do you want us to do? We've got *kids*. When you've got a family, you need a *home*. What's your problem with that?"'

Conor ran a hand up his jaw, hard enough that it left a red streak. 'We were yelling. Back where we grew up, there'd have been half a dozen old ones sticking their noses out the doors by now. Out there, nothing even moved. I go, "If you can't buy something you actually want, then keep renting till you can." Pat goes, "Sweet Jesus, Conor, that's not how it *works*! We need to get on the property ladder!" I go, "Like this? By going a million miles into debt for some dive that might never be a decent place to live? What if the wind changes and you get stuck like that?"

'Jenny tucks her hand in my elbow and she goes, "Conor, it's fine, honest to God it is. I know you're just trying to look out for us or whatever, but you're being totally old-fashioned. Everyone's doing it these days. *Everyone*."

He laughed, a single dry scrape. 'She said it like that meant something. Like that was the argument over, end of story. I couldn't believe what I was hearing.'

Richie said quietly, 'She was right. Our generation, how many of them were doing the exact same thing? Thousands, man. Thousands and thousands.'

'*So?* Who gives a fuck what everyone else does? They were buying a *house*, not a T-shirt. Not an *investment*. A *home*. If you let other people decide what you think about something like that, if you just follow along because it's trendy, then who are you? When the flock changes direction tomorrow, what, you just throw away everything you think and start over, because other people said so? Then what are you, underneath? You're nothing. You're no one.'

That fury, dense and cold as stone. I thought of the kitchen, smashed and bloody. 'Is that what you said to Jenny?'

'I couldn't say anything. Pat – he must've seen it on my face – Pat goes, "It's true, man. Ask anyone in the country: ninety-nine per cent of them would say we're doing the right thing."'

That raw scrape of a laugh again. 'Stood there with my mouth open, staring. I couldn't . . . Pat was never like that. Never. Not when we were *sixteen*. Yeah, sometimes he'd have a smoke or a spliff just because everyone at the party was, but underneath he knew who he *was*. He'd never have done anything full-on brain-dead, got into a car where the driver was pissed or anything like that, just because someone tried to pressure him into it. And now here he was, a fucking grown man, bleating on about "Everyone *else* is doing it!"'

I said, 'So what did you say?'

Conor shook his head. 'There wasn't anything to say. I knew that already. The two of them . . . I didn't have a clue who they were, any more. They weren't people I wanted anything to do with. I tried anyway – fucking eejit. I went, "What the fuck's happened to you two?"'

'Pat says, "We grew up. That's what happened. This is what being an adult is *like*. You play by the rules."'

'I go, "*No it's fucking well not.* If you're an adult, you think for your fucking self. Are you insane? Are you a zombie? What are you?"'

'We were squared up like we were about to beat the shite out of each other. I thought we were; I thought he was going to punch me, any second. But then Jenny grabs my elbow again and pulls me around, and she yells, "You shut up! Just shut up! You're going to ruin the whole thing. I can't stand it, all this negativity – I don't want that anywhere *near* the kids, I don't want it anywhere near us, I don't *want* it! It's *sick*. If everyone starts thinking like you, the whole country's going to go down the toilet and then we *will* be in trouble. *Then* will you be happy?"'

Conor ran a hand over his mouth again; I saw him bite down on the flesh of his palm. 'She was crying. I started to say something, I don't even know what, but Jenny slapped her hands over her ears and walked off, fast, down the road. Pat looked at me like I was dirt. He said, "Thanks, man. That was great." And he went after her.'

I said, 'And what did you do?'

'I walked away. Walked around that shithole estate for a couple of hours, looking for something that'd make me ring Pat and say *Sorry, man, I was so wrong, this place is gonna be paradise.* All I found was more shithole. In the end I rang this other mate of mine and got him to pick me up. Didn't hear from them again. Didn't try to get in touch, either.'

'Hmm,' I said. I leaned back in my chair, tapping my pen off my teeth, and considered that. 'I suppose I've heard of friendships breaking up over some weird stuff, all right. But property values? Seriously?'

'I turned out to be right, didn't I?'

'Were you pleased about that?'

'*No.* I'd have loved to be wrong.'

'Because you cared about Pat. Not to mention Jenny. You cared about Jenny.'

'About all four of them.'

'Especially Jenny. No, hang on: I'm not done. I'm a simple guy, Conor. Ask my partner here, he'll tell you: I always go for the simplest solution, and it usually turns out to be the right one. So I'm thinking you *could* have fought with the Spains over their choice of house and the size of their mortgage and what it meant about their world view and whatever else you just said – I lost track of some of it, you can remind me later. But it's a lot simpler, given the background, that you guys fought because you were still in love with Jenny Spain.'

'That never even came up. We hadn't talked about it since that one time, after Fiona broke up with me.'

I said, 'So you were still in love with her.'

After a moment Conor said, quietly and painfully, 'I've never known anyone like her.'

'Which is why your girlfriends never last. Right?'

'I don't throw years of my life into something I don't want. No matter who tells me I should. I saw Pat and Jenny; I know what the real thing looks like. Why would I go after anything else?'

I said, 'But you're trying to tell me that's not what the argument was about.'

A flash of narrow, disgusted grey eyes. 'It wasn't. You think I'd've let them guess, either of them?'

'They did before.'

'Because I was younger. I was shite at hiding stuff, back then.'

I laughed out loud. 'Just one big open book, yeah? Looks like Pat and Jenny weren't the only ones who changed when they grew up.'

'I got more sense. I got more control. I didn't turn into a different *person*.'

I said, 'Does that mean you're still in love with Jenny?'

'I haven't talked to her in years.'

Which was a whole different question, but both of them could wait. 'Maybe not. But you've seen plenty of her, from your little hideout. How did that start, while we're at it?'

I expected Conor to dodge around that, but he answered fast and easily, like he welcomed it: any subject was better than his feelings for Jenny Spain. 'By accident, almost. Things weren't going great, the end of last year. Work had dried up. It was the start of the crash – no one was saying it, not then, you were a traitor to the country if you noticed it, but I knew. Freelancers like me, we were the first ones that felt it. I was pretty much skint. Had to move out of my apartment, get a shite bedsit – you've probably seen it. Haven't you?'

Neither of us answered – in his corner Richie was staying still and melting into the background, leaving me a clear shot. The corner of Conor's mouth twisted. 'Hope you liked it. You can see why I don't hang out there if I can help it.'

'But you didn't sound like you were wild about Ocean View, either. How'd you end up hanging out there?'

He shrugged. 'I had time on my hands, I was down . . . I kept thinking about Pat and Jenny. They were who I'd always talked to, if anything was bad. I missed them. I just . . . I wanted to see how they were getting on. I just started wondering.'

I said, 'Well, that much I can get. But your average Joe, if he wants to reconnect with old mates, he doesn't set up camp outside their back window. He picks up the phone. Sorry if it's a stupid question, old son, but that didn't occur to you?'

'Didn't know if they'd want to talk to me. Didn't even know if we still had enough in common that we'd get on. I couldn't have taken finding out that we didn't.' For a second he sounded like a teenager, fragile and raw. 'Yeah, I could've rung Fiona and asked after them, but I didn't know how much they'd told her, didn't want to put her in the middle . . . One weekend I just figured I'd head out to Brianstown, see if I could get a look at them, go home. That was all.'

'And you got your look.'

'Yeah. Went up into that house, where you found me. I was only thinking I might catch them coming out into the back garden or something, but the windows in that kitchen . . . I could see everything. The four of them at the table. Jenny putting an elastic in Emma's hair so it wouldn't get in her lunch. Pat telling some story. Jack laughing, food all over his face.'

I asked, 'How long did you stay up there?'

'Maybe an hour. It was nice; the nicest thing I'd seen in I don't know how long.' The memory smoothed the tension out of Conor's voice, gentled it. 'Peaceful. I went home peaceful.'

'So you came back for another fix.'

'Yeah. A couple of weeks later. Emma had her dolls out in the garden, making them take turns to do some dance, showing them how. Jenny was hanging out her washing. Jack was being an airplane.'

'And that was peaceful too. So you kept coming back.'

'Yeah. What else was I going to do all day? Sit in that bedsit, staring at the telly?'

I said, 'Next thing you know, you're all set up with a sleeping bag and a pair of binoculars.'

Conor said, 'I know it sounds crazy. You don't have to tell me.'

'It does. But so far, fella, it also sounds harmless. Where it goes into full-on psycho is where you start breaking into their gaff. Want to tell us your version of that part?'

He still didn't think twice. Even breaking and entering was safer ground than Jenny. 'I found the back-door key, like I told you. I wasn't planning on doing anything with it; I just liked having it. But one morning they were all out, I'd been there all night, I was damp, I was bloody freezing – that was before I got the decent sleeping bag. I thought, *Why not, just for five minutes, just to warm up* . . . But it was good, in there. It smelled like ironing, and tea and baking, and some kind of flowery thing. Everything was clean, sparkly. It'd been a long time since I'd been in a place like that. A home.'

'When was this?'

'Spring. I don't remember the date.'

'And then you just kept coming back,' I said. 'You're not much good at resisting temptation, are you, old son?'

'I wasn't doing any harm.'

'No? So what did you do in there?'

Shrug. Conor had his arms folded and his eyes cut away from us: he was getting embarrassed. 'Nothing much. Had a cup of tea and a biscuit. Sometimes a sandwich.' Jenny's vanishing ham slices. 'Sometimes I'd . . .' That flush was rising on his cheeks. 'I'd close the curtains in the sitting room, so the arsehole neighbours couldn't see, and watch a bit of telly. Stuff like that.'

I said, 'You were pretending you lived there.'

Conor didn't answer.

'Ever go upstairs? Into the bedrooms?'

Silence again.

'Conor.'

'A couple of times.'

'What'd you do?'

'Just looked into Emma's room, and Jack's. Stood at the door, looked. I just wanted to be able to picture them.'

'And Pat and Jenny's room? Did you go in there?'

'Yeah.'

'And?'

'Not what you're thinking. I lay down in their bed – I took off my shoes first. Just for a minute. Closed my eyes. That's all.'

He wasn't looking at us. He was falling away into the memory; I could feel the sadness rising off him, like cold off ice. I said, sharply, 'It didn't occur to you that you could be scaring the living shite out of the Spains? Or was that a bonus?'

That brought him back. 'I wasn't scaring them. I always made sure I got out of there way before they were due back. Put everything back just like I found it: washed my cup, dried it, put it away. Cleaned the floor, if I'd tracked in dirt. The stuff I took was all tiny; no one's going to miss a couple of elastic bands. No one would've known I'd been there.'

'Except that we did know,' I said. 'Keep that in mind. Tell me something, Conor – and remember, no bullshitting. You were jealous as hell, weren't you? Of the Spains. Of Pat.'

Conor shook his head, an impatient jerk like he was shaking off a fly. '*No.* You're not getting it. Same as the stuff when we were eighteen: it wasn't the way you mean.'

'Then what way was it?'

'I didn't want anything bad to happen to them, ever. I just . . . I know I gave them shit about doing what everyone else did. But when I started watching them . . .'

A long breath. The heating had cut off again. Without its hum the room felt silent as a vacuum; the thin sounds of our breathing were sucked into that silence, dissolved away to nothing. 'From the outside their life looked exactly like everyone else's, something out of some nightmare clone film. But once you saw it from the inside, you saw . . . Like, Jenny used to put on the same idiot fake-tan shite that all the girls use, make herself look exactly like everyone else – but afterwards she'd bring the bottle into the kitchen, and her and the kids would get little paintbrushes and draw on their hands. Stars or smiley faces, or their initials – once she put tiger stripes all up Jack's arms; he was over the moon, being a tiger all week. Or after the kids were in bed Jenny'd be tidying up their crap, her and every other housewife in the world, only sometimes Pat would come give her a hand and they'd end up playing with the toys – like they'd be having a fight with the stuffed toys, and laughing, and when they got tired they'd lie on the floor together and look out the window at the moon. From up there, you could see they were still them. Still who they were when we were sixteen.'

Conor's arms had loosened; his hands were cupped on the table, palms upturned, and his lips had parted. He was watching some slow procession of images move past a lit window, faraway and untouchable, glowing richly as enamel and gold.

'Nights last longer, when you're outside on your own. You get to thinking strange things. I could see other lights, in other houses across the estate. Sometimes I heard music – someone used to play old rock 'n' roll, top volume; someone else had a flute, used to practise. I started thinking about all the other people living there. All those different lives. Even if they were all just cooking dinner, one guy could be making his kid's favourite to cheer her up after a bad day at school, some couple could be celebrating finding out she was pregnant . . . Every one of them, making dinner out there, every one of them was thinking something all their own. Loving someone all their own. Every time I was up there, it hit me harder. That kind of life: it's beautiful, after all.'

Conor caught another deep breath and laid his hands flat on the table, palms down. He said, 'That's all. Not jealous. Just . . . that.'

Richie said, from his corner, 'The Spains' lives didn't stay beautiful, though. Not after Pat lost his job.'

'They were grand.'

The instant edge to Conor's voice – straight to Pat's defence – set that unease ricocheting around inside me again. Richie came off the wall and leaned his arse on the table, too close to Conor. 'Last time we talked, you said it wrecked Pat's head. What'd you mean by that, exactly?'

'Nothing. I know Pat. I knew he'd hate being out of work. That's all.'

'Man, the poor bastard was in tatters. OK? You're not giving away anything we don't already know. So what'd you see? Him acting weird? Crying? Fighting with Jenny?'

'No.' A short, tight pause, as Conor weighed up what to give us. His arms were folded across his chest again. 'At first he was fine. After a few months – like over the summer – he started staying up late, sleeping late. He didn't go out as much. He used to go running every day, but that went out the window. Some days he didn't bother getting dressed, or shaving.'

'Sounds like depression to me.'

'He was down. So? Do you blame him?'

Richie said, 'But you still didn't think about actually getting in touch, no? When things went bad for you, you wanted Pat and Jenny. You never thought they might want you, when things got tough?'

Conor said, 'Yeah. I did. I thought about it a lot. Thought maybe I could help – head out with Pat for a couple of pints and a laugh, mind the kids while the two of them got some time together . . . But I couldn't do it. It would've been like saying, *Ha-ha, told you this would all go to shite.* Would've made things worse, not better.'

'Jaysus, man. How much worse could he have got?'

'A lot. So he didn't get enough exercise, big deal. That doesn't mean he was falling apart.'

The defensive snap was still there. I said, 'You can't have been happy that Pat wasn't going out. If he was home, no tea and sand-wiches for you. Did you still get chances to spend time in the house, the last couple of months?'

He turned towards me fast, giving Richie his shoulder, like I was saving him. 'Less. Maybe once a week, though, they'd all be out, like they'd all pick up Emma from school and then go to the shops. Pat wasn't *scared* to go out the door – he just wanted to be in so he could keep an eye out for that mink or whatever. He didn't have a phobia, nothing like that.'

I didn't look at Richie, but I felt him freeze. Conor shouldn't have known about Pat's animal.

I said easily, before he could realise, 'Did you ever see the animal?'

'Like I said. I wasn't in the house much.'

'Sure you were. I'm not talking just the last couple of months; I'm talking about the whole time you were popping in and out. Did you see it? Hear it?'

Conor was starting to turn wary, even if he wasn't sure why. 'I heard scratching, a couple of times. Thought it was mice, maybe, or a bird that had got into the attic.'

'What about at night? That's when the animal would have been doing its hunting or shagging or whatever it's into, and you were right outside, with your little binoculars. Ever see a mink, on your travels? An otter? Even a rat?'

'There's stuff living out there, yeah. I heard plenty of things moving around, at night. Some of them were big. No clue what they were, because I didn't see any of them. It was dark.'

'That didn't worry you? You're out there in the middle of nowhere, surrounded by wildlife you can't see, nothing to protect yourself with?'

Conor shrugged. 'Animals don't bother me.'

'Brave man,' I said approvingly.

Richie said – rubbing his head, confused, the bewildered newbie trying to get things straight – 'Hang on a sec there. I'm after missing a bit. How'd you know Pat was looking out for this animal?'

Conor's mouth opened for an instant; then he shut down, thinking fast. 'What's the big deal?' I demanded. 'It's not a complicated question. Any reason you don't want to tell us?'

'No. I just don't remember how I found out.'

Richie and I looked at each other and started to laugh. 'Beautiful,' I said. 'Honest to God, no matter how long I do this job, that one never gets old.' Conor's jaw had hardened: he didn't like being laughed at. 'Sorry, fella. But you've got to understand, we see an awful lot of amnesia around here. Sometimes I worry that the government's putting something in the water. Want to try again?'

His mind was revving. Richie said, with the grin still in his voice, 'Ah, come on, man. What harm?'

Conor said, 'Listened at the kitchen window, one night. Heard Pat and Jenny talking about it.'

No street lighting, no outside lights in the Spains' garden: once it got dark, he could have come over the wall and spent his evenings pressed against their windows, listening. Privacy should have been the least of the Spains' problems, out among rubble and creeping vines and sea-sounds, miles of motorway from anyone who gave a damn about them. Instead, not one thing had been their own. Conor wandering through their house, pressing up against their late-night wine and cuddles; the Gogans' greasy fingers pawing over their arguments, poking into the soft crevices of their marriage. The walls of their home had been tissue paper, ripping and melting to nothing.

'Interesting,' I said. 'And how did the conversation sound to you?'

'What d'you mean?'

'Who said what? Were they worried? Upset? Arguing? Yelling and screaming? What?'

Conor's face had gone blank. He hadn't planned for this. 'I didn't hear all of it. Pat said something about a trap not working. And I guess Jenny said something about trying different bait, and Pat said if he could just get a look at the animal then he'd know what to use. They didn't seem upset, nothing like that. Bit concerned, maybe, but so would anyone be. It definitely wasn't an argument. It didn't sound like a big deal.'

'Right. And when was this?'

'Don't remember. Sometime this summer, probably. Could've been later.'

'Interesting stuff,' I said, shoving my chair back from the table. 'Hold that thought, fella. We're going outside to talk about you for a while. Interview suspended; Detectives Kennedy and Curran leaving the room.'

Conor said, 'Wait. How's Jenny? Is she . . . ?' He couldn't finish.

'Ah,' I said, swinging my jacket over my shoulder. 'I was waiting for that. You did well, Conor old son: you hung in there a good long time before you just had to ask. I thought you'd be begging inside sixty seconds. I underestimated you.'

'I answered everything you asked.'

'You did, didn't you? Give or take. Good boy.' I arched an inquiring eyebrow at Richie, who shrugged, sliding off the table. 'Why not, I suppose. Jenny's alive, chum. She's out of danger. Another few days and she should be out of the hospital.'

I expected either relicf or fear, maybe even anger. Instead he took that in with a quick hissing breath and a curt nod, and said nothing.

I said, 'She's given us some very interesting information.'

'What did she say?'

'Come on, fella. You know we can't share that. Let's just say, though, you'd want to be very careful about telling us any lies that Jenny Spain can contradict. You think about that, while we're gone. Think good and hard.'

I caught a last look at Conor while I held the door open for Richie. He was staring at nothing and breathing through his teeth, and just like I had told him to, he was thinking hard.

In the corridor I said, 'Did you hear that? There's a motive in there somewhere. It's there after all, thank Jesus. And I'm going to get at it, if I have to beat it out of that freak.'

My heart was hammering; I wanted to hug Richie, bang on the door to make Conor jump, I couldn't tell what. Richie was running a fingernail back and forth across the battered green paint of the wall and watching the door. He said, 'You figure, yeah?'

'I figure *hell* yeah. The second he made that slip about the animal, he started bullshitting us again. That conversation about traps and bait, that never happened. If there was a shouting match going on and Conor practically had his ear to the window, probably he could have heard a lot of it; but the Spains had double glazing, remember. Throw in the sound of the sea, and even from right up close, no way would he have been able to hear a normal conversation. Maybe he's just lying about the tone – they were having a screaming row, and he doesn't feel like telling us, for whatever reason. But if that's not how he found out about the animal, then how?'

Richie said, 'He found the computer up and running, one of the times he broke in. Had a read.'

'Could be. It makes more sense than this crap he's feeding us. But why not say it straight out?'

'He doesn't know we've recovered anything off the computer. Doesn't want us knowing Pat was losing the plot, in case we cop on that he's covering for Pat.'

'*If* he is. *If.*' I had known Richie wasn't on side yet, but hearing it out loud set me pacing tight circles in the corridor. Every muscle in me was twitching from making myself sit still at that table for so long. 'Has it occurred to you how else he could have known?'

Richie said, 'Him and Jenny were having an affair. Jenny told him about the animal.'

'Yes. Maybe. Could be. We'll find out. But that's not what I've got in mind. *Losing the plot*, you said: Pat was losing the plot. What if that was what Pat was supposed to think, too?'

Richie shoved himself back against the wall and tucked his hands in his pockets. He said, 'Go on.'

I said, 'Remember what that hunter guy on the internet said, the one who recommended the trap? He wanted to know if there was any chance Pat's kids were messing about with it. Now, we know the kids were too little for that, but there's someone else who wasn't. Someone who had access.'

'You think Conor let the animal out of the trap? Took the bait mouse away?'

I couldn't stop circling. I wished we had an observation room, somewhere I could move fast and not have to keep my voice down. 'Maybe that. Maybe even more than that. Fact: to begin with, at least, Conor was fucking with Jenny's head. Eating her food, nicking her bits and pieces – he can keep telling us till the cows come home that he didn't want to scare her, but the fact is, that's what he did: freaked the shit out of her. He had Fiona thinking Jenny was losing her mind; probably he had Jenny thinking the same thing. What if he did the same to Pat?'

'How, like?'

'Whatshisname, Dr Dolittle, he said he couldn't swear there had ever been an animal in that attic. You took that to mean that Pat Spain was imagining the whole thing. What if there never was an animal because it was all Conor's doing?'

That sent something vivid shooting across Richie's face: scepticism, defensiveness, I couldn't tell what. I said, 'Every sign Pat talked about, everything we've seen, could have been faked by anyone who had access to that house. You heard Dr Dolittle, what he said about that robin: an animal's teeth could have taken its head off, but so could a knife. Those gouges on the attic beam: could be claw-marks, could be blade-marks or nail-marks. The skeletons: an animal isn't the only thing that can strip a couple of squirrels to bones.'

'The noises?'

'Oh, yeah. Let's not forget the noises. Remember what Pat posted, way back on the Wildwatcher board? There's a space about eight inches deep between the attic floor and the ceiling below. How hard would it be to get a remote-controlled MP3 player and a good set of speakers, plant them in that space, and switch on a track of scratching and banging every time you see Pat going upstairs? Hide them behind bits of insulation, so that if he goes looking around the space with a torch – like he did – he'll see nothing. It's not like he'll be looking for an electronic gadget, anyway; he'll be looking for hairs, droppings, an animal, and no fear of him spotting any of those. If you want a little extra fun, then you switch off the track whenever Jenny's around, so she starts to wonder if Pat's going off his trolley. Swap the batteries every time you break in – or just find a way to run the system off the house electricity – and your little game can keep going for as long as it takes.'

Richie pointed out, 'It didn't stay in the attic, but. The animal – if there was an animal. It went down in the walls. Pat heard it in every room, just about.'

'He *thought* he did. Remember what else he posted? He couldn't be sure where the animal was, because the acoustics in the house were strange. Say Conor's shifting the speakers every now and then, just to keep Pat on his toes, make it sound like the animal's moving around the attic. Then one day he realises that, when he positions the speakers just right, the sound goes down through the wall cavities so it sounds like it's coming from a downstairs room . . . Even the house played straight into Conor's hands.'

Richie was biting a nail, thinking. 'Long way from that hide to the attic. Would a remote control even work?'

I couldn't slow down. 'I'm sure you can get one that would. Or, if you can't, then you come out of the hide. After dark, you sit in the Spains' garden and push buttons; during the day, you work the remote from the attic next door, and you only play the track when you know Jenny's going to be out or cooking. It's a little less precise, since you can't watch the Spains, but it'll get the job done in the end.'

'Lot of hassle.'

'It would be, yeah. So was setting up that hide.'

'The Bureau lads didn't find anything like that. No MP3 player, no speakers, nothing.'

'So Conor took his system away and bunged it in a bin some-where. Before he killed the Spains – if it had been after, he'd have left blood-smears. And that means the murders were planned. Carefully planned.'

'Nasty,' Richie said, almost absently. He was still chewing on that nail. 'Why, but? Why invent an animal?'

I said, 'Because he's still mad about Jenny, and he figured she would be more likely to run off with him if Pat was losing his mind. Because he wanted to show them what morons they'd been to buy in Brianstown. Because he had nothing better to do.'

'Thing is, though: Conor cared about Pat, as well as Jenny. You said it yourself, right from the beginning. You think he'd try to drive Pat round the twist?'

'Caring about them didn't stop him from killing them.' Richie's eyes met mine for a second and flicked away, but he said nothing. I said, 'You still don't think he did that, either.'

'I think he loved them. All I'm saying.'

'"Loved" doesn't mean the same thing to Conor as it does to you and me. You heard him in there: he wanted to *be* Pat Spain. He's wanted that since they were teenagers. That's why he threw a tantrum when Pat started making decisions he didn't like: he felt like Pat's life was his. Like he owned it.' As I passed the interview-room door I gave it a kick, harder than I meant to. 'Last year, when Conor's own life went to shit, he finally had to face it. The more he watched the Spains, the harder it hit home that, no matter how much he bitched about Stepford and zombies, that was what he wanted: the sweet kids, the nice home, the steady job, Jenny. Pat's life.' The thought moved me faster and faster. 'Up there in his own little world, Conor *was* Pat Spain. And when Pat's life went arse-ways, Conor felt like *he* was being robbed of all that.'

'And that's the motive? Revenge?'

'More complicated than that. Pat isn't doing what Conor signed on for any more. Conor isn't getting his transfusion of second-hand happy-ever-after, and he's desperate for it. So he decides he's going to step in and put things back on track. It's up to him to fix things for Jenny and the kids. Maybe not for Pat, but that doesn't matter. In Conor's mind, Pat's broken the contract: he's not doing his job. He doesn't deserve his perfect life any more. It should go to someone who's going to make the most of it.'

'So, not revenge,' Richie said. His voice was neutral: he was listening, but he wasn't convinced. 'Salvage.'

'Salvage. Probably Conor's got a whole elaborate fantasy about sweeping Jenny and the kids off to California, Australia, some-where a web designer can get a good job and keep a lovely family in style and sunshine. But in order to step in, he needs to get Pat out of the way. He needs to break up that marriage. And I'll give him this: he was clever about it. Pat and Jenny are already under pressure, the cracks are starting to show, so Conor uses what's to hand: he steps up that pressure. He finds ways to make them both paranoid – about their home, about each other, about themselves. He's got a knack, this guy. He takes his time over the job, he ratchets things up little step by little step, and before you know it, there's no place left where Pat and Jenny feel safe. Not with each other, not in their own home, not in their own minds.'

I realised, with a kind of detached surprise, that my hands were shaking. I shoved them into my pockets. 'He was clever, all right,' I said. 'He was good.'

Richie took his nail out of his mouth. 'I'll tell you what's bothering me,' he said. 'What happened to the simplest solution?'

'What are you on about?'

'Stick with the answer that needs the fewest extras. That's what you said. MP3 player, speakers, remote control; extra break-ins to move them around; a load of luck so Jenny never hears the noises . . . Man, that's a lot of extras.'

I said, 'It's easier to assume that Pat was a fruitcake.'

'Not easier. Simpler. It's simpler to assume that he was imagining the whole thing.'

'Is it? And the guy who was stalking them, wandering around their house eating their ham slices, at exactly the same time as Pat was turning from a sensible guy into a looper: that's just a coincidence? A coincidence that size, my friend, that's one hell of an extra.'

Richie was shaking his head. 'The recession got to both of them; no big coincidence there. This thing with the MP3, though: that'd be a one-in-a-million shot, making sure Pat hears the noises and Jenny never does. You're talking about day and night, for months; and that house, it's not some massive mansion where people can be miles apart. No matter how careful you were, sooner or later she'd hear something.'

'Yeah,' I said. 'You're probably right.' I realised that I had stopped moving, what felt like a long time ago. 'So maybe she did.'

'What d'you mean?'

'Maybe the two of them were in it together: Conor and Jenny.

That makes everything a whole lot simpler, doesn't it? No need for Conor to worry about keeping the noises away from Jenny: if Pat asks her, "Do you hear that?" all she has to do is look blank and say, "Hear what?" No need to worry if the kids hear, either: Jenny can convince them they're just imagining things, and they shouldn't talk about it in front of Daddy. And no need for Conor to break in and move equipment around: Jenny can look after all that.'

Under the white fluorescents, Richie's face looked like it had in the stripped morning light outside the morgue: bleached white, eroded down to the bone. He didn't like this.

I said, 'That explains why she's playing down Pat's state of mind. It explains why she didn't tell him, or the local uniforms, about the break-ins. It explains why Conor wiped the animal off the computer. It explains why he confessed: protecting his girlfriend. It explains why she's not grassing him up: guilt. In fact, old son, I'd say it explains just about everything.' I could hear the pieces falling into place all around me, a small neat patter like soft raindrops. I wanted to lift my face to it, wash myself clean in it, drink it down.

Richie didn't move and for a moment I knew he felt it too, but then he caught a quick breath and shook his head. 'I don't see it.'

'It's clear as day. It's beautiful. You don't see it because you don't want to see it.'

'It's not that. How do you get from there to the murders? If Conor was aiming to send Pat mental, it was working great: the poor bastard's head was melted. Why would Conor dump all his plans and kill him? And if Jenny and the kids are what he's after, what's he doing killing them too?'

I said, 'Come on.' I was already striding down the corridor, as fast as I could go without breaking into a run. Richie had to trot to keep up. 'Remember that JoJo's badge?'

'Yeah.'

'The little fuck,' I said. I took the stairs down to the evidence room two at a time.

*     *     *

Conor was still in his chair, but there were red marks around one thumb where he had been chewing on it. He knew he had fucked up, even if he wasn't sure how. Finally, and about time, he was nervous as hell.

Neither of us bothered to sit down. Richie told the camera, 'Detective Kennedy and Detective Curran resuming interview with Conor Brennan'; then he leaned back in a corner at the edge of Conor's vision, folded his arms and bumped one heel off the wall in a slow, nagging rhythm. I didn't even try to stay still: I circled the room, fast, shoving chairs out of my way. Conor tried to watch both of us at once.

'Conor,' I said. 'We need to talk.'

Conor said, 'I want to go back to the cell.'

'And I want a date with Anna Kournikova. Life's a bitch. Do you know what else I want, Conor?'

He shook his head.

'I want to know why this happened. I want to know why Jenny Spain is in the hospital and her family's in the morgue. Do you want to do this the easy way, and just tell me now?'

Conor said, 'You've got everything you need. I told you I did it. Who cares why?'

'I care. So does Detective Curran. So do plenty of other people, but we're the ones you need to worry about right now.'

He shrugged. As I passed behind him, I pulled the evidence bag out of my pocket and threw it down on the table in front of him, hard enough that it bounced. 'Explain this.'

Conor didn't flinch: he had been ready for this. 'It's a badge.'

'No, Einstein. It's not *a* badge. It's *this* badge.' I leaned in over his shoulder, slapped down the summer ice-cream photo and stayed there, practically cheek to cheek with him. He smelled of harsh jail soap. 'This badge right here, that you're wearing in this photo right here. We found it in Jenny's stuff. Where did she get it?'

He pointed at the photo with his chin. 'There. She's wearing it. We all had them.'

'You're the only one who had this one. Photo analysis shows that the image on yours is off-centre, to exactly the same degree as the image on this one here. None of the others match. So let's try again: how did your badge get into Jenny Spain's stuff?'

I love *CSI*: our techs don't need to work miracles these days, because all the civilians think they can. After a moment Conor shifted away from me. He said, 'I left it in their house.'

'Where?'

'Kitchen counter.'

I moved in again. 'I thought you said you weren't trying to scare the Spains. I thought you said no one would ever have known you were in the house. So what the hell is this? You figured they'd think it had materialised out of thin air? What?'

Conor's hand came out to cover the badge, like it was private. 'I figured Jenny would find it. She's always the first one down in the mornings.'

'Get your hands off the evidence. Find it and *what*? Think the fairies had left it?'

'No.' His hand hadn't moved. 'I knew she'd guess it was me. I wanted her to.'

'Why?'

'Because. Just so she'd know she wasn't on her own, out there. So she'd know I was still around. Still cared about her.'

'Oh, God. And then she'd dump Pat, run into your arms and live happily ever after. Are you on drugs, chum?'

A quick, vicious flash of disgust, before Conor's eyes slid away from mine again. 'Nothing like that. I just thought it'd make Jenny happy. OK?'

'This is how you make her happy?' I slapped his hand away and sent the evidence bag skidding across the table, out of reach. 'Not with a card in the post, not with an e-mail that says, *Hey, thinking of you*: by breaking into her house and leaving her some rusty piece of shit that she's probably completely forgotten. No wonder you're single, sonny.'

Conor said, with absolute certainty, 'She hadn't forgotten. That summer, in that photo: we were happy. All of us. I think it was the happiest I've ever been. You don't forget that. This was to remind Jenny of being happy.'

Richie said, from his corner, 'Why, man?'

'What d'you mean, why?'

'Why did she need reminding? Why did she need telling that someone cared about her? She had Pat. Didn't she?'

'He was a bit down. I told you.'

'You told us he'd been a bit down for months, but you weren't into getting in touch in case it made things worse. What changed?'

Conor had tightened up. He was where we wanted him: dancing, second-guessing each step for booby traps. 'Nothing. I just changed my mind.'

I leaned across him, whipped the evidence bag off the table and started circling the room again, tossing the bag from hand to hand. 'You didn't happen to notice an awful lot of baby monitors set up around the place, did you? While you were having your tea and sandwiches.'

'That's what those were?' Conor's face was a careful blank again: he had prepared for this one, too. 'I thought they were walkie-talkies or something. Some game Pat and Jack were having, maybe.'

'They weren't. Can you tell me why you think Pat and Jenny might have had half a dozen baby monitors spread around the house?'

Shrug. 'Wouldn't know.'

'Right. What about the holes in the walls? Did you notice those?'

'Yeah. Saw those. I knew all along that gaff was made of shite. They should've sued the scumbag that built it, only he's probably declared bankruptcy and retired to the Costa del Sol to spend more time with his offshore accounts.'

'You can't blame this one on the builders, sonny. Pat smashed those holes in his own walls, because he was going off the deep end trying to catch this mink or whatever it was. He covered the place with video monitors because he was obsessed with getting a look at this thing that was tap-dancing over his head. You're trying to tell us, in all your hours of spying, you somehow failed to notice that?'

'I knew about the animal. I told you that.'

'Too bloody right, you knew. But you skipped the part where Pat was losing his fucking mind.' I dropped the bag, scooped it up with a toe and kicked it up to my hand again. 'Oops.'

Richie pulled out a chair and sat down, across the table from Conor. 'Man, we've recovered all the info off the computer. We know what state he was in. "Depressed" doesn't begin to cover it.'

Conor was breathing faster, nostrils flaring. 'Computer?'

I said, 'Let's skip the part where you play dumb. It's boring, it's pointless and it puts me in a very fucking bad mood.' I gave the evidence bag a vicious bounce off the wall. 'That OK with you?'

He kept his mouth shut. Richie said, 'So let's go again, yeah? Something changed, to make you leave that yoke for Jenny.' I waved the bag at Conor, between throws. 'It was Pat, wasn't it? He was getting worse.'

'If you already know, what are you asking me for?'

Richie said easily, 'Standard procedure, man. We're just checking that your story matches up with what we've got from other sources. If it all fits, then happy days, we believe you. If you're telling us one thing and the evidence is telling us another . . .' He shrugged. 'Then we've got a problem, and we've got to keep digging till we sort it. You get me?'

After a moment Conor said, 'OK. Pat was getting worse. He wasn't *mental*, not yelling at this animal to come out and fight, nothing like that. He was just having a tough time. OK?'

'But something must've happened. Something made you get in touch with Jenny, all of a sudden.'

Conor said simply, 'She just looked so lonely. Pat hadn't said a word to her in, like, two days – not that I saw. He was spending all his time sitting at the kitchen table with those monitors lined up in front of him, just staring. She'd tried to talk to him a couple of times, but he didn't even look up. Wasn't like they'd been catching up at night, either: the night before, he'd slept in the kitchen, on that beanbag.'

Conor had been up in that hide practically twenty-four-seven, by the end. I stopped playing with the evidence bag and stood still, behind him.

'Jenny . . . I saw her in the kitchen, waiting for the kettle to boil. Leaning her hands on the countertop, like she was too wrecked to stand up. Staring at nothing. Jack was pulling at her leg, trying to show her something; she didn't even notice. She looked forty; more. Lost. I almost jumped straight down out of that house, straight over the wall, to put my arms around her.'

I said, keeping it expressionless, 'So you decided what she really needed, at this difficult time in her life, was to find out she had a stalker.'

'I was just trying to help. I thought about calling in, or ringing up, or e-mailing her, but Jenny . . .' He shook his head heavily. 'When things aren't great, she doesn't want to talk about it. She wouldn't've wanted a chat, not with Pat all . . . So I just thought: something to let her know I was there. I went home and got the badge. Maybe I called it wrong. Sue me. It seemed like a good idea at the time.'

I asked, 'At what time, exactly?'

'What?'

'When did you leave this in the Spains' house?'

Conor had taken a breath to answer, but something caught him: I saw the sudden stiffening of his shoulders. He said, 'I don't remember.'

'Don't even try that, chum. It's not funny any more. When did you leave the badge?'

After a moment Conor said, 'Sunday night.'

My eyes met Richie's, across his head. I said, 'This Sunday night just gone.'

'Yeah.'

'What time?'

'Five in the morning, maybe.'

'With all the Spains at home and asleep, a few yards away. I'll say this for you, chum: you've certainly got a pair.'

'I just went in the back door, put it on the counter and left. I waited till Pat had gone to bed – he didn't stay downstairs that night. No big deal.'

'What about the alarm?'

'I know the code. Watched Pat typing it in.'

Surprise, surprise. 'Still,' I said. 'It was risky. You must have been pretty desperate to get this done, am I right?'

'I wanted her to have it.'

'Of course you did. And twenty-four hours later, Jenny's dying and her family's dead. Don't even try to tell me that's a coincidence, Conor.'

'I'm not trying to tell you anything.'

'So what happened? She wasn't happy with your little present? Wasn't grateful enough? She shoved it in a drawer instead of wearing it?'

'She put it in her pocket. Don't know what she did with it after that, and I don't care. I just wanted her to have it.'

I got both hands on the back of Conor's chair and said, low and hard and straight into his ear, 'You're so full of shit you make me want to flush your head down the jacks. You know damn well what Jenny thought of the badge. You knew it wasn't going to scare her, because you put it into her hand yourself. Is that how you were working it, the two of you? She'd sneak downstairs late at night, leave Pat sleeping, and the two of you would fuck on the kids' beanbag?'

He whipped round to face me, eyes like shards of ice. He wasn't leaning back away from me, not this time; our faces were almost touching. 'You make me sick. If you think that, if you honest to God think that, there's something wrong with you.'

He wasn't afraid. It came as a shock: you get used to people being afraid of you, guilty or innocent. Maybe, whether we admit it or not, all of us like it. Conor had no reason left to be afraid of me.

I said, 'Fine: so it wasn't on the beanbag. In your hideout? What are we going to find, when we swab that sleeping bag?'

'You swab away. Knock yourself out. She was never there.'

'Then where, Conor? On the beach? In Pat's bed? Where did you and Jenny bump your uglies?'

He had his fists clenched on the folds of his jeans to stop himself from punching me. That couldn't last, and I couldn't wait. 'I'd never have touched her. She'd never have touched me. Never. Are you too thick to get that?'

I laughed in his face. 'Of course you would have. Oh, poor little lonely Jenny, stuck out there in that nasty estate: she just needed to know someone cared about her. Isn't that what you said? You were gagging to be that guy. All that shite about her being sooo lonely, that was just a handy excuse so you could bang her without feeling guilty about Pat. When did it start?'

'Never. You'd do it, then that's your problem. You've never had a real friend, never been in love, then that's your problem.'

'Some real friend you were. That animal that was sending Pat over the edge: that was you, all along.'

That icy, incredulous stare again. 'What are you—'

'How'd you do it? I'm not bothered about the noises – we're going to trace the place where you bought the sound system, sooner or later – but I'd love to know just how you got the flesh off those squirrels. Knife? Boiling water? Your teeth?'

'I haven't got a clue what you're on about.'

'Fine. I'll let our lab fill me in on the squirrels. Here's the thing I really want to know: was it just you, this animal? Or was Jenny in on it too?'

Conor shoved back his chair, hard enough that it went tumbling, and stalked off across the room. I went after him so fast I didn't even feel myself move. My rush backed him against the wall. 'You don't fucking walk away from me. I'm talking to you, sonny boy. When I talk, you fucking listen.'

His face was rigid, a mask carved from hard wood. He was staring past me, eyes narrowed and focused on nothing.

'She was helping you, wasn't she? Did the two of you have a laugh about it, up in your little hideout? That eejit Pat, that sucker, falling for every piece of crap you fed him—'

'Jenny did nothing.'

'Everything was going so well, wasn't it? Pat getting crazier every day, Jenny snuggling up closer to you. And then this happened.' I shoved the evidence bag at him, so close that I felt it brush his cheek. I just managed not to grind it into his face.

'Turned out to be a big mistake, didn't it? You thought it'd be a lovely romantic gesture, but all it did was send Jenny on a massive guilt trip. Like you said, she was happy, that summer. Happy with Pat. And you went and reminded her of it. All of a sudden, she felt like shit about slutting around on him. She decided it had to stop.'

'She wasn't slutting—'

'How did she tell you? A note in your hideout? She didn't even bother to break it off face to face, did she?'

'There was nothing *to* break off. She didn't even know I was—'

I threw the evidence bag somewhere and slammed my hands against the wall on either side of Conor's head, pinning him in. My voice was rising and I didn't care. 'Did you decide right then that you were going to kill them all? Or were you just going to get Jenny, and then you figured what the hell, might as well go the whole hog? Or was this how you planned it all along: Pat and the kids dead, Jenny alive and in hell?'

Nothing. I banged my hands off the wall; he didn't even jump.

'All this, Conor, all of this, because you wanted Pat's life instead of getting your own. Was it worth it? How good a fuck is this woman?'

'I never—'

'Shut the fuck up. I *know* you were banging her. I know it. I know it for a fact. I know it because that's the only way this whole fucking nightmare makes any sense.'

'Get away from me.'

'Make me. Come on, Conor. Hit me. Push me away. Just one shove.' I was shouting, straight into his face. My palms hit the wall again and again and the judders ran up through my bones, but if there was pain I didn't feel it. I had never done anything like this before and I couldn't remember why because it felt incredible, it felt like pure savage joy. 'You were a big man when you were fucking your best mate's wife, big man when you were smothering a three-year-old – where's the big man now that you're up against someone your own size? Come on, big man, show me what you've got—'

Conor wasn't moving a muscle, those narrow eyes were still fixed on the nothing over my shoulder. We were almost touching from faces to shoes, inches between us, less. I knew the video camera would never catch it, just one jab to the stomach, one lift of the knee, Richie would back me up— 'Come on, you mother-fucker, you cocksucker, hit me, I'm begging you, give me an excuse—'

One thing was warm and solid: something on my shoulder, holding me in place, holding my feet down on the ground. I almost threw it off before I understood that it was Richie's hand. 'Detective Kennedy,' his voice said mildly, in my ear. 'This fella's definite that there was nothing going on between him and Jenny. I figure that's fair enough. Don't you?'

I stared at him like an idiot, mouth open. I didn't know whether to punch him or clutch at him for dear life.

Richie said matter-of-factly, 'I'd love a quick chat with Conor. Is that all right?'

I still couldn't speak. I nodded and backed away. The walls had printed their ragged texture deep into my palms.

Richie turned two chairs away from the table to face each other, just a couple of feet apart. 'Conor,' he said, motioning to one of them. 'Have a seat.'

Conor didn't move. His face still had that rigidity. I couldn't tell if he had heard the words.

'Go on. I'm not gonna ask about your motive, and I don't think you and Jenny were doing the bold thing. Swear to God. I just need to clear up a couple of bits and pieces, just for myself. OK?'

After a moment Conor dropped into the chair. Something in the movement – the sudden looseness of it, as if his legs had gone under him – made me realise: I had been getting to him, after all. He had been a hairsbreadth from breaking: howling at me, hitting me, I would never know what. I could have been a hairsbreadth from the answer.

I wanted to roar, send Richie flying and get my hands around Conor's throat. Instead I stood there, with my hands hanging at my sides and my mouth open, gawking uselessly at the pair of them. After a moment I saw the evidence bag, crumpled in a corner, and bent to get it. The movement sent heartburn shooting up my throat, hot and corrosive.

Richie asked Conor, 'You all right?'

Conor had his elbows braced on his knees and his hands clasped tight. 'I'm fine.'

'Would you have a cup of tea? Coffee? Water?'

'I'm fine.'

'Good,' Richie said peacefully, taking the other chair and shifting himself comfortable. 'I just want to make sure I'm clear on a few things. OK?'

'Whatever.'

'Deadly. Just to start with: how bad did Pat get, exactly?'

'He was depressed. He wasn't going up the walls, but yeah, he was down. I said that.'

Richie scraped at something on the knee of his trousers, tilted his head to squint at it. He said, 'Tell you something I've noticed. Every time we start talking about Pat, you're straight in to tell us he wasn't crazy. Did you notice that?'

'Because he wasn't.'

Richie nodded, still inspecting his trousers. He said, 'When you went in, Monday night. Was the computer on?'

Conor examined that from every angle before he answered. 'No. Off.'

'It had a password. How'd you get past that?'

'Guessed. Once, back before Jack was born, I gave Pat shit about using "Emma" for some password. He just laughed, said it'd be grand. I figured there was a decent chance any password since Jack came along would be "EmmaJack".'

'Fair play to you. So you turned on the computer, wiped all the internet stuff. Why?'

'It was none of your business.'

'Is that where you'd found out about the animal, yeah? On the computer?'

Conor's eyes, empty of everything except wariness, came up to meet Richie's. Richie didn't blink. He said steadily, 'We've read the lot. We already know.'

Conor said, 'I went in one day, a couple of months back. The computer was on. Some board full of hunters, all trying to figure out what was in Pat and Jenny's gaff. I went through the browser history: more of the same.'

'Why didn't you tell us to start with?'

'Didn't want you getting the wrong idea.'

Richie said, 'You mean you didn't want us thinking Pat went mental and killed his family. Am I right?'

'Because he didn't. I did.'

'Fair enough. But the stuff on the computer, that had to tell you Pat wasn't in great shape. Didn't it?'

Conor's head moved. 'It's the internet. You can't go by what people say on there.'

'Still, but. If that was one of my mates, I'd've been worried.'

'I was.'

'I figured that, all right. Ever see him crying?'

'Yeah. Twice.'

'Arguing with Jenny?'

'Yeah.'

'Giving her a slap?' Conor's chin shot up angrily, but Richie had a hand raised, silencing him. 'Hang on. I'm not just pulling this out of my arse. We've got evidence that says he was hitting her.'

'That's a load of—'

'Just give me a sec, yeah? I want to be sure I say this right. Pat had been following the rules all along, doing everything he was told, and then the rules dropped him in the shite, big-time. Like you said yourself: who was he, once that happened? People who don't know who they are, man, they're dangerous. They could do anything. I don't think anyone'd be shocked if Pat lost the run of himself, now and then. I'm not excusing it or nothing; just saying I can see how it could happen even to a good guy.'

Conor said, 'Can I answer now?'

'Go ahead.'

'Pat *never* hurt Jenny. Never hurt the kids, either. Yeah, he was in tatters. Yeah, I saw him punch a wall a couple of times – the last time, he couldn't use that hand for days after; probably it was bad enough that he should've gone to the hospital. But her, the kids . . . *never.*'

Richie asked, 'Why didn't you get in touch with him, man?'

He sounded genuinely curious. Conor said, 'I wanted to. Thought about it all the time. But Pat, he's a stubborn bollix. If things had been going great for him, then he'd have been delighted to hear from me again. But with everything gone to shite, with me having been right . . . he'd have slammed the door in my face.'

'You could've tried anyway.'

'Yeah. I could've.'

The bitterness in his voice burned. Richie was leaning forward, his head bent close to Conor's. 'And you feel bad about that, right? About not even trying.'

'Yeah. I feel like shit.'

'So would I, man. What would you do to make up for it?'

'Whatever. Anything.'

Richie's clasped hands were almost touching Conor's. He said, very gently, 'You've done great for Pat. You've been a good mate; you've taken good care of him. If there's someplace after we die, he's thanking you now.'

Conor stared at the floor and bit down on his lips, hard. He was trying not to cry.

'But Pat's dead, man. Where he is now, there's nothing left that can hurt him. Whatever people know about him, whatever people think: it doesn't matter to him now.'

Conor caught his breath, one great raw heave, and bit down again.

'Time to tell me, man. You were up in your hide, and you saw Pat going for Jenny. You legged it down there, but you were too late. That's what happened, isn't it?'

Another heave, wrenching his body like a sob.

'I know you wish you'd done more, but it's time to stop making up for that. You don't need to protect Pat any more. He's safe. It's OK.'

He sounded like a best friend, like a brother, like the one person in the world who cared. Conor managed to look up, open-mouthed and gasping. In that moment I was sure Richie had him. I couldn't tell which one was strongest: the relief, or the shame, or the fury.

Then Conor leaned back in the chair and dragged his hands over his face. He said, through his fingers, 'Pat never touched them.'

After a moment Richie eased backwards too. 'OK,' he said, nodding. 'OK. Grand. Just one more question, and I'll fuck off and leave you alone. Answer me this and Pat's in the clear. What did you do to the kids?'

'Get your doctors to tell you.'

'They have. Like I told you before: cross-checking.'

No one had gone upstairs from the kitchen, after the bloodshed began. If Conor had come running when he saw the struggle, he had come through the back door, into the kitchen, and he had left the same way, without ever going upstairs. If he knew how Emma and Jack had died, it was because he was our man.

Conor folded his arms, braced a foot against the table and shoved his chair around to face me, giving Richie his back. His eyes were red. He said, to me, 'I did it because I was mad for Jenny and she wouldn't go near me. That's the motive. Put that in a statement. I'll sign.'

The corridor felt cold as a ruin. We needed to take Conor's statement and send him back to his cell, update the Super and the floaters, write up our reports. Neither of us moved away from the interview-room door.

Richie said, 'You all right?'

'Yeah.'

'Was that OK? What I did. I wasn't sure if . . .'

He let it trail off. I said, without looking at him, 'Thanks. I appreciate it.'

'No problem.'

'You were good, in there. I thought you had him.'

Richie said, 'So did I.' His voice sounded strange. We were both near the end of our strength.

I found my comb and tried to get my hair back in place, but I had no mirror and I couldn't focus. I said, 'That motive he's giving us, that's crap. He's still lying to us.'

'Yeah.'

'There's still something we're missing. We've got all of tomorrow, and most of tomorrow night if we need it.' The thought made me close my eyes.

Richie said, 'You wanted to be sure.'

'Yeah.'

'Are you?'

I groped for that feeling, that sweet patter of things falling into all the right places. It was nowhere; it felt like some pathetic fantasy, like a child's stories about his stuffed toys fighting off the monsters in the dark. 'No,' I said. My eyes were still closed. 'I'm not sure.'

That night I woke up hearing the ocean. Not the restless, insistent shove and tug of the waves on Broken Harbour; this was a sound like a great hand stroking my hair, the miles-wide roll of breakers on some gentle Pacific beach. It was coming from outside my bedroom door.

*Dina*, I told myself, feeling my heartbeat in the roof of my mouth. *Dina watching something on the TV, to put herself to sleep.* The relief took my breath away. Then I remembered: Dina was somewhere else, on Jezzer's flea-ridden sofa, in a reeking laneway. For an upside-down second my stomach jerked with pure terror, like I was the one on my own with nobody to keep down the wilds of my mind, like she was the one who had been protecting me.

I kept my eyes on the door and eased open the drawer of my bedside table. The cold weight of my gun was comforting, solid. Outside the door the waves soothed on, unperturbed.

I had the bedroom door open, my back against the wall and my gun up and ready all in one move. The living room was empty and dark, wan rectangles of off-black in the windows, my coat huddled over the arm of the sofa. There was a thin line of white light around the kitchen door. The sound of waves surged louder. It was coming from the kitchen.

I bit down on the inside of my cheek till I tasted blood. Then I moved across the living room, carpet prickling at the soles of my feet, and kicked the kitchen door open.

The fluorescent strip light under the cupboards was on, giving an alien glow to a knife and half an apple I had forgotten on the countertop. The roar of the ocean rose up and rolled over me, blood-warm and skin-soft, like I could have dropped my gun and let myself fall forwards into it, let myself be carried away.

The radio was off. All the appliances were off, only the fridge humming grimly to itself – I had to lean close to catch the sound, under the waves. When I could hear that and the snap of my fingers, I knew there was nothing wrong with my hearing. I pressed my ear against the neighbours' wall: nothing. I pressed harder, hoping for a murmur of voices or a snip of a television show, something to prove that my apartment hadn't transformed into something weightless and free-floating, that I was still anchored in a solid building, surrounded by warm life. Silence.

I waited for a long time for the sound to fade. When I understood that it wasn't going to, I switched off the strip light, closed the kitchen door and went back to my bedroom. I sat on the edge of the bed, pressing circles into my palm with the barrel of the gun and wishing for something I could shoot, listening to the waves sigh like some great sleeping animal and trying to remember turning the strip light on.

# 17

I slept through my alarm. My first look at the clock – almost nine – shot me out of bed with my heart drumming. I couldn't remember the last time I had done that, no matter how wrecked I was; I have myself trained to be awake and sitting up at the first tone. I threw on my clothes and left, no shower or shave or breakfast. The dream, or whatever it was, had snagged in a corner of my mind, scrabbling at me like something terrible happening just out of sight. When the traffic backed up – it was raining hard – I had to fight the urge to leave my car where it was and run the rest of the way. The dash from the car park to HQ left me dripping.

Quigley was on the first landing, spread out along a railing, wearing a hideous checked jacket and crackling a brown paper evidence bag between his fingers. On a Saturday I should have been safe from Quigley – it wasn't like he was working some huge case that needed twenty-four-seven attention – but he's always behind on his paperwork; probably he had come in to try and bully one of my floaters into doing it for him. 'Detective Kennedy,' he said. 'Could we have a little word?'

He had been waiting for me. That should have been my first warning. 'I'm in a hurry,' I said.

'This is me doing you a favour, Detective. Not the other way round.'

The echo sent his voice spinning up the stairwell, even though he was keeping the volume down. That sticky, hushed tone should have been my second warning, but I was soaked and rushed and I had bigger things than Quigley on my mind. I almost kept walking. It was the evidence bag that stopped me. It was one of the small ones, the size of my palm; I couldn't see the window, it could have

held anything. If Quigley had got hold of something to do with the
case, and if I didn't fluff his slimy little ego, he could make sure a
filing glitch kept that bag from getting to me for weeks. 'Fire away,'
I said, keeping one shoulder pointed towards the next flight of
stairs so he knew this chat wasn't a long one.

'That's a good choice, Detective. Do you happen to know a
young female, twenty-five to thirty-five, about five foot four, very
slim build, chin-length dark hair? I should probably say very
attractive, if you don't mind them a bit scruffy-like.'

For a second I thought I would have to grab the banister.
Quigley's jab slid right off me; all I could think of was a Jane
Doe with my number on her phone, a ring pulled off a cold finger
and tossed in an evidence bag for identification. 'What's happened
to her?'

'So you do know her?'

'Yeah. I know her. What's happened?'

Quigley stretched it out, arching his eyebrows and trying to
look enigmatic, till the precise second before I would have slammed
him against the wall. 'She came waltzing in here first thing this
morning. Wanted to see Mikey Kennedy right away, *if* you don't
mind; wouldn't take no for an answer. *Mikey*, is it? I would've bet
you'd like them cleaner, more respectable, but there's no accounting for tastes.'

He smirked at me. I couldn't answer. The relief felt like it had
sucked out my insides.

'Bernadette told her you weren't in and she should take a seat
and wait, but that wasn't good enough for Little Miss Emergency.
She was giving terrible hassle, raising her voice and all. Shocking
carry-on. I suppose some people like the drama queens, but this is
a Garda building, not a nightclub.'

I said, 'Where is she?'

'Your girlfriends aren't my responsibility, Detective Kennedy. I
just happened to be on my way in, and I saw the ruckus she was
causing. I thought I'd give you a helping hand, show the young
woman that she can't be coming in here like the Queen of Sheba
demanding this, that and the other. So I let her know that I was a

friend of yours, and anything she wanted to say to you, she could say to me.'

I had my hands stuffed in my coat pockets to hide my clenched fists. I said, 'You mean you bullied her into talking to you.'

Quigley's lips vanished. 'You don't want to take that tone with me, Detective. I didn't *bully* her into anything. I brought her into an interview room and we had a wee chat. She took a bit of convincing, but in the end she realised that you're always better off following Garda orders.'

I said, keeping my voice level, 'You threatened to arrest her.' The thought of being locked up would have sent Dina into an animal panic; I could almost hear the wild jabber surging up inside her mind. I kept my fists where they were and focused on the thought of filing every complaint in the book on Quigley's flabby arse. I didn't give a damn if he had the chief commissioner in his pocket and I ended up investigating sheep rustlers in Leitrim for the rest of my life, as long as I took this lump of shit down with me.

Quigley said virtuously, 'She was holding stolen police property. I couldn't ignore that, could I, now? If she refused to hand it over, it was my duty to place her under arrest.'

'What are you talking about? What stolen police property?' I tried to think what I could have brought home, a file, a photo, what on earth I wouldn't have missed by now. Quigley gave me a nauseating little smile and held up the evidence bag.

I tilted it towards the weak, pearly light from the landing window – he didn't let go. For a second I didn't understand what I was seeing. It was a woman's fingernail, neatly filed and manicured, painted a smooth pinkish-beige. It had been ripped off at the quick. Caught in a crack was a wisp of rose-pink wool.

Quigley was saying something, somewhere, but I couldn't hear him. The air had turned dense and savage, pounding at my skull, gibbering in a thousand mindless voices. I needed to turn my face away, shove Quigley to the floor and run. I couldn't move. My eyes felt like they had been pinned wide open.

The handwriting on the evidence-bag label was familiar, firm and forward-slanting, not Quigley's semi-literate scrawl. *Collected sitting room, residence of Conor Brennan* . . . Cold air, smell of apples, Richie's drawn face.

When I could hear again, Quigley was still talking. The stairwell turned his voice sibilant and disembodied. 'At first I thought, well, holy God, the great Scorcher Kennedy leaving evidence lying around for his bit of fluff to pick up on her way out: who would've thought it?' He gave a snigger. I could almost feel it, dripping down my face like stale grease. 'But then, while I was waiting for you to honour us, I had a wee read of your case file – I'd never intrude, but you can see why I needed to know where this yoke here might fit in, so I could decide on the right thing to do. And didn't I spot something interesting? That handwriting there: it's not yours – sure, I know yours, after all this time – but it shows up an awful lot, in the file.' He tapped his temple. 'They don't call me a detective for nothing, amn't I right?'

I wanted to crush the bag in my hand till it crumbled to dust and vanished, till even the image of it was squashed out of my mind. Quigley said, 'I knew you'd got thick as thieves, yourself and young Curran, but I never guessed you were sharing *that* much.' The snigger again. 'So I'm wondering, now: did the young lady get this off you, or off Curran?'

Somewhere far inside my mind, one corner was moving again, methodically as a machine. Twenty-five years' worth of working my arse off to learn control. Friends have slagged me for it, newbies have rolled their eyes when I gave them the speech. Fuck them all. It was worth it, for that conversation on a draughty landing when I held it together. When this case sets its claws scrabbling circles around the inside of my skull, the only thing I have left to tell myself is that it could have been worse.

Quigley was loving this, every second, and I could use that. I heard myself say, cool as ice, 'Don't tell me you forgot to ask her.'

I had been right: he couldn't resist. 'Holy God, the drama. Wouldn't give me her name, wouldn't give me any information on where and how she came into possession of this here – when I put the pressure on, just gently, like, she went only hysterical. I'm not joking you: she pulled out a great clump of her hair by the roots, screamed at me that she was going to tell you I'd done it. Now, I wasn't worried about that – any sensible man would take the word of an officer over the say-so of some young one – but the girl's mad as a bag of cats. I could have got her talking easily enough, but there was no point: I couldn't rely on a word she said. I'm telling you, it doesn't matter how tasty she is, that one belongs in a straitjacket.'

I said, 'Shame you didn't have one handy.'

'I'd have been doing you a favour, so I would.'

The squad-room door slammed open above us and three of the lads headed down the corridor towards the canteen, bitching colourfully about some witness who had suddenly developed amnesia. Quigley and I pressed back against the wall, like conspirators, until their voices faded. I said, 'What did you do with her instead?'

'I told her she needed to get a hold of herself and she was free to go, and off she flounced. Gave Bernadette the finger on the way out. Lovely.' With his arms folded and his chins tucked in sourly, he looked like a fat old woman bitching about wanton modern youth. That icy, detached corner of me almost wanted to smile. Dina had scared the shit out of Quigley. Every now and then, the crazy comes in useful. 'Your girlfriend, is she? Or a little treat you bought for yourself? How much do you think she'd have wanted for this yoke, if she'd found you this morning?'

I wagged a finger at him. 'Be nice, chum. She's a lovely girl.'

'She's a very *lucky* girl that I didn't place her under arrest for the theft. Just as a favour to you, that was. I think you owe me a nice polite thank-you.'

'Sounds like she brightened up a boring morning. Maybe you're the one who should be thanking me.'

This conversation wasn't going the way Quigley had planned. 'So,' he said, trying to get it back. He held up the evidence bag and gave the top a little squeeze between those fat white fingers. 'Tell us, Detective. This yoke here. How bad do you need it?'

He hadn't worked it out. The relief rushed over me like a

breaker. I brushed rain off my sleeve and shrugged. 'Who knows? Thanks for getting it off the young woman, and all that, but I can't see it being exactly make-or-break stuff.'

'You'd want to be sure, wouldn't you? Because as soon as the story goes on the record, it's no good to you any more.'

We forget to hand in evidence, every once in a while. It's not supposed to happen, but it does: you're taking off your suit at night and find a bulge in your pocket where you shoved an envelope when a witness asked for a word, or you open your car boot and there's the bag you meant to hand in the night before. As long as no one else has had access to your pockets or keys to your car, it's not the end of the world. But Dina had had this in her possession, for hours or days. If we ever tried to bring it into court, a defence lawyer would argue that she could have done anything from breathing on the evidence to exchanging it for something completely different.

Evidence doesn't always come to us pristine from the crime scene: witnesses hand it in weeks later, it lies in a field getting rained on for months until a dog noses it out. We work with what we've got and find ways to head off the defence arguments. This was different. We had tainted this ourselves, and so it tainted everything else we had touched. If we tried to bring it in, then every move we had made in this investigation would be up for grabs: that could have been planted, he could have been bullied, we could have invented that to suit ourselves. We had broken the rules once. Why should anyone believe that had been the only time?

I gave the bag a dismissive flick with one finger – touching it made my spine leap. 'It might've been fun to have, if it turned out to link our suspect to the crime scene. But we've got plenty of stuff that does that anyway. I think we'll survive.'

Quigley's sharp little eyes crawled over my face, checking. 'Either way,' he said, in the end. He was trying to hide a pissed-off note. I had convinced him. 'Even if this doesn't turn your case to shite, it could have done. The Super'll hit the roof when he hears one of his dream team's been handing out evidence like sweeties

– and on this case, out of all the ones in the world. Those poor little kiddies.' He shook his head, clicked his tongue reproachfully. 'You're fond of young Curran, aren't you? You wouldn't want to see him reverted to uniform before he even gets off the starting blocks. All that promise, all that great *working relationship* the two of you have, all wasted. Wouldn't that be a shame?'

'Curran's a big boy. He can take care of himself.'

'A-ha,' Quigley said smugly, pointing at me, like I had slipped up and revealed some big secret. 'Will I take that to mean he's the bold lad, after all?'

'Take it whatever way you like it, chum. And if you like it, take it again.'

'It doesn't matter, sure. Even if it was Curran that did it, he's only on probation; you're the one that's meant to be minding him. If anyone were to find out about this . . . Wouldn't that be dreadful timing, and you just on your way back up?' Quigley had edged close enough that I could see the wet glisten of his lips, the sheen of dirt and grease grained into his jacket collar. 'No one wants that to happen. I'm sure we can come to an arrangement.'

For an instant I thought he meant money. For an even briefer, disgraceful splinter of time I thought of saying yes. I have savings, in case something were to happen to me and Dina needed looking after; not a lot, but enough to shut Quigley's mouth, save Richie, save myself, set the ricocheting world back in its orbit and let us all keep going as if nothing had happened.

Then I understood: it was me he wanted, and there was no way back to safe. He wanted to work with me on the good cases, take credit for anything I came up with, and offload the no-hopers onto me; he wanted to bask while I sang his praises to O'Kelly, warn me with a meaningful eyebrow-lift when something wasn't good enough, soak up the sight of Scorcher Kennedy at his mercy. It would never end.

I want to believe that that wasn't the reason I turned Quigley down. I know how many people would take it for granted that it was just that simple, that my ego wouldn't let me spend the rest of my career coming running to his whistle and making sure I got his coffee just right. I still pray to believe that I said no because it was the right thing to do.

I said, 'I wouldn't come to an arrangement with you if you had a bomb strapped to my chest.'

That pushed Quigley back a step, out of my face, but he wasn't going to give up that easily. His prize was so close he was practically drooling. 'Don't be saying anything you'll regret, Detective Kennedy. No one needs to know where this was last night. You can sort your bit of fluff; she won't say a word. Neither will Curran, if he's got any sense in his head. This can go straight to the evidence room, like nothing ever happened.' He shook the bag; I heard the dry rattle of the fingernail on paper. 'It'll be our wee secret. You have a think about that, before you go disrespecting me.'

'There's nothing to think about.'

After a moment, Quigley leaned back against the railing. 'I'll tell you something for nothing, Kennedy,' he said. His tone had changed; all the creamy fake-buddy coating had fallen away. 'I knew you were going to fuck this case up. The second you came back from seeing the Super, Tuesday, I knew. You always thought you were something special, didn't you? Mr Perfect, never put a toe out of line. And look at you now.' That smirk again, this time halfway to a snarl, alive with malice that he wasn't bothering to hide any more. 'I'd only love to know: what was it made you cross the line on this one? Was it just that you've been a saint so long, you figured you could get away with anything you like, no one would ever suspect the great Scorcher Kennedy?'

Not paperwork after all, not the chance to borrow one of my floaters. Quigley had come in to work on a Saturday morning because God forbid he should miss the moment when I went arse over tip. I said, 'I wanted to make your day, old son. Looks like I succeeded.'

'You always took me for a fool. Let's all take the piss out of Quigley, the great thick eejit, sure he won't even notice. Go on and tell me: if you're the hero and I'm the fool, then how come you're the one that's deep in the shit, and I'm the one that saw it coming all along?'

He was wrong. I had never underestimated him. I had always known about Quigley's one skill: his hyena nose, the instinct that pulls him snuffling and salivating towards shaky suspects, frightened witnesses, wobbly-legged newbies, anything that flashes soft spots or smells of blood. Where I had gone wrong was in believing that didn't mean me. All those years of endless excruciating therapy sessions, of staying vigilant over every move and word and thought; I had been sure I was mended, all the breaks healed, all the blood washed away. I knew I had earned my way to safety. I had believed, beyond any doubt, that that meant I was safe.

The moment I said *Broken Harbour* to O'Kelly, every faded scar in my mind had lit up like a beacon. I had walked the glittering lines of those scars, obedient as a farm animal, from that moment straight to this one. I had moved through this case shining like Conor Brennan had shone on that dark road, a blazing signal for predators and scavengers far and wide.

I said, 'You're not a fool, Quigley. You're a disgrace. I could fuck up every hour on the hour, from now till I retire, and still be a better cop than you'll ever be. I'm ashamed to be on the same squad as you.'

'You're in luck, then, aren't you? You might not have to put up with me much longer. Not once the Super sees this.'

I said, 'I'll take it from here.'

I held out a hand for the bag, but Quigley whipped it out of reach. He prissed up his mouth and deliberated, swinging the bag between finger and thumb. 'I'm not sure I can give you this, now. How do I know where it'll end up?'

When I got my breath back, I said, 'You make me sick.'

Quigley's face curdled, but he saw something in mine that shut him up. He dropped the bag into my hand like it was filthy. 'I'll be submitting a full report,' he informed me. 'As soon as possible.'

I said, 'You do that. Just stay out of my way.' I shoved the evidence bag into my pocket and left him there.

\*    \*    \*

I went up to the top floor, shut myself in a cubicle in the gents' and leaned my forehead against the clammy plastic of the door. My mind had turned slippery and treacherous as black ice, I couldn't get purchase; every thought seemed to send me lurching through into freezing water, grabbing for solid ground and finding nothing. When my hands finally stopped shaking, I opened the door and went downstairs to the incident room.

It was overheated and buzzing, floaters taking calls, updating the whiteboard, drinking coffee and laughing at a dirty joke and having some kind of debate about blood-spatter patterns. All the energy made me dizzy. I picked my way through it feeling like my legs might go at any second.

Richie was at his desk, shirtsleeves rolled up, messing around with report sheets and not seeing them. I threw my sodden coat over the back of my chair, leaned over to him and said quietly, 'We're going to collect a few pieces of paper each and leave the room, like we're in a hurry, but without making a big deal of it. Let's go.'

He stared for a second. His eyes were bloodshot; he looked like shit. Then he nodded, picked up a handful of reports and pushed back his chair.

There's an interview room, down at the far end of the top-floor corridor, that we never use unless we have to. The heating doesn't work – even in the heart of summer the room feels chilled, subterranean – and something wrong with the wiring means that the strip lights give off a raw, eye-splitting blaze and burn out every week or two. We went there.

Richie closed the door behind us. He stayed beside it, sheaf of pointless paper hanging forgotten from one hand, eyes skittery as a corner boy's. That was what he looked like: some malnourished scumbag hunched against a graffitied wall, standing lookout for small-time dealers in exchange for a fix. I had been beginning to think of this man as my partner. His skinny shoulder braced against mine had begun to feel like something that belonged. The feeling had been a good one, a warm one. Both of us made me sick.

I took the evidence bag out of my pocket and put it down on the table.

Richie bit down on both his lips, but he didn't flinch or startle. The last scatter of hope blew out of me. He had been expecting this.

The silence went on forever. Probably Richie thought I was using it to bear down on him, the way I would have with a suspect. I felt as if the air of the room had turned crystalline, brittle, and when I spoke it would shatter into a million razor-edged shards and rain down on our heads, slice us both to rags.

Finally I said, 'A woman handed it in this morning. The description matches my sister.'

That hit Richie. His head snapped up and he stared at me, sick-faced and forgetting to breathe. I said, 'I'd like to know how the fuck she got her hands on this.'

'Your *sister*?'

'The woman you saw waiting for me outside here, on Tuesday night.'

'I didn't know she was your sister. You never said.'

'And I didn't know it was any of your business. How did she get hold of this?'

Richie slumped back against the door and ran a hand across his mouth. 'She showed up at my gaff,' he said, without looking at me. 'Last night.'

'How did she know where you live?'

'I don't know. I walked home, yesterday – I needed a chance to think.' A glance – a quick one, like it hurt – at the table. 'I figure she must've been waiting outside here again, either for me or for you. She must've seen me come out, followed me home. I was only in the door five minutes when I heard the bell.'

'And you invited her in for a cup of tea and a nice chat? Is that what you normally do when strange women show up at your door?'

'She asked could she come in. She was freezing; I could see her shivering. And she wasn't some randomer. I remembered her, from Tuesday night.' Of course he had. Men, in particular, don't forget Dina in a hurry. 'I wasn't going to let a mate of yours freeze on my doorstep.'

'You're a real saint. It didn't occur to you to, I don't know, *ring me* and tell me she was there?'

'It *did* occur to me. I was going to. But she was . . . she wasn't in great shape, man. She was holding on to my arm and going, over and over, "Don't tell Mikey I'm here, don't you dare tell Mikey, he'll freak out . . ." I would've done it anyway, only she didn't give me a chance. Even when I went to the jacks, she made me leave my phone with her – and my flatmates were down the pub, it wasn't like I could drop them a hint or get her talking to one of them while I texted you. In the end I thought, no harm done, she's somewhere safe for the night, you and me could talk in the morning.'

'"No harm done,"' I said. 'Is that what you call this?'

A short, twisting silence. I said, 'What did she want?'

Richie said, 'She was worried about you.'

I laughed loud enough to startle both of us. 'Oh, she was, was she? That's a fucking riot. I think you know Dina well enough at this stage to have spotted that, if anyone needs worrying about, it's *her*. You're a detective, chum. That means you're supposed to notice the bleeding obvious. My sister is as mad as a hatter. She's five beers short of a six-pack. She's up the wall and swinging from the chandelier. Please don't tell me you missed that.'

'She didn't seem crazy to me. Upset, yeah, up to ninety, but that was because she was worried about you. Properly worried, like. Freaking-out worried.'

'That's exactly what I'm talking about. That *is* crazy. Worried about *what*?'

'This case. What it was doing to you. She said—'

'The only thing Dina knows about this case is that it *exists*. That's it. And even that was enough to send her off the fucking deep end.' I never tell anyone that Dina is crazy. People have raised the possibility to me before, on occasion; none of them made that mistake twice. 'Do you want to know how I spent Tuesday night? Listening to her rave about how she couldn't sleep in her flat because her shower curtain was ticking like a grandfather clock. Want to know how I spent Wednesday evening? Trying to convince her not to set fire to the heap of paper that she had left of my books.'

Richie shifted, uneasily, against the door. 'I don't know about any of that. She wasn't like that at my place.'

Something in my stomach clamped tight. 'Of course she bloody well wasn't. She knew you'd be on the phone to me in a heartbeat, and that didn't suit her plans. She's crazy, not stupid. And she's got some serious willpower, when she feels like it.'

'She said she'd been over at yours the last few nights, talking to you, and the case had your head melted. She . . .' He glanced at me. He was picking his words carefully. 'She said you weren't OK. She said you'd always been good to her, never once been anything but gentle, even when she didn't deserve it – that's what she said – but the other night she startled you, when she showed up, and you pulled your gun. She said she left because you told her she should kill herself.'

'And you believed that.'

'I figured she was exaggerating. But still . . . She wasn't making it up about you being stressed, man. She said you were coming apart, this case was taking you apart, and there was no way you'd put it down.'

I couldn't tell, through all this dark snarled mess, whether this was Dina's revenge for something real or imaginary that I had done to her, or whether she had seen something I had missed, something that had sent her banging on Richie's door like a panicked bird beating against a window. I couldn't tell, either, which one would be worse.

'She said to me, "You're his partner, he trusts you. You have to look after him. He won't let me, he won't let his family, maybe he might let you."'

I said, 'Did you sleep with her?'

I had been trying not to ask. The fraction of silence, after Richie opened his mouth, told me everything I needed to know. I said, 'Don't bother answering that.'

'Listen, man, listen – you never said she was your sister. Neither did she. I swear to God, if I'd've known—'

I had come within a hairsbreadth of telling him. I had held back because, God help me, I thought it would make me vulnerable. 'What did you think she was? My girlfriend? My ex? My daughter? How exactly would any of those have made it better?'

'She said she was an old mate of yours. She said she knew you from back when you were kids – your family and her family used to get caravans together at Broken Harbour, for the summer. That's what she told me. Why would I think she was lying?'

'How about because she's fucking nutso? She comes in babbling about a case she hasn't got a clue about, drowning you in bullshit about me having a nervous breakdown. Ninety per cent of what she says is gibberish. It doesn't even occur to you that the other ten per cent might not be on the level?'

'It wasn't gibberish, but. She was dead right: this case, it's been getting to you. I thought that from the start, almost.'

Every breath hurt on its way in. 'That's sweet. I'm touched. So you felt the appropriate response was to fuck my sister.'

Richie looked like he would happily saw his own arm off if it would make this conversation go away. 'It wasn't like that.'

'How in the name of sweet jumping Jesus was it *not like that*? Did she drug you? Handcuff you to the bedpost?'

'I didn't go in there planning to . . . I don't think she did either.'

'Are you seriously trying to tell me how my sister thinks? After one night?'

'*No*. I'm just saying—'

'Because I know her a lot better than you do, chum, and even I struggle for any clue about what goes on in her head. I think it's more than possible that she went to your house planning on doing exactly what she did. I'm one hundred per cent positive that this was her idea, not yours. That doesn't mean you had to play along. What the holy hell were you thinking?'

'Honest to God, it was just one thing led to another. She was scared this case would mess you up, she was going in circles around my sitting room, crying – she couldn't sit down, she was that upset. I gave her a hug, just to settle her—'

'And that's where you shut up. I don't need the graphic details.' I didn't; I could see exactly how it had gone down. It's so, so lethally easy to get dragged into Dina's crazy. One minute you're only going to dip your toes at the edge, just so you can grab her hand and pull her out; the next minute you're full fathom five and flailing for air.

'I'm only telling you. It just happened.'

'Your partner's sister,' I said. Suddenly I was exhausted, exhausted and sick to my stomach, something rising and burning in my throat. I leaned my head back against the wall and pressed my fingers into my eyes. 'Your partner's crazy sister. How could that seem OK?'

Richie said quietly, 'It doesn't.'

The dark behind my fingers was deep and restful. I didn't want to open my eyes on that harsh, biting light. 'And when you woke up this morning,' I said, 'Dina was gone, and so was the evidence bag. Where had it been?'

A moment's silence. 'On my bedside table.'

'In plain view of anyone who happened to wander in. Flatmates, burglars, one-night stands. Brilliant, old son.'

'My bedroom door locks. And during the day I kept it on me. In my jacket pocket.'

All those arguments we'd had, Conor versus Pat, half-real animals, old love stories: Richie's side had been bullshit. He had been holding the answer the whole time, close enough that I could have reached out and put my hand on it. I said, 'And didn't that work out well?'

'I never thought of her taking it. She—'

'You weren't thinking at all. Not by the time she got into your bedroom.'

'She was your *mate* – or I thought she was. I didn't think about her *robbing* stuff, specially not that. She cared about you, like a lot; that was obvious. Why would she want to fuck up your case?'

'Oh, no, no. She wasn't the one who fucked up this case.' I took my hands away from my face. Richie was scarlet. 'She swiped this envelope because she changed her mind about you, chum. And she's not the only one. Once she spotted this, it struck her that you might not be the wonderful, trustworthy, stand-up guy she'd been picturing, which meant you might not in fact be the best person to *take care* of me. So she figured her only option was to do it herself, by bringing me the evidence that my partner had decided to run off with. Two for one: I get my case back, and I get to find out the truth about who I'm dealing with. Seems to me that, crazy or no, she was on to something.'

Richie, focusing on his shoes, said nothing. I asked, 'Were you ever planning to tell me?'

That snapped him straight. 'Yeah, I was. When I first found that yoke, I was, practically definitely. That's why I bagged it and tagged it. If I hadn't been planning on telling you, I could've just flushed it down the jacks.'

'Well, congratulations, old son. What do you want, a medal?' I nodded towards the evidence envelope. I couldn't look at it; in the corner of my eye it seemed crammed tight with something alive and raging, a great insect thrumming against the thin paper and plastic, straining to split the seams and attack. '"Collected in sitting room, residence of Conor Brennan." While I was outside, on the phone to Larry. Is that right?'

Richie stared at the papers in his hand, blankly, like he couldn't remember what they were. He opened his hand and let them scatter on the floor. 'Yeah,' he said.

'Where was it?'

'Must've been on the carpet. I was putting back all that stuff that had been on the sofa, and this was hanging off the sleeve of a jumper. It wasn't there when we took the clothes off the sofa – we gave them all a proper going-over, remember, in case any of them had blood on. The jumper must've picked it up off the floor.'

I asked, 'What colour jumper?' I already knew I would remember if Conor Brennan's wardrobe had included rose-pink knitwear.

'Green. Khaki, like.'

And the carpet had been cream, with dirty green and yellow swirls. Larry's lads could go over the flat with magnifying glasses, looking for a match to that wisp of pink, and find nothing. I had known, the moment I saw that fingernail, where the match was.

I asked, 'And how did you interpret this find?'

There was a silence. Richie was looking at nothing. I said, 'Detective Curran.'

He said, 'The fingernail – the shape and the polish – it matches Jenny Spain's. The wool that's caught in it—' A corner of his mouth spasmed. 'Looked to me like it matched the embroidery on the pillow that smothered Emma.'

The sodden thread that Cooper had fished out of her throat, while he held her frail jaw open between thumb and finger. 'And what did you take that to mean?'

Richie said, evenly and very quietly, 'I took it to mean that Jennifer Spain could be our woman.'

'Not could be. Is.'

His shoulders moved restlessly, against the door. 'It's not definite. She could've picked up the wool some other way. Earlier on, when she put Emma to bed—'

'Jenny keeps herself groomed. Not a hair out of place. You think she'd have left a broken nail to snag on things all evening, gone to bed with it still ragged? Left a piece of wool caught in it for hours?'

'Or it could've been a transfer off Pat. He gets the bit of wool on his pyjama top when he's using the pillow on Emma; then, when he's struggling with Jenny, she breaks a nail, the wool catches in it . . .'

'That one specific fibre, out of the thousands and thousands in his pyjamas, on his pyjamas, in her own pyjamas, all over the kitchen. What are the odds?'

'It could happen. We can't just drop the whole thing on Jenny. Cooper was positive, remember? Her injuries weren't self-inflicted.'

'I know that,' I said. 'I'll talk to her.' The thought of having to deal with the world outside this room felt like a baton to the back of the knees. I sat down heavily at the table; I couldn't stand up any more.

Richie had caught that: *I'll talk to her*, not *We*. He opened his mouth and then shut it again, looking for the right question.

I said, 'Why didn't you tell me?' I heard the raw note of pain, but I didn't care.

Richie's eyes fell away from mine. He knelt on the floor and started picking up the papers he had dropped. He said, 'Because I knew what you'd want to do.'

'What? Arrest Jenny? Not charge Conor with a triple murder he didn't commit? What, Richie? What part of that is so fucking terrible that you just couldn't let it happen?'

'Not terrible. Just . . . Arresting her: I don't know, man. I'm not sure that's the right thing to do here.'

'That's what we *do*. We arrest murderers. If you have a problem with the job description, you should've got a different fucking job.'

That brought Richie up on his feet again. 'That right there, that's why I didn't tell you. I knew that was what you'd say. I knew it. With you, man, everything's black and white. No questions; just stick to the rules and go home. I needed to think about it because I knew the second I told you, it'd be too late.'

'Damn right it's black and white. You slaughter your family, you go to prison. Where the fuck are you seeing shades of grey?'

'Jenny's in hell. Every second of her life, she's going to be in the kind of pain I don't even want to think about. You think prison's going to punish her any worse than her own head? There's nothing she can do, or we can do, to fix what she did, and it's not like we need to lock her up to stop her doing it again. What's a life sentence going to do here?'

Here I had thought it was Richie's knack, his special gift: coaxing witnesses and suspects into believing, absurd and impossible though it was, that he saw them as human beings. I had been so impressed by the way he convinced the Gogans they were more than random irritating scumbags to him, the way he convinced Conor Brennan he was more than just another wild animal we needed to get off the street. I should have known, that night in the hide when we became just two guys talking, I should have known then and I should have seen the danger: it wasn't an act.

I said, 'So that's why you were all over Pat Spain. And here I thought it was all in the name of truth and justice. Silly me.'

Richie had the grace to flush. 'It wasn't like that. At first I honestly thought it must've been him – Conor didn't work for me, it didn't look like there was anyone else. And then, once I saw that yoke there, I thought . . .'

His voice trailed off. I said, 'The idea of arresting Jenny offended your delicate sensibilities, but you figured it might just be a bad idea to slap Conor in prison for life for something he didn't do. Sweet of you to care. So you decided to find a way to dump the whole mess on Pat. That lovely little performance with Conor, yesterday: that's where you were trying to take him. He almost bit, too. It must have ruined your day when he decided not to take the bait.'

'Pat's *dead*, man. It can't hurt him. I know what you said about everyone thinking he was a murderer; but you remember what he said on that board, about just wanting to take care of Jenny. If he had the choice, what do you think he'd pick? Take the blame, or put her away for life? He'd be begging us to call him a killer, man. He'd beg us on his knees.'

'And that's what you were doing with the Gogan bitch, too. And with Jenny. All that bullshit about whether Pat was losing his temper more, was he having a nervous breakdown, were you afraid he'd hurt you . . . You were trying to get Jenny to throw Pat under a bus. Only it turns out a triple murderer has more sense of honour than you do.'

Richie's face flared brighter. He didn't answer. I said, 'Let's just say for one second that we do it your way. Throw that thing in the shredder, shove the blame on Pat, close the file and let Jenny walk out of the hospital. What do you figure happens next? Whatever went down that night, she loved her kids. She loved her husband. What do you think she's going to do, the second she's strong enough?'

Richie put the reports on the table, a safe distance from the envelope, and squared off the edges of the pile. He said, 'She's going to finish the job.'

'Yes,' I said. The light was burning the air, turning the room into a white haze, a jumble of incandescent outlines hanging in midair. 'That's exactly what she'll do. And this time she won't fuck it up. If we let her out of that hospital, inside forty-eight hours she'll be dead.'

'Yeah. Probably.'

'How the hell are you OK with that?' One of his shoulders lifted in something like a shrug. 'Is it revenge? She deserves to die, we don't have the death penalty, what the hell, let her do it herself. Is that what you're thinking?'

Richie's eyes came up to meet mine. He said, 'It's the best thing left that could happen to her.'

I nearly came out of my chair and grabbed him by the shirt front. '*You can't say that.* Jenny's got how many years left, fifty, sixty? You think the best thing she can do with them is get in the bath and slice her wrists open?'

'Sixty years, yeah, maybe. Half of them in prison.'

'Which is the best place for her. The woman needs treatment. She needs therapy, drugs, I don't know what, but there are doctors who do. If she's inside, she'll get all of that. She'll pay her debt to society, get her head fixed, and come out with some kind of life in front of her.'

Richie was shaking his head, hard. 'No, she won't. She won't. Are you crazy? There's nothing in front of her. She killed her *kids.* She held them down till she felt them stop fighting. She stabbed her husband and then lay there with him while he bled out. Every doctor in the *world* couldn't fix that. You saw the state of her. She's already gone, man. Let her go. Have a bit of mercy.'

'You want to talk about mercy? Jenny Spain isn't the only person in this story. Remember Fiona Rafferty? Remember their mother? Got any mercy for them? Think about what they've already lost. Then look at me and tell me they deserve to lose Jenny as well.'

'They didn't deserve *any* of this. You think it'd be easier on them to know what she did? They lose her either way. At least this way it'll be over and done with.'

'It won't be over,' I said. Saying the words sucked my breath out, left me hollow, like my chest was folding in on itself. 'It's never going to be over for them.'

That shut Richie up. He sat down opposite me and watched his fingers square off the reports, again and again. After a while he said, 'Her debt to society: I don't know what that means. Tell me one person who's better off if Jenny sits in prison for twenty-five years.'

I said, 'Shut the hell up. You don't even get to *ask* that question. The judge hands down sentences, not us. That's what the whole bloody system is *for*: to stop arrogant little pricks like you from playing God, handing out death sentences whenever they feel like it. You just stick to the fucking rules, hand in the fucking evidence and let the fucking system do its job. You don't get to throw Jenny Spain away.'

'It's not about throwing her away. Making her spend years in this kind of pain . . . That's torture, man. It's wrong.'

'No. *You* think it's wrong. Who knows why you think that? Because you're right, or because this case breaks your heart, because you're feeling guilty as hell, because Jenny reminds you of Miss Kelly who taught you when you were five? That's why we have rules to begin with, Richie: because you can't trust your mind to tell you what's right and what's wrong. Not on something like this. The consequences if you make a mistake are too huge and too horrible even to think about, never mind live with. The rules say we put Jenny away. Everything else is bullshit.'

He was shaking his head. 'It's still wrong. I'll trust my own mind on this one.'

I could have laughed, or howled. 'Yeah? Just look where that's got you. Rule Zero, Richie, the rule to end all rules: your mind is garbage. It's a weak, broken, fucked-up mess that will let you down at every worst moment there is. Don't you think my sister's mind told her she was doing the right thing when she followed you home? Don't you think Jenny believed she was doing the right thing, Monday night? If you trust your mind, you will fuck up and you will fuck up big. Every single thing I've done right in my life, it's been because I don't trust my mind.'

Richie lifted his head to look at me. It took an effort. He said, 'Your sister told me about your mother.'

In that second I almost punched his face in. I saw him brace for it, saw the blast of fear or hope. By the time my fists would unclench and I could breathe again, the silence had got long.

I said, 'What exactly did she tell you?'

'That your mam drowned, the summer you were fifteen. When yous were down at Broken Harbour.'

'Did she happen to mention the manner of death?'

He wasn't looking at me any more. 'Yeah. She said your mam went into the water herself. On purpose, like.'

I waited, but he was done. I said, 'And you figured that meant I was one strap away from a straitjacket. Is that right?'

'I didn't—'

'No, old son, I'm curious. Go ahead and tell me: what was the line of thinking that led you to that conclusion? Did you assume I was so scarred for life that going within a mile of Broken Harbour was sending me off on some kind of psychotic break? Did you figure the crazy was hereditary, and I might suddenly get the urge to strip and start screaming about lizard people from the rooftops? Were you worried that I was going to blow my brains out on your time? I think I deserve to know.'

Richie said, 'I never thought you were crazy. I never thought that. But the way you were about Brennan . . . That worried me, even before . . . before last night. I said it to you, sure. I thought you were overboard.'

I was itching to shove back my chair and start circling the room, but I knew if I got any closer to Richie I was going to hit him, and I knew that would be bad even if I was having trouble remembering why. I stayed put. 'Right. So you said. And once you talked to Dina, you figured you knew why. Not just that: you figured you had a free hand to play about with the evidence. That sucker, you thought, that burnt-out old lunatic, he'll never work this out himself. He's too busy hugging his pillow and sobbing about his dead mummy. Is that right, Richie? Is that about the size of it?'

'No. *No.* I thought . . .' He caught a quick, deep breath. 'I thought maybe we were gonna be partners for a good while, like. I know that sounds like, who do I think I am, but I just . . . I felt like it was working. I was hoping . . .' I stared him out of it until he let the sentence fall away. Instead he said, 'This week, anyway, we were partners. And partners means if you've got a problem, I've got a problem.'

'That would be adorable, only I *don't* have a fucking problem, chum. Or at least, I didn't, up until you decided to get smart with evidence. My mother has *nothing* to do with this. Do you understand? Is that sinking in?'

His shoulders twisted. 'I'm only saying. I figured maybe . . . I can see why you wouldn't like the idea of Jenny finishing the job.'

'I don't like the idea of *people getting fucking killed*. By themselves or anyone else. That's what I'm *doing* here. That doesn't require some deep psychological explanation. The part that's begging for a good therapist is the part where you're sitting there arguing that we should help Jenny Spain take a header off a tall building.'

'Come on, man. That's stupid talk. No one's saying to help her. I'm just saying . . . let nature take its course.'

In a way, it was a relief; a small, bitter one, but a relief all the same. He would never have made a detective. If it hadn't been this, if I hadn't been stupid and weak and pathetic enough to see just what I wanted to see and let the rest slide by, sooner or later it would have been something else. I said, 'I'm not David fucking Attenborough. I don't sit back on the sidelines and watch *nature take its course*. If I ever caught myself thinking that way, I'd be the one finding myself a tall building.' I heard the vicious flick of disgust in my voice and saw Richie flinch, but all I felt was a cold pleasure. 'Murder is nature. Hadn't you noticed that? People maiming each other, raping each other, killing each other, doing all the stuff that animals do: that's nature in action. Nature is the devil I'm fighting, chum. Nature is my worst enemy. If it isn't yours, then you're in the wrong fucking gig.'

Richie didn't answer. His head was down and he was running a fingernail over the table in tense, invisible geometric patterns – I remembered him doodling on the window of the observation room, like it had been a long, long time ago. After a moment he asked, 'So what are you planning on doing? Just hand in that envelope to the evidence room like nothing ever happened, take it from there?'

*You*, not *we*. I said, 'Even if that was how I roll, I don't have the option. When Dina got here this morning, I wasn't in yet. She gave this to Quigley instead.'

Richie stared. He said, like the breath had been punched out of him, 'Oh, fuck.'

'Yeah: oh, fuck. Believe me, Quigley's got no intention of letting this slide. What did I say to you, just a couple of days ago? *Quigley would love a chance to throw the pair of us under a bus. Don't play into his hands.*'

He had gone even whiter. Some sadistic part of me, creeping out of its dark storeroom because I had no energy left to keep it locked away, was loving the sight of him. He asked, 'What do we do?'

His voice shook. His palms were upturned towards me, like I was the shining hero who could fix this hideous mess, make it all go away. I said, '*We* don't do anything. You go home.'

Richie watched me, uncertain, trying to work out what I meant. The cold room had him shivering in his shirtsleeves, but he didn't seem to notice. I said, 'Get your things and go home. Stay there till I tell you to come back in. You can use the time to think about how you'll justify your actions to the Super, if you want, although I doubt it'll make much difference.'

'What are you going to do?'

I stood up, leaning my weight on the table like an old man. 'That's not your problem.'

After a moment, Richie asked, 'What'll happen to me?'

It was one small thing to his credit, that this was the first time he had asked. I said, 'You'll be reverted back to uniform. You'll stay there.'

I was still staring down at my hands planted on the table, but in my peripheral vision I could see him nodding, repetitive meaningless nods, trying to take in everything that that meant. I said, 'You were right. We worked well together. We would have made good partners.'

'Yeah,' Richie said. The tide of grief in his voice almost rocked me on my feet. 'We would.'

He picked up his sheaf of reports and got up, but he didn't move towards the door. I didn't look up. After a minute he said, 'I want to apologise. I know that counts for fuck-all, at this stage, but still: I'm really, really sorry. For everything.'

I said, 'Go home.'

I kept staring at my hands, till they slipped out of focus and turned into strange white things crouched on the table, deformed and maggoty, waiting to pounce. Finally I heard the door close. The light raked at me from every direction, ricocheted off the envelope's plastic window to spike at my eyes. I had never been in a room that felt so savagely bright, or so empty.

# 18

There have been so many of them. Run-down rooms in tiny mountain-country stations, smelling of mould and feet; sitting-rooms crammed with flowered upholstery, simpering holy cards, all the shining medals of respectability; council-flat kitchens where the baby whined through a bottle of Coke and the ashtray over-flowed onto the cereal-crusted table; our own interview rooms, still as sanctuaries, so familiar that blindfolded I could have put my hand on that piece of graffiti, that crack in the wall. They are the rooms where I have come eye to eye with a killer and said, *You. You did this.*

I remember every one. I save them up, a deck of richly coloured collector's cards to be kept in velvet and thumbed through when the day has been too long for sleep. I know whether the air was cool or warm against my skin, how light soaked into worn yellow paint or ignited the blue of a mug, whether the echoes of my voice slid up into high corners or fell muffled by heavy curtains and shocked china ornaments. I know the grain of wooden chairs, the drift of a cobweb, the soft drip of a tap, the give of carpet under my shoes. *In my father's house there are many mansions:* if somehow I earn one, it will be the one I have built out of these rooms.

I have always loved simplicity. *With you, everything's black and white,* Richie had said, like an accusation; but the truth is that almost every murder case is, if not simple, capable of simplicity, and that this is not only necessary but breathtaking, that if there are miracles then this is one. In these rooms, the world's vast hissing tangle of shadows burns away, all its treacherous greys are honed to the stark purity of a bare blade, two-edged: cause and effect, good and evil. To me, these rooms are beautiful. I go into them the way a boxer goes into the ring: intent, invincible, home.

Jenny Spain's hospital room was the only one I have ever been afraid of. I couldn't tell whether it was because the darkness inside was honed sharper than I had ever touched, or because something told me that it hadn't been honed at all, that those shadows were still crisscrossing and multiplying, and this time there was no way to make them stop.

They were both there, Jenny and Fiona. Their heads turned to the door when I opened it, but no conversation cut off in mid-sentence: they hadn't been talking, just sitting there, Fiona by the bedside in an undersized plastic chair, her hand and Jenny's clasped together on the threadbare blanket. They stared at me, thin faces worn away in grooves where the pain was settling in to stay, blank blue eyes. Someone had found a way to wash Jenny's hair – without the straighteners, it was soft and flyaway as a little girl's – and her fake tan had worn away, leaving her even paler than Fiona. For the first time I saw a resemblance there.

'I'm sorry to disturb you,' I said. 'Ms Rafferty, I need a few words with Mrs Spain.'

Fiona's hand clamped tight around Jenny's. 'I'll stay.'

She knew. 'I'm afraid that's not an option,' I said.

'Then she doesn't want to talk to you. She's not in any state to talk, anyway. I'm not going to let you bully her.'

'I don't plan to bully anyone. If Mrs Spain wants a solicitor to be present during the interview, she can request one, but I can't have anyone else in the room. I'm sure you understand that.'

Jenny disengaged her hand, gently, and put Fiona's on the arm of the chair. 'It's OK,' she said. 'I'm fine.'

'No you're *not*.'

'I am. Honestly, I am.' The doctors had dialled down the pain-killers. Jenny's movements still had an underwater quality and her face looked unnaturally calm, almost slack, as if some crucial muscles had been severed; but her eyes were focusing, and the words came out slow and thin but clear. She was lucid enough to give a statement, if I got her that far. 'Go on, Fi. Come back in a bit.'

I held the door open till Fiona got up, reluctantly, and pulled her coat off the chair. As she put it on I said, 'Please do come back. I'll need to talk with you, as well, once your sister and I are done here. It's important.'

Fiona didn't answer. Her eyes were still on Jenny. When Jenny nodded, Fiona brushed past me and headed off down the corridor. I waited till I was sure she was gone before I closed the door.

I put my briefcase down by the bed, took off my coat and arranged it on the back of the door, pulled the chair so close to Jenny that my knees nudged her blanket. She watched me tiredly, incuriously, like I was another doctor bustling around her with things that beeped and flashed and hurt. The thick pad of bandage on her cheek had been replaced by a slim, neat strip; she was wearing something soft and blue, a T-shirt or a pyjama top, with long sleeves that wrapped around her hands. A thin rubber tube ran from a hanging IV bag into one sleeve. Outside the window, a tall tree spun pinwheels of glowing leaves against a thin-stretched blue sky.

'Mrs Spain,' I said. 'I think we need to talk.'

She watched me, leaning her head back on the pillow. She was waiting patiently for me to finish and go away, leave her to hypnotise herself with the moving leaves until she could dissolve into them, a flicker of tossed light, a breath of breeze, gone.

'How are you feeling?' I asked.

'Better. Thanks.'

She looked better. Her lips were parched from hospital air, but the thick hoarseness had faded from her voice, leaving it high and sweet as a girl's, and her eyes weren't red any more: she had stopped crying. If she had been distraught, howling, I would have been less frightened for her. 'That's good to hear,' I said. 'When are the doctors planning to let you go home?'

'They said maybe day after tomorrow. Maybe the day after that.'

I had less than forty-eight hours. The ticking clock, and the

nearness of her, were hammering at me to hurry. 'Mrs Spain,' I said,
'I came to tell you that there's been some progress in the investigation. We've arrested someone for the attack on you and your family.'

That ignited a startled sputter of life in Jenny's eyes. I said,
'Your sister didn't tell you?'

She shook her head. 'You've . . . ? Arrested *who?*'

'This may come as a bit of a shock, Mrs Spain. It's someone
you know – someone you were very close to, for a long time.' The
sputter caught, flared into fear. 'Can you tell me any reason why
Conor Brennan would want to hurt your family?'

'*Conor?*'

'We've arrested him for the crimes. He'll be charged this
weekend. I'm sorry.'

'Oh my God— No. No no no. You've got it all *wrong*. Conor
would never hurt us. He'd never hurt anyone.' Jenny was struggling to lift herself off the pillow; one hand stretched towards
mine, tendons standing out like an old woman's, and I saw those
broken nails. 'You have to let him out.'

'Believe it or not,' I said, 'I'm with you on this one: I don't think
Conor is a killer either. Unfortunately, though, all the evidence
points to him, and he's confessed to the crimes.'

'*Confessed?*'

'I can't ignore that. Unless someone can give me concrete proof
that Conor didn't kill your family, I've got no choice but to file the
charges against him – and believe me, the case will stand up in
court. He's going to prison for a very long time.'

'I was there. It wasn't him. Is that concrete enough?'

I said gently, 'I thought you didn't remember that night.'

That only threw her for a second. 'I don't. And if it had been
Conor, I'd remember that. So it wasn't.'

I said, 'We're past that kind of game, Mrs Spain. I'm almost
sure I know what happened that night. I'm very sure that you do.
And I'm pretty sure that no one else alive does, except Conor.
That makes you the only person who can get him off the hook.
Unless you want him convicted of murder, you need to tell me
what happened.'

Tears started in Jenny's eyes. She blinked them back. 'I don't remember.'

'Take a minute and think about what you'll be doing to Conor if you keep that up. He cares about you. He's loved you and Pat for a very long time – I think you know just how much he loves you. How will he feel, if he finds out you're willing to let him spend the rest of his life in prison for something he didn't do?'

Her mouth wobbled, and for a second I thought I had her, but then it set hard. 'He won't go to prison. He didn't do anything wrong. You'll see.'

I waited, but she was done. Richie and I had been right. She was planning her note. She cared about Conor, but her chance at death meant more to her than anyone left alive.

I leaned over to my briefcase, flicked it open and pulled out Emma's drawing, the one we had found stashed away in Conor's flat. I laid it on the blanket on Jenny's lap. For a second I thought I smelled the cool harvest sweetness of wood and apples.

Jenny's eyes slammed tight. When they opened she stared out the window again, her body twisted away from the drawing as if it might leap for her.

I said, 'Emma drew this the day before she died.'

That spasm again, jerking her eyes closed. Then nothing. She gazed at the leaves turning the light, like I wasn't there.

'This animal in the tree. What is it?'

Nothing at all, this time. Everything Jenny had left was going into shutting me out. Soon she wouldn't hear me any more.

I leaned in, so close I could smell the chemical flowers of her shampoo. The nearness of her made the hairs on the back of my neck rise in a slow cold wave. It was like leaning cheek to cheek with a wraith. 'Mrs Spain,' I said. I put my finger on the plastic evidence envelope, on the sinuous black thing draped along a branch. It smiled out at me, orange-eyed, mouth wide to show triangular white teeth. 'Look at the drawing, Mrs Spain. Tell me what this is.'

My breath on her cheek made her lashes flicker. 'A cat.'

That was what I had thought. I couldn't believe I had ever seen it like that, as some soft, harmless thing. 'You don't have a cat. Neither do any of your neighbours.'

'Emma wanted one. So she drew one.'

'That doesn't look like a cuddly house pet to me. That looks like a wild animal. Something savage. Not something any little girl would want snuggled up on her bed. What is it, Mrs Spain? Mink? Wolverine? What?'

'I don't know. Something Emma made up. What does it matter?'

'It matters because, from everything I've heard about Emma, she liked pretty things. Soft, fluffy, pink things. So where did she come up with something like this?'

'I don't have a clue. School, maybe. On the telly.'

'No, Mrs Spain. She found this at home.'

'No she *didn't*. I wouldn't let my kids near some wild animal. Go ahead: look through our house. You won't find anything like that.'

I said, 'I've already found it. Did you know Pat was posting to internet discussion boards?'

Jenny's head whipped around so fast I flinched. She stared at me, eyes frozen wide. 'No he wasn't.'

'We've found his posts.'

'No you haven't. It's the internet; anyone can say they're anyone. Pat didn't go online. Only to e-mail his brother and look for jobs.'

She had started shaking, a tiny unstoppable tremor that juddered her head and her hands. I said, 'We found the posts via your home computer, Mrs Spain. Someone tried to delete the internet history, but he didn't do a very good job: it took our lads no time to get the info back. For months before he died, Pat was looking for ways to catch, or at least identify, the predator living inside his walls.'

'That was a joke. He was bored, he had time on his hands – he was messing about, just to see what people online would say. That's all.'

'And the wolf trap in your attic? The holes in your walls? The video monitors? Were those jokes too?'

'I don't know. I don't remember. The holes in the walls just

happened, those houses are built from crap, they're all falling to
bits – the monitors, those were just Pat and the kids playing, just
to see if—'

'Mrs Spain,' I said, 'listen to me. We're the only ones here. I'm
not recording anything. I haven't cautioned you. Anything you say
can never be used as evidence.'

Plenty of detectives take this gamble on a regular basis, betting
that if the suspect talks once, the second time will come easier,
or that the unusable confession will point them towards something they can use. I don't like gambles, but I had nothing and no
time to lose. Jenny was never going to give me a confession under
caution, not in a hundred years. I had nothing to offer her that
she wanted more than the sweet cold of razor blades, the cleans-
ing fire of ant poison, the calling sea, and nothing to brandish
that was more terrifying than the thought of sixty years on this
earth.

If her mind had held even the smallest chance of a future, she
would have had no reason to tell me anything at all, whether or not
it could send her to prison. But this is what I know about people
getting ready to walk off the edges of their own lives: they want
someone to know how they got there. Maybe they want to know
that when they dissolve into earth and water, that last fragment
will be saved, held in some corner of someone's mind; or maybe
all they want is a chance to dump it pulsing and bloody into
someone else's hands, so it won't weigh them down on the journey.
They want to leave their stories behind. No one in all the world
knows that better than I do.

That was the one thing I had to offer Jenny Spain: a place to put
her story. I would have sat there while that blue sky dimmed into
night, sat there while over the hills in Broken Harbour the grinning jack-o'-lanterns faded and the Christmas lights started to
flash out their defiant celebrations, if that was how long it took her
to tell me. As long as she was talking, she was alive.

Silence, while Jenny let that move around her mind. The shaking
had stopped. Slowly her hands uncurled from the soft sleeves and
reached out for the drawing on her lap; her fingers moved like a

blind woman's over the four yellow heads, the four smiles, the block-lettered EMMA in the bottom corner.

She said, just a thin thread of whisper trickling through the still air, 'It was getting out.'

Slowly, so as not to spook her, I leaned back in my chair and gave her room. It was only when I moved back that I realised how hard I had been trying not to breathe the air around her, and how light-headed it had left me. 'Let's go from the beginning,' I said. 'How did it start?'

Jenny's head moved on the pillow, heavily, from side to side. 'If I knew that, I could've stopped it. I've been lying here just thinking and thinking, but I can't put my finger on it.'

'When did you first notice that something was bothering Pat?'

'Way back. Ages ago. May? The start of June? I'd say something to him and he wouldn't answer; when I looked at him, he'd be there staring into space, like he was listening for something. Or the kids would start making noise, and Pat would whip round and go, "Shut up!" – and when I asked him what the problem was, because that totally wasn't like him, he'd be like, "Nothing, just I should be able to get some bloody peace and quiet in my own home, that's the only problem." It was just tiny stuff – no one else would have even noticed – and he said he was fine, but I knew Pat. I knew him inside out. I knew there was something wrong.'

I said, 'But you didn't know what it was.'

'How would I have known?' Jenny's voice had a sudden defensive edge. 'He'd said a few times about hearing scratching noises up in the attic, but I never heard anything. I thought probably it was a bird going in and out. I didn't think it was a big deal – like, why would it be? I figured Pat was depressed about being out of work.'

Meanwhile, Pat had slowly turned more and more afraid that she thought he was hearing things. He had taken it for granted that the animal was preying on her mind too. I said, 'Unemployment had been getting to him?'

'Yeah. A lot. We were . . .' Jenny shifted restlessly in the bed, caught her breath sharply as some wound pulled. 'We'd been having problems about that. We never used to fight, ever. But Pat loved providing for all of us – he was over the moon when I quit working, he was so proud that he could afford for me to do that. When he lost his job . . . At first he was all positive, all, "Don't worry, babes, I'll have something else before you know it, you go buy that new top you were wanting and don't worry for one second." I thought he'd get something, too – I mean, he's good at what he does, he works like mad, of *course* he would, right?'

She was still shifting, running a hand through her hair, tugging harder and harder at tangles. 'That's how it *works*. Everyone knows: if you don't have a job, it's because you're crap at what you do, or because you don't actually want one. End of story.'

I said, 'There's a recession on. During a recession, there are exceptions to most rules.'

'It just made *sense* that he'd find something, you know? But things don't make sense any more. It didn't matter what Pat deserved: there just weren't any jobs out there. By the time that started hitting us, though, we were pretty much broke.'

The word sent a hot, raw red creeping up her neck. I said, 'And that was putting a strain on you both.'

'Yeah. Having no money . . . it's *awful*. I said that to Fiona once, but she didn't get it. She was all, "So what? Sooner or later, one of you'll get another job. Till then, you're not starving, you've got plenty of clothes, the kids don't even know the difference. You'll be fine." I mean, maybe to her and her arty friends, money isn't a big deal, but to most of us out here in the real world, it actually does make a difference. To actual real things.'

Jenny flashed me a defiant look, like she didn't expect the old guy to get it. I said, 'What kind of things?'

'Everything. *Everything.* Like, before, we used to have people over for dinner parties, or barbecues in the summer – but you can't *do* that if all you can afford to give them is tea and Aldi biscuits. Maybe Fiona would, but I'd've died of embarrassment. Some of the people we know, they can be total bitches – they'd have been like, "Oh my God, did you see the label on the wine? Did you see, the SUV's gone? Did you see she was wearing last year's stuff? Next time we come over, they'll be in shiny tracksuits, living on McDonald's." Even the ones who wouldn't have been like that, they'd have felt sorry for us, and I wasn't going to take that. If we couldn't do it right, I wasn't going to do it at all. We just didn't invite people around any more.'

That hot red had filled up her face, turning it swollen-looking and tender. 'And it wasn't like we could afford to go out, either. So we basically stopped ringing people – it was *humiliating*, having this nice normal chat with someone and then, when they'd say, "So when do you want to meet up?" having to come up with some excuse about Jack having the flu. And after a few rounds of excuses, people stopped ringing us, too. Which I was actually glad about – it made things way easier – but all the same . . .'

I said, 'It must have been lonely.'

The red deepened, as if that was something shameful too. She tucked her head down so that a haze of hair hid her face. 'It was, yeah. Really lonely. If we'd been in town then I could've met other mums at the park, stuff like that, but out there . . . Sometimes I went a whole week without saying a word to another adult except Pat, only "Thanks" at the shop. Back when we first got married we were going out three, four nights a week, our weekends were always packed, we were *popular*; and now here we were, staring at each other like a pair of no-mates losers.'

Her voice was speeding up. 'We were starting to bitch at each other about little things, stupid things – how I folded the washing, or how loud he had the telly. And every single thing turned into a fight about money – I don't even know how, but it always did. So I figured that had to be what was bothering Pat. All that stuff.'

'You didn't ask him?'

'I didn't want to push him about it. It was obviously a big deal already; I didn't want to make it even bigger. So I just went, *Right. OK. I'm going to make everything lovely for him. I'm going to show him we're fine.*' Jenny's chin came up, remembering, and I caught that flash of steel. 'I'd always had the house nice, but I started keeping it totally perfect, like not a crumb anywhere – even if I was wrecked, I cleaned the whole kitchen before I went to bed, so when Pat came down for breakfast it'd be spotless. I'd take the kids picking wildflowers so we'd have something to put in the vases. When the kids needed clothes I got them secondhand, off eBay – nice clothes, but God, a couple of years ago I'd've *died* sooner than put them in secondhand stuff – but it meant I had enough money left to get decent food that Pat liked, steak for dinner sometimes. It was like, *Look, everything's OK, see? We can totally handle this; it's not like we're going to turn into skangers overnight. We're still us.'*

Probably Richie would have seen a spoilt middle-class princess whose sense of herself was too shallow to survive without pesto salad and designer shoes. I saw a frail, doomed gallantry that broke my heart. I saw a girl who thought she had built a fortress against the wild sea, braced at the door with all her pathetic weapons, fighting her heart out while the water seeped past her.

I said, 'But everything wasn't OK.'

'No. It so wasn't OK. By, like, the beginning of July . . . Pat kept getting jumpier, and more – not even like he was ignoring me and the kids, exactly; like he forgot we existed, because there was something huge on his mind. He talked about the noises in the attic a bunch more times, he even rigged up this old video baby monitor, but I still didn't connect it up. I just thought . . . guys with gadgets, you know? I thought Pat was just finding ways to fill up all that spare time. By that stage I did know it wasn't just being out of work that was getting to him, but . . . He was spending more and more time on the computer, or hanging around upstairs on his own when I had the kids downstairs. I was scared that he was addicted to some kind of weird porn, or having one of those online affairs, or like sexting someone on his phone?'

Jenny made a sound halfway between a laugh and a sob, harsh and sore enough that it made me jump. 'God, if only. Probably I should've copped on to the monitor thing, but . . . I don't know. I had my own stuff on my mind, too.'

'The break-ins.'

An uncomfortable shift of her shoulders. 'Yeah. Well, or whatever they were. They started around then – or I started noticing them, anyway. It made it hard to think straight. I was all the time looking for anything going missing, or anything moved, but if I actually spotted something, I worried that I was just being paranoid – and then I got worried that I was being paranoid about Pat, too . . .'

And Fiona's doubts hadn't helped. I wondered whether Fiona had sensed, deep down, that she was nudging Jenny further off balance, or whether it had been innocent honesty; whether anything within families is ever innocent.

'So I just tried to ignore it all and keep going. I didn't know what else to do. I cleaned the house even more; the second the kids got something messy, I'd tidy it away, or wash it – I was mopping the kitchen floor like three times a day. It wasn't just to cheer Pat up any more. I needed to keep everything perfect, so that if anything was ever out of place, I'd know straightaway. I mean' – a flash of wariness – 'it wasn't a big deal, or anything. Like I told you before, I knew it was probably Pat moving stuff and forgetting. I was just making sure.'

And here I had thought she was shielding Conor. It had never even occurred to her that he was involved. She was positive that she had been hallucinating; all she could think about was the nightmare chance that the doctors would find out she was crazy and keep her here. What she was protecting was the most precious thing she had left: her plan.

'I understand,' I said. Under cover of shifting position, I checked my watch: we had been there around twenty minutes. Sooner or later, Fiona – especially if I was right about her – wouldn't be able to make herself wait any longer. 'And then . . . ? What changed?'

'Then,' Jenny said. The room was stifling and getting worse, but she had her arms wrapped around her body as if she was cold. 'This one night, late, I went into the kitchen and Pat practically knocked the computer off the desk, trying to switch away from whatever he was doing. So I sat down next to him and I was like, "OK, you need to tell me what's going on. I don't care what it is, we can work through it, but I have to know." At first he was all, "Oh, everything's fine, I've got it all under control, don't worry about it." Of course that put me into a total panic – I was like, "Oh my God, what? What? Neither of us moves from this desk till you tell me what's going on." And Pat, when he saw how scared I was, it just came *pouring* out of him: "I didn't want to freak you out, I thought I could catch it and you'd never even have to know . . ." And all this stuff about minks and polecats, and bones in the attic, and people online having ideas . . .'

That raw half-laugh again. 'You know something? I was over the *moon*. I was like, "Wait, this is *it*? *This* is all that's wrong?" Here I'd been worrying about affairs and, I don't know, terminal *diseases*, and Pat's telling me we might have a *rat* or something. I practically burst into tears, I was so relieved. I went, "So we'll ring an exterminator tomorrow. I don't care if we have to get a bank loan, it'll be worth it."

'But Pat was all, "No, listen, you don't understand." He said he'd already tried an exterminator, but the guy told him whatever we had was way out of his league. I was like, "Oh my *God*, Pat, and you just let us keep living here? Are you insane?" He looked at me like a little kid who's brought you his new drawing and you threw it in the bin. He went, "You think I'd let you and the kids stay if it wasn't safe? I'm *on* it. We don't need some exterminator guy messing around with poison and charging us a few grand. *I'm* going to get this thing."

Jenny shook her head. 'I was like, "Um, hello? So far you haven't even managed to get a *look* at it," and he went, "Well, yeah, but that's because I couldn't do anything that might tip you off. Now that you know, there's all kinds of stuff I can do. God, Jen, this is such a massive relief!"

'He was laughing: flopped back in his chair, rubbing his head so his hair went all messy, and laughing. Personally I didn't exactly see anything to laugh about, but still . . .' Something that might have been a smile, if it had been less crammed with sadness. 'It was nice to see him like that, you know? Really nice. So I went, "What kind of stuff?"

'Pat leaned his elbows on the desk, all settled in like when we used to plan out a holiday or something, and he went, "Well, the monitor in the attic obviously isn't working, right? The animal's dodging it – maybe it doesn't like the infrared, I don't know. So what we have to do is think like the animal. See what I mean?"

'I went, "Totally not," and he laughed again. He went, "OK, what does it *want*? We're not sure – could be food, warmth, even company. But whatever it is, the animal thinks it's going to find it in this house, or it wouldn't be here, right? It wants something that it thinks it's going to get from *us*. So we have to give it the chance to get closer."

'I was like, "Oh hell *no*," but Pat went, "No no no, don't worry, not that close! I'm talking about a *controlled* chance. *We* control it, all the way. I rig up a monitor on the landing, pointing at the attic hatch, right? I leave the hatch open, but with wire mesh nailed over it, so the animal can't get down into the house. We'll keep the landing light on, so there'll be enough light that I won't need to use the infrared, in case that's what's scaring it away. And then we just have to wait. Sooner or later, it's going to get tempted, it's going to need to get closer to us, it's going to head for the hatch – and boom-boom, caught on camera. See? It's perfect!"'

Jenny's palms turned up helplessly. 'It didn't exactly sound perfect to me. But, I mean . . . I'm supposed to support my husband, right? And like I said, this was the happiest he'd looked in months. So I went, "OK, fine. Off you go."'

This story should have been gibberish, incoherent fragments gasped out between sobs. Instead, it was crystal-clear. She was telling it with the same relentless, iron-willed precision that had forced her house to perfection every night, before she could sleep. Maybe I should have admired her control, or at least been grateful for it: I had thought, before that first interview, that Jenny dissolved in howling grief was my worst nightmare. This flat still voice, like a disembodied thing waking you deep in the night to whisper on and on in your ear, was much worse.

I said – I had to clear my throat before the words would come out – 'When was this conversation?'

'Like the end of July? God—' I saw her swallow. 'Less than three months. I can't believe . . . It feels like three *years*.'

The end of July tallied with Pat's discussion-board posts. I said, 'Did you assume that the animal existed? Or did it occur to you, even just as a possibility, that your husband might be imagining it?'

Jenny said, sharply and instantly, 'Pat's not crazy.'

'I've never thought he was. But you've just told me he was under a lot of stress. In the circumstances, anyone's imagination could get a little overactive.'

Jenny stirred restlessly. She said, 'I don't know. Maybe I wondered, sort of. I mean, I'd never heard anything, so . . .' A shrug. 'But I didn't even really care. All I cared about was getting back to normal. I figured once Pat put up the camera, things would get better. Either he'd get a look at this animal or he'd work out it wasn't there – because it had gone somewhere else, or because it was never there to start with. And either way, he'd feel better because he was doing something and because he was talking to me, right? I still think that makes sense. That wasn't a crazy thing to think, was it? Anyone would've thought that. Right?'

Her eyes were on me, huge with pleading. 'That's exactly what I would have thought,' I said. 'But that's not what happened?'

'Things got *worse*. Pat still didn't see anything, but instead of just giving up, he decided the animal knew the monitor was there. I was like, "OK, hello, *how*?" He was like, "Whatever it is, it's not stupid. It's very far from stupid." He said he kept hearing the scratching in the sitting room, when he was watching telly, so he figured the animal had got scared by the camera and worked its way into the *walls*. He was like, "That hatch is way too exposed. I don't have a clue what I was thinking; no wild animal's going to come out into the open like that. Of *course* it's moved into the walls. What I really need to do is get a camera pointed inside the sitting-room wall."

'I went, "No. No way," but Pat went, "Ah, come on, Jen, we're only talking about a tiny little hole. I'll put it out of sight, in by the sofa; you won't even know it's there. Just for a few days, maybe a week tops; just till we get a look at this thing. If we don't sort it now, the animal could get stuck inside the walls and die there, and then I'd have to rip up half the place to get it out. You don't want that, do you?"'

Jenny's fingers tugged at the hem of the bedsheet, pleating it into little folds. 'To be honest, I wasn't all that worried about that. Maybe you're right: maybe deep down I thought there was nothing there. But just in case . . . And it meant so much to him. So I said OK.' Her fingers were moving faster. 'Maybe that was my mistake; that was where I went wrong. Maybe if I'd put my foot down right then, he'd have forgotten about it. Do you think?'

It felt like something scalding into my skin, that desperate plea, like something I would never be able to scrape off. I said, 'I doubt he would have forgotten about it.'

'You think? You don't think if I'd just said no, everything would have been OK?'

I couldn't bear her eyes. I said, 'So Pat made a hole in the wall?'

'Yeah. Our lovely house, that we'd worked like crazy to buy and keep nice, that we used to *love*, and now he was smashing it to pieces. I wanted to cry. Pat saw my face and he went, really *grim*, "What's it matter? A couple more months and it'll be the bank's anyway." He'd never said anything like that before. Before, we'd both always been all, "We'll find a way, it'll be OK . . ." And the look on his face . . . There was nothing I could say. I just turned around and walked out and left him there, hammering the wall. It fell apart like it was made out of nothing.'

I checked my watch again, out of the corner of my eye. For all I knew Fiona already had her ear pressed to the door, trying to work out whether to burst in. I shifted my chair even closer to Jenny – it made the hair at the top of my head lift – so she wouldn't raise her voice.

She said, 'And then the new camera didn't catch anything, either. And a week later the kids and I got back from the shops and there was another hole, in the hall. I went, "What's this?" and Pat was like, "Give me the car keys. I need another monitor, quick. It's moving back and forth between the sitting room and the hall – I swear it's deliberately screwing with me. One more monitor and I've got the bastard!" Maybe I could have put my foot down then, maybe that was when I should've done it, but Emma was all, "What? What? What's moving, Daddy?" and Jack was yelling "Bastard bastard bastard!" and I just wanted to get Pat out of there so I could sort them. I gave him the keys, and he practically ran out the door.'

A bitter little smile, one-sided. 'More excited than he'd been in months. I told the kids, "Your daddy thinks we might have a mouse, don't worry about it." And when Pat got back – with *three* video monitors, just in case, when Jack's wearing secondhand jeans – I said to him, "You need to not talk about this around the kids, or they'll get nightmares. I'm serious." He was all, "Yeah, course, you're right as usual, no problem." That lasted, what, two hours? That *same evening* I was in the playroom, reading to the kids, and Pat came running in with one of those bloody monitors, going, "Jen, listen, it's making this mad hissing noise in there, listen!" I gave him the daggers but he didn't even notice, not till I said, "We'll talk about it later," and then he actually looked pissed off.'

Her voice was rising. I could have kicked myself for not bringing someone, anyone, even Richie, to stand guard outside the door. 'And the next afternoon he's on the computer and the kids are *right there*, I'm making their snack, and Pat goes, "Wow, Jen, listen to this! Some guy in Slovenia, he's bred this giant mink, like the size of a dog, I wonder if one could've escaped and—" And 'cause the kids were there I had to go, "That's really interesting, why don't you tell me about it later on," when inside I was just like, *I don't care! I don't give a fuck! All I want is for you to shut up around the kids!*'

Jenny tried to take a deep breath, but her muscles were too tense to let her. 'So of course the kids figured it out – Emma did, anyway. A couple of days later we were in the car, her and me and Jack, and she was like, "Mum, what's a mink?" I went, "It's an animal," and she went, "Is there one inside our wall?"

'I went, all casual, "Oh, I don't think so. If there is, though, your daddy's going to get rid of it." The kids seemed OK with that, but I could've *hit* Pat. I got home and told him – I was yelling, I'd sent the kids out to the garden so they wouldn't hear – and Pat just went, "Oops, shit, sorry. Tell you what, though: now they know, maybe they could help. I can't keep an eye on all these monitors at once, I keep worrying that I'm missing something. Maybe the kids could hang on to one each?" Which was just so *wrong* I could hardly *talk*. I just went, "No. No. No bloody way. Don't you ever suggest that again," and he didn't, but still. And of course even though he said he had too many monitors he got nothing out of the hallway wall so he made more holes, he set up more monitors, every time I looked *around* there was another hole in our *home*!'

I made some meaningless reassuring noise. Jenny didn't notice. 'And that was all he did: watch those monitors. He got this *trap* – not just a mousetrap, but this massive horrible thing with teeth that he put in the attic – I mean, I guess you've seen it. He acted like it was some big *mystery*, he was all, "Don't worry about it, babe, what you don't know won't hurt you," but he was totally over the moon with it, like this was a brand-new Porsche or some magic wand that was going to fix all our problems forever. He would've watched that trap twenty-four-seven if he could've. He wouldn't play with the kids any more – I couldn't even leave Jack with him while I took Emma to school, or I'd come home and find Jack, like, painting the kitchen floor with tomato sauce while Pat sat there, three feet away, staring at these little screens with his mouth open. I tried to get him to turn them off in front of the kids, and mostly he would, but that just meant the second the kids were in bed Pat had to sit in front of those things all evening long. A couple of times I tried making a fancy dinner, with candles and flowers and the nice silver, and dressing up – like a date night, you know? – but he just lined up the monitors in front of his plate and stared at them the whole time we were eating. He said it was important: the thing got hyper when it smelled food, he had to be ready. I mean, I thought *we* were important too, but no, apparently not.'

I thought of the frantic message-board posts, *She doesn't understand, she doesn't get it* . . . I asked, 'Did you try telling Pat how you felt?'

Jenny's hands flew up and out, the IV line swinging from that great purple bruise. '*How?* He literally wouldn't *have* a conversation, in case he missed something on those *fucking* monitors. When I tried to say anything to him, even just asking him to get something off a shelf, he'd *shush* me. He'd never done that before. I couldn't tell if I should give out, or if that would make Pat blow up at me, or pull away from me even more. And I couldn't tell *why* I couldn't tell – whether it was because I was so stressed out I wasn't thinking straight, or whether there just wasn't a right answer—'

I said soothingly, 'I understand. I wasn't implying—' Jenny didn't stop.

'And anyway, we practically didn't even *see* each other any more. Pat said the thing was "more active" at night, so he was staying up late and sleeping half the day. We always used to go to bed together, always, but the kids get up early, so I couldn't stay up with him. He wanted me to – he kept being like, "Come on, I know tonight's the night we get a look at it, I can feel it" – he was always having some idea that was definitely going to catch the thing, like some new bait, or some tent-type thing over the hole and the camera so the animal would *feel safe*. And he'd be like, "Please, Jenny, please, I'm begging you – all it'll take is one look and you'll be so much happier, you won't be worrying about me any more. I know you don't believe me, but just stay up this one night and you'll see . . ."'

'And did you?' I kept my voice low and hoped Jenny would take the hint, but hers looped higher and higher.

'I *tried*! I hated even *looking* at those holes, I hated them so *much*, but I thought if Pat was right then I owed it to him, and if he was wrong then I might as well be sure, you know? And either way, at least we'd be doing *something* together, even if it wasn't exactly a romantic dinner. But I was getting so exhausted, a couple of times I thought I was going to fall asleep when I was driving; I couldn't do it any more. So I'd go to bed at midnight, and Pat would come up whenever he got too tired to keep his eyes open. At first it was like two o'clock, but then it was three, four, five, sometimes not even then – in the morning I'd find him crashed out on the sofa, with all the monitors lined up on the coffee table. Or in the chair by the computer, because he'd spent the whole night online reading up on animals.'

I said, '"If he was right." By this point, you had doubts.'

Jenny caught a breath and for a second I thought she was going to snap at me again, but then her spine sagged and she slumped back against the pillows.

She said quietly, 'No. By then I knew. I knew there was nothing there. If there had been, how come I never heard anything? All those cameras, how come we never once saw anything? I tried to tell myself it could still maybe be real, but I knew. But by then it was too late. Our house bashed to bits, me and Pat hardly talking any more; I couldn't remember the last time we'd even kissed, like properly kissed. The kids keyed up all the time, hyper, even if they didn't understand why.'

Her head moved from side to side, blindly. 'I knew I should do something, stop the whole thing – I'm not thick, I'm not insane; I did know that, by that stage. But I didn't know what to do. There's no self-*help* book for this; there's no internet group. They didn't tell us what to do about this on our marriage guidance course.'

I said, 'You didn't consider talking to anyone?'

That flash of steel. 'No. No way. Are you joking?'

'It was a difficult situation. A lot of people might have felt that talking to someone would help.'

'Talking to who?'

'Your sister, maybe.'

'Fiona . . .' A wry twist of Jenny's mouth. 'Um, I don't think so. I love Fi, but like I said before, there's stuff she just doesn't get. And anyway, she was always . . . I mean, sisters get jealous. Fi always felt like I had things easy; like stuff just fell into my lap, while she was working her arse off for everything. If I'd said something to her, part of her would've had to be like, *Ha-ha, now you know how it feels*. She wouldn't've said it, but I'd've known. How would that have helped anything?'

'What about friends?'

'I don't have those kind of friends, not any more. And, like, what would I say? *Hi, Pat's hallucinating some animal that lives in our walls, I think he's going loop-the-loop?* Yeah, right. I'm not stupid. Once you tell one person, it gets out. I told you, no way was I going to have people laughing at us – or, even worse, feeling *sorry* for us.' The thought had her chin out, ready for a fight. 'I kept thinking about this girl Shona, we used to hang out when we were kids – she's turned into a total bitch now. We're not in touch any more, but if she'd heard about this, she'd have been on the phone to me like a shot. Whenever I got tempted to say something to Fi or whoever, that's what I'd hear: Shona. *Jenny! Hi! Oh my God, I heard Pat's totally lost it, like he's seeing pink elephants on the ceiling? Everyone's just like, wow, who would've guessed? I remember we all thought you guys were the perfect couple, Mr and Mrs Boring, happy ever after . . . Like, how wrong were we? Gotta go, time for my hot stone massage, just had to say sooo sorry it all went tits-up for you! Byeee!*'

Jenny was rigid in the bed, palms pressed down on the blanket, fingers digging in. 'That was the *one* thing we still had going for us: nobody knew. I kept on telling myself over and over, *At least we've got that.* As long as people thought we were doing great, we had a chance of getting back up and doing great again. If people think you're some kind of lunatic losers, they start *treating* you like lunatic losers, and then you're screwed. Totally screwed.'

*If that's how everyone treats you,* I had said to Richie, *then that's how you feel. How is that different?* I said, 'There are professionals. Counsellors, therapists. Anything you said to someone like that would have been confidential.'

'And have him say Pat was nuts, and cart him off to some loony bin where he actually would have gone crazy? No. Pat didn't need a therapist. All Pat needed was a *job*, so he wouldn't have all this time to freak out about nothing, so he'd have to go to bed at a decent hour instead of . . .' Jenny shoved the drawing away, so violently that it fluttered off the bed, glided to rest by my foot with an ugly rasping sound. 'I just had to hold things together till he could get a job again. That was all. And I couldn't *do* that if everyone knew. When I'd pick up Emma from school, and her teacher would smile at me and be like, "Oh, isn't Emma's reading getting so much better," or whatever, just like I was a normal mummy going home to a normal house – that was the only time I *felt* normal. I *needed* that. That was the only thing getting me through. If she'd given me some awful sympathetic smile and a pat on the arm, because she'd found out that Emma's daddy was in a nuthouse, I'd have curled up and died, right there on the class-room floor.'

The air felt solid with heat. For a stab of a second I saw me and Dina, maybe fourteen and five, me jerking her arm behind her back at the school gates: *Shut up, you shut up, you don't ever talk about Mum outside the house or I'll break your arm*— The high steam-whistle shriek out of her, and the stomach-turning free-fall pleasure of yanking her wrist higher. I leaned down to pick up the drawing, so I could hide my face.

Jenny said, 'I never wanted all that much. I wasn't one of those ambitious types who want to be a pop star or a CEO or an It girl. All I wanted was to be normal.'

All the force had ebbed out of her voice, leaving it drained and wan. I laid the drawing back on the bed; she didn't seem to notice. 'That's why you didn't send Jack back to preschool, isn't it?' I said. 'Not because of the money. Because he was saying he'd heard the animal, and you were afraid he'd say it there.'

Jenny flinched like I had raised a hand to her. 'He kept on and *on* saying it! Back at the beginning of summer it was just once in a while, and it was only because Pat was encouraging him – they'd come downstairs and Pat would be all, "See, Jen, I'm not going loopy. Jack heard it just now, didn't you, Jack the lad?" And of course Jack would be like, "Yeah, Mummy, I heard the aminal in the ceiling!" If you tell a three-year-old he's heard something, and if he knows you *want* him to have heard it, then yeah, of *course* he'll end up convinced that he did. Back then I didn't even think it was a big deal. I just went, "Don't worry about it, it's only a bird, it'll go out again in a minute." But then . . .'

Something jerked her body, so hard that I thought she was going to be sick. It took me a second to realise it had been a shudder. 'Then he started saying it more and more. "Mum, the aminal went scratch scratch scratch in my wall! Mum, the aminal jumped up and down like this! Mum, the aminal, the aminal, the . . ." And then this one afternoon in I guess August, towards the end of August, I took him over to play at his friend Karl's house, and when I got back to pick him up, the two of them were in the garden, yelling and pretending to whack something with sticks. Aisling – that's Karl's mum – she said to me, "Jack was talking about a big animal that growls, and Karl said they should kill it, so that's what they've been doing. Is that OK? You don't mind?"'

That racking shudder again. 'Oh, God. I thought I was going to faint. Thank God, Aisling took it for granted it was just something Jack had made up – she was just worried in case I thought she was encouraging them to be cruel to animals, or something. I don't know how I got out of there. I took Jack home and I sat down on the sofa with him on my lap – that's what we do for serious talks. I went, "Jack, look at me. Remember how we talked about the Big Bad Wolf not being real? This animal you told Karl about, it's the same kind as the Big Bad Wolf: it's makey-up. You know there's no real animal, don't you? You know it's only pretend. Don't you?"'

'He wouldn't look at me. He kept wiggling, trying to get down – Jack always hated staying still, but it wasn't just that. I held onto his arms harder – I was terrified I was actually hurting him, but I had to hear him say yes. I had to. Finally he yelled, "No! It makes growls inside the wall! I hate you!" And he kicked me in the stomach and pulled away, and ran.'

Jenny smoothed the blanket carefully over her knees. 'So,' she said, 'I rang the preschool and told them Jack wasn't coming back. I could tell they thought it was the money – I wasn't happy about that, but I couldn't think of anything better. When Aisling rang after that, I didn't answer the phone. She left messages, but I just deleted them. After a while she stopped ringing.'

'And Jack,' I said. 'Did he keep talking about the animal?'

'Not after that. Once or twice, just little mentions, but the same way he'd talk about Baloo or Elmo, you know? Not like it was in his actual life. I knew that could be just because he could tell I didn't want to hear it, but that was OK. Jack was only little. As long as he knew not to act like it was real, it didn't matter so much whether he knew why. Once everything was over, he'd forget all about it.'

I asked, carefully, 'And Emma?'

'Emma,' Jenny said, so gently, like she wanted to cup the word in her two hands and keep it safe from spilling. 'I was so scared about Emma. She was still little enough that I knew she could end up believing in this thing, if Pat went on about it enough; but she wasn't little enough that anyone would figure it was just a game, like Aisling did with Jack. And I couldn't take her out of school, either. And Emma – when something upsets her, she can't let go of it; she'll stay upset for weeks and keep bringing it up over and over. If she started getting sucked in, I didn't know *what* I was going to do. When I tried to think about it, my mind just blanked out.

'So when I was putting her to bed, that night in August after I talked to Jack, I tried to explain. I went, "Sweetie, you know that animal Daddy talks about? The one in the attic?"

'Emma gave me this quick little careful look. It totally broke my heart – she shouldn't ever have to watch herself around me – but at the same time I was actually glad, that she knew to be careful. She went, "Yeah. The one that scratches." I went, "Have you ever heard it?" and she shook her head and went, "No."'

Jenny's chest rose and fell. 'The relief; Jesus, the relief. Emma's not a great liar; I'd have known. I said, "That's right. That's because it's not really there. Daddy's just a little confused right now. Sometimes people think silly things when they're not feeling great. Remember when you had the flu and you were calling all your dolls the wrong names, because everything got all mixed up in your head? That's how Daddy's feeling right now. So we just have to take good care of him and wait for him to get better."

'Emma got that – she liked helping me take care of Jack when he was sick. She went, "Probably he needs some medicine and chicken soup." I went, "OK, we'll try that. But if it doesn't work straightaway, you know what's the most important thing you can do to help? Not tell anybody. Not anybody at all, ever. Daddy's going to get better soon, and when he does, it's really important that no one knows about this, or they'll think he was very silly. The animal has to be a family secret. Do you understand that?"'

Her thumb moved on the sheet, stroking, a tiny tender movement. 'Emma went, "But it's definitely not there?" and I went, "*Definitely* definitely. It's just a bit of silliness, and so we're not going to talk about it, ever. OK?"

'Emma looked a lot happier. She snuggled down in her bed and went, "OK. Shhh." And she put her finger up to her mouth and smiled at me, over it—'

Jenny caught her breath, and her head whipped back. Her eyes were wild, ricocheting. I said, quickly, 'And she didn't mention it again?'

She didn't hear me. 'I was just trying to keep the kids OK. That was all I could do. Just keep the house clean, keep the kids safe, and keep getting up in the morning. Some days I didn't think I was going to manage even that. I knew Pat wasn't going to get better – nothing was going to get better. He'd stopped even applying for jobs, and anyway who'd hire him, in the state he was in? And we needed money, but even if I could've got work, how could I leave the kids with him?'

I tried to make some kind of soothing noise; I don't know what came out. Jenny didn't stop. 'You know what it was like? It was like being in a blizzard. You can't see what's right in front of your face, you can't hear anything except this white-noise roar that never lets up, you don't have a clue where you are or where you're heading, and it keeps just coming at you from every direction, just coming and coming and coming. All you can do is keep on taking the next step – not because it'll actually get you anywhere, just so that you don't lie down and die. That was what it was like.'

Her voice was ripe and swollen with remembered nightmare, like some dark rotten thing ready to burst. I said – for her sake or my own, I didn't know and didn't care – 'Let's move forward. This was August?'

I was just thin meaningless sounds, yammering at the rim of that blizzard. 'I was having dizzy fits – I'd be going up the stairs and all of a sudden my head would be spinning; I'd have to sit down on the step and put my head on my knees till it went away. And I started forgetting stuff, stuff that had just *happened*. Like I'd say to the kids, "Get your coats on, we're going to the shop," and Emma would give me this weird look and say, "But we went this morning," and I'd look in the cupboards and yeah, everything I thought we needed would be right there, but I still couldn't remember anything – putting it there, or buying it, or even going out. Or I'd go to take a shower, and when I was taking off my top I'd realise my hair was wet: I'd just *had* a shower, like it had to be less than an hour ago, but I couldn't remember it. I would've thought I was losing it, except I didn't have room to worry about that. I couldn't keep hold of anything except the second that was actually happening.'

In that moment I thought of Broken Harbour: of my summer haven, awash with the curves of water and the loops of seabirds and the long falls of silver-gold light through sweet air; of muck and craters and raw-edged walls where human beings had beat their retreat. For the first time in my life, I saw the place for what it was: lethal, shaped and honed for destruction as expertly as the trap lurking in the Spains' attic. The menace of it left me blinded, sang like hornets in the bones of my skull. We need straight lines to keep us safe, we need walls; we build solid concrete boxes, sign-posts, packed skylines, because we need them. Without any of that to hold them down, Pat's mind and Jenny's had flown wild, zigzagging in unmapped space, tied to nothing.

Jenny said, 'The worst part was talking to Fi. We always talked every morning; if I'd stopped, she'd have known something was wrong. But it was so *hard*. There was so much stuff to remember – like I had to make sure Jack was out in the garden or up in his room before she called, because I wasn't about to tell her he wasn't in preschool, so I couldn't have her hearing him. And I had to try and remember what I'd said to her before – for a while I used to take notes while we talked, so I could have them there the next day and make sure I got it right, but I got paranoid about Pat or the kids finding them and wanting to know what the story was. And I had to sound *cheerful* all the time, even if Pat was conked out on the sofa because he'd been sitting there till five in the morning staring at a hole in the bloody wall. It was awful. It got . . .'

She swiped a tear off her face, absently, like someone batting at a fly. 'It got to where I woke up dreading that phone call. Isn't that terrible? My own sister that I love to bits, and I used to daydream about how I could pick some fight bad enough that she'd stop speaking to me. I'd have done it, except I couldn't concentrate long enough to come up with anything.'

'Mrs Spain,' I said, louder, putting a snap into my voice. 'When did things reach this point?'

After a moment her face turned towards me. 'What? . . . I'm not sure. It felt like I kept on going for ages like that, years, but . . . I don't know. September? Sometime in September?'

I braced my feet hard against the floor and said, 'Let's move on to this Monday.'

'Monday,' Jenny said. Her eyes skidded away to the window and for a sinking second I thought I had lost her again, but then she drew a long breath and wiped off another tear. 'Yeah. OK.'

Outside the window the light had moved; it fired the whirling leaves with a translucent orange glow, turned them into blazing danger-flags that made my adrenaline leap. Inside the air felt stripped of oxygen, as if the heat and the disinfectants had seared it all away, left the room dried hollow. Everything I was wearing itched fiercely against my skin.

Jenny said, 'It wasn't a good day. Emma got up on the wrong side of the bed – her toast tasted funny, and the tag in her shirt bothered her, and whine whine whine . . . And Jack picked up on it, so he was being awful too. He kept going on and *on* about how he wanted to be an animal for Halloween. I had a pirate costume all made for him, he'd been running around with a scarf round his head saying he was a pirate for *weeks*, but all of a sudden he decided he was going to be "Daddy's big scary animal". He wouldn't shut up about it, all day long. I was trying everything to distract him, giving him biscuits and letting him watch the telly and promising he'd get crisps when we went to the shop – I know I sound like a terrible mum, but he never gets that stuff normally; I just couldn't listen to it, not that day.'

It was so homely, the anxious note in her voice, the little furrow between her eyebrows as she looked at me; so ordinary. No woman wants some stranger thinking she's a bad mother for bribing her little boy with junk food. I had to hold back a shudder. 'I understand,' I said.

'But he wouldn't *stop*. In the shop, even, he was telling the girl at the till about the animal – I swear I would've told him to shut up, and I never do that either, only I didn't want her to see me make a big deal of it. Once we got outside I wouldn't say a word to Jack all the way home, and I wouldn't give him his crisps – he howled so loud he nearly broke my and Emma's eardrums, but I just ignored him. It was all I could do just to get us home without crashing the car. Probably I could've handled it better, only . . .' Jenny's head turned uneasily on the pillow. 'I wasn't in great form either.'

*Sunday night. To remind her of being happy.* I said, 'Something had happened. That morning, when you first came downstairs.'

She didn't ask how I knew. The boundaries of her life had been turning ragged and permeable for so long, another invader was nothing strange. 'Yeah. I went to put the kettle on, and right beside it, on the countertop, there was . . . there was this pin. Like a badge, like kids pin on their jackets? It said, "I go to JoJo's." I used to have one like that, but I hadn't seen it in *years* – I probably threw it away when I moved out of home, I don't even remember. No *way* had it been there the night before. I'd tidied up, last thing; the place was spotless. No *way*.'

'So how did you think it had got there?'

The memory had her breathing faster. 'I couldn't think *anything*. I just stood there like an eejit, staring at it with my mouth open. Pat used to have one of them too, so I was trying to tell myself he must have found it somewhere and put it there for me to find, like a romantic thing, like to remind me about the good times, to apologise for how awful things had got? It's the kind of thing he would've done, before . . . Only he doesn't keep stuff like that either. And even if he had, it would've been in a box in the attic, and that stupid wire was still nailed over the attic hatch; how could he have got it down without me noticing?'

She was searching my face, scanning for any particle of doubt. 'I swear to God, I didn't imagine it. You can look. I wrapped the pin up in a piece of tissue – I didn't even want to touch it – and stuck it in my pocket. When Pat woke up I was praying he'd say something about it, like, "Oh, did you find your present?" but of course he didn't. So I took it upstairs and folded it in a jumper, in my bottom drawer. Go look. It's there.'

'I know,' I said gently. 'We found it.'

'See? See? It was real! I actually . . .' Jenny's face ducked away from mine for a second; her voice, when she started talking again, had a muffled sound to it. 'I actually wondered, at first. I was . . . I told you what things had been like. I thought I could actually be seeing things. So I stuck the pin into my thumb, deep – it bled for ages. I knew I couldn't be imagining that, right? All day, I couldn't think about anything else – I went straight through a red light on the way to get Emma. But at least when I started getting scared that I'd hallucinated the whole thing, I could look at my thumb and go, *OK, a hallucination didn't do that.*'

'But you were still upset.'

'Well, *yeah*, obviously I was. I could only come up with two answers, and they were both . . . they were bad. Either that same person had broken in again and left it there – except I checked the alarm, and it was on; and anyway, how would anyone know about JoJo's? It would have to be someone who'd been stalking me, finding out everything about my whole entire life, and now they wanted me to *know* they knew—' She shuddered. 'I felt like a crazy person even thinking about it. Stuff like that doesn't happen, except in the movies. But the only other thing I could think of was that I actually still had my badge somewhere, and I had done the whole thing myself – gone and dug it out, put it down in the kitchen. And I didn't remember anything about it. And that would mean . . .'

Jenny stared up at the ceiling, blinking to keep the tears back. 'It's one thing doing everyday stuff, autopilot stuff, and forgetting about it – going to the shop or taking a shower, things I would've done anyway. But if I was doing stuff like digging out that badge, crazy stuff that didn't make any sense . . . then I could do anything. Anything. I could get up one morning and look in the mirror and realise I'd shaved my head or painted my face green. I could go to pick Emma up from school one day and find the teacher and all the other mums not talking to me, and I wouldn't have a clue why.'

She was panting, working for each breath like the wind had been knocked out of her. 'And the *kids*. Oh, God, the kids. How was I supposed to *protect* them, if I couldn't tell what I was going to do the next second? How would I even know if I'd been keeping them safe or if I'd, I'd— I couldn't even tell what I was scared of doing, because I wouldn't know till it *happened*. Thinking about it made me want to get sick. It was like I could feel the pin upstairs, wiggling, trying to get out of the drawer. Every time I put my hand in my pocket, I was terrified I'd find it there.'

*To remind her of being happy.* Conor, floating in his cold concrete bubble, with nothing to moor him but the bright silent images of the Spains moving across their windows and the thick-twined anchor rope of his love for them: he had never dreamed that his gift might not do exactly what he wanted it to, that Jenny might not react the way he had planned; that, with all the best intentions in the world, he might smash down the frail scaffolding that kept her standing. I said, 'So what you told me the first time we met, about that evening being an ordinary one – you and Pat giving the children their bath, and Pat making Jack laugh by playing with Emma's dress: that wasn't true.'

A wan, bitter half-smile. 'God, that. I forgot I said that. I didn't want you thinking we were . . . It should've been true. We used to do that, back before. But no: I washed the kids, Pat stayed down in the sitting room – he said he had "high hopes" for the hole by the sofa. He had such high hopes, he hadn't even eaten dinner with us, in case the hole did something amazing meanwhile. He said he wasn't hungry, he'd get a sandwich or something later. Back when we were first married, we used to lie in bed and talk about someday when we had kids: what they'd look like, what we'd name them; Pat used to joke about how we'd all have family dinner round the table together every night, no matter what, even when the kids were horrible teenagers and they hated our guts . . .'

Jenny was still staring up at the ceiling and blinking hard, but a tear escaped, trickled down into the soft hair at her temple. 'And now here we were, with Jack banging his fork on the table and yelling, "Daddy Daddy Daddy come here!" over and over, because Pat was in the sitting room, still in his pyjamas from last night, staring at a hole. And Emma with her fingers in her ears screaming at Jack to shut up, and me not even trying to make them both be quiet because I didn't have the energy. I was just trying so hard to make it through the rest of the day without doing anything else insane. I just wanted to sleep.'

Me and Richie, on that first torch-lit walkthrough, spotting the rumpled duvet and knowing someone had been in bed when it all turned bad. I said, 'So you bathed the children and put them to bed. And then . . . ?'

'I just went to bed too. I could hear Pat moving around downstairs, but I couldn't face him — I couldn't handle hearing all about what the animal was doing, not that night — so I stayed upstairs. I tried to read my book for a while, but I couldn't concentrate. I wanted to put something in front of the drawer where the pin was, like something heavy, but I knew that would be a crazy thing to do. So in the end I switched off the light and I tried to go to sleep.'

Jenny stopped. Neither of us wanted her to go on. I said, 'And then?'

'Emma started crying. I don't know what time it was; I was dozing off and on, waiting for Pat to come up, listening out for what he was doing downstairs. Emma's always had nightmares, ever since she was tiny. I thought that was all it was, just a nightmare. I got up and went in to her, and she was sitting up in bed, totally *terrified*. She was crying so hard she could barely breathe; she was trying to say something, but she couldn't talk. I sat down on the bed and I hugged her — she was clinging on to me, sobbing her poor little heart out. When she calmed down a bit I said, "What's wrong, sweetie? Tell Mummy and I'll fix it." And she said . . .'

Jenny caught a deep, open-mouthed gasp of breath. 'She said . . . "It's in my wardrobe, Mum. It was going to come get me."

'I said, "What's in your wardrobe, sweetie?" I still thought it was just a dream or maybe a spider, she hates spiders. But Emma went, she went, "*The animal.* Mummy, the animal, it's the animal, it's laughing at me with its teeth—" She was starting to go to bits again. I said, "There's no animal here; it was just a dream," and she *wailed*, this awful high noise that didn't even sound human. I grabbed her, I even shook her – I've never done that before, ever. I was scared she was going to wake Jack, but it wasn't just that. I was . . .' That great gasp again. 'I was scared of the animal. That it would hear her and come after her. I knew there was nothing there. I knew that. But I still – the thought of it, Jesus, I had to make Emma shut up before . . . She stopped wailing, thank God, but she was still crying and clutching at me, and she was pointing at her schoolbag – it was on the floor by her bed. All I could make out was "in there, in there," so I switched on the bedside lamp and dumped everything out of the bag. When Emma saw that . . .'

Jenny's finger hovered over the drawing. 'This. She went, "*That!* Mummy, that! It's in my wardrobe!"'

The gasping was gone; her voice had stilled, slowed, just a small pinpoint of life scratching at the thick silence of the room. 'The bedside lamp's only little, and the paper was in a shadow. All I could see was the eyes and the teeth, in the middle of black. I said, "What is it, sweetie?" But I already knew.

'Emma said – she was starting to get her breath back, but she was still doing that hiccuppy thing – she said, "The animal. The animal Daddy wants to catch. I'm sorry, Mummy, I'm so so sorry—"

'I put on my sensible voice and I went, "Don't be silly. There's nothing to be sorry for. But we've talked about that animal before. It isn't real, remember? It's just a game Daddy plays. He's just a bit confused. You know that."

'She looked so wretched. Emma's sensitive; things she doesn't understand, they just rip her up inside. She knelt up in bed and hugged me around the neck, and she whispered – right into my ear, like she was scared something would hear her – "I see it. For days and days now. I'm sorry, Mummy, I tried not to . . ."

'I wanted to die. I wanted to just melt into a little puddle and soak away into the carpet. I thought I'd kept them *safe*. That was all I ever wanted. But that animal, that *thing*, it had got everywhere. It was inside Emma, inside her head. I would have killed it if I could have, I'd have done it with my bare hands, but I couldn't do that because it didn't *exist*. Emma was going, "I know I wasn't meant to tell about it, but Miss Carey said draw your home and it just came out, I'm sorry, I'm sorry . . ." I knew I had to get the kids away, but there was nowhere I could take them. It had escaped; it had got outside the house, too. There wasn't anywhere left that was safe. And nothing I could do was worth anything, because I couldn't trust myself to do things right any more.'

Jenny laid her fingertips on the drawing, lightly and with a kind of bleak wonder: this tiny thing, this slip of paper and crayon that had changed the world.

'I kept so calm. I said to Emma, "It's all right, sweetie. I know you tried. Mummy's going to make it all OK. You go to sleep now. I'll stay right here so the animal can't get you. OK?" I opened her wardrobe and looked in all the corners, so she could see there was nothing there. I put all her things back in her schoolbag. Then I switched off the lamp again and I sat there on the bed, holding her hand, till she fell asleep – it took a while, she kept opening her eyes to double-check that I was still there, but she was exhausted from getting so freaked out; in the end she went off. And then I took the drawing and I went downstairs to find Pat.

'He was on the kitchen floor. He had the cupboard door open, this cupboard where he'd made a hole at the back, and he was *crouching* in front of it like an animal, like this great big animal waiting to pounce. He had one of his hands in the cupboard, spread out on the shelf. In the other hand he had this vase, this silver vase, it was our wedding present from my grandmother – I used to put it on the windowsill in our bedroom with pink roses in it, like I had in my bouquet, to remind us of our wedding day . . . Pat was holding it by the neck, holding it up like he was about to smash something with it. And there was this *knife*, one of these really sharp cooking knives that we bought back when we used to do Gordon Ramsay recipes, it was on the floor right next to him. I said, "What are you *doing*?"

'Pat said, "Shut up. Listen." I listened but I couldn't hear anything, there was nothing *there*! So I said that: "There's nothing there."

'Pat laughed – he didn't even look at me, he was just staring into this *cupboard* – and he said, he said, "That's what it wants you to think. It's right there, inside the wall, I can hear it, if you'd shut up for a second you'd hear it too. It's smart, it keeps very quiet till I'm just about ready to give up and right then it does a quick little scrabble, just to keep me on my toes, it's like it's laughing at me. Well fuck that, I'm smarter than it is. I'm staying one step ahead. Yeah, so it's got plans, but I've got plans too. I'm keeping my eye on the prize. I'm ready to rumble."

'I go, "What are you talking about?" and Pat goes – he's hunched over towards me, practically whispering, like he thinks this thing can *understand* him – "I finally figured out what it wants. It wants *me*. The kids too, and you, it wants all of us, but most of all it wants me. That's what it's after. No wonder I couldn't catch it before, fucking about with peanut butter and hamburger— So here I am. Come on, motherfucker, I'm right here, come and get me!" He's like *beckoning* at the hole with the hand in the cupboard, like a guy trying to get another guy to go for him. He goes, "It can smell me, I'm so close it can practically taste me, and that's driving it wild. It's smart, all right, it's careful, but sooner or later – no, sooner, I can feel it, any minute – it's going to want me so bad that it can't be careful any more. It's going to lose control and it's going to stick its head out of that hole and take a big bite of my hand and then I'll grab it and *bam bam bam not so smart now motherfucker not so smart now are you—*"'

Jenny was shaking with the memory. 'His face was all red, all covered in sweat, his eyes were practically popping out – he was smashing the vase down over and over, like he was hitting something. He looked *insane*. I yelled at him to shut up, I was like, "This has to stop, I've had enough, look at this, *look*—" and I shoved this thing in his face.' She had both palms on the drawing, pressing it into the blanket. 'I was trying to keep it down because I didn't want to wake up the babies, I couldn't let them see their dad like that, but I guess I was loud enough that at least I got Pat's attention. He stopped waving the vase around and grabbed this and stared at it for a while, and then he was like, "So?"

'I said, "Emma drew that. She drew it in school." He was still looking at me like, "What's the big deal?" I wanted to *scream* at him. Pat and I don't have screaming rows, we're not like that – weren't. But he was just squatting there looking at me like all this was totally normal, and it made me – I could barely even stand to look at him. I knelt down next to him on the floor, and I said, "Pat. Listen to me. You have to listen to me. This stops now. There's *nothing there*. There never *was* anything there. Before the kids wake up tomorrow morning, you fill in every single one of these bloody holes, and I'll take these bloody monitors down to the beach and I'll throw them in the sea. And then we'll forget this whole thing and we'll never mention it again, *ever ever ever*."

'I actually thought I'd got through. Pat put down the vase and he brought his *bait* hand out of the cupboard, and he leaned over and took hold of my hands, and I thought . . .' A quick breath that caught Jenny off guard, juddered her whole body. 'They just felt so warm, his hands. So strong, just like always, just like they've always felt since we were teenagers. He was looking straight at me, properly – he looked like Pat again. For that one second, I thought it was OK. I thought Pat was going to give me a hug, a big long hug, and then we'd find a way to fix the holes together, and then we'd go to bed and sleep wrapped round each other. And someday, when we were old, we'd have a laugh about the whole insane thing. I actually thought that.'

The pain in her voice went so deep that I had to look away in case I saw it open up in front of me, a blackness gaping right down to the core of the earth. Bubbles in the magnolia paint on the wall. Red leaves rattling and scraping at the window.

'Except then Pat goes, "Jenny. My sweetheart. My lovely little missus. I know I've been a crap husband the last while. God, I totally know that. I haven't been able to look after you, I haven't been able to look after the kids, and you guys have stood by me while I sat here and let us fall deeper into the shite every day."

'I tried to tell him it wasn't about money, money didn't even matter any more, but he wouldn't let me. He shook his head and went, "Shhh. Hang on. I need to say this, OK? I know you don't deserve to live like this. You deserve all the fancy clothes and expensive curtains in the world. Emma deserves dance lessons. Jack deserves tickets to Man U. And it's been killing me that I can't give you that stuff. But this, at least, this one thing, *this* I can do. I can get this little fucker. We'll have it stuffed and mount it on the sitting-room wall. How's that?"

'He was stroking my hair, my cheek, and he was *smiling* at me, actually smiling – he looked honest-to-God happy. *Joyful,* like the answer to all our problems was shining right there in front of him and he knew exactly how to catch it. He went, "Trust me. Please. I finally know what I'm doing. Our lovely house, Jen, it's going to be all safe again. The kids, they're going to be safe. Don't worry, baby. It's OK. I won't let this thing get you."'

Jenny's voice was rocking wildly; her hands were fisted in the bedclothes. 'I didn't know how to say it to him: that was *exactly* what he was doing. He was letting this *thing*, this animal, this stupid insane *imaginary it was never even there* animal, he was letting it eat Jack and Emma alive. Every second he sat there staring at that hole, he was giving it another bite out of their minds. If he didn't want it to have them, *all he had to do* was get up! Fix the holes! Put the bloody vase *away*!'

Her voice was so thick with damage and tears and rising hysteria, I could barely make out the words. Maybe someone else would have patted her shoulder and come out with the perfect thing to say. I couldn't touch her. I took the glass of water from her bedside table and held it out. Jenny buried her face in it, choking and coughing, until she got some water down and the terrible noises subsided.

She said, down to the glass, 'So then I just sat there next to him, on the floor. It was freezing cold, but I couldn't get up. I was too dizzy, it was the worst it's ever been, everything kept sliding and tilting. I thought if I tried to stand up I'd fall over face-first and smash my head on one of the cupboards, and I knew I couldn't do that. I think we sat there for a couple of hours, I don't know. I just held onto this thing' – the drawing, spattered with drops of water now – 'and I stared at it. I was *terrified* that if I stopped looking at it even for a second, I'd forget it had ever existed, and then I'd forget that I needed to do something about it.'

She wiped at her face, for water or for tears, I couldn't tell. 'I kept thinking about that JoJo's pin, up in my drawer. How happy we were back then. How that had to be why I'd dug it out of some box: because I was trying to find something happy. All I could think was *How did we get here?* I felt like there had to be something we had done, me and Pat, to make this happen, and if I could just find that, then maybe I could change it and everything would be different. But I couldn't find it. I thought right back to the first time we kissed, when we were sixteen – it was on the beach in Monkstown, it was evening but it was summer so it was still bright and so warm, the warm air on my arms. We were sitting on a rock talking, and Pat just leaned over to me and . . . I went through every moment I could remember, every single one, but I couldn't find anything. I couldn't work out how we had ever got here, this kitchen floor, from where we started out.'

She had quieted. Behind the fine gold haze of hair, her face was still, turned inwards. Her voice was steady. I was the one who was afraid.

Jenny said, 'Everything looked so weird. It felt like the light kept getting brighter, till it turned into searchlights everywhere; or like there had been something wrong with my eyes for months, some kind of haze blurring them up, and all of a sudden it was gone and I could see again. Everything looked so shiny and so sharp it hurt, and it was all so *beautiful* – just ordinary stuff like the fridge and the toaster and the table, they looked like they were made out of light, floating, like they were angel things that would blow you to atoms if you touched them. And then I started floating too, I was floating up off the ground, and I knew I had to do something fast, before I just drifted away through the window, and the kids and Pat were left there to get eaten up alive. I said, "Pat, we have to get out now" – at least I think I did, I'm not sure. He didn't hear me, either way. He didn't notice when I got up, didn't even notice I was leaving – he was whispering something to that hole, I couldn't hear what . . . Going up the stairs took forever because my feet weren't touching the ground, I couldn't move forward, I kept hanging there trying to go up in slow motion. I knew I should be scared that I wasn't going to get there in time, but I wasn't; I didn't feel anything at all, just numb and sad. So sad.'

The thin bloodied thread of her voice, winding through the dark of that night to its monstrous heart. The tears had stopped; this place was far beyond tears. 'I gave them kisses, Emma and Jack. I said to them, "It's OK. It's OK. Mummy loves you so much. I'm coming. Wait for me; I'll be there as soon as I can."'

Maybe I should have made her say it. I couldn't open my mouth. The humming was a fretsaw whining at my skull; if I moved, breathed, I would split into a thousand pieces. My mind was flailing for something else, anything. Dina. Quigley. Richie, white-faced.

'Pat was still on the kitchen floor. The knife was right there beside him. I picked it up and he turned around and I stuck it into his chest. He stood up and he went, "What . . . ?" He was staring at his chest and he looked so amazed, like he couldn't work out what had happened, he just couldn't understand. I said, "Pat we have to go," and I did it again and then he grabbed me, my wrists, and we were fighting, all over the kitchen – he was trying not to hurt me, just hold me, but he was so much stronger and I was so scared he would get the knife away – I was kicking him, I was screaming, "Pat hurry we have to hurry . . ." He was going, "Jenny Jenny Jenny" – he looked like Pat again, he was looking at me properly and it was terrible, why couldn't he have looked at me like that before?'

O'Kelly. Geri. My father. I slid my eyes out of focus till Jenny was just a blur of white and gold. Her voice in my ears stayed mercilessly clear, that fine thread pulling me onwards, slicing deep.

'There was blood all over. It felt like he was getting weaker, but so was I – I was so *tired* . . . I went, "Please, Pat, please stop, we have to go find the kids, we can't leave them alone there," and he just froze, stopped still in the middle of the floor and stared at me. I could hear us both breathing, these big ugly gasping noises. Pat said – his voice, Jesus, the sound in his voice – he went, 'Oh, God. What did you do?''

'His hands had gone all loose on my wrists. I got away and I hit him with the knife again. He didn't even notice. He started to head for the kitchen door, and then he fell over. He just fell. He was trying to crawl for a second, but he stopped.'

Jenny's eyes shut for a second. So did mine. The one thing I had been hoping for Pat, the one thing that had been left to hope, was that he had never known about the children.

Jenny said, 'I sat down beside him and I stuck the knife in my chest and then in my stomach, but it didn't *work* – my hands were all, they were all slippy and I was shaking so hard and I wasn't *strong* enough! I was crying and I tried my face and my throat and everywhere, but it was no good: my arms were like jelly. I couldn't even sit up any more, I was lying on the floor, but I was still *there*. I . . . Oh, God.' The shudder galvanised her whole body. 'I thought I was going to get stuck there. I thought the neighbours would have heard us fighting and called the cops, and an ambulance was going to come and . . . I've never been so frightened. Never. Never.'

She was rigid, staring into the folds and valleys of that worn blanket, seeing things. She said, 'I prayed. I knew I didn't have any right to, but I did anyway. I thought maybe God would strike me dead for it, but that was what I was praying for anyway. I prayed to the Virgin Mary; I thought maybe she might understand. I said the Hail Mary – I couldn't remember half the words, it was so long since I'd said it, but I said the bits I could remember. I said *Please*, over and over. *Please.*'

I said, 'And that's when Conor arrived.'

Jenny's head came up and she stared at me, confused, as if she had forgotten I was there. After a moment she shook her head. 'No. Conor didn't do anything. I haven't seen Conor for, since, for years—'

'Mrs Spain, we can prove he was in the house that night. We can prove that some of your wounds weren't self-inflicted. That puts at least part of the attack on Conor. Right now, he's going down for three murders and one attempted. If you want to get him out of trouble, the best thing you can do for him is tell me exactly what happened.'

I couldn't get any force into my voice. It felt like a struggle underwater, slowed, weary; both of us were too drained to remember why we were fighting each other, but we kept going because there was nothing else. I asked, 'How long did it take him to get there?'

Jenny was more exhausted than I was. Her fight ran out first. After a moment her eyes drifted away again, and she said, 'I don't know. It felt like ages.'

Out of the sleeping bag, down the scaffolding, over the wall, up the garden and turn the key in the back door: a minute, maybe two, tops. Conor must have been drowsing, wrapped snug and warm in his sleeping bag and in the certainty of the Spains' lives sailing onwards below him, in their shining little boat. Maybe the fighting had woken him: Jenny's muffled screams, Pat's shouts, the faint bangs of overturning furniture. I wondered what he had seen when he leaned to the windowsill, yawning and rubbing his eyes; how long it had taken him to understand what was happening, and to realise that he was real enough to smash through the wall of glass that had held him away from his best friends for so long.

Jenny said, 'He must have come in through the back door; I felt the wind on me when it opened. It smelled like the sea. He picked me up off the floor, my head, he pulled me into his lap. He was making this sound, like whining or moaning, like a dog that's got hit by a car. At first I didn't even recognise him – he'd got so thin and so white, and he looked so terrible; his face was all the wrong shapes, he didn't even look like a human being. I thought he was something else – like an angel maybe, because I'd prayed so hard, or something awful that had come up out of the sea. Then he said, "Oh Jesus, oh Jenny, oh Jesus, what happened?" And his voice was the same as always. The same as when we were kids.'

She made a vague motion towards her stomach. 'He was pulling at me, here, at my pyjamas – I guess he was trying to see . . . There was blood all over him but I couldn't understand why, when I didn't hurt anywhere. I went, "Conor, help me, you have to help me." At first he didn't understand, he went, "It's OK, it's OK, I'll get an ambulance," and he was trying to go for the phone, but I screamed. I grabbed hold of him and I screamed, "No!" till he stopped.'

And the fingernail that had split as Emma fought for her life, that had snagged for an instant on the pink wool of her embroi-dered cushion, tore away in the thick weave of Conor's jumper. Neither he nor Jenny had noticed – how could they? And later, at home, when Conor wrenched off his bloody clothes and threw them on the floor, he would never have seen that fragment falling away into the carpet. He had been blinded, seared, just praying that someday he would be able to see something other than that kitchen.

'I went, "You don't understand. No ambulance. I don't want an ambulance." He was going, "You're going to be fine, they'll get you fixed up in no time—" He was holding me so tight – he had my face pressed into his jumper. It felt like it took me forever to get away enough that I could talk to him.'

Jenny was still watching nothing, but her lips were parted, loose as a child's, and her face was almost tranquil. For her, the bad part was over; this had looked like a happy ending. 'I wasn't frightened any more. I knew exactly what needed doing, like it was all written out in front of me. The drawing was there on the floor, Emma's awful drawing, and I said, "That thing there, take it away. Put it in your pocket and burn it when you get home." Conor jammed it into his pocket – I don't think he even saw it, he just did what I said. If anyone had found it they could have guessed, like you guessed, and I couldn't let anyone find out, could I? They'd think Pat was crazy. He didn't deserve that.'

'No,' I said. 'He didn't.' But when Conor had found the drawing, later, at home, he hadn't been able to burn it. This last message from his godchild: he had saved it, one final souvenir.

'Then,' Jenny said, 'then I told him what I needed him to do. I said, "Here, here's the knife, do it, Conor, please, you have to." And I shoved the knife into his hand.

'His eyes. He looked at the knife and then he looked down at me like he was afraid of me, like I was the most terrifying thing he had ever seen. He went, "You're not thinking straight," but I was like, "Yes, I am. I am" – I was trying to scream at him again, but it came out just a whisper. I went, "Pat's dead, I stabbed him and now he's dead—"

'Conor went, "*Why?* Jenny, Christ, what *happened?*"'

Jenny made a painful scraping sound that could have been some kind of laugh. 'If we'd had a month or two, then maybe . . . I just went, "No ambulance. Please." Conor went, "Wait. Hang on. Hang on," and he laid me down and crawled over to Pat. He turned Pat's head and he did something, I don't know what, tried to open his eyes or something – he didn't say anything but I saw his face, I saw the look on his face, so I knew. I was glad about that, at least.'

I wondered how many times Conor had re-run those few minutes in his head, staring at the ceiling of his cell, changing a different tiny thing each time: *If I hadn't fallen asleep. If I had got up the second I heard noises. If I had run faster. If I hadn't fumbled getting the key in the door.* If he had made it into that kitchen just a few minutes earlier, he would have been in time to save Pat, at least.

Jenny said, 'But then Conor – he started trying to stand up. He was trying to pull himself up on the computer desk – he kept falling back, like he was slipping on the blood or maybe he was dizzy, but I could tell he was aiming for the kitchen door. He was trying to go upstairs. I got hold of him, the leg of his trousers, and I went, "No. Don't go up there. They're dead, too. I had to get them out." Conor – he just went down on his hands and knees. He said – he had his head down, but I heard him anyway – he said, "Ah, Jesus Christ."'

Up until then he must have thought it was a domestic fight turned terrible, love transformed under all those tons of pressure into something diamond-hard that sliced flesh and bone. Maybe he had even thought it was self-defence, that Pat's mind had boiled over at last and he had gone for Jenny. Once she told him about the children, there had been no place left for answers, for comfort, for ambulances or doctors or tomorrows.

'I went, "I need to be with the babies. I need to be with Pat. Please, Conor, please, get me out of here."

'Conor made this coughing noise, like he was going to get sick. He said, "I can't." He sounded like he was hoping this was all some kind of nightmare, like he was trying to find some way to wake up and make it all go away. I managed to get over closer to him – I had to drag myself, my legs had gone all numb and shaky. I got hold of his wrist and I went, "Conor, you have to. I can't stay here. Please hurry. Please."'

Jenny's voice was fading, barely more than a hoarse flicker of sound; she was at the end of her strength. 'He sat down beside me, and he turned my head so my face was against his chest again. He said, "It's OK. It's OK. Close your eyes." He was stroking my hair. I said, "Thank you," and I shut my eyes.'

Jenny spread her hands, palms up, on the blanket. She said simply, 'That's all.'

Conor had believed it was the last thing he would ever do for Jenny. And before he left, he had done two last things for Pat: wiped the computer, and taken the weapons. No wonder the delete job had been fast and messy; every second Conor stayed in that house had been shredding his mind. But he had known that if we read the flood of madness on that computer, and if there was no evidence that anyone else had been in the house, we would never look beyond Pat.

He must have known, too, that if he shoved it all onto Pat he would walk away safe, or at least safer. But Conor had believed the same thing I believed: you can't do that. He had missed his chance to save the life that Pat should have had. Instead, he had put himself on the line to save those twenty-nine years from being branded with a lie.

When we came to get him, he had trusted in silence, in his gloves, in the hope that we couldn't prove anything. Then I had told him that Jenny was alive; and he had done one more thing for her, before I could force the truth out of her. Probably a part of him had welcomed the chance.

Jenny said, 'See? Conor only did what I wanted him to do.'

Her hand was struggling across the blanket again, reaching for me, and there was a flare of urgency in her voice. I said, 'He assaulted you. By both of your accounts, he was trying to kill you. That's a crime. Consent isn't a defence to attempted murder.'

'I *made* him do it. You can't put him in jail for that.'

I said, 'That depends. If you testify to all of this in court, then yes, there's an excellent chance Conor will walk away. Juries are only human; sometimes they bend the rules and go with their own consciences instead. Even if you give me an official statement, I can probably do something with that. But as it stands, all we've got to go on is the evidence and Conor's confession. Those make him a triple murderer.'

'But he didn't *kill* anyone! I *told* you what happened. You said, if I told you—'

'You told me your version. Conor told me his. The evidence doesn't rule out either one, and Conor's the one who's willing to go on the record. That means his version carries a lot more weight than yours.'

'But you believe me. Right? If you believe me—'

Her hand had reached mine. She clutched my fingers like a child. Hers were so thin I could feel the bones moving, and terribly cold.

I said, 'Even if I do, there's nothing I can do about it. I'm not a layperson on a jury; I don't have the luxury of acting on my conscience. My job is to follow the evidence. If you don't want Conor going to jail, Mrs Spain, then you need to be in court to save him. After what he did for you, I think you owe him that much.'

I heard myself: pompous, self-righteous, vapid, the kind of puffed-up little prick who spends his schooldays lecturing his classmates on the evils of alcohol and getting his head slammed into locker doors. If I believed in curses, I would believe that this is mine: when it matters most, in the moments when I know with the greatest clarity exactly what needs to be done, everything I say comes out wrong.

Jenny said – to the machines and the walls and the air, as much as to me – 'He'll be all right.'

She was planning her note again. 'Mrs Spain,' I said. 'I understand a little of what you're going through. I know you probably don't believe me, but I swear on everything that's holy, it's the truth. I understand what you want to do. But there are still people who need you. There are still things you need to do. You can't just let go of those. They're yours.'

Just for a second, I thought Jenny had heard me. Her eyes met mine, startled and clear, as if in that instant she had caught a glimpse of the world still turning, outside this sealed room: children outgrowing their clothes and old people forgetting old hurts, lovers coming together and coming apart, tides wearing rock away to sand, leaves falling to cover seeds germinating deep in the cold earth. For a second I thought that, by some miracle, I had found the right words.

Then her eyes fell away and she twisted her hand out of mine – I hadn't realised, until then, that I was squeezing it tight enough to hurt. She said, 'I don't even know what Conor was doing there. When I woke up in here, when I started remembering what happened, I thought probably he was never there at all; probably I'd imagined him. Right up until you said it today, I thought that. What was he . . . ? How did he get there?'

I said, 'He had been spending a bit of time in Brianstown. When he saw that you and Pat were in trouble, he came to help.'

I saw the pieces start falling into place, slowly and painfully. 'The pin,' Jenny said. 'The JoJo's pin. Was that . . . ? Was that *Conor*?'

I had too little mind left to figure out which answer was the most likely to hold her, or the least cruel. The second of silence told her. 'Oh, God. And I thought . . .' A quick, high gasp, like a hurt child's. 'The break-ins, too?'

'I can't go into that.'

Jenny nodded. That surge of fight had used up the last of her strength; she looked almost past moving. After a while she said quietly, 'Poor Conor.'

'Yes,' I said. 'I suppose so.'

We sat there for a long time. Jenny didn't speak, didn't look at me; she was done. She leaned her head back on the pillows and watched her fingers tracing the creases in the sheet, slowly, steadily, over and over. After a while her eyes closed.

In the corridor two women passed by talking and laughing, shoes clicking briskly on the tiled floor. My throat hurt from the dry air. Outside the window, the light had moved on; I didn't remember hearing rain, but the leaves looked dark and drenched, shivering against a mottled, sulky sky. Jenny's head fell to one side. Small ragged shudders caught at her chest, until gradually the ebb and flow of her breath smoothed them away.

I still don't know why I stayed there. Maybe my legs wouldn't move, or maybe I was afraid to leave Jenny alone; or maybe some part of me was still hoping that she would turn in her sleep and murmur the secret password, the thing that would unlock the code, magic the gibbering mess of shadows to black and white, and show me how all of this made sense.

# 19

Fiona was in the corridor, hunched in one of the plastic chairs that were scattered along the wall, wrapping a ratty striped scarf around her wrists. Beyond her, the waxy green shine of the floor stretched on for what seemed like miles.

Her head snapped up when I clicked the door shut behind me. 'How's Jenny? Is she OK?'

'She's asleep.' I pulled up another chair and sat down next to her. The red duffel coat smelled of cold air and smoke: she had been outside for a cigarette.

'I should go in. She gets freaked out if no one's there when she wakes up.'

I said, 'How long have you known?'

Instantly Fiona's face went blank. 'Known what?'

There were a thousand clever ways I could have done it. I had nothing left for any of them. 'Your sister just confessed to the murders of her family. I'm pretty sure this isn't a big surprise to you.'

The blank look didn't budge. 'She's off her head on painkillers. She hasn't got a clue what she's talking about.'

'Believe me, Ms Rafferty, she knew exactly what she was saying. All the details of her story match the evidence.'

'You bullied her into it. The state she's in, you could make her say anything. I could report you.'

She was as exhausted as I was; she couldn't even manage to put a tough edge on it. 'Ms Rafferty,' I said. 'Please, let's not do this. Anything you say to me here is off the record; I can't even prove we ever had this conversation. The same goes for your sister's confession: legally, it doesn't exist. I'm just trying to find a way to end this mess before any more damage gets done.'

Fiona scanned my face, tired red eyes trying to focus. The harsh lights turned her skin greyish and pitted; she looked older and sicker than Jenny. Down the corridor a child was crying, immense bereft sobs, like the world had shattered around him.

Something, I don't know what, told Fiona I meant it. Unusual, I had thought when we interviewed her, perceptive; back then I hadn't been pleased, but it worked for me in the end. The fight went out of her body, and her head fell back against the wall. She said, 'Why did she . . . ? She loved them so *much*. What the hell . . . ? *Why?*'

'I can't tell you that. When did you know?'

After a moment Fiona said, 'When you told me Conor said he'd done it. I knew he hadn't. No matter what had happened to him since I saw him, no matter if he had another fight with Pat and Jenny, even if he'd completely lost his mind: he wouldn't do that.'

There was no doubt in her voice, not a thread. For a strange, exhausted moment I envied them both, her and Conor Brennan. Just about everything in this life is treacherous, ready to twist and shape-shift at any second; it seemed to me that the whole world would be a different place if you had someone you were certain of, certain to the bone, or if you could be that to someone else. I know husbands and wives who are that to each other. I know partners.

Fiona said, 'At first I thought you were making it up, but I'm mostly pretty good at telling when people are lying. So I tried to think why Conor would say that. Probably he'd have done it to protect Pat, to keep him out of jail; but Pat was dead. That left Jenny.'

I heard the small, painful sound of her swallowing. 'So,' she said, 'I knew.'

'That's why you didn't tell Jenny that Conor had been arrested.'

'Yeah. I didn't know what she'd do – if she'd try to own up, if she'd freak out and have a relapse or something . . .'

I said, 'You were sure she was guilty, straightaway. You were positive Conor would never do this, but you didn't feel the same way about your own sister.'

'You think I should have.'

'I don't know what you should have thought,' I said. Rule Number Something: suspects and witnesses need to believe you're omniscient; you never let them see you being anything other than sure. I couldn't remember, any more, why it mattered. 'I'm just wondering what made the difference.'

She twisted the scarf around her hand, trying to find the words. After a moment she said, 'Jenny does everything right, and everything goes right for her. That's how her life's always worked. When something finally went wrong, when Pat was out of work . . . She didn't know how to handle it. That's why I was scared that she was going crazy, back when she said that about someone breaking in. I'd been worried ever since Pat lost his job. And I was right: she was going to pieces. Is that . . . ? Was that why she . . . ?'

I didn't answer. Fiona said, low and fierce, pulling the scarf tighter, 'I should have known. She did a good job of hiding it, after that, but if I'd been paying more attention, if I'd been out there more . . .'

There was nothing she could have done. I didn't tell her that; I needed her guilt. Instead I said, 'Have you brought this up with Jenny?'

'*No.* Jesus, no. Either she'd tell me to fuck off and never come back, or she'd tell me . . .' A flinch. 'You think I want to hear her talk about it?'

'How about with anyone else?'

'No. Like who? This isn't exactly something you tell your flatmates. And I don't want my mum to know. Ever.'

'Do you have any proof that you're right? Anything Jenny's said, anything you've seen? Or is it just instinct?'

'No. No proof. If I'm wrong, I'll be – God, I'd be so happy.'

I said, 'I don't think you're wrong. But here's the problem: I don't have proof either. Jenny's confession to me can't be used in court. The evidence we've got isn't enough to arrest her, never mind convict her. Unless I can get something more, she's going to walk out of here a free woman.'

'Good.' Fiona caught something in my face, or thought she did, and shrugged wearily. 'What do you expect? I know probably she should go to prison, but I don't care. She's my sister; I love her. And if she got arrested, my mum would find out. I know I'm not supposed to hope someone gets away with this, but I do. There you go.'

'And what about Conor? You told me you still care about him. Are you seriously going to let him spend the rest of his life in prison? Not that it'll be long. Do you know what other criminals think of child-killers? Do you want to know what they do to them?'

Her eyes had widened. 'Hang on. You're not going to send Conor to *jail*. You know he didn't *do* this.'

'Not me, Ms Rafferty. The system. I can't just ignore the fact that I've got more than enough evidence to charge him; whether he's convicted or not is up to the lawyers, the judge and the jury. I just work with what I've got. If I've got nothing on Jenny, then I'll have to go with Conor.'

Fiona shook her head. 'You won't do it,' she said.

That certainty rang in her voice again, clear as struck bronze. It felt like a strange gift, warm as a tiny flame, in this cold place where I would never have expected to find it. This woman I shouldn't even have been talking to, this woman I didn't even like: for her, of all people, I was certainty.

'No,' I said. I couldn't make myself lie to her. 'I won't.'

She nodded. 'Good,' she said, on a small tired sigh.

I said, 'Conor isn't the one you should be worrying about. Your sister's planning to kill herself, first chance she gets.'

I made it as brutal as I could. I expected shock maybe, panic, but Fiona didn't even look around; she kept staring off down the corridor, at the dingy posters proclaiming the saving power of hand sanitiser. She said, 'As long as she's in the hospital, she won't do anything.'

She already knew. It hit me that she could actually want it to happen – as a mercy, like Richie had, or as punishment, or out of some ferocious sister-tangle of emotions that not even she would ever understand. I said, 'So what are you planning to do when they let her out?'

'Watch her.'

'Just you? Twenty-four-seven?'

'Me and my mum. She doesn't know, but she figures after what happened, Jenny might . . .' Fiona's head jerked, and she focused harder on the posters. She said again, 'We'll watch her.'

I said, 'For how long? A year, two, ten? And what about when you need to go to work, and your mother needs to have a shower or get some sleep?'

'You can get nurses. Carers.'

'If you've won the Lotto, you can. Have you checked how much they cost?'

'We'll find the money if we have to.'

'From Pat's life insurance?' That silenced her. 'And what happens when Jenny fires the nurse? She's a free adult: if she doesn't want someone looking after her, and we both know she won't, there's not a bloody thing you can do about it. Rock and a hard place, Ms Rafferty: you can't keep her safe unless you get her locked up.'

'Prison isn't exactly safe. We'll look after her.'

The sharp edge to her voice said I was getting to her. I said, 'You probably will, for a while. You might manage weeks, or even months. But sooner or later, you're going to take your eye off the ball. Maybe your boyfriend will ring you up wanting to chat, or your friends will be on at you to come out for a drink and a laugh, and you'll think: *Just this once. Just this once, life will let me off the hook; it won't punish me for wanting to be a normal human being, just for an hour or two. I've earned it.* Maybe you'll only leave Jenny for a minute. A minute is all it takes to find the disinfectant or the razor blades. If someone's serious enough about killing herself, she will find a way to do it. And if it happens on your watch, you'll spend the rest of your life ripping yourself to shreds.'

Fiona shoved her hands deep into the opposite sleeves of her coat. She said, 'What do you want?'

I said, 'I need Conor Brennan to come clean about what happened that night. I want you to explain to him exactly what he's doing. He's not just perverting the course of justice, he's kicking it in the teeth: he's letting Pat and Emma and Jack go into the ground while the person who murdered them walks away scot-free. And he's leaving Jenny to die.' It's one thing to do what Conor had done in a nightmare moment of howling panic and horror, Jenny clutching him with her bloody hands and begging; it's another to stand by, in the cold light of day, and let someone you love walk in front of a bus. 'If it comes from me, he'll think I'm just trying to mess with his head. From you, he'll take it on board.'

The corner of Fiona's mouth twitched in what was almost a bitter little smile. She said, 'You don't really get Conor, do you?'

I could have laughed. 'I'm pretty sure I don't, no.'

'He doesn't give a damn about the course of justice, or Jenny's debt to society, or any of that stuff. He just cares about Jenny. He has to know what she wants to do. If he confessed to you guys, that's why: so she can get the chance.' That twitch again. 'Probably he'd think I'm being selfish, trying to save her just because I want her here. Maybe I am. I don't care.'

*Trying to save her.* She was on my side, if I could just find a way to use that. 'Then tell him Jenny's already dead. He knows she'll be out of hospital any day: tell him they let her out, and she took the first chance she got. If she's not there to be protected any more, he might as well go ahead and save his own arse.'

Fiona was already shaking her head. 'He'd know I was lying. He knows Jenny. There's no way she'd . . . She wouldn't go without leaving a note to get him out. No way.'

We had lowered our voices, like conspirators. I said, 'Then do you think you could convince Jenny to make an official statement? Beg her, guilt-trip her, talk about the children, about Pat, about Conor; say whatever you need to say. I've had no luck, but coming from you—'

She was still shaking her head. 'She's not going to listen to me. Would you, if you were her?'

Both our eyes went to that closed door. 'I don't know,' I said. I would have been boiling over with frustration – for a second I thought of Dina, gnawing at her arm – if I had had anything left. 'I haven't got a clue.'

'I don't want her to die.'

All of a sudden Fiona's voice was thick and wobbling. She was about to cry. I said, 'Then we need evidence.'

'You said you don't *have* any.'

'I don't. And at this point, we're not going to get any.'

'Then what do we *do*?' She pressed her fingers to her cheeks, swiped away tears.

When I took a breath, it felt like it was made of something more volatile and violent than air, something that burned its way through membranes into my blood. I said, 'There's only one possible solution that I can think of.'

'Then do it. Please.'

'It's not a good solution, Ms Rafferty. But very occasionally, desperate times can call for desperate measures.'

'Like what?'

'Rarely, and I'm talking *very* rarely, a crucial piece of evidence shows up through the back door. Through channels that you could call less than one hundred per cent legit.'

Fiona was staring at me. Her cheeks were still wet, but she had forgotten about crying. She said, 'You mean you could—' She stopped, started again more carefully. 'OK. What do you mean?'

It happens. Not often, nowhere near as often as you probably think, but it happens. It happens because a uniform lets some little smart-arse get under his skin; it happens because a lazy prick like Quigley gets jealous of the real detectives and our solve rates; it happens because a detective knows for a fact that this guy is about to put his wife in hospital or pimp a twelve-year-old. It happens because someone decides to trust his own mind over the rules we've sworn to follow.

I had never done it. I had always believed that if you can't get your solve the straight way, you don't deserve to get it at all. I had never even been the guy who looks the other way while the blood-stained tissue moves to the right place, or the wrap of coke gets dropped, or the witness gets coached. No one had ever asked me, probably in case I turned them in to Internal Affairs, and I had been grateful to them for not making me do it. But I knew.

I said, 'If you were to bring me a piece of evidence that linked

Jenny to the crime, soon – say, this afternoon – then I could place her under arrest before she's released from the hospital. From that moment on, she'd be under suicide watch.' All that silent time watching Jenny sleep, I had been thinking about this.

I saw the fast blink as it went in. After a long moment Fiona said, 'Me?'

'If I could come up with a way to do this without your help, I wouldn't be talking to you.'

Her face was tight, watchful. 'How do I know you're not setting me up?'

'What for? If I just wanted a solve and I was looking for someone to take the fall, I wouldn't need you: I've got Conor Brennan, all packaged up and good to go.' A porter shoved a clanging trolley past the end of the corridor, and we both jumped. I said, even more quietly, 'And I'm taking at least as much of a risk as you are. If you ever decide to tell anyone about this – tomorrow, or next month, or ten years down the line – then I'm facing an Internal Affairs investigation at the very least, and at the worst I'm looking at a review of every case I've ever touched and criminal charges of my own. I'm putting everything I've got in your hands, Ms Rafferty.'

Fiona said, 'Why?'

There were too many answers. Because of that moment, still flickering small and searingly bright inside me, when she had told me she was certain of me. Because of Richie. Because of Dina, her lips stained dark with red wine, telling me *There isn't any why.* In the end I gave her the only one I could stand to share. 'We had one piece of evidence that might have been enough, but it got destroyed. It was my fault.'

After a moment Fiona said, 'What'll they do to her? If she gets arrested. How long . . . ?'

'She'll be sent to a psychiatric hospital, at least at first. If she's found fit to stand trial, her defence will plead either not guilty or insanity. If the jury finds she was insane, then she'll go back to the hospital until the doctors decide she's no longer a danger to herself or others. If she's found guilty, then she'll probably be in prison for ten or fifteen years.' Fiona winced. 'I know it sounds like a long time, but we can make sure she gets the treatment she needs, and by the time she's my age she'll be out. She can start over, with you and Conor there to help her.'

The PA squealed into life, ordered Dr Something to Accident and Emergency please; Fiona didn't move. Finally she nodded. Every muscle in her was still stretched taut, but that wariness had gone out of her face. 'OK,' she said. 'I'm on.'

'I need you to be sure.'

'I'm sure.'

'Then here's what we're going to do,' I said. The words felt heavy as stones, sinking me. 'You're going to mention to me that you're heading out to Ocean View, to pick up supplies for your sister – her dressing gown, toiletries, her iPod, books, whatever you think she might need. I'm going to tell you that the house is still sealed and you can't go in there. Instead, I'll offer to drive out myself, go into the house and pick up whatever Jenny needs – I'll bring you along, so that you can make sure I get the right things. You can make me a list on the way. Write it out, so I've got it to show anyone who asks.'

Fiona nodded. She was watching me like a floater at a briefing, alert and attentive, memorising every word.

'Seeing the house again is going to jog your memory. All of a sudden you'll remember that, on the morning when you and the uniformed officers found the bodies, when you followed the officers into the house, you picked up something that was lying at the bottom of the stairs. You did it automatically: the house was always so tidy that anything on the floor seemed out of place, so you tucked it in your coat pocket without even realising what you were doing – your mind was on other things, after all. Does this all hang together for you?'

'The thing I picked up. What is it?'

'Jenny's got a handful of bracelets in her jewellery box. Is there one she wears a lot? Not one of those solid things, what do you call them, bangles; we need a chain. A strong one.'

Fiona thought. 'She's got a charm bracelet. It's a gold chain, a thick one; it looks pretty strong. Pat gave it to Jenny for her twenty-first, and after that he gave her charms when anything important happened – like a heart when they got married, and initials when the kids were born, and a little house when they bought the house. Jenny wears it a lot.'

'Perfect. That's the other reason why you picked it up: you knew it meant a lot to Jenny, she wouldn't want it lying around on the floor. When you saw what had happened, that blew the bracelet right out of your mind. Naturally enough, you haven't thought of it since. But while you're waiting for me to come out of the house, it'll come back to you. You'll go through your coat pockets and find it. When I get back to the car, you'll hand it over to me, on the off-chance that it might come in useful.'

Fiona said, 'How's that going to help?'

I said, 'If everything had happened exactly the way I'm describing, then you wouldn't have any way of knowing how the bracelet would fit into our investigation. So it's better you don't know it now. Less chance of you slipping up. You're going to have to trust me.'

She said, 'You're sure, too, right? This will work. It's not going to go all wrong. You're sure.'

'It isn't perfect. Some people, possibly including the prosecutor, are going to think that you knew all along and deliberately held back. And some people are going to wonder if the whole thing is just a little too convenient to be true – department politics; you don't need to know the details. I can make sure you don't get into any actual trouble – you won't be arrested for concealing evidence or obstruction of justice, nothing like that – but I can't make sure you won't get a tough time from the prosecutor, or the defender if it gets that far. They may even try to imply that you should be a suspect, given that you'd have been the beneficiary if Jenny had died.'

Fiona's eyes snapped wide. 'Don't worry,' I said. 'I promise, there's no way that could go anywhere. You're not going to get in trouble. I'm just telling you in advance: this isn't perfect. But it's the best I can do.'

'OK,' Fiona said, on a deep breath. She pulled herself upright in the chair and pushed hair off her face with both hands, ready for action. 'What comes now?'

'We need to do it, conversations and all. If we go through every step, then you'll remember the details when you give your statement, or when you're cross-examined. You'll sound truthful, because you'll be telling the truth.'

She nodded. 'So,' I said. 'Where are you off to, Ms Rafferty?'

'If Jenny's asleep, I should drive down to Brianstown. She needs some things from the house.'

Her voice was wooden and empty, nothing left in it but a sediment of sadness. I said, 'I'm afraid you can't go into the house. It's still a crime scene. If it would help, I can take you down there and get out whatever you need.'

'That'd be good. Thanks.'

I said, 'Let's go.'

I stood up, bracing myself against the wall like an old man. Fiona buttoned her coat, wrapped the scarf around her neck and tugged it tight. The child had stopped crying. We stood there in the corridor for a moment, listening by Jenny's door for a call, a movement, anything that would keep us there, but nothing came.

For the rest of my life I will remember that journey. It was the last moment when I could have turned back: picked up Jenny's bits and pieces, told Fiona I had spotted a flaw in my grand plan, dropped her back at the hospital and said goodbye. On the way to Broken Harbour that day, I was what I had given all my adult life to becoming: a murder detective, the finest on the squad, the one who got the solves and got them on the straight and narrow. By the time I left, I was something else.

Fiona huddled against the passenger door, staring out the window. When we got onto the motorway I took one hand off the wheel, found my notebook and pen and passed them to her. She balanced the notebook on her knee and I kept my speed steady while she wrote. When she was done she passed them back to me. I took a quick glance at the page: her handwriting was clear and rounded, with fast little flourishes on the tails. *Moisturiser (whatever's on bedside table or in bathroom). Jeans. Top. Jumper. Bra. Socks. Shoes (trainers). Coat. Scarf.*

Fiona said, 'She'll need clothes to leave the hospital in. Wherever she's going next.'

'Thanks,' I said.

'I can't believe I'm doing this.'

*You're doing the right thing.* It almost came out automatically. Instead I said, 'You're saving your sister's life.'

'I'm putting her in prison.'

'You're doing the best you can. That's all any of us can do.'

She said suddenly, as if the words had forced their way out, 'When we were kids I used to pray that Jenny would do something awful. I was always in trouble – nothing major, I wasn't some delinquent, just little stuff like giving my mum cheek or talking in class. Jenny never did anything bad, ever. She wasn't a goody-goody; it just came natural to her. I used to pray she'd do something really terrible, just once. Then I would tell and she'd get in trouble, and everyone would be like, "Well done, Fiona. You did the right thing. Good girl."'

She had her hands clasped together in her lap, tightly, like a child at confession. I said, 'Don't tell that story again, Ms Rafferty.'

My voice came out sharper than I meant it to. Fiona went back to staring out the window. 'I wouldn't.'

After that we didn't talk. As I turned into Ocean View a man swung out from a side road, running hard; I slammed on the brakes, but it was a jogger, eyes staring and unseeing, nostrils flaring like a runaway horse's. For a second I thought I heard the great gasps of his breath, through the glass; then he was gone. He was the only person we saw. The wind coming off the sea shook the chain-link fences, held the tall weeds in the gardens at a steep slant, shoved at the car windows.

Fiona said, 'I read in the paper they're talking about bulldozing these places, the ghost estates. Just smash them down to the ground, walk away and pretend it never happened.'

For one last second, I saw Broken Harbour the way it should

have been. The lawnmowers buzzing and the radios blasting sweet fast beats while men washed their cars in the drives, the little kids shrieking and swerving on scooters; the girls out jogging with their ponytails bouncing, the women leaning over the garden fences to swap news, the teenagers shoving and giggling and flirting on every corner; colour exploding from geranium pots and new cars and children's toys, smell of fresh paint and barbecue blowing on the sea wind. The image leaped out of the air, so strong that I saw it more clearly than all the rusting pipes and potholed dirt. I said, 'That's a shame.'

'It's good riddance. It should've happened four years ago, before this place was ever built: burn the plans and walk away. Better late than never.'

I had got the hang of the estate: I got us to the Spains' house on the first try, without asking Fiona for directions – she had vanished into her mind again, and I was happy to leave her there. When I parked the car and opened my door, the wind roared in, filling my ears and my eyes like cold water.

I said, 'I'll be back in a few minutes. Go through the motions of finding something in your pocket, just in case someone's watching.' The Gogans' curtains hadn't moved, but it was only a matter of time. 'If anyone comes over to you, don't talk to them.' Fiona nodded, out the window.

The padlock was still in place: the souvenir hunters and ghouls were biding their time. I found the key I had taken off Dr Dolittle. When I stepped inside out of the wind, the instant silence rang in my ears.

I rummaged through kitchen cupboards, not bothering to stay clear of the blood spatter, till I found a bin-liner. I took it upstairs and threw things into it, working fast – Sinéad Gogan was presumably glued to her front window by now, and would be happy to tell anyone who asked exactly how long I had spent in here. When I was done, I put on my gloves and opened Jenny's jewellery box.

The charm bracelet was laid out in a little compartment all its own, ready to put on. The golden heart, the tiny golden house, glowing in the soft light drifting through the cream lampshade;

the curly E, chips of diamond sparkling; the J, enamelled in red; the diamond drop that must have been for Jenny's twenty-first. There was plenty of room left on the chain, for all the wonderful things that had still been going to happen.

I left the bin-liner on the floor and took the bracelet into Emma's room. I switched on the light – I wasn't about to do this with the curtains open. The room was the way Richie and I had left it when we finished searching: tidy, full of thought and love and pink, only the stripped bed to tell you something had happened here. On the bedside table the monitor was flashing a warning: *12°. TOO COLD.*

Emma's hairbrush – pink, with a pony on the back – was on her chest of drawers. I picked out the hairs carefully, matching the lengths, holding them up – they were so fine and fair, at the wrong angle they vanished into the light – to find the ones with roots and skin tags still attached where a careless sweep of the brush had tugged too hard. In the end I had eight.

I smoothed them together into a tiny lock, held the roots between thumb and finger and wound the other end into the charm bracelet. It took me a few tries – on the chain, the clasp, the little gold heart – before it caught tightly enough, in the loop holding the enamelled J, that a tug jerked the hairs free of my fingers and left them fluttering against the gold.

I put the bracelet around one hand and pulled till a link bent open. It left a red mark across my palm, but Jenny's wrists had been covered with bruises and abrasions where Pat had tried to hold her off. Any one of them, blurred by the others, could have come from the bracelet.

Emma had fought; Cooper had told us that already. For a moment she had managed to pull the pillow off her head. As Jenny scrabbled to get it back into place, her bracelet had snagged in Emma's whipping hair. Emma had grabbed hold of it, yanked till a weak link bent, then lost her grip; her hand had been trapped under the pillow again, nothing left in it but a few strands of her own hair.

The bracelet had stayed on Jenny's wrist while she finished

what she was doing. As she went downstairs to find Pat, the bent link had slipped loose.

Probably it wouldn't be enough for a conviction. Emma's hair could have snagged in the bracelet as Jenny brushed it before bed, that last evening; the link could have caught on a door handle as she rushed downstairs to see what the commotion was. The whole thing was dripping with reasonable doubt. But together with everything else, it would be enough to arrest her, charge her, to keep her on remand while she waited for trial.

That can take a year or more. By then Jenny would have spent plenty of time with various psychiatrists and psychologists, who would shower her with meds and counselling and everything else that would give her a chance of stepping back from that wind-swept edge. If she changed her mind about dying, she would plead guilty: there was nothing else she needed to get out for, and a guilty plea would take the shadow off Pat and Conor both. If she didn't change her mind, then someone would spot what she was planning – in spite of what some people think, most mental-health professionals know their job – and do what they could to keep her somewhere safe. I had told Fiona the truth: it wasn't perfect, far from it, but there was no place left for perfect in this case.

Before I left Emma's room I pulled back one of her curtains and stood at the window, looking out at the rows of half-houses and the beach beyond them. The winter was starting to draw in; it was barely three o'clock, but already the light was gathering that evening melancholy and the blue had leached out of the sea, leaving it a restless grey streaked with white foam. In Conor's hide, the plastic sheeting thrummed with the wind; the houses around it threw crazy shadows on the unpaved road. The place looked like Pompeii, like some archaeological discovery preserved to let tourists wander through it – open-mouthed and neck-craning, trying to picture the disaster that had wiped it bare of life – for a brief few years, until it collapsed to dust, until anthills grew up in the middle of kitchen floors and ivy twined around light fixtures.

I closed Emma's door behind me, gently. On the landing floor, next to a coil of power cable running into the bathroom, Richie's precious video camera pointed up at the attic hatch and blinked a tiny red eye to show that it was recording. A little grey spider had already built a hammock of web between the camera and the wall.

Up in the attic, the wind poured in at the hole under the eaves with a high fluttering wail like a fox or a banshee. I squinted up into the open hatch. For an instant I thought I saw something move – a shifting and coalescing of the black, a deliberate muscled ripple – but when I blinked, there was only darkness and the flood of cold air.

The next day, once the case was closed, I would send Richie's tech back out to collect the camera, inspect every frame of the footage and write me a report in triplicate about anything he saw. There was no reason why I shouldn't have flipped up the little built-in monitor and fast-forwarded through the footage myself, kneeling there on the landing, but I didn't do it. I already knew there was nothing there.

Fiona was leaning against the passenger door, staring blankly at the skeleton house where we had talked to her that first day, with a cigarette sending up a thin thread of smoke between her fingers. As I reached her she threw the cigarette into a pothole half-full of murky water.

'Here are your sister's things,' I said, holding up the bin-liner. 'Are these what you had in mind, or would you like anything different?'

'That stuff's fine. Thanks.'

She hadn't even glanced over. For a dizzy second I thought she had changed her mind. I said, 'Are you all right?'

Fiona said, 'Looking at the house reminded me. The day we found them – Jenny and Pat and the kids – I picked this up.'

She brought her hand out of her pocket, curled as if she were holding something. I held out my palm, cupped close around the bracelet to shield it from watchers and from the wind, and she opened her empty one above it.

I said, 'You should touch it, just in case.'

She clasped her hand around the bracelet, tight, for a moment. Even through my gloves, I could feel the cold of her fingers.

I said, 'Where did you get this?'

'When the policemen went in the house, that morning, I followed them. I wanted to know what was going on. I saw this at the bottom of the stairs, like right up against the bottom stair. I picked it up – Jenny wouldn't want it getting kicked around the floor. I put it in my coat pocket. There's a hole in my pocket; this went down into the lining. I forgot about it, till now.'

Her voice was thin and flat; the ceaseless roar of the wind scudded it away, into the raw concrete and rusted metal. 'Thank you,' I said. 'I'll look into it.'

I went round to the driver's side and opened the door. Fiona didn't move. It wasn't until I had put the bracelet into an evidence envelope, labelled it carefully and tucked it into my coat pocket that she straightened up and got into the car. She still didn't look at me.

I started the car and drove us out of Broken Harbour, manoeuvring around the potholes and the straggles of wire, with the wind still slamming against the windows like a wrecking ball. It was that easy.

The caravan site was farther up the beach than the Spains' house, maybe a hundred yards to the north. When Richie and I had walked through the dark to Conor Brennan's hide, and back again with him between us and our case all solved, we had probably crossed over the spot where my family's caravan used to stand.

The last time I saw my mother was outside that caravan, on our last evening at Broken Harbour. My family had gone up to Whelan's for a big farewell dinner; I had made myself a couple of quick ham sandwiches in our kitchenette and I was getting ready to go out, to meet the gang down at the beach. We had flagons of cider and packets of cigarettes stashed in the sand dunes, flagged by blue plastic bags tied in the marram grass; someone was going to bring a guitar; my parents had said I could stay out till midnight. The smell of Lynx Musk deodorant hanging in the caravan, the low rich light through the windows hitting the mirror so that I had to duck sideways to gel my hair into careful spikes; Geri's case open and already half-packed on her bunk, Dina's little white hat and sunglasses thrown on hers. Somewhere kids were laughing and a mother was calling them in to dinner; a faraway radio was playing 'Every Little Thing She Does Is Magic' and I sang along, under my breath in my new deep voice, and thought of the way Amelia pushed back her hair.

Jeans jacket on, running down the caravan steps, and then I stopped. My mother was sitting outside, in one of the little folding chairs, her head tilted back to watch the sky turning peach and gold. Her nose was sunburned and her soft fair hair was falling out of its bun from a day of lying in the sun, building sand castles with Dina, walking by the waterline hand in hand with my father. The hem of her long skirt, pale-blue cotton dotted with white flowers, lifted and swirled in the breeze.

*Mikey,* she said, smiling up at me. *You're looking very handsome.*

*I thought you were up at the pub.*

*Too many people.* That should have been my first clue. *It's so lovely here. So peaceful. Look.*

I shot a token glance at the sky. *Yeah. Pretty. I'm going down to the beach, remember I said? I'll be—*

*Sit down here with me a minute.* She reached out a hand, beckoning.

*I've got to go. The lads are—*

*I know. Just a few minutes.*

I should have known. But she had seemed so happy, all those two weeks. She was always happy at Broken Harbour. Those were the only two weeks of the year when I could be just a normal guy: nothing to guard against except saying something stupid in front of the lads, no secrets prowling the back of my mind except the thoughts of Amelia that turned me red at all the wrong moments, nothing to watch for except big Dean Gorry who fancied her too. I had relaxed into it. All year long, I had watched and worked so hard; I thought I deserved this. I had forgotten that God, or the world, or whatever carves the rules in stone, doesn't give you time off for good behaviour.

I sat on the edge of the other chair and tried not to jiggle. Mum leaned back and sighed, a contented, dreamy sound. *Look at that,* she said, and stretched out her arms towards the flirt and rush of the water. It was a soft evening, lavender waves lapping and the air sweet and salty as caramel, only a high thin haze in the sunset to say that the wind might turn on us and bite down sometime in the night. *There's nowhere like here, sure there isn't. I wish I never had to go home. Don't you?*

*Yeah. Probably. It's nice.*

*Tell me something. That blonde girl, the one with the nice dad who gave us milk that day we ran out. Is she your girlfriend?*

*Jesus! Mum!* I was twisting with embarrassment.

She didn't notice. *Good. That's good. Sometimes I worry that you don't have girlfriends because* . . . Another small sigh, as she brushed hair off her forehead. *Ah, that's good. She's a lovely girl; she's got a lovely smile.*

*Yeah.* Amelia's smile, the way her eyes came up sideways to meet mine; the curve of her lip that made me want to bite it. *I guess.*

*Take good care of her. Your dad's always taken good care of me.* My mother smiled, reached across the gap between the chairs to pat my hand. *So have you. I hope that girl knows how lucky she is.*

*We've only been going out a few days.*

*Are you going to keep on seeing each other?*

I shrugged. *Don't know. She's from Newry.* In my head I was already sending Amelia mix tapes, writing out the address in my best handwriting, picturing the girl-bedroom where she would listen to them.

*Stay in touch. You'd have beautiful children.*

*Mum! We've only known each other—*

*You never know.* Something skimmed across her face, something swift and frail as the shadow of a bird on water. *You never know, in this life.*

Dean had a million little brothers and sisters, his parents didn't care where he was; he would be down on the beach already, ready and waiting to leap on his chance. *Mum, I have to go. OK? Can I?*

I was half off my seat, legs braced ready to shoot me off through the dunes. Her hand reached across the gap again, caught hold of mine. *Not yet. I don't want to be on my own.*

I glanced up the path towards Whelan's, praying, but it was empty. *Dad and the girls'll be back any minute.*

We both knew it would be longer than that. Whelan's was where all the caravan-park families went: Dina would be running around playing catch and shrieking with the other little kids, Dad would get into a game of darts, Geri would sit on the wall outside flirting for just one more minute. Mum's hand was still wrapped around mine. *There are things I need to talk to you about. Things. It's important.*

My head was full up with Amelia, with Dean, with the wild sea-smell surging in my blood, with the whole cider-tasting world of night and laughter and mystery that was waiting for me in those dunes. I thought she wanted to talk about love, girls, maybe God forbid sex. *Yeah, OK, just not* now. *Tomorrow, when we get home – just I have to go, Mum, seriously, I'm meeting Amelia—*

*She'll wait for you. Stay with me. Don't leave me on my own.*

The first note of desperation rising through her voice, tainting the air like toxic smoke. I whipped my hand out from under hers as if it had burned me. Tomorrow at home I would have been ready for this, but not here, not now. The unfairness of it slashed like a whip across the face, left me stunned, outraged, blinded. *Mum. Just don't.*

Her hand still outstretched towards mine, ready to clutch. *Please, Mikey. I need you.*

*So what?* It exploded out of me, took all my breath and left me panting. I wanted to punch her out of my way, out of my world. *I'm so fucking* sick *of taking care of you! You're the one who's supposed to be taking care of* me!

Her face, stricken, open-mouthed. The sunset light gilding away the grey in her hair, turning her young and shimmering, ready to vanish into its blinding brightness. *Oh, Mike. Oh, Mike, I'm so sorry—*

*Yeah. I know. Me too.* I was shifting on the chair, scarlet with shame and defiance and hideous embarrassment, dying to get out of there even more. *Just forget it. I didn't mean it.*

*You did. I know you did. And you're right. You shouldn't have to . . . Oh, God. Oh, love, I'm so sorry.*

*It's OK. It's fine.* Bright flashes of colour were moving in the dunes, long-legged shadows stretching in front of them as they ran towards the water. A girl laughed; I couldn't tell whether it was Amelia. *Can I go?*

*Yes. Of course. Go.* Her hand twisting among the flowers of her skirt. *Don't worry, Mike, love. I won't do this to you again. I promise. You have a gorgeous evening.*

As I jumped up – already putting up a hand to gingerly triple-check my hair, running my tongue over my teeth to make sure they were clean – she caught me by the sleeve. *Mum, I have to—*

*I know. Just a second.* She pulled me down, pressed her hands to my cheeks and kissed my forehead. She smelled of coconut suntan oil, of salt, of summer, of my mother.

Afterwards people blamed my father. We had done a good job, he and I and Geri, of keeping our secret locked safe inside our own four walls; too good. No one had ever suspected the days when my mother couldn't stop crying, the weeks when she lay in bed staring at the wall; but back then neighbours watched out for each other, or watched each other, I'm not sure which it was. The whole road knew there had been weeks when she didn't come out of the house, days when she could only manage a faint hello or when she tucked her head down and scurried away from their curious eyes.

The adults tried to be subtle, but every condolence had a question swaying in the undercurrent; the guys in school didn't even try, half the time. They all wanted to know the same things. When she kept her head down, was she hiding black eyes? When she stayed indoors, was she waiting for ribs to heal? When she went into the water, was it because my father had sent her there?

I shut the adults up with a cold blank stare; I beat the shit out of classmates who got too blatant, right up until the day when my sympathy points got used up and teachers started giving me detention for fighting. I needed to get home on time, to help Geri with Dina and the house – my father couldn't do it, he could barely talk. I couldn't afford detention. That was when I started learning control.

Deep down, I didn't blame them for asking. It looked like plain salacious nosiness, but even then I understood that it was more. They needed to know. Like I told Richie, cause and effect isn't a luxury. Take it away and we're left paralysed, clinging to some tiny raft lurching wild and random on endless black sea. If my mother could go into the water just because, then so could theirs, any night, any minute; so could they. When we can't see a pattern, we fit pieces together until one takes shape, because we have to.

I fought them because the pattern they were seeing was the wrong one, and I couldn't make myself tell them any other way. I knew they were right about this much: things don't happen for no reason. I was the only one in the world who knew that the reason was me.

I had learned how to live with that. I had found a way, slowly and with immense amounts of work and pain. I had no way to live without it.

_There isn't any why._ If Dina was right, then the world was unlivable. If she was wrong, if – and this needed to be true – if the world was sane and it was only the strange galaxy inside her head that was spinning reasonless off any axis, then all of this was because of me.

I dropped Fiona outside the hospital. As I pulled up the car, I said, 'I'll need you to come in and give an official statement about finding the bracelet.'

I saw her eyes shut for a second. 'When?'

'Now, if you don't mind. I can wait here while you drop off your sister's things.'

'When are you going to . . . ?' Her chin tilted towards the building. 'To tell her?'

To arrest her. 'As soon as possible. Probably tomorrow.'

'Then I'll come in after that. I'll stay with Jenny till then.'

I said, 'It might be easier on you to come in this evening. You might find it tough, being with Jenny right now.'

Fiona said tonelessly, 'I might, yeah.' Then she climbed out of the car and walked away, holding the bin-liner in both arms, leaning backwards as if it weighed too much to carry.

I handed the Beemer in to the car pool and waited outside the castle wall, lurking in shadows like a corner boy, until the shift was over and the lads had gone home. Then I went to find the Super.

O'Kelly was still at his desk, head bent in a circle of lamplight, running his pen along the lines of a statement sheet. He had his reading glasses on the end of his nose. The cosy yellow light brought out the deep creases around his eyes and mouth, the white streaks growing in his hair; he looked like some kind old man in a storybook, the wise grandfather who knows how to fix it all.

Outside the window the sky was a rich winter black, and shadows were starting to pile up around the ragged stacks of files leaning in corners. The office felt like a place I had dreamed about once when I was a kid and spent years trying to find, a place whose every priceless detail I should have been hoarding in my memory; a place that was already dissolving through my fingers, already lost.

I moved in the doorway, and O'Kelly raised his head. For a split second he looked tired and sad. Then all that was wiped away and his face turned blank, utterly expressionless.

'Detective Kennedy,' he said, taking off his reading glasses. 'Shut the door.'

I closed it behind me, stayed standing until O'Kelly pointed his pen at a chair. He said, 'Quigley was in to me this morning.'

I said, 'He should have left it to me.'

'That's what I told him. He put on his nun-face and said he didn't trust you to come clean.'

The little fuckwad. 'Wanted to get his version in first, more like.'

'He couldn't wait to drop you in the shite. Practically came in his kacks at the chance. Here's the thing, though: Quigley'll twist a story to suit himself, all right, but I've never known him make one up from scratch. Too careful of his own arse.'

I said, 'He wasn't making it up.' I found the evidence bag in my pocket – it felt like days since I had put it there – and laid it on O'Kelly's desk.

He didn't pick it up. He said, 'Give me your version. I'll need it in a written statement, but I want to hear it first.'

'Detective Curran found this in Conor Brennan's flat, while I was outside making a phone call. The nail polish matches Jennifer Spain's. The wool matches the pillow that was used to suffocate Emma Spain.'

O'Kelly whistled. 'Sweet fuck. The mammy. Are you sure?'

'I spent the afternoon with her. She won't confess under caution, but she gave me a full account off the record.'

'Which is bugger-all use to us, without this.' He nodded at the envelope. 'How'd it get into Brennan's flat, if he's not our man?'

'He was at the scene. He's the one who tried to finish off Jennifer Spain.'

'Thank Jaysus for that. At least you didn't arrest a holy innocent. That's one less lawsuit, anyway.' O'Kelly thought that over, grunted. 'Go on. Curran finds this, clicks what it means. And then? Why the hell didn't he hand it in?'

'He was in two minds. In his view, Jennifer Spain's suffered enough, and no purpose would be served by her arrest: the best solution would be to release Conor Brennan and close the file, with the implication that Patrick Spain was the perpetrator.'

O'Kelly snorted. 'Beautiful. That's only beautiful. The fucking gobshite. So out he walks, cool as a cucumber, with this yoke in his pocket.'

'He was holding on to the evidence while he decided what to do with it. Last night, a woman who's also known to me was at Detective Curran's house. She spotted that envelope and thought it shouldn't be there, so she took it away with her. She tried to hand it in to me this morning, but Quigley intercepted her.'

'This young one,' O'Kelly said. He was clicking the top of his pen with his thumb, watching it like it was fascinating stuff. 'Quigley tried to tell me ye were all having some mad three-way – said he was concerned because the squad should be upholding morals, all that altar-boy shite. What's the real story?'

O'Kelly has always been good to me. 'She's my sister,' I said.

That got his attention. 'Holy God. I'd say Curran is missing a few teeth now, is he?'

'He didn't know.'

'That's no excuse. Dirty little whoremaster.'

I said, 'Sir, I'd like to keep my sister out of this, if possible. She's not well.'

'That's what Quigley said, all right.' Only presumably not in those words. 'No need to bring her into it. IA might want to talk to her, but I'll tell them there's nothing she can add. You make sure she doesn't go chatting to some media bastard, and she'll be grand.'

'Thank you, sir.'

O'Kelly nodded. 'This,' he said, flicking the envelope with his pen. 'Can you swear you never saw it till today?'

I said, 'I swear, sir. I didn't know it existed till Quigley waved it in my face.'

'When did Curran pick it up?'

'Thursday morning.'

'Thursday morning,' O'Kelly repeated. Something ominous was building in his voice. 'So he kept it to himself for the bones of two days. The two of ye are spending every waking moment together, you're talking about nothing only this case – or at least I hope you are – and Curran's got the answer in the pocket of his shiny tracksuit the whole time. Tell me, Detective: how the sweet living fuck did you miss that?'

'I was focused on the case. I did notice—'

O'Kelly exploded. 'Sweet Jesus! What does this yoke look like to you? Chopped liver? This *is* the fucking case. And it's not some piece-of-shite druggie case where nobody cares if you take your eye off the ball. There are murdered *kids* here. You didn't think this might be a good time to act like a bloody detective and keep an eye on what's going on around you?'

I said, 'I knew something was on Curran's mind, sir. I didn't
miss that. But I thought it was because we weren't on the same
page. I thought Brennan was our man, and looking anywhere else
was a waste of time; Curran thought – said he thought – that
Patrick Spain was a better suspect and we should spend more
time on him. I thought that was all it was.'

O'Kelly took a breath to keep bollocking me, but his heart
wasn't in it. 'Either Curran deserves an Oscar,' he said, but the
heat had gone out of his voice, 'or you deserve a good kicking.' He
rubbed his eyes with thumb and finger. 'Where is the little prick,
anyway?'

'I sent him home. I wasn't about to let him touch anything else.'

'Too bloody right. Get onto him, tell him to report to me first
thing in the morning. If he survives that, I'll find him a nice desk
where he can file paperwork till IA's done with him.'

'Yes, sir.' I would text him. I had no desire to talk to Richie, ever
again.

O'Kelly said, 'If your sister hadn't nicked the evidence, would
Curran have handed it over, in the end? Or would he have flushed
it down the jacks, kept his mouth shut for good? You knew him
better than I did. What do you figure?'

*He'd have handed it in today, sir, I'd bet my month's salary on
it* . . . All those partners I had envied would have done it without a
second thought, but Richie wasn't my partner any more, if he ever
had been. 'I don't know,' I said. 'I don't have a clue.'

O'Kelly grunted. 'Not like it matters either way. Curran's
through. I'd boot him back to whatever council flat he came from,
if I could do it without IA and the brass and the media crawling
up my arse; since I can't, he'll be reverted to uniform, and I'll find
him some lovely shithole full of addicts and handguns where he
can wait for his pension. If he knows what's good for him, he'll
keep his mouth shut and take it.'

He left a space in case I wanted to put up a fight. His eye told
me it would be pointless, but I wouldn't have done it anyway. I
said, 'I think that's the right outcome.'

'Hold your horses there. IA and the brass aren't going to be happy with you, either. Curran's still on probation; you're the man in charge. If this investigation's gone down the jacks, that's all yours.'

'I accept that, sir. But I don't think it's down the jacks just yet. While I was at the hospital with Jennifer Spain, I ran into Fiona Rafferty – that's the sister. She picked this up in the Spains' hallway, the morning we were called to the scene. She'd forgotten about it until today.'

I found the envelope with the bracelet in it and put it on the desk, next to the other one. A tiny detached part of me was able to be pleased at how steady my hand was. 'She's identified the bracelet as Jennifer Spain's. Going by colour and length, the hair caught in it could belong to either Jennifer or Emma, but the techs should have no trouble telling us which one: Jennifer's hair is lightened. If this is Emma's – and I'd bet it is – then we've still got our case.'

O'Kelly watched me for a long time, clicking the top of his pen, those sharp little eyes steady on mine. He said, 'That's very bloody convenient.'

It was a question. I said, 'Just very lucky, sir.'

After another long moment, he nodded. 'Better play the Lotto tonight. You're the luckiest man in Ireland. Do you need me to tell you how much shit you'd have been in if this yoke hadn't shown up?'

Scorcher Kennedy, the straightest straight arrow, twenty years' service and never put a toe over the line: after that one wisp of suspicion, O'Kelly believed I was as pure as the driven snow. So would everyone else. Even the defence wouldn't waste their time trying to impeach the evidence. Quigley would bitch and hint, but nobody listens to Quigley. 'No, sir,' I said.

'Hand it in to the evidence room, quick, before you find a way to bollix it up. Then go home. Get some sleep. You'll need your wits about you for IA on Monday.' He jammed his reading glasses onto his nose and bent his head over the statement sheet again. We were done.

I said, 'Sir, there's something else you should know.'

'Oh, Jesus. If there's any more fucking shite to do with this mess, I don't want to hear it.'

'Nothing like that, sir. When this case is wound up, I'll be putting in my papers.'

That brought O'Kelly's head up. 'Why?' he asked, after a moment.

'I think it's time for a change.'

Those sharp eyes poked at me. He said, 'You don't have your thirty. You'll get no pension till you're sixty years of age.'

'I know, sir.'

'What'll you do instead?'

'I don't know yet.'

He watched me, tapping his pen on the page in front of him. 'I put you back on the pitch too early. I thought you were fighting fit again. Could've sworn you were only dying to get off the bench.'

There was something in his voice that could have been concern, or maybe even compassion. I said, 'I was.'

'I should've spotted that you weren't ready. Now this mess is after shaking your nerve. That's all it is. A few good nights' kip, a few pints with the lads, you'll be grand.'

'It's not that simple, sir.'

'Why not? You won't be spending the next few years sharing a desk with Curran, if that's what you're worried about. This was my mistake. I'll say that to the brass. I don't want you booted onto desk duty, any more than you do; leave me stuck with that shower of eejits out there.' O'Kelly jerked his head towards the squad room. 'I won't see you shafted. You'll take a bollocking, you'll lose a few days' holidays – sure, you've plenty saved up anyway, am I right? – and everything'll be back to normal.'

'Thank you, sir,' I said. 'I appreciate that. But I've got no problem taking whatever's coming my way. You're right: I should have caught this.'

'Is that it? You're sulking because you missed a trick? For Christ's sake, man, we've all done it. So you'll get some slagging from the lads – Detective Perfect hitting a banana skin and going arse over tip, they'd want to be saints to turn down a chance like this. You'll survive. Get a grip on yourself and don't be giving me the big farewell speech.'

It wasn't just that I had tainted everything I would ever touch – if this came out, then no solve with my name on it would be safe. It wasn't just that I knew, somewhere deeper than logic, that I was going to lose the next case, and the next, and the one after that. It was that I was dangerous. Stepping over the line had come so easily, once there was no other way; so naturally. You can tell yourself as much as you want *It was only this once, it'll never happen again, this was different.* There will always be another once-off, another special case that needs just one little step further. All it takes is that first tiny hole in the levee, so tiny it does no harm to anything. The water will find it. It will nose into the crack, pushing, eroding, mindless and ceaseless, until the levee you built collapses to dust and the whole sea comes roaring over you. The only chance to stop that is at the beginning.

I said, 'It's not a sulk, sir. When I ballsed up before, I took the slaggings; I didn't enjoy it, but I survived. Maybe you're right: maybe my nerve's gone. All I can say is, this isn't the right place for me any more.'

O'Kelly rolled his pen across his knuckles and watched me for what I wasn't telling him. 'You'd want to be bloody sure. If you have second thoughts once you're gone, you've got no right to come back. Think about that. Think long and hard.'

'I will, sir. I won't go until Jennifer Spain's trial is over and done with.'

'Good. Meantime, I won't say this to anyone else. Come back to me and tell me you've changed your mind, any time you like, and we'll say no more about it.'

We both knew I wasn't going to change my mind. 'Thanks, sir. I appreciate that.'

O'Kelly nodded. 'You're a good cop,' he said. 'You picked the wrong case to fuck up, all right, but you're a good cop. Don't forget that.'

I took one last look at the office, before I closed the door behind me. The light was gentle on the massive green mug that O'Kelly has had since I joined the squad, on the golf trophies he keeps on his bookshelf, on the brass nameplate saying DET. SUPT. G. O'KELLY. I used to hope that that would be my office, someday. I had pictured it so many times: the framed photos of Laura and of Geri's kids on my desk, my musty old criminology books on the shelves, maybe a bonsai tree or a little aquarium for tropical fish. Not that I was wishing O'Kelly gone, I wasn't, but you need to keep your dreams vivid, or they'll get lost along the way. That had been mine.

I got in my car and drove to Dina's place. I tried her flat and all the other flats in her fleapit building, shoved my ID in the hairy losers' faces: none of them had seen her in days. I tried four of her exes' places, got everything from a slammed-down intercom to 'When she shows, tell her to give me a call'. I went through every corner of Geri's neighbourhood, trying every pub where the lighted windows might have caught Dina's eye, every green space that might have looked soothing. I tried my place, and all the nearby laneways where vile subhumans sell every vile thing they can get their hands on. I tried Dina's phone, a couple of dozen times. I thought of trying Broken Harbour, but Dina can't drive and it was too far for a taxi.

Instead I drove around the city centre, leaning out of my car window to check the face of every girl I passed – it was a cold night, everyone wrapped tight in hats and scarves and hoods, a dozen times some slim graceful girl's walk almost choked me with hope before I craned my neck far enough to catch a glimpse of her face. When a tiny dark girl with stilettos and a cigarette yelled at me to fuck off, I realised that it was after midnight, and what I looked like. I pulled in at the side of the road and sat there for a long time, listening to Dina's voicemail and watching my breath turn to smoke in the cold of the car, before I could make myself give up and go home.

Sometime after three o'clock in the morning, when I had been lying in bed for a long time, I heard fumbling at the door of my apartment. After a few tries a key turned in the lock, and a band of whitish light from the corridor widened on my sitting-room floor. 'Mikey?' Dina whispered.

I stayed still. The band of light shrank to nothing, and the door clicked closed. Careful steps across the floor, stage-tiptoeing; then her silhouette in my bedroom doorway, a slim condensation of blackness, swaying a little with uncertainty.

'Mikey,' she said, just above a whisper this time. 'Are you awake?'

I closed my eyes and breathed evenly. After a while Dina sighed, a small exhausted sound like a child after a long day playing outside. 'It's raining,' she said, almost to herself.

I heard her sitting down on the floor and pulling off her boots, the thump of each of them on the laminate flooring. She climbed into bed beside me and pulled the duvet over us, tucking the edges in tight. She nudged her back against my chest, insistently, until I put my arm around her. Then she sighed again, snuggled her head deeper into the pillow and tucked the point of her coat collar into her mouth, ready for sleep.

All those hours Geri and I had spent asking her questions, over all those years, that was the one we had never been able to ask. *Did you pull away, at the edge of the water, waves already wrapping round your ankles; did you twist your arm out of her warm fingers and run back, into the dark, into the hissing marram grass that closed around you and hid you tight from her calling? Or was that the last thing she did, before she stepped off that far edge: did she open her hand and let you go, did she scream to you to run, run?* I could have asked, that night. I think Dina would have answered.

I listened to the small noises of her sucking on her collar, to her breathing slowing and deepening into sleep. She smelled of wild cold air, cigarettes and blackberries. Her coat was sodden with rain, soaking through my pyjamas and chilling my skin. I lay still, looking into the dark and feeling her hair wet against my cheek, waiting for the dawn.

In the best books, the ending often comes as a shock.
Not just because of that one last twist in the tale,
but because you have been so absorbed in their world,
that coming back to the harsh light of reality is a jolt.

If that describes you now, then perhaps you should track down
some new leads, and find new suspense in other worlds.

Join us at www.hodder.co.uk, or follow us on
Twitter @hodderbooks, and you can tap in to a
community of fellow thrill-seekers.

Whether you want to find out more about this book,
or a particular author, watch trailers and interviews, have
the chance to win early limited editions, or simply browse
our expert readers' selection of the very best books,
we think you'll find what you're looking for.

And if you don't, that's the place to tell us what's missing.

**We love what we do, and we'd love you to be part of it.**

www.hodder.co.uk

 @hodderbooks

 HodderBooks

HodderBooks